PENGUIN CLASSICS

SELECTED TALES

HENRY JAMES was born in 1843 in New York City, of Scottish and Irish ancestry. His father was a prominent theologian and philosopher, and his elder brother, William, is also famous as a philosopher. He attended schools in New York and later in London, Paris and Geneva, entering the Law School at Harvard in 1862. In 1865 he began to contribute reviews and short stories to American journals. In 1875, after two prior visits to Europe, he settled for a year in Paris, where he met Flaubert, Turgenev and other literary figures. However, the next year he moved to London, where he became so popular in society that in the winter of 1878–9 he confessed to accepting 107 invitations. In 1898 he left London and went to live at Lamb House, Rye, Sussex. Henry James became a British citizen in 1915, was awarded the Order of Merit, and died in 1916.

Henry James wrote some twenty novels, the first published being *Roderick Hudson* (1875). Other titles include *The Europeans*, *Washington Square*, *The Portrait of a Lady*, *The Bostonians*, *The Princess Casamassima*, *The Tragic Muse*, *The Spoils of Poynton*, *The Awkward Age*, *The Ambassadors* and *The Golden Bowl*.

JOHN LYON is Senior Lecturer in English at the University of Bristol and Gillespie Visiting Professor at the College of Wooster, Ohio. He is a Founding Fellow of the English Association. He is the author of a book-length study of *The Merchant of Venice*, and publishes on the novel and on contemporary poetry. He has also edited Rudyard Kipling's *The Light That Failed*, Joseph Conrad's *Youth/Heart of Darkness/The End of the Tether* and Henry James's *The Sacred Fount* for Penguin.

HENRY JAMES

SELECTED TALES

Edited with an Introduction and Notes by
JOHN LYON

PENGUIN BOOKS

PENGUIN BOOKS

Published by the Penguin Group
Penguin Books Ltd, 80 Strand, London WC2R 0RL, England
Penguin Putnam Inc., 375 Hudson Street, New York, New York 10014, USA
Penguin Books Australia Ltd, 250 Camberwell Road, Camberwell, Victoria 3124, Australia
Penguin Books Canada Ltd, 10 Alcorn Avenue, Toronto, Ontario, Canada M4V 3B2
Penguin Books India (P) Ltd, 11 Community Centre, Panchsheel Park, New Delhi – 110 017, India
Penguin Books (NZ) Ltd, Cnr Rosedale and Airborne Roads, Albany, Auckland, New Zealand
Penguin Books (South Africa) (Pty) Ltd, 24 Sturdee Avenue, Rosebank 2196, South Africa

Penguin Books Ltd, Registered Offices: 80 Strand, London WC2R 0RL, England

www.penguin.com

This collection published in Penguin Classics 2001
2

Editorial material copyright © John Lyon, 2001
All rights reserved

The moral right of the editor has been asserted

Set in 9.5/11.5 pt Monotype Octavian
Typeset by Rowland Phototypesetting Ltd, Bury St Edmunds, Suffolk
Printed in England by Clays Ltd, St Ives plc

CONTENTS

ACKNOWLEDGEMENTS

This edition would not have been possible without the help of my friends – George and Mary Donaldson, Penny Fielding, Tim Kendall and Fiona Mathews, John Lee, Peter McDonald and Karen O'Brien, Carol Meale, and Helen Small. At Penguin, Hilary Laurie has proved an exemplary editor, not least in her patience and kindness; and the text is all the better for Lindeth Vasey's characteristic and scrupulous copy editing.

INTRODUCTION

EVER SO MANY THINGS

'It is like starting a zoo in a closet: the giraffe alone takes up more space than one has for the collection.'[1] So the distinguished poet and critic Randall Jarrell lamented the task of selecting an anthology of short stories. The Jamesian zoo which we are sampling here is indeed vast, running to some 112 fine specimens – with a profusion of giraffes and elephants, and some extraordinary supernatural beasts. If Jamesian tales are not always tall, they are often very large for, despite the pressures of publishers and magazine editors, Henry James was never to be persuaded of the 'blank misery'[2] that stories ought, always or even usually, to be short. The works I have been selecting from here vary between 5,000 and 45,000 words. They encompass brief stories, which James referred to as anecdotes, and longer works, which he called *nouvelles*, and they are all most usefully subsumed under the general title which their author himself favoured – tales. Remarkably numerous, highly various both in subject matter and in style, often very long: mundane facts like these about Jamesian tales put further constraints even on a volume as large as this in its attempt to be adequate to his diversity and variety. Such an attempt, the least that readers have a right to expect from any selection of any author, is an altogether greater requirement in the case of Henry James, where diversity and variety are the very heart of the matter, the message as well as the medium.

Moreover, this great abundance of tales is itself only part of the story of Jamesian art. James cherished, and unquestionably realized, his dream of becoming one of the world's greatest novelists – although by the time of the 'late phase' (James's twentieth-century writing), his art had travelled far from the realism of those nineteenth-century novelists, such as Balzac and George Eliot, whom he had come to Europe to admire and to emulate. James cherished, and by his own account humiliatingly failed in, an ambition to be a successful dramatist. James produced essays, criticism, travel writing, autobiography and a vast, incessant flow of letters. Yet throughout his artistic career, from his first creative publication of 'A Tragedy of Error' in 1864 to his continuing revision of tales even in the final months of his life, James was writing and revising tales – anecdotes and *nouvelles*

– with a regularity and profusion which might allow us to map out his artistic life as a life of tales. When his roles of novelist or of dramatist came under pressure, or his novels and dramas failed the public or the public failed them, then his commitment to tales, and the thinking behind such a commitment, were formulated with particular force. At such times, James apparently felt that he could be more imaginatively adequate to the world's rich and varying possibilities by way of a seemingly endless accumulation of comparative smallnesses rather than by containing that rich variousness in a single large work, however magisterial. In his *Notebooks* – the great gathering place of the sources for so many of his writings – in 1889 and 1891, at a time when he was struggling both with large novelistic attempts at social realism and with ambitions for a career as playwright in the London theatre, he was drawn repeatedly and in recompense to the multiplicity and freedom of opportunities which the tale afforded him:

reviving, refreshing, confirming, consecrating, as it were, the wish and dream that have lately grown stronger than ever in me – the desire that the literary heritage, such as it is, poor thing, that I may leave, shall consist of a large number of perfect *short* things, *nouvelles* and tales, illustrative of ever so many things in life – in the life I see and know and feel – and of all the deep and the delicate – and of London, and of art, and of everything: and that they shall be fine, rare, strong, wise – eventually perhaps even recognized.

. . . by doing short things I can do so many, touch so many subjects, break out in so many places, handle so many of the threads of life.[3]

The plurality of James's stories, together with the selectivity and compression necessary within each one of them, declare implicitly that there are other ways to tell each tale, and other tales to be told: taken together, his many tales approach the Jamesian dream of 'everything', a vast magnanimous inclusiveness of seeing and knowing and feeling, a great grasping of 'the threads of life'.

In this selection, doubtless, individual inclusions and exclusions will disappoint individual readers. However, this volume, if it is not to fail, must give some sense of the imaginative, liberating largesse of this prolific and generous writer. The present introduction, too, will have gone wrong if it attempts what James himself does altogether better: here, then, in place of any attempt to summarize or 'tell' the stories which follow (although some plot details will be revealed), are some observations and contexts which readers may test against their experiences of the tales in this selection.

CREATING THE RECORD

Henry James embraced what some other writers in the nineteenth century feared: what Matthew Arnold had described as a growing awareness of the 'world's multitudinousness'.[4] For James was uniquely placed to recognize, from the start, that the world was not reducible to a single understanding, however complex and capacious. Born in New York in 1843, as a child Henry James travelled with his family in Europe, receiving an idiosyncratic education. He crossed the Atlantic again, as a young adult travelling alone in England, France and Italy, before settling in England in 1876. But his toings and froings to the Continent and across the Atlantic, his literal and his imaginative voyagings, his comparings and contrastings, were never really over: even on his deathbed by the Thames in Chelsea, James continued to travel far and wide in his imagination, rearranging the entire world in his tenacious but now fragmenting mind. His elder brother, the philosopher William James, was led to conclude that Henry was 'really . . . a native of the James family, and has no other country',[5] but even this may be too fraternally appropriative: Henry James was unique, an internationalist at a time when this signified, not today's bland homogeneity and erosion of difference, but comedies and tragedies of distinctiveness and divergence. The tales, particularly the earlier works such as 'Four Meetings', 'Daisy Miller' and 'The Pension Beaurepas' here, are the lasting record of James's appreciation of the international. Other tales here realize the fuller implications, beyond any literal contrast of European and American perspectives, of this international vision, and of the challenge which such a vision represents for the writer.

How is a writer to depict worlds so various? In 1884, in his great, ever hesitating, ever qualifying essay, 'The Art of Fiction', Henry James spoke up for fiction as history, for fiction as what we rather glibly call 'realism'. He declared that the writer of fiction must 'possess the sense of reality'. But *which* reality? James himself immediately expands into a wondering, complicating celebration of the mind's relation with its worlds:

Humanity is immense, and reality has a myriad forms . . . Experience is never limited, and it is never complete; it is an immense sensibility, a kind of huge spider-web of the finest silken threads suspended in the chamber of consciousness, and catching every air-borne particle in its tissue. It is the very atmosphere of the mind; and when the mind is imaginative – much more when it happens to be that of a man of genius – it takes to itself the faintest hints of life, it converts the very pulses of the air into revelations . . . The power to guess the unseen from the seen, to trace the implication of things, to judge the whole piece by the pattern, the condition of feeling life in general so completely that you are well on your way to knowing any particular corner of it – this cluster of gifts may almost be said to constitute experience . . . If experience consists of impressions, it may be said that impressions *are* experience, just as (have we not seen it?) they are the very air we breathe . . .[6]

'Experience' flows into 'sensibility', into 'consciousness'; 'experience' is related to, and then equated with, 'impressions'. From here James goes on, all gently and benignly, to proffer to the intending writer a piece of advice which perhaps only a Henry James could fulfil, a piece of advice baffling, exhausting, well-nigh impossible: 'Try to be one of the people on whom nothing is lost!'[7]

The terms for the great Jamesian drama – the encounter between the mind and the world, the romantic and the realistic, vision and fact, art and life – are already declaring themselves here; and he is already varying his emphasis and his priority, just as each of his tales varies in its particular configuration of that drama. Near the end of James's life, H. G. Wells's mocked 'the elaborate copious emptiness' of Jamesian style and described, with cruel comedy, James's narrative as 'a magnificent but painful hippopotamus resolved at any cost, even at the cost of its dignity, upon picking up a pea'.[8] In reply and rebuke, Henry James declared: 'It is art that *makes* life, makes interest, makes importance, for our consideration and application of these things, and I know of no substitute for the force and beauty of its process.'[9] However, it was a few years earlier, in the Preface to the volume in the important New York Edition of those tales centred particularly on 'the literary life' (represented in this selection by 'The Lesson of the Master', 'The Death of the Lion' and 'The Figure in the Carpet'), that James was to elaborate more publicly and more fully the argument for art in opposition to, and in rebuke of, actuality; he argued for imaginative possibilities above reality's probabilities. Faced with the accusation that such tales focused on 'supersubtle fry' who were without precedent in real life, James defended an art which 'implies and projects the possible other case, the case rich and edifying where actuality is pretentious and vain'. If art and life were not in accord, then 'so much the worse for that life'. And James warmed to his audacious argument with his disbelieving reader:

What does your contention of non-existent conscious *exposures*, in the midst of all the stupidity and vulgarity and hypocrisy, imply but that we have been, nationally, so to speak, graced with no instance of recorded sensibility fine enough to react against these things? – an admission too distressing. What one would accordingly fain do is to baffle any such calamity, to *create* the record, in default of any other enjoyment of it; to imagine, in a word, the honourable, the producible case. What better example than this of the high and helpful public and, as it were, civic use of the imagination? . . . How can one consent to make a picture of the preponderant futilities and vulgarities and miseries of life without the impulse to exhibit as well from time to time, in its place, some fine example of the reaction, the opposition or the escape?[10]

However, in the stories here, we can also often find James taking a sharp look at 'all the stupidity and vulgarity and hypocrisy . . . the preponderant futilities and vulgarities and miseries of life', including those realities of the world of work and of ordinary people with which his writing is not usually associated. James himself worried that his talent did not stretch 'downtown', to the world of business, but was confined 'uptown', in New York and elsewhere, with the ladies. Nevertheless, the figure of Mr Ruck is the most sympathetic portrait in 'The Pension Beaurepas', an informed observation of a New York businessman, on unhappy holiday, failing in health and failing financially, as his wife and daughter continue only too well in *their* roles, spending his wealth in the 'stores' of Europe. The ugly horror of American business emerges again, in ghostly form, in 'The Jolly Corner'. On the other side of the Atlantic, 'The Birthplace' begins with a wonderfully economical and sharp-eyed depiction of genteel poverty in Blackport-on-Dwindle. But the great work in this respect is 'In the Cage', combining an extraordinary particularity in its realization of the ordinary woman at work with – in a *nouvelle* notorious for its cryptic difficulties – an astonishingly direct diagnosis and denunciation of the late nineteenth-century aristocracy. The telegraphist hates them: 'They're *too* real! They're selfish brutes.'

What could still remain fresh in her daily grind was the immense disparity, the difference and contrast, from class to class, of every instant and every motion . . . What twisted the knife in her vitals was the way the profligate rich scattered about them, in extravagant chatter over their extravagant pleasures and sins, an amount of money that would have held the stricken household of her frightened childhood, her poor pinched mother and tormented father and lost brother and starved sister, together for a lifetime.

This is not to suggest that the revelation of 'stupidity and vulgarity and hypocrisy' is limited to matters of class; when James turns to the life of the family, his attention appears similarly unremitting. The vileness of the Moreen parents in 'The Pupil' is hard to match; the children of 'Greville Fane' are pitilessly selfish, in fact murderous.

But James was never content merely to depict and to diagnose vain actuality. His tales also celebrate creative reaction. 'Daisy Miller' has been attacked for failing on both accounts, attacked both for its unpatriotic satirizing of the American girl and for its idealizing of her. Within the tale, Daisy Miller is the victim, among the expatriate American community in Europe, of too dogmatic, too confident, too single-minded readings: in this respect, the tale itself was to suffer from readings analogous to those inflicted on its eponymous heroine. In his Preface to this story James recalls how 'in Italy again . . . in Venice . . . on the Grand Canal', he was the recipient of such criticism. There two friends – again American expatriates – voice opposing views about the tale: one identifies in two young American girls they are watching on the terrace of a Venetian hotel 'a couple of attesting Daisy Millers'. The other friend, however, protests that, in his portrayal of Daisy Miller, James 'quite falsified . . . the thing you had had, to satiety, the chance of "observing"'. On this account, James has failed to produce a realistic and satiric diagnosis of the Daisy Miller type; he has misled critical judgement and indeed rendered a judgemental attitude impossible; he has been led astray by his 'incurable prejudice in favour of grace'. The culmination of the attack and James's reply reveal that, by the time he writes this Preface in the first decade of the twentieth century, he has become relaxed and explicit about an art which is not content merely to serve realism:

'. . . Is it that you've after all too much imagination? Those awful young women capering at the hotel-door, *they* are the real little Daisy Millers that were; whereas yours in the tale is such a one, more's the pity, as – for pitch of the ingenuous, for quality of the artless – couldn't have been at all.' My answer to all which bristled of course with more professions than I can or need report here; the chief of them inevitably to the effect that my supposedly typical little figure was of course pure poetry, and had never been anything else; since this is what helpful imagination, in however slight a dose, ever directly makes for.[11]

Both Morris Gedge in 'The Birthplace' and the telegraphist of 'In the Cage' might be said to exhibit 'all too much imagination'. At the end of the latter *nouvelle*, the telegraphist finally sees 'in the whole business . . . the vivid reflexion of her own dreams and delusions and her own return to reality', and it falls, not to our telegraphist whose imaginings we have followed throughout this long tale, but to the butler Mr Drake to reveal the truth about the shabby amatory intriguings of the tale's various telegram-sending aristocrats. In 'The Birthplace' Morris Gedge almost loses his job as guide and caretaker because of his initial inability to play along with the tourists' need for stories about Shakespeare's birthplace, and then, abandoning his critical sense for the creative, triumphantly does his job only too well in vastly embellishing the Shakespearean legend. We might read these two tales as satire, indeed as punitive revelations of illusion. Thus 'In the Cage' might take its place in the tradition of prose fiction – of which Jane Austen and George Eliot are famous exponents – which judges the delusions of young women led astray by reading cheap, romantic fiction. 'The Birthplace' is a trenchant and prescient critique of the ways in which culture has come to serve cynical commercial tourism: James predicted with extraordinary accuracy the dismal 'Show' of present-day Stratford, even down to the catering franchises, the '*buffet* farmed out to a great firm'. But this story, as it initially occurred to James and is recorded in his *Notebooks*,[12] ends with the protagonist denying Shakespeare, refusing to play to the needs of the tourists and being dismissed: wouldn't that be enough to secure James's satirical point – without need of the tale's glorious, imaginative coda? And, in the case of 'In the Cage', would we as readers really prefer what the butler saw – the shoddy aristocratic connivings told to us by Mr Drake? There is an imaginative excess in both these tales, an excess centred on their protagonists, which compels our admiration. Both Morris Gedge – described as 'really a genius' – and the telegraphist are artists, and if their imaginings exhibit something of what James in 'The Middle Years' calls 'the madness of art', they are nonetheless artists of a kind remarkably close to James himself. In particular, the action of 'In the Cage' is, according to James, 'simply the girl's "subjective" adventure – that of her quite definitely winged intelligence'; and, like the reader, he too wonders that such a seemingly unpromising adventure should have 'whirled us so far'.[13] The telegraphist creates a huge adventure from mere scraps – the truncated staccato words and numbers of telegram messages. This ability to make so much out of so little proves to be an especially close parallel to Henry James's own typical practice as a writer. It was often the case that others – at the dinner table and in other sociable circumstances – would give him ideas or 'germs' for stories and he himself wanted to hear them, but not too much of them – there was a limit to what he wanted to hear or to know since 'anything more than the minimum . . . spoils the [creative] operation'.[14]

The tales here are a full and varied record of the worlds of the later nineteenth and early twentieth centuries, but they also resist those worlds to pursue 'the reaction, the opposition or the escape' and to cultivate an artistic consciousness in despite of and in rebuke of reality. They are of an inclusiveness which accommodates both the real and the imaginary, the actual and the creative.

A DRAMA OF SIGNS AND LANGUAGES

In 'Four Meetings', prior to what amounts, especially in pre-aircraft days, to her comically, pathetically brief day-trip – a mere thirteen hours – in Europe, the American heroine, Caroline Spencer, asks of our narrator: 'Do you know the foreign languages?' It is a question, variously posed and variously answered, which will structure the tale. The diverse replies received in the course of the story are revealingly equivocal: 'After a fashion'; 'Some kinds'; 'I do, madam – *tant bien que mal.*' James's early stories play over what is literally a diverse array of European languages, but all his stories are dramas of translation. Realist novels often invite readers to enter their imaginatively realized worlds and, as it were, to leave words behind: language is offered merely as a transparent window on the world. By contrast, James's novels and tales are always linguistically self-conscious. Writing on 'The Question of Our Speech', he explained the primacy of language:

All life therefore comes back to the question of our speech, the medium through which we communicate with each other; for all life comes back to the question of our relations with each other. These relations are made possible, are registered, are verily constituted, by our speech, and are successful . . . in proportion as our speech is worthy of its great human and social function; is developed, delicate, flexible, rich – an adequate accomplished fact. The more it suggests and expresses the more we live by it – the more it promotes and enhances life. Its quality, its authenticity, its security, are hence supremely important for the general multifold opportunity, for the dignity and integrity, of our existence.[15]

James tells stories through words but he also tells stories about words. They are the very stuff of his tales; quotation marks, italics and repetitions isolate words and phrases as objects in themselves to be held inquiringly up to the light, as it were, wondered at and puzzled over. Characters are forever picking up on each other's words, repeating them and questioning them ('The Pension Beaurepas' offers such dialogue in particularly pure form). Such linguistic self-consciousness makes for a habit of voice in James's tales which, even in the smallest details, calls the reader's attention to different ways of thinking and to the different cultures represented by different languages, signs, idioms and conventions. A lot may be lost in translation. People may be lost in translation. Opportunities and constraints cannot always be translated. Signs may all too easily be misread or mistranslated. Above all, too dogmatic and single-minded a reading of people's words and actions, of the people who speak and act – and, by extension, of stories about such people, can be deadening and destructive: that is the one message, the 'figure in the carpet', which these open and exploratory tales consistently offer their readers.

Is a 'jeune fille' the same thing as an 'American girl'? And what is to become of Aurora Church ('The Pension Beaurepas') who is in the particular – and perhaps false – position of being neither? Aurora speaks four languages, but is she entirely sure that she knows (American) English? How does a 'flirt' differ from a 'coquette'? How is Winterbourne to interpret Daisy Miller's various sayings and doings? And how, in turn, are we to understand Winterbourne? Winterbourne will never be more wrong than when he believes that Daisy Miller was 'easy to read'. Henry St George, the Master of 'The Lesson of the Master', is a 'text . . . a style considerably involved, a language not easy to translate at sight'. His is a text which neither we nor the narrator shall ever satisfactorily resolve. Morgan Moreen, 'The Pupil', is 'as puzzling as a page in an unknown language . . . Indeed the whole mystic volume in which the boy had been amateurishly bound demanded some practice in translation.' Morgan's baffling family speak 'Ultramoreen', 'an ingenious dialect of their own, an elastic spoken cipher'. The greatest interpretative challenge among these tales is perhaps the compressed words and numbers of the telegrams which make for the drama of 'In the Cage'. The greatest joke is 'The Figure in the Carpet', where as readers we are invited to worry over the interpretation of writings which are entirely withheld from us.

At the centre of this concern with reading and with languages is an obsession with names and naming.[16] James's *Notebooks* are often nothing more and nothing less than long lists of names, often gathered from real life – from the pages of that day's *Times* for example – to be put to fictional use. Perhaps the peculiarities of his own name contributed to his fascination. Born into the burden of a famous family name, Henry James nevertheless had in one sense no name of his own but, until he was nearly forty years of age, was merely his father's second son and namesake, Henry (or Harry) James Junior: the later title of 'Master' or 'cher Maître' which younger writers accorded him was clearly a welcome compensation.

Are Jamesian names telltale? Are names in direct accord with the realities they offer to describe? Or is the relation instead an ironic and inverted one? Or is there no such relation at all? James does not use names to fix character but, in keeping with his imaginative generosity, deploys names interrogatively and teasingly as part of the comic play of a story's interpretative possibilities. Daisy Miller seems doubly ordinary – a common but pretty flower; a worthy but mundane occupation – and is mocked as such in Mrs Costello's deliberate misrememberings of Daisy's name as Miss Baker or Miss Chandler. But, in the course of the tale and at great cost, does not Daisy prove herself *extra*ordinary under the cold eyes of Winterbourne? There is, moreover, another ironic naming in the same tale in the figure of Mrs Walker who does not in fact walk but travels by carriage and who, in one of the narrative's great moments of confrontation, wishes that Daisy would do likewise. In 'In the Cage' names multiply riotously – the camply priapic Everard who is also the Captain, Philip, Phil, the Count, William, 'the Pink 'Un' and – an especial confusion – Mudge; Lady Bradeen at Twindle and Doctor Buzzard at Brickwood; Lady Ventnor, Mrs Bubb and Lord Rye; Fritz and Gussy and Mary and Cissy; Miss Dolman for whom it is always Cooper's and never Burfield's; the Mr Mudge who is *not* Captain Everard; Mr Buckton, Mr Drake, Mr Cocker and 'Mr Cocker's young men'. Yet the story's heroine remains without a name just as she remains largely unnoticed and without an identity for her many customers throughout the tale. The only role which awaits her proves to be that of Mrs Mudge, a muddy smudge of a name. Yet her patient fiancé is greater – both more generous and more heroic – than his name. Like the telegraphist, Shakespeare goes unnamed in 'The Birthplace' – but for quite other reasons. The eponymous, much engaged heroine of 'Julia Bride' is destined, it seems, never to fulfil her name, beset as she is by the damaging attentions of the likes of Mrs George Maule in a very proper New York 'not in sympathy with the old American freedom'. The 'waning April days' will see the failure of any relationship between John Marcher and May Bartram in 'The Beast in the Jungle'.

James seems to take particular delight in the naming of artists, and in their soubriquets and pseudonyms. He relishes, for example, the suggestions of the vain and the feigning in the work of the novelist Greville Fane, who 'wrote only from the elbow down' and whose 'real' name – Mrs Stormer – is no less expressive. In 'The Death of the Lion', the lion in question, Neil Paraday, hovers between parody and paragon, while James has great fun with the aggressive futurity of the gossip columnist, Mr Morrow, and the cross-gendered novelists, Guy Walsingham, 'a pretty little girl', and Dora Forbes, the male, red-moustached author of *The Other Way Round*. Even the tales' titles may involve naming jokes. This is the case with the misnomer of 'Fordham Castle', as we shall see below. It is true too of 'The Pension Beaurepas' where the plot, such as it is, turns on the eating of an ice-cream.

THE LIFE OF THE ARTIST

James's writing gathers its energy from increasing uncertainty – at times empowering, at times frightening – about what life is, and what life should be, and about how that life should be represented in art. It is unsurprising in such circumstances that his art should become self-conscious and that so many of the tales here centre on the life of the artist. As the nineteenth century progressed, the artist's claim to representation, and in particular to realistic representation, was being challenged by new media and by new technology: newspapers, advertising, photography. The written word, which assumed an intimacy between the individual writer and the individual reader, was challenged by the telegraph, which compressed eloquence into staccato phrases, numbers, and indeed mere clicks of sound and electrical impulses, and sent them over great distances, across oceans, rendering them at once more public, more anonymous and more cryptic. The telephone soon followed. In the tales here, in addition to the profusion of telegrams in 'In the Cage', one telegram precipitates 'Greville Fane' and another effects a major turn in the plot of 'The Pupil'. Journalism, advertising and photography press in on and harry the various artists in, for example, 'The Real Thing', 'The Death of the Lion', 'The Lesson of the Master' and 'Broken Wings'. The real thing became doubly problematic: the artist was unsure of the reality of his subject, and unsure of the adequacy of his medium in representing that subject. Print proliferated, yet the elegy for a written and verbal culture had begun.

'The Real Thing', with a double focus on the dilemma of the painter and on that of the socially displaced, is a humane and wittily paradoxical exposition of such matters. The artist narrator discovers that, as a source of inspiration for his art, he prefers his professional models to the '*immensely*' photographed Monarchs, the 'real thing'. When he works from the Monarchs, his art suffers. Yet Major Monarch and his wife, 'the Beautiful Statue', reduced to seeking paid work as artists' models, are no more what they appear to be, no more the 'real thing', than are the professional models. The impoverished Monarchs are now hard pressed to keep up appearances and, as Major Monarch well knows, the couple are merely two among the many 'thousands as good as yourself already on the ground' and in straitened circumstances. The ironically named Monarchs go on to prove inadequate models, and serve momentarily as servants before being finally bought off and dismissed from the narrator's sight. The social instability of which they are a symptom compounds the challenge of representation which the artist faces, and the story delights in the paradoxes and contradictions which such a challenge throws up. So the distinguished appearance of Major Monarch 'would have struck me as a celebrity if celebrities often were striking'. The narrator learns that 'a figure with a good deal of frontage was, as one might say, almost never a public institution'. The tale begins in a comic confusion over who – artist or models – is going to pay whom. The narrator declares a Wildean 'preference for the represented subject over the real one: the defect of the real one was so apt to be a lack of representation'. Artistic drawings of Mrs Monarch turn out, topsy turvy, to look like nothing more than 'a copy of a photograph'. And the narrative puns zanily on figures physical, artistic and financial, on what fits and is fitting, on copies and copiousness. In the course of the tale, the 'real thing' proves itself to be 'the wrong thing': reality and aesthetic rightness are no longer in any easy relation.

If life and art are in difficulties, then what of life and the artist? At the close of 'The Middle Years' the dying novelist Dencombe announces oddly but movingly: 'We work in the dark – we do what we can – we give what we have. Our doubt is our passion and our passion is our task. The rest is the madness of art.' Few of James's artists have an easy time of it. It is remarkable how many tales here involve the death of the artist: 'Greville Fane', 'The Middle Years', 'The Death of the Lion', 'The Figure in the Carpet', 'The Real Right Thing' and – stretching the term 'artist' to include men of letters – 'The Abasement of the Northmores'. While death comes all too often and all too soon, life, in the form of reciprocated and realized love, seems to elude the artist. Or perhaps the artist deliberately evades love, or he is tricked by others into such evasion – as might be the case in 'The Lesson of the Master'. Is such evasion motivated by a concern to preserve the fineness of high art? Is it perhaps a reflection of a fear of life, and a fear of sexuality in particular? The artist tales here are a set of variations on such questions, James repeatedly configuring and reconfiguring the problems, the pressures and the pleasures of the artistic life.

ON NOT BEING THE NOVEL

One way of thinking of these tales is as jokes at the novel's expense, the tales enjoying a freedom and a fleetingness which the nineteenth-century novel in its vast interrelatedness is always denied. That joke is there in the very title of 'Fordham Castle': the narrative promises us a place and then never gets there. As a novelist James often enmeshed his writing in the vast complicating history which the great family house carries – one thinks pre-eminently of Isabel Archer in *The Portrait of a Lady*, but also of *The Spoils of Poynton* and *The Golden Bowl*. He thus enmeshed himself in a novelistic tradition which goes back through George Eliot, the Brontës, Austen (as, for example, the very title *Mansfield Park* declares) to Henry Fielding and the eighteenth century and which goes forward to D. H. Lawrence and E. M. Forster. But the tale 'Fordham Castle' is a comic misnomer, avoiding the English castle and instead putting itself out 'at board' in an anonymous Swiss *pension*. The tale ends with one of its protagonists finally setting off for a minor part in the novelistic Fordham Castle; the other promises to follow – but only 'as the ghost'. The encumbrances of marriage and paternity (or, more accurately, maternity) – the very stuff of the novel – are in this tale radically and abruptly dissolved. For example, Abel Taker's identity flickers in the dark in the 'little momentary flame' of a struck match. Identities in such tales have a freedom and an elusiveness more modern, more frightening and more free than the novel traditionally can accommodate: names quickly change and multiply; gender seems fluid; even the distinction between being alive or dead is put in question; and pages crowd with alter egos, alibis, doubles and ghosts.

'Broken Wings' too is a joke at the novel's expense: it is the story, not of a failed relationship, but of something which fails to be a relationship – and the curious final reparation in the coming together of Stuart Straith and Mrs Harvey in a mutuality of failure at the tale's close. In the wonderfully elaborated joke of the tale's opening, the protagonists hover uncertainly at the periphery of the novelistic events of a country-house weekend, but the meetings characteristic of novels do not get underway, since throughout luncheon and dinner 'no sound and no sign from the other had been picked up by either'. Indeed Straith is left wondering at 'the special oddity – for it was nothing else – of his being there at all'. 'Broken Wings' is, moreover, a vengeful snub to another great art form: our two characters go to the theatre, attending the opening night of a play set to run for three years and more, and manage to take in precisely nothing of the drama playing before them. These tales suggest versions and histories alternative to those which the novel and the theatre provide. 'Greville Fane' and 'The Death of the Lion' are stories told after the public story has been despatched by their respective narrators to newspapers and magazines. Victims in the publicly accredited world of the novel are allowed, in these stories, their private sorrows – and their private victories. Furthermore, such victories are not without an element of revenge, as in the case of 'The Abasement of the Northmores' where the widowed Mrs Hope spares Lady Northmore further public humiliation, but nonetheless cherishes her privately printed volume of intimate letters and – either selflessly or else perversely – wishes for her own death. It is precisely the element of vengefulness, the admission of negative feelings, which gives so many of these tales, predominantly of generosity and self-abnegation, their edge.

Typically these tales – even the early 'Four Meetings' – afford not the novelistic continuities of day-to-day living, but brief meetings, casual or formal, by arrangement or by chance, leaping over wide gaps of time and spanning vast distances among diverse locations. The tales put the eventfulnesses and significances of the nineteenth-century novel in question. 'The Beast in the Jungle' here, the story of a man in whose life precisely nothing is to happen, is the pre-eminent case. Even when they attempt what James once called 'the large in a small dose',[17] his tales are without the solidity and continuity of specification which we associate with the novel. They speak instead of a more modern world – a various, uncertain and often uncanny world, one of potential and opportunity, but also of terror and waste.

AGAINST INTERPRETATION

In the light of such diversity and uncertainty, perhaps we should not be too quick in fixing these tales' meanings. Particular tales here are salutary for the interpreter. Even to speak of 'The Figure in the Carpet' – the story of the monomaniacal pursuit of Hugh Vereker's literary meaning – is to become embroiled in its joke: we can become as sophisticated as we like – and critics have proved themselves extraordinarily sophisticated and ingenious – but, whatever we say, we are inevitably positing *some* figure in the carpet. It may be a secret, an absence, a misapprehension, even, as I would have it, a caution against over-zealous interpretation, but it still is a figure.[18] The interpreters within the tale are nightmarish reflections of ourselves as readers: they turn the world upside down in their obsessive pursuit of literary meaning. Marriages, engagements, illnesses of brothers, deaths of mothers, husbands and best friends are subordinate, merely a means to interpretative fulfilment. Sexuality is displaced into hermeneutics. In this crazy world the narrator sees the revelation of the literary secret as the wedding night's consummation – 'For what else but that ceremony had the nuptials taken place?' – and looks for signs of (intellectual) pregnancy in husbands:

Never, for a marriage in literary circles – so the newspapers described the alliance – had a lady been so bravely dowered. I began with due promptness to look for the fruit of the affair – that fruit, I mean, of which the premonitory symptoms would be peculiarly visible in the husband.

Both life *and* literature suffer as the narrator reveals that his obsession with Vereker's meaning 'damaged my liking', destroying the pleasures of the texts: 'Instead of being a pleasure the more they became a resource the less.'

In another cautionary tale for readers, 'The Death of the Lion', Neil Paraday, the literary lion in question, endures a fate perhaps worse than the ultimate one which awaits him at the tale's close. He is made 'a contemporary': 'the poor man was to be squeezed into his horrible age'. Such ostensible popularity involves remaking the artist to serve society's image. It involves *not* reading him, and indeed literally losing the one copy of Paraday's latest and last manuscript somewhere between Lady Augusta's maid and Lord Dorimont's man. It is perhaps inevitable that to appropriate an author, to render him *our* contemporary, is also, in some sense, to lose him. At present, academic criticism of James is focused on matters of gender, and James's writings are daring to speak their homosexuality. Of May Bartram's relationship with John Marcher in 'The Beast in the Jungle', the narrative records: 'The rest of the world of course thought him queer, but she, she only, knew how, and above all why, queer; which was precisely what enabled her to dispose the concealing veil in the right folds.'[19] Among the tales here, the veil is currently being professionally lifted in the cases of 'The Pupil', 'The Middle Years', 'In the Cage', 'The Beast in the Jungle' and 'The Jolly Corner'; and while these are strong and plausible readings they are also somewhat disappointing. They insist on the possible fact of a homosexual interpretation; they are less persuasive that the tales are saying anything distinctive and particular about homosexuality. While politically radical they are in method critically old-fashioned and somewhat oppressive: what is proffered initially as a possible meaning of a tale very quickly becomes *the* meaning. For all the political liberation they appear to offer, they narrow the possibilities of interpretation, and the pleasures of James's texts are somehow lost amidst our contemporary political zeal.[20]

In 1964 the American critic and thinker Susan Sontag published a wonderful polemical essay 'Against Interpretation'.[21] Her argument is particularly apposite to the short story and to Henry James's tales, where the comparative brevity of these writings, and their diverse plurality, ask that we respect their reticence and their refusal to have the final authoritative say. We can bring various contexts – biographical, historical and critical – to bear on James's tales; we can, for example, read them as marginal and illuminating commentary on the fulsome major novels; but we damage these tales, for ourselves and for future readers, if we fix their meanings, squeeze them into our own age and our own intellectual and political agendas. In place of interpretation Sontag argued for an 'erotics of art' – a phrase we might presently misunderstand because of our current emphasis on the sexualities of writing and on the politics of desire. But her emphasis was intended to return us to the *experiential* nature of art, to the 'sensory experience' as it unfolds in time. What we experience as we read Henry James – from individual sentences to the whole works which these sentences go to make up – is a delicate play of multiplying, ever transforming interpretative possibilities, an entangling, puzzling, pleasurable play of meaning.

James himself knew the value of the *experience* of reading; he repeatedly advised readers to take him slowly; and in his last tale, 'A Round of Visits', he wrote of 'a momentary watcher – which is indeed what I can but invite the reader to become'.[22] It is now time for the reader to take up that invitation and, given that it comes from a tale not reprinted here, eventually perhaps to extend the acquaintance with James's tales even beyond those in this substantial volume.

NOTES

1. Randall Jarrell, 'Stories' (first published 1962), in *The New Short Story Theories*, ed. Charles E. May (Athens: Ohio University Press, 1994), p. 8.

2. Henry James, Preface to 'The Lesson of the Master' (1908), in *Literary Criticism: French Writers; Other European Writers; The Prefaces to the New York Edition* (New York: Library of America, 1984), p. 1227.

3. *The Complete Notebooks of Henry James*, ed. Leon Edel and Lyall H. Powers (New York and Oxford: Oxford University Press, 1987), pp. 54, 57.

4. *The Letters of Matthew Arnold to Arthur Hugh Clough*, ed. Howard Foster Lowry (Oxford: Clarendon Press, 1932), p. 97.

5. F. O. Matthiessen, *The James Family: A Group Biography* (1947; New York: Vintage Books, 1980), p. 303.

6. Henry James, 'The Art of Fiction' (1884), in *Literary Criticism: Essays on Literature; American Writers; English Writers* (New York: Library of America, 1984), pp. 52–3.

7. Ibid., p. 53.

8. *Henry James and H. G. Wells: A Record of their Friendship, their Debate on the Art of Fiction, and their Quarrel*, ed. Leon Edel and Gordon N. Ray (London: Rupert Hart-Davis, 1958), pp. 248, 249.

9. *Henry James: A Life in Letters*, ed. Philip Horne (London: Allen Lane, 1999), p. 555.

10. Henry James, Preface to 'The Lesson of the Master', in *Literary Criticism: French Writers*, pp. 1229–30.

11. Henry James, Preface to 'Daisy Miller' (1909), in *Literary Criticism: French Writers*, pp. 1270–71.

12. *Complete Notebooks*, ed. Edel and Powers, p. 195.

13. Henry James, Preface to *What Maisie Knew* (1908), in *Literary Criticism: French Writers*, pp. 1170–71.

14. Henry James, Preface to *The Spoils of Poynton* (1908), in *Literary Criticism: French Writers*, p. 1138.

15. Henry James, *The Question of Our Speech; The Lesson of Balzac: Two Lectures* (Boston and New York: Houghton Mifflin, 1905), p. 10.

16. On the comedy of names generally, see Anne Barton, *The Names of Comedy* (Toronto: University of Toronto Press, 1990); on James's playful naming – and in particular on the implications for sexuality and gender of such play, see Hugh Stevens, *Henry James and Sexuality* (Cambridge: Cambridge University Press, 1998).

17. Henry James, 'The Story-Teller at Large: Mr Henry Harland' (1898), in *Literary Criticism: Essays on Literature*, p. 285.

18. For the important and influential argument that James's narratives are dependent on a secret or an absent cause, see Tzvetan Todorov, 'The Secret of Narrative', *The Poetics of Prose*, trans. Richard Howard (Ithaca, NY: Cornell University Press, 1977), pp. 143–78.

19. In *Twentieth Century Words* (Oxford: Oxford University Press, 1999), p. 166, John Ayto dates 'queer' meaning 'homosexual' to 1922 and states that the usage did not become widespread until the 1930s. This is, of course, long after James. However, evidence of word usage is never conclusive – not least in the case of language naming controversial or taboo subjects.

20. See, for example, Eve Kosofsky Sedgwick, 'The Beast in the Closet: James and the Writing of Homosexual Panic', *Epistemology of the Closet* (London: Harvester Wheatsheaf, 1990), pp. 182–212. Philip Horne has taken the pains to point out the inadequacies of such readings in his 'The Master and the "Queer Affair" of "The Pupil" ', in *Henry James: The Shorter Fiction – Reassessments* (Basingstoke: Macmillan, 1997), pp. 114–37.

21. Susan Sontag, 'Against Interpretation' (1964), in *A Susan Sontag Reader* (Harmondsworth: Penguin, 1983), pp. 95–104.

22. Henry James, 'A Round of Visits' (1910), in *The Complete Tales of Henry James*, ed. Leon Edel, Vol. 12, 1903–1910 (London: Rupert Hart-Davis, 1964), p. 449.

FURTHER READING

BIBLIOGRAPHY

Edel, Leon and Dan H. Laurence, *A Bibliography of Henry James*, 3rd edn. (Oxford: Clarendon Press, 1982)

LIFE AND LETTERS

A Small Boy and Others (New York: Scribner's, 1913); *Notes of a Son and Brother* (New York: Scribner's, 1914); and *The Middle Years* (Glasgow: Collins, 1917) (autobiographies)

Henry James: A Life in Letters, ed. Philip Horne (London: Allen Lane, 1999)

The Letters of Henry James, ed. Percy Lubbock, 2 vols. (London: Macmillan, 1920); *Selected Letters of Henry James*, ed. Leon Edel (London: Rupert Hart-Davis, 1956); and *Henry James Letters*, ed. Leon Edel, 4 vols. (Cambridge, Mass.: Belknap Press, 1974–84) (these volumes overlap to some extent)

The Correspondence of Henry James and Henry Adams 1877–1914, ed. George Monteiro (Baton Rouge: Louisiana State University Press, 1992)

Letters, Fictions, Lives: Henry James and William Dean Howells, ed. Michael Anesko (New York and Oxford: Oxford University Press, 1997)

The Correspondence of Henry James and the House of Macmillan, 1877–1914, ed. Rayburn S. Moore (Basingstoke: Macmillan, 1993)

Henry James and Robert Louis Stevenson: A Record of Friendship and Criticism, ed. Janet Adam Smith (London: Rupert Hart-Davis, 1948)

Henry James and H. G. Wells: A Record of their Friendship, their Debate on the Art of Fiction, and their Quarrel, ed. Leon Edel and Gordon N. Ray (London: Rupert Hart-Davis, 1958)

Henry James and Edith Wharton: Letters 1900–1915, ed. Lyall H. Powers (London: Weidenfeld and Nicolson, 1990)

JAMES'S WRITINGS

The Novels and Tales of Henry James, 24 vols. (New York: Charles Scribner's Sons, 1907–9; London: Macmillan, 1908–9) (New York Edition)

The Complete Tales of Henry James, ed. Leon Edel, 12 vols. (London: Rupert Hart-Davis, 1962–4) (prints the texts of the first book publications)

The Tales of Henry James, ed. Maqbool Aziz (Oxford: Clarendon Press, 1973–   ), 3 vols. to date (prints the texts of the first publication, usually in magazines)

The Art of the Novel, ed. R. P. Blackmur (New York: Scribner's, 1962) (Collected Prefaces to the New York Edition)

The Critical Muse: Selected Literary Criticism, ed. Roger Gard (London: Penguin, 1987)

Literary Criticism: French Writers; Other European Writers; The Prefaces to the New York Edition (New York: Library of America, 1984)

Literary Criticism: Essays on Literature; American Writers; English Writers (New York: Library of America, 1984)

The Complete Notebooks of Henry James, ed. Leon Edel and Lyall H. Powers (New York and Oxford: Oxford University Press, 1987)

BIOGRAPHY

Edel, Leon, *Henry James*, 5 vols. (London: Rupert Hart-Davis, 1953–72)

Kaplan, Fred, *Henry James: The Imagination of Genius* (London: Hodder and Stoughton, 1992)

Lewis, R. W. B., *The Jameses: A Family Narrative* (London: André Deutsch, 1991)

Matthiessen, F. O., *The James Family: A Group Biography* (1947; New York: Vintage Books, 1980)

CRITICISM

Albers, Christina E., *A Reader's Guide to the Short Stories of Henry James* (New York: Hall, 1997)

Anesko, Michael, *'Friction with the Market': Henry James and the Profession of Authorship* (New York: Oxford University Press, 1986)

Banta, Martha, *Henry James and the Occult: The Great Extension* (Bloomington: Indiana University Press, 1972)

Bishop, George, *When the Master Relents: The Neglected Short Fictions of Henry James* (Ann Arbor: UMI, 1988)

Buelens, Gert (ed.), *Enacting History in Henry James: Narrative, Power, and Ethics* (Cambridge: Cambridge University Press, 1997)

Chambers, Ross, 'Not for the Vulgar? The Question of Readership in "The Figure in the Carpet"', *Story and Situation: Narrative Seduction and the Power of Fiction* (Minneapolis and Manchester: University of Minnesota and Manchester University Press, 1984), pp. 151–80

Chapman, Sara S., *Henry James's Portrait of the Writer as Hero* (Basingstoke: Macmillan, 1990)

Freedman, Jonathan, *The Cambridge Companion to Henry James* (Cambridge: Cambridge University Press, 1998)

Gage, Richard P., *Order and Design: Henry James' Titled Story Sequences* (New York: Peter Lang, 1988)

Gard, Roger (ed.), *Henry James: The Critical Heritage* (London: Routledge, 1982)

Goode, John (ed.), *The Air of Reality: New Essays on Henry James* (London: Methuen, 1972)

Hocks, Richard A., *Henry James: A Study of the Short Fiction* (Boston: Twayne, 1990)

Horne, Philip, *Henry James and Revision* (Oxford: Clarendon Press, 1990)

Jolly, Roslyn, *Henry James: History, Narrative, Fiction* (Oxford: Clarendon Press, 1993)

Kappeler, Susanne, *Reading and Writing in Henry James* (London: Macmillan, 1980)

Lustig, T. J., *Henry James and the Ghostly* (Cambridge: Cambridge University Press, 1994)

McWhirter, David (ed.), *Henry James's New York Edition: The Construction of Authorship* (Stanford: Stanford University Press, 1995)

Poole, Adrian, *Henry James* (London: Harvester Wheatsheaf, 1991)

Putt, S. Gorley, *A Reader's Guide to Henry James* (London: Thames and Hudson, 1966)

Reeve, N. H. (ed.), *Henry James: The Shorter Fiction – Reassessments* (Basingstoke: Macmillan, 1997)

Rimmon, Shlomith, *The Concept of Ambiguity: The Example of Henry James* (Chicago: University of Chicago Press, 1977)

Rowe, John Carlos, *The Theoretical Dimensions of Henry James* (Madison and London: University of Wisconsin Press, 1984)

Rowe, John Carlos, *The Other Henry James* (Durham and London: Duke University Press, 1998)

Sedgwick, Eve Kosofsky, 'The Beast in the Closet: James and the Writing of Homosexual Panic', *Epistemology of the Closet* (London: Harvester Wheatsheaf, 1990), pp. 182–212

Stevens, Hugh, *Henry James and Sexuality* (Cambridge: Cambridge University Press, 1998)

Tanner, Tony (ed.), *Henry James: Modern Judgements* (London: Macmillan, 1968)

Tanner, Tony, *Henry James: The Writer and his Work* (Amherst: University of Massachusetts Press, 1985) (originally published as three pamphlets by the British Council, 1979–81)

Tanner, Tony, *The Reign of Wonder: Naivety and Reality in American Literature* (Cambridge: Cambridge University Press, 1965)

Todorov, Tzvetan, 'The Secret of Narrative' and 'The Ghosts of Henry James', *The Poetics of Prose*, trans. Richard Howard (Ithaca, NY: Cornell University Press, 1977), pp. 143–78 and 179–89 respectively

Vaid, Krishna Baldev, *Technique in the Tales of Henry James* (Cambridge: Harvard University Press, 1964)

Wagenknecht, Edward, *The Tales of Henry James* (New York: Frederick Ungar, 1984)

West, Rebecca, *Henry James* (London: Nisbet and Co., 1916)

JOURNAL AND INTERNET

The *Henry James Review* (1979–) is published three times a year. The Henry James Scholar's Guide to Web Sites (www.newpaltz.edu/~hathaway/) publishes electronic texts of James's works and provides information on conferences and discussion groups.

A HENRY JAMES CHRONOLOGY

The titles of tales in this volume are marked by asterisks and at the first date of publication.

1843   Born 15 April, Washington Place, New York, the second son of Henry and Mary James. (Elder brother William – future philosopher and author of *The Varieties of Religious Experience* – born 1842.)

1843–4   Family travelling in Europe. Father experiences nervous breakdown and spiritual resurrection, and becomes a Swedenborgian.

1844–55 Childhood in Albany and then New York City; birth of brothers (Garth Wilkinson or 'Wilky', 1845; Robertson, 1847) and sister (Alice, 1848). Father, frequently visited by Ralph Waldo Emerson and others of the Transcendentalist group, despairs of American education for his children.

1855–8   Family travelling in Europe. Henry educated in France, England and Switzerland, and by private tutor.

1858   Family resident at Newport, Rhode Island. Henry befriends Francophile and painter John La Farge.

1859   Family travelling in Europe. Henry at school in Geneva (engineering at his parents' insistence; later in the humanities) and Bonn (studying German).

1860–62 Family returns to Newport. La Farge introduces Henry to contemporary French literature; Henry discovers Hawthorne. Henry injured while extinguishing a fire, which prevents active service in the Civil War (1861–5). Wilky and Robertson enlist as officers in black Massachusetts regiments; Wilky, wounded at Gettysburg, recuperates at home.

1862–4   Term at Harvard Law School; drops law in favour of a literary career. Family moves to Boston. Henry hears spiritualist lecturer, Cora L. V. Hatch, at New York, November 1863. First published tale, 'A Tragedy of Error', appears anonymously, February 1864. Begins to write book reviews for *North American Review*.

1865   'The Story of a Year' appears under his name. Writes reviews for
        Nation. Wilky and Robertson start a cotton plantation in Florida,
        employing freed slaves.

1866   Family moves to Cambridge, the Harvard University suburb.

1869–70 Travels in Europe: England, France, Switzerland and Italy. Meets George
        Eliot. Death of Minny Temple (b. 1845), his much-loved cousin.

1871   Returns to Cambridge. First novel, *Watch and Ward*, serialized in
        Atlantic Monthly.

1872–4 Travelling in Europe, at first with his aunt and sister. Writing travel
        sketches, tales and reviews in preparation for his first 'big' novel. Begins
        to become self-supporting as a writer.

1875–6 First consolidation: *Transatlantic Sketches* (travel). *A Passionate Pil-
        grim* (tales) and first important novel *Roderick Hudson* all published in
        USA. In Paris writing correspondence for *New York Tribune*. Mingles
        in the Parisian literary scene and meets Turgenev, Flaubert, Daudet,
        Zola and Maupassant. Resigns from *Tribune*, moves to England and
        settles in Piccadilly, London.

1877   *'Four Meetings'. *The American*. Again travelling in France and Italy.

1878   First English publication: *French Poets and Novelists*. *'Daisy Miller'
        published in *Cornhill Magazine*, earning real fame in England and
        USA. 'An International Episode' and *The Europeans* also reflect this
        'international theme'. Elected to the Reform Club, London, and begins
        punishing schedule of social engagements and country-house visits.

1879   *'The Pension Beaurepas'. *Hawthorne*, which disparages American
        literary culture.

1881   'Middle phase' inaugurated by successful novels *Washington Square*
        and *The Portrait of a Lady*.

1881–2 Travels to USA. Much fêted in New York; visits Washington (and
        President Chester A. Arthur). Recalled to Cambridge by his mother's
        death, January 1882. Alice and father move back to Boston. Returns to
        England in May. Travels in France. Called back to Boston by his
        father's death, December.

1883   In America dealing with his family affairs. Fourteen-volume Collective
        Edition of novels and tales published. Returns to London in September.
        Wilky dies, November.

1884   Revisits Paris and Daudet and Zola. *A Little Tour in France, Tales of
        Three Cities* and important statement of novelistic principles, 'The Art
        of Fiction', published. Starts writing *The Bostonians* in Dover, August.
        Invalid sister comes to live in England.

1886   *The Bostonians*. *The Princess Casamassima*. Moves to Chelsea.

1887	Travelling in Italy.
1888	*'The Lesson of the Master'. *The Reverberator, The Aspern Papers*.
1890	*The Tragic Muse*. Turns his attention to the theatre.
1891	*'The Pupil'. Dramatization of *The American* enjoys success in London.
1892	*'The Real Thing'. *'Greville Fane'. Alice dies, March. Still writing unproduced plays.
1893	*'The Middle Years'.
1894	*Theatricals: Two Comedies* and *Theatricals: Second Series*.
1895	*'The Death of the Lion'. Disastrous failure of play *Guy Domville* in London. Returns to fiction.
1896	*'The Figure in the Carpet'.
1897	*The Spoils of Poynton. What Maisie Knew*. Begins to compose by dictation.
1898	*'In the Cage'. Moves to Lamb House, Rye, Sussex. 'The Turn of the Screw', his most appreciated publication since 'Daisy Miller'.
1899	*'The Real Right Thing'. 'Late phase' inaugurated by *The Awkward Age*. New agent and business arrangements refresh sense of vocation.
1900	*'Broken Wings'. *'The Abasement of the Northmores'.
1901	*The Sacred Fount*.
1902	*The Wings of the Dove*.
1903	*'The Beast in the Jungle'. *'The Birth Place'. *The Ambassadors*.
1904	*'Fordham Castle'. *The Golden Bowl*.
1904–5	Travels and lectures in the USA after twenty-year absence; elected to American Academy of Arts and Letters.
1906	Writes eighteen prefaces for new collection of his fiction.
1907	*The American Scene*. Publication begins of the New York Edition, 24 vols. (1907–9).
1908	*'Julia Bride'. *'The Jolly Corner'. Depressed by poor sales of New York Edition and various illnesses. Burns private papers. *Italian Hours* (travel).
1910	Still profoundly depressed. Travels in Germany with ailing William; they return to the USA after death of Robertson, June. William dies, August. Spends winter in America.
1911–12	Honorary degree from Harvard. Returns to England and takes flat in Chelsea. Honorary degree from Oxford.
1913	Presented with a golden bowl by admirers, and has his portrait painted by John Singer Sargent, both as part of seventieth birthday celebrations. First volume of autobiography. *A Small Boy and Others*.
1914	*Notes of a Son and Brother*. Profoundly disturbed by outbreak of the Great War, visits wounded and refugees in hospital. *Notes on Novelists* (mainly the nineteenth-century French realists) published.

1915   Becomes a British subject to change his status as wartime 'alien'. Suffers stroke in December.

1916   Awarded Order of Merit by George V, New Year's Day. Dies, 28 February. Funeral in Chelsea Old Church; ashes buried in family grave, Cambridge, Massachusetts.

1917   Publication of *The Middle Years* (autobiography) and works of fiction – *The Ivory Tower* and *The Sense of the Past*, both incomplete.

1921–3   Complete edition of novels and tales published by Macmillan.

A NOTE ON THE TEXTS

Typically James would publish a tale in a magazine, revise it for publication as part of a collection of tales and revise again for subsequent publications, including the great but commercially unsuccessful 24-volume New York Edition (1907–9). It is the texts of the New York Edition which are printed here. Any choice of one text over another involves losses as well as gains. What is lost here is the possibility first, to have direct experience of James the young writer and secondly, to see, moving from early tales to late, a broad view of his development as a writer. However, the latter has already been forfeited by the drastic selection of a mere 19 stories out of 112. The gain, in choosing the texts of the New York Edition, lies, first, in being true to the fact of revision as a central aspect of James's creativity (never merely as an afterthought), and secondly – this point is admittedly contentious, a matter of taste and for critical argument – in printing what the present editor believes are, by and large, better versions than their earlier incarnations. Jamesian revision is overwhelmingly improvement; he did *not* convert earlier lucidities into what some feel to be the indirect obscurities of the late style, and indeed, many of the revisions serve greater precision, clarity and vividness. Here the reader will find in the Notes of 'Four Meetings' and 'Daisy Miller' a selection of wording variants between the first magazine publication and the New York Edition, so he or she can get a sense of James as reviser. However, other large changes are less easily represented in notes – in particular, the general lightening of punctuation in the New York Edition. Its much scantier use of the comma diminishes the controlling, shaping and placing that such punctuation often entails. The reader thus is more involved in a *continuous* experience of wondering and puzzling, has perhaps to work harder in making provisional sense of the story as it unfolds, but is rewarded by a more thoroughgoing engagement in interpretative play.

Penguin house-styling has been minimized: double quotation marks are made singles (and vice versa), stops in personal titles and abbreviations are dropped (Mr, Mrs, Dr, St), dashes are spaced en-dashes, vowels are not ligatured and punctuation following a single italic word is not italicized. The unusual spaced contractions of the New York Edition (e.g. I'd, would n't) have been regularized, but its spelling and punctuation have been retained. James's frequent lists of adjectives and adverbs without commas (e.g. 'the large simple scared foolish fond woman' and 'the long lean loose slightly cadaverous gentleman' in 'Fordham Castle') are left intact, but in about half a dozen instances the omission of a necessary comma has been rectified. In fewer than a dozen instances has consistency of hyphenation or italicization been imposed, and one spelling has been corrected. The apparent error of a section number 'I' at the start of 'The Middle Years' (with no 'II') has been omitted, although some critics have argued ingeniously that this is a deliberate joke, alluding to the fact that there is to be no second chance for Dencombe.

SELECTION PRINCIPLES

Any selection should include some account of the principles on which it was made. My aim has been to represent something of the diversity, in both style and subject matter, of James as a writer of tales, and to offer some compromise between the familiar and expected and the less well-known. The emphasis has rightly fallen on the former category, but it is hoped that some of the tales here – 'The Pension Beaurepas', 'Greville Fane', 'In the Cage', 'Broken Wings', 'The Abasement of the Northmores', 'The Birthplace', 'Fordham Castle' – will be less familiar and neither less interesting nor less enjoyable for that. 'The Turn of the Screw' (1898) and 'The Aspern Papers' (1888) have been excluded simply because they are long and very familiar and are already available in Penguin editions. A few works were excluded on the unfashionable grounds that they seemed to the present editor not to merit their current reputations: at worst, such a view may merely be a provocation to readers to see for themselves in the case of, for example, 'The Altar of the Dead' (1895), 'Glasses' (1896), 'The Great Good Place' (1900) and 'The Bench of Desolation' (1909–10). Beyond these points, principles of selection give way merely to a list of regrets. In particular, it is regrettable that only lack of space has led to the exclusion of any tale earlier than 1877. Here 'A Landscape Painter' (1866), James's extraordinary modern reading of *Hamlet*, 'Master Eustace' (1871), 'The Madonna of the Future' (1873) and 'Madame de Mauves' (1874) all have strong claims on our attention. Above all, one regrets that absence of the long and admittedly somewhat meandering 'A Passionate Pilgrim' (1871), in which an American confronts the ghost of what it might have meant to stay in Europe in a way which anticipates 'A Jolly Corner', Spencer Brydon's confrontation with the ghostly self who has stayed in America. Here, as in pairing 'Daisy Miller' and 'Julia Bride', late James is in mirroring dialogue with his earlier self in ways which further substantiate the claim made in the Introduction that Henry James's creative life may been read as a life of tales. Perhaps finally one must recognize that a selection justifies itself only in the dissatisfactions it induces in readers – and in the stimulus it affords them to seek more of the author's tales.

Four Meetings

I saw her but four times, though I remember them vividly; she made her impression on me. I thought her very pretty and very interesting – a touching specimen of a type with which I had had other and perhaps less charming associations. I'm sorry to hear of her death, and yet when I think of it why *should* I be? The last time I saw her she was certainly not – ! But it will be of interest to take our meetings in order.

I

The first was in the country, at a small tea-party, one snowy night of some seventeen years ago. My friend Latouche, going to spend Christmas with his mother, had insisted on my company, and the good lady had given in our honour the entertainment of which I speak. To me it was really full of savour – it had all the right marks: I had never been in the depths of New England at that season. It had been snowing all day and the drifts were knee-high. I wondered how the ladies had made their way to the house; but I inferred that just those general rigours rendered any assembly[1] offering the attraction of two gentlemen from New York worth a desperate effort.

Mrs Latouche in the course of the evening asked me if I 'didn't want to' show the photographs to some of the young ladies. The photographs were in a couple of great portfolios, and had been brought home by her son, who, like myself, was lately returned from Europe. I looked round and was struck with the fact that most of the young ladies were provided with an object of interest more absorbing than the most vivid sun-picture. But there was a person alone near the mantel-shelf who looked round the room with a small vague smile, a discreet, a disguised yearning, which seemed somehow at odds with her isolation. I looked at her a moment and then chose. 'I should like to show them to that young lady.'

'Oh yes,' said Mrs Latouche, 'she's just the person. She doesn't care for flirting

– I'll speak to her.' I replied that if she didn't care for flirting she wasn't perhaps just the person; but Mrs Latouche had already, with a few steps, appealed to her participation. 'She's delighted,' my hostess came back to report; 'and she's just the person – so quiet and so bright.' And she told me the young lady was by name Miss Caroline Spencer – with which she introduced me.

Miss Caroline Spencer was not quite a beauty, but was none the less, in her small odd way, formed to please. Close upon thirty, by every presumption, she was made almost like a little girl and had the complexion of a child. She had also the prettiest head, on which her hair was arranged as nearly as possible like the hair of a Greek bust, though indeed it was to be doubted if she had ever seen a Greek bust. She was 'artistic,' I suspected, so far as the polar influences of North Verona[2] could allow for such yearnings or could minister to them. Her eyes were perhaps just too round and too inveterately surprised,[3] but her lips had a certain mild decision and her teeth, when she showed them, were charming. About her neck she wore what ladies call, I believe, a 'ruche'[4] fastened with a very small pin of pink coral, and in her hand she carried a fan made of plaited straw and adorned with pink ribbon. She wore a scanty black silk dress. She spoke with slow soft neatness, even without smiles showing the prettiness of her teeth, and she seemed extremely pleased, in fact quite fluttered, at the prospect of my demonstrations. These went forward very smoothly after I had moved the portfolios out of their corner and placed a couple of chairs near a lamp. The photographs were usually things I knew – large views of Switzerland, Italy and Spain, landscapes, reproductions of famous buildings, pictures and statues. I said what I could for them, and my companion, looking at them as I held them up, sat perfectly still, her straw fan raised to her under-lip and gently, yet, as I could feel, almost excitedly, rubbing it. Occasionally, as I laid one of the pictures down, she said without confidence, which would have been too much: 'Have you seen that place?' I usually answered that I had seen it several times – I had been a great traveller, though I was somehow particularly admonished not to swagger – and then I felt her look at me askance for a moment with her pretty eyes. I had asked her at the outset whether she had been to Europe; to this she had answered 'No, no, no' – almost as much below her breath as if the image of such an event scarce, for solemnity, brooked phrasing. But after that, though she never took her eyes off the pictures, she said so little that I feared she was at last bored. Accordingly when we had finished one portfolio I offered, if she desired it, to desist. I rather guessed the exhibition really held her, but her reticence puzzled me and I wanted to make her speak. I turned round to judge better and then saw a faint flush in each of her cheeks. She kept waving her little fan to and fro. Instead of looking at me she fixed her eyes on the remainder of the collection, which leaned, in its receptacle, against the table.

'Won't you show me that?' she quavered, drawing the long breath of a person launched and afloat but conscious of rocking a little.[5]

'With pleasure,' I answered, 'if you're really not tired.'

'Oh I'm not tired a bit. I'm just fascinated.' With which as I took up the other portfolio she laid her hand on it, rubbing it softly. 'And have you been here too?'

On my opening the portfolio it appeared I had indeed been there. One of the first photographs was a large view of the Castle of Chillon[6] by the Lake of Geneva. 'Here,' I said, 'I've been many a time. Isn't it beautiful?' And I pointed to the perfect reflexion of the rugged rocks and pointed towers in the clear still water. She didn't say 'Oh enchanting!' and push it away to see the next picture. She looked a while and then asked if it weren't where Bonnivard, about whom Byron wrote,[7] had been confined. I assented, trying to quote Byron's verses, but not quite bringing it off.

She fanned herself a moment and then repeated the lines correctly, in a soft flat voice but with charming conviction. By the time she had finished, she was nevertheless blushing. I complimented her and assured her she was perfectly equipped for visiting Switzerland and Italy. She looked at me askance again, to see if I might be serious, and I added that if she wished to recognise Byron's descriptions she must go abroad speedily – Europe was getting sadly dis-Byronised. 'How soon must I go?' she thereupon enquired.

'Oh I'll give you ten years.'

'Well, I guess I can go in *that* time,' she answered as if measuring her words.

'Then you'll enjoy it immensely,' I said; 'you'll find it of the highest interest.' Just then I came upon a photograph of some nook in a foreign city which I had been very fond of and which recalled tender memories. I discoursed (as I suppose) with considerable spirit; my companion sat listening breathless.

'Have you been *very* long over there?' she asked some time after I had ceased.

'Well, it mounts up, put all the times together.'

'And have you travelled everywhere?'

'I've travelled a good deal. I'm very fond of it and happily have been able.'

Again she turned on me her slow shy scrutiny. 'Do you know the foreign languages?'

'After a fashion.'

'Is it hard to speak them?'

'I don't imagine you'd find it so,' I gallantly answered.

'Oh I shouldn't want to speak – I should only want to listen.' Then on a pause she added: 'They say the French theatre's so beautiful.'

'Ah the best in the world.'

'Did you go there very often?'

'When I was first in Paris I went every night.'

'Every night!' And she opened her clear eyes very wide. 'That to me is' – and her expression hovered – 'as if you tell me a fairy-tale.' A few minutes later she put to me: 'And which country do you prefer?'

'There's one I love beyond any. I think you'd do the same.'

Her gaze rested as on a dim revelation and then she breathed 'Italy?'

'Italy,' I answered softly too; and for a moment we communed over it. She looked as pretty as if instead of showing her photographs I had been making love to her. To increase the resemblance she turned off blushing. It made a pause which she broke at last by saying: 'That's the place which – in particular – I thought of going to.'

'Oh that's the place – that's the place!' I laughed.

She looked at two or three more views in silence. 'They say it's not very dear.'

'As some other countries? Well, one gets back there one's money. That's not the least of the charms.'

'But it's *all* very expensive, isn't it?'

'Europe, you mean?'

'Going there and travelling. That has been the trouble. I've very little money. I teach, you know,' said Miss Caroline Spencer.

'Oh of course one must have money,' I allowed; 'but one can manage with a moderate amount judiciously spent.'

'I think I should manage. I've saved and saved up, and I'm always adding a little to it. It's all for that.' She paused a moment, and then went on with suppressed eagerness, as if telling me the story were a rare, but possibly an impure satisfaction. 'You see it hasn't been only the money – it has been everything. Everything has acted against it. I've waited and waited. It has been my castle in the air. I'm almost afraid to talk about it. Two or three times it has come a little nearer, and then I've talked about it and it has melted away. I've talked about it too much,' she said hypocritically – for I saw such talk was now a small tremulous ecstasy. 'There's a lady who's a great friend of mine – she doesn't want to go, but I'm always at her about it. I think I must tire her dreadfully. She told me just the other day she didn't know what would become of me. She guessed I'd go crazy if I didn't sail, and yet certainly I'd go crazy if I did.'

'Well,' I laughed, 'you haven't sailed up to now – so I suppose you *are* crazy.'

She took everything with the same seriousness. 'Well, I guess I must be. It seems as if I couldn't think of anything else – and I don't require photographs to work me up! I'm always right *on* it. It kills any interest in things nearer home – things I ought to attend to. That's a kind of craziness.'

'Well then the cure for it's just to go,' I smiled – 'I mean the cure for this kind. Of course you may have the other kind worse,' I added – 'the kind you get over there.'

'Well, I've a faith that I'll go *some* time all right!' she quite elatedly cried. 'I've a relative right there on the spot,' she went on, 'and I guess he'll know how to control me.' I expressed the hope that he would, and I forget whether we turned over more photographs; but when I asked her if she had always lived just where I found her, 'Oh no sir,' she quite eagerly replied; 'I've spent twenty-two months and a half[8] in Boston.' I met it with the inevitable joke that in this case foreign lands might prove a disappointment to her, but I quite failed to alarm her. 'I know more about them than you might think' – her earnestness resisted even that. 'I mean by reading – for I've really read considerable. In fact I guess I've prepared my mind about as much as you *can* – in advance. I've not only read Byron – I've read histories and guide-books and articles and lots of things. I know I shall rave about everything.'

' "Everything" is saying much, but I understand your case,' I returned. 'You've the great American disease, and you've got it "bad" – the appetite, morbid and monstrous, for colour and form, for the picturesque and the romantic at any price. I don't know whether we come into the world with it – with the germs implanted and antecedent to experience; rather perhaps we catch it early, almost before developed consciousness – we *feel*, as we look about, that we're going (to save our souls, or at least our senses) to be thrown back on it hard. We're like travellers in the desert – deprived of water and subject to the terrible mirage, the torment of illusion, of the thirst-fever.[9] They hear the plash of fountains, they see green gardens and orchards that are hundreds of miles away. So we with *our* thirst – except that with us it's *more* wonderful: we have before us the beautiful old things we've never seen at all, and when we do at last see them – if we're lucky – we simply recognise them. What experience does is merely to confirm and consecrate our confident dream.'[10]

She listened with her rounded eyes. 'The way you express it's too lovely, and I'm sure it will be just like that. I've dreamt of everything – I'll know it all!'

'I'm afraid,' I pretended for harmless comedy, 'that you've wasted a great deal of time.'

'Oh yes, that has been my great wickedness!' The people about us had begun to scatter; they were taking their leave. She got up and put out her hand to me, timidly, but as if quite shining and throbbing.

'I'm going back there – one *has* to,' I said as I shook hands with her. 'I shall look out for you.'

Yes, she fairly glittered with her fever of excited faith. 'Well, I'll tell you if I'm disappointed.' And she left me, fluttering all expressively her little straw fan.

II

A few months after this I crossed the sea eastward again and some three years elapsed. I had been living in Paris and, toward the end of October, went from that city to the Havre, to meet a pair of relatives who had written me they were about to arrive there. On reaching the Havre I found the steamer already docked – I was two or three hours late. I repaired directly to the hotel, where my travellers were duly established. My sister had gone to bed, exhausted and disabled by her voyage; she was the unsteadiest of sailors and her sufferings on this occasion had been extreme. She desired for the moment undisturbed rest and was able to see me but five minutes – long enough for us to agree to stop over, restoratively, till the morrow. My brother-in-law, anxious about his wife, was unwilling to leave her room; but she insisted on my taking him a walk for aid to recovery of his spirits and his land-legs.

The early autumn day was warm and charming, and our stroll through the bright-coloured busy streets of the old French seaport beguiling enough. We walked along the sunny noisy quays and then turned into a wide pleasant street which lay half in sun and half in shade – a French provincial street that resembled an old water-colour drawing: tall grey steep-roofed red-gabled many-storied houses; green shutters on windows and old scroll-work above them; flower-pots in balconies and white-capped women in doorways. We walked in the shade; all this stretched away on the sunny side of the vista and made a picture. We looked at it as we passed along; then suddenly my companion stopped – pressing my arm and staring. I followed his gaze and saw that we had paused just before reaching a café where, under an awning, several tables and chairs were disposed upon the pavement. The windows were open behind; half a dozen plants in tubs were ranged beside the door; the pavement was besprinkled with clean bran. It was a dear little quiet old-world café; inside, in the comparative dusk, I saw a stout handsome woman, who had pink ribbons in her cap, perched up with a mirror behind her back and smiling at some one placed out of sight. This, to be exact, I noted afterwards; what I first observed was a lady seated alone, outside, at one of the little marble-topped tables. My brother-in-law had stopped to look at her. Something had been put before her, but she only leaned back, motionless and with her hands folded, looking down the street and away from us. I saw her but in diminished profile; nevertheless I was sure I knew on the spot that we must already have met.

'The little lady of the steamer!' my companion cried.

'Was she on your steamer?' I asked with interest.

'From morning till night. She was never sick. She used to sit perpetually at the side of the vessel with her hands crossed that way, looking at the eastward horizon.'

'And are you going to speak to her?'

'I don't know her. I never made acquaintance with her. I wasn't in form to make up to ladies. But I used to watch her and – I don't know why – to be interested in her. She's a dear little Yankee woman. I've an idea she's a school-mistress taking a holiday – for which her scholars have made up a purse.'

She had now turned her face a little more into profile, looking at the steep grey house-fronts opposite. On this I decided. 'I shall speak to her myself.'

'I wouldn't – she's very shy,' said my brother-in-law.

'My dear fellow, I know her. I once showed her photographs at a tea-party.' With which I went up to her, making her, as she turned to look at me, leave me in no doubt of her identity. Miss Caroline Spencer had achieved her dream. But she was less quick to recognize me and showed a slight bewilderment. I pushed a chair to the table and sat down. 'Well,' I said, 'I hope you're not disappointed!'

She stared, blushing a little – then gave a small jump and placed me. 'It was you who showed me the photographs – at North Verona.'

'Yes, it was I. This happens very charmingly, for isn't it quite for me to give you a formal reception here – the official welcome? I talked to you so much about Europe.'

'You didn't say too much. I'm so intensely happy!' she declared.

Very happy indeed she looked. There was no sign of her being older; she was as gravely, decently, demurely pretty as before. If she had struck me then as a thin-stemmed mild-hued flower of Puritanism it may be imagined whether in her present situation this clear bloom was less appealing. Beside her an old gentleman was drinking absinthe; behind her the *dame de comptoir*[11] in the pink ribbons called 'Alcibiade, Alcibiade!' to the long-aproned waiter. I explained to Miss Spencer that the gentleman with me had lately been her shipmate, and my brother-in-law came up and was introduced to her. But she looked at him as if she had never so much as seen him, and I remembered he had told me her eyes were always fixed on the eastward horizon. She had evidently not noticed him, and, still timidly smiling, made no attempt whatever to pretend the contrary. I stayed with her on the little terrace of the café while he went back to the hotel and to his wife. I remarked to my friend that this meeting of ours at the first hour of her landing partook, among all chances, of the miraculous, but that I was delighted to be there and receive her first impressions.

'Oh I can't tell you,' she said – 'I feel so much in a dream. I've been sitting here an hour and I don't want to move. Everything's so delicious and romantic. I don't know whether the coffee has gone to my head – it's *so* unlike the coffee of my dead past.'

'Really,' I made answer, 'if you're so pleased with this poor prosaic Havre you'll have no admiration left for better things. Don't spend your appreciation all the first day – remember it's your intellectual letter of credit.[12] Remember all the beautiful places and things that are waiting for you. Remember that lovely Italy we talked about.'

'I'm not afraid of running short,' she said gaily, still looking at the opposite houses. 'I could sit here all day – just saying to myself that here I am at last. It's so dark and strange – so old and different.'

'By the way then,' I asked, 'how come you to be encamped in this odd place? Haven't you gone to one of the inns?' For I was half-amused, half-alarmed at the good conscience with which this delicately pretty woman had stationed herself in conspicuous isolation on the edge of the sidewalk.

'My cousin brought me here and – a little while ago – left me,' she returned. 'You know I told you I had a relation over here. He's still here – a real cousin. Well,' she pursued with unclouded candour, 'he met me at the steamer this morning.'

It was absurd – and the case moreover none of my business; but I felt somehow disconcerted. 'It was hardly worth his while to meet you if he was to desert you so soon.'

'Oh he has only left me for half an hour,' said Caroline Spencer. 'He has gone to get my money.'

I continued to wonder. 'Where *is* your money?'

She appeared seldom to laugh, but she laughed for the joy of this. 'It makes me feel very fine to tell you! It's in circular notes.'[13]

'And where are your circular notes?'

'In my cousin's pocket.'[14]

This statement was uttered with such clearness of candour that – I can hardly say why – it gave me a sensible chill. I couldn't at all at the moment have justified my lapse from ease, for I knew nothing of Miss Spencer's cousin. Since he stood in that relation to her – dear respectable little person – the presumption was in his favour. But I found myself wincing at the thought that half an hour after her landing her scanty funds should have passed into his hands. 'Is he to travel with you?' I asked.

'Only as far as Paris. He's an art-student in Paris – I've always thought that so splendid. I wrote to him that I was coming, but I never expected him to come off to the ship. I supposed he'd only just meet me at the train in Paris. It's very kind of him. But he *is*,' said Caroline Spencer, 'very kind – and very bright.'

I felt at once a strange eagerness to see this bright kind cousin who was an art-student. 'He's gone to the banker's?' I enquired.

'Yes, to the banker's. He took me to an hotel – such a queer quaint cunning little place, with a court in the middle and a gallery all round, and a lovely landlady in such a beautifully fluted cap[15] and such a perfectly fitting dress! After a while we came out to walk to the banker's, for I hadn't any French money. But I was very dizzy from the motion of the vessel and I thought I had better sit down. He found this place for me here – then he went off to the banker's himself. I'm to wait here till he comes back.'

Her story was wholly lucid and my impression perfectly wanton, but it passed through my mind that the gentleman would never come back. I settled myself in a chair beside my friend and determined to await the event. She was lost in the vision and the imagination of everything near us and about us – she observed, she recognized and admired, with a touching intensity. She noticed everything that was brought before us by the movement of the street – the peculiarities of costume, the shapes of vehicles, the big Norman horses, the fat priests, the shaven poodles. We talked of these things, and there was something charming in her freshness of perception and the way her book-nourished fancy sallied forth for the revel.

'And when your cousin comes back what are you going to do?' I went on.

For this she had, a little oddly, to think. 'We don't quite know.'

'When do you go to Paris? If you go by the four o'clock train I may have the pleasure of making the journey with you.'

'I don't think we shall do that.' So far she was prepared. 'My cousin thinks I had better stay here a few days.'

'Oh!' said I – and for five minutes had nothing to add. I was wondering what our absentee was, in vulgar parlance, 'up to.' I looked up and down the street, but saw nothing that looked like a bright and kind American art-student. At last I took the liberty of observing that the Havre was hardly a place to choose as one of the aesthetic stations of a European tour. It was a place of convenience, nothing more; a place of transit, through which transit should be rapid. I recommended her to go to Paris by the afternoon train and meanwhile to amuse herself by driving to the ancient fortress at the mouth of the harbour – that remarkable circular structure which bore the name of Francis the First and figured a sort of small Castle of Saint Angelo.[16] (I might really have foreknown that it was to be demolished.)

She listened with much interest – then for a moment looked grave. 'My cousin told me that when he returned he should have something particular to say to me, and that we could do nothing or decide nothing till I should have heard it. But I'll make him tell me right off, and then we'll go to the ancient fortress. Francis the First, did you say? Why, that's lovely. There's no hurry to get to Paris; there's plenty of time.'

She smiled with her softly severe little lips as she spoke those last words, yet, looking at her with a purpose, I made out in her eyes, I thought, a tiny gleam of apprehension. 'Don't tell me,' I said, 'that this wretched man's going to give you bad news!'

She coloured as if convicted of a hidden perversity, but she was soaring too high to drop. 'Well, I guess it's a *little* bad, but I don't believe it's *very* bad. At any rate I must listen to it.'

I usurped an unscrupulous authority. 'Look here; you didn't come to Europe to listen — you came to *see*!' But now I was sure her cousin would come back; since he had something disagreeable to say to her he'd infallibly turn up. We sat a while longer and I asked her about her plans of travel. She had them on her fingers' ends and told over the names as solemnly as a daughter of another faith might have told over the beads of a rosary: from Paris to Dijon and to Avignon, from Avignon to Marseilles and the Cornice road; thence to Genoa, to Spezia, to Pisa, to Florence, to Rome. It apparently had never occurred to her that there could be the least incommodity in her travelling alone; and since she was unprovided with a companion I of course civilly abstained from disturbing her sense of security.

At last her cousin came back. I saw him turn toward us out of a side-street, and from the moment my eyes rested on him I knew he could but be the bright, if not the kind, American art-student. He wore a slouch hat[17] and a rusty black velvet jacket, such as I had often encountered in the Rue Bonaparte.[18] His shirt-collar displayed a stretch of throat that at a distance wasn't strikingly statuesque. He was tall and lean, he had red hair and freckles. These items I had time to take in while he approached the café, staring at me with natural surprise from under his romantic brim. When he came up to us I immediately introduced myself as an old acquaintance of Miss Spencer's, a character she serenely permitted me to claim. He looked at me hard with a pair of small sharp eyes, then he gave me a solemn wave, in the 'European' fashion, of his rather rusty sombrero.

'You weren't on the ship?' he asked.

'No, I wasn't on the ship. I've been in Europe these several years.'

He bowed once more, portentously, and motioned me to be seated again. I sat down, but only for the purpose of observing him an instant — I saw it was time I should return to my sister. Miss Spencer's European protector was, by my measure, a very queer quantity. Nature hadn't shaped him for a Raphaelesque or Byronic attire,[19] and his velvet doublet and exhibited though not columnar throat weren't in harmony with his facial attributes. His hair was cropped close to his head; his ears were large and ill-adjusted to the same. He had a lackadaisical carriage and a sentimental droop which were peculiarly at variance with his keen conscious strange-coloured eyes — of a brown that was almost red. Perhaps I was prejudiced, but I thought his eyes too shifty. He said nothing for some time; he leaned his hands on his stick and looked up and down the street. Then at last, slowly lifting the stick and pointing with it, 'That's a very nice bit,' he dropped with a certain flatness. He had his head to one side – he narrowed his ugly lids. I followed the direction of his stick; the object it indicated was a red cloth hung out of an old window. 'Nice bit of colour,' he continued; and without moving his head transferred his half-closed gaze to me. 'Composes well. Fine old tone. Make a nice thing.' He spoke in a charmless vulgar voice.

'I see you've a great deal of eye,' I replied. 'Your cousin tells me you're studying art.' He looked at me in the same way, without answering, and I went on with deliberate urbanity: 'I suppose you're at the studio of one of those great men.' Still on this he continued to fix me, and then he named one of the greatest of that day; which led me to ask him if he liked his master.

'Do you understand French?' he returned.

'Some kinds.'

He kept his little eyes on me; with which he remarked: 'Je suis fou de la peinture!'[20]

'Oh I understand that kind!' I replied. Our companion laid her hand on his arm with a small pleased and fluttered movement; it was delightful to be among people who were on such easy terms with foreign tongues. I got up to take leave and asked her where, in Paris, I might have the honour of waiting on her. To what hotel would she go?

She turned to her cousin enquiringly and he favoured me again with his little languid leer. 'Do you know the Hôtel des Princes?'

'I know where it is.'

'Well, that's the shop.'

'I congratulate you,' I said to Miss Spencer. 'I believe it's the best inn in the world; but, in case I should still have a moment to call on you here, where are you lodged?'

'Oh it's such a pretty name,' she returned gleefully. 'A la Belle Normande.'

'I guess I know my way round!' her kinsman threw in; and as I left them he gave me with his swaggering head-cover a great flourish that was like the wave of a banner over a conquered field.

III

My relative, as it proved, was not sufficiently restored to leave the place by the afternoon train; so that as the autumn dusk began to fall I found myself at liberty to call at the establishment named to me by my friends. I must confess that I had spent much of the interval in wondering what the disagreeable thing was that the less attractive of these had been telling the other. The *auberge*[21] of the Belle Normande proved an hostelry in a shady by-street, where it gave me satisfaction to think Miss Spencer must have encountered local colour in abundance. There was a crooked little court, where much of the hospitality of the house was carried on; there was a staircase climbing to bedrooms on the outer side of the wall; there was a small trickling fountain with a stucco statuette set in the midst of it; there was a little boy in a white cap and apron cleaning copper vessels at a conspicuous kitchen door; there was a chattering landlady, neatly laced, arranging apricots and grapes into an artistic pyramid upon a pink plate. I looked about, and on a green bench outside of an open door labelled Salle-à-Manger,[22] I distinguished Caroline Spencer. No sooner had I looked at her than I was sure something had happened since the morning. Supported by the back of her bench, with her hands clasped in her lap, she kept her eyes on the other side of the court where the landlady manipulated the apricots.

But I saw that, poor dear, she wasn't thinking of apricots or even of landladies. She was staring absently, thoughtfully; on a nearer view I could have certified she had been crying. I had seated myself beside her before she was aware; then, when she had done so, she simply turned round without surprise and showed me her sad face. Something very bad indeed had happened; she was completely changed, and I immediately charged her with it. 'Your cousin has been giving you bad news. You've had a horrid time.'

For a moment she said nothing, and I supposed her afraid to speak lest her tears should again rise. Then it came to me that even in the few hours since my leaving her she had shed them all — which made her now intensely, stoically composed. 'My poor cousin has been having one,' she replied at last. 'He has had great worries. His news was bad.' Then after a dismally conscious wait: 'He was in dreadful want of money.'

'In want of yours, you mean?'

'Of any he could get — honourably of course. Mine *is* all — well, that's available.'

Ah it was as if I had been sure from the first! 'And he has taken it from you?'

Again she hung fire, but her face meanwhile was pleading. 'I gave him what I had.'

I recall the accent of those words as the most angelic human sound I had ever listened to — which is exactly why I jumped up almost with a sense of personal outrage. 'Gracious goodness, madam, do you call that his getting it "honourably"?'

I had gone too far — she coloured to her eyes. 'We won't speak of it.'

'We *must* speak of it,' I declared as I dropped beside her again. 'I'm your friend — upon my word I'm your protector; it seems to me you need one. What's the matter with this extraordinary person?'

She was perfectly able to say. 'He's just badly in debt.'

'No doubt he is! But what's the special propriety of your – in such tearing haste! – paying for that?'

'Well, he has told me all his story. I *feel* for him so much.'

'So do I, if you come to that! But I hope,' I roundly added, 'he'll give you straight back your money.'

As to this she was prompt. 'Certainly he will – as soon as ever he can.'

'And when the deuce will that be?'

Her lucidity maintained itself. 'When he has finished his great picture.'

It took me full in the face. 'My dear young lady, damn his great picture! Where is this voracious man?'

It was as if she must let me feel a moment that I did push her! – though indeed, as appeared, he was just where he'd naturally be. 'He's having his dinner.'

I turned about and looked through the open door into the salle-à-manger. There, sure enough, alone at the end of a long table, was the object of my friend's compassion – the bright, the kind young art-student. He was dining too attentively to notice me at first, but in the act of setting down a well-emptied wine-glass he caught sight of my air of observation. He paused in his repast and, with his head on one side and his meagre jaws slowly moving, fixedly returned my gaze. Then the landlady came brushing lightly by with her pyramid of apricots.

'And that nice little plate of fruit is for him?' I wailed.

Miss Spencer glanced at it tenderly. 'They seem to arrange everything so nicely!' she simply sighed.

I felt helpless and irritated. 'Come now, really,' I said; 'do you think it right, do you think it decent, that that long strong fellow should collar your funds?' She looked away from me – I was evidently giving her pain. The case was hopeless; the long strong fellow had 'interested' her.

'Pardon me if I speak of him so unceremoniously,' I said. 'But you're really too generous, and he hasn't, clearly, the rudiments of delicacy. He made his debts himself – he ought to pay them himself.'

'He has been foolish,' she obstinately said – 'of course I know that. He has told me everything. We had a long talk this morning – the poor fellow threw himself on my charity. He has signed notes to a large amount.'

'The more fool he!'

'He's in real distress – and it's not only himself. It's his poor young wife.'

'Ah he has a poor young wife?'

'I didn't know – but he made a clean breast of it. He married two years since – secretly.'

'Why secretly?'

My informant took precautions as if she feared listeners. Then with low impressiveness: 'She was a Countess!'

'Are you very sure of that?'

'She has written me the most beautiful letter.'

'Asking you – whom she has never seen – for money?'

'Asking me for confidence and sympathy' – Miss Spencer spoke now with spirit. 'She has been cruelly treated by her family – in consequence of what she has done for him. My cousin has told me every particular, and she appeals to me in her own lovely way in the letter, which I've here in my pocket. It's such a wonderful old-world romance,' said my prodigious friend. 'She was a beautiful young widow[23] – her first husband was a Count, tremendously high-born, but really most wicked, with whom she hadn't been happy and whose death had left her ruined after he had deceived her in all sorts of ways. My poor cousin, meeting her in that situation and perhaps a little too recklessly pitying her and charmed with her, found her, don't you see?' – Caroline's appeal on this head was amazing! – 'but too ready to trust a better man after all she had been through. Only when her "people," as he says – and I do like the word! – understood she *would* have him, poor gifted young American art-student though he simply was, because she just adored him, her great-aunt, the old Marquise, from whom she had expectations of wealth which she could yet sacrifice for her love, utterly cast her off and wouldn't so much as speak to her, much less to *him*, in their dreadful haughtiness and pride. They *can* be haughty over here, it seems,' she ineffably developed – 'there's no mistake about that! It's like something in some famous old book. The family, my cousin's wife's,' she by this time almost complacently wound up, 'are of the oldest Provençal noblesse.'

I listened half-bewildered. The poor woman positively found it so interesting to be swindled by a flower of that stock – if stock or flower or solitary grain of truth was really concerned in the matter – as practically to have lost the sense of what the forfeiture of her hoard meant for her. 'My dear young lady,' I groaned, 'you don't want to be stripped of every dollar for such a rigmarole!'

She asserted, at this, her dignity – much as a small pink shorn lamb might have done. 'It isn't a rigmarole, and I shan't be stripped. I shan't live any worse than I *have* lived, don't you see? And I'll come back before long to stay with them. The Countess – he still gives her, he says, her title, as they do to noble widows, that is to 'dowagers,' don't you know? in England – insists on a visit from me *some* time. So I guess for *that* I can start afresh – and meanwhile I'll have recovered my money.'

It was all too heart-breaking. 'You're going home then at once?'

I felt the faint tremor of voice she heroically tried to stifle. 'I've nothing left for a tour.'

'You gave it *all* up?'

'I've kept enough to take me back.'

14

I uttered, I think, a positive howl, and at this juncture the hero of the situation, the happy proprietor of my little friend's sacred savings and of the infatuated *grande dame*[24] just sketched for me, reappeared with the clear consciousness of a repast bravely earned and consistently enjoyed. He stood on the threshold an instant, extracting the stone from a plump apricot he had fondly retained; then he put the apricot into his mouth and, while he let it gratefully dissolve there, stood looking at us with his long legs apart and his hands thrust into the pockets of his velvet coat. My companion got up, giving him a thin glance that I caught in its passage and which expressed at once resignation and fascination – the last dregs of her sacrifice and with it an anguish of upliftedness. Ugly vulgar pretentious dishonest as I thought him, and destitute of every grace of plausibility, he had yet appealed successfully to her eager and tender imagination. I was deeply disgusted, but I had no warrant to interfere, and at any rate felt that it would be vain. He waved his hand meanwhile with a breadth of appreciation. 'Nice old court. Nice mellow old place. Nice crooked old staircase. Several pretty things.'

Decidedly I couldn't stand it, and without responding I gave my hand to my friend. She looked at me an instant with her little white face and rounded eyes, and as she showed her pretty teeth I suppose she meant to smile. 'Don't be sorry for me,' she sublimely pleaded; 'I'm very sure I shall see something of this dear old Europe yet.'

I refused however to take literal leave of her – I should find a moment to come back next morning. Her awful kinsman, who had put on his sombrero again, flourished it off at me by way of a bow – on which I hurried away.

On the morrow early I did return, and in the court of the inn met the landlady, more loosely laced than in the evening. On my asking for Miss Spencer, '*Partie*, monsieur,' the good woman said. 'She went away last night at ten o'clock, with her – her – not her husband, eh? – in fine her Monsieur. They went down to the American ship.' I turned off – I felt the tears in my eyes. The poor girl had been some thirteen hours in Europe.

IV

I myself, more fortunate, continued to sacrifice to opportunity as I myself met it. During this period – of some five years – I lost my friend Latouche, who died of a malarious fever during a tour in the Levant.[25] One of the first things I did on my return to America was to go up to North Verona on a consolatory visit to his poor mother. I found her in deep affliction and sat with her the whole of the morning that followed my arrival – I had come in late at night – listening to her tearful descant and singing the praises of my friend. We talked of nothing else, and our conversation ended only with the arrival of a quick little woman who drove herself up to the door in a 'carry-all'[26] and whom I saw toss the reins to the horse's back with the briskness of a startled sleeper throwing off the bedclothes. She jumped out of the carry-all and she jumped into the room. She proved to be the minister's wife and the great town-gossip, and she had evidently, in the latter capacity, a choice morsel to communicate. I was as sure of this as I was that poor Mrs Latouche was not absolutely too bereaved to listen to her. It seemed to me discreet to retire, and I described myself as anxious for a walk before dinner.

'And by the way,' I added, 'if you'll tell me where my old friend Miss Spencer lives I think I'll call on her.'

The minister's wife immediately responded. Miss Spencer lived in the fourth house beyond the Baptist church; the Baptist church was the one on the right, with that queer green thing over the door; they called it a portico, but it looked more like an old-fashioned bedstead swung in the air. 'Yes, do look up poor Caroline,' Mrs Latouche further enjoined. 'It will refresh her to see a strange face.'

'I should think she had had enough of strange faces!' cried the minister's wife.

'To see, I mean, a charming visitor' – Mrs Latouche amended her phrase.

'I should think she had had enough of charming visitors!' her companion returned. 'But you don't mean to stay ten years,' she added with significant eyes on me.

'Has she a visitor of that sort?' I asked in my ignorance.

'You'll make out the sort!' said the minister's wife. 'She's easily seen; she generally sits in the front yard. Only take care what you say to her, and be very sure you're polite.'

'Ah she's so sensitive?'

The minister's wife jumped up and dropped me a curtsey – a most sarcastic curtsey. 'That's what she is, if you please. "Madame la Comtesse!"'

And pronouncing these titular words with the most scathing accent, the little woman seemed fairly to laugh in the face of the lady they designated. I stood staring, wondering, remembering.

'Oh I shall be very polite!' I cried; and, grasping my hat and stick, I went on my way.

I found Miss Spencer's residence without difficulty. The Baptist church was easily identified, and the small dwelling near it, of a rusty white, with a large central chimney-stack and a Virginia creeper, seemed naturally and properly the abode of a withdrawn old maid with a taste for striking effects inexpensively obtained. As I approached I slackened my pace, for I had heard that some one was always sitting in the front yard, and I wished to reconnoitre. I looked cautiously over the low white fence that separated the small garden-space from the unpaved street, but I descried nothing in the shape of a Comtesse. A small straight path led up to the crooked door-step, on either side of which was a little grass-plot fringed with currant-bushes. In the middle of the grass, right and left, was a large quince-tree, full of antiquity and contortions, and beneath one of the quince-trees were placed a small table and a couple of light chairs. On the table lay a piece of unfinished embroidery and two or three books in bright-coloured paper covers. I went in at the gate and paused halfway along the path, scanning the place for some further token of its occupant, before whom − I could hardly have said why − I hesitated abruptly to present myself. Then I saw the poor little house to be of the shabbiest and felt a sudden doubt of my right to penetrate, since curiosity had been my motive and curiosity here failed of confidence. While I demurred a figure appeared in the open doorway and stood there looking at me. I immediately recognized Miss Spencer, but she faced me as if we had never met. Gently, but gravely and timidly, I advanced to the door-step, where I spoke with an attempt at friendly banter.

'I waited for you over there to come back, but you never came.'

'Waited where, sir?' she quavered, her innocent eyes rounding themselves as of old. She was much older; she looked tired and wasted.

'Well,' I said, 'I waited at the old French port.'

She stared harder, then recognised me, smiling, flushing, clasping her two hands together. 'I remember you now − I remember that day.' But she stood there, neither coming out nor asking me to come in. She was embarrassed.

I too felt a little awkward while I poked at the path with my stick. 'I kept looking out for you year after year.'

'You mean in Europe?' she ruefully breathed.

'In Europe of course! Here apparently you're easy enough to find.'

She leaned her hand against the unpainted door-post and her head fell a little to one side. She looked at me thus without speaking, and I caught the expression visible in women's eyes when tears are rising. Suddenly she stepped out on the cracked slab of stone before her threshold and closed the door. Then her strained smile prevailed and I saw her teeth were as pretty as ever. But there had been tears too. 'Have you been there ever since?' she lowered her voice to ask.

'Until three weeks ago. And you − you never came back?'

Still shining at me as she could, she put her hand behind her and reopened the door. 'I'm not very polite,' she said. 'Won't you come in?'

'I'm afraid I incommode you.'

'Oh no!' − she wouldn't hear of it now. And she pushed back the door with a sign that I should enter.

I followed her in. She led the way to a small room on the left of the narrow

17

hall, which I supposed to be her parlour, though it was at the back of the house, and we passed the closed door of another apartment which apparently enjoyed a view of the quince-trees. This one looked out upon a small wood-shed and two clucking hens. But I thought it pretty until I saw its elegance to be of the most frugal kind; after which, presently, I thought it prettier still, for I had never seen faded chintz and old mezzotint engravings, framed in varnished autumn leaves, disposed with so touching a grace. Miss Spencer sat down on a very small section of the sofa, her hands tightly clasped in her lap. She looked ten years older, and I needn't now have felt called to insist on the facts of her person. But I still thought them interesting, and at any rate I was moved by them. She was peculiarly agitated. I tried to appear not to notice it; but suddenly, in the most inconsequent fashion – it was an irresistible echo of our concentrated passage in the old French port – I said to her: 'I do incommode you. Again you're in distress.'

She raised her two hands to her face and for a moment kept it buried in them. Then taking them away, 'It's because you remind me,' she said.

'I remind you, you mean, of that miserable day at the Havre?'

She wonderfully shook her head. 'It wasn't miserable. It was delightful.'

Ah was it? my manner of receiving this must have commented. 'I never was so shocked as when, on going back to your inn the next morning, I found you had wretchedly retreated.'

She waited an instant, after which she said: 'Please let us not speak of that.'

'Did you come straight back here?' I nevertheless went on.

'I was back here just thirty days after my first start.'

'And here you've remained ever since?'

'Every minute of the time.'

I took it in; I didn't know what to say, and what I presently said had almost the sound of mockery. 'When then are you going to make that tour?' It might be practically aggressive; but there was something that irritated me in her depths of resignation, and I wished to extort from her some expression of impatience.

She attached her eyes a moment to a small sun-spot on the carpet; then she got up and lowered the window-blind a little to obliterate it. I waited, watching her with interest – as if she had still something more to give me. Well, presently, in answer to my last question, she gave it. 'Never!'

'I hope at least your cousin repaid you that money,' I said.

At this again she looked away from me. 'I don't care for it now.'

'You don't care for your money?'

'For ever going to Europe.'

'Do you mean you wouldn't go if you could?'

'I can't – I can't,' said Caroline Spencer. 'It's all over. Everything's different. I never think of it.'

'The scoundrel never repaid you then!' I cried.

'Please, please –!' she began.

But she had stopped – she was looking toward the door. There had been a rustle and a sound of steps in the hall.

I also looked toward the door, which was open and now admitted another person – a lady who paused just within the threshold. Behind her came a young man. The lady looked at me with a good deal of fixedness – long enough for me to rise to a vivid impression of herself. Then she turned to Caroline Spencer and, with a smile and a strong foreign accent, *'Pardon, ma chère!* I didn't know you had company,' she said. 'The gentleman came in so quietly.' With which she again gave me the benefit of her attention. She was very strange, yet I was at once sure I had seen her before. Afterwards I rather put it that I had only seen ladies remarkably like her. But I had seen them very far away from North Verona, and it was the oddest of all things to meet one of them in that frame. To what quite other scene did the sight of her transport me? To some dusky landing before a shabby Parisian *quatrième*[27] – to an open door revealing a greasy ante-chamber and to Madame leaning over the banisters while she holds a faded wrapper together and bawls down to the portress to bring up her coffee. My friend's guest was a very large lady, of middle age, with a plump dead-white face and hair drawn back *à la chinoise*.[28] She had a small penetrating eye and what is called in French *le sourire agréable*.[29] She wore an old pink cashmere dressing-gown covered with white embroideries, and, like the figure in my momentary vision, she confined it in front with a bare and rounded arm and a plump and deeply-dimpled hand.

'It's only to spick about my café,' she said to her hostess with her *sourire agréable*. 'I should like it served in the garden under the leetle tree.'

The young man behind her had now stepped into the room, where he also stood revealed, though with rather less of a challenge. He was a gentleman of few inches but a vague importance, perhaps the leading man of the world of North Verona. He had a small pointed nose and a small pointed chin; also, as I observed, the most diminutive feet and a manner of no point at all. He looked at me foolishly and with his mouth open.

'You shall have your coffee,' said Miss Spencer as if an army of cooks had been engaged in the preparation of it.

'C'est bien!'[30] said her massive inmate. 'Find your bouk' – and this personage turned to the gaping youth.

He gaped now at each quarter of the room. 'My grammar, d'ye mean?'

The large lady however could but face her friend's visitor while persistently engaged with a certain laxity in the flow of her wrapper. 'Find your bouk,' she more absently repeated.

'My poetry, d'ye mean?' said the young man, who also couldn't take his eyes off me.

'Never mind your bouk' – his companion reconsidered. 'To-day we'll just talk. We'll make some conversation. But we mustn't interrupt Mademoiselle's. Come, come' – and she moved off a step. 'Under the leetle tree,' she added for the benefit of Mademoiselle. After which she gave me a thin salutation, jerked a measured 'Monsieur!' and swept away again with her swain following.

I looked at Miss Spencer, whose eyes never moved from the carpet, and I spoke, I fear, without grace. 'Who in the world's that?'

'The Comtesse – that *was*: my *cousine* as they call it in French.'

'And who's the young man?'

'The Countess's pupil, Mr Mixter.' This description of the tie uniting the two persons who had just quitted us must certainly have upset my gravity; for I recall the marked increase of my friend's own as she continued to explain. 'She gives lessons in French and music, the simpler sorts – '

'The simpler sorts of French?' I fear I broke in.

But she was still impenetrable, and in fact had now an intonation that put me vulgarly in the wrong. 'She has had the worst reverses – with no one to look to. She's prepared for any exertion – and she takes her misfortunes with gaiety.'

'Ah well,' I returned – no doubt a little ruefully, 'that's all I myself am pretending to do. If she's determined to be a burden to nobody, nothing could be more right and proper.'

My hostess looked vaguely, though I thought quite wearily enough, about: she met this proposition in no other way. 'I must go and get the coffee,' she simply said.

'Has the lady many pupils?' I none the less persisted.

'She has only Mr Mixter. She gives him all her time.' It might have set me off again, but something in my whole impression of my friend's sensibility urged me to keep strictly decent. 'He pays very well,' she at all events inscrutably went on. 'He's not very bright – as a pupil; but he's very rich and he's very kind. He has a buggy – with a back, and he takes the Countess to drive.'

'For good long spells I hope,' I couldn't help interjecting – even at the cost of her so taking it that she had still to avoid my eyes. 'Well, the country's beautiful for miles,' I went on. And then as she was turning away: 'You're going for the Countess's coffee?'

'If you'll excuse me a few moments.'

'Is there no one else to do it?'

She seemed to wonder who there should be. 'I keep no servants.'

'Then can't I help?' After which, as she but looked at me, I bettered it. 'Can't she wait on herself?'

Miss Spencer had a slow headshake – as if that too had been a strange idea. 'She isn't used to *manual* labour.'

The discrimination was a treat, but I cultivated decorum. 'I see – and you *are*.' But at the same time I couldn't abjure curiosity. 'Before you go, at any rate, please tell me this: who *is* this wonderful lady?'

'I told you just who in France – that extraordinary day. She's the wife of my cousin, whom you saw there.'

'The lady disowned by her family in consequence of her marriage?'

'Yes; they've never seen her again. They've completely broken with her.'

'And where's her husband?'

'My poor cousin's dead.'

I pulled up, but only a moment. 'And where's your money?'

The poor thing flinched – I kept her on the rack. 'I don't know,' she woefully said.

I scarce know what it didn't prompt me to – but I went step by step. 'On her husband's death this lady at once came to you?'

It was as if she had had too often to describe it. 'Yes, she arrived one day.'

'How long ago?'

'Two years and four months.'

'And has been here ever since?'

'Ever since.'

I took it all in. 'And how does she like it?'

'Well, not *very* much,' said Miss Spencer divinely.

That too I took in. 'And how do *you* –?'

She laid her face in her two hands an instant as she had done ten minutes before. Then, quickly, she went to get the Countess's coffee.

Left alone in the little parlour I found myself divided between the perfection of my disgust and a contrary wish to see, to learn more. At the end of a few minutes the young man in attendance on the lady in question reappeared as for a fresh gape at me. He was inordinately grave – to be dressed in such parti-coloured flannels;[31] and he produced with no great confidence on his own side the message with which he had been charged. 'She wants to know if you won't come right out.'

'Who wants to know?'

'The Countess. That French lady.'

'She has asked you to bring me?'

'Yes sir,' said the young man feebly – for I may claim to have surpassed him in stature and weight.

I went out with him, and we found his instructress seated under one of the small quince-trees in front of the house; where she was engaged in drawing a fine needle with a very fat hand through a piece of embroidery not remarkable for freshness. She pointed graciously to the chair beside her and I sat down. Mr Mixter glanced about him and then accommodated himself on the grass at her feet; whence he gazed upward more gapingly than ever and as if convinced that between us something wonderful would now occur.

'I'm sure you spick French,' said the Countess, whose eyes were singularly protuberant as she played over me her agreeable smile.

'I do, madam – *tant bien que mal*,'[32] I replied, I fear, more dryly.

'Ah voilà!' she cried as with delight. 'I knew it as soon as I looked at you. You've been in my poor dear country.'

'A considerable time.'

'You love it then, *mon pays de France*?'

'Oh it's an old affection.' But I wasn't exuberant.

'And you know Paris well?'

'Yes, *sans me vanter*,[33] madam, I think I really do.' And with a certain conscious purpose I let my eyes meet her own.

She presently, hereupon, moved her own and glanced down at Mr Mixter. 'What are we talking about?' she demanded of her attentive pupil.

He pulled his knees up, plucked at the grass, stared, blushed a little. 'You're talking French,' said Mr Mixter.

'*La belle découverte!*' mocked the Countess. 'It's going on ten months,' she explained to me, 'since I took him in hand. Don't put yourself out not to say he's *la bêtise même*,'[34] she added in fine style. 'He won't in the least understand you.'

A moment's consideration of Mr Mixter, awkwardly sporting at our feet, quite assured me that he wouldn't. 'I hope your other pupils do you more honour,' I then remarked to my entertainer.

'I have no others. They don't know what French – or what anything else – is in this place; they don't want to know. You may therefore imagine the pleasure it is to me to meet a person who speaks it like yourself.' I could but reply that my own pleasure wasn't less, and she continued to draw the stitches through her embroidery with an elegant curl of her little finger. Every few moments she put her eyes, near-sightedly, closer to her work – this as if for elegance too. She inspired me with no more confidence than her late husband, if husband he was, had done, years before, on the occasion with which this one so detestably matched: she was coarse, common, affected, dishonest – no more a Countess than I was a Caliph. She had an assurance – based clearly on experience; but this couldn't have been the experience of 'race.' Whatever it was indeed it did now, in a yearning fashion, flare out of her. 'Talk to me of Paris, *mon beau Paris* that I'd give my eyes to see. The very name of it *me fait languir*.[35] How long since you were there?'

'A couple of months ago.'

'*Vous avez de la chance!*[36] Tell me something about it. What were they doing? Oh for an hour of the Boulevard!'

'They were doing about what they're always doing – amusing themselves a good deal.'

'At the theatres, *hein?*' sighed the Countess. 'At the cafés-concerts? *sous ce beau ciel*[37] – at the little tables before the doors? *Quelle existence!* You know I'm a Parisienne, monsieur,' she added, 'to my finger-tips.'

'Miss Spencer was mistaken then,' I ventured to return, 'in telling me you're a Provençale.'

She stared a moment, then put her nose to her embroidery, which struck me as having acquired even while we sat a dingier and more desultory air. 'Ah I'm a Provençale by birth, but a Parisienne by – inclination.' After which she pursued: 'And by the saddest events of my life – as well as by some of the happiest, hélas!'[38]

'In other words by a varied experience!' I now at last smiled.

She questioned me over it with her hard little salient eyes. 'Oh experience! – I could talk of that, no doubt, if I wished. *On en a de toutes les sortes*[39] – and I never dreamed that mine, for example, would ever have *this* in store for me.' And she indicated with her large bare elbow and with a jerk of her head all surrounding objects; the little white house, the pair of quince-trees, the rickety paling, even the rapt Mr Mixter.

I took them all bravely in. 'Ah if you mean you're decidedly in exile –!'

'You may imagine what it is. These two years of my *épreuve – elles m'en ont données, des heures, des heures!*[40] One gets used to things' – and she raised her shoulders to the highest shrug ever accomplished at North Verona; 'so that I sometimes think I've got used to this. But there are some things that are always beginning again. For example my coffee.'

I so far again lent myself. 'Do you always have coffee at this hour?'

Her eyebrows went up as high as her shoulders had done. 'At what hour would you propose to me to have it? I must have my little cup after breakfast.'

'Ah you breakfast at this hour?'

'At mid-day – *comme cela se fait.*[41] Here they breakfast at a quarter past seven. That "quarter past" is charming!'

'But you were telling me about your coffee,' I observed sympathetically.

'My *cousine* can't believe in it; she can't understand it. C'est une fille charmante, but that little cup of black coffee with a drop of "*fine*,"[42] served at this hour – they exceed her comprehension. So I have to break the ice each day, and it takes the coffee the time you see to arrive. And when it does arrive, monsieur –! If I don't press it on *you* – though monsieur here sometimes joins me! – it's because you've drunk it on the Boulevard.'

I resented extremely so critical a view of my poor friend's exertions, but I said nothing at all – the only way to be sure of my civility. I dropped my eyes on Mr Mixter, who, sitting cross-legged and nursing his knees, watched my companion's foreign graces with an interest that familiarity had apparently done little to restrict. She became aware, naturally, of my mystified view of him and faced the question with all her boldness. 'He adores me, you know,' she murmured with her nose again in her tapestry – 'he dreams of becoming *mon amoureux*. Yes, *il me fait une cour acharnée*[43] – such as you see him. That's what we've come to. He has read some French novel – it took him six months. But ever since that he has thought himself a hero and me – such as I am, monsieur – *je ne sais quelle dévergondée!* '[44]

Mr Mixter may have inferred that he was to that extent the object of our reference; but of the manner in which he was handled he must have had small suspicion – preoccupied as he was, as to my companion, with the ecstasy of contemplation. Our hostess moreover at this moment came out of the house, bearing a coffee-pot and three cups on a neat little tray. I took from her eyes, as she approached us, a brief but intense appeal – the mute expression, as I felt, conveyed in the hardest little look she had yet addressed me, of her longing to know what, as a man of the world in general and of the French world in particular, I thought of these allied forces now so encamped on the stricken field of her life. I could only 'act' however, as they said at North Verona, quite impenetrably – only make no answering sign. I couldn't intimate, much less could I frankly utter, my inward sense of the Countess's probable past,[45] with its measure of her virtue, value and accomplishments, and of the limits of the consideration to which she could properly pretend. I couldn't give my friend a hint of how I myself personally 'saw' her interesting pensioner – whether as the runaway wife of a too-jealous hair-dresser or of a too-morose pastry-cook, say; whether as a very small bourgeoise, in fine, who had vitiated her case beyond patching up, or even as some character, of the nomadic sort, less edifying still. I couldn't let in, by the jog of a shutter, as it were, a hard informing ray and then, washing my hands of the business, turn my back for ever. I could on the contrary but save the situation, my own at least, for the moment, by pulling myself together with a master hand and appearing to ignore everything but that the dreadful person between us *was* a 'grande dame.' This effort was possible indeed but as a retreat in good order and with all the forms of courtesy. If I couldn't speak, still less could I stay, and I think I must, in spite of everything, have turned black with disgust to see Caroline Spencer stand there like a waiting-maid. I therefore won't answer for the shade of success that may have attended my saying to the Countess, on my feet and as to leave her: 'You expect to remain some time in these *parages?*'[46]

What passed between us, as from face to face, while she looked up at me, *that*

24

at least our companion may have caught, that at least may have sown, for the after-time, some seed of revelation. The Countess repeated her terrible shrug. 'Who knows? I don't see my way —! It isn't an existence, but when one's in misery —! *Chère belle*,' she added as an appeal to Miss Spencer, 'you've gone and forgotten the "*fine*"!'

I detained that lady as, after considering a moment in silence the small array, she was about to turn off in quest of this article. I held out my hand in silence — I had to go. Her wan set little face, severely mild and with the question of a moment before now quite cold in it, spoke of extreme fatigue, but also of something else strange and conceived — whether a desperate patience still, or at last some other desperation, being more than I can say. What was clearest on the whole was that she was glad I was going. Mr Mixter had risen to his feet and was pouring out the Countess's coffee. As I went back past the Baptist church I could feel how right my poor friend had been in her conviction at the other, the still intenser, the now historic crisis, that she should still see something of that dear old Europe.

Daisy Miller

At the little town of Vevey,[1] in Switzerland, there is a particularly comfortable hotel; there are indeed many hotels, since the entertainment of tourists is the business of the place, which, as many travellers will remember, is seated upon the edge of a remarkably blue lake – a lake that it behoves every tourist to visit. The shore of the lake presents an unbroken array of establishments of this order, of every category, from the 'grand hotel' of the newest fashion, with a chalk-white front, a hundred balconies, and a dozen flags flying from its roof, to the small Swiss pension of an elder day, with its name inscribed in German-looking lettering upon a pink or yellow wall and an awkward summer-house in the angle of the garden. One of the hotels at Vevey, however, is famous, even classical, being distinguished from many of its upstart neighbours by an air both of luxury and of maturity. In this region, through the month of June, American travellers are extremely numerous; it may be said indeed that Vevey assumes at that time some of the characteristics of an American watering-place. There are sights and sounds that evoke a vision, an echo, of Newport and Saratoga.[2] There is a flitting hither and thither of 'stylish' young girls, a rustling of muslin flounces, a rattle of dance-music in the morning hours, a sound of high-pitched voices at all times. You receive an impression of these things at the excellent inn of the 'Trois Couronnes,'[3] and are transported in fancy to the Ocean House or to Congress Hall. But at the 'Trois Couronnes,' it must be added, there are other features much at variance with these suggestions: neat German waiters who look like secretaries of legation; Russian princesses sitting in the garden; little Polish boys walking about, held by the hand, with their governors; a view of the snowy crest of the Dent du Midi and the picturesque towers of the Castle of Chillon.[4]

I hardly know whether it was the analogies or the differences that were uppermost in the mind of a young American, who, two or three years ago, sat in the garden of the 'Trois Couronnes,' looking about him rather idly at some of the graceful objects I have mentioned. It was a beautiful summer morning, and in whatever fashion the young American looked at things they must have seemed to him charming. He had come from Geneva the day before, by the little steamer, to see his aunt, who was staying at the hotel – Geneva having been for a long time his place of residence. But his aunt had a headache – his aunt had almost always a headache – and she was now shut up in her room smelling camphor, so that he was at liberty to wander about. He was some seven-and-twenty years of age; when his friends spoke of him they usually said that he was at Geneva 'studying.' When his enemies spoke of him they said – but after all he had no enemies: he was extremely amiable and generally liked. What I should say is simply that when certain persons spoke of him they conveyed that the reason of his spending so much time at Geneva was that he was extremely devoted to a lady who lived there – a foreign lady, a person older than himself. Very few Americans – truly I think none – had ever seen this lady, about whom there were some singular stories. But Winterbourne had an old attachment for the little capital of Calvinism;[5] he had been put to school there as a boy and had afterwards even gone, on trial – trial of the grey old 'Academy'[6] on the steep and stony hillside – to college there; circumstances which had led to his forming a great many youthful friendships. Many of these he had kept, and they were a source of great satisfaction to him.

After knocking at his aunt's door and learning that she was indisposed he had taken a walk about the town and then he had come in to his breakfast. He had now finished that repast, but was enjoying a small cup of coffee which had been served him on a little table in the garden by one of the waiters who looked like *attachés*. At last he finished his coffee and lit a cigarette. Presently a small boy came walking along the path – an urchin of nine or ten. The child, who was diminutive for his years, had an aged expression of countenance, a pale complexion and sharp little features. He was dressed in knickerbockers and had red stockings that displayed his poor little spindle-shanks; he also wore a brilliant red cravat. He carried in his hand a long alpenstock,[7] the sharp point of which he thrust into everything he approached – the flower-beds, the garden-benches, the trains of the ladies' dresses. In front of Winterbourne he paused, looking at him with a pair of bright and penetrating little eyes.

'Will you give me a lump of sugar?' he asked in a small sharp hard voice – a voice immature and yet somehow not young.

Winterbourne glanced at the light table near him, on which his coffee-service rested, and saw that several morsels of sugar remained. 'Yes, you may take one,' he answered; 'but I don't think too much sugar good for little boys.'

This little boy stepped forward and carefully selected three of the coveted fragments, two of which he buried in the pocket of his knickerbockers, depositing the other as promptly in another place. He poked his alpenstock, lance-fashion, into Winterbourne's bench and tried to crack the lump of sugar with his teeth.

'Oh blazes; it's har-r-d!' he exclaimed, divesting vowel and consonants, pertinently enough, of any taint of softness.

Winterbourne had immediately gathered that he might have the honour of claiming him as a countryman. 'Take care you don't hurt your teeth,' he said paternally.

'I haven't got any teeth to hurt. They've all come out. I've only got seven teeth. Mother counted them last night, and one came out right afterwards. She said she'd slap me if any more came out. I can't help it. It's this old Europe. It's the climate that makes them come out. In America they didn't come out. It's these hotels.'

Winterbourne was much amused. 'If you eat three lumps of sugar your mother will certainly slap you,' he ventured.

'She's got to give me some candy then,' rejoined his young interlocutor. 'I can't get any candy here – any American candy. American candy's the best candy.'

'And are American little boys the best little boys?' Winterbourne asked.

'I don't know. *I'm* an American boy,' said the child.

'I see you're one of the best!' the young man laughed.

'Are you an American man?' pursued this vivacious infant. And then on his friend's affirmative reply, 'American men are the best,' he declared with assurance.

His companion thanked him for the compliment, and the child, who had now got astride of his alpenstock, stood looking about him while he attacked another lump of sugar. Winterbourne wondered if he himself had been like this in his infancy, for he had been brought to Europe at about the same age.

'Here comes my sister!' cried his young compatriot. 'She's an American girl, you bet!'

Winterbourne looked along the path and saw a beautiful young lady advancing. 'American girls are the best girls,' he thereupon cheerfully remarked to his visitor.

'My sister ain't the best!' the child promptly returned. 'She's always blowing at me.'

'I imagine that's your fault, not hers,' said Winterbourne. The young lady meanwhile had drawn near. She was dressed in white muslin, with a hundred frills and flounces and knots of pale-coloured ribbon. Bareheaded, she balanced in her hand a large parasol with a deep border of embroidery; and she was strikingly, admirably pretty. 'How pretty they are!' thought our friend, who straightened himself in his seat as if he were ready to rise.

The young lady paused in front of his bench, near the parapet of the garden, which overlooked the lake. The small boy had now converted his alpenstock into a vaulting-pole, by the aid of which he was springing about in the gravel and kicking it up not a little. 'Why Randolph,' she freely began, 'what *are* you doing?'

'I'm going up the Alps!' cried Randolph. 'This is the way!' And he gave another extravagant jump, scattering the pebbles about Winterbourne's ears.

'That's the way they come down,' said Winterbourne.

'He's an American man!' proclaimed Randolph in his harsh little voice.

The young lady gave no heed to this circumstance, but looked straight at her brother. 'Well, I guess you'd better be quiet,' she simply observed.

It seemed to Winterbourne that he had been in a manner presented. He got up and stepped slowly toward the charming creature, throwing away his cigarette. 'This little boy and I have made acquaintance,' he said with great civility. In Geneva, as he had been perfectly aware, a young man wasn't at liberty to speak to a young unmarried lady save under certain rarely-occurring conditions; but here at Vevey what conditions could be better than these? – a pretty American girl coming to stand in front of you in a garden with all the confidence in life. This pretty American girl, whatever that might prove, on hearing Winterbourne's observation simply glanced at him; she then turned her head and looked over the parapet, at the lake and the opposite mountains. He wondered whether he had gone too far, but decided that he must gallantly advance rather than retreat. While he was thinking of something else to say the young lady turned again to the little boy, whom she addressed quite as if they were alone together. 'I should like to know where you got that pole.'

'I bought it!' Randolph shouted.

'You don't mean to say you're going to take it to Italy!'

'Yes, I'm going to take it t'Italy!' the child rang out.

She glanced over the front of her dress and smoothed out a knot or two of ribbon. Then she gave her sweet eyes to the prospect again. 'Well, I guess you'd better leave it somewhere,' she dropped after a moment.

'Are you going to Italy?' Winterbourne now decided very respectfully to enquire.

She glanced at him with lovely remoteness. 'Yes, sir,' she then replied. And she said nothing more.

'And are you – a – thinking of the Simplon?'[8] he pursued with a slight drop of assurance.

'I don't know,' she said. 'I suppose it's some mountain. Randolph, what mountain are we thinking of?'

'Thinking of?' – the boy stared.

'Why going right over.'

'Going to where?' he demanded.

'Why right down to Italy' – Winterbourne felt vague emulations.

'I don't know,' said Randolph. 'I don't want to go t'Italy. I want to go to America.'

'Oh Italy's a beautiful place!' the young man laughed.

'Can you get candy there?' Randolph asked of all the echoes.

'I hope not,' said his sister. 'I guess you've had enough candy, and mother thinks so too.'

'I haven't had any for ever so long – for a hundred weeks!' cried the boy, still jumping about.

The young lady inspected her flounces and smoothed her ribbons again; and Winterbourne presently risked an observation on the beauty of the view. He was ceasing to be in doubt, for he had begun to perceive that she was really not in the least embarrassed. She might be cold, she might be austere, she might even be prim; for that was apparently – he had already so generalised – what the most 'distant' American girls did: they came and planted themselves straight in front of you to show how rigidly unapproachable they were. There hadn't been the slightest flush in her fresh fairness however; so that she was clearly neither offended nor fluttered. Only she was composed – he had seen that before too – of charming little parts that didn't match and that made no *ensemble*; and if she looked another way when he spoke to her, and seemed not particularly to hear him, this was simply her habit, her manner, the result of her having no idea whatever of 'form' (with such a tell-tale appendage as Randolph where in the world would she have got it?) in any such connexion. As he talked a little more and pointed out some of the objects of interest in the view, with which she appeared wholly unacquainted, she gradually, none the less, gave him more of the benefit of her attention; and then he saw that act unqualified by the faintest shadow of reserve. It wasn't however what would have been called a 'bold' front that she presented, for her expression was as decently limpid as the very cleanest water. Her eyes were the very prettiest conceivable, and indeed Winterbourne hadn't for a long time seen anything prettier than his fair countrywoman's various features – her complexion, her nose, her ears, her teeth. He took a great interest generally in that range of effects and was addicted to noting and, as it were, recording them; so that in regard to this young lady's face he made several observations. It wasn't at all insipid, yet at the same time wasn't pointedly – what point, on earth, could she ever make? – expressive; and though it offered such a collection of small finenesses and neatnesses he mentally accused it – very forgivingly – of a want of finish. He thought nothing more likely than that its wearer would have had her own experience of the action of her charms, as she would certainly have acquired a resulting confidence; but even should she depend on this for her main amusement her bright sweet superficial little visage gave out neither mockery nor irony. Before long it became clear that, however these things might be, she was much disposed to conversation. She remarked to Winterbourne that they were going to Rome for the winter – she and her mother and Randolph. She asked him if he was a 'real American'; she wouldn't have taken him for one;

he seemed more like a German — this flower was gathered as from a large field of comparison — especially when he spoke. Winterbourne, laughing, answered that he had met Germans who spoke like Americans, but not, so far as he remembered, any American with the resemblance she noted. Then he asked her if she mightn't be more at ease should she occupy the bench he had just quitted. She answered that she liked hanging round, but she none the less resignedly, after a little, dropped to the bench. She told him she was from New York State — 'if you know where that is'; but our friend really quickened this current by catching hold of her small slippery brother and making him stand a few minutes by his side.

'Tell me your honest name, my boy.' So he artfully proceeded.

In response to which the child was indeed unvarnished truth. 'Randolph C. Miller. And I'll tell you hers.' With which he levelled his alpenstock at his sister.

'You had better wait till you're asked!' said this young lady quite at her leisure.

'I should like very much to know *your* name,' Winterbourne made free to reply.

'Her name's Daisy Miller!' cried the urchin. 'But that ain't her real name; that ain't her name on her cards.'

'It's a pity you haven't got one of my cards!' Miss Miller quite as naturally remarked.

'Her real name's Annie P. Miller,' the boy went on.

It seemed, all amazingly, to do her good. 'Ask him *his* now' — and she indicated their friend.

But to this point Randolph seemed perfectly indifferent; he continued to supply information with regard to his own family. 'My father's name is Ezra B. Miller. My father ain't in Europe — he's in a better place than Europe.' Winterbourne for a moment supposed this the manner in which the child had been taught to intimate that Mr Miller had been removed to the sphere of celestial rewards. But Randolph immediately added: 'My father's in Schenectady.[9] He's got a big business. My father's rich, you bet.'

'Well!' ejaculated Miss Miller, lowering her parasol and looking at the embroidered border. Winterbourne presently released the child, who departed, dragging his alpenstock along the path. 'He don't like Europe,'[10] said the girl as with an artless instinct for historic truth. 'He wants to go back.'

'To Schenectady, you mean?'

'Yes, he wants to go right home. He hasn't got any boys here. There's one boy here, but he always goes round with a teacher. They won't let him play.'

'And your brother hasn't any teacher?' Winterbourne enquired.

It tapped, at a touch, the spring of confidence. 'Mother thought of getting him one — to travel round with us. There was a lady told her of a very good teacher; an American lady — perhaps you know her — Mrs Sanders. I think she came from

Boston. She told her of this teacher, and we thought of getting him to travel round with us. But Randolph said he didn't want a teacher travelling round with us. He said he wouldn't have lessons when he was in the cars.[11] And we *are* in the cars about half the time. There was an English lady we met in the cars – I think her name was Miss Featherstone; perhaps you know her. She wanted to know why I didn't give Randolph lessons – give him "instruction," she called it. I guess he could give me more instruction than I could give him. He's very smart.'

'Yes,' said Winterbourne; 'he seems very smart.'

'Mother's going to get a teacher for him as soon as we get t'Italy. Can you get good teachers in Italy?'

'Very good, I should think,' Winterbourne hastened to reply.

'Or else she's going to find some school. He ought to learn some more. He's only nine. He's going to college.' And in this way Miss Miller continued to converse upon the affairs of her family and upon other topics. She sat there with her extremely pretty hands, ornamented with very brilliant rings, folded in her lap, and with her pretty eyes now resting upon those of Winterbourne, now wandering over the garden, the people who passed before her and the beautiful view. She addressed her new acquaintance as if she had known him a long time. He found it very pleasant. It was many years since he had heard a young girl talk so much. It might have been said of this wandering maiden who had come and sat down beside him upon a bench that she chattered. She was very quiet, she sat in a charming tranquil attitude; but her lips and her eyes were constantly moving. She had a soft slender agreeable voice, and her tone was distinctly sociable. She gave Winterbourne a report of her movements and intentions, and those of her mother and brother, in Europe, and enumerated in particular the various hotels at which they had stopped. 'That English lady in the cars,' she said – 'Miss Featherstone – asked me if we didn't all live in hotels in America. I told her I had never been in so many hotels in my life as since I came to Europe. I've never seen so many – it's nothing but hotels.' But Miss Miller made this remark with no querulous accent; she appeared to be in the best humour with everything. She declared that the hotels were very good when once you got used to their ways and that Europe was perfectly entrancing. She wasn't disappointed – not a bit. Perhaps it was because she had heard so much about it before. She had ever so many intimate friends who had been there ever so many times, and that way she had got thoroughly posted. And then she had had ever so many dresses and things from Paris. Whenever she put on a Paris dress she felt as if she were in Europe.

'It was a kind of a wishing-cap,' Winterbourne smiled.

'Yes,' said Miss Miller at once and without examining this analogy; 'it always made me wish I was here. But I needn't have done that for dresses. I'm sure they send all the pretty ones to America; you see the most frightful things here. The only thing I don't like,' she proceeded, 'is the society. There ain't any society – or if there is I don't know where it keeps itself. Do you? I suppose there's some society somewhere, but I haven't seen anything of it. I'm very fond of society and I've always had plenty of it. I don't mean only in Schenectady, but in New York. I used to go to New York every winter. In New York I had lots of society. Last winter I had seventeen dinners given me, and three of them were by gentlemen,' added Daisy Miller. 'I've more friends in New York than in Schenectady – more gentlemen friends; and more young lady friends too,' she resumed in a moment. She paused again for an instant; she was looking at Winterbourne with all her prettiness in her frank gay eyes and in her clear rather uniform smile. 'I've always had,' she said, 'a great deal of gentlemen's society.'

Poor Winterbourne was amused and perplexed – above all he was charmed. He had never yet heard a young girl express herself in just this fashion; never at least save in cases where to say such things was to have at the same time some rather complicated consciousness about them. And yet was he to accuse Miss Daisy Miller of an actual or a potential *arrière-pensée*,[12] as they said at Geneva? He felt he had lived at Geneva so long as to have got morally muddled; he had lost the right sense for the young American tone. Never indeed since he had grown old enough to appreciate things had he encountered a young compatriot of so 'strong' a type as this. Certainly she was very charming, but how extraordinarily communicative and how tremendously easy! Was she simply a pretty girl from New York State – were they all like that, the pretty girls who had had a good deal of gentlemen's society? Or was she also a designing, an audacious, in short an expert young person? Yes, his instinct for such a question had ceased to serve him, and his reason could but mislead. Miss Daisy Miller looked extremely innocent. Some people had told him that after all American girls *were* exceedingly innocent, and others had told him that after all they weren't. He must on the whole take Miss Daisy Miller for a flirt – a pretty American flirt. He had never as yet had relations with representatives of that class. He had known here in Europe two or three women – persons older than Miss Daisy Miller and provided, for respectability's sake, with husbands – who were great coquettes; dangerous terrible women with whom one's light commerce might indeed take a serious turn. But this charming apparition wasn't a coquette in that sense; she was very unsophisticated; she was only a pretty American flirt. Winterbourne was almost grateful for having found the formula that applied to Miss Daisy Miller. He leaned back in his seat; he remarked to himself that she had the finest little nose he had ever seen; he wondered what were the regular conditions and limitations of one's intercourse with a pretty American flirt. It presently became apparent that he was on the way to learn.

'Have you been to that old castle?' the girl soon asked, pointing with her parasol to the far-shining walls of the Château de Chillon.

'Yes, formerly, more than once,' said Winterbourne. 'You too, I suppose, have seen it?'

'No, we haven't been there. I want to go there dreadfully. Of course I mean to go there. I wouldn't go away from here without having seen that old castle.'

'It's a very pretty excursion,' the young man returned, 'and very easy to make. You can drive, you know, or you can go by the little steamer.'

'You can go in the cars,' said Miss Miller.

'Yes, you can go in the cars,' Winterbourne assented.

'Our courier[13] says they take you right up to the castle,' she continued. 'We were going last week, but mother gave out. She suffers dreadfully from dyspepsia. She said she couldn't any more go –!' But this sketch of Mrs Miller's plea remained unfinished. 'Randolph wouldn't go either; he says he don't think much of old castles. But I guess we'll go this week if we can get Randolph.'

'Your brother isn't interested in ancient monuments?' Winterbourne indulgently asked.

He now drew her, as he guessed she would herself have said, every time. 'Why no, he says he don't care much about old castles. He's only nine. He wants to stay at the hotel. Mother's afraid to leave him alone, and the courier won't stay with him; so we haven't been to many places. But it will be too bad if we don't go up there.' And Miss Miller pointed again at the Château de Chillon.

'I should think it might be arranged,' Winterbourne was thus emboldened to reply. 'Couldn't you get some one to stay – for the afternoon – with Randolph?'

Miss Miller looked at him a moment, and then with all serenity, 'I wish *you'd* stay with him!' she said.

He pretended to consider it. 'I'd much rather go to Chillon with you.'

'With me?' she asked without a shadow of emotion.

She didn't rise blushing, as a young person at Geneva would have done; and yet, conscious that he had gone very far, he thought it possible she had drawn back. 'And with your mother,' he answered very respectfully.

But it seemed that both his audacity and his respect were lost on Miss Daisy Miller. 'I guess mother wouldn't go – for *you*,' she smiled. 'And she ain't much *bent* on going, anyway. She don't like to ride round in the afternoon.' After which she familiarly proceeded: 'But did you really mean what you said just now – that you'd like to go up there?'

'Most earnestly I meant it,' Winterbourne declared.

'Then we may arrange it. If mother will stay with Randolph I guess Eugenio will.'

'Eugenio?' the young man echoed.

'Eugenio's our courier. He doesn't like to stay with Randolph – he's the most fastidious man I ever saw. But he's a splendid courier. I guess he'll stay at home with Randolph if mother does, and then we can go to the castle.'

Winterbourne reflected for an instant as lucidly as possible: 'we' could only mean Miss Miller and himself. This prospect seemed almost too good to believe; he felt as if he ought to kiss the young lady's hand. Possibly he would have done so, – and quite spoiled his chance; but at this moment another person – presumably Eugenio – appeared. A tall handsome man, with superb whiskers and wearing a velvet morning-coat and a voluminous watch-guard, approached the young lady, looking sharply at her companion. 'Oh Eugenio!' she said with the friendliest accent.

Eugenio had eyed Winterbourne from head to foot; he now bowed gravely to Miss Miller. 'I have the honour to inform Mademoiselle that luncheon's on table.'

Mademoiselle slowly rose. 'See here, Eugenio, I'm going to that old castle anyway.'

'To the Château de Chillon, Mademoiselle?' the courier enquired. 'Mademoiselle has made arrangements?' he added in a tone that struck Winterbourne as impertinent.

Eugenio's tone apparently threw, even to Miss Miller's own apprehension, a slightly ironical light on her position. She turned to Winterbourne with the slightest blush. 'You won't back out?'

'I shall not be happy till we go!' he protested.

'And you're staying in this hotel?' she went on. 'And you're really American?'

The courier still stood there with an effect of offence for the young man so far as the latter saw in it a tacit reflexion on Miss Miller's behaviour and an insinuation that she 'picked up' acquaintances. 'I shall have the honour of presenting to you a person who'll tell you all about me,' he said, smiling, and referring to his aunt.

'Oh well, we'll go some day,' she beautifully answered; with which she gave him a smile and turned away. She put up her parasol and walked back to the inn beside Eugenio. Winterbourne stood watching her, and as she moved away, drawing her muslin furbelows over the walk, he spoke to himself of her natural elegance.[14]

II

He had, however, engaged to do more than proved feasible in promising to present his aunt, Mrs Costello, to Miss Daisy Miller. As soon as that lady had got better of her headache he waited on her in her apartment and, after a show of the proper solicitude about her health, asked if she had noticed in the hotel an American family – a mamma, a daughter and an obstreperous little boy.

'An obstreperous little boy and a preposterous big courier?' said Mrs Costello. 'Oh yes, I've noticed them. Seen them, heard them and kept out of their way.' Mrs Costello was a widow of fortune, a person of much distinction and who frequently intimated that if she hadn't been so dreadfully liable to sick-headaches she would probably have left a deeper impress on her time. She had a long pale face, a high nose and a great deal of very striking white hair, which she wore in large puffs[15] and over the top of her head. She had two sons married in New York and another who was now in Europe. This young man was amusing himself at Homburg[16] and, though guided by his taste, was rarely observed to visit any particular city at the moment selected by his mother for her appearance there. Her nephew, who had come to Vevey expressly to see her, was therefore more attentive than, as she said, her very own. He had imbibed at Geneva the idea that one must be irreproachable in all such forms. Mrs Costello hadn't seen him for many years and was now greatly pleased with him, manifesting her approbation by initiating him into many of the secrets of that social sway which, as he could see she would like him to think, she exerted from her stronghold in Forty-Second Street. She admitted that she was very exclusive, but if he had been better acquainted with New York he would see that one had to be. And her picture of the minutely hierarchical constitution of the society of that city, which she presented to him in many different lights, was, to Winterbourne's imagination, almost oppressively striking.

He at once recognised from her tone that Miss Daisy Miller's place in the social scale was low. 'I'm afraid you don't approve of them,' he pursued in reference to his new friends.

'They're horribly common' – it was perfectly simple. 'They're the sort of Americans that one does one's duty by just ignoring.'

'Ah you just ignore them?' – the young man took it in.

'I can't not, my dear Frederick. I wouldn't if I hadn't to, but I have to.'

'The little girl's very pretty,' he went on in a moment.

'Of course she's very pretty. But she's of the last crudity.'

'I see what you mean of course,' he allowed after another pause.

'She has that charming look they all have,' his aunt resumed. 'I can't think where they pick it up; and she dresses in perfection – no, you don't know how well she dresses. I can't think where they get their taste.'

'But, my dear aunt, she's not, after all, a Comanche savage.'

'She is a young lady,' said Mrs Costello, 'who has an intimacy with her mamma's courier?'

'An "intimacy" with him?' Ah there it was!

'There's no other name for such a relation. But the skinny little mother's just as bad! They treat the courier as a familiar friend – as a gentleman and a scholar. I shouldn't wonder if he dines with them. Very likely they've never seen a man with such good manners, such fine clothes, so *like* a gentleman – or a scholar. He probably corresponds to the young lady's idea of a count. He sits with them in the garden of an evening. I think he smokes in their faces.'

Winterbourne listened with interest to these disclosures; they helped him to make up his mind about Miss Daisy. Evidently she was rather wild. 'Well,' he said, 'I'm not a courier and I didn't smoke in her face, and yet she was very charming to me.'

'You had better have mentioned at first,' Mrs Costello returned with dignity, 'that you had made her valuable acquaintance.'

'We simply met in the garden and talked a bit.'

'By appointment – no? Ah that's still to come! Pray what did you say?'

'I said I should take the liberty of introducing her to my admirable aunt.'

'Your admirable aunt's a thousand times obliged to you.'

'It was to guarantee my respectability.'

'And pray who's to guarantee hers?'

'Ah you're cruel!' said the young man. 'She's a very innocent girl.'

'You don't say that as if you believed it,' Mrs Costello returned.

'She's completely uneducated,' Winterbourne acknowledged, 'but she's wonderfully pretty, and in short she's very nice. To prove I believe it I'm going to take her to the Château de Chillon.'

Mrs Costello made a wondrous face. 'You two are going off there together? I should say it proved just the contrary. How long had you known her, may I ask, when this interesting project was formed? You haven't been twenty-four hours in the house.'

'I had known her half an hour!' Winterbourne smiled.

'Then she's just what I supposed.'

'And what do you suppose?'

'Why that she's a horror.'

Our youth was silent for some moments. 'You really think then,' he presently began, and with a desire for trustworthy information, 'you really think that –' But he paused again while his aunt waited.

'Think what, sir?'

'That she's the sort of young lady who expects a man sooner or later to – well, we'll call it carry her off?'

'I haven't the least idea what such young ladies expect a man to do. But I really consider you had better not meddle with little American girls who are uneducated, as you mildly put it. You've lived too long out of the country. You'll be sure to make some great mistake. You're too innocent.'

'My dear aunt, not so much as that comes to!' he protested with a laugh and a curl of his moustache.

'You're too guilty then!'

He continued all thoughtfully to finger the ornament in question. 'You won't let the poor girl know you then?' he asked at last.

'Is it literally true that she's going to the Château de Chillon with you?'

'I've no doubt she fully intends it.'

'Then, my dear Frederick,' said Mrs Costello, 'I must decline the honour of her acquaintance. I'm an old woman, but I'm not too old – thank heaven – to be honestly shocked!'

'But don't they all do these things – the little American girls at home?' Winterbourne enquired.

Mrs Costello stared a moment. 'I should like to see my granddaughters 'do them!' she then grimly returned.

This seemed to throw some light on the matter, for Winterbourne remembered to have heard his pretty cousins in New York, the daughters of this lady's two daughters, called 'tremendous flirts.' If therefore Miss Daisy Miller exceeded the liberal licence allowed to these young women it was probable she did go even by the American allowance rather far. Winterbourne was impatient to see her again, and it vexed, it even a little humiliated him, that he shouldn't by instinct appreciate her justly.

Though so impatient to see her again he hardly knew what ground he should give for his aunt's refusal to become acquainted with her; but he discovered promptly enough that with Miss Daisy Miller there was no great need of walking on tiptoe. He found her that evening in the garden, wandering about in the warm starlight after the manner of an indolent sylph and swinging to and fro the largest fan he had ever beheld. It was ten o'clock. He had dined with his aunt, had been sitting with her since dinner, and had just taken leave of her till the morrow. His young friend frankly rejoiced to renew their intercourse; she pronounced it the stupidest evening she had ever passed.

'Have you been all alone?' he asked with no intention of an epigram and no effect of her perceiving one.

'I've been walking round with mother. But mother gets tired walking round,' Miss Miller explained.

'Has she gone to bed?'

'No, she doesn't like to go to bed. She doesn't sleep scarcely any – not three hours. She says she doesn't know how she lives. She's dreadfully nervous. I guess she sleeps more than she thinks. She's gone somewhere after Randolph; she wants to try to get him to go to bed. He doesn't like to go to bed.'

The soft impartiality of her *constatations*,[17] as Winterbourne would have termed them, was a thing by itself – exquisite little fatalist as they seemed to make her. 'Let us hope she'll persuade him,' he encouragingly said.

'Well, she'll talk to him all she can – but he doesn't like her to talk to him': with which Miss Daisy opened and closed her fan. 'She's going to try to get Eugenio to talk to him. But Randolph ain't afraid of Eugenio. Eugenio's a splendid courier, but he can't make much impression on Randolph! I don't believe he'll go to bed before eleven.' Her detachment from any invidious judgement of this was, to her companion's sense, inimitable; and it appeared that Randolph's vigil was in fact triumphantly prolonged, for Winterbourne attended her in her stroll for some time without meeting her mother. 'I've been looking round for that lady you want to introduce me to,' she resumed – 'I guess she's your aunt.' Then on his admitting the fact and expressing some curiosity as to how she had learned it, she said she had heard all about Mrs Costello from the chambermaid. She was very quiet and very *comme il faut*;[18] she wore white puffs; she spoke to no one and she never dined at the common table.[19] Every two days she had a headache. 'I think that's a lovely description, headache and all!' said Miss Daisy, chattering along in her thin gay voice. 'I want to know her ever so much. I know just what *your* aunt would be; I know I'd like her. She'd be very exclusive. I like a lady to be exclusive; I'm dying to be exclusive myself. Well, I guess we *are* exclusive, mother and I. We don't speak to any one – or they don't speak to us. I suppose it's about the same thing. Anyway, I shall be ever so glad to meet your aunt.'

Winterbourne was embarrassed – he could but trump up some evasion. 'She'd be most happy, but I'm afraid those tiresome headaches are always to be reckoned with.'

The girl looked at him through the fine dusk.

'Well, I suppose she doesn't have a headache every day.'

He had to make the best of it. 'She tells me she wonderfully does.' He didn't know what else to say.

Miss Miller stopped and stood looking at him. Her prettiness was still visible in the darkness; she kept flapping to and fro her enormous fan. 'She doesn't want to know me!' she then lightly broke out. 'Why don't you say so? You needn't be afraid. *I'm* not afraid!' And she quite crowed for the fun of it.

Winterbourne distinguished however a wee false note in this: he was touched, shocked, mortified by it. 'My dear young lady, she knows no one. She goes through life immured. It's her wretched health.'

The young girl walked on a few steps in the glee of the thing. 'You needn't be afraid,' she repeated. 'Why should she want to know me?' Then she paused again; she was close to the parapet of the garden, and in front of her was the starlit lake. There was a vague sheen on its surface, and in the distance were dimly-seen mountain forms. Daisy Miller looked out at these great lights and shades and again proclaimed a gay indifference — 'Gracious! she *is* exclusive!' Winterbourne wondered if she were seriously wounded and for a moment almost wished her sense of injury might be such as to make it becoming in him to reassure and comfort her. He had a pleasant sense that she would be all accessible to a respectful tenderness at that moment. He felt quite ready to sacrifice his aunt — conversationally; to acknowledge she was a proud rude woman and to make the point that they needn't mind her. But before he had time to commit himself to this questionable mixture of gallantry and impiety, the young lady, resuming her walk, gave an exclamation in quite another tone. 'Well, here's mother! I guess she *hasn't* got Randolph to go to bed.' The figure of a lady appeared, at a distance, very indistinct in the darkness; it advanced with a slow and wavering step and then suddenly seemed to pause.

'Are you sure it's your mother? Can you make her out in this thick dusk?' Winterbourne asked.

'Well,' the girl laughed, 'I guess I know my own mother! And when she has got on my shawl too. She's always wearing my things.'

The lady in question, ceasing now to approach, hovered vaguely about the spot at which she had checked her steps.

'I'm afraid your mother doesn't see you,' said Winterbourne. 'Or perhaps,' he added — thinking, with Miss Miller, the joke permissible — 'perhaps she feels guilty about your shawl.'

'Oh it's a fearful old thing!' his companion placidly answered. 'I told her she could wear it if she didn't mind looking like a fright. She won't come here because she sees you.'

'Ah then,' said Winterbourne, 'I had better leave you.'

'Oh no — come on!' the girl insisted.

'I'm afraid your mother doesn't approve of my walking with you.'

She gave him, he thought, the oddest glance. 'It isn't for me; it's for you — that is it's for *her*. Well, I don't know who it's for! But mother doesn't like any of my gentlemen friends. She's right down timid. She always makes a fuss if I introduce a gentleman. But I *do* introduce them — almost always. If I didn't introduce my gentlemen friends to mother,' Miss Miller added, in her small flat monotone, 'I shouldn't think I was natural.'

'Well, to introduce me,' Winterbourne remarked, 'you must know my name.' And he proceeded to pronounce it.

'Oh my – I can't say all that!' cried his companion, much amused. But by this time they had come up to Mrs Miller, who, as they drew near, walked to the parapet of the garden and leaned on it, looking intently at the lake and presenting her back to them. 'Mother!' said the girl in a tone of decision – upon which the elder lady turned round. 'Mr Frederick Forsyth Winterbourne,'[20] said the latter's young friend, repeating his lesson of a moment before and introducing him very frankly and prettily. 'Common' she might be, as Mrs Costello had pronounced her; yet what provision was made by that epithet for her queer little native grace?

Her mother was a small spare light person, with a wandering eye, a scarce perceptible nose, and, as to make up for it, an unmistakeable forehead, decorated – but too far back, as Winterbourne mentally described it – with thin much-frizzled hair. Like her daughter Mrs Miller was dressed with extreme elegance; she had enormous diamonds in her ears. So far as the young man could observe, she gave him no greeting – she certainly wasn't looking at him. Daisy was near her, pulling her shawl straight. 'What are you doing, poking round here?' this young lady enquired – yet by no means with the harshness of accent her choice of words might have implied.

'Well, I don't know' – and the new-comer turned to the lake again.

'I shouldn't think you'd want that shawl!' Daisy familiarly proceeded.

'Well – I do!' her mother answered with a sound that partook for Winterbourne of an odd strain between mirth and woe.

'Did you get Randolph to go to bed?' Daisy asked.

'No, I couldn't induce him' – and Mrs Miller seemed to confess to the same mild fatalism as her daughter. 'He wants to talk to the waiter. He *likes* to talk to that waiter.'

'I was just telling Mr Winterbourne,' the girl went on; and to the young man's ear her tone might have indicated that she had been uttering his name all her life.

'Oh yes!' he concurred – 'I've the pleasure of knowing your son.'

Randolph's mamma was silent; she kept her attention on the lake. But at last a sigh broke from her. 'Well, I don't see how he lives!'

'Anyhow, it isn't so bad as it was at Dover,' Daisy at least opined.

'And what occurred at Dover?' Winterbourne desired to know.

'He wouldn't go to bed at all. I guess he sat up all night – in the public parlour. He wasn't in bed at twelve o'clock: it seemed as if he couldn't budge.'

'It was half-past twelve when *I* gave up,' Mrs Miller recorded with passionless accuracy.

It was of great interest to Winterbourne. 'Does he sleep much during the day?'

'I guess he doesn't sleep *very* much,' Daisy rejoined.

'I wish he just *would!*' said her mother. 'It seems as if he *must* make it up somehow.'

'Well, I guess it's we that make it up. I think he's real tiresome,' Daisy pursued.

After which, for some moments, there was silence. 'Well, Daisy Miller,' the elder lady then unexpectedly broke out, 'I shouldn't think you'd want to talk against your own brother!'

'Well, he *is* tiresome, mother,' said the girl, but with no sharpness of insistence.

'Well, he's only nine,' Mrs Miller lucidly urged.

'Well, he wouldn't go up to that castle, anyway,' her daughter replied as for accommodation. 'I'm going up there with Mr Winterbourne.'

To this announcement, very placidly made, Daisy's parent offered no response. Winterbourne took for granted on this that she opposed such a course; but he said to himself at the same time that she was a simple easily-managed person and that a few deferential protestations would modify her attitude. 'Yes,' he therefore interposed, 'your daughter has kindly allowed me the honour of being her guide.'

Mrs Miller's wandering eyes attached themselves with an appealing air to her other companion, who, however, strolled a few steps further, gently humming to herself. 'I presume you'll go in the cars,' she then quite colourlessly remarked.

'Yes, or in the boat,' said Winterbourne.

'Well, of course I don't know,' Mrs Miller returned. 'I've never been up to that castle.'

'It is a pity you shouldn't go,' he observed, beginning to feel reassured as to her opposition. And yet he was quite prepared to find that as a matter of course she meant to accompany her daughter.

It was on this view accordingly that light was projected for him. 'We've been thinking ever so much about going, but it seems as if we couldn't. Of course Daisy – she wants to go round everywhere. But there's a lady here – I don't know her name – she says she shouldn't think we'd want to go to see castles *here*; she should think we'd want to wait till we got t'Italy. It seems as if there would be so many there,' continued Mrs Miller with an air of increasing confidence. 'Of course we only want to see the principal ones. We visited several in England,' she presently added.

'Ah yes, in England there are beautiful castles,' said Winterbourne. 'But Chillon here is very well worth seeing.'

'Well, if Daisy feels up to it – ' said Mrs Miller in a tone that seemed to break under the burden of such conceptions. 'It seems as if there's nothing she won't undertake.'

'Oh I'm pretty sure she'll enjoy it!' Winterbourne declared. And he desired more and more to make it a certainty that he was to have the privilege of a *tête-à-tête* with the young lady who was still strolling along in front of them and softly vocalising. 'You're not disposed, madam,' he enquired, 'to make the so interesting excursion yourself?'

So addressed Daisy's mother looked at him an instant with a certain scared obliquity and then walked forward in silence. Then, 'I guess she had better go alone,' she said simply.

It gave him occasion to note that this was a very different type of maternity from that of the vigilant matrons who massed themselves in the forefront of social intercourse in the dark old city at the other end of the lake.[21] But his meditations were interrupted by hearing his name very distinctly pronounced by Mrs Miller's unprotected daughter. 'Mr Winterbourne!' she piped from a considerable distance.

'Mademoiselle!' said the young man.

'Don't you want to take me out in a boat?'

'At present?' he asked.

'Why of course!' she gaily returned.

'Well, Annie Miller!' exclaimed her mother.

'I beg you, madam, to let her go,' he hereupon eagerly pleaded; so instantly had he been struck with the romantic side of this chance to guide through the summer starlight a skiff freighted with a fresh and beautiful young girl.

'I shouldn't think she'd want to,' said her mother. 'I should think she'd rather go indoors.'

'I'm sure Mr Winterbourne wants to *take* me,' Daisy declared. 'He's so awfully devoted!'

'I'll row you over to Chillon under the stars.'

'I don't believe it!' Daisy laughed.

'Well!' the elder lady again gasped, as in rebuke of this freedom.

'You haven't spoken to me for half an hour,' her daughter went on.

'I've been having some very pleasant conversation with your mother,' Winterbourne replied.

'Oh pshaw! I want you to take me out in a boat!' Daisy went on as if nothing else had been said. They had all stopped and she had turned round and was looking at her friend. Her face wore a charming smile, her pretty eyes gleamed in the darkness, she swung her great fan about. No, he felt, it was impossible to be prettier than that.

'There are half a dozen boats moored at that landing-place,' and he pointed to a range of steps that descended from the garden to the lake. 'If you'll do me the honour to accept my arm we'll go and select one of them.'

She stood there smiling; she threw back her head; she laughed as for the drollery of this. 'I like a gentleman to be formal!'

'I assure you it's a formal offer.'

'I was bound I'd make you say something,' Daisy agreeably mocked.

'You see it's not very difficult,' said Winterbourne. 'But I'm afraid you're chaffing me.'

'I think not, sir,' Mrs Miller shyly pleaded.

'Do then let me give you a row,' he persisted to Daisy.

'It's quite lovely, the way you say that!' she cried in reward.

'It will be still more lovely to do it.'

'Yes, it would be lovely!' But she made no movement to accompany him; she only remained an elegant image of free light irony.

'I guess you'd better find out what time it is,' her mother impartially contributed.

'It's eleven o'clock, Madam,' said a voice with a foreign accent out of the neighbouring darkness; and Winterbourne, turning, recognised the florid person-age he had already seen in attendance. He had apparently just approached.

'Oh Eugenio,' said Daisy, 'I'm going out with Mr Winterbourne in a boat!'

Eugenio bowed. 'At this hour of the night, Mademoiselle?'

'I'm going with Mr Winterbourne,' she repeated with her shining smile. 'I'm going this very minute.'

'Do tell her she can't, Eugenio,' Mrs Miller said to the courier.

'I think you had better not go out in a boat, Mademoiselle,' the man declared.

Winterbourne wished to goodness this pretty girl were not on such familiar terms with her courier; but he said nothing, and she meanwhile added to his ground. 'I suppose you don't think it's proper! My!' she wailed; 'Eugenio doesn't think anything's proper.'

'I'm nevertheless quite at your service,' Winterbourne hastened to remark.

'Does Mademoiselle propose to go alone?' Eugenio asked of Mrs Miller.

'Oh no, with this gentleman!' cried Daisy's mamma for reassurance.

'I *meant* alone with the gentleman.' The courier looked for a moment at Winterbourne — the latter seemed to make out in his face a vague presumptuous intelligence as at the expense of their companions — and then solemnly and with a bow, 'As Mademoiselle pleases!' he said.

But Daisy broke off at this. 'Oh I hoped you'd make a fuss! I don't care to go now.'

'Ah but I myself shall make a fuss if you don't go,' Winterbourne declared with spirit.

'That's all I want — a little fuss!' With which she began to laugh again.

'Mr Randolph has retired for the night!' the courier hereupon importantly announced.

'Oh Daisy, now we can go then!' cried Mrs Miller.

Her daughter turned away from their friend, all lighted with her odd perversity. 'Good-night — I hope you're disappointed or disgusted or something!'

He looked at her gravely, taking her by the hand she offered. 'I'm puzzled, if you want to know!' he answered.

'Well, I hope it won't keep you awake!' she said very smartly; and, under the escort of the privileged Eugenio, the two ladies passed toward the house.

Winterbourne's eyes followed them; he was indeed quite mystified. He lingered beside the lake a quarter of an hour, baffled by the question of the girl's sudden familiarities and caprices. But the only very definite conclusion he came to was that he should enjoy deucedly 'going off' with her somewhere.

Two days later he went off with her to the Castle of Chillon. He waited for her in the large hall of the hotel, where the couriers, the servants, the foreign tourists were lounging about and staring. It wasn't the place he would have chosen for a tryst, but she had placidly appointed it. She came tripping downstairs, buttoning her long gloves, squeezing her folded parasol against her pretty figure, dressed exactly in the way that consorted best, to his fancy, with their adventure. He was a man of imagination and, as our ancestors used to say, of sensibility; as he took in her charming air and caught from the great staircase her impatient confiding step the note of some small sweet strain of romance, not intense but clear and sweet, seemed to sound for their start. He could have believed he was *really* going 'off' with her. He led her out through all the idle people assembled – they all looked at her straight and hard: she had begun to chatter as soon as she joined him. His preference had been that they should be conveyed to Chillon in a carriage, but she expressed a lively wish to go in the little steamer – there would be such a lovely breeze upon the water and they should see such lots of people. The sail wasn't long, but Winterbourne's companion found time for many characteristic remarks and other demonstrations, not a few of which were, from the extremity of their candour, slightly disconcerting. To the young man himself their small excursion showed so for delightfully irregular and incongruously intimate that, even allowing for her habitual sense of freedom, he had some expectation of seeing her appear to find in it the same savour. But it must be confessed that he was in this particular rather disappointed. Miss Miller was highly animated, she was in the brightest spirits; but she was clearly not at all in a nervous flutter – as she should have been to match *his* tension; she avoided neither his eyes nor those of any one else; she neither coloured from an awkward consciousness when she looked at him nor when she saw that people were looking at herself. People continued to look at her a great deal, and Winterbourne could at least take pleasure in his pretty companion's distinguished air. He had been privately afraid she would talk loud, laugh overmuch, and even perhaps desire to move extravagantly about the boat. But he quite forgot his fears; he sat smiling with his eyes on her face while, without stirring from her place, she delivered herself of a great number of original reflexions. It was the most charming innocent prattle he had ever heard, for, by his own experience hitherto, when young persons were so ingenuous they were less articulate and when they were so confident were more sophisticated. If he had assented to the idea that she was 'common,' at any rate, *was* she proving so, after all, or was he simply getting used to her commonness? Her discourse was for the most part of what immediately and superficially surrounded them, but there were moments when it threw out a longer look or took a sudden straight plunge.

'What on *earth* are you so solemn about?' she suddenly demanded, fixing her agreeable eyes on her friend's.

'*Am* I solemn?' he asked. 'I had an idea I was grinning from ear to ear.'

'You look as if you were taking me to a prayer-meeting or a funeral. If that's a grin your ears are very near together.'

'Should you like me to dance a hornpipe on the deck?'

'Pray do, and I'll carry round your hat. It will pay the expenses of our journey.'

'I never was better pleased in my life,' Winterbourne returned.

She looked at him a moment, then let it renew her amusement. 'I like to make you say those things. You're a queer mixture!'

In the castle, after they had landed, nothing could exceed the light independence of her humour. She tripped about the vaulted chambers, rustled her skirts in the corkscrew staircases, flirted back with a pretty little cry and a shudder from the edge of the oubliettes[22] and turned a singularly well-shaped ear to everything Winterbourne told her about the place. But he saw she cared little for mediaeval history and that the grim ghosts of Chillon loomed but faintly before her. They had the good fortune to have been able to wander without other society than that of their guide; and Winterbourne arranged with this companion that they shouldn't be hurried — that they should linger and pause wherever they chose. He interpreted the bargain generously — Winterbourne on his side had been generous — and ended by leaving them quite to themselves. Miss Miller's observations were marked by no logical consistency; for anything she wanted to say she was sure to find a pretext. She found a great many, in the tortuous passages and rugged embrasures of the place, for asking her young man sudden questions about himself, his family, his previous history, his tastes, his habits, his designs, and for supplying information on corresponding points in her own situation. Of her own tastes, habits and designs the charming creature was prepared to give the most definite and indeed the most favourable account.

'Well, I hope you know enough!' she exclaimed after Winterbourne had sketched for her something of the story of the unhappy Bonnivard.[23] 'I never saw a man that knew so much!' The history of Bonnivard had evidently, as they say, gone into one ear and out of the other. But this easy erudition struck her none the less as wonderful, and she was soon quite sure she wished Winterbourne would travel with them and 'go round' with them; they too in that case might learn something about something. 'Don't you want to come and teach Randolph?' she asked; 'I guess he'd improve with a gentleman teacher.' Winterbourne was certain that nothing could possibly please him so much, but that he had unfortunately other occupations. 'Other occupations? I don't believe a speck of it!' she protested. 'What do you mean now? You're not in business.' The young man allowed that he was not in business, but he had engagements which even within a day or two would necessitate his return to Geneva. 'Oh bother!' she panted, 'I don't believe it!' and she began to talk about something else. But a few moments later, when he was pointing out to her the interesting design of an antique fireplace, she broke out irrelevantly: 'You don't mean to say you're going back to Geneva?'

'It is a melancholy fact that I shall have to report myself there to-morrow.'

She met it with a vivacity that could only flatter him. 'Well, Mr Winterbourne, I think you're horrid!'

'Oh don't say such dreadful things!' he quite sincerely pleaded — 'just at the last.'

'The last?' the girl cried; 'I call it the very first! I've half a mind to leave you here and go straight back to the hotel alone.' And for the next ten minutes she did nothing but call him horrid. Poor Winterbourne was fairly bewildered; no young lady had as yet done him the honour to be so agitated by the mention of his personal plans. His companion, after this, ceased to pay any attention to the curiosities of Chillon or the beauties of the lake; she opened fire on the special charmer in Geneva whom she appeared to have instantly taken it for granted that he was hurrying back to see. How did Miss Daisy Miller know of that agent of his fate in Geneva? Winterbourne, who denied the existence of such a person, was quite unable to discover; and he was divided between amazement at the rapidity of her induction and amusement at the directness of her criticism. She struck him afresh, in all this, as an extraordinary mixture of innocence and crudity. 'Does she never allow you more than three days at a time?' Miss Miller wished ironically to know. 'Doesn't she give you a vacation in summer? there's no one so hard-worked but they can get leave to go off somewhere at this season. I suppose if you stay another day she'll come right after you in the boat. Do wait over till Friday and I'll go down to the landing to see her arrive!' He began at last even to feel he had been wrong to be disappointed in the temper in which his young lady had embarked. If he had missed the personal accent, the personal accent was now making its appearance. It sounded very distinctly, toward the end, in her telling him she'd stop 'teasing' him if he'd promise her solemnly to come down to Rome that winter.

'That's not a difficult promise to make,' he hastened to acknowledge. 'My aunt has taken an apartment in Rome from January and has already asked me to come and see her.'

'I don't want you to come for your aunt,' said Daisy; 'I want you just to come for me.' And this was the only allusion he was ever to hear her make again to his invidious kinswoman. He promised her that at any rate he would certainly come, and after this she forbore from teasing. Winterbourne took a carriage and they drove back to Vevey in the dusk; the girl at his side, her animation a little spent, was now quite distractingly passive.

In the evening he mentioned to Mrs Costello that he had spent the afternoon at Chillon with Miss Daisy Miller.

'The Americans — of the courier?' asked this lady.

'Ah happily the courier stayed at home.'

'She went with you all alone?'

'All alone.'

Mrs Costello sniffed a little at her smelling-bottle. 'And that,' she exclaimed, 'is the little abomination you wanted me to know!'

III

Winterbourne, who had returned to Geneva the day after his excursion to Chillon, went to Rome toward the end of January. His aunt had been established there a considerable time and he had received from her a couple of characteristic letters. 'Those people you were so devoted to last summer at Vevey have turned up here, courier and all,' she wrote. 'They seem to have made several acquaintances, but the courier continues to be the most *intime*.[24] The young lady, however, is also very intimate with various third-rate Italians, with whom she rackets about in a way that makes much talk. Bring me that pretty novel of Cherbuliez's — "Paule Méré"[25] — and don't come later than the 23d.'

Our friend would in the natural course of events, on arriving in Rome, have presently ascertained Mrs Miller's address at the American banker's and gone to pay his compliments to Miss Daisy. 'After what happened at Vevey I certainly think I may call upon them,' he said to Mrs Costello.

'If after what happens — at Vevey and everywhere — you desire to keep up the acquaintance, you're very welcome. Of course you're not squeamish — a man may know every one. Men are welcome to the privilege!'

'Pray what is it then that "happens" — here for instance?' Winterbourne asked.

'Well, the girl tears about alone with her unmistakeably low foreigners. As to what happens further you must apply elsewhere for information. She has picked up half a dozen of the regular Roman fortune-hunters of the inferior sort and she takes them about to such houses as she may put *her* nose into. When she comes to a party – such a party as she can come to – she brings with her a gentleman with a good deal of manner and a wonderful moustache.'

'And where's the mother?'

'I haven't the least idea. They're very dreadful people.'

Winterbourne thought them over in these new lights. 'They're very ignorant – very innocent only, and utterly uncivilised. Depend on it they're not "bad."'

'They're hopelessly vulgar,' said Mrs Costello. 'Whether or no being hopelessly vulgar is being "bad" is a question for the metaphysicians. They're bad enough to blush for, at any rate; and for this short life that's quite enough.'

The news that his little friend the child of nature of the Swiss lakeside was now surrounded by half a dozen wonderful moustaches checked Winterbourne's impulse to go straightway to see her. He had perhaps not definitely flattered himself that he had made an ineffaceable impression upon her heart, but he was annoyed at hearing of a state of affairs so little in harmony with an image that had lately flitted in and out of his own meditations; the image of a very pretty girl looking out of an old Roman window and asking herself urgently when Mr Winterbourne would arrive. If, however, he determined to wait a little before reminding this young lady of his claim to her faithful remembrance, he called with more promptitude on two or three other friends. One of these friends was an American lady who had spent several winters at Geneva, where she had placed her children at school. She was a very accomplished woman and she lived in Via Gregoriana.[26] Winterbourne found her in a little crimson drawing-room on a third floor; the room was filled with southern sunshine. He hadn't been there ten minutes when the servant, appearing in the doorway, announced complacently 'Madame Mila!' This announcement was presently followed by the entrance of little Randolph Miller, who stopped in the middle of the room and stood staring at Winterbourne. An instant later his pretty sister crossed the threshold; and then, after a considerable interval, the parent of the pair slowly advanced.

'I guess I know you!' Randolph broke ground without delay.

'I'm sure you know a great many things' – and his old friend clutched him all interestedly by the arm. 'How's your education coming on?'

Daisy was engaged in some pretty babble with her hostess, but when she heard Winterbourne's voice she quickly turned her head with a 'Well, I declare!' which he met smiling. 'I told you I should come, you know.'

'Well, I didn't believe it,' she answered.

'I'm much obliged to you for that,' laughed the young man.

'You might have come to see me then,' Daisy went on as if they had parted the week before.

'I arrived only yesterday.'

'I don't believe any such thing!' the girl declared afresh.

Winterbourne turned with a protesting smile to her mother, but this lady evaded his glance and, seating herself, fixed her eyes on her son. 'We've got a bigger place than this,' Randolph hereupon broke out. 'It's all gold on the walls.'

Mrs Miller, more of a fatalist apparently than ever, turned uneasily in her chair. 'I told you if I was to bring you you'd say something!' she stated as for the benefit of such of the company as might hear it.

'I told *you!*' Randolph retorted. 'I tell *you,* sir!' he added jocosely, giving Winterbourne a thump on the knee. 'It *is* bigger too!'

As Daisy's conversation with her hostess still occupied her Winterbourne judged it becoming to address a few words to her mother – such as 'I hope you've been well since we parted at Vevey.'

Mrs Miller now certainly looked at him – at his chin. 'Not very well, sir,' she answered.

'She's got the dyspepsia,' said Randolph. 'I've got it too. Father's got it bad. But I've got it worst!'

This proclamation, instead of embarrassing Mrs Miller, seemed to soothe her by reconstituting the environment to which she was most accustomed. 'I suffer from the liver,' she amiably whined to Winterbourne. 'I think it's this climate; it's less bracing than Schenectady, especially in the winter season. I don't know whether you know we reside at Schenectady. I was saying to Daisy that I certainly hadn't found any one like Dr Davis and I didn't believe I *would.* Oh up in Schenectady, he stands first; they think everything of Dr Davis. He has so much to do, and yet there was nothing he wouldn't do for *me.* He said he never saw anything like my dyspepsia, but he was bound to get at it. I'm sure there was nothing he wouldn't try, and I didn't care what he did to me if he only brought me relief. He was just going to try something new, and I just longed for it, when we came right off. Mr Miller felt as if he wanted Daisy to see Europe for herself. But I couldn't help writing the other day that I supposed it was all right for Daisy, but that I didn't know as I *could* get on much longer without Dr Davis. At Schenectady he stands at the very top; and there's a great deal of sickness there too. It affects my sleep.'

Winterbourne had a good deal of pathological gossip with Dr Davis's patient, during which Daisy chattered unremittingly to her own companion. The young man asked Mrs Miller how she was pleased with Rome. 'Well, I must say I'm disappointed,' she confessed. 'We had heard so much about it – I suppose we had heard too much. But we couldn't help that. We had been led to expect something different.'

Winterbourne, however, abounded in reassurance. 'Ah wait a little, and you'll grow very fond of it.'

'I hate it worse and worse every day!' cried Randolph.

'You're like the infant Hannibal,'[27] his friend laughed.

'No I ain't – like any infant!' Randolph declared at a venture.

'Well, that's so – and you never *were*!' his mother concurred. 'But we've seen places,' she resumed, 'that I'd put a long way ahead of Rome.' And in reply to Winterbourne's interrogation, 'There's Zürich[28] – up there in the mountains,' she instanced; 'I think Zürich's real lovely, and we hadn't heard half so much about it.'

'The best place we've seen's the *City of Richmond*!' said Randolph.

'He means the ship,' Mrs Miller explained. 'We crossed in that ship. Randolph had a good time on the *City of Richmond*.'

'It's the best place *I've* struck,' the child repeated. 'Only it was turned the wrong way.'

'Well, we've got to turn the right way sometime,' said Mrs Miller with strained but weak optimism. Winterbourne expressed the hope that her daughter at least appreciated the so various interest of Rome, and she declared with some spirit that Daisy was quite carried away. 'It's on account of the society – the society's splendid. She goes round everywhere; she has made a great number of acquaintances. Of course she goes round more than I do. I must say they've all been very sweet – they've taken her right in. And then she knows a great many gentlemen. Oh she thinks there's nothing like Rome. Of course it's a great deal pleasanter for a young lady if she knows plenty of gentlemen.'

By this time Daisy had turned her attention again to Winterbourne, but in quite the same free form. 'I've been telling Mrs Walker how mean you were!'

'And what's the evidence you've offered?' he asked, a trifle disconcerted, for all his superior gallantry, by her inadequate measure of the zeal of an admirer who on his way down to Rome had stopped neither at Bologna nor at Florence, simply because of a certain sweet appeal to his fond fancy, not to say to his finest curiosity. He remembered how a cynical compatriot had once told him that American women – the pretty ones, and this gave a largeness to the axiom – were at once the most exacting in the world and the least endowed with a sense of indebtedness.

'Why you were awfully mean up at Vevey,' Daisy said. 'You wouldn't do most anything. You wouldn't stay there when I asked you.'

'Dearest young lady,' cried Winterbourne, with generous passion, 'have I come all the way to Rome only to be riddled by your silver shafts?'

'Just hear him say that!' – and she gave an affectionate twist to a bow on her hostess's dress. 'Did you ever hear anything so quaint?'

'So "quaint," my dear?' echoed Mrs Walker more critically – quite in the tone of a partisan of Winterbourne.

'Well, I don't know' – and the girl continued to finger her ribbons. 'Mrs Walker, I want to tell you something.'

'Say, mother-r,' broke in Randolph with his rough ends to his words,[29] 'I tell you you've got to go. Eugenio'll raise something!'

'I'm not afraid of Eugenio,' said Daisy with a toss of her head. 'Look here, Mrs Walker,' she went on, 'you know I'm coming to your party.'

'I'm delighted to hear it.'

'I've got a lovely dress.'

'I'm very sure of that.'

'But I want to ask a favour – permission to bring a friend.'

'I shall be happy to see any of your friends,' said Mrs Walker, who turned with a smile to Mrs Miller.

'Oh they're not my friends,' cried that lady, squirming in shy repudiation. 'It seems as if they didn't take to *me* – I never spoke to one of them!'

'It's an intimate friend of mine, Mr Giovanelli,' Daisy pursued without a tremor in her young clearness or a shadow on her shining bloom.

Mrs Walker had a pause and gave a rapid glance at Winterbourne. 'I shall be glad to see Mr Giovanelli,' she then returned.

'He's just the finest kind of Italian,' Daisy pursued with the prettiest serenity. 'He's a great friend of mine and the handsomest man in the world – except Mr Winterbourne! He knows plenty of Italians, but he wants to know some Americans. It seems as if he was crazy about Americans. He's tremendously bright. He's perfectly lovely!'

It was settled that this paragon should be brought to Mrs Walker's party, and then Mrs Miller prepared to take her leave. 'I guess we'll go right back to the hotel,' she remarked with a confessed failure of the larger imagination.

'You may go back to the hotel, mother,' Daisy replied, 'but I'm just going to walk round.'

'She's going to go it with Mr Giovanelli,' Randolph unscrupulously commented.

'I'm going to go it on the Pincio,'[30] Daisy peaceably smiled, while the way that she 'condoned' these things almost melted Winterbourne's heart.

'Alone, my dear – at this hour?' Mrs Walker asked. The afternoon was drawing to a close – it was the hour for the throng of carriages and of contemplative pedestrians. 'I don't consider it's safe, Daisy,' her hostess firmly asserted.

'Neither do I then,' Mrs Miller thus borrowed confidence to add. 'You'll catch the fever[31] as sure as you live. Remember what Dr Davis told you!'

'Give her some of that medicine before she starts in,' Randolph suggested.

The company had risen to its feet; Daisy, still showing her pretty teeth, bent over and kissed her hostess. 'Mrs Walker, you're too perfect,' she simply said. 'I'm not going alone; I'm going to meet a friend.'

'Your friend won't keep you from catching the fever even if it *is* his own second nature,' Mrs Miller observed.

'Is it Mr Giovanelli that's the dangerous attraction?' Mrs Walker asked without mercy.

Winterbourne was watching the challenged girl; at this question his attention quickened. She stood there smiling and smoothing her bonnet-ribbons; she glanced at Winterbourne. Then, while she glanced and smiled, she brought out all affirmatively and without a shade of hesitation: 'Mr Giovanelli – the beautiful Giovanelli.'

'My dear young friend' – and, taking her hand, Mrs Walker turned to pleading – ' don't prowl off to the Pincio at this hour to meet a beautiful Italian.'

'Well, he speaks first-rate English,' Mrs Miller incoherently mentioned.

'Gracious me,' Daisy piped up, 'I don't want to do anything that's going to affect my health – or my character either! There's an easy way to settle it.' Her eyes continued to play over Winterbourne. 'The Pincio's only a hundred yards off, and if Mr Winterbourne were as polite as he pretends he'd offer to walk right in with me!'

Winterbourne's politeness hastened to proclaim itself, and the girl gave him gracious leave to accompany her. They passed downstairs before her mother, and at the door he saw Mrs Miller's carriage drawn up, with the ornamental courier whose acquaintance he had made at Vevey seated within. 'Goodbye, Eugenio,' cried Daisy; 'I'm going to take a walk!' The distance from Via Gregoriana to the beautiful garden at the other end of the Pincian Hill is in fact rapidly traversed. As the day was splendid, however, and the concourse of vehicles, walkers and loungers numerous, the young Americans found their progress much delayed. This fact was highly agreeable to Winterbourne, in spite of his consciousness of his singular situation. The slow-moving, idly-gazing Roman crowd bestowed much attention on the extremely pretty young woman of English race who passed through it, with some difficulty, on his arm; and he wondered what on earth had been in Daisy's mind when she proposed to exhibit herself unattended to its appreciation. His own mission, to her sense, was apparently to consign her to the hands of Mr Giovanelli; but, at once annoyed and gratified, he resolved that he would do no such thing.

'Why haven't you been to see me?' she meanwhile asked. 'You can't get out of that.'

'I've had the honour of telling you that I've only just stepped out of the train.'

'You must have stayed in the train a good while after it stopped!' she derisively cried. 'I suppose you were asleep. You've had time to go to see Mrs Walker.'

'I knew Mrs Walker – ' Winterbourne began to explain.

'I know where you knew her. You knew her at Geneva. She told me so. Well, you knew me at Vevey. That's just as good. So you ought to have come.' She asked him no other question than this; she began to prattle about her own affairs. 'We've got splendid rooms at the hotel; Eugenio says they're the best rooms in Rome. We're going to stay all winter – if we don't die of the fever; and I guess we'll stay then! It's a great deal nicer than I thought; I thought it would be fearfully quiet – in fact I was sure it would be deadly pokey. I foresaw we should be going round all the time with one of those dreadful old men who explain about the pictures and things. But we only had about a week of that, and now I'm enjoying myself. I know ever so many people, and they're all so charming. The society's extremely select. There are all kinds – English and Germans and Italians. I think I like the English best. I like their style of conversation. But there are some lovely Americans. I never saw anything so hospitable. There's something or other every day. There's not much dancing – but I must say I never thought dancing was everything. I was always fond of conversation. I guess I'll have plenty at Mrs Walker's – her rooms are so small.' When they had passed the gate of the Pincian Gardens Miss Miller began to wonder where Mr Giovanelli might be. 'We had better go straight to that place in front, where you look at the view.'[32]

Winterbourne at this took a stand. 'I certainly shan't help you to find him.'

'Then I shall find him without you,' Daisy said with spirit.

'You certainly won't leave me!' he protested.

She burst into her familiar little laugh. 'Are you afraid you'll get lost – or run over? But there's Giovanelli leaning against that tree. He's staring at the women in the carriages: did you ever see anything so cool?'

Winterbourne descried hereupon at some distance a little figure that stood with folded arms and nursing its cane. It had a handsome face, a hat artfully poised, a glass in one eye and a nosegay in its button-hole. Daisy's friend looked at it a moment and then said: 'Do you mean to speak to that thing?'

'Do I mean to speak to him? Why you don't suppose I mean to communicate by signs!'

'Pray understand then,' the young man returned, 'that I intend to remain with you.'

Daisy stopped and looked at him without a sign of troubled consciousness, with nothing in her face but her charming eyes, her charming teeth and her happy dimples. 'Well, she's a cool one!' he thought.

'I don't like the way you say that,' she declared. 'It's too imperious.'

'I beg your pardon if I say it wrong. The main point's to give you an idea of my meaning.'

The girl looked at him more gravely, but with eyes that were prettier than ever. 'I've never allowed a gentleman to dictate to me or to interfere with anything I do.'

'I think that's just where your mistake has come in,' he retorted. 'You should sometimes listen to a gentleman – the right one.'

At this she began to laugh again. 'I do nothing but listen to gentlemen! Tell me if Mr Giovanelli is the right one.'

The gentleman with the nosegay in his bosom had now made out our two friends and was approaching Miss Miller with obsequious rapidity. He bowed to Winterbourne as well as to the latter's compatriot; he seemed to shine, in his coxcombical way, with the desire to please and the fact of his own intelligent joy, though Winterbourne thought him not a bad-looking fellow. But he nevertheless said to Daisy: 'No, he's not the right one.'

She had clearly a natural turn for free introductions; she mentioned with the easiest grace the name of each of her companions to the other. She strolled forward with one of them on either hand; Mr Giovanelli, who spoke English very cleverly – Winterbourne afterwards learned that he had practised the idiom upon a great many American heiresses – addressed her a great deal of very polite nonsense. He had the best possible manners, and the young American, who said nothing, reflected on that depth of Italian subtlety, so strangely opposed to Anglo-Saxon simplicity, which enables people to show a smoother surface in proportion as they're more acutely displeased. Giovanelli of course had counted upon something more intimate – he had not bargained for a party of three; but he kept his temper in a manner that suggested far-stretching intentions. Winterbourne flattered himself he had taken his measure. 'He's anything but a gentleman,' said the young American; 'he isn't even a very plausible imitation of one. He's a music-master or a penny-a-liner[33] or a third-rate artist. He's awfully on his good behaviour, but damn his fine eyes!' Mr Giovanelli had indeed great advantages; but it was deeply disgusting to Daisy's other friend that something in her shouldn't have instinctively discriminated against such a type. Giovanelli chattered and jested and made himself agreeable according to his honest Roman lights. It was true that if he was an imitation the imitation was studied. 'Nevertheless,' Winterbourne said to himself, 'a nice girl ought to know!' And then he came back to the dreadful question of whether this *was* in fact a nice girl. Would a nice girl – even allowing for her being a little American flirt – make a rendezvous with a presumably low-lived foreigner? The rendezvous in this case indeed had been in broad daylight and in the most crowded corner of Rome; but wasn't it possible to regard the choice of these very circumstances as a proof more of vulgarity than of anything else? Singular though it may seem, Winterbourne was vexed that the girl, in joining her *amoroso*,[34] shouldn't appear more impatient of his own company, and he was vexed precisely because of his inclination. It was impossible to regard her as a wholly unspotted flower – she lacked a certain indispensable fineness; and it would therefore much simplify the situation to be able to treat her as the subject of one of the visitations known to romancers as 'lawless passions.' That she should seem to wish to get rid of him would have helped him to think more lightly of her, just as to be able to think more lightly of her would have made her less perplexing. Daisy at any rate continued on this occasion to present herself as an inscrutable combination of audacity and innocence.

She had been walking some quarter of an hour, attended by her two cavaliers and responding in a tone of very childish gaiety, as it after all struck one of them, to the pretty speeches of the other, when a carriage that had detached itself from the revolving train[35] drew up beside the path. At the same moment Winterbourne noticed that his friend Mrs Walker – the lady whose house he had lately left – was seated in the vehicle and was beckoning to him. Leaving Miss Miller's side, he hastened to obey her summons – and all to find her flushed, excited, scandalised. 'It's really too dreadful' – she earnestly appealed to him. 'That crazy girl mustn't do this sort of thing. She mustn't walk here with you two men. Fifty people have remarked her.'

Winterbourne – suddenly and rather oddly rubbed the wrong way by this – raised his grave eyebrows. 'I think it's a pity to make too much fuss about it.'

'It's a pity to let the girl ruin herself!'

'She's very innocent,' he reasoned in his own troubled interest.

'She's very reckless,' cried Mrs Walker, 'and goodness knows how far – left to itself – it may go. Did you ever,' she proceeded to enquire, 'see anything so blatantly imbecile as the mother? After you had all left me just now I couldn't sit still for thinking of it. It seemed too pitiful not even to attempt to save them. I ordered the carriage and put on my bonnet and came here as quickly as possible. Thank heaven I've found you!'

'What do you propose to do with us?' Winterbourne uncomfortably smiled.

'To ask her to get in, to drive her about here for half an hour – so that the world may see she's not running absolutely wild – and then take her safely home.'

'I don't think it's a very happy thought,' he said after reflexion, 'but you're at liberty to try.'

Mrs Walker accordingly tried. The young man went in pursuit of their young lady who had simply nodded and smiled, from her distance, at her recent patroness in the carriage and then had gone her way with her own companion. On learning, in the event, that Mrs Walker had followed her, she retraced her steps, however, with a perfect good grace and with Mr Giovanelli at her side. She professed herself 'enchanted' to have a chance to present this gentleman to her good friend, and immediately achieved the introduction; declaring with it, and as if it were of as little importance, that she had never in her life seen anything so lovely as that lady's carriage-rug.

'I'm glad you admire it,' said her poor pursuer, smiling sweetly. 'Will you get in and let me put it over you?'

'Oh no, thank you!' – Daisy knew her mind. 'I'll admire it ever so much more as I see you driving round with it.'

'Do get in and drive round *with* me,' Mrs Walker pleaded.

'That would be charming, but it's so fascinating just as I am!' – with which the girl radiantly took in the gentlemen on either side of her.

'It may be fascinating, dear child, but it's not the custom here,' urged the lady of the victoria,[36] leaning forward in this vehicle with her hands devoutly clasped.

'Well, it ought to be then!' Daisy imperturbably laughed. 'If I didn't walk I'd expire.'

'You should walk with your mother, dear,' cried Mrs Walker with a loss of patience.

'With my mother dear?' the girl amusedly echoed. Winterbourne saw she scented interference. 'My mother never walked ten steps in her life. And then, you know,' she blandly added, 'I'm more than five years old.'

'You're old enough to be more reasonable. You're old enough, dear Miss Miller, to be talked about.'

Daisy wondered to extravagance. 'Talked about? What do you mean?'

'Come into my carriage and I'll tell you.'

Daisy turned shining eyes again from one of the gentlemen beside her to the other. Mr Giovanelli was bowing to and fro, rubbing down his gloves and laughing irresponsibly; Winterbourne thought the scene the most unpleasant possible. 'I don't think I want to know what you mean,' the girl presently said. 'I don't think I should like it.'

Winterbourne only wished Mrs Walker would tuck up her carriage-rug and drive away; but this lady, as she afterwards told him, didn't feel she could 'rest there.' 'Should you prefer being thought a very reckless girl?' she accordingly asked.

'Gracious me!' exclaimed Daisy. She looked again at Mr Giovanelli, then she turned to her other companion. There was a small pink flush in her cheek; she was tremendously pretty. 'Does Mr Winterbourne think,' she put to him with a wonderful bright intensity of appeal, 'that – to save my reputation – I ought to get into the carriage?'

It really embarrassed him; for an instant he cast about – so strange was it to hear her speak that way of her 'reputation.' But he himself in fact had to speak in accordance with gallantry. The finest gallantry here was surely just to tell her the truth; and the truth, for our young man, as the few indications I have been able to give have made him known to the reader, was that his charming friend should listen to the voice of civilised society. He took in again her exquisite prettiness and then said the more distinctly: 'I think you should get into the carriage.'

Daisy gave the rein to her amusement. 'I never heard anything so stiff! If this is improper, Mrs Walker,' she pursued, 'then I'm *all* improper, and you had better give me right up. Good-bye; I hope you'll have a lovely ride!' – and with Mr Giovanelli, who made a triumphantly obsequious salute, she turned away.

Mrs Walker sat looking after her, and there were tears in Mrs Walker's eyes. 'Get in here, sir,' she said to Winterbourne, indicating the place beside her. The young man answered that he felt bound to accompany Miss Miller; whereupon the lady of the victoria declared that if he refused her this favour she would never speak to him again. She was evidently wound up. He accordingly hastened to overtake Daisy and her more faithful ally, and, offering her his hand, told her that Mrs Walker had made a stringent claim on his presence. He had expected her to answer with something rather free, something still more significant of the perversity from which the voice of society, through the lips of their distressed friend, had so earnestly endeavoured to dissuade her. But she only let her hand slip, as she scarce looked at him, through his slightly awkward grasp; while Mr Giovanelli, to make it worse, bade him farewell with too emphatic a flourish of the hat.

Winterbourne was not in the best possible humour as he took his seat beside the author of his sacrifice. 'That was not clever of you,' he said candidly, as the vehicle mingled again with the throng of carriages.

'In such a case,' his companion answered, 'I don't want to be clever – I only want to be *true*!'

'Well, your truth[37] has only offended the strange little creature – it has only put her off.'

'It has happened very well' – Mrs Walker accepted her work. 'If she's so perfectly determined to compromise herself the sooner one knows it the better – one can act accordingly.'

'I suspect she meant no great harm, you know,' Winterbourne maturely opined.

'So I thought a month ago. But she has been going too far.'

'What has she been doing?'

'Everything that's not done here. Flirting with any man she can pick up; sitting in corners with mysterious Italians; dancing all the evening with the same partners; receiving visits at eleven o'clock at night. Her mother melts away when the visitors come.'

'But her brother,' laughed Winterbourne, 'sits up till two in the morning.'

'He must be edified by what he sees. I'm told that at their hotel every one's talking about her and that a smile goes round among the servants when a gentleman comes and asks for Miss Miller.'

'Ah we needn't mind the servants!' Winterbourne compassionately signified. 'The poor girl's only fault,' he presently added, 'is her complete lack of education.'

'She's naturally indelicate,' Mrs Walker, on her side, reasoned. 'Take that example this morning. How long had you known her at Vevey?'

'A couple of days.'

'Imagine then the taste of her making it a personal matter that you should have left the place!'

He agreed that taste wasn't the strong point of the Millers – after which he was silent for some moments; but only at last to add: 'I suspect, Mrs Walker, that you and I have lived too long at Geneva!' And he further noted that he should be glad to learn with what particular design she had made him enter her carriage.

'I wanted to enjoin on you the importance of your ceasing your relations with Miss Miller; that of your not appearing to flirt with her; that of your giving her no further opportunity to expose herself; that of your in short letting her alone.'

'I'm afraid I can't do anything quite so enlightened as *that*,' he returned. 'I like her awfully, you know.'

'All the more reason you shouldn't help her to make a scandal.'

'Well, there shall be nothing scandalous in my attentions to her,' he was willing to promise.

'There certainly will be in the way she takes them. But I've said what I had on my conscience,' Mrs Walker pursued. 'If you wish to rejoin the young lady I'll put you down. Here, by the way, you have a chance.'

The carriage was engaged in that part of the Pincian drive which overhangs the wall of Rome and overlooks the beautiful Villa Borghese.[38] It is bordered by a large parapet, near which are several seats. One of these, at a distance, was occupied by a gentleman and a lady, toward whom Mrs Walker gave a toss of her head. At the same moment these persons rose and walked to the parapet. Winterbourne had asked the coachman to stop; he now descended from the carriage. His companion looked at him a moment in silence and then, while he raised his hat, drove majestically away. He stood where he had alighted; he had turned his eyes toward Daisy and her cavalier. They evidently saw no one; they were too deeply occupied with each other. When they reached the low garden-wall they remained a little looking off at the great flat-topped pine-clusters of Villa Borghese; then the girl's attendant admirer seated himself familiarly on the broad ledge of the wall. The western sun in the opposite sky sent out a brilliant shaft through a couple of cloud-bars; whereupon the gallant Giovanelli took her parasol out of her hands and opened it. She came a little nearer and he held the parasol over her; then, still holding it, he let it so rest on her shoulder that both of their heads were hidden from Winterbourne. This young man stayed but a moment longer; then he began to walk. But he walked – not toward the couple united beneath the parasol, rather toward the residence of his aunt Mrs Costello.

IV

He flattered himself on the following day that there was no smiling among the servants when he at least asked for Mrs Miller at her hotel. This lady and her daughter, however, were not at home; and on the next day after, repeating his visit, Winterbourne again was met by a denial. Mrs Walker's party took place on the evening of the third day, and in spite of the final reserves that had marked his last interview with that social critic our young man was among the guests. Mrs Walker was one of those pilgrims from the younger world who, while in contact with the elder, make a point, in their own phrase, of studying European society; and she had on this occasion collected several specimens of diversely-born humanity to serve, as might be, for text-books. When Winterbourne arrived the little person he desired most to find wasn't there; but in a few moments he saw Mrs Miller come in alone, very shyly and ruefully. This lady's hair, above the dead waste of her temples, was more frizzled than ever. As she approached their hostess Winterbourne also drew near.

'You see I've come all alone,' said Daisy's unsupported parent. 'I'm so frightened I don't know what to do; it's the first time I've ever been to a party alone – especially in this country. I wanted to bring Randolph or Eugenio or some one, but Daisy just pushed me off by myself. I ain't used to going round alone.'

'And doesn't your daughter intend to favour us with her society?' Mrs Walker impressively enquired.

'Well, Daisy's all dressed,' Mrs Miller testified with that accent of the dispassionate, if not of the philosophic, historian with which she always recorded the current incidents of her daughter's career. 'She got dressed on purpose before dinner. But she has a friend of hers there; that gentleman – the handsomest of the Italians – that she wanted to bring. They've got going at the piano – it seems as if they couldn't leave off. Mr Giovanelli does sing splendidly. But I guess they'll come before very long,' Mrs Miller hopefully concluded.

'I'm sorry she should come – in that particular way,' Mrs Walker permitted herself to observe.

'Well, I told her there was no use in her getting dressed before dinner if she was going to wait three hours,' returned Daisy's mamma. 'I didn't see the use of her putting on such a dress as that to sit round with Mr Giovanelli.'

'This is most horrible!' said Mrs Walker, turning away and addressing herself to Winterbourne. '*Elle s'affiche, la malheureuse*.[39] It's her revenge for my having ventured to remonstrate with her. When she comes I shan't speak to her.'

Daisy came after eleven o'clock, but she wasn't, on such an occasion, a young lady to wait to be spoken to. She rustled forward in radiant loveliness, smiling and chattering, carrying a large bouquet and attended by Mr Giovanelli. Every one stopped talking and turned and looked at her while she floated up to Mrs Walker. 'I'm afraid you thought I never was coming, so I sent mother off to tell you. I wanted to make Mr Giovanelli practise some things before he came; you know he sings beautifully, and I want you to ask him to sing. This is Mr Giovanelli; you know I introduced him to you; he's got the most lovely voice and he knows the most charming set of songs. I made him go over them this evening on purpose; we had the greatest time at the hotel.' Of all this Daisy delivered herself with the sweetest brightest loudest confidence, looking now at her hostess and now at all the room, while she gave a series of little pats, round her very white shoulders, to the edges of her dress. 'Is there any one I know?' she as undiscourageably asked.

'I think every one knows you!' said Mrs Walker as with a grand intention; and she gave a very cursory greeting to Mr Giovanelli. This gentleman bore himself gallantly; he smiled and bowed and showed his white teeth, he curled his moustaches and rolled his eyes and performed all the proper functions of a handsome Italian at an evening party. He sang, very prettily, half a dozen songs, though Mrs Walker afterwards declared that she had been quite unable to find out who asked him. It was apparently not Daisy who had set him in motion – this young lady being seated a distance from the piano and though she had publicly, as it were, professed herself his musical patroness or guarantor, giving herself to gay and audible discourse while he warbled.

'It's a pity these rooms are so small; we can't dance,' she remarked to Winterbourne as if she had seen him five minutes before.

'I'm not sorry we can't dance,' he candidly returned. 'I'm incapable of a step.'

'Of course you're incapable of a step,' the girl assented. 'I should think your legs *would* be stiff cooped in there so much of the time in that victoria.'

'Well, they were very restless there three days ago,' he amicably laughed; 'all they really wanted was to dance attendance on you.'

'Oh my other friend – my friend in need[40] – stuck to me; he seems more at one with his limbs than you are – I'll say that for him. But did you ever hear anything so cool,' Daisy demanded, 'as Mrs Walker's wanting me to get into her carriage and drop poor Mr Giovanelli, and under the pretext that it was proper? People have different ideas! It would have been most unkind; he had been talking about that walk for ten days.'

'He shouldn't have talked about it at all,' Winterbourne decided to make answer on this: 'he would never have proposed to a young lady of this country to walk about the streets of Rome with him.'

'About the streets?' she cried with her pretty stare. 'Where then would he have proposed to her to walk? The Pincio ain't the streets either, I guess; and I besides, thank goodness, am not a young lady of this country. The young ladies of this country have a dreadfully pokey time of it, by what I can discover; I don't see why I should change my habits for *such* stupids.'

'I'm afraid your habits are those of a ruthless flirt,' said Winterbourne with studied severity.

'Of course they are!' – and she hoped, evidently, by the manner of it, to take his breath away. 'I'm a fearful frightful flirt! Did you ever hear of a nice girl that wasn't? But I suppose you'll tell me now I'm not a nice girl.'

He remained grave indeed under the shock of her cynical profession. 'You're a very nice girl, but I wish you'd flirt with me, and me only.'

'Ah thank you, thank you very much: you're the last man I should think of flirting with. As I've had the pleasure of informing you, you're too stiff.'

'You say that too often,' he resentfully remarked.

Daisy gave a delighted laugh. 'If I could have the sweet hope of making you angry I'd say it again.'

'Don't do that – when I'm angry I'm stiffer than ever. But if you won't flirt with me do cease at least to flirt with your friend at the piano. They don't,' he declared as in full sympathy with 'them,' 'understand that sort of thing here.'

'I thought they understood nothing else!' Daisy cried with startling world-knowledge.

'Not in young unmarried women.'

'It seems to me much more proper in young unmarried than in old married ones,' she retorted.

'Well,' said Winterbourne, 'when you deal with natives you must go by the custom of the country. American flirting is a purely American silliness; it has – in its ineptitude of innocence – no place in *this* system. So when you show yourself in public with Mr Giovanelli and without your mother –'

'Gracious, poor mother!' – and she made it beautifully unspeakable.

Winterbourne had a touched sense for this, but it didn't alter his attitude. 'Though *you* may be flirting Mr Giovanelli isn't – he means something else.'

'He isn't preaching at any rate,' she returned. 'And if you want very much to know, we're neither of us flirting – not a little speck. We're too good friends for that. We're real intimate friends.'

He was to continue to find her thus at moments inimitable. 'Ah,' he then judged, 'if you're in love with each other it's another affair altogether!'

She had allowed him up to this point to speak so frankly that he had no thought of shocking her by the force of his logic; yet she now none the less immediately rose, blushing visibly and leaving him mentally to exclaim that the name of little American flirts was incoherence. 'Mr Giovanelli at least,' she answered, sparing but a single small queer glance for it, a queerer small glance, he felt, than he had ever yet had from her – 'Mr Giovanelli never says to me such very disagreeable things.'

It had an effect on him – he stood staring. The subject of their contention had finished singing; he left the piano, and his recognition of what – a little awkwardly – didn't take place in celebration of this might nevertheless have been an acclaimed operatic tenor's series of repeated ducks before the curtain. So he bowed himself over to Daisy. 'Won't you come to the other room and have some tea?' he asked – offering Mrs Walker's slightly thin refreshment as he might have done all the kingdoms of the earth.[41]

Daisy at last turned on Winterbourne a more natural and calculable light. He was but the more muddled by it, however, since so inconsequent a smile made nothing clear – it seemed at the most to prove in her a sweetness and softness that reverted instinctively to the pardon of offences. 'It has never occurred to Mr Winterbourne to offer me any tea,' she said with her finest little intention of torment and triumph.

'I've offered you excellent advice,' the young man permitted himself to growl.

'I prefer weak tea!' cried Daisy, and she went off with the brilliant Giovanelli. She sat with him in the adjoining room, in the embrasure of the window, for the rest of the evening. There was an interesting performance at the piano, but neither of these conversers gave heed to it. When Daisy came to take leave of Mrs Walker this lady conscientiously repaired the weakness of which she had been guilty at the moment of the girl's arrival – she turned her back straight on Miss Miller and left her to depart with what grace she might. Winterbourne happened to be near the door; he saw it all. Daisy turned very pale and looked at her mother, but Mrs Miller was humbly unconscious of any rupture of any law or of any deviation from any custom. She appeared indeed to have felt an incongruous impulse to draw attention to her own striking conformity. 'Good-night, Mrs Walker,' she said; 'we've had a beautiful evening. You see if I let Daisy come to parties without me I don't want her to go away without me.' Daisy turned away, looking with a small white prettiness, a blighted grace, at the circle near the door: Winterbourne saw that for the first moment she was too much shocked and puzzled even for indignation. He on his side was greatly touched.

'That was very cruel,' he promptly remarked to Mrs Walker.

But this lady's face was also as a stone. 'She never enters my drawing-room again.'

Since Winterbourne then, hereupon, was not to meet her in Mrs Walker's drawing-room he went as often as possible to Mrs Miller's hotel. The ladies were rarely at home, but when he found them the devoted Giovanelli was always present. Very often the glossy little Roman, serene in success, but not unduly presumptuous, occupied with Daisy alone the florid salon enjoyed by Eugenio's care, Mrs Miller being apparently ever of the opinion that discretion is the better part of solicitude. Winterbourne noted, at first with surprise, that Daisy on these occasions was neither embarrassed nor annoyed by his own entrance; but he presently began to feel that she had no more surprises for him and that he really liked, after all, not making out what she was 'up to.' She showed no displeasure for the interruption of her *tête-à-tête* with Giovanelli; she could chatter as freshly and freely with two gentlemen as with one, and this easy flow had ever the same anomaly for her earlier friend that it was so free without availing itself of its freedom. Winterbourne reflected that if she was seriously interested in the Italian it was odd she shouldn't take more trouble to preserve the sanctity of their interviews, and he liked her the better for her innocent-looking indifference and her inexhaustible gaiety. He could hardly have said why, but she struck him as a young person not formed for a troublesome jealousy. Smile at such a betrayal though the reader may, it was a fact with regard to the women who had hitherto interested him that, given certain contingencies, Winterbourne could see himself afraid – literally afraid – of these ladies. It pleased him to believe that even were twenty other things different and Daisy should love him and he should know it and like it, he would still never be afraid of Daisy. It must be added that this conviction was not altogether flattering to her: it represented that she was nothing every way if not light.

But she was evidently very much interested in Giovanelli. She looked at him whenever he spoke; she was perpetually telling him to do this and to do that; she was constantly chaffing and abusing him. She appeared completely to have forgotten that her other friend had said anything to displease her at Mrs Walker's entertainment. One Sunday afternoon, having gone to Saint Peter's[42] with his aunt, Winterbourne became aware that the young woman held in horror by that lady was strolling about the great church under escort of her coxcomb of the Corso.[43] It amused him, after a debate, to point out the exemplary pair – even at the cost, as it proved, of Mrs Costello's saying when she had taken them in through her eye-glass: 'That's what makes you so pensive in these days, eh?'

'I hadn't the least idea I was pensive,' he pleaded.

'You're very much preoccupied; you're always thinking of something.'

'And what is it,' he asked, 'that you accuse me of thinking of?'

'Of that young lady's, Miss Baker's, Miss Chandler's – what's her name? – Miss Miller's intrigue with that little barber's block.'[44]

'Do you call it an intrigue,' he asked – 'an affair that goes on with such peculiar publicity?'

'That's their folly,' said Mrs Costello, 'it's not their merit.'

'No,' he insisted with a hint perhaps of the preoccupation to which his aunt had alluded – 'I don't believe there's anything to be called an intrigue.'

'Well' – and Mrs Costello dropped her glass – 'I've heard a dozen people speak of it: they say she's quite carried away by him.'

'They're certainly as thick as thieves,' our embarrassed young man allowed.

Mrs Costello came back to them, however, after a little; and Winterbourne recognized in this a further illustration – than that supplied by his own condition – of the spell projected by the case. 'He's certainly very handsome. One easily sees how it is. She thinks him the most elegant man in the world, the finest gentleman possible. She has never seen anything like him – he's better even than the courier. It was the courier probably who introduced him, and if he succeeds in marrying the young lady the courier will come in for a magnificent commission.'

'I don't believe she thinks of marrying him,' Winterbourne reasoned, 'and I don't believe he hopes to marry her.'

'You may be very sure she thinks of nothing at all. She romps on from day to day, from hour to hour, as they did in the Golden Age.[45] I can imagine nothing more vulgar,' said Mrs Costello, whose figure of speech scarcely went on all fours.[46] And at the same time,' she added, 'depend upon it she may tell you any moment that she is "engaged."'

'I think that's more than Giovanelli really expects,' said Winterbourne.

'And who is Giovanelli?'

'The shiny – but, to do him justice, not greasy – little Roman. I've asked questions about him and learned something. He's apparently a perfectly respectable little man. I believe he's in a small way a *cavaliere avvocato*.[47] But he doesn't move in what are called the first circles. I think it really not absolutely impossible the courier introduced him. He's evidently immensely charmed with Miss Miller. If she thinks him the finest gentleman in the world, he, on his side, has never found himself in personal contact with such splendour, such opulence, such personal daintiness, as this young lady's. And then she must seem to him wonderfully pretty and interesting. Yes, he can't really hope to pull it off. That must appear to him too impossible a piece of luck. He has nothing but his handsome face to offer, and there's a substantial, a possibly explosive Mr Miller in that mysterious land of dollars and six-shooters. Giovanelli's but too conscious that he hasn't a title to offer. If he were only a count or a *marchese*![48] What on earth can he make of the way they've taken him up?'

'He accounts for it by his handsome face and thinks Miss Miller a young lady *qui se passe ses fantaisies*!'[49]

'It's very true,' Winterbourne pursued, 'that Daisy and her mamma haven't yet risen to that stage of – what shall I call it? – of culture, at which the idea of catching a count or a *marchese* begins. I believe them intellectually incapable of that conception.'

'Ah but the *cavaliere avvocato* doesn't believe them!' cried Mrs Costello.

Of the observation excited by Daisy's 'intrigue' Winterbourne gathered that day at Saint Peter's sufficient evidence. A dozen of the American colonists in Rome came to talk with his relative, who sat on a small portable stool at the base of one of the great pilasters. The vesper-service was going forward in splendid chants and organ-tones in the adjacent choir, and meanwhile, between Mrs Costello and her friends, much was said about poor little Miss Miller's going really 'too far.' Winterbourne was not pleased with what he heard; but when, coming out upon the great steps of the church, he saw Daisy, who had emerged before him, get into an open cab with her accomplice and roll away through the cynical streets of Rome, the measure of her course struck him as simply there to take. He felt very sorry for her – not exactly that he believed she had completely lost her wits, but because it was painful to see so much that was pretty and undefended and natural sink so low in human estimation. He made an attempt after this to give a hint to Mrs Miller. He met one day in the Corso a friend – a tourist like himself – who had just come out of the Doria Palace,[50] where he had been walking through the beautiful gallery. His friend 'went on' for some moments about the great portrait of Innocent X, by Velasquez, suspended in one of the cabinets of the palace, and then said: 'And in the same cabinet, by the way, I enjoyed sight of an image of a different kind; that little American who's so much more a work of nature than of art and whom you pointed out to me last week.' In answer to Winterbourne's enquiries his friend narrated that the little American – prettier now than ever – was seated with a companion in the secluded nook in which the papal presence is enshrined.

'All alone?' the young man heard himself disingenuously ask.

'Alone with a little Italian who sports in his button-hole a stack of flowers. The girl's a charming beauty, but I thought I understood from you the other day that she's a young lady *du meilleur monde*.'[51]

'So she is!' said Winterbourne; and having assured himself that his informant had seen the interesting pair but ten minutes before, he jumped into a cab and went to call on Mrs Miller. She was at home, but she apologised for receiving him in Daisy's absence.

'She's gone out somewhere with Mr Giovanelli. She's always going round with Mr Giovanelli.'

'I've noticed they're intimate indeed,' Winterbourne concurred.

'Oh it seems as if they couldn't live without each other!' said Mrs Miller. 'Well, he's a real gentleman anyhow. I guess I have the joke on Daisy – that she *must* be engaged!'

'And how does your daughter *take* the joke?'

'Oh she just says she ain't. But she might as *well* be!' this philosophic parent resumed. 'She goes on as if she was. But I've made Mr Giovanelli promise to tell me if Daisy don't. I'd want to write to Mr Miller about it – wouldn't you?'

Winterbourne replied that he certainly should; and the state of mind of Daisy's mamma struck him as so unprecedented in the annals of parental vigilance that he recoiled before the attempt to educate at a single interview either her conscience or her wit.

After this Daisy was never at home and he ceased to meet her at the houses of their common acquaintance, because, as he perceived, these shrewd people had quite made up their minds as to the length she must have gone. They ceased to invite her, intimating that they wished to make, and make strongly, for the benefit of observant Europeans, the point that though Miss Daisy Miller was a pretty American girl all right, her behaviour wasn't pretty at all – was in fact regarded by her compatriots as quite monstrous. Winterbourne wondered how she felt about all the cold shoulders that were turned upon her, and sometimes found himself suspecting with impatience that she simply didn't feel and didn't know. He set her down as hopelessly childish and shallow, as such mere giddiness and ignorance incarnate as was powerless either to heed or to suffer. Then at other moments he couldn't doubt that she carried about in her elegant and irresponsible little organism a defiant, passionate, perfectly observant consciousness of the impression she produced. He asked himself whether the defiance would come from the consciousness of innocence or from her being essentially a young person of the reckless class. Then it had to be admitted, he felt, that holding fast to a belief in her 'innocence' was more and more but a matter of gallantry too fine-spun for use. As I have already had occasion to relate, he was reduced without pleasure to this chopping of logic and vexed at his poor fallibility, his want of instinctive certitude as to how far her extravagance was generic and national and how far it was crudely personal. Whatever it was he had helplessly missed her, and now it was too late. She was 'carried away' by Mr Giovanelli.

A few days after his brief interview with her mother he came across her at that supreme seat of flowering desolation known as the Palace of the Caesars.[52] The early Roman spring had filled the air with bloom and perfume, and the rugged surface of the Palatine was muffled with tender verdure. Daisy moved at her ease over the great mounds of ruin that are embanked with mossy marble and paved with monumental inscriptions. It seemed to him he had never known Rome so lovely as just then. He looked off at the enchanting harmony of line and colour that remotely encircles the city – he inhaled the softly humid odours and felt the freshness of the year and the antiquity of the place reaffirm themselves in deep interfusion. It struck him also that Daisy had never showed to the eye for so utterly charming; but this had been his conviction on every occasion of their meeting. Giovanelli was of course at her side, and Giovanelli too glowed as never before with something of the glory of his race.

'Well,' she broke out upon the friend it would have been such mockery to designate as the latter's rival, 'I should think you'd be quite lonesome!'

'Lonesome?' Winterbourne resignedly echoed.

'You're always going round by yourself. Can't you get any one to walk with you?'

'I'm not so fortunate,' he answered, 'as your gallant companion.'

Giovanelli had from the first treated him with distinguished politeness; he listened with a deferential air to his remarks; he laughed punctiliously at his pleasantries; he attached such importance as he could find terms for to Miss Miller's cold compatriot. He carried himself in no degree like a jealous wooer; he had obviously a great deal of tact; he had no objection to any one's expecting a little humility of him. It even struck Winterbourne that he almost yearned at times for some private communication in the interest of his character for common sense; a chance to remark to him as another intelligent man that, bless him, *he* knew how extraordinary was their young lady and didn't flatter himself with confident – at least *too* confident and too delusive – hopes of matrimony and dollars. On this occasion he strolled away from his charming charge to pluck a sprig of almond-blossom which he carefully arranged in his button-hole.

'I know why you say that,' Daisy meanwhile observed. 'Because you think I go round too much with *him*!' And she nodded at her discreet attendant.

'Every one thinks so – if you care to know,' was all Winterbourne found to reply.

'Of course I care to know!' – she made this point with much expression. 'But I don't believe a word of it. They're only pretending to be shocked. They don't really care a straw what I do. Besides, I don't go round so much.'

'I think you'll find they do care. They'll show it – disagreeably,' he took on himself to state.

Daisy weighed the importance of that idea. 'How – disagreeably?'

'Haven't you noticed anything?' he compassionately asked.

'I've noticed *you*. But I noticed you've no more "give" than a ramrod the first time ever I saw you.'

'You'll find at least that I've more "give" than several others,' he patiently smiled.

'How shall I find it?'

'By going to see the others.'

'What will they do to me?'

'They'll show you the cold shoulder. Do you know what that means?'

Daisy was looking at him intently; she began to colour. 'Do you mean as Mrs Walker did the other night?'

'Exactly as Mrs Walker did the other night.'

She looked away at Giovanelli, still titivating with his almond-blossom. Then with her attention again on the important subject: 'I shouldn't think you'd let people be so unkind!'

'How can I help it?'

'I should think you'd want to say something.'

'I do want to say something' – and Winterbourne paused a moment. 'I want to say that your mother tells me she believes you engaged.'

'Well, I guess she does,' said Daisy very simply.

The young man began to laugh. 'And does Randolph believe it?'

'I guess Randolph doesn't believe anything.' This testimony to Randolph's scepticism excited Winterbourne to further mirth, and he noticed that Giovanelli was coming back to them. Daisy, observing it as well, addressed herself again to her countryman. 'Since you've mentioned it,' she said, 'I *am* engaged.' He looked at her hard – he had stopped laughing. 'You don't believe it!' she added.

He asked himself, and it was for a moment like testing a heart-beat; after which, 'Yes, I believe it!' he said.

'Oh no, you don't,' she answered. 'But *if* you possibly do,' she still more perversely pursued – 'well, I ain't!'

Miss Miller and her constant guide were on their way to the gate of the enclosure, so that Winterbourne, who had but lately entered, presently took leave of them. A week later on he went to dine at a beautiful villa on the Caelian Hill,[53] and, on arriving, dismissed his hired vehicle. The evening was perfect and he promised himself the satisfaction of walking home beneath the Arch of Constantine and past the vaguely-lighted monuments of the Forum.[54] Above was a moon half-developed, whose radiance was not brilliant but veiled in a thin cloud-curtain that seemed to diffuse and equalise it. When on his return from the villa at eleven o'clock he approached the dusky circle of the Colosseum[55] the sense of the romantic in him easily suggested that the interior, in such an atmosphere, would well repay a glance. He turned aside and walked to one of the empty arches, near which, as he observed, an open carriage – one of the little Roman street-cabs – was stationed. Then he passed in among the cavernous shadows of the great structure and emerged upon the clear and silent arena. The place had never seemed to him more impressive. One half of the gigantic circus was in deep shade while the other slept in the luminous dusk. As he stood there he began to murmur Byron's famous lines out of 'Manfred';[56] but before he had finished his quotation he remembered that if nocturnal meditation thereabouts was the fruit of a rich literary culture it was none the less deprecated by medical science. The air of other ages surrounded one; but the air of other ages, coldly analysed, was no better than a villainous miasma. Winterbourne sought, however, toward the middle of the arena, a further reach of vision, intending the next moment a hasty retreat. The great cross in the centre[57] was almost obscured; only as he drew near did he make it out distinctly. He thus also distinguished two persons stationed on the low steps that formed its base. One of these was a woman seated; her companion hovered before her.

Presently the sound of the woman's voice came to him distinctly in the warm night-air. 'Well, he looks at us as one of the old lions or tigers may have looked at the Christian martyrs!' These words were winged with their accent, so that they fluttered and settled about him in the darkness like vague white doves. It was Miss Daisy Miller who had released them for flight.

'Let us hope he's not very hungry' — the bland Giovanelli fell in with her humour. 'He'll have to take *me* first; you'll serve for dessert.'

Winterbourne felt himself pulled up with final horror now — and, it must be added, with final relief. It was as if a sudden clearance had taken place in the ambiguity of the poor girl's appearances and the whole riddle of her contradictions had grown easy to read. She was a young lady about the *shades* of whose perversity a foolish puzzled gentleman need no longer trouble his head or his heart. That once questionable quantity *had* no shades — it was a mere black little blot. He stood there looking at her, looking at her companion too, and not reflecting that though he saw them vaguely he himself must have been more brightly presented. He felt angry at all his shiftings of view — he felt ashamed of all his tender little scruples and all his witless little mercies. He was about to advance again, and then again checked himself; not from the fear of doing her injustice, but from a sense of the danger of showing undue exhilaration for this disburdenment of cautious criticism. He turned away toward the entrance of the place; but as he did so he heard Daisy speak again.

'Why it was Mr Winterbourne! He saw me and he cuts me dead!'

What a clever little reprobate she was, he was amply able to reflect at this, and how smartly she feigned, how promptly she sought to play off on him, a surprised and injured innocence! But nothing would induce him to cut her either 'dead' or to within any measurable distance even of the famous 'inch' of her life. He came forward again and went toward the great cross. Daisy had got up and Giovanelli lifted his hat. Winterbourne had now begun to think simply of the madness, on the ground of exposure and infection, of a frail young creature's lounging away such hours in a nest of malaria. What if she *were* the most plausible of little reprobates? That was no reason for her dying of the *perniciosa*.[58]

'How long have you been "fooling round" here?' he asked with conscious roughness.

Daisy, lovely in the sinister silver radiance, appraised him a moment, roughness and all. 'Well, I guess all the evening.' She answered with spirit and, he could see even then, with exaggeration. 'I never saw anything so quaint.'

'I'm afraid,' he returned, 'you'll not think a bad attack of Roman fever very quaint. This is the way people catch it. I wonder,' he added to Giovanelli, 'that you, a native Roman, should countenance such extraordinary rashness.'

'Ah,' said this seasoned subject, 'for myself I have no fear.'

'Neither have I − for you!' Winterbourne retorted in French. 'I'm speaking for this young lady.'

Giovanelli raised his well-shaped eyebrows and showed his shining teeth, but took his critic's rebuke with docility. 'I assured Mademoiselle it was a grave indiscretion, but when was Mademoiselle ever prudent?'

'I never was sick, and I don't mean to be!' Mademoiselle declared. 'I don't look like much, but I'm healthy! I was bound to see the Colosseum by moonlight − I wouldn't have wanted to go home without *that*; and we've had the most beautiful time, haven't we, Mr Giovanelli? If there has been any danger Eugenio can give me some pills.[59] Eugenio has got some splendid pills.'

'*I* should advise you then,' said Winterbourne, 'to drive home as fast as possible and take one!'

Giovanelli smiled as for the striking happy thought. 'What you say is very wise. I'll go and make sure the carriage is at hand.' And he went forward rapidly.

Daisy followed with Winterbourne. He tried to deny himself the small fine anguish of looking at her, but his eyes themselves refused to spare him, and she seemed moreover not in the least embarrassed. He spoke no word; Daisy chattered over the beauty of the place: 'Well, I *have* seen the Colosseum by moonlight − that's one thing I can rave about!' Then noticing her companion's silence she asked him why he was so stiff − it had always been her great word. He made no answer, but he felt his laugh an immense negation of stiffness. They passed under one of the dark archways; Giovanelli was in front with the carriage. Here Daisy stopped a moment, looking at her compatriot. '*Did* you believe I was engaged the other day?'

'It doesn't matter now what I believed the other day!' he replied with infinite point.

It was a wonder how she didn't wince for it. 'Well, what do you believe now?'

'I believe it makes very little difference whether you're engaged or not!'

He felt her lighted eyes fairly penetrate the thick gloom of the vaulted passage − as if to seek some access to him she hadn't yet compassed. But Giovanelli, with

71

a graceful inconsequence, was at present all for retreat. 'Quick, quick; if we get in by midnight we're quite safe!'

Daisy took her seat in the carriage and the fortunate Italian placed himself beside her. 'Don't forget Eugenio's pills!' said Winterbourne as he lifted his hat.

'I don't care,' she unexpectedly cried out for this, 'whether I have Roman fever or not!' On which the cab-driver cracked his whip and they rolled across the desultory patches of antique pavement.

Winterbourne – to do him justice, as it were – mentioned to no one that he had encountered Miss Miller at midnight in the Colosseum with a gentleman; in spite of which deep discretion, however, the fact of the scandalous adventure was known a couple of days later, with a dozen vivid details, to every member of the little American circle, and was commented accordingly. Winterbourne judged thus that the people about the hotel had been thoroughly empowered to testify, and that after Daisy's return there would have been an exchange of jokes between the porter and the cab-driver. But the young man became aware at the same moment of how thoroughly it had ceased to ruffle him that the little American flirt should be 'talked about' by low-minded menials. These sources of current criticism a day or two later abounded still further: the little American flirt was alarmingly ill and the doctors now in possession of the scene. Winterbourne, when the rumour came to him, immediately went to the hotel for more news. He found that two or three charitable friends had preceded him and that they were being entertained in Mrs Miller's salon by the all-efficient Randolph.

'It's going round at night that way, you bet – that's what has made her so sick. She's always going round at night. I shouldn't think she'd want to – it's so plaguey dark over here. You can't see anything over here without the moon's right up. In America they don't go round by the moon!' Mrs Miller meanwhile wholly surrendered to her genius for unapparent uses; her salon knew her less than ever, and she was presumably now at least giving her daughter the advantage of her society. It was clear that Daisy was dangerously ill.

Winterbourne constantly attended for news from the sick-room, which reached him, however, but with worrying indirectness, though he once had speech, for a moment, of the poor girl's physician and once saw Mrs Miller, who, sharply alarmed, struck him as thereby more happily inspired than he could have conceived and indeed as the most noiseless and lighthanded of nurses. She invoked a good deal the remote shade of Dr Davis, but Winterbourne paid her the compliment of taking her after all for less monstrous a goose. To this indulgence indeed something she further said perhaps even more insidiously disposed him. 'Daisy spoke of you the other day quite pleasantly. Half the time she doesn't know what she's saying, but that time I think she did. She gave me a message – she told me to tell you.

She wanted you to know she never was engaged to that handsome Italian who was always round. I'm sure I'm very glad; Mr Giovanelli hasn't been near us since she was taken ill. I thought he was so much of a gentleman, but I don't call that very polite! A lady told me he was afraid I hadn't approved of his being round with her so much evenings. Of course it ain't as if their evenings were as pleasant as ours – since *we* don't seem to feel that way about the poison. I guess I *don't* see the point now; but I suppose he knows I'm a lady and I'd scorn to raise a fuss. Anyway, she wants you to realize she ain't engaged. I don't know why she makes so much of it, but she said to me three times "Mind you tell Mr Winterbourne." And then she told me to ask if you remembered the time you went up to that castle in Switzerland. But I said I wouldn't give any such messages as *that*. Only if she ain't engaged I guess I'm glad to realise it too.'

But, as Winterbourne had originally judged, the truth on this question had small actual relevance. A week after this the poor girl died; it had been indeed a terrible case of the *perniciosa*. A grave was found for her in the little Protestant cemetery,[60] by an angle of the wall of imperial Rome, beneath the cypresses and the thick spring-flowers. Winterbourne stood there beside it with a number of other mourners; a number larger than the scandal excited by the young lady's career might have made probable. Near him stood Giovanelli, who came nearer still before Winterbourne turned away. Giovanelli, in decorous mourning, showed but a whiter face; his button-hole lacked its nosegay and he had visibly something urgent – and even to distress – to say, which he scarce knew how to 'place.' He decided at last to confide it with a pale convulsion to Winterbourne. 'She was the most beautiful young lady I ever saw, and the most amiable.' To which he added in a moment: 'Also – naturally! – the most innocent.'

Winterbourne sounded him with hard dry eyes, but presently repeated his words, 'The most innocent?'

'The most innocent!'

It came somehow so much too late that our friend could only glare at its having come at all. 'Why the devil,' he asked, 'did you take her to that fatal place?'

Giovanelli raised his neat shoulders and eyebrows to within suspicion of a shrug. 'For myself I had no fear; and *she* – she did what she liked.'[61]

Winterbourne's eyes attached themselves to the ground. 'She did what she liked!'

It determined on the part of poor Giovanelli a further pious, a further candid, confidence. 'If she had lived I should have got nothing. She never would have married me.'

It had been spoken as if to attest, in all sincerity, his disinterestedness, but Winterbourne scarce knew what welcome to give it. He said, however, with a grace inferior to his friend's: 'I dare say not.'

The latter was even by this not discouraged. 'For a moment I hoped so. But no. I'm convinced.'

Winterbourne took it in; he stood staring at the raw protuberance among the April daisies. When he turned round again his fellow mourner had stepped back.

He almost immediately left Rome, but the following summer he again met his aunt Mrs Costello at Vevey. Mrs Costello extracted from the charming old hotel there a value that the Miller family hadn't mastered the secret of. In the interval Winterbourne had often thought of the most interesting member of that trio – of her mystifying manners and her queer adventure. One day he spoke of her to his aunt – said it was on his conscience he had done her injustice.

'I'm sure I don't know' – that lady showed caution. 'How did your injustice affect her?'

'She sent me a message before her death which I didn't understand at the time. But I've understood it since. She would have appreciated one's esteem.'

'She took an odd way to gain it! But do you mean by what you say,' Mrs Costello asked, 'that she would have reciprocated one's affection?'

As he made no answer to this she after a little looked round at him – he hadn't been directly within sight; but the effect of that wasn't to make her repeat her question. He spoke, however, after a while. 'You were right in that remark that you made last summer. I was booked to make a mistake. I've lived too long in foreign parts.' And this time she herself said nothing.

Nevertheless he soon went back to live at Geneva, whence there continue to come the most contradictory accounts of his motives of sojourn: a report that he's 'studying' hard – an intimation that he's much interested in a very clever foreign lady.

The Pension Beaurepas

I was not rich – on the contrary; and I had been told the Pension Beaurepas[1] was cheap. I had further been told that a boarding-house is a capital place for the study of human nature. I was inclined to a literary career and a friend had said to me: 'If you mean to write you ought to go and live in a boarding-house: there's no other such way to pick up material.' I had read something of this kind in a letter addressed by the celebrated Stendhal to his sister:[2] 'I have a passionate desire to know human nature, and a great mind to live in a boarding-house, where people can't conceal their real characters.' I was an admirer of 'La Chartreuse de Parme,' and easily believed one couldn't do better than follow in the footsteps of its author. I remembered, too, the magnificent boarding-house in Balzac's 'Père Goriot' – the 'pension bourgeoise des deux sexes et autres,' kept by Madame Vauquer, née de Conflans.[3] Magnificent, I mean, as a piece of portraiture; the establishment, as an establishment, was certainly sordid enough, and I hoped for better things from the Pension Beaurepas. This institution was one of the most esteemed in Geneva and, standing in a little garden of its own not far from the lake, had a very homely comfortable sociable aspect. The regular entrance was, as one might say, at the back, which looked upon the street, or rather upon a little *place*[4] adorned, like every *place* in Geneva, great or small, with a generous cool fountain. That approach was not prepossessing, for on crossing the threshold you found yourself more or less in the kitchen – amid the 'offices'[5] and struck with their assault on your nostril. This, however, was no great matter, for at the Pension Beaurepas things conformed frankly to their nature and the whole mechanism lay bare. It was rather primitive, the mechanism, but it worked in a friendly homely regular way. Madame Beaurepas was an honest little old woman – she was far advanced in life and had been keeping a pension for more than forty years – whose only faults were that she was slightly deaf, that she was fond of a surreptitious pinch of snuff, and that, at the age of seventy-four, she wore stacks of flowers in her cap. There was a legend in the house that she wasn't so deaf as she pretended and that she feigned this infirmity in order to possess herself of the secrets of her lodgers. I never indeed subscribed to this theory, convinced as I became that Madame Beaurepas had outlived the period of indiscreet curiosity. She dealt with the present and the future in the steady light of a long experience; she had been having lodgers for nearly half a century and all her concern with them was that they should pay their bills, fold their napkins and make use of the doormat. She cared very little for their secrets. 'J'en ai vus de toutes les couleurs,'[6] she said to me. She had quite ceased to trouble about individuals; she cared only for types and clear categories. Her large observation had made her acquainted with a number of these and her mind become a complete collection of 'heads.'[7] She flattered herself that she knew at a glance where to pigeonhole a new-comer, and if she made mistakes her deportment never betrayed them. I felt that as regards particular persons – once they conformed to the few rules – she had neither likes nor dislikes; but she was capable of expressing esteem or contempt for a species. She had her own ways, I suppose, of manifesting her approval, but her manner of indicating the reverse was simple and unvarying. 'Je trouve que c'est déplacé'[8] – this exhausted her view of the matter. If one of her inmates had put arsenic into the *pot-au-feu*[9] I believe Madame Beaurepas would have been satisfied to remark that this receptacle was not the place for arsenic. She could have imagined it otherwise and suitably applied. The line of misconduct to which she most objected was an undue assumption of gentility; she had no patience with boarders who gave themselves airs. 'When people come chez moi[10] it isn't to cut a figure in the world; I've never so flattered myself,' I remember hearing her say; 'and when you pay seven francs a day, tout compris,[11] it comprises everything but the right to look down on the others. Yet there are people who, the less they pay, take themselves the more au sérieux.[12] My most difficult boarders have always been those who've fiercely bargained and had the cheapest rooms.'

Madame Beaurepas had a niece, a young woman of some forty odd years; and the two ladies, with the assistance of a couple of thick-waisted red-armed peasant-women, kept the house going. If on your exits and entrances you peeped into the kitchen it made very little difference; as Célestine the cook shrouded herself in no mystery and announced the day's fare, amid her fumes, quite with the resonance of the priestess of the tripod [13] foretelling the future. She was always at your service with a grateful grin: she blacked your boots; she trudged off to fetch a cab; she would have carried your baggage, if you had allowed her, on her broad little back. She was always tramping in and out between her kitchen and the fountain in the *place*, where it often seemed to me that a large part of the preparation for our meals went forward – the wringing-out of towels and table-cloths, the washing of potatoes and cabbages, the scouring of saucepans and cleansing of water-bottles. You enjoyed from the door-step a perpetual back-view of Célestine and of her large loose woollen ankles as she craned, from the waist, over into the fountain and dabbled in her various utensils. This sounds as if life proceeded but in a makeshift fashion at the Pension Beaurepas – as if we suffered from a sordid tone. But such was not at all the case. We were simply very bourgeois; we practised the good old Genevese principle of not sacrificing to appearances. Nothing can be better than that principle when the rich real underlies it. We had the rich real at the Pension Beaurepas: we had it in the shape of soft short beds equipped with fluffy *duvets*; of admirable coffee, served to us in the morning by Célestine in person as we lay recumbent on these downy couches; of copious wholesome succulent dinners, conformable to the best provincial tra-ditions. For myself, I thought the Pension Beaurepas local colour, and this, with me, at that time, was a grand term. I was young and ingenuous and had just come from America. I wished to perfect myself in the French tongue and innocently believed it to flourish by Lake Leman.[14] I used to go to lectures at the Academy, the nursing mother of the present University,[15] and come home with a violent appetite. I always enjoyed my morning walk across the long bridge – there was only one just there in those days – which spans the deep blue out-gush of the lake, and up the dark steep streets of the old Calvinistic city. The garden faced this way, toward the lake and the old town, and gave properest access to the house. There was a high wall with a double gate in the middle and flanked by a couple of ancient massive posts; the big rusty grille bristled with old-fashioned iron-work. The garden was rather mouldy and weedy, tangled and untended; but it contained a small thin-flowing fountain, several green benches, a rickety little table of the same complexion, together with three orange-trees in tubs disposed as effectively as possible in front of the windows of the salon.

II

As commonly happens in boarding-houses the rustle of petticoats was at the Pension Beaurepas the most familiar form of the human tread. We enjoyed the usual allowance of economical widows and old maids and, to maintain the balance of the sexes, could boast but of a finished old Frenchman and an obscure young American. It hardly made the matter easier that the old Frenchman came from Lausanne. He was a native of that well-perched place, but had once spent six months in Paris, where he had tasted of the tree of knowledge; he had got beyond Lausanne, whose resources he pronounced inadequate. Lausanne, as he said, ʼ*manquait d'agréments.*ʼ[16] When obliged, for reasons he never specified, to bring his residence in Paris to a close, he had fallen back on Geneva; he had broken his fall at the Pension Beaurepas. Geneva was after all more like Paris, and at a

Genevese boarding-house there was sure to be plenty of Americans who might be more or less counted on to add to the resemblance. M. Pigeonneau[17] was a little lean man with a vast narrow nose, who sat a great deal in the garden and bent his eyes, with the aid of a large magnifying glass, on a volume from the *cabinet de lecture*.[18]

One day a fortnight after my adoption of the retreat I describe I came back rather earlier than usual from my academic session; it wanted half an hour of the midday breakfast. I entered the salon with the design of possessing myself of the day's *Galignani*[19] before one of the little English old maids should have removed it to her virginal bower – a privilege to which Madame Beaurepas frequently alluded as one of the attractions of the establishment. In the salon I found a new-comer, a tall gentleman in a high black hat, whom I immediately recognised as a compatriot. I had often seen him, or his equivalent, in the hotel-parlours of my native land. He apparently supposed himself to be at the present moment in an hotel-parlour; his hat was on his head or rather half off it – pushed back from his forehead and more suspended than poised. He stood before a table on which old newspapers were scattered; one of these he had taken up and, with his eye-glass on his nose, was holding out at arm's length. It was that honourable but extremely diminutive sheet the *Journal de Genève*, a newspaper then of about the size of a pocket-handkerchief. As I drew near, looking for my *Galignani*, the tall gentleman gave me, over the top of his eyeglass, a sad and solemn stare. Presently, however, before I had time to lay my hand on the object of my search, he silently offered me the *Journal de Genève*.

'It appears,' he said, 'to be the paper of the country.'

'Yes,' I answered, 'I believe it's the best.'

He gazed at it again, still holding it at arm's-length as if it had been a looking-glass. 'Well,' he concluded, 'I suppose it's natural a small country should have small papers. You could wrap this one up, mountains and all, in one of our dailies!'

I found my *Galignani* and went off with it into the garden, where I seated myself on a bench in the shade. Presently I saw the tall gentleman in the hat appear at one of the open windows of the salon and stand there with his hands in his pockets and his legs a little apart. He looked infinitely bored, and – I don't know why – I immediately felt sorry for him. He hadn't at all – as M. Pigeonneau, for instance, in his way, had it – the romantic note; he looked just a jaded faded absolutely voided man of business. But after a little he came into the garden and began to stroll about; and then his restless helpless carriage and the vague unacquainted manner in which his eyes wandered over the place seemed to make it proper that, as an older resident, I should offer him a certain hospitality. I addressed him some remark founded on our passage of a moment before, and he came and sat down beside me on my bench, clasping one of his long knees in his hands.

'When is it this big breakfast[20] of theirs comes off?' he enquired. 'That's what I call it – the little breakfast and the big breakfast. I never thought I should live to see the time when I'd want to eat two breakfasts. But a man's glad to do anything over here.'

'For myself,' I dropped, 'I find plenty to do.'

He turned his head and glanced at me with an effect of bottomless wonder and dry despair. 'You're getting used to the life, are you?'

'I like the life very much,' I laughed.

'How long have you tried it?'

'Do you mean this place?'

'Well, I mean anywhere. It seems to me pretty much the same all over.'

'I've been in this house only a fortnight,' I said.

'Well, what should you say, from what you've seen?' my companion asked.

'Oh you can see all there is at once. It's very simple.'

'Sweet simplicity, eh? Well then I guess my two ladies will know right off what's the matter with it.'

'Oh everything's very good,' I hastened to explain. 'And Madame Beaurepas is a charming old woman. And then it's very cheap.'

'Cheap, is it?' my friend languidly echoed.

'Doesn't it strike you so?' I thought it possible he hadn't enquired the terms. But he appeared not to have heard me; he sat there, clasping his knee and absently blinking at the sunshine.

'Are you from the United States, sir?' he presently demanded, turning his head again.

'Well, I guess I am, sir,' I felt it indicated to reply; and I mentioned the place of my nativity.

'I presumed you were American or English. I'm from the United States myself – from New York City. Many of our people here?' he went on.

'Not so many as I believe there have sometimes been. There are two or three ladies.'

'Well,' my interlocutor observed, 'I'm very fond of ladies' society. I think when it's really nice there's nothing comes up to it. I've got two ladies here myself. I must make you acquainted with them.' And then after I had rejoined that I should be delighted and had enquired of him if he had been long in Europe: 'Well, it seems precious long, but my time's not up yet. We've been here nineteen weeks and a half.'

'Are you travelling for pleasure?' I hazarded.

Once more he inclined his face to me – his face that was practically so odd a comment on my question, and I so felt his unspoken irony that I soon also turned and met his eyes. 'No, sir. Not much, sir,' he added after a considerable interval.

'Pardon me,' I said; for his desolation had a little the effect of a rebuke.

He took no notice of my appeal; he simply continued to look at me. 'I'm travelling,' he said at last, 'to please the doctors. They seemed to think *they'd* enjoy it.'

'Ah they sent you abroad for your health?'

'They sent me abroad because they were so plaguey muddled they didn't know what else to do.'

'That's often the best thing,' I ventured to remark.

'It was a confession of medical bankruptcy; they wanted to stop my run on them. They didn't know enough to cure me, as they had originally pretended they did, and that's the way they thought they'd get round it. I wanted to be cured — I didn't want to be transported.[21] I hadn't done any harm.' I could but assent to the general proposition of the inefficiency of doctors, and put to my companion that I hoped he hadn't been seriously ill. He only shook his foot at first, for some time, by way of answer; but at last, 'I didn't get natural rest,' he wearily observed.

'Ah that's very annoying. I suppose you were overworked.'

'I didn't have a natural appetite — nor even an unnatural, when they fixed up things for me. I took no interest in my food.'

'Well, I guess you'll both eat and sleep here,' I felt justified in remarking.

'I couldn't hold a pen,' my neighbour went on. 'I couldn't sit still. I couldn't walk from my house to the cars[22] — and it's only a little way. I lost my interest in business.'

'You needed a good holiday,' I concluded.

'That's what the doctors said. It wasn't so very smart of them. I had been paying strict attention to business for twenty-three years.'

'And in all that time you had never let up?' I cried in horror.

My companion waited a little. 'I kind o' let up Sundays.'

'Oh that's nothing — because our Sundays themselves never let up.'

'I guess they do over here,' said my friend.

'Yes, but you weren't over here.'

'No, I wasn't over here. I shouldn't have been where I was three years ago if I had spent my time travelling round Europe. I was in a very advantageous position. I did a very large business. I was considerably interested in lumber.' He paused, bending, though a little hopelessly, about to me again. 'Have you any business interests yourself?' I answered that I had none, and he proceeded slowly, mildly and deliberately. 'Well sir, perhaps you're not aware that business in the United States is not what it was a short time since. Business interests are very insecure.

There seems to be a general falling-off. Different parties offer different explanations of the fact, but so far as I'm aware none of their fine talk has set things
going again.' I ingeniously intimated that if business was dull the time was good
for coming away; whereupon my compatriot threw back his head and stretched
his legs a while. 'Well sir, that's one view of the matter certainly. There's
something to be said for that. These things should be looked at all round. That's
the ground my wife took. That's the ground,' he added in a moment, 'that a lady
would naturally take.' To which he added a laugh as ghostly as a dried flower.

'You think there's a flaw in the reasoning?' I asked.

'Well sir, the ground I took was that the worse a man's business is the more it
requires looking after. I shouldn't want to go out to recreation – not even to go
to church – if my house was on fire. My firm's not doing the business it was; it's
like a sick child – it requires nursing. What I wanted the doctors to do was to fix
me up so that I could go on at home. I'd have taken anything they'd have given
me, and as many times a day. I wanted to be right there; I had my reasons; I
have them still. But I came off all the same,' said my friend with a melancholy
smile.

I was a great deal younger than he, but there was something so simple and
communicative in his tone, so expressive of a desire to fraternise and so exempt
from any theory of human differences, that I quite forgot his seniority and found
myself offering him paternal advice. 'Don't think about all that. Simply enjoy
yourself, amuse yourself, get well. Travel about and see Europe. At the end of a
year, by the time you're ready to go home, things will have improved over there,
and you'll be quite well and happy.'

He laid his hand on my knee; his wan kind eyes considered me, and I thought
he was going to say 'You're very young!' But he only brought out: '*You've* got
used to Europe anyway!'

III

At breakfast I encountered his ladies – his wife and daughter. They were placed,
however, at a distance from me, and it was not until the pensionnaires[23] had
dispersed and some of them, according to custom, had come out into the garden,
that he had an opportunity of carrying out his offer.

'Will you allow me to introduce you to my daughter?' he said, moved apparently
by a paternal inclination to provide this young lady with social diversion. She
was standing with her mother in one of the paths, where she looked about with
no great complacency, I inferred, at the homely characteristics of the place. Old

M. Pigeonneau meanwhile hovered near, hesitating apparently between the desire to be urbane and the absence of a pretext. 'Mrs Ruck, Miss Sophy Ruck' – my friend led me up.

Mrs Ruck was a ponderous light-coloured person with a smooth fair face, a somnolent eye and an arrangement of hair, with forehead-tendrils, water-waves and other complications, that reminded me of those framed 'capillary' tributes to the dead[24] which used long ago to hang over artless mantel-shelves between the pair of glass domes protecting wax flowers. Miss Sophy was a girl of one-and-twenty, tiny and pretty and lively, with no more maiden shyness than a feminine terrier in a tinkling collar. Both of these ladies were arrayed in black silk dresses, much ruffled and flounced, and if elegance were *all* a matter of trimming they would have been elegant.

'Do you think highly of this pension?' asked Mrs Ruck after a few preliminaries.

'It's a little rough,' I made answer, 'but it seems to me comfortable.'

'Does it take a high rank in Geneva?'

'I imagine it enjoys a very fair fame.'

'I should never dream of comparing it to a New York boarding-house,' Mrs Ruck pursued.

'It's quite in a different style,' her daughter observed. Miss Ruck had folded her arms; she held her elbows with a pair of small white hands and tapped the ground with a pretty little foot.

'We hardly expected to come to a pension,' said Mrs Ruck, who looked considerably over my head and seemed to confide the truth in question, as with an odd austerity or chastity, a marked remoteness, to the general air. 'But we thought we'd try; we had heard so much about Swiss pensions. I was saying to Mr Ruck that I wondered if this is a favourable specimen. I was afraid we might have made a mistake.'

'Well, we know some people who have been here; they think everything of Madame Beaurepas,' said Miss Sophy. 'They say she's a real friend.'

Mrs Ruck, at this, drew down a little. 'Mr and Mrs Parker – perhaps you've heard her speak of them.'

'Madame Beaurepas has had a great many Americans; she's very fond of Americans,' I replied.

'Well, I must say I should think she would be if she compares them with some others.'

'Mother's death on comparing,' remarked Miss Ruck.

'Of course I like to study things and to see for myself,' the elder lady returned. 'I never had a chance till now; I never knew my privileges. Give me an American!' And, recovering her distance again, she seemed to impose this tax on the universe.

'Well, I must say there are some things I like over here,' said Miss Sophy with courage. And indeed I could see that she was a young woman of sharp affirmations.

Her father gave one of his ghostly grunts. 'You like the stores – that's what you like most, I guess.'

The young lady addressed herself to me without heeding this charge. 'I suppose you feel quite at home here.'

'Oh he likes it – he has got used to the life. He says you *can*!' Mr Ruck proclaimed.

'I wish you'd teach Mr Ruck then,' said his wife. 'It seems as if he couldn't get used to anything.'

'I'm used to you, my dear,' he retorted, but with his melancholy eyes on me.

'He's intensely restless,' continued Mrs Ruck. 'That's what made me want to come to a pension. I thought he'd settle down more.'

'Well, lovey,' he sighed, 'I've had hitherto mainly to settle up!'

In view of a possible clash between her parents I took refuge in conversation with Miss Ruck, who struck me as well out in the open[25] – as leaning, subject to any swing, so to speak, on the easy gate of the house of life. I learned from her that with her companions, after a visit to the British islands, she had been spending a month in Paris and that she thought she should have died on quitting that city. 'I hung out of the carriage, when we left the hotel – I assure you I did. And I guess mother did too.'

'Out of the other window, I hope,' said I.

'Yes, one out of each window' – her promptitude was perfect. 'Father had hard work, I can tell you. We hadn't half-finished – there were ever so many other places we wanted to go to.'

'Your father insisted on coming away?'

'Yes – after we had been there about a month he claimed he had had enough. He's fearfully restless; he's very much out of health. Mother and I took the ground that if he was restless in Paris he needn't hope for peace anywhere. We don't mean to let up on him till he takes us back.' There was an air of keen resolution in Miss Ruck's pretty face, of the lucid apprehension of desirable ends, which made me, as she pronounced these words, direct a glance of covert compassion toward her poor recalcitrant sire. He had walked away a little with his wife, and I saw only his back and his stooping patient-looking shoulders, whose air of acute resignation was thrown into relief by the cold serenity of his companion. 'He'll have to take us back in September anyway,' the girl pursued; 'he'll have to take us back to get some things we've ordered.'

I had an idea it was my duty to draw her out. 'Have you ordered a great many things?'

'Well, I guess we've ordered *some*. Of course we wanted to take advantage of being in Paris – ladies always do. We've left the most important ones till we go back. Of course that's the principal interest for ladies. Mother said she'd feel so shabby if she just passed through. We've promised all the people to be right there in September, and I never broke a promise yet. So Mr Ruck has got to make his plans accordingly.'

'And what are his plans?' I continued, true to my high conception.

'I don't know; he doesn't seem able to make any. His great idea was to get to Geneva, but now that he has got here he doesn't seem to see the point. It's the effect of bad health. He used to be so bright and natural, but now he's quite subdued. It's about time he should improve, anyway. We went out last night to look at the jewellers' windows[26] – in that street behind the hotel. I had always heard of those jewellers' windows. We saw some lovely things, but it didn't seem to rouse father. He'll get tired of Geneva sooner than he did of Paris.'

'Ah,' said I, 'there are finer things here than the jewellers' windows. We're very near some of the most beautiful scenery in Europe.'

'I suppose you mean the mountains. Well, I guess we've seen plenty of mountains at home. We used to go to the mountains every summer. We're familiar enough with the mountains. Aren't we, mother?' my young woman demanded, appealing to Mrs Ruck, who, with her husband, had drawn near again.

'Aren't we what?' enquired the elder lady.

'Aren't we familiar with the mountains?'

'Well, I hope so,' said Mrs Ruck.

Mr Ruck, with his hands in his pockets, gave me a sociable wink. 'There's nothing much you can *tell* them!'

The two ladies stood face to face a few moments, surveying each other's garments. Then the girl put her mother a question. 'Don't you want to go out?'

'Well, I think we'd better. We've got to go up to that place.'

'To what place?' asked Mr Ruck.

'To that jeweller's – to that big one.'

'They all seemed big enough – they were *too* big!' And he gave me another dry wink.

'That one where we saw the blue cross,' said his daughter.

'Oh come, what do you want of that blue cross?' poor Mr Ruck demanded.

'She wants to hang it on a black velvet ribbon and tie it round her neck,' said his wife.

'A black velvet ribbon? Not much!' cried the young lady. 'Do you suppose I'd wear that cross on a black velvet ribbon? On a nice little gold chain, if you please – a little narrow gold chain like an old-fashioned watch-chain. That's the proper thing for that blue cross. I know the sort of chain I mean; I'm going to look for one. When I want a thing,' said Miss Ruck with decision, 'I can generally find it.'

'Look here, Sophy,' her father urged, 'you don't want that blue cross.'

'I do want it — I happen to want it.' And her light laugh, with which she glanced at me, was like the flutter of some gage of battle.

The grace of this demonstration, in itself marked, suggested that there were various relations in which one might stand to Miss Ruck; but I felt that the sharpest of the strain would come on the paternal. 'Don't worry the poor child,' said her mother.

She took it sharply up. 'Come on, mother.'

'We're going to look round a little,' the elder lady explained to me by way of taking leave.

'I know what that means,' their companion dropped as they moved away. He stood looking at them while he raised his hand to his head, behind, and rubbed it with a movement that displaced his hat. (I may remark in parenthesis that I never saw a hat more easily displaced than Mr Ruck's.) I supposed him about to exhale some plaint, but I was mistaken. Mr Ruck was unhappy, but he was a touching fatalist. 'Well, they want to pick up something,' he contented himself with recognising. 'That's the principal interest for ladies.'

IV

He distinguished me, as the French say; he honoured me with his esteem and, as the days elapsed, with no small share of his confidence. Sometimes he bored me a little, for the tone of his conversation was not cheerful, tending as it did almost exclusively to a melancholy dirge over the financial prostration of our common country. 'No sir, business in the United States is not what it once was,' he found occasion to remark several times a day. 'There's not the same spring — there's not the same hopeful feeling. You can see it in all departments.' He used to sit by the hour in the little garden of the pension with a roll of American newspapers in his lap and his high hat pushed back, swinging one of his long legs and reading the *New York Herald*.[27] He paid a daily visit to the American banker's on the other side of the Rhône[28] and remained there a long time, turning over the old papers on the green velvet table in the centre of the Salon des Etrangers[29] and fraternising with chance compatriots. But in spite of these diversions the time was heavy on his hands. I used at times to propose him a walk, but he had a mortal horror of any use of his legs other than endlessly dangling or crossing them, and regarded my direct employment of my own as a morbid form of activity. 'You'll kill yourself if you don't look out,' he said, 'walking all over the country. I don't want to stump round that way — I ain't a postman!' Briefly speaking, Mr Ruck had few resources. His wife and daughter, on the other hand, it was to be supposed, were possessed of a good many that couldn't be apparent to an unobtrusive young man. They also sat a great deal in the garden or in the salon, side by side, with folded hands, taking in, to vague ends, material objects, and were remarkably independent of most of the usual feminine aids to idleness – light literature, tapestry, the use of the piano. They lent themselves to complete displacement, however, much more than their companion, and I often met them, in the Rue du Rhône[30] and on the quays, loitering in front of the jewellers' windows. They might have had a cavalier in the person of old M. Pigeonneau, who professed a high appreciation of their charms, but who, owing to the absence of a common idiom, was deprived, in the connexion, of the pleasures of intimacy. He knew no English, and Mrs Ruck and her daughter had, as it seemed, an incurable mistrust of the beautiful tongue which, as the old man endeavoured to impress upon them, was pre-eminently the language of conversation.

'They have a tournure de princesse[31] – a distinction suprême,' he said to me. 'One's surprised to find them in a little pension bourgeoise at seven francs a day.'

'Oh they don't come for economy. They must be rich.'

'They don't come for my beaux yeux – for mine,' said M. Pigeonneau sadly. 'Perhaps it's for yours, young man. Je vous recommande la maman!'[32]

I considered the case. 'They came on account of Mr Ruck – because at hotels he's so restless.'

M. Pigeonneau gave me a knowing nod. 'Of course he is, with such a wife as that! – a femme superbe. She's preserved in perfection – a miraculous fraîcheur. I like those large fair quiet women; they're often, dans l'intimité, the most agreeable. I'll warrant you that at heart Madame Roque is a finished coquette.' And then as I demurred: 'You suppose her cold? Ne vous y fiez pas!'[33]

'It's a matter in which I've nothing at stake.'

'You young Americans are droll,' said M. Pigeonneau: 'you never have anything at stake! But the little one, for example; I'll warrant you she's not cold. Toute menue[34] as she is she's admirably made.'

'She's very pretty.'

' "She's very pretty"! Vous dites cela d'un ton![35] When you pay compliments to Mees Roque I hope that's not the way you do it.'

'I don't pay compliments to Miss Ruck.'

'Ah decidedly,' said M. Pigeonneau, 'you young Americans are droll!'

I should have suspected that these two ladies wouldn't especially commend themselves to Madame Beaurepas; that as a maîtresse de salon,[36] which she in some degree aspired to be, she would have found them wanting in a certain colloquial ease. But I should have gone quite wrong: Madame Beaurepas had no fault at all to find with her new pensionnaires. 'I've no observation whatever to make about them,' she said to me one evening. 'I see nothing in those ladies at all déplacé. They don't complain of anything; they don't meddle; they take what's given them; they leave me tranquil. The Americans are often like that. Often, but not always,' Madame Beaurepas pursued. 'We're to have a specimen tomorrow of a very different sort.'

'An American?' I was duly interested.

'Two Américaines — a mother and a daughter. There are Americans and Americans: when you're difficiles you're more so than any one, and when you've pretensions — ah, par exemple, it's serious. I foresee that with this little lady everything will be serious, beginning with her café au lait. She has been staying at the Pension Chamousset — my concurrente,[37] you know, further up the street; but she's coming away because the coffee's bad. She holds to her coffee, it appears. I don't know what liquid Madame Chamousset may dispense under that name, but we'll do the best we can for her. Only I know she'll make me des histoires about something else. She'll demand a new lamp for the salon; vous allez voir cela.[38] She wishes to pay but eleven francs a day for herself and her daughter, tout compris; and for their eleven francs they expect to be lodged like princesses. But she's very "ladylike" — isn't that what you call it in English? Oh, pour cela, she's ladylike!'

I caught a glimpse on the morrow of the source of these portents, who had presented herself at our door as I came in from a walk. She had come in a cab, with her daughter and her luggage; and with an air of perfect softness and serenity she now disputed the fare as she stood on the steps and among her boxes. She addressed her cabman in a very English accent, but with extreme precision and correctness. 'I wish to be perfectly reasonable, but don't wish to encourage you in exorbitant demands. With a franc and a half you're sufficiently paid. It's not the custom at Geneva to give a pour-boire[39] for so short a drive. I've made enquiries and find it's not the custom even in the best families. I'm a stranger, yes, but I always adopt the custom of the native families. I think it my duty to the natives.'

'But I'm a native too, moi!' cried the cabman in high derision.

'You seem to me to speak with a German accent,' continued the lady. 'You're probably from Basel.[40] A franc and a half are sufficient. I see you've left behind the little red bag I asked you to hold between your knees; you'll please to go back to the other house and get it. Very well, si vous me manquez[41] I'll make a complaint of you to-morrow at the administration. Aurora, you'll find a pencil in the outer pocket of my embroidered satchel; please write down his number — 87; do you see it distinctly? — in case we should forget it.'

The young lady so addressed — a slight fair girl holding a large parcel of umbrellas – stood at hand while this allocution went forward, but apparently gave no heed to it. She stood looking about her in a listless manner – looking at the front of the house, at the corridor, at Célestine tucking back her apron in the doorway, at me as I passed in amid the disseminated luggage; her mother's parsimonious attitude seeming to produce in Miss Aurora neither sympathy nor embarrassment. At dinner the two ladies were placed on the same side of the table as myself and below Mrs Ruck and her daughter – my own position being on the right of Mr Ruck. I had therefore little observation of Mrs Church – such I learned to be her name – but I occasionally heard her soft distinct voice.

'White wine, if you please; we prefer white wine. There's none on the table? Then you'll please get some and remember to place a bottle of it always here between my daughter and myself.'

'That lady seems to know what she wants,' said Mr Ruck, 'and she speaks so I can understand her. I can't understand every one over here. I'd like to make that lady's acquaintance. Perhaps she knows what *I* want too: it seems so hard to find out! But I don't want any of their sour white wine; that's one of the things I don't want. I guess she'll be an addition to the pension.'

Mr Ruck made the acquaintance of Mrs Church that evening in the parlour, being presented to her by his wife, who presumed on the rights conferred upon herself by the mutual proximity, at table, of the two ladies. I seemed to make out that in Mrs Church's view Mrs Ruck presumed too far. The fugitive from the Pension Chamousset, as M. Pigeonneau called her, was a little fresh plump comely woman, looking less than her age, with a round bright serious face. She was very simply and frugally dressed, not at all in the manner of Mr Ruck's companions, and had an air of quiet distinction which was an excellent defensive weapon. She exhibited a polite disposition to listen to what Mr Ruck might have to say, but her manner was equivalent to an intimation that what she valued least in boarding-house life was its social opportunities. She had placed herself near a lamp, after carefully screwing it and turning it up, and she had opened in her lap, with the assistance of a large embroidered marker, an octavo[42] volume which I perceived to be in German. To Mrs Ruck and her daughter she was evidently a puzzle; they were mystified beyond appeal by her frugal attire and expensive culture. The two younger ladies, however, had begun to fraternise freely, and Miss Ruck presently went wandering out of the room with her arm round the waist of Miss Church. It was a warm evening; the long windows of the salon stood wide open to the garden, and, inspired by the balmy darkness, M. Pigeonneau and Mademoiselle Beaurepas, a most obliging little woman who lisped and always wore a huge cravat, declared they would organise a fête de nuit.[43] They engaged in this enterprise, and the fête developed itself on the lines of half a dozen red paper lanterns hung about in the trees, and of several glasses of *sirop* carried on a tray by the stout-armed Célestine. As the occasion deepened to its climax I went out into the garden, where M. Pigeonneau was master of ceremonies.

'But where are those charming young ladies,' he cried, 'Mees Roque and the new-comer, l'aimable transfuge?[44] Their absence has been remarked and they're wanting to the brilliancy of the scene. Voyez, I have selected a glass of syrup – a generous glass – for Mees Roque, and I advise you, my young friend, if you wish to make a good impression, to put aside one which you may offer to the other young lady. What's her name? Mees Cheurche? I see; it's a singular name. Ça veut dire "église," n'est-ce-pas?[45] Voilà a church where I'd willingly worship!'

Mr Ruck presently came out of the salon, having concluded his interview with the elder of the pair. Through the open window I saw that accomplished woman seated under the lamp with her German octavo, while Mrs Ruck established empty-handed in an armchair near her, fairly glowered at her for fascination.

'Well, I told you she'd know what I want,' he promptly observed to me. 'She says I want to go right up to Appenzell,[46] wherever that is; that I want to drink whey and live in a high latitude – what did she call it? – a high altitude. She seemed to think we ought to leave for Appenzell to-morrow; she'd got it all fixed. She says this ain't a high enough lat— a high enough altitude. And she says I mustn't go too high either; that would be just as bad; she seems to know just the right figure. She says she'll give me a list of the hotels where we must stop on the way to Appenzell. I asked her if she didn't want to go with us, but she says she'd rather sit still and read. I guess she's a big reader.'

The daughter of this devotee now reappeared, in company with Miss Ruck, with whom she had been strolling through the outlying parts of the garden; and that young lady noted with interest the red paper lanterns. 'Good gracious,' she enquired, 'are they trying to stick the flower-pots into the trees?'

'It's an illumination in honour of our arrival,' her companion returned. 'It's a triumph over Madame Chamousset.'

'Meanwhile, at the Pension Chamousset,' I ventured to suggest, 'they've put out their lights – they're sitting in darkness and lamenting your departure.'

She smiled at me – she was standing in the light that came from the house. M. Pigeonneau meanwhile, who had awaited his chance, advanced to Miss Ruck with his glass of syrup. 'I've kept it for you, mademoiselle,' he said; 'I've jealously guarded it. It's very delicious!'

Miss Ruck looked at him and his syrup without making any motion to take the glass. 'Well, I guess it's sour,' she dropped with a small shake of her head.

M. Pigeonneau stood staring, his syrup in his hand; then he slowly turned away. He looked about at the rest of us as to appeal from Miss Ruck's insensibility, and went to deposit his rejected tribute on a bench. 'Won't you give it to me?' asked Miss Church in faultless French. 'J'adore le sirop, moi.'

M. Pigeonneau came back with alacrity and presented the glass with a very low bow. 'I adore good manners.'

This incident caused me to look at Miss Church with quickened interest. She was not strikingly pretty, but in her charming irregular face was a light of ardour. Like her mother, though in a less degree, she was simply dressed.

'She wants to go to America,[47] and her mother won't let her' – Miss Sophy explained to me her friend's situation.

'I'm very sorry – for America,' I responsively laughed.

'Well, I don't want to say anything against your mother, but I think it's shameful,' Miss Ruck pursued.

'Mamma has very good reasons. She'll tell you them all.'

'Well, I'm sure I don't want to hear them,' said Miss Ruck. 'You've got a right to your own country; every one has a right to their own country.'

'Mamma's not very patriotic,' Aurora was at any rate not too spiritless to mention.

'Well, I call that dreadful,' her companion declared. 'I've heard there are some Americans like that, but I never believed it.'

'Oh there are all sorts of Americans.'

'Aurora's one of the right sort,' cried Miss Ruck, ready, it seemed, for the closest comradeship.

'Are you very patriotic,' I asked of the attractive exile.

Miss Ruck, however, promptly answered for her. 'She's right down homesick – she's dying to go. If you were me,' she went on to her friend, 'I guess your mother would *have* to take me.'

'Mamma's going to take me to Dresden.'[48]

'Well, I never heard of anything so cold-blooded!' said Miss Ruck. 'It's like something in a weird story.'

'I never heard Dresden was so awful a fate,' I ventured to interpose.

Miss Ruck's eyes made light of me. 'Well, I don't believe *you're* a good American,' she smartly said, 'and I never supposed you were. You'd better go right in there and talk to Mrs Church.'

'Dresden's really very nice, isn't it?' I asked of her companion.

'It isn't nice if you happen to prefer New York,' Miss Ruck at once returned. 'Miss Church prefers New York. Tell him you're dying to see New York; it will make him mad,' she went on.

'I've no desire to make him mad,' Aurora smiled.

'It's only Miss Ruck who can do that,' I hastened to state. 'Have you been a long time in Europe?' I added.

'As long as I can remember.'

'I call that wicked!' Miss Ruck declared.

'You might be in a worse place,' I continued. 'I find Europe very interesting.'

Miss Ruck fairly snorted. 'I was just *saying* that you wanted to pass for a European.'

Well, I saw my way to admit it. 'Yes, I want to pass for a Dalmatian.'[49]

Miss Ruck pounced straight. 'Then you had better not come home. We know how to treat your sort.'

'Were you born in these countries?' I asked of Aurora Church.

'Oh no – I came to Europe a small child. But I remember America a little, and it seems delightful.'

'Wait till you see it again. It's just too lovely,' said Miss Ruck.

'The grandest country in all the world,' I added.

Miss Ruck began to toss her head. 'Come away, my dear. If there's a creature I despise it's a man who tries to say funny things about his own country.'

But Aurora lingered while she all appealingly put it to me. 'Don't you think one can be tired of Europe?'

'Well – as one may be tired of life.'[50]

'Tired of the life?' cried Miss Ruck. 'Father was tired of it after three weeks.'

'I've been here sixteen years,' her friend went on, looking at me as for some charming intelligence. 'It used to be for my education. I don't know what it's for now.'

'She's beautifully educated,' Miss Ruck guaranteed. 'She knows four languages.'

'I'm not very sure I know English!'

'You should go to Boston!' said our companion. 'They speak splendidly in Boston.'

'C'est mon rêve,'[51] said Aurora, still looking at me.

'Have you been all over Europe,' I asked – 'in all the different countries?'

She consulted her reminiscences. 'Everywhere you can find a pension. Mamma's devoted to pensions. We've lived at one time or another in every pension in Europe – say at some five or six hundred.'

'Well, I should think you had seen about enough!' Miss Ruck exhaled.

'It's a delightful way of seeing Europe' – our friend rose to a bright high irony. 'You may imagine how it has attached me to the different countries. I have such charming souvenirs! There's a pension awaiting us now at Dresden – eight francs a day, without wine. That's so much beyond our mark that mamma means to make them give us wine. Mamma's a great authority on pensions; she's known, that way, all over Europe. Last winter we were in Italy, and she discovered one at Piacenza[52] – four francs a day. We made economies.'

'Your mother doesn't seem to mingle much,' observed Miss Ruck, who had glanced through the window at Mrs Church's concentration.

'No, she doesn't mingle, except in the native society. Though she lives in pensions she detests our vulgar life.'

'"Vulgar"?' cried Miss Ruck. 'Why then does she skimp so?' This young woman had clearly no other notion of vulgarity.

'Oh because we're so poor; it's the cheapest way to live. We've tried having a cook, but the cook always steals. Mamma used to set me to watch her; that's the way I passed my jeunesse – my belle jeunesse.[53] We're frightfully poor,' she went on with the same strange frankness – a curious mixture of girlish grace and conscious cynicism. 'Nous n'avons pas le sou.[54] That's one of the reasons we don't go back to America. Mamma says we could never afford to live there.'

'Well, any one can see that you're an American girl,' Miss Ruck remarked in a consolatory manner. 'I can tell an American girl a mile off. You've got the natural American style.'

'I'm afraid I haven't the natural American clothes,' said Aurora in tribute to the other's splendour.

'Well, your dress was cut in France; any one can see that.'

'Yes,' our young lady laughed, 'my dress was cut in France – at Avranches.'[55]

'Well, you've got a lovely figure anyway,' pursued her companion.

'Ah,' she said for the pleasantry of it, 'at Avranches too my figure was admired.' And she looked at me askance and with no clear poverty of intention. But I was an innocent youth and I only looked back at her and wondered. She was a great deal nicer than Miss Ruck, and yet Miss Ruck wouldn't have said that in that way. 'I try to be the American girl,' she continued; 'I do my best, though mamma doesn't at all encourage it. I'm very patriotic. I try to strike for freedom, though mamma has brought me up à la française; that is as much as one can in pensions. For instance I've never been out of the house without mamma – oh never never! But sometimes I despair; American girls do come out so with things. I can't come out, I can't rush in, like that. I'm awfully pinched, I'm always afraid. But I do what I can, as you see. Excusez du peu!'[56]

I thought this young lady of an inspiration at least as untrammelled as her unexpatriated sisters, and her despondency in the true note of much of their predominant prattle. At the same time she had by no means caught, as it seemed to me, what Miss Ruck called the natural American style. Whatever her style was, however, it had a fascination – I knew not what (as I called it) distinction, and yet I knew not what odd freedom.

The young ladies began to stroll about the garden again, and I enjoyed their society until M. Pigeonneau's conception of a 'high time' began to languish.

V

Mr Ruck failed to take his departure for Appenzell on the morrow, in spite of the eagerness to see him off quaintly attributed by him to Mrs Church. He continued on the contrary for many days after to hang about the garden, to wander up to the banker's and back again, to engage in desultory conversation with his fellow boarders, and to endeavour to assuage his constitutional restlessness by perusal of the American journals. But it was at least on the morrow that I had the honour of making Mrs Church's acquaintance. She came into the salon after the midday breakfast, her German octavo under her arm, and appealed to me for assistance in selecting a quiet corner.

'Would you very kindly,' she said, 'move that large fauteuil[57] a little more this way? Not the largest; the one with the little cushion. The fauteuils here are very insufficient; I must ask Madame Beaurepas for another. Thank you; a little more to the left, please; that will do. Are you particularly engaged?' she enquired after she had seated herself. 'If not I should like briefly to converse with you. It's some time since I've met a young American of your – what shall I call it? – affiliations. I've learned your name from Madame Beaurepas; I must have known in other days some of your people. I ask myself what has become of all my friends. I used to have a charming little circle at home, but now I meet no one I either know or desire to know. Don't you think there's a great difference between the people one meets and the people one would like to meet? Fortunately, sometimes,' my patroness graciously added, 'there's no great difference. I suppose you're a specimen – and I take you for a good one,' she imperturbably went on – 'of modern young America. Tell me then what modern young America is thinking of in these strange days of ours. What are its feelings, its opinions, its aspirations? What is its *ideal*?' I had seated myself and she had pointed this interrogation with the gaze of her curiously bright and impersonal little eyes. I felt it embarrassing to be taken for a superior specimen of modern young America and to be expected to answer for looming millions. Observing my hesitation Mrs Church clasped her hands on the open page of her book and gave a dismal, a desperate smile. '*Has* it an ideal?' she softly asked. 'Well, we must talk of this,' she proceeded without insisting. 'Speak just now for yourself simply. Have you come to Europe to any intelligent conscious end?'

'No great end to boast of,' I said. 'But I seem to feel myself study a little.'

'Ah I'm glad to hear that. You're gathering up a little European culture; that's what we lack, you know, at home. No individual can do much, of course; but one mustn't be discouraged – every little so counts.'

'I see that you at least are doing your part,' I bravely answered, dropping my eyes on my companion's learned volume.

'Ah yes, I go as straight as possible to the sources. There's no one after all like the Germans. That is for digging up the facts and the evidence. For conclusions I frequently diverge. I form my opinions myself. I'm sorry to say, however,' Mrs Church continued, 'that I don't do much to spread the light. I'm afraid I'm sadly selfish; I do little to irrigate the soil. I belong – I frankly confess it – to the class of impenitent absentees.'

'I had the pleasure, last evening,' I said, 'of making the acquaintance of your daughter. She tells me you've been a long time in Europe.'

She took it blandly. 'Can one ever be *too* long? You see it's *our* world, that of us few real fugitives from the rule of the mob. We shall never go back to that.'

'Your daughter nevertheless fancies she yearns!' I replied.

'Has she been taking you into her confidence? She's a more sensible young lady than she sometimes appears. I've taken great pains with her; she's really – I may be permitted to say it – superbly educated.'

'She seemed to me to do you honour,' I made answer. 'And I hear she speaks fluently four languages.'

'It's not only that,' said Mrs Church in the tone of one sated with fluencies and disillusioned of diplomas. 'She has made what we call *de fortes études*[58] – such as I suppose you're making now. She's familiar with the results of modern science; she keeps pace with the new historical school.'

'Ah,' said I, 'she has gone much further than I!'

She seemed to look at me a moment as for the tip of the ear of irony. 'You doubtless think I exaggerate, and you force me therefore to mention the fact that I speak of such matters with a certain intelligence.'

'I should never dream of doubting it,' I returned, 'but your daughter nevertheless strongly holds that you ought to take her home.' I might have feared that these words would practically represent treachery to the young lady, but I was reassured by seeing them produce in her mother's placid surface no symptom whatever of irritation.

'My daughter has her little theories,' that lady observed; 'she has, I may say, her small fond illusions and rebellions. And what wonder! What would youth be without its Sturm und Drang?[59] Aurora says to herself – all at her ease – that she would be happier in their dreadful New York, in their dreary Boston, in their desperate Philadelphia, than in one of the charming old cities in which our lot is cast. But she knows not what she babbles of – that's all. We must allow our children their yearning to make mistakes, mustn't we? But we must keep the mistakes down to as few as possible.'

Her soft sweet positiveness, beneath which I recognised all sorts of really hard rigours of resistance and aggression, somehow breathed a chill on me. 'American cities,' I none the less threw off, 'are the paradise of the female young.'

'Do you mean,' she enquired, 'that the generations reared in those places are angels?'

'Well,' I said resolutely, 'they're the nicest of all girls.'

'This young lady — what's her odd name? — with whom my daughter has formed a somewhat precipitate acquaintance: is Miss Ruck an angel and one of the nicest of all? But I won't,' she amusedly added, 'force you to describe her as she deserves. It would be too cruel to make a single exception.'

'Well,' I at any rate pleaded, 'in America they've the easiest lot and the best time. They've the most innocent liberty.'

My companion laid her hand an instant on my arm. 'My dear young friend, I know America, I know the conditions of life there down to the ground. There's perhaps no subject on which I've reflected more than on our national idiosyncrasies.'

'To the effect, I see, of your holding them in horror,' I said a little roughly.

Rude indeed as was my young presumption Mrs Church had still her cultivated patience, even her pity, for it. 'We're very crude,' she blandly remarked, 'and we're proportionately indigestible.' And lest her own refined strictures should seem to savour of the vice she deprecated she went on to explain. 'There are two classes of minds, you know — those that hold back and those that push forward. My daughter and I are not pushers; we move with the slow considerate steps to which a little dignity may still cling. We like the old trodden paths; we like the old old world.'

'Ah,' said I, 'you know what you like. There's a great virtue in that.'

'Yes, we like Europe; we prefer it. We like the opportunities of Europe; we like the *rest*. There's so much in that, you know. The world seems to me to be hurrying, pressing forward so fiercely, without knowing in the least where it's going. "Whither?" I often ask in my little quiet way. But I've yet to learn that any one can tell me.'

'You're a grand old conservative,' I returned while I wondered whether I myself might have been able to meet her question.

Mrs Church gave me a smile that was equivalent to a confession. 'I wish to retain a wee bit — just a wee bit. Surely we've done so much we might rest a while; we might pause. That's all my feeling — just to stop a little, to wait, to take breath. I've seen so many changes. I want to draw in, to draw in — to hold back, to hold back.'

'You shouldn't hold your daughter back!' I laughed as I got up. I rose not by way of closing our small discussion, for I felt my friend's exposition of her views to be by no means complete, but in order to offer a chair to Miss Aurora, who at this moment drew near. She thanked me and remained standing, but without at first, as I noticed, really facing her parent.

'You've been engaged with your new acquaintance, my dear?' this lady enquired.

'Yes, mamma,' said the girl with a sort of prompt sweet dryness.

'Do you find her very edifying?'

Aurora had a silence; then she met her mother's eyes. 'I don't know, mamma. She's very fresh.'

I ventured a respectful laugh. 'Your mother has another word for that. But I must not,' I added, 'be indigestibly raw.'

'Ah, vous m'en voulez?'[60] Mrs Church serenely sighed. 'And yet I can't pretend I said it in jest. I feel it too much. We've been having a little social discussion,' she said to her daughter. 'There's still so much to be said. And I wish,' she continued, turning to me, 'that I could give you our point of view. Don't you wish, Aurora, that we could give him our point of view?'

'Yes, mamma,' said Aurora.

'We consider ourselves very fortunate in our point of view, don't we, dearest?' mamma demanded.

'Very fortunate indeed, mamma.'

'You see we've acquired an insight into European life,' the elder lady pursued. 'We've our place at many a European fireside. We find so much to esteem – so much to enjoy. Don't we find delightful things, my daughter?'

'So very delightful, mamma,' the girl went on with her colourless calm. I wondered at it; it offered so strange a contrast to the mocking freedom of her tone the night before; but while I wondered I desired to testify to the interest at least with which she inspired me.

'I don't know what impression you ladies may have found at European firesides,' I again ventured, 'but there can be very little doubt of the impression you must have made there.'

Mrs Church got in motion to acknowledge my compliment. 'We've spent some charming hours. And that reminds me that we've just now such an occasion in prospect. We're to call upon some Genevese friends – the family of the Pasteur Galopin. They're to go with us to the old library at the Hôtel de Ville,[61] where there are some very interesting documents of the period of the Reformation: we're promised a glimpse of some manuscripts of poor Servetus, the antagonist and victim, you know, of the dire Calvin.[62] Here of course one can only speak of ce monsieur under one's breath, but some day when we're more private' – Mrs Church looked round the room – 'I'll give you my view of him. I think it has a force of its own. Aurora's familiar with it – aren't you, my daughter, familiar with my view of the evil genius of the Reformation?'

'Yes, mamma – very,' said Aurora with docility – and also, as I thought, with subtlety – while the two ladies went to prepare for their visit to the Pasteur Galopin.

VI

'She has demanded a new lamp: I told you she would!' This communication was made me by Madame Beaurepas a couple of days later. 'And she has asked for a new tapis de lit,[63] and she has requested me to provide Célestine with a pair of light shoes. I remarked to her that, as a general thing, domestic drudges aren't shod with satin. That brave Célestine!'

'Mrs Church may be exacting,' I said, 'but she's a clever little woman.'

'A lady who pays but five francs and a half shouldn't be too clever. C'est déplacé. I don't like the type.'

'What type then,' I asked, 'do you pronounce Mrs Church's?'

'Mon Dieu,' said Madame Beaurepas, 'c'est une de ces mamans, comme vous en avez, qui promènent leur fille.'[64]

'She's trying to marry her daughter? I don't think she's of that sort.'

But Madame Beaurepas shrewdly held to her idea. 'She's trying it in her own way; she does it very quietly. She doesn't want an American; she wants a foreigner. And she wants a mari sérieux.[65] But she's travelling over Europe in search of one. She would like a magistrate.'

'A magistrate?'

'A gros bonnet[66] of some kind; a professor or a deputy.'

'I'm awfully sorry for the poor girl,' I found myself moved to declare.

'You needn't pity her too much; she's a fine mouche[67] – a sly thing.'

'Ah for that, no!' I protested. 'She's no fool, but she's an honest creature.'

My hostess gave an ancient grin. 'She has hooked you, eh? But the mother won't have you.'

I developed my idea without heeding this insinuation. 'She's a charming girl, but she's a shrewd politician. It's a necessity of her case. She's less submissive to her mother than she has to pretend to be. That's in self-defence. It's to make her life possible.'

'She wants to get away from her mother' – Madame Beaurepas so far confirmed me. 'She wants to courir les champs.'[68]

'She wants to go to America, her native country.'

'Precisely. And she'll certainly manage it.'

'I hope so!' I laughed.

'Some fine morning – or evening – she'll go off with a young man; probably with a young American.'

'Allons donc!'[69] I cried with disgust.

'That will be quite America enough,' pursued my cynical hostess. 'I've kept a boarding-house for nearly half a century. I've seen that type.'

'Have such things as that happened chez vous?' I asked.

'Everything has happened chez moi. But nothing has happened more than once. Therefore this won't happen here. It will be at the next place they go to, or the next. Besides, there's here no young American pour la partie[70] – none except you, monsieur. You're susceptible but you're too reasonable.'

'It's lucky for you I'm reasonable,' I answered. 'It's thanks to my cold blood you escape a scolding!'

One morning about this time, instead of coming back to breakfast at the pension after my lectures at the Academy, I went to partake of this meal with a fellow student at an ancient eating-house in the collegiate quarter. On separating from my friend I took my way along that charming public walk known in Geneva as the Treille,[71] a shady terrace, of immense elevation, overhanging a stretch of the lower town. Here are spreading trees and well-worn benches, and over the tiles and chimneys of the *ville basse*[72] a view of the snow-crested Alps. On the other side, as you turn your back to the view, the high level is overlooked by a row of tall sober-faced *hôtels*, the dwellings of the local aristocracy. I was fond of the place, resorting to it for stimulation of my sense of the social scene at large. Presently, as I lingered there on this occasion, I became aware of a gentleman seated not far from where I stood, his back to the Alpine chain, which this morning was all radiant, and a newspaper unfolded in his lap. He wasn't reading, however; he only stared before him in gloomy contemplation. I don't know whether I recognised first the newspaper or its detainer; one, in either case, would have helped me to identify the other. One was the *New York Herald* – the other of course was Mr Ruck. As I drew nearer he moved his eyes from the stony succession, the grey old high-featured house-masks, on the other side of the terrace, and I knew by the expression of his face just how he had been feeling about these distinguished abodes. He had made up his mind that their proprietors were a 'mean' narrow-minded unsociable company that plunged its knotted roots into a superfluous past. I endeavoured therefore, as I sat down beside him, to strike a pleasanter note.

'The Alps, from here, do make a wondrous show!'

'Yes sir,' said Mr Ruck without a stir, 'I've examined the Alps. Fine thing in its way, the view – fine thing. Beauties of nature – that sort of thing. We came up on purpose to look at it.'

'Your ladies then have been with you?'

'Yes – I guess they're fooling round. They're awfully restless. They keep saying *I'm* restless, but I'm as quiet as a sleeping child to *them*. It takes,' he added in a moment dryly, 'the form of an interest in the stores.'

'And are the stores what they're after now?'

'Yes – unless this is one of the days the stores don't keep. They regret them, but I wish there were more of them! They told me to sit here a while and they'd just have a look. I generally know what that means – it's *their* form of scenery. But that's the principal interest for ladies,' he added, retracting his irony. 'We thought we'd come up here and see the cathedral;[73] Mrs Church seemed to think it a dead loss we shouldn't see the cathedral, especially as we hadn't seen many yet. And I had to come up to the banker's anyway. Well, we certainly saw the cathedral. I don't know as we're any the better for it, and I don't know as I should know it again. But we saw it anyway, stone by stone – and heard about it century by century. I don't know as I should want to go there regularly, but I suppose it will give us in conversation a kind of hold on Mrs Church, hey? I guess we want something of that kind. Well,' Mr Ruck continued, 'I stepped in at the banker's to see if there wasn't something, and they handed me out an old *Herald*.'

'Well, I hope the *Herald*'s full of good news,' I returned.

'Can't say it is. Damned bad news.'

'Political,' I enquired, 'or commercial?'

'Oh hang politics! It's business, sir. There *ain't* any business. It's all gone to –' and Mr Ruck became profane. 'Nine failures in one day, and two of them in our locality. What do you say to that?'

'I greatly hope they haven't inconvenienced you,' was all I could gratify him with.

'Well, I guess they haven't affected me quite desirably. So many houses on fire, that's all. If they happen to take place right where you live they don't increase the value of your own property. When mine catches I suppose they'll write and tell me – one of these days when they get round to me. I didn't get a blamed letter this morning; I suppose they think I'm having such a good time over here it's a pity to break in. If I could attend to business for about half an hour I'd find out something. But I can't, and it's no use talking. The state of my health was never so unsatisfactory as it was about five o'clock this morning.'

'I'm very sorry to hear that,' I said, 'and I recommend you strongly not to think of business.'

'I don't,' Mr Ruck replied. 'You can't *make* me. I'm thinking of cathedrals. I'm thinking of the way they used to chain you up under them or burn you up in front of them – in those high old times. I'm thinking of the beauties of nature too,' he went on, turning round on the bench and leaning his elbow on the parapet. 'You can get killed over there I suppose also' – and he nodded at the shining crests. 'I'm thinking of going over – because, whatever the danger, I seem more afraid not to. That's why I do most things. How do you get over?' he sighed.

'Over to Chamouni?'

'Over to those hills. Don't they run a train right up?'

'You can go to Chamouni,'[74] I said. 'You can go to Grindelwald and Zermatt[75] and fifty other places. You can't go by rail, but you can drive.'

'All right, we'll drive – you can't tell the difference in these cars. Yes,' Mr Ruck proceeded, 'Chamouni's one of the places we put down. I hope there are good stores in Chamouni.' He spoke with a quickened ring and with an irony more pointed than commonly served him. It was as if he had been wrought upon, and yet his general submission to fate was still there. I judged he had simply taken, in the face of disaster, a sudden sublime resolution not to worry. He presently twisted himself about on his bench again and began to look out for his companions. 'Well, they *are* taking a look,' he resumed; 'I guess they've struck something somewhere. And they've got a carriage waiting outside of that archway too. They seem to do a big business in archways here, don't they? They like to have a carriage to carry home the things – those ladies of mine. Then they're sure they've got 'em.' The ladies, after this, to do them justice, were not very long in appearing. They came toward us from under the archway to which Mr Ruck had somewhat invidiously alluded, slowly and with a jaded air. My companion watched them as they advanced. 'They're right down tired. When they look like that it kind o' foots up.'[76]

'Well,' said Mrs Ruck, 'I'm glad you've had some company.' Her husband looked at her, in silence, through narrowed eyelids, and I suspected that her unusually gracious observation was prompted by the less innocent aftertaste of her own late pastime.

Her daughter glanced at me with the habit of straighter defiance. 'It would have been more proper if *we* had had the company. Why didn't you come after us instead of sneaking there?' she asked of Mr Ruck's companion.

'I was told by your father,' I explained, 'that you were engaged in sacred rites.' If Miss Ruck was less conciliatory it would be scarcely, I felt sure, because she had been more frugal. It was rather because her conception of social intercourse appeared to consist of the imputation to as many persons as possible – that is to as many subject males – of some scandalous neglect of her charms and her claims. 'Well, for a gentleman there's nothing so sacred as ladies' society,' she replied in the manner of a person accustomed to giving neat retorts.

'I suppose you refer to the cathedral,' said her mother. 'Well, I must say we didn't go back there. I don't know what it may be for regular attendants, but it doesn't meet my idea of a really pleasant place of worship. Few of these old buildings do,' Mrs Ruck further mentioned.

'Well, we discovered a little lace-shop, where I guess I could regularly attend!' her daughter took occasion to announce without weak delay.

Mr Ruck looked at his child; then he turned about again, leaning on the parapet and gazing away at the 'hills.'

'Well, the place was certainly not expensive,' his wife said with her eyes also on the Alps.

'We're going up to Chamouni,' he pursued. 'You haven't any call for lace up there.'

'Well, I'm glad to hear you've decided to go somewhere,' Mrs Ruck returned. 'I don't want to be a fixture at an old pension.'

'You can wear lace anywhere,' her daughter reminded us, 'if you put it on right. That's the great thing with lace. I don't think they know how to wear lace in Europe. I know how I mean to wear mine; but I mean to keep it till I get home.'

Mr Ruck transferred his melancholy gaze to her elaborately-appointed little person; there was a great deal of very new-looking detail in Miss Ruck's appearance. Then in a tone of voice quite out of consonance with his facial despondency, 'Have you purchased a great deal?' he enquired.

'I've purchased enough for you to make a fuss about.'

'He can't make a fuss about *that*,' said Mrs Ruck.

'Well, you'll see!' – the girl had unshaken confidence.

The subject of this serenity, however, went on in the same tone: 'Have you got it in your pocket? Why don't you put it on – why don't you hang it round you?'

'I'll hang it round *you* if you don't look out!' cried Miss Ruck.

'Don't you want to show it off to this gentleman?' he sociably continued.

'Mercy, how you do carry on!' his wife sighed.

'Well, I want to be lively. There's every reason for it. We're going up to Chamouni.'

'You're real restless – that's what's the matter with you.' And Mrs Ruck roused herself from her own repose.

'No, I ain't,' said her husband. 'I never felt so quiet. I feel as peaceful as a little child.'

Mrs Ruck, who had no play of mind, looked at her daughter and at me. 'Well, I hope you'll improve,' she stated with a certain flatness.

'Send in the bills,' he went on, rising to match. 'Don't let yourself suffer from want, Sophy. I don't care what you do now. We can't be more than gay, and we can't be worse than broke.'

Sophy joined her mother with a little toss of her head, and we followed the ladies to the carriage, where the younger addressed her father. 'In your place, Mr Ruck, I wouldn't want to flaunt my meanness quite so much before strangers.'

He appeared to feel the force of this rebuke, surely deserved by a man on whom the humiliation of seeing the main ornaments of his hearth betray the ascendency of that character had never yet been laid. He flushed and was silent; his companions got into their vehicle, the front seat of which was adorned with a large parcel. Mr Ruck gave the parcel a poke with his umbrella and turned to me with a grimly penitent smile. 'After all, for the ladies, that's the principal interest.'

VII

Old M. Pigeonneau had more than once offered me the privilege of a walk in his company, but his invitation had hitherto, for one reason or another, always found me hampered. It befell, however, one afternoon that I saw him go forth for a vague airing with an unattended patience that attracted my sympathy. I hastily overtook him and passed my hand into his venerable arm, an overture that produced in the good old man so rejoicing a response that he at once proposed we should direct our steps to the English Garden:[77] no scene less consecrated to social ease was worthy of our union. To the English Garden accordingly we went; it lay beyond the bridge and beside the lake. It was always pretty and now was really recreative; a band played furiously in the centre and a number of discreet listeners sat under the small trees on benches and little chairs or strolled beside the blue water. We joined the strollers, we observed our companions and conversed on obvious topics. Some of these last of course were the pretty women who graced the prospect and who, in the light of M. Pigeonneau's comprehensive criticism, appeared surprisingly numerous. He seemed bent upon our making up our minds as to which might be prettiest, and this was an innocent game in which I consented to take a hand.

Suddenly my companion stopped, pressing my arm with the liveliest emotion. 'La voilà, la voilà, the prettiest!' he quickly murmured; 'coming toward us in a blue dress with the other.' It was at the other I was looking, for the other, to my surprise, was our interesting fellow pensioner, the daughter of the most systematic of mothers. M. Pigeonneau meanwhile had redoubled his transports – he had recognised Miss Ruck. 'Oh la belle rencontre, nos aimables convives[78] – the prettiest girl in the world in effect!' And then after we had greeted and joined the young ladies, who, like ourselves, were walking arm in arm and enjoying the scene, he addressed himself to the special object of his admiration, Mees Roque. 'I was citing you with enthusiasm to my young friend here even before I had recognised you, mademoiselle.'

'I don't believe in French compliments,' remarked Miss Sophy, who presented her back to the smiling old man.

'Are you and Miss Ruck walking alone?' I asked of her companion. 'You had better accept M. Pigeonneau's gallant protection, to say nothing of mine.'

Aurora Church had taken her hand from Miss Ruck's arm; she inclined her head to the side and shone at me while her open parasol revolved on her shoulder. 'Which is most improper – to walk alone or to walk with gentlemen that one picks up? I want to do what's most improper.'

'What perversity,' I asked, 'are you, with an ingenuity worthy of a better cause, trying to work out?'

'He thinks you can't understand him when he talks like that,' said Miss Ruck. 'But I *do* understand you,' she flirted at me – 'always!'

'So I've always ventured to hope, my dear Miss Ruck.'

'Well, if I didn't it wouldn't be much loss!' cried this young lady.

'Allons, en marche!'[79] trumpeted M. Pigeonneau, all gallant urbanity and undiscouraged by her impertinence. 'Let us make together the tour of the garden.' And he attached himself to Miss Ruck with a respectful elderly grace which treated her own lack even of the juvenile form of that attraction as some flower of alien modesty, and was ever sublimely conscious of a mission to place modesty at its ease. This ill-assorted couple walked in front, while Aurora Church and I strolled along together.

'I'm sure this is more improper,' said my companion; 'this is delightfully improper. I don't say that as a compliment to you,' she added. 'I'd say it to any clinging man, no matter how stupid.'

'Oh I'm clinging enough,' I answered; 'but I'm as stupid as you could wish, and this doesn't seem to me wrong.'

'Not for you, no; only for me. There's nothing that a man can do that's wrong, is there? *En morale*,[80] you know, I mean. Ah yes, he can kill and steal; but I think there's nothing else, is there?'

'Well, it's a nice question. One doesn't know how those things are taken till after one has done them. Then one's enlightened.'

'And you mean you've never been enlightened? You make yourself out very good.'

'That's better than making one's self out very bad, as you do.'

'Ah,' she explained, 'you don't know the consequences of a false position.'

I was amused at her great formula. 'What do you mean by yours being one?'

'Oh I mean everything. For instance I've to pretend to be a jeune fille. I'm not a jeune fille; no American girl's a jeune fille; an American girl's an intelligent responsible creature. I've to pretend to be idiotically innocent, but I'm not in the least innocent.'

This, however, was easy to meet. 'You don't in the least pretend to be innocent; you pretend to be – what shall I call it? – uncannily wise.'

'That's no pretence. I *am* uncannily wise. You could call it nothing more true.'

I went along with her a little, rather thrilled by this finer freedom. 'You're essentially not an American girl.'

She almost stopped, looking at me; there came a flush to her cheek. 'Voilà!' she said. 'There's my false position. I want to be an American girl, and I've been hideously deprived of that immense convenience, that beautiful resource.'

'Do you want me to tell you?' I pursued with interest. 'It would be utterly impossible to an American girl — I mean unperverted, and that's the whole point — to talk as you're talking to me now.'

The expressive eagerness she showed for this was charming. 'Please tell me then! How would she talk?'

'I can't tell you all the things she'd say, but I think I can tell you most of the things she wouldn't. She wouldn't reason out her conduct as you seem to me to do.'

Aurora gave me the most flattering attention. 'I see. She would be simpler. To do very simply things not at all simple — that's the American girl!'

I greatly enjoyed our intellectual relation. 'I don't know whether you're a French girl, or what you are, but, you know, I find you witty.'

'Ah you mean I strike false notes!' she quite comically wailed. 'See how my whole sense for such things has been ruined. False notes are just what I want to avoid. I wish you'd always tell me.'

The conversational union between Miss Ruck and her neighbour, in front of us, had evidently not borne fruit. Miss Ruck suddenly turned round to us with a question. 'Don't you want some ice-cream?'

'She doesn't strike false notes,' I declared.

We had come into view of a manner of pavilion or large kiosk, which served as a café and at which the delicacies generally procurable at such an establishment were dispensed. Miss Ruck pointed to the little green tables and chairs set out on the gravel; M. Pigeonneau, fluttering with a sense of dissipation, seconded the proposal, and we presently sat down and gave our order to a nimble attendant. I managed again to place myself next Aurora; our companions were on the other side of the table.

My neighbour rejoiced to extravagance in our situation. 'This is best of all — I never believed I should come to a café with two strange and possibly depraved men! Now you can't persuade me this isn't wrong.'

'To make it wrong,' I returned, 'we ought to see your mother coming down that path.'

'Ah my mother makes everything wrong,' she cried, attacking with a little spoon in the shape of a spade the apex of a pink ice. And then she returned to her idea of a moment before. 'You must promise to tell me — to warn me in some way — whenever I strike a false note. You must give a little cough, like that — ahem!'

'You'll keep me very busy and people will think I'm in a consumption.'

'Voyons,' she continued, 'why have you never talked to me more? Is that a false note? Why haven't you been "attentive"? That's what American girls call it; that's what Miss Ruck calls it.'

I assured myself that our companions were out of ear-shot and that Miss Ruck was much occupied with a large vanilla cream. 'Because you're always interlaced with that young lady. There's no getting near you.'

Aurora watched her friend while the latter devoted herself to her ice. 'You wonder, no doubt, why I should care for her at all. So does mamma; elle s'y perd. I don't like her particularly; je n'en suis pas folle.[81] But she gives me information; she tells me about her – your – everything but *my* – extraordinary country. Mamma has always tried to prevent my knowing anything about it, and I'm all the more devoured with curiosity. And then Miss Ruck's so very fresh.'

'I may not be so fresh as Miss Ruck,' I said, 'but in future, when you want information, I recommend you to come to me for it.'

'Ah but our friend offers to take me there; she invites me to go back with her, to stay with her. You couldn't do that, could you?' And my companion beautifully faced me on it. 'Bon, a false note! I can see it by your face; you remind me of an outraged maître de piano.'[82]

'You overdo the character – the poor American girl,' I said. 'Are you going to stay with that delightful family?'

'I'll go and stay with any one who will take me or ask me. It's a real nostalgie. She says that in New York – in Thirty-Seventh Street near Fourth Avenue – I should have the most lovely time.'

'I've no doubt you'd enjoy it.'

'Absolute liberty to begin with.'

'It seems to me you've a certain liberty here,' I returned.

'Ah *this*? Oh I shall pay for this. I shall be punished by mamma and lectured by Madame Galopin.'

'The wife of the pasteur?'

'His digne épouse.[83] Madame Galopin, for mamma, is the incarnation of European opinion. That's what vexes me with mamma, her thinking so much of people like Madame Galopin. Going to see Madame Galopin – mamma calls that being in European society. European society! I'm so sick of that expression; I've heard it since I was six years old. Who's Madame Galopin – who the devil thinks anything of her here? She's nobody; she's the dreariest of frumps; she's perfectly third-rate. If I like your America better than mamma I also know my Europe better.'

'But your mother, certainly,' I objected a trifle timidly – for my young lady was excited and had a charming little passion in her eye – 'your mother has a great many social relations all over the continent.'

'She thinks so, but half the people don't care for us. They're not so good as we and they know it – I'll do them that justice – so that they wonder why we should care for them. When we're polite to them they think the less of us; there are plenty of people like that. Mamma thinks so much of them simply because they're foreigners. If I could tell you all the ugly stupid tenth-rate people I've had to talk to for no better reason than that they were *de leur pays*![84] – Germans, French, Italians, Turks, everything. When I complain mamma always says that at any rate it's practice in the language. And she makes so much of the most impossible English too; I don't know what *that's* practice in.'

Before I had time to suggest an hypothesis as regards this latter point I saw something that made me rise – I fear with an undissimulated start – from my chair. This was nothing less than the neat little figure of Mrs Church – a perfect model of the femme comme il faut[85] – approaching our table with an impatient step and followed most unexpectedly in her advance by the pre-eminent form of Mr Ruck, whose high hat had never looked so high. She had evidently come in search of her daughter, and if she had commanded this gentleman's attendance it had been on no more intimate ground than that of his unenvied paternity to her guilty child's accomplice. My movement had given the alarm and my young friend and M. Pigeonneau got up; Miss Ruck alone didn't, in the local phrase, derange herself. Mrs Church, beneath her modest little bonnet, looked thoroughly resolute though not at all agitated; she came straight to her daughter, who received her with a smile, and then she took the rest of us in very fixedly and tranquilly and without bowing. I must do both these ladies the justice that neither of them made the least little 'scene.'

'I've come for you, dearest,' said the mother.

'Yes, dear mamma.'

'Come for you – come for you,' Mrs Church repeated, looking down at the relics of our little feast, on which she seemed somehow to shed at once the lurid light of the disreputable. 'I was obliged to appeal to Mr Ruck's assistance. I was much perplexed. I thought a long time.'

'Well Mrs Church, I was glad to see you perplexed once in your life!' cried Mr Ruck with friendly jocosity. 'But you came pretty straight for all that. I had hard work to keep up with you.'

'We'll take a cab, Aurora,' Mrs Church went on without heeding this pleasantry – 'a closed one;[86] we'll enter it at once. Come, ma fille.'

'Yes, dear mamma.' The girl had flushed for humiliation, but she carried it bravely off; and her grimace as she looked round at us all and her eyes met mine didn't keep her, I thought, from being beautiful. 'Good-bye. I've had a ripping time.'

'We mustn't linger,' said her mother; 'it's five o'clock. We're to dine, you know, with Madame Galopin.'

'I had quite forgotten,' Aurora declared. 'That will be even more charming.'

'Do you want me to assist you to carry her back, ma'am?' asked Mr Ruck.

Mrs Church covered him for a little with her coldest contemplation. 'Do you prefer then to leave your daughter to finish the evening with these gentlemen?'

Mr Ruck pushed back his hat and scratched the top of his head. 'Well, I don't know. How'd you like that, Sophy?'

'Well, I never!' gasped Sophy as Mrs Church marched off with her daughter.

VIII

I had half-expected a person of so much decision, and above all of so much consistency, would make me feel the weight of her disapproval of my own share in that little act of revelry by the most raffish part of the lakeside. But she maintained her claim to being a highly reasonable woman – I couldn't but admire the justice of this pretension – by recognizing my practical detachment. I had taken her daughter as I found her, which was, according to Mrs Church's view, in a very equivocal position. The natural instinct of a young man in such a situation is not to protest but to profit; and it was clear to Mrs Church that I had had nothing to do with Miss Aurora's appearing in public under the compromising countenance, as she regarded the matter, of Miss Ruck. Besides, she liked to converse, and she apparently did me the honour to consider that of all the inmates of the Pension Beaurepas I was the best prepared for that exercise. I found her in the salon a couple of evenings after the incident I have just narrated, and I approached her with a view to making my peace with her if this should prove necessary. But Mrs Church was as gracious as I could have desired; she put her marker into her inveterate volume and folded her plump little hands on the cover. She made no specific allusion to the English Garden; she embarked rather on those general considerations in which her cultivated mind was so much at home.

'Always at your deep studies, Mrs Church,' I didn't hesitate freely to observe.

'Que voulez-vous, monsieur?[87] To say studies is to say too much; one doesn't study in the parlour of a boarding-house of this character. But I do what I can; I've always done what I can. That's all I've ever claimed.'

'No one can do more, and you appear to have done a great deal.'

'Do you know my secret?' she asked with an air of brightening confidence. And this treasure hung there a little temptingly before she revealed it. 'To care only for the *best*! To do the best, to know the best – to have, to desire, to recognise, only the best. That's what I've always done in my little quiet persistent way. I've gone through Europe on my devoted little errand, seeking, seeing, heeding, only the best. And it hasn't been for myself alone – it has been for my daughter. My daughter has had the best. We're not rich, but I can say that.'

'She has had *you*, madam,' I pronounced finely.

'Certainly, such as I am, I've been devoted. We've got something everywhere; a little here, a little there. That's the real secret – to get something everywhere; you always can if you *are* devoted. Sometimes it has been a little music, sometimes a little deeper insight into the history of art; sometimes into that of literature, politics, economics: every little counts, you know. Sometimes it has been just a glimpse, a view, a lovely landscape, a mere impression. We've always been on the lookout. Sometimes it has been a valued friendship, a delightful social tie.'

'Here comes the "European society," the poor daughter's bugbear,' I said to myself. 'Certainly,' I remarked aloud – I admit rather hypocritically – 'if you've lived a great deal in pensions you must have got acquainted with lots of people.'

Mrs Church dropped her eyes an instant; taking it up, however, as one for whom discrimination was always at hand. 'I think the European pension system in many respects remarkable and in some satisfactory. But of the friendships that we've formed few have been contracted in establishments of this stamp.'

'I'm sorry to hear that!' I ruefully laughed.

'I don't say it for you, though I might say it for some others. We've been interested in European *homes*.'

'Ah there you're beyond me!'

'Naturally' – she quietly assented. 'We have the entrée of the old Genevese society. I like its tone. I prefer it to that of Mr Ruck,' added Mrs Church calmly; 'to that of Mrs Ruck and Miss Ruck. To that of Miss Ruck in particular.'

'Ah the poor Rucks *have* no tone,' I pleaded. 'That's just the point of them. Don't take them more seriously than they take themselves.'

Well, she would see what she could do. But she bent grave eyes on me. 'Are they really fair examples?'

'Examples of what?'

'Of our American tendencies.'

'Tendencies' is a big word, dear lady; tendencies are difficult to calculate.' I used even a greater freedom. 'And you shouldn't abuse those good Rucks, who have been so kind to your daughter. They've invited her to come and stay with them in Thirty-Seventh Street near Fourth Avenue.'

'Aurora has told me. It might be very serious.'

'It might be very droll,' I said.

'To me,' she declared, 'it's all too terrible. I think we shall have to leave the Pension Beaurepas. I shall go back to Madame Chamousset.'

'On account of the Rucks?' I asked.

'Pray why don't they go themselves? I've given them some excellent addresses

– written down the very hours of the trains. They were going to Appenzell; I thought it was arranged.'

'They talk of Chamouni now,' I said; 'but they're very helpless and undecided.'

'I'll give them some Chamouni addresses. Mrs Ruck will send for a *chaise à porteurs*;[88] I'll give her the name of a man who lets them lower than you get them at the hotels. After that they *must* go.'

She had thoroughly fixed it, as we said; but her large assumptions ruffled me. 'I nevertheless doubt,' I returned, 'if Mr Ruck will ever really be seen on the Mer de Glace[89] – great as might be the effect there of that high hat. He's not like you; he doesn't value his European privileges. He takes no interest. He misses Wall Street[90] all the time. As his wife says, he's deplorably restless, but I guess Chamouni won't quiet him. So you mustn't depend too much on the effect of your addresses.'

'Is it, in its strange mixture of the barbaric and the effete, a frequent type?' asked Mrs Church with all the force of her noble appetite for knowledge.

'I'm afraid so. Mr Ruck's a broken-down man of business. He's broken-down in health and I think he must be broken-down in fortune. He has spent his whole life in buying and selling and watching prices, so that he knows how to do nothing else. His wife and daughter have spent their lives, not in selling, but in buying – with a considerable indifference to prices – and they on their side know how to do nothing else. To get something in a "store" that they can put on their backs – that's their one idea; they haven't another in their heads. Of course they spend no end of money, and they do it with an implacable persistence, with a mixture of audacity and of cunning. They do it in his teeth and they do it behind his back; the mother protects the daughter, while the daughter eggs on the mother. Between them they're bleeding him to death.'

'Ah what a picture!' my friend calmly sighed. 'I'm afraid they're grossly illiterate.'

'I share your fears. We make a great talk at home about education, but see how little that ideal has ever breathed on them. The vision of fine clothes rides them like a fury. They haven't an idea of any sort – not even a worse one – to compete with it. Poor Mr Ruck, who's a mush of personal and private concession – I don't know what he may have been in the business world – strikes me as a really tragic figure. He's getting bad news every day from home; his affairs may be going to the dogs. He's unable, with his lost nerve, to apply himself; so he has to stand and watch his fortunes ebb. He has been used to doing things in a big way and he feels "mean" if he makes a fuss about bills. So the ladies keep sending them in.'

'But haven't they common sense? Don't they know they're marching to ruin?'

'They don't believe it. The duty of an American husband and father is to keep them going. If he asks them how, that's his own affair. So by way of not being mean, of being a good American husband and father, poor Ruck stands staring at bankruptcy.'

Mrs Church, with her cold competence, picked my story over. 'Why if Aurora were to go to stay with them she mightn't even have a good *nourriture*.'[91]

'I don't on the whole recommend,' I smiled, 'that your daughter should pay a visit to Thirty-Seventh Street.'

She took it in – with its various bearings – and had after all, I think, to renounce the shrewd view of a contingency. 'Why should I be subjected to such trials – so sadly éprouvée?'[92] From the moment nothing at all was to be got from the Rucks – not even eventual gratuitous board – she washed her hands of them altogether. 'Why should a daughter of mine like that dreadful girl?'

'*Does* she like her?'

She challenged me nobly. 'Pray do you mean that Aurora's such a hypocrite?'

I saw no reason to hesitate. 'A little, since you enquire. I think you've forced her to be.'

'I?' – she was shocked. 'I *never* force my daughter!'

'She's nevertheless in a false position,' I returned. 'She hungers and thirsts for her own great country; she wants to "come out" in New York, which is certainly, socially speaking, the El Dorado[93] of young ladies. She likes any one, for the moment, who will talk to her of that and serve as a connecting-link with the paradise she imagines there. Miss Ruck performs this agreeable office.'

'Your idea is then that if she were to go with such a person to America she could drop her afterwards?'

I complimented Mrs Church on her quickly-working mind, but I explained that I prescribed no such course. 'I can't imagine her – when it should come to the point – embarking with the famille Roque. But I wish she might go nevertheless.'

Mrs Church shook her head lucidly – she found amusement in my inappropriate zeal. 'I trust my poor child may never be guilty of so fatal a mistake. She's completely in error; she's wholly unadapted to the peculiar conditions of American life. It wouldn't please her. She wouldn't sympathise. My daughter's ideal's not the ideal of the class of young women to which Miss Ruck belongs. I fear they're very numerous; they pervade the place, they give the tone.'

'It's you who are mistaken,' I said. 'There are plenty of Miss Rucks, and she has a terrible significance – though largely as the product of her weak-kneed sire and his "absorption in business." But there are other forms. Go home for six months and see.'

'I've not, unfortunately, the means to make costly experiments. My daughter,' Mrs Church pursued, 'has had great advantages – rare advantages – and I should be very sorry to believe that *au fond*[94] she doesn't appreciate them. One thing's certain: I must remove her from this pernicious influence. We must part company with this deplorable family. If Mr Ruck and his ladies can't be induced to proceed to Chamouni – a journey from which no traveller with the smallest self-respect can dispense himself – my daughter and I shall be obliged to retire from the field. *We* shall go to Dresden.'

'To Dresden?' I submissively echoed.

'The capital of Saxony. I had arranged to go there for the autumn, but it will be simpler to go immediately. There are several works in the gallery with which Aurora has not, I think, sufficiently familiarised herself. It's especially strong in the seventeenth-century schools.'

As my companion offered me this information I caught sight of Mr Ruck, who lounged in with his hands in his pockets and his elbows making acute angles. He had his usual anomalous appearance of both seeking and avoiding society, and he wandered obliquely toward Mrs Church, whose last words he had overheard. 'The seventeenth-century schools,' he said as if he were slowly weighing some very small object in a very large pair of scales. 'Now do you suppose they *had* schools at that period?'

Mrs Church rose with a good deal of majesty, making no answer to this incongruous jest. She clasped her large volume to her neat little bosom and looked at our luckless friend more in pity than in anger, though more in edification than in either. 'I had a letter this morning from Chamouni.'

'Well,' he made answer, 'I suppose you've got friends all round.'

'I've friends at Chamouni, but they're called away. To their great regret.' I had got up too; I listened to this statement and wondered. I'm almost ashamed to mention my wanton thought. I asked myself whether this mightn't be a mere extemporised and unestablished truth – a truth begotten of a deep desire; but the point has never been cleared. 'They're giving up some charming rooms; perhaps you'd like them. I would suggest your telegraphing. The weather's glorious,' continued Mrs Church, 'and the highest peaks are now perceived with extraordinary distinctness.'

Mr Ruck listened, as he always listened, respectfully. 'Well,' he said, 'I don't know as I want to go up Mount Blank. That's the principal attraction, ain't it?'

'There are many others. I thought I would offer you an exceptional opportunity.'

'Well,' he returned, 'I guess you know, and if I could *let* you fix me we'd probably have some big times. But I seem to strike opportunities – well, in excess of my powers. I don't seem able to respond.'

'It only needs a little decision,' remarked Mrs Church with an air that was a perfect example of this virtue. 'I wish you good-night, sir.' And she moved noiselessly away.

Mr Ruck, with his long legs apart, stood staring after her; then he transferred his perfectly quiet eyes to me. 'Does she own a hotel over there? Has she got any stock in Mount Blank?' Indeed in view of the way he had answered her I thought the dear man – to whom I found myself becoming hourly more attached – had beautiful manners.

IX

The next day Madame Beaurepas held out to me with her own venerable fingers a missive which proved to be a telegram. After glancing at it I let her know that it appeared to call me away. My brother had arrived in England and he proposed I should meet him there; he had come on business and was to spend but three weeks in Europe. 'But my house empties itself!' the old woman cried on this. 'The famille Roque talks of leaving me and Madame Cheurche nous fait la révérence.'[95]

'Mrs Church is going away?'

'She's packing her trunk; she's a very extraordinary person. Do you know what she asked me this morning? To invent some combination by which the famille Roque should take itself off. I assured her I was no such inventor. That poor famille Roque! "Oblige me by getting rid of them," said Madame Cheurche – quite as she would have asked Célestine to remove a strong cheese. She speaks as if the world were made for Madame Cheurche. I hinted that if she objected to the company there was a very simple remedy – and at present elle fait ses paquets.'[96]

'She really asked you to get the Rucks out of the house?'

'She asked me to tell them that their rooms had been let three months ago to another family. She has an aplomb!'

Mrs Church's aplomb caused me considerable diversion; I'm not sure that it wasn't in some degree to laugh at my leisure that I went out into the garden that evening to smoke a cigar. The night was dark and not particularly balmy, and most of my fellow pensioners, after dinner, had remained indoors. A long straight walk conducted from the door of the house to the ancient grille I've described, and I stood here for some time looking through the iron bars at the silent empty street. The prospect was not enlivening and I presently turned away. At this moment I saw in the distance the door of the house open and throw a shaft of lamplight into the darkness. Into the lamplight stepped the figure of an apparently circumspect female, as they say in the old stories, who presently closed the door behind her. She disappeared in the dusk of the garden and I had seen her but an instant; yet I remained under the impression that Aurora Church, on the eve of departure, had come out to commune, like myself, with isolation.

I lingered near the gate, keeping the red tip of my cigar turned toward the house, and before long a slight but interesting figure emerged from among the shadows of the trees and encountered the rays of a lamp that stood just outside the gate. My fellow solitary was in fact Aurora Church, who acknowledged my presence with an impatience not wholly convincing.

'Ought I to retire – to return to the house?'

'If you ought,' I replied, 'I should be very sorry to tell you so.'

'But we're all alone. There's no one else in the garden.'

'It's not the first time then that I've been alone with a young lady. I'm not at all terrified.'

'Ah but I?' she wailed to extravagance. 'I've *never* been alone –!' Quickly, however, she interrupted herself. 'Bon, there's another false note!'

'Yes, I'm obliged to admit that one's very false.'

She stood looking at me. 'I'm going away tomorrow; after that there will be no one to tell me.'

'That will matter little,' I presently returned. 'Telling you will do no good.'

'Ah why do you say that?' she all ruefully asked.

I said it partly because it was true, but I said it for other reasons, as well, which I found hard to define. Standing there bareheaded in the night air, in the vague light, this young lady took on an extreme interest, which was moreover not diminished by a suspicion on my own part that she had come into the garden knowing me to be there. I thought her charming, I thought her remarkable and felt very sorry for her; but as I looked at her the terms in which Madame Beaurepas had ventured to characterise her recurred to me with a certain force. I had professed a contempt for them at the time, but it now came into my head that perhaps this unfortunately situated, this insidiously mutinous young creature was in quest of an effective preserver. She was certainly not a girl to throw herself at a man's head, but it was possible that in her intense – her almost morbid – desire to render operative an ideal charged perhaps after all with as many fallacies as her mother affirmed, she might do something reckless and irregular – something in which a sympathetic compatriot, as yet unknown, would find his profit. The image, unshaped though it was, of this sympathetic compatriot filled me with a semblance of envy. For some moments I was silent, conscious of these things; after which I answered her question. 'Because some things – some differences – are felt, not learned. To you liberty's not natural; you're like a person who has bought a repeating watch and is, in his satisfaction, constantly taking it out of his pocket to hear it sound. To a real American girl her liberty's a very vulgarly-ticking old clock.'

'Ah you mean then,' said my young friend, 'that my mother has ruined me?'

'Ruined you?'

'She has so perverted my mind that when I try to be natural I'm necessarily indecent.'

I threw up hopeless arms. 'That again's a false note!'

She turned away. 'I think you're cruel.'

'By no means,' I declared; 'because, for my own taste, I prefer you as – as –'

On my hesitating she turned back. 'As what?'

'As you are!'

She looked at me a while again, and then she said in a little reasoning tone that reminded me of her mother's, only that it was conscious and studied, 'I wasn't aware that I'm under any particular obligation to please you!' But she also gave a clear laugh, quite at variance with this stiffness. Suddenly I thought her adorable.

'Oh there's no obligation,' I said, 'but people sometimes have preferences. I'm very sorry you're going away.'

'What does it matter to you? You are going yourself.'

'As I'm going in a different direction, that makes all the greater separation.'

She answered nothing; she stood looking through the bars of the tall gate at the empty dusky street. 'This grille is like a cage,' she said at last.

'Fortunately it's a cage that will open.' And I laid my hand on the lock.

'Don't open it'; and she pressed the gate close. 'If you should open it I'd go out. There you'd be, monsieur – for I should never return.'

I treated it as wholly thrilling, and indeed I quite found it so. 'Where should you go?'

'To America.'

'Straight away?'

'Somehow or other. I'd go to the American consul. I'd beg him to give me money – to help me.'

I received this assertion without a smile; I was not in a smiling humour. On the contrary I felt singularly excited and kept my hand on the lock of the gate. I believed, or I thought I believed, what my companion said, and I had – absurd as it may appear – an irritated vision of her throwing herself on consular tenderness. It struck me for a moment that to pass out of that gate with this yearning straining young creature would be to pass to some mysterious felicity. If I were only a hero of romance I would myself offer to take her to America.

In a moment more perhaps I should have persuaded myself that I *was* one, but at this juncture I heard a sound hostile to the romantic note. It was nothing less than the substantial tread of Célestine, the cook, who stood grinning at us as we turned about from our colloquy.

'I ask bien pardon,' said Célestine. 'The mother of mademoiselle desires that mademoiselle should come in immediately. M. le Pasteur Galopin has come to make his adieux to ces dames.'[97]

Aurora gave me but one glance, the memory of which I treasure. Then she surrendered to Célestine, with whom she returned to the house.

The next morning, on coming into the garden, I learned that Mrs Church and her daughter had effectively quitted us. I was informed of this fact by old M. Pigeonneau, who sat there under a tree drinking his café au lait at a little green table.

'I've nothing to envy you,' he said; 'I had the last glimpse of that charming Mees Aurore.'

'I had a very late glimpse,' I answered, 'and it was all I could possibly desire.'

'I've always noticed,' rejoined M. Pigeonneau, 'that your desires are more under control than mine. Que voulez-vous? I'm of the old school. Je crois que cette race se perd. I regret the departure of that attractive young person; she has an enchanting smile. Ce sera une femme d'esprit. For the mother, I can console myself. I'm not sure *she* was a femme d'esprit, though she wished so prodigiously to pass for one. Round, rosy, potelée, she yet had not the temperament of her appearance; she was a femme austère[98]—I made up my mind to that. I've often noticed that contradiction in American ladies. You see a plump little woman with a speaking eye and the contour and complexion of a ripe peach, and if you venture to conduct yourself in the smallest degree in accordance with these *indices*,[99] you discover a species of Methodist – of what do you call it? – of Quakeress. On the other hand, you encounter a tall lean angular form without colour, without grace, all elbows and knees, and you find it's a nature of the tropics! The women of duty look like coquettes, and the others look like alpenstocks! However, we've still la belle Madame Roque – a real femme de Rubens, celle-là.[100] It's very true that to talk to her one must know the Flemish tongue!'

I had determined in accordance with my brother's telegram to go away in the afternoon; so that, having various duties to perform, I left M. Pigeonneau to his ethnic studies. Among other things I went in the course of the morning to the banker's, to draw money for my journey, and there I found Mr Ruck with a pile of crumpled letters in his lap, his chair tipped back and his eyes gloomily fixed on the fringe of the green plush table-cloth. I timidly expressed the hope that he had got better news from home; whereupon he gave me a look in which, considering his provocation, the habit of forlorn patience was conspicuous.

He took up his letters in his large hand and, crushing them together, held it out to me. 'That stack of postal matter,' he said, 'is worth about five cents. But I guess,' he added, rising, 'that I know where I am by this time.' When I had drawn my money I asked him to come and breakfast with me at the little brasserie, much favoured by students, to which I used to resort in the old town. 'I couldn't eat, sir,' he frankly pleaded, 'I couldn't eat. Bad disappointments strike at the seat of the appetite. But I guess I'll go with you, so as not to be on show down there at the pension. The old woman down there accuses me of turning up my nose at her food. Well, I guess I shan't turn up my nose at anything now.'

We went to the little brasserie, where poor Mr Ruck made the lightest possible déjeuner. But if he ate very little he still moved his lean jaws – he mumbled over his spoilt repast of apprehended facts; strange tough financial fare into which I was unable to bite. I was very sorry for him, I wanted to ease him off; but the only thing I could do when we had breakfasted was to see him safely back to the Pension Beaurepas. We went across the Treille and down the Corraterie, out of which we turned into the Rue du Rhône. In this latter street, as all the world knows, prevail those shining shop-fronts of the watchmakers and jewellers for its long list of whom Geneva is famous. I had always admired these elegant exhibitions and never passed them without a lingering look. Even on this occasion, preoccupied as I was with my impending departure and with my companion's troubles, I attached my eyes to the precious tiers that flashed and twinkled behind the huge clear plates of glass. Thanks to this inveterate habit I recorded a fresh observation. In the largest and most irresistible of these repositories I distinguished two ladies, seated before the counter with an air of absorption which sufficiently proclaimed their identity. I hoped my companion wouldn't see them, but as we came abreast of the door, a little beyond, we found it open to the warm summer air. Mr Ruck happened to glance in, and he immediately recognized his wife and daughter. He slowly stopped, his eyes fixed on them; I wondered what he would do. A salesman was in the act of holding up a bracelet before them on its velvet cushion and flashing it about in a winsome manner.

Mr Ruck said nothing, but he presently went in; whereupon, feeling that I mustn't lose him, I did the same. 'It will be an opportunity,' I remarked as cheerfully as possible, 'for me to bid good-bye to the ladies.'

They turned round on the approach of their relative, opposing an indomitable front. 'Well, you'd better get home to breakfast – that's what *you'd* better do,' his wife at once remarked. Miss Sophy resisted in silence; she only took the bracelet from the attendant and gazed at it all fixedly. My friend seated himself on an empty stool and looked round the shop. 'Well, we've been here before, and you ought to know it.' Mrs Ruck a trifle guiltily contended. 'We were here the first day we came.'

The younger lady held out to me the precious object in her hand. 'Don't you think that's sweet?'

I looked at it a moment. 'No, I think it's ugly.'

She tossed her head as at a challenge to a romp. 'Well, I don't believe you've any taste.'

'Why sir, it's just too lovely,' said her mother.

'You'll see it some day *on* me, anyway,' piped Miss Ruck.

'Not very much,' said Mr Ruck quietly.

'It will be his own fault then,' Miss Sophy returned.

'Well, if we're going up to Chamouni we want to get something here,' said Mrs Ruck. 'We mayn't have another chance.'

Her husband still turned his eyes over the shop, whistling half under his breath. 'We ain't going up to Chamouni. We're going back to New York City straight.'

'Well, I'm glad to hear that,' she made answer. 'Don't you suppose we want to take something home?'

'If we're going straight back I must have that bracelet,' her daughter declared. 'Only I don't want a velvet case; I want a satin case.'

'I must bid you good-bye,' I observed all irrelevantly to the ladies. 'I'm leaving Geneva in an hour or two.'

'Take a good look at that bracelet, so you'll know it when you see it,' was hereupon Miss Sophy's form of farewell to me.

'She's bound to have something!' her mother almost proudly attested.

Mr Ruck still vaguely examined the shop; he still just audibly whistled. 'I'm afraid he's not at all well,' I took occasion to intimate to his wife.

She twisted her head a little and glanced at him; she had a brief but pregnant pause. 'Well, I must say I wish he'd improve!'

'A satin case, and a nice one!' cried Miss Ruck to the shopman.

I bade her other parent good-bye. 'Don't wait for me,' he said, sitting there on his stool and not meeting my eye. 'I've got to see this thing through.'

I went back to the Pension Beaurepas, and when an hour later I left it with my luggage these interesting friends had not returned.

The Lesson of the Master

I

He had been told the ladies were at church, but this was corrected by what he saw from the top of the steps – they descended from a great height in two arms, with a circular sweep of the most charming effect – at the threshold of the door which, from the long bright gallery, overlooked the immense lawn. Three gentlemen, on the grass, at a distance, sat under the great trees, while the fourth figure showed a crimson dress that told as a 'bit of colour' amid the fresh rich green. The servant had so far accompanied Paul Overt as to introduce him to this view, after asking him if he wished first to go to his room. The young man declined that privilege, conscious of no disrepair from so short and easy a journey and always liking to take at once a general perceptive possession of a new scene. He stood there a little with his eyes on the group and on the admirable picture, the wide grounds of an old country-house near London – that only made it better – on a splendid Sunday in June. 'But that lady, who's *she?*' he said to the servant before the man left him.

'I think she's Mrs St George, sir.'

'Mrs St George the wife of the distinguished –' Then Paul Overt checked himself, doubting if a footman would know.

'Yes, sir – probably, sir,' said his guide, who appeared to wish to intimate that a person staying at Summersoft would naturally be, if only by alliance, distinguished. His tone, however, made poor Overt himself feel for the moment scantly so.

'And the gentlemen?' Overt went on.

'Well, sir, one of them's General Fancourt.'

'Ah yes, I know; thank you.' General Fancourt was distinguished, there was no doubt of that, for something he had done, or perhaps even hadn't done – the young man couldn't remember which – some years before in India.[1] The servant went away, leaving the glass doors open into the gallery, and Paul Overt remained at the head of the wide double staircase, saying to himself that the place was sweet and promised a pleasant visit, while he leaned on the balustrade of fine old ironwork which, like all the other details, was of the same period as the house. It all went together and spoke in one voice – a rich English voice of the early part of the eighteenth century. It might have been church-time on a summer's day in the reign of Queen Anne:[2] the stillness was too perfect to be modern, the nearness counted so as distance, and there was something so fresh and sound in the originality of the large smooth house, the expanse of beautiful brickwork that showed for pink rather than red and that had been kept clear of messy creepers by the law under which a woman with a rare complexion disdains a veil. When Paul Overt became aware that the people under the trees had noticed him he turned back through the open doors into the great gallery which was the pride of the place. It marched across from end to end and seemed – with its bright colours, its high panelled windows, its faded flowered chintzes, its quickly-recognized portraits and pictures, the blue-and-white china of its cabinets and the attenuated festoons and rosettes of its ceiling – a cheerful upholstered avenue into the other century.

Our friend was slightly nervous; that went with his character as a student of fine prose, went with the artist's general disposition to vibrate; and there was a particular thrill in the idea that Henry St George might be a member of the party. For the young aspirant he had remained a high literary figure, in spite of the lower range of production to which he had fallen after his three first great successes, the comparative absence of quality in his later work. There had been moments when Paul Overt almost shed tears for this; but now that he was near him – he had never met him – he was conscious only of the fine original source and of his own immense debt. After he had taken a turn or two up and down the gallery he came out again and descended the steps. He was but slenderly supplied with a certain social boldness – it was really a weakness in him – so that, conscious of a want of acquaintance with the four persons in the distance, he gave way to motions recommended by their not committing him to a positive approach. There was a fine English awkwardness in this – he felt that too as he sauntered vaguely and obliquely across the lawn, taking an independent line. Fortunately there was an equally fine English directness in the way one of the gentlemen presently rose and made as if to 'stalk' him, though with an air of conciliation and reassurance. To this demonstration Paul Overt instantly responded, even if the gentleman were not his host. He was tall, straight and elderly and had, like the great house itself, a pink smiling face, and into the bargain a white moustache. Our young man met him halfway while he laughed and said: 'Er – Lady Watermouth told us you were coming; she asked me just to look after you.' Paul Overt thanked him, liking him on the spot, and turned round with him to walk toward the others. 'They've all gone to church – all except us,' the stranger continued as they went; 'we're just sitting here – it's so jolly.' Overt pronounced it jolly indeed: it was such a lovely place. He mentioned that he was having the charming impression for the first time.

'Ah you've not been here before?' said his companion. 'It's a nice little place – not much to *do*, you know.' Overt wondered what he wanted to 'do' – he felt that he himself was doing so much. By the time they came to where the others sat he had recognized his initiator for a military man and – such was the turn of Overt's imagination – had found him thus still more sympathetic. He would naturally have a need for action, for deeds at variance with the pacific pastoral scene. He was evidently so good-natured, however, that he accepted the inglorious hour for what it was worth. Paul Overt shared it with him and with his companions for the next twenty minutes; the latter looked at him and he looked at them without knowing much who they were, while the talk went on without much telling him even what it meant. It seemed indeed to mean nothing in particular; it wandered, with casual pointless pauses and short terrestrial flights, amid names of persons and places – names which, for our friend, had no great power of evocation. It was all sociable and slow, as was right and natural of a warm Sunday morning.

His first attention was given to the question, privately considered, of whether one of the two younger men would be Henry St George. He knew many of his distinguished contemporaries by their photographs, but had never, as happened, seen a portrait of the great misguided novelist. One of the gentlemen was unimaginable – he was too young; and the other scarcely looked clever enough, with such mild undiscriminating eyes. If those eyes were St George's the problem presented by the ill-matched parts of his genius would be still more difficult of solution. Besides, the deportment of their proprietor was not, as regards the lady in the red dress, such as could be natural, toward the wife of his bosom, even to a writer accused by several critics of sacrificing too much to manner. Lastly Paul Overt had a vague sense that if the gentleman with the expressionless eyes bore the name that had set his heart beating faster (he also had contradictory conventional whiskers – the young admirer of the celebrity had never in a mental vision seen *his* face in so vulgar a frame) he would have given him a sign of recognition or of friendliness, would have heard of him a little, would know something about 'Ginistrella,' would have an impression of how that fresh fiction had caught the eye of real criticism. Paul Overt had a dread of being grossly proud, but even morbid modesty might view the authorship of 'Ginistrella' as constituting a degree of identity. His soldierly friend became clear enough: he was 'Fancourt,' but was also 'the General'; and he mentioned to the new visitor in the course of a few moments that he had but lately returned from twenty years' service abroad.

'And now you remain in England?' the young man asked.

'Oh yes; I've bought a small house in London.'

'And I hope you like it,' said Overt, looking at Mrs St George.

'Well, a little house in Manchester Square³ – there's a limit to the enthusiasm *that* inspires.'

'Oh I meant being at home again – being back in Piccadilly.'⁴

'My daughter likes Piccadilly – that's the main thing. She's very fond of art and music and literature and all that kind of thing. She missed it in India and she finds it in London, or she hopes she'll find it. Mr St George has promised to help her – he has been awfully kind to her. She has gone to church – she's fond of that too – but they'll all be back in a quarter of an hour. You must let me introduce you to her – she'll be so glad to know you. I dare say she has read every blest word you've written.'

'I shall be delighted – I haven't written so very many,' Overt pleaded, feeling, and without resentment, that the General at least was vagueness itself about that. But he wondered a little why, expressing this friendly disposition, it didn't occur to the doubtless eminent soldier to pronounce the word that would put him in relation with Mrs St George. If it was a question of introductions Miss Fancourt – apparently as yet unmarried – was far away, while the wife of his illustrious confrère⁵ was almost between them. This lady struck Paul Overt as altogether pretty, with a surprising juvenility and a high smartness of aspect, something that – he could scarcely have said why – served for mystification. St George certainly had every right to a charming wife, but he himself would never have imagined the important little woman in the aggressively Parisian dress the partner for life, the *alter ego*, of a man of letters. That partner in general, he knew, that second self, was far from presenting herself in a single type: observation had taught him that she was not inveterately, not necessarily plain. But he had never before seen her look so much as if her prosperity had deeper foundations than an ink-spotted study-table littered with proof-sheets. Mrs St George might have been the wife of a gentleman who 'kept' books rather than wrote them, who carried on great affairs in the City⁶ and made better bargains than those that poets mostly make with publishers. With this she hinted at a success more personal – a success peculiarly stamping the age in which society, the world of conversation, is a great drawing-room with the City for its antechamber. Overt numbered her years at first as some thirty, and then ended by believing that she might approach her fiftieth. But she somehow in this case juggled away the excess and the difference – you only saw them in a rare glimpse, like the rabbit in the conjuror's sleeve. She was extraordinarily white, and her every element and item was pretty; her eyes, her ears, her hair, her voice, her hands, her feet – to which her relaxed attitude in her wicker chair gave a great publicity – and the numerous ribbons and trinkets with which she was bedecked. She looked as if she had put on her best clothes to go to church and then had decided they were too good for that and had stayed at home. She told a story of some length about the shabby way Lady

Jane had treated the Duchess, as well as an anecdote in relation to a purchase she had made in Paris – on her way back from Cannes;[7] made for Lady Egbert, who had never refunded the money. Paul Overt suspected her of a tendency to figure great people as larger than life, until he noticed the manner in which she handled Lady Egbert, which was so sharply mutinous that it reassured him. He felt he should have understood her better if he might have met her eye; but she scarcely so much as glanced at him. 'Ah here they come – all the good ones!' she said at last; and Paul Overt admired at his distance the return of the churchgoers – several persons, in couples and threes, advancing in a flicker of sun and shade at the end of a large green vista formed by the level grass and the overarching boughs.

'If you mean to imply that *we're* bad, I protest,' said one of the gentlemen – 'after making one's self agreeable all the morning!'

'Ah if they've found you agreeable –!' Mrs St George gaily cried. 'But if we're good the others are better.'

'They must be angels then,' said the amused General.

'Your husband was an angel, the way he went off at your bidding,' the gentleman who had first spoken declared to Mrs St George.

'At my bidding?'

'Didn't you make him go to church?'

'I never made him do anything in my life but once – when I made him burn up a bad book. That's all!' At her 'That's all!' our young friend broke into an irrepressible laugh; it lasted only a second, but it drew her eyes to him. His own met them, though not long enough to help him to understand her; unless it were a step towards this that he saw on the instant how the burnt book – the way she alluded to it! – would have been one of her husband's finest things.

'A bad book?' her interlocutor repeated.

'I didn't like it. He went to church because your daughter went,' she continued to General Fancourt. 'I think it my duty to call your attention to his extraordinary demonstrations to your daughter.'

'Well, if you don't mind them I don't!' the General laughed.

'Il s'attache à ses pas.[8] But I don't wonder – she's so charming.'

'I hope she won't make him burn any books!' Paul Overt ventured to exclaim.

'If she'd make him write a few it would be more to the purpose,' said Mrs St George. 'He has been of a laziness of late –!'

Our young man stared – he was so struck with the lady's phraseology. Her 'Write a few' seemed to him almost as good as her 'That's all.' Didn't she, as the wife of a rare artist, know what it was to produce *one* perfect work of art? How in the world did she think they were turned off? His private conviction was that, admirably as Henry St George wrote, he had written for the last ten years, and

especially for the last five, only too much, and there was an instant during which
he felt inwardly solicited to make this public. But before he had spoken a diversion
was effected by the return of the absentees. They strolled up dispersedly – there
were eight or ten of them – and the circle under the trees rearranged itself as they
took their place in it. They made it much larger, so that Paul Overt could feel –
he was always feeling that sort of thing, as he said to himself – that if the
company had already been interesting to watch the interest would now become
intense. He shook hands with his hostess, who welcomed him without many
words, in the manner of a woman able to trust him to understand and conscious
that so pleasant an occasion would in every way speak for itself. She offered him
no particular facility for sitting by her, and when they had all subsided again he
found himself still next General Fancourt, with an unknown lady on his other
flank.

'That's my daughter – that one opposite,' the General said to him without loss
of time. Overt saw a tall girl, with magnificent red hair, in a dress of a pretty
grey-green tint and of a limp silken texture, a garment that clearly shirked every
modern effect. It had therefore somehow the stamp of the latest thing, so that our
beholder quickly took her for nothing if not contemporaneous.

'She's very handsome – very handsome,' he repeated while he considered her.
There was something noble in her head, and she appeared fresh and strong.

Her good father surveyed her with complacency, remarking soon: 'She looks
too hot – that's her walk. But she'll be all right presently. Then I'll make her
come over and speak to you.'

'I should be sorry to give you that trouble. If you were to take me over *there* –!'
the young man murmured.

'My dear sir, do you suppose I put myself out that way? I don't mean for you,
but for Marian,' the General added.

'*I* would put myself out for her soon enough,' Overt replied; after which he
went on: 'Will you be so good as to tell me which of those gentlemen is Henry
St George?'

'The fellow talking to my girl. By Jove, he *is* making up to her – they're going
off for another walk.'

'Ah is that he – really?' Our friend felt a certain surprise, for the personage
before him seemed to trouble a vision which had been vague only while not
confronted with the reality. As soon as the reality dawned the mental image,
retiring with a sigh, became substantial enough to suffer a slight wrong. Overt,
who had spent a considerable part of his short life in foreign lands, made now,
but not for the first time, the reflexion that whereas in those countries he had
almost always recognized the artist and the man of letters by his personal 'type,'[9]
the mould of his face, the character of his head, the expression of his figure and

even the indications of his dress, so in England this identification was as little as possible a matter of course, thanks to the greater conformity, the habit of sinking the profession instead of advertising it, the general diffusion of the air of the gentleman – the gentleman committed to no particular set of ideas. More than once, on returning to his own country, he had said to himself about people met in society: 'One sees them in this place and that, and one even talks with them; but to find out what they *do* one would really have to be a detective.' In respect to several individuals whose work he was the opposite of 'drawn to' – perhaps he was wrong – he found himself adding 'No wonder they conceal it – when it's so bad!' He noted that oftener than in France and in Germany his artist looked like a gentleman – that is like an English one – while, certainly outside a few exceptions, his gentleman didn't look like an artist. St George was not one of the exceptions; that circumstance he definitely apprehended before the great man had turned his back to walk off with Miss Fancourt. He certainly looked better behind than any foreign man of letters – showed for beautifully correct in his tall black hat and his superior frock coat. Somehow, all the same, these very garments – he wouldn't have minded them so much on a weekday – were disconcerting to Paul Overt, who forgot for the moment that the head of the profession was not a bit better dressed than himself. He had caught a glimpse of a regular face, a fresh colour, a brown moustache and a pair of eyes surely never visited by a fine frenzy, and he promised himself to study these denotements on the first occasion. His superficial sense was that their owner might have passed for a lucky stockbroker – a gentleman driving eastward every morning from a sanitary suburb in a smart dog-cart.[10] That carried out the impression already derived from his wife. Paul's glance, after a moment, travelled back to this lady, and he saw how her own had followed her husband as he moved off with Miss Fancourt. Overt permitted himself to wonder a little if she were jealous when another woman took him away. Then he made out that Mrs St George wasn't glaring at the indifferent maiden. Her eyes rested but on her husband, and with unmistakeable serenity. That was the way she wanted him to be – she liked his conventional uniform. Overt longed to hear more about the book she had induced him to destroy.

II

As they all came out from luncheon General Fancourt took hold of him with an 'I say, I want you to know my girl!' as if the idea had just occurred to him and he hadn't spoken of it before. With the other hand he possessed himself all paternally of the young lady. 'You know all about him. I've seen you with his books. She reads everything – everything!' he went on to Paul. The girl smiled at him and then laughed at her father. The General turned away and his daughter spoke – 'Isn't papa delightful?'

'He is indeed, Miss Fancourt.'

'As if I read you because I read "everything"!'

'Oh I don't mean for saying that,' said Paul Overt. 'I liked him from the moment he began to be kind to me. Then he promised me this privilege.'

'It isn't for you he means it – it's for me. If you flatter yourself that he thinks of anything in life but me you'll find you're mistaken. He introduces every one. He thinks me insatiable.'

'You speak just like him,' laughed our youth.

'Ah but sometimes I want to' – and the girl coloured. 'I don't read everything – I read very little. But I *have* read you.'

'Suppose we go into the gallery,' said Paul Overt. She pleased him greatly, not so much because of this last remark – though that of course was not too disconcerting – as because, seated opposite to him at luncheon, she had given him for half an hour the impression of her beautiful face. Something else had come with it – a sense of generosity, of an enthusiasm which, unlike many enthusiasms, was not all manner. That was not spoiled for him by his seeing that the repast had placed her again in familiar contact with Henry St George. Sitting next her this celebrity was also opposite our young man, who had been able to note that he multiplied the attentions lately brought by his wife to the General's notice. Paul Overt had gathered as well that this lady was not in the least discomposed by these fond excesses and that she gave every sign of an unclouded spirit. She had Lord Masham on one side of her and on the other the accomplished Mr Mulliner, editor of the new high-class lively evening paper which was expected to meet a want felt in circles increasingly conscious that Conservatism must be made amusing, and unconvinced when assured by those of another political colour that it was already amusing enough. At the end of an hour spent in her company Paul Overt thought her still prettier than at the first radiation, and if her profane allusions to her husband's work had not still rung in his ears he should have liked her – so far as it could be a question of that in connexion with a woman to whom he had not yet spoken and to whom probably he should never speak if it were left to her. Pretty women were a clear need to this genius, and for the hour it was Miss Fancourt who supplied the want. If Overt had promised himself a closer view the occasion was now of the best, and it brought consequences felt by the young man as important. He saw more in St George's face, which he liked the better for its not having told its whole story in the first three minutes. That story came out as one read, in short instalments – it was excusable that one's analogies should be somewhat professional – and the text was a style considerably involved, a language not easy to translate at sight. There were shades of meaning in it and a vague perspective of history which receded as you advanced. Two facts Paul had particularly heeded. The first of these was that he liked the measured mask much better at inscrutable rest than in social agitation; its almost convulsive smile above all displeased him (as much as any impression from that source could), whereas the quiet face had a charm that grew in proportion as stillness settled again. The change to the expression of gaiety excited, he made out, very much the private protest of a person sitting gratefully in the twilight when the lamp is brought in too soon. His second reflexion was that, though generally averse to the flagrant use of ingratiating arts by a man of age 'making up' to a pretty girl, he was not in this case too painfully affected: which seemed to prove either that St George had a light hand or the air of being younger than he was, or else that Miss Fancourt's own manner somehow made everything right.

Overt walked with her into the gallery, and they strolled to the end of it, looking at the pictures, the cabinets, the charming vista, which harmonised with the prospect of the summer afternoon, resembling it by a long brightness, with great divans and old chairs that figured hours of rest. Such a place as that had the added merit of giving those who came into it plenty to talk about. Miss Fancourt sat down with her new acquaintance on a flowered sofa, the cushions of which, very numerous, were tight ancient cubes of many sizes, and presently said: 'I'm so glad to have a chance to thank you.'

'To thank me –?' He had to wonder.

'I liked your book so much. I think it splendid.'

She sat there smiling at him, and he never asked himself which book she meant; for after all he had written three or four. That seemed a vulgar detail, and he wasn't even gratified by the idea of the pleasure she told him – her handsome bright face told him – he had given her. The feeling she appealed to, or at any rate the feeling she excited, was something larger, something that had little to do with any quickened pulsation of his own vanity. It was responsive admiration of the life she embodied, the young purity and richness of which appeared to imply that real success was to resemble *that*, to live, to bloom, to present the perfection of a fine type, not to have hammered out headachy fancies with a bent back at an ink-stained table. While her grey eyes rested on him – there was a wideish space between these, and the division of her rich-coloured hair, so thick that it ventured to be smooth, made a free arch above them – he was almost ashamed of that exercise of the pen which it was her present inclination to commend. He was conscious he should have liked better to please her in some other way. The lines of her face were those of a woman grown, but the child lingered on in her complexion and in the sweetness of her mouth. Above all she was natural – that was indubitable now; more natural than he had supposed at first, perhaps on account of her aesthetic toggery, which was conventionally unconventional, suggesting what he might have called a tortuous spontaneity. He had feared that sort of thing in other cases, and his fears had been justified; for, though he was an artist to the essence, the modern reactionary nymph, with the brambles of the woodland caught in her folds and a look as if the satyrs had toyed with her hair, made him shrink not as a man of starch and patent leather, but as a man potentially himself a poet or even a faun. The girl was really more candid than her costume, and the best proof of it was her supposing her liberal character suited by any uniform. This was a fallacy, since if she was draped as a pessimist he was sure she liked the taste of life. He thanked her for her appreciation – aware at the same time that he didn't appear to thank her enough and that she might think him ungracious. He was afraid she would ask him to explain something he had written, and he always winced at that – perhaps too timidly – for to his own ear the explanation of a work of art sounded fatuous. But he liked her so much as to feel a confidence that in the long run he should be able to show her he wasn't rudely evasive. Moreover she surely wasn't quick to take offence, wasn't irritable; she could be trusted to wait. So when he said to her 'Ah don't talk of anything I've done, don't talk of it *here*; there's another man in the house who's the actuality!' – when he uttered this short sincere protest it was with the sense that she would see in the words neither mock humility nor the impatience of a successful man bored with praise.

'You mean Mr St George – isn't he delightful?'

Paul Overt met her eyes, which had a cool morning-light that would have half-broken his heart if he hadn't been so young. 'Alas I don't know him. I only admire him at a distance.'

'Oh you *must* know him – he wants so to talk to you,' returned Miss Fancourt, who evidently had the habit of saying the things that, by her quick calculation, would give people pleasure. Paul saw how she would always calculate on everything's being simple between others.

'I shouldn't have supposed he knew anything about me,' he professed.

'He does then – everything. And if he didn't I should be able to tell him.'

'To tell him everything?' our friend smiled.

'You talk just like the people in your book,' she answered.

'Then they must all talk alike.'

She thought a moment, not a bit disconcerted. 'Well, it must be so difficult. Mr St George tells me it *is* – terribly. I've tried too – and I find it so. I've tried to write a novel.'

'Mr St George oughtn't to discourage you,' Paul went so far as to say.

'You do much more – when you wear that expression.'

'Well, after all, why try to be an artist?' the young man pursued. 'It's so poor — so poor!'

'I don't know what you mean,' said Miss Fancourt, who looked grave.

'I mean as compared with being a person of action — as living your works.'

'But what's art but an intense life — if it be real?' she asked. 'I think it's the only one — everything else is so clumsy!' Her companion laughed, and she brought out with her charming serenity what next struck her. 'It's so interesting to meet so many celebrated people.'

'So I should think — but surely it isn't new to you.'

'Why I've never seen any one — any one: living always in Asia.'

The way she talked of Asia somehow enchanted him. 'But doesn't that continent swarm with great figures? Haven't you administered provinces in India and had captive rajahs and tributary princes chained to your car?'[11]

It was as if she didn't care even *should* he amuse himself at her cost. 'I was with my father, after I left school to go out there. It was delightful being with him — we're alone together in the world, he and I — but there was none of the society I like best. One never heard of a picture — never of a book, except bad ones.'

'Never of a picture? Why, wasn't all life a picture?'

She looked over the delightful place where they sat. 'Nothing to compare to this. I adore England!' she cried.

It fairly stirred in him the sacred chord. 'Ah of course I don't deny that we must do something with her, poor old dear, yet!'

'She hasn't been touched, really,' said the girl.

'Did Mr St George say that?'

There was a small and, as he felt, harmless spark of irony in his question; which, however, she answered very simply, not noticing the insinuation. 'Yes, he says England hasn't been touched — not considering all there is,' she went on eagerly. 'He's so interesting about our country. To listen to him makes one want so to do something.'

'It would make *me* want to,' said Paul Overt, feeling strongly, on the instant, the suggestion of what she said and that of the emotion with which she said it, and well aware of what an incentive, on St George's lips, such a speech might be.

'Oh you — as if you hadn't! I should like so to hear you talk together,' she added ardently.

'That's very genial of you; but he'd have it all his own way. I'm prostrate before him.'

She had an air of earnestness. 'Do you think then he's so perfect?'

'Far from it. Some of his later books seem to me of a queerness —!'

'Yes, yes — he knows that.'

Paul Overt stared. 'That they seem to me of a queerness —?'

'Well yes, or at any rate that they're not what they should be. He told me he didn't esteem them. He has told me such wonderful things – he's so interesting.'

There was a certain shock for Paul Overt in the knowledge that the fine genius they were talking of had been reduced to so explicit a confession and had made it, in his misery, to the first comer; for though Miss Fancourt was charming what was she after all but an immature girl encountered at a country-house? Yet precisely this was part of the sentiment he himself had just expressed: he would make way completely for the poor peccable great man not because he didn't read him clear, but altogether because he did. His consideration was half composed of tenderness for superficialities which he was sure their perpetrator judged privately, judged more ferociously than any one, and which represented some tragic intellectual secret. He would have his reasons for his psychology *à fleur de peau*,[12] and these reasons could only be cruel ones, such as would make him dearer to those who already were fond of him. 'You excite my envy. I have my reserves, I discriminate – but I love him,' Paul said in a moment. 'And seeing him for the first time this way is a great event for me.'

'How momentous – how magnificent!' cried the girl. 'How delicious to bring you together!'

'*Your* doing it – that makes it perfect,' our friend returned.

'He's as eager as you,' she went on. 'But it's so odd you shouldn't have met.'

'It's not really so odd as it strikes you. I've been out of England so much – made repeated absences all these last years.'

She took this in with interest. 'And yet you write of it as well as if you were always here.'

'It's just the being away perhaps. At any rate the best bits, I suspect, are those that were done in dreary places abroad.'

'And why were they dreary?'

'Because they were health-resorts – where my poor mother was dying.'

'Your poor mother?' – she was all sweet wonder.

'We went from place to place to help her to get better. But she never did. To the deadly Riviera, (I hate it!) to the high Alps, to Algiers, and far away – a hideous journey – to Colorado.'

'And she isn't better?' Miss Fancourt went on.

'She died a year ago.'

'Really? – like mine! Only that's years since. Some day you must tell me about your mother,' she added.

He could at first, on this, only gaze at her. 'What right things you say! If you say them to St George I don't wonder he's in bondage.'

It pulled her up for a moment. 'I don't know what you mean. He doesn't make speeches and professions at all – he isn't ridiculous.'

'I'm afraid you consider then that I am.'

'No, I don't' – she spoke it rather shortly. And then she added: 'He understands – understands everything.'

The young man was on the point of saying jocosely: 'And I don't – is that it?' But these words, in time, changed themselves to others slightly less trivial. 'Do you suppose he understands his wife?'

Miss Fancourt made no direct answer, but after a moment's hesitation put it: 'Isn't she charming?'

'Not in the least!'

'Here he comes. Now you must know him,' she went on. A small group of visitors had gathered at the other end of the gallery and had been there overtaken by Henry St George, who strolled in from a neighbouring room. He stood near them a moment, not falling into the talk but taking up an old miniature from a table and vaguely regarding it. At the end of a minute he became aware of Miss Fancourt and her companion in the distance; whereupon, laying down his miniature, he approached them with the same procrastinating air, his hands in his pockets and his eyes turned, right and left, to the pictures. The gallery was so long that this transit took some little time, especially as there was a moment when he stopped to admire the fine Gainsborough.[13] 'He says Mrs St George has been the making of him,' the girl continued in a voice slightly lowered.

'Ah he's often obscure!' Paul laughed.

'Obscure?' she repeated as if she heard it for the first time. Her eyes rested on her other friend, and it wasn't lost upon Paul that they appeared to send out great shafts of softness. 'He's going to speak to us!' she fondly breathed. There was a sort of rapture in her voice, and our friend was startled. 'Bless my soul, does she care for him like *that*? – is she in love with him?' he mentally enquired. 'Didn't I tell you he was eager?' she had meanwhile asked of him.

'It's eagerness dissimulated,' the young man returned as the subject of their observation lingered before his Gainsborough. 'He edges toward us shyly. Does he mean that she saved him by burning that book?'

'That book? what book did she burn?' The girl quickly turned her face to him.

'Hasn't he told you then?'

'Not a word.'

'Then he doesn't tell you everything!' Paul had guessed that she pretty much supposed he did. The great man had now resumed his course and come nearer; in spite of which his more qualified admirer risked a profane observation. 'St George and the Dragon[14] is what the anecdote suggests!'

His companion, however, didn't hear it; she smiled at the dragon's adversary. 'He *is* eager – he is!' she insisted.

'Eager for you – yes.'

But meanwhile she had called out: 'I'm sure you want to know Mr Overt. You'll be great friends, and it will always be delightful to me to remember I was here when you first met and that I had something to do with it.'

There was a freshness of intention in the words that carried them off; nevertheless our young man was sorry for Henry St George, as he was sorry at any time for any person publicly invited to be responsive and delightful. He would have been so touched to believe that a man he deeply admired should care a straw for him that he wouldn't play with such a presumption if it were possibly vain. In a single glance of the eye of the pardonable master he read – having the sort of divination that belonged to his talent – that this personage had ever a store of friendly patience, which was part of his rich outfit, but was versed in no printed page of a rising scribbler. There was even a relief, a simplification, in that: liking him so much already for what he had done, how could one have liked him any more for a perception which must at the best have been vague? Paul Overt got up, trying to show his compassion, but at the same instant he found himself encompassed by St George's happy personal art – a manner of which it was the essence to conjure away false positions. It all took place in a moment. Paul was conscious that he knew him now, conscious of his handshake and of the very quality of his hand; of his face, seen nearer and consequently seen better, of a general fraternising assurance, and in particular of the circumstance that St George didn't dislike him (as yet at least) for being imposed by a charming but too gushing girl, attractive enough without such danglers.[15] No irritation at any rate was reflected in the voice with which he questioned Miss Fancourt as to some project of a walk – a general walk of the company round the park. He had soon said something to Paul about a talk – 'We must have a tremendous lot of talk; there are so many things, aren't there?' – but our friend could see this idea wouldn't in the present case take very immediate effect. All the same he was extremely happy, even after the matter of the walk had been settled – the three presently passed back to the other part of the gallery, where it was discussed with several members of the party; even when, after they had all gone out together, he found himself for half an hour conjoined with Mrs St George. Her husband had taken the advance with Miss Fancourt, and this pair were quite out of sight. It was the prettiest of rambles for a summer afternoon – a grassy circuit, of immense extent, skirting the limit of the park within. The park was completely surrounded by its old mottled but perfect red wall, which, all the way on their left, constituted in itself an object of interest. Mrs St George mentioned to him the surprising number of acres thus enclosed, together with numerous other facts relating to the property and the family, and the family's other properties: she couldn't too strongly urge on him the importance of seeing their other houses.

She ran over the names of these and rang the changes on them with the facility of practice, making them appear an almost endless list. She had received Paul Overt very amiably on his breaking ground with her by the mention of his joy in having just made her husband's acquaintance, and struck him as so alert and so accommodating a little woman that he was rather ashamed of his *mot*[16] about her to Miss Fancourt; though he reflected that a hundred other people, on a hundred occasions, would have been sure to make it. He got on with Mrs St George, in short, better than he expected; but this didn't prevent her suddenly becoming aware that she was faint with fatigue and must take her way back to the house by the shortest cut. She professed that she hadn't the strength of a kitten and was a miserable wreck; a character he had been too preoccupied to discern in her while he wondered in what sense she could be held to have been the making of her husband. He had arrived at a glimmering of the answer when she announced that she must leave him, though this perception was of course provisional. While he was in the very act of placing himself at her disposal for the return the situation underwent a change; Lord Masham had suddenly turned up, coming back to them, overtaking them, emerging from the shrubbery – Overt could scarcely have said how he appeared – and Mrs St George had protested that she wanted to be left alone and not to break up the party. A moment later she was walking off with Lord Masham. Our friend fell back and joined Lady Watermouth, to whom he presently mentioned that Mrs St George had been obliged to renounce the attempt to go further.

'She oughtn't to have come out at all,' her ladyship rather grumpily remarked. 'Is she so very much of an invalid?'

'Very bad indeed.' And his hostess added with still greater austerity: 'She oughtn't really to come to one!' He wondered what was implied by this, and presently gathered that it was not a reflexion on the lady's conduct or her moral nature: it only represented that her strength was not equal to her aspirations.

III

The smoking-room at Summersoft was on the scale of the rest of the place – high light commodious and decorated with such refined old carvings and mouldings that it seemed rather a bower for ladies who should sit at work at fading crewels[17] than a parliament of gentlemen smoking strong cigars. The gentlemen mustered there in considerable force on the Sunday evening, collecting mainly at one end, in front of one of the cool fair fireplaces of white marble, the entablature of which was adorned with a delicate little Italian 'subject.' There was another in the wall that faced it, and, thanks to the mild summer night, a fire in neither; but a nucleus for aggregation was furnished on one side by a table in the chimney-corner laden with bottles, decanters and tall tumblers. Paul Overt was a faithless smoker; he would puff a cigarette for reasons with which tobacco had nothing to do. This was particularly the case on the occasion of which I speak; his motive was the vision of a little direct talk with Henry St George. The 'tremendous' communion of which the great man had held out hopes to him earlier in the day had not yet come off, and this saddened him considerably, for the party was to go its several ways immediately after breakfast on the morrow. He had, however, the disappointment of finding that apparently the author of 'Shadowmere' was not disposed to prolong his vigil. He wasn't among the gentlemen assembled when Paul entered, nor was he one of those who turned up, in bright habiliments,[18] during the next ten minutes. The young man waited a little, wondering if he had only gone to put on something extraordinary; this would account for his delay as well as contribute further to Overt's impression of his tendency to do the approved superficial thing. But he didn't arrive — he must have been putting on something more extraordinary than was probable. Our hero gave him up, feeling a little injured, a little wounded, at this loss of twenty coveted words. He wasn't angry, but he puffed his cigarette sighingly, with the sense of something rare possibly missed. He wandered away with his regret and moved slowly round the room, looking at the old prints on the walls. In this attitude he presently felt a hand on his shoulder and a friendly voice in his ear 'This is good. I hoped I should find you. I came down on purpose.' St George was there without a change of dress and with a fine face — his graver one — to which our young man all in a flutter responded. He explained that it was only for the Master — the idea of a little talk — that he had sat up, and that, not finding him, he had been on the point of going to bed.

'Well, you know, I don't smoke — my wife doesn't let me,' said St George, looking for a place to sit down. 'It's very good for me — very good for me. Let us take that sofa.'

'Do you mean smoking's good for you?'

'No no — her not letting me. It's a great thing to have a wife who's so sure of all the things one can do without. One might never find them out one's self. She doesn't allow me to touch a cigarette.' They took possession of a sofa at a distance from the group of smokers, and St George went on: 'Have you got one yourself?'

'Do you mean a cigarette?'

'Dear no — a wife!'

'No; and yet I'd give up my cigarette for one.'

'You'd give up a good deal more than that,' St George returned. 'However, you'd get a great deal in return. There's a something to be said for wives,' he added, folding his arms and crossing his outstretched legs. He declined tobacco altogether and sat there without returning fire. His companion stopped smoking, touched by his courtesy; and after all they were out of the fumes, their sofa was in a faraway corner. It would have been a mistake, St George went on, a great mistake for them to have separated without a little chat; 'for I know all about you,' he said, 'I know you're very remarkable. You've written a very distinguished book.'

'And how do you know it?' Paul asked.

'Why, my dear fellow, it's in the air, it's in the papers, it's everywhere.' St George spoke with the immediate familiarity of a confrère – a tone that seemed to his neighbour the very rustle of the laurel.[19] 'You're on all men's lips and, what's better, on all women's. And I've just been reading your book.'

'Just? You hadn't read it this afternoon,' said Overt.

'How do you know that?'

'I think you should know how I know it,' the young man laughed.

'I suppose Miss Fancourt told you.'

'No indeed – she led me rather to suppose you had.'

'Yes – that's much more what she'd do. Doesn't she shed a rosy glow over life? But you didn't believe her?' asked St George.

'No, not when you came to us there.'

'Did I pretend? did I pretend badly?' But without waiting for an answer to this St George went on: 'You ought always to believe such a girl as that – always, always. Some women are meant to be taken with allowances and reserves; but you must take *her* just as she is.'

'I like her very much,' said Paul Overt.

Something in his tone appeared to excite on his companion's part a momentary sense of the absurd; perhaps it was the air of deliberation attending this judgement. St George broke into a laugh to reply. 'It's the best thing you can do with her. She's a rare young lady! In point of fact, however, I confess I hadn't read you this afternoon.'

'Then you see how right I was in this particular case not to believe Miss Fancourt.'

'How right? how can I agree to that when I lost credit by it?'

'Do you wish to pass exactly for what she represents you? Certainly you needn't be afraid,' Paul said.

'Ah, my dear young man, don't talk about passing – for the likes of me! I'm passing away – nothing else than that. She has a better use for her young imagination (isn't it fine?) than in "representing" in any way such a weary wasted used-up animal!' The Master spoke with a sudden sadness that produced a protest on Paul's part; but before the protest could be uttered he went on, reverting to the latter's striking novel: 'I had no idea you were so good – one hears of so many things. But you're surprisingly good.'

'I'm going to be surprisingly better,' Overt made bold to reply.

'I see that, and it's what fetches me. I don't see so much else – as one looks about – that's going to be surprisingly better. They're going to be consistently worse – most of the things. It's so much easier to be worse – heaven knows I've found it so. I'm not in a great glow, you know, about what's breaking out all over the place. But you *must* be better, you really must keep it up. I haven't of course. It's very difficult – that's the devil of the whole thing, keeping it up. But I see you'll be able to. It will be a great disgrace if you don't.'

'It's very interesting to hear you speak of yourself; but I don't know what you mean by your allusions to your having fallen off,' Paul Overt observed with pardonable hypocrisy. He liked his companion so much now that the fact of any decline of talent or of care had ceased for the moment to be vivid to him.

'Don't say that – don't say that,' St George returned gravely, his head resting on the top of the sofa-back and his eyes on the ceiling. 'You know perfectly what I mean. I haven't read twenty pages of your book without seeing that you can't help it.'

'You make me very miserable,' Paul ecstatically breathed.

'I'm glad of that, for it may serve as a kind of warning. Shocking enough it must be, especially to a young fresh mind, full of faith – the spectacle of a man meant for better things sunk at my age in such dishonour.' St George, in the same contemplative attitude, spoke softly but deliberately, and without perceptible emotion. His tone indeed suggested an impersonal lucidity that was practically cruel – cruel to himself – and made his young friend lay an argumentative hand on his arm. But he went on while his eyes seemed to follow the graces of the eighteenth-century ceiling: 'Look at me well, take my lesson to heart – for it *is* a lesson. Let that good come of it at least that you shudder with your pitiful impression, and that this may help to keep you straight in the future. Don't become in your old age what I have in mine – the depressing, the deplorable illustration of the worship of false gods!'

'What do you mean by your old age?' the young man asked.

'It has made me old. But I like your youth.'

Paul answered nothing – they sat for a minute in silence. They heard the others going on about the governmental majority. Then 'What do you mean by false gods?' he enquired.

His companion had no difficulty whatever in saying, 'The idols of the market; money and luxury and "the world"; placing one's children and dressing one's wife; everything that drives one to the short and easy way. Ah the vile things they make one do!'

'But surely one's right to want to place one's children.'

'One has no business to have any children,' St George placidly declared. 'I mean of course if one wants to do anything good.'

'But aren't they an inspiration – an incentive?'

'An incentive to damnation, artistically speaking.'

'You touch on very deep things – things I should like to discuss with you,' Paul said. 'I should like you to tell me volumes about yourself. This is a great feast for *me*!'

'Of course it is, cruel youth. But to show you I'm still not incapable, degraded as I am, of an act of faith, I'll tie my vanity to the stake for you and burn it to ashes. You must come and see me – you must come and see us,' the Master quickly substituted. 'Mrs St George is charming; I don't know whether you've had any opportunity to talk with her. She'll be delighted to see you; she likes great celebrities, whether incipient or predominant. You must come and dine – my wife will write to you. Where are you to be found?'

'This is my little address' – and Overt drew out his pocketbook and extracted a visiting-card. On second thoughts, however, he kept it back, remarking that he wouldn't trouble his friend to take charge of it but would come and see him straightway in London and leave it at his door if he should fail to obtain entrance.

'Ah you'll probably fail; my wife's always out – or when she isn't out is knocked up from having *been* out. You must come and dine – though that won't do much good either, for my wife insists on big dinners.' St George turned it over further, but then went on: 'You must come down and see us in the country, that's the best way; we've plenty of room and it isn't bad.'

'You've a house in the country?' Paul asked enviously.

'Ah not like this! But we have a sort of place we go to – an hour from Euston.[20] That's one of the reasons.'

'One of the reasons?'

'Why my books are so bad.'

'You must tell me all the others!' Paul longingly laughed.

His friend made no direct rejoinder to this, but spoke again abruptly. 'Why have I never seen you before?'

The tone of the question was singularly flattering to our hero, who felt it to imply the great man's now perceiving he had for years missed something. 'Partly, I suppose, because there has been no particular reason why you should see me. I haven't lived in the world – in your world. I've spent many years out of England, in different places abroad.'

'Well, please don't do it any more. You must do England – there's such a lot of it.'

'Do you mean I must write about it?' – and Paul struck the note of the listening candour of a child.

'Of course you must. And tremendously well, do you mind? That takes off a little of my esteem for this thing of yours – that it goes on abroad. Hang "abroad"! Stay at home and do things here – do subjects we can measure.'

'I'll do whatever you tell me,' Overt said, deeply attentive. 'But pardon me if I say I don't understand how you've been reading my book,' he added. 'I've had you before me all the afternoon, first in that long walk, then at tea on the lawn, till we went to dress for dinner, and all the evening at dinner and in this place.'

St George turned his face about with a smile. 'I gave it but a quarter of an hour.'

'A quarter of an hour's immense, but I don't understand where you put it in. In the drawing-room after dinner you weren't reading – you were talking to Miss Fancourt.'

'It comes to the same thing, because we talked about "Ginistrella." She described it to me – she lent me her copy.'

'Lent it to you?'

'She travels with it.'

'It's incredible,' Paul blushed.

'It's glorious for you, but it also turned out very well for me. When the ladies went off to bed she kindly offered to send the book down to me. Her maid brought it to me in the hall, and I went to my room with it. I hadn't thought of coming here, I do that so little. But I don't sleep early, I always have to read an hour or two. I sat down to your novel on the spot, without undressing, without taking off anything but my coat. I think that's a sign my curiosity had been strongly roused about it. I read a quarter of an hour, as I tell you, and even in a quarter of an hour I was greatly struck.'

'Ah the beginning isn't very good – it's the whole thing!' said Overt, who had listened to this recital with extreme interest. 'And you laid down the book and came after me?' he asked.

'That's the way it moved me. I said to myself "I see it's off his own bat, and he's there, by the way, and the day's over, and I haven't said twenty words to him." It occurred to me that you'd probably be in the smoking-room and that it wouldn't be too late to repair my omission. I wanted to do something civil to you, so I put on my coat and came down. I shall read your book again when I go up.'

Our friend faced round in his place – he was touched as he had scarce ever been by the picture of such a demonstration in his favour. 'You're really the kindest of men. Cela s'est passé comme ça?[21] – and I've been sitting here with you all this time and never apprehended it and never thanked you!'

'Thank Miss Fancourt – it was she who wound me up. She has made me feel as if I had read your novel.'

'She's an angel from heaven!' Paul declared.

'She is indeed. I've never seen any one like her. Her interest in literature's touching – something quite peculiar to herself; she takes it all so seriously. She feels the arts and she wants to feel them more. To those who practise them it's almost humiliating – her curiosity, her sympathy, her good faith. How can anything be as fine as she supposes it?'

'She's a rare organisation,' the younger man sighed.

'The richest I've ever seen – an artistic intelligence really of the first order. And lodged in such a form!' St George exclaimed.

'One would like to represent such a girl as that,' Paul continued.

'Ah there it is – there's nothing like life!' said his companion. 'When you're finished, squeezed dry and used up and you think the sack's empty, you're still appealed to, you still get touches and thrills, the idea springs up – out of the lap of the actual – and shows you there's always something to be done. But I shan't do it – she's not for me!'

'How do you mean, not for you?'

'Oh it's all over – she's for you, if you like.'

'Ah much less!' said Paul. 'She's not for a dingy little man of letters; she's for the world, the bright rich world of bribes and rewards. And the world will take hold of her – it will carry her away.'

'It will try – but it's just a case in which there may be a fight. It would be worth fighting, for a man who had it in him, with youth and talent on his side.'

These words rang not a little in Paul Overt's consciousness – they held him briefly silent. 'It's a wonder she has remained as she is; giving herself away so – with so much to give away.'

'Remaining, you mean, so ingenuous – so natural? Oh she doesn't care a straw – she gives away because she overflows. She has her own feelings, her own standards; she doesn't keep remembering that she must be proud. And then she hasn't been here long enough to be spoiled; she has picked up a fashion or two, but only the amusing ones. She's a provincial – a provincial of genius,' St George went on; 'her very blunders are charming, her mistakes are interesting. She has come back from Asia with all sorts of excited curiosities and unappeased appetites. She's first-rate herself and she expends herself on the second-rate. She's life herself and she takes a rare interest in imitations. She mixes all things up, but there are none in regard to which she hasn't perceptions. She sees things in a perspective – as if from the top of the Himalayas – and she enlarges everything she touches. Above all she exaggerates – to herself, I mean. She exaggerates you and me!'

There was nothing in that description to allay the agitation caused in our younger friend by such a sketch of a fine subject. It seemed to him to show the art of St George's admired hand, and he lost himself in gazing at the vision – this hovered there before him – of a woman's figure which should be part of the glory of a novel. But at the end of a moment the thing had turned into smoke, and out of the smoke – the last puff of a big cigar – proceeded the voice of General Fancourt, who had left the others and come and planted himself before the gentlemen on the sofa. 'I suppose that when you fellows get talking you sit up half the night.'

'Half the night? – jamais de la vie!²² I follow a hygiene' – and St George rose to his feet.

'I see – you're hothouse plants,' laughed the General. 'That's the way you produce your flowers.'

'I produce mine between ten and one every morning – I bloom with a regularity!' St George went on.

'And with a splendour!' added the polite General, while Paul noted how little the author of 'Shadowmere' minded, as he phrased it to himself, when addressed as a celebrated story-teller. The young man had an idea *he* should never get used to that; it would always make him uncomfortable – from the suspicion that people would think they had to – and he would want to prevent it. Evidently his great colleague had toughened and hardened – had made himself a surface. The group of men had finished their cigars and taken up their bedroom candlesticks; but before they all passed out Lord Watermouth invited the pair of guests who had been so absorbed together to 'have' something.²⁴ It happened that they both declined; upon which General Fancourt said: 'Is that the hygiene? You don't water the flowers?'

'Oh I should drown them!' St George replied; but, leaving the room still at his young friend's side, he added whimsically, for the latter's benefit, in a lower tone: 'My wife doesn't let me.'

'Well I'm glad I'm not one of you fellows!' the General richly concluded.

The nearness of Summersoft to London had this consequence, chilling to a person who had had a vision of sociability in a railway-carriage, that most of the company, after breakfast, drove back to town, entering their own vehicles, which had come out to fetch them, while their servants returned by train with their luggage. Three or four young men, among whom was Paul Overt, also availed themselves of the common convenience; but they stood in the portico of the house and saw the others roll away. Miss Fancourt got into a victoria²⁵ with her father after she had shaken hands with our hero and said, smiling in the frankest way in the world, 'I *must* see you more. Mrs St George is so nice; she has promised to ask us both to dinner together.' This lady and her husband took their places in a perfectly-appointed brougham – she required a closed carriage[26] – and as our young man waved his hat to them in response to their nods and flourishes he reflected that, taken together, they were an honourable image of success, of the material rewards and the social credit of literature. Such things were not the full measure, but he nevertheless felt a little proud for literature.

IV

Before a week had elapsed he met Miss Fancourt in Bond Street,[27] at a private view of the works of a young artist in 'black-and-white'[28] who had been so good as to invite him to the stuffy scene. The drawings were admirable, but the crowd in the one little room was so dense that he felt himself up to his neck in a sack of wool. A fringe of people at the outer edge endeavoured by curving forward their backs and presenting, below them, a still more convex surface of resistance to the pressure of the mass, to preserve an interval between their noses and the glazed mounts of the pictures; while the central body, in the comparative gloom projected by a wide horizontal screen hung under the skylight and allowing only a margin for the day, remained upright dense and vague, lost in the contemplation of its own ingredients. This contemplation sat especially in the sad eyes of certain female heads, surmounted with hats of strange convolution and plumage, which rose on long necks above the others. One of the heads, Paul perceived, was much the most beautiful of the collection, and his next discovery was that it belonged to Miss Fancourt. Its beauty was enhanced by the glad smile she sent him across surrounding obstructions, a smile that drew him to her as fast as he could make his way. He had seen for himself at Summersoft that the last thing her nature contained was an affectation of indifference; yet even with this circumspection he took a fresh satisfaction in her not having pretended to await his arrival with composure. She smiled as radiantly as if she wished to make him hurry, and as soon as he came within earshot she broke out in her voice of joy: 'He's here – he's here; he's coming back in a moment!'

'Ah your father?' Paul returned as she offered him her hand.

'Oh dear no, this isn't in my poor father's line. I mean Mr St George. He has just left me to speak to some one – he's coming back. It's he who brought me – wasn't it charming?'

'Ah that gives him a pull over me – I couldn't have "brought" you, could I?'

'If you had been so kind as to propose it – why not you as well as he?' the girl returned with a face that, expressing no cheap coquetry, simply affirmed a happy fact.

'Why he's a *père de famille*.[29] They've privileges,' Paul explained. And then quickly: 'Will you go to see places with *me*?' he asked.

'Anything you like,' she smiled. 'I know what you mean, that girls have to have a lot of people —!' Then she broke off: 'I don't know; I'm free. I've always been like that — I can go about with any one. I'm so glad to meet you,' she added with a sweet distinctness that made those near her turn round.

'Let me at least repay that speech by taking you out of this squash,' her friend said. 'Surely people aren't happy here!'

'No, they're awfully *mornes*,[30] aren't they? But I'm very happy indeed and I promised Mr St George to remain on this spot till he comes back. He's going to take me away. They send him invitations for things of this sort — more than he wants. It was so kind of him to think of me.'

'They also send me invitations of this kind — more than *I* want. And if thinking of *you* will do it —!' Paul went on.

'Oh I delight in them — everything that's life, everything that's London!'

'They don't have private views in Asia, I suppose,' he laughed. 'But what a pity that for this year, even in this gorged city, they're pretty well over.'

'Well, next year will do, for I hope you believe we're going to be friends always. Here he comes!' Miss Fancourt continued before Paul had time to respond.

He made out St George in the gaps of the crowd, and this perhaps led to his hurrying a little to say: 'I hope that doesn't mean I'm to wait till next year to see you.'

'No, no — aren't we to meet at dinner on the twenty-fifth?' she panted with an eagerness as happy as his own.

'That's almost next year. Is there no means of seeing you before?'

She stared with all her brightness. 'Do you mean you'd *come*?'

'Like a shot, if you'll be so good as to ask me!'

'On Sunday then — this next Sunday?'

'What have I done that you should doubt it?' the young man asked with delight.

Miss Fancourt turned instantly to St George, who had now joined them, and announced triumphantly: 'He's coming on Sunday — this next Sunday!'

'Ah my day — my day too!' said the famous novelist, laughing, to their companion.

'Yes, but not yours only. You shall meet in Manchester Square; you shall talk — you shall be wonderful!'

'We don't meet often enough,' St George allowed, shaking hands with his disciple. 'Too many things — ah too many things! But we must make it up in the country in September. You won't forget you've promised me that?'

'Why he's coming on the twenty-fifth — you'll see him then,' said the girl.

'On the twenty-fifth?' St George asked vaguely.

'We dine with you; I hope you haven't forgotten. He's dining out that day,' she added gaily to Paul.

'Oh bless me, yes – that's charming! And you're coming? My wife didn't tell me,' St George said to him. 'Too many things – too many things!' he repeated.

'Too many people – too many people!' Paul exclaimed, giving ground before the penetration of an elbow.

'You oughtn't to say that. They all read you.'

'Me? I should like to see them! Only two or three at most,' the young man returned.

'Did you ever hear anything like that? He knows, haughtily, how good he is!' St George declared, laughing, to Miss Fancourt. 'They read *me*, but that doesn't make me like them any better. Come away from them, come away!' And he led the way out of the exhibition.

'He's going to take me to the Park,'[31] Miss Fancourt observed to Overt with elation as they passed along the corridor that led to the street.

'Ah does he go there?' Paul asked, taking the fact for a somewhat unexpected illustration of St George's *moeurs*.[32]

'It's a beautiful day – there'll be a great crowd. We're going to look at the people, to look at types,' the girl went on. 'We shall sit under the trees; we shall walk by the Row.'[33]

'I go once a year – on business,' said St George, who had overheard Paul's question.

'Or with a country cousin, didn't you tell me? I'm the country cousin!' she continued over her shoulder to Paul as their friend drew her toward a hansom[34] to which he had signalled. The young man watched them get in; he returned, as he stood there, the friendly wave of the hand with which, ensconced in the vehicle beside her, St George took leave of him. He even lingered to see the vehicle start away and lose itself in the confusion of Bond Street. He followed it with his eyes; it put to him embarrassing things. 'She's not for *me*!' the great novelist had said emphatically at Summersoft; but his manner of conducting himself toward her appeared not quite in harmony with such a conviction. How could he have behaved differently if she *had* been for him? An indefinite envy rose in Paul Overt's heart as he took his way on foot alone; a feeling addressed alike, strangely enough, to each of the occupants of the hansom. How much he should like to rattle about London with such a girl! How much he should like to go and look at 'types' with St George!

The next Sunday at four o'clock he called in Manchester Square, where his secret wish was gratified by his finding Miss Fancourt alone. She was in a large bright friendly occupied room, which was painted red all over, draped with the quaint cheap florid stuffs that are represented as coming from southern and eastern countries, where they are fabled to serve as the counterpanes of the peasantry, and bedecked with pottery of vivid hues, ranged on casual shelves, and with many water-colour drawings from the hand (as the visitor learned) of the young lady herself, commemorating with a brave breadth the sunsets, the mountains, the temples and palaces of India. He sat an hour – more than an hour, two hours – and all the while no one came in. His hostess was so good as to remark, with her liberal humanity, that it was delightful they weren't interrupted: it was so rare in London, especially at that season, that people got a good talk. But luckily now, of a fine Sunday, half the world went out of town, and that made it better for those who didn't go, when these others were in sympathy. It was the defect of London – one of two or three, the very short list of those she recognised in the teeming world-city she adored – that there were too few good chances for talk: you never had time to carry anything far.

'Too many things, too many things!' Paul said, quoting St George's exclamation of a few days before.

'Ah yes, for him there are too many – his life's too complicated.'

'Have you seen it *near*? That's what I should like to do; it might explain some mysteries,' her visitor went on. She asked him what mysteries he meant, and he said: 'Oh peculiarities of his work, inequalities, superficialities. For one who looks at it from the artistic point of view it contains a bottomless ambiguity.'

She became at this, on the spot, all intensity. 'Ah do describe that more – it's so interesting. There are no such suggestive questions. I'm so fond of them. He thinks he's a failure – fancy!' she beautifully wailed.

'That depends on what his ideal may have been. With his gifts it ought to have been high. But till one knows what he really proposed to himself –! Do *you* know by chance?' the young man broke off.

'Oh he doesn't talk to me about himself. I can't make him. It's too provoking.'

Paul was on the point of asking what then he did talk about, but discretion checked it and he said instead: 'Do you think he's unhappy at home?'

She seemed to wonder. 'At home?'

'I mean in his relations with his wife. He has a mystifying little way of alluding to her.'

'Not to me,' said Marian Fancourt with her clear eyes. 'That wouldn't be right, would it?' she asked gravely.

'Not particularly; so I'm glad he doesn't mention her to you. To praise her might bore you, and he has no business to do anything else. Yet he knows you better than me.'

'Ah but he respects *you*!' the girl cried as with envy.

Her visitor stared a moment, then broke into a laugh. 'Doesn't he respect you?'

'Of course, but not in the same way. He respects what you've done – he told me so the other day.'

Paul drank it in, but retained his faculties. 'When you went to look at types?'

'Yes – we found so many: he has such an observation of them! He talked a great deal about your book. He says it's really important.'

'Important! Ah the grand creature!' – and the author of the work in question groaned for joy.

'He was wonderfully amusing, he was inexpressibly droll, while we walked about. He sees everything; he has so many comparisons and images, and they're always exactly right. C'est d'un trouvé,[35] as they say!'

'Yes, with his gifts, such things as he ought to have done!' Paul sighed.

'And don't you think he *has* done them?'

Ah it was just the point. 'A part of them, and of course even that part's immense. But he might have been one of the greatest. However, let us not make this an hour of qualifications. Even as they stand,' our friend earnestly concluded, 'his writings are a mine of gold.'

To this proposition she ardently responded, and for half an hour the pair talked over the Master's principal productions. She knew them well – she knew them even better than her visitor, who was struck with her critical intelligence and with something large and bold in the movement in her mind. She said things that startled him and that evidently had come to her directly; they weren't picked-up phrases – she placed them too well. St George had been right about her being first-rate, about her not being afraid to gush, not remembering that she must be proud. Suddenly something came back to her, and she said: 'I recollect that he did speak of Mrs St George to me once. He said, apropos of something or other, that she didn't care for perfection.'

'That's a great crime in an artist's wife,' Paul returned.

'Yes, poor thing!' and the girl sighed with a suggestion of many reflexions, some of them mitigating. But she presently added: 'Ah perfection, perfection – how one ought to go in for it! I wish *I* could.'

'Every one can in his way,' her companion opined.

'In *his* way, yes – but not in hers. Women are so hampered – so condemned! Yet it's a kind of dishonour if you don't, when you want to *do* something, isn't it?' Miss Fancourt pursued, dropping one train in her quickness to take up another, an accident that was common with her. So these two young persons sat discussing high themes in their eclectic drawing-room, in their London 'season'[36] – discussing, with extreme seriousness, the high theme of perfection. It must be said in extenuation of this eccentricity that they were interested in the business. Their tone had truth and their emotion beauty; they weren't posturing for each other or for some one else.

The subject was so wide that they found themselves reducing it; the perfection to which for the moment they agreed to confine their speculations was that of the valid, the exemplary work of art. Our young woman's imagination, it appeared, had wandered far in that direction, and her guest had the rare delight of feeling in their conversation a full interchange. This episode will have lived for years in his memory and even in his wonder; it had the quality that fortune distils in a single drop at a time – the quality that lubricates many ensuing frictions. He still, whenever he likes, has a vision of the room, the bright red sociable talkative room with the curtains that, by a stroke of successful audacity, had the note of vivid blue. He remembers where certain things stood, the particular book open on the table and the almost intense odour of the flowers placed, at the left, somewhere behind him. These facts were the fringe, as it were, of a fine special agitation which had its birth in those two hours and of which perhaps the main sign was in its leading him inwardly and repeatedly to breathe 'I had no idea there was any one like this! – I had no idea there was any one like this!' Her freedom amazed him and charmed him – it seemed so to simplify the practical question. She was on the footing of an independent personage – a motherless girl who had passed out of her teens and had a position and responsibilities, who wasn't held down to the limitations of a little miss. She came and went with no dragged duenna,[37] she received people alone, and, though she was totally without hardness, the question of protection or patronage had no relevancy in regard to her. She gave such an impression of the clear and the noble combined with the easy and the natural that in spite of her eminent modern situation she suggested no sort of sisterhood with the 'fast' girl.[38] Modern she was indeed, and made Paul Overt, who loved old colour, the golden glaze of time, think with some alarm of the muddled palette of the future. He couldn't get used to her interest in the arts he cared for; it seemed too good to be real – it was so unlikely an adventure to tumble into such a well of sympathy. One might stray into the desert easily – that was on the cards and that was the law of life; but it was too rare an accident to stumble on a crystal well. Yet if her aspirations seemed at one moment too extravagant to be real they struck him at the next as too intelligent to be false. They were both high and lame, and, whims for whims, he preferred them to any he had met in a like relation. It was probable enough she would leave them behind – exchange them for politics or 'smartness' or mere prolific maternity, as was the custom of scribbling daubing educated flattered girls in an age of luxury and a society of leisure. He noted that the water-colours on the walls of the room she sat in had mainly the quality of being naïves, and reflected that naïveté in art is like a zero in a number: its importance depends on the figure it is united with. Meanwhile, however, he had fallen in love with her. Before he went away, at any rate, he said to her: 'I thought St George was coming to see you to-day, but he doesn't turn up.'

For a moment he supposed she was going to cry 'Comment donc?[39] Did you come here only to meet him?' But the next he became aware of how little such a speech would have fallen in with any note of flirtation he had as yet perceived in her. She only replied: 'Ah yes, but I don't think he'll come. He recommended me not to expect him.' Then she gaily but all gently added: 'He said it wasn't fair to you. But I think I could manage two.'

'So could I,' Paul Overt returned, stretching the point a little to meet her. In reality his appreciation of the occasion was so completely an appreciation of the woman before him that another figure in the scene, even so esteemed a one as St George, might for the hour have appealed to him vainly. He left the house wondering what the great man had meant by its not being fair to him; and, still more than that, whether he had actually stayed away from the force of that idea. As he took his course through the Sunday solitude of Manchester Square, swinging his stick and with a good deal of emotion fermenting in his soul, it appeared to him he was living in a world strangely magnanimous. Miss Fancourt had told him it was possible she should be away, and that her father should be, on the following Sunday, but that she had the hope of a visit from him in the other event. She promised to let him know should their absence fail, and then he might act accordingly. After he had passed into one of the streets that open from the Square he stopped, without definite intentions, looking sceptically for a cab. In a moment he saw a hansom roll through the place from the other side and come a part of the way toward him. He was on the point of hailing the driver when he noticed a 'fare' within; then he waited, seeing the man prepare to deposit his passenger by pulling up at one of the houses. The house was apparently the one he himself had just quitted; at least he drew that inference as he recognised Henry St George in the person who stepped out of the hansom. Paul turned off as quickly as if he had been caught in the act of spying. He gave up his cab – he preferred to walk; he would go nowhere else. He was glad St George hadn't renounced his visit altogether – that would have been too absurd. Yes, the world was magnanimous, and even he himself felt so as, on looking at his watch, he noted but six o'clock, so that he could mentally congratulate his successor on having an hour still to sit in Miss Fancourt's drawing-room. He himself might use that hour for another visit, but by the time he reached the Marble Arch[40] the idea of such a course had become incongruous to him. He passed beneath that architectural effort and walked into the Park till he had got upon the spreading grass. Here he continued to walk; he took his way across the elastic turf and came out by the Serpentine.[41] He watched with a friendly eye the diversions of the London people, he bent a glance almost encouraging on the young ladies paddling their sweethearts about the lake and the guardsmen tickling tenderly with their bearskins the artificial flowers in the Sunday hats of their partners. He prolonged his meditative walk;

he went into Kensington Gardens, he sat upon the penny chairs, he looked at the little sail-boats launched upon the round pond and was glad he had no engagement to dine. He repaired for this purpose, very late, to his club, where he found himself unable to order a repast and told the waiter to bring whatever there was. He didn't even observe what he was served with, and he spent the evening in the library of the establishment, pretending to read an article in an American magazine. He failed to discover what it was about; it appeared in a dim way to be about Marian Fancourt.

Quite late in the week she wrote to him that she was not to go into the country – it had only just been settled. Her father, she added, would never settle anything, but put it all on her. She felt her responsibility – she had to – and since she was forced this was the way she had decided. She mentioned no reasons, which gave our friend all the clearer field for bold conjecture about them. In Manchester Square on this second Sunday he esteemed his fortune less good, for she had three or four other visitors. But there were three or four compensations; perhaps the greatest of which was that, learning how her father had after all, at the last hour, gone out of town alone, the bold conjecture I just now spoke of found itself becoming a shade more bold. And then her presence was her presence, and the personal red room was there and was full of it, whatever phantoms passed and vanished, emitting incomprehensible sounds. Lastly, he had the resource of staying till every one had come and gone and of believing this grateful to her, though she gave no particular sign. When they were alone together he came to his point. 'But St George did come – last Sunday. I saw him as I looked back.'

'Yes, but it was the last time.'

'The last time?'

'He said he would never come again.'

Paul Overt stared. 'Does he mean he wishes to cease to see you?'

'I don't know, what he means,' the girl bravely smiled. 'He won't at any rate see me here.'

'And pray why not?'

'I haven't the least idea,' said Marian Fancourt, whose visitor found her more perversely sublime than ever yet as she professed this clear helplessness.

V

'Oh I say, I want you to stop a little,' Henry St George said to him at eleven o'clock the night he dined with the head of the profession. The company – none of it indeed *of* the profession – had been numerous and was taking its leave; our young man, after bidding good-night to his hostess, had put out his hand in farewell to the master of the house. Besides drawing from the latter the protest I have cited this movement provoked a further priceless word about their chance now to have a talk, their going into his room, his having still everything to say. Paul Overt was all delight at this kindness; nevertheless he mentioned in weak jocose qualification the bare fact that he had promised to go to another place which was at a considerable distance.

'Well then you'll break your promise, that's all. You quite awful humbug!' St George added in a tone that confirmed our young man's ease.

'Certainly I'll break it – but it was a real promise.'

'Do you mean to Miss Fancourt? You're following her?' his friend asked.

He answered by a question. 'Oh is *she* going?'

'Base impostor!' his ironic host went on. 'I've treated you handsomely on the article of that young lady: I won't make another concession. Wait three minutes – I'll be with you.' He gave himself to his departing guests, accompanied the long-trained ladies to the door. It was a hot night, the windows were open, the sound of the quick carriages and of the linkmen's[42] call came into the house. The affair had rather glittered; a sense of festal things was in the heavy air: not only the influence of that particular entertainment, but the suggestion of the wide hurry of pleasure which in London on summer nights fills so many of the happier quarters of the complicated town. Gradually Mrs St George's drawing-room emptied itself; Paul was left alone with his hostess, to whom he explained the motive of his waiting. 'Ah yes, some intellectual, some *professional*, talk,' she leered; 'at this season doesn't one miss it? Poor dear Henry, I'm so glad!' The young man looked out of the window a moment, at the called hansoms that lurched up, at the smooth broughams that rolled away. When he turned round Mrs St George had disappeared; her husband's voice rose to him from below – he was laughing and talking, in the portico, with some lady who awaited her carriage. Paul had solitary possession, for some minutes, of the warm deserted rooms where the covered tinted lamplight was soft, the seats had been pushed about and the odour of flowers lingered. They were large, they were pretty, they contained objects of value; everything in the picture told of a 'good house.' At the end of five minutes a servant came in with a request from the Master that he would join him downstairs; upon which, descending, he followed his conductor through a long passage to an apartment thrown out, in the rear of the habitation, for the special requirements, as he guessed, of a busy man of letters.

St George was in his shirt-sleeves in the middle of a large high room – a room without windows, but with a wide skylight at the top, that of a place of exhibition. It was furnished as a library, and the serried bookshelves rose to the ceiling, a surface of incomparable tone produced by dimly-gilt 'backs' interrupted here and there by the suspension of old prints and drawings. At the end furthest from the door of admission was a tall desk, of great extent, at which the person using it could write only in the erect posture of a clerk in a counting-house; and stretched from the entrance to this structure was a wide plain band of crimson cloth, as straight as a garden-path and almost as long, where, in his mind's eye, Paul at once beheld the Master pace to and fro during vexed hours – hours, that is, of admirable composition. The servant gave him a coat, an old jacket with a hang of experience, from a cupboard in the wall, retiring afterwards with the garment he had taken off. Paul Overt welcomed the coat; it was a coat for talk, it promised confidences – having visibly received so many – and had tragic literary elbows. 'Ah we're practical – we're practical!' St George said as he saw his visitor look the place over. 'Isn't it a good big cage for going round and round? My wife invented it and she locks me up here every morning.'

Our young man breathed – by way of tribute – with a certain oppression. 'You don't miss a window – a place to look out?'

'I did at first awfully; but her calculation was just. It saves time, it has saved me many months in these ten years. Here I stand, under the eye of day – in London of course, very often, it's rather a bleared old eye – walled in to my trade. I can't get away – so the room's a fine lesson in concentration. I've learnt the lesson, I think; look at that big bundle of proof and acknowledge it.' He pointed to a fat roll of papers, on one of the tables, which had not been undone.

'Are you bringing out another –?' Paul asked in a tone the fond deficiencies of which he didn't recognize till his companion burst out laughing, and indeed scarce even then.

'You humbug, you humbug!' – St George appeared to enjoy caressing him, as it were, with that opprobrium. 'Don't I know what you think of them?' he asked, standing there with his hands in his pockets and with a new kind of smile. It was as if he were going to let his young votary see him all now.

'Upon my word in that case you know more than I do!' the latter ventured to respond, revealing a part of the torment of being able neither clearly to esteem nor distinctly to renounce him.

'My dear fellow,' said the more and more interesting Master, 'don't imagine I talk about my books specifically; they're not a decent subject – il ne manquerait plus que ça![43] I'm not so bad as you may apprehend. About myself, yes, a little, if you like; though it wasn't for that I brought you down here. I want to ask you something – very much indeed; I value this chance. Therefore sit down. We're practical, but there *is* a sofa, you see – for she does humour my poor bones so far. Like all really great administrators and disciplinarians she knows when wisely to relax.' Paul sank into the corner of a deep leathern couch, but his friend remained standing and explanatory. 'If you don't mind, in this room, this is my habit. From the door to the desk and from the desk to the door. That shakes up my imagination gently; and don't you see what a good thing it is that there's no window for her to fly out of? The eternal standing as I write (I stop at that bureau and put it down, when anything comes, and so we go on) was rather wearisome at first, but we adopted it with an eye to the long run: you're in better order – if your legs don't break down! – and you can keep it up for more years. Oh we're practical – we're practical!' St George repeated, going to the table and taking up all mechanically the bundle of proofs. But, pulling off the wrapper, he had a change of attention that appealed afresh to our hero. He lost himself a moment, examining the sheets of his new book, while the younger man's eyes wandered over the room again.

'Lord, what good things I should do if I had such a charming place as this to do them in!' Paul reflected. The outer world, the world of accident and ugliness, was so successfully excluded, and within the rich protecting square, beneath the patronising sky, the dream-figures, the summoned company, could hold their particular revel. It was a fond prevision of Overt's rather than an observation on actual data, for which occasions had been too few, that the Master thus more closely viewed would have the quality, the charming gift, of flashing out, all surprisingly, in personal intercourse and at moments of suspended or perhaps even of diminished expectation. A happy relation with him would be a thing proceeding by jumps, not by traceable stages.

'Do you read them – really?' he asked, laying down the proofs on Paul's enquiring of him how soon the work would be published. And when the young man answered 'Oh yes, always,' he was moved to mirth again by something he caught in his manner of saying that. 'You go to see your grandmother on her birthday – and very proper it is, especially as she won't last for ever. She has lost every faculty and every sense; she neither sees, nor hears, nor speaks; but all customary pieties and kindly habits are respectable. Only you're strong if you *do* read 'em! *I* couldn't, my dear fellow. You *are* strong, I know; and that's just a part of what I wanted to say to you. You're very strong indeed. I've been going into your other things – they've interested me immensely. Some one ought to have told me about them before – some one I could believe. But whom can one believe? You're wonderfully on the right road – it's awfully decent work. Now do you mean to keep it up? – that's what I want to ask you.'

'Do I mean to do others?' Paul asked, looking up from his sofa at his erect inquisitor and feeling partly like a happy little boy when the schoolmaster is gay, and partly like some pilgrim of old who might have consulted a world-famous oracle. St George's own performance had been infirm, but as an adviser he would be infallible.

'Others – others? Ah the number won't matter; one other would do, if it were really a further step — a throb of the same effort. What I mean is have you it in your heart to go in for some sort of decent perfection?'

'Ah decency, ah perfection —!' the young man sincerely sighed. 'I talked of them the other Sunday with Miss Fancourt.'

It produced on the Master's part a laugh of odd acrimony. 'Yes, they'll "talk" of them as much as you like! But they'll do little to help one to them. There's no obligation of course; only you strike me as capable,' he went on. 'You must have thought it all over. I can't believe you're without a plan. That's the sensation you give me, and it's so rare that it really stirs one up — it makes you remarkable. If you haven't a plan, if you *don't* mean to keep it up, surely you're within your rights; it's nobody's business, no one can force you, and not more than two or three people will notice you don't go straight. The others — *all* the rest, every blest soul in England, will think you do — will think you *are* keeping it up: upon my honour they will! I shall be one of the two or three who know better. Now the question is whether you can do it for two or three. Is that the stuff you're made of?'

It locked his guest a minute as in closed throbbing arms. 'I could do it for one, if you were the one.'

'Don't say that; I don't deserve it; it scorches me,' he protested with eyes suddenly grave and glowing. 'The "one" is of course one's self, one's conscience, one's idea, the singleness of one's aim. I think of that pure spirit as a man thinks of a woman he has in some detested hour of his youth loved and forsaken. She haunts him with reproachful eyes, she lives for ever before him. As an artist, you know, I've married for money.' Paul stared and even blushed a little, confounded by this avowal; whereupon his host, observing the expression of his face, dropped a quick laugh and pursued: 'You don't follow my figure. I'm not speaking of my dear wife, who had a small fortune — which, however, was not my bribe. I fell in love with her, as many other people have done. I refer to the mercenary muse whom I led to the altar of literature. Don't, my boy, put your nose into *that* yoke. The awful jade will lead you a life!'

Our hero watched him, wondering and deeply touched. 'Haven't you been happy!'

'Happy? It's a kind of hell.'

'There are things I should like to ask you,' Paul said after a pause.

'Ask me anything in all the world. I'd turn myself inside out to save you.'

'To "save" me?' he quavered.

'To make you stick to it — to make you see it through. As I said to you the other night at Summersoft, let my example be vivid to you.'

'Why your books are not so bad as that,' said Paul, fairly laughing and feeling that if ever a fellow had breathed the air of art —!

'So bad as what?'

'Your talent's so great that it's in everything you do, in what's less good as well as in what's best. You've some forty volumes to show for it – forty volumes of wonderful life, of rare observation, of magnificent ability.'

'I'm very clever, of course I know that' – but it was a thing, in fine, this author made nothing of. 'Lord, what rot they'd all be if I hadn't been! I'm a successful charlatan,' he went on – 'I've been able to pass off my system. But do you know what it is? It's *carton-pierre*.'[44]

'*Carton-pierre?*' Paul was struck, and gaped.

'Lincrusta-Walton!'[45]

'Ah don't say such things – you make me bleed!' the younger man protested. 'I see you in a beautiful fortunate home, living in comfort and honour.'

'Do you call it honour?' – his host took him up with an intonation that often comes back to him. 'That's what I want *you* to go in for. I mean the real thing. This is brummagem.'[46]

'Brummagem?' Paul ejaculated while his eyes wandered, by a movement natural at the moment, over the luxurious room.

'Ah they make it so well to-day – it's wonderfully deceptive!'

Our friend thrilled with the interest and perhaps even more with the pity of it. Yet he wasn't afraid to seem to patronise when he could still so far envy. 'Is it deceptive that I find you living with every appearance of domestic felicity – blest with a devoted, accomplished wife, with children whose acquaintance I haven't yet had the pleasure of making, but who *must* be delightful young people, from what I know of their parents?'

St George smiled as for the candour of his question. 'It's all excellent, my dear fellow – heaven forbid I should deny it. I've made a great deal of money; my wife has known how to take care of it, to use it without wasting it, to put a good bit of it by, to make it fructify. I've got a loaf on the shelf; I've got everything in fact but the great thing.'

'The great thing?' Paul kept echoing.

'The sense of having done the best – the sense which is the real life of the artist and the absence of which is his death, of having drawn from his intellectual instrument the finest music that nature had hidden in it, of having played it as it should be played. He either does that or he doesn't – and if he doesn't he isn't worth speaking of. Therefore, precisely, those who really know *don't* speak of him. He may still hear a great chatter, but what he hears most is the incorruptible silence of Fame. I've squared her, you may say, for my little hour – but what's my little hour? Don't imagine for a moment,' the Master pursued, 'that I'm such a cad as to have brought you down here to abuse or to complain of my wife to you. She's a woman of distinguished qualities, to whom my obligations are immense; so that, if you please, we'll say nothing about her. My boys – my children are all boys – are straight and strong, thank God, and have no poverty of growth about them, no penury of needs. I receive periodically the most satisfactory attestation from Harrow, from Oxford, from Sandhurst[47] – oh we've done the best for them! – of their eminence as living thriving consuming organisms.'

'It must be delightful to feel that the son of one's loins is at Sandhurst,' Paul remarked enthusiastically.

'It is – it's charming. Oh I'm a patriot!'

The young man then could but have the greater tribute of questions to pay. 'Then what did you mean – the other night at Summersoft – by saying that children are a curse?'

'My dear youth, on what basis are we talking?' and St George dropped upon the sofa at a short distance from him. Sitting a little sideways he leaned back against the opposite arm with his hands raised and interlocked behind his head. 'On the supposition that a certain perfection's possible and even desirable – isn't it so? Well, all I say is that one's children interfere with perfection. One's wife interferes. Marriage interferes.'

'You think then the artist shouldn't marry?'

'He does so at his peril – he does so at his cost.'

'Not even when his wife's in sympathy with his work?'

'She never is – she can't be! Women haven't a conception of such things.'

'Surely they on occasion work themselves,' Paul objected.

'Yes, very badly indeed. Oh of course, often, they think they understand, they think they sympathise. Then it is they're most dangerous. Their idea is that you shall do a great lot and get a great lot of money. Their great nobleness and virtue, their exemplary conscientiousness as British females, is in keeping you up to that. My wife makes all my bargains with my publishers for me, and has done so for twenty years. She does it consummately well – that's why I'm really pretty well off. Aren't you the father of their innocent babes, and will you withhold from them their natural sustenance? You asked me the other night if they're not an immense incentive. Of course they are – there's no doubt of that!'

Paul turned it over: it took, from eyes he had never felt open so wide, so much looking at. 'For myself I've an idea I need incentives.'

'Ah well then, n'en parlons plus!'[48] his companion handsomely smiled.

'*You* are an incentive, I maintain,' the young man went on. 'You don't affect me in the way you'd apparently like to. Your great success is what I see – the pomp of Ennismore Gardens!'

'Success?' – St George's eyes had a cold fine light. 'Do you call it success to be spoken of as you'd speak of me if you were sitting here with another artist –

a young man intelligent and sincere like yourself? Do you call it success to make you blush – as you *would* blush! – if some foreign critic (some fellow, of course I mean, who should know what he was talking about and should have shown you he did, as foreign critics like to show it) were to say to you: "He's the one, in this country, whom they consider the most perfect, isn't he?" Is it success to be the occasion of a young Englishman's having to stammer as you would have to stammer at such a moment for old England? No, no; success is to have made people wriggle to another tune. Do try it!'

Paul continued all gravely to glow. 'Try what?'

'Try to do some really good work.'

'Oh I want to, heaven knows!'

'Well, you can't do it without sacrifices – don't believe that for a moment,' the Master said. 'I've made none. I've had everything. In other words I've missed everything.'

'You've had the full rich masculine human general life, with all the responsibilities and duties and burdens and sorrows and joys – all the domestic and social initiations and complications. They must be immensely suggestive, immensely amusing,' Paul anxiously submitted.

'Amusing?'

'For a strong man – yes.'

'They've given me subjects without number, if that's what you mean; but they've taken away at the same time the power to use them. I've touched a thousand things, but which one of them have I turned into gold?[50] The artist has to do only with that – he knows nothing of any baser metal. I've led the life of the world, with my wife and my progeny; the clumsy conventional expensive materialised vulgarised brutalised life of London. We've got everything handsome, even a carriage – we're perfect Philistines and prosperous hospitable eminent people. But, my dear fellow, don't try to stultify yourself and pretend you don't know what we *haven't* got. It's bigger than all the rest. Between artists – come!' the Master wound up. 'You know as well as you sit there that you'd put a pistol-ball into your brain if you had written my books!'

It struck his listener that the tremendous talk promised by him at Summersoft had indeed come off, and with a promptitude, a fulness, with which the latter's young imagination had scarcely reckoned. His impression fairly shook him and he throbbed with the excitement of such deep soundings and such strange confidences. He throbbed indeed with the conflict of his feelings – bewilderment and recognition and alarm, enjoyment and protest and assent, all commingled with tenderness (and a kind of shame in the participation) for the sores and bruises exhibited by so fine a creature, and with a sense of the tragic secret nursed under his trappings. The idea of *his*, Paul Overt's, becoming the occasion of such an act of humility made him flush and pant, at the same time that his consciousness was in certain directions too much alive not to swallow – and not intensely to taste – every offered spoonful of the revelation. It had been his odd fortune to blow upon the deep waters, to make them surge and break in waves of strange eloquence. But how couldn't he give out a passionate contradiction of his host's last extravagance, how couldn't he enumerate to him the parts of his work he loved, the splendid things he had found in it, beyond the compass of any other writer of the day? St George listened a while, courteously; then he said, laying his hand on his visitor's: 'That's all very well; and if your idea's to do nothing better there's no reason you shouldn't have as many good things as I – as many human and material appendages, as many sons or daughters, a wife with as many gowns, a house with as many servants, a stable with as many horses, a heart with as many aches.' The Master got up when he had spoken thus – he stood a moment – near the sofa looking down on his agitated pupil. 'Are you possessed of any property?' it occurred to him to ask.

'None to speak of.'

'Oh well then there's no reason why you shouldn't make a goodish income – if you set about it the right way. Study *me* for that – study me well. You may really have horses.'

Paul sat there some minutes without speaking. He looked straight before him – he turned over many things. His friend had wandered away, taking up a parcel of letters from the table where the roll of proofs had lain. 'What was the book Mrs St George made you burn – the one she didn't like?' our young man brought out.

'The book she made me burn – how did you know that?' The Master looked up from his letters quite without the facial convulsion the pupil had feared.

'I heard her speak of it at Summersoft.'

'Ah yes – she's proud of it. I don't know – it was rather good.'

'What was it about?'

'Let me see.' And he seemed to make an effort to remember. 'Oh yes – it was about myself.' Paul gave an irrepressible groan for the disappearance of such a production, and the elder man went on: 'Oh but *you* should write it – *you* should do me.' And he pulled up – from the restless motion that had come upon him; his fine smile a generous glare. 'There's a subject, my boy: no end of stuff in it!'

Again Paul was silent, but it was all tormenting. 'Are there no women who really understand – who can take part in a sacrifice?'

'How can they take part? They themselves are the sacrifice. They're the idol and the altar and the flame.'

'Isn't there even *one* who sees further?' Paul continued.

For a moment St George made no answer; after which, having torn up his letters, he came back to the point all ironic. 'Of course I know the one you mean. But not even Miss Fancourt.'

'I thought you admired her so much.'

'It's impossible to admire her more. Are you in love with her?' St George asked.

'Yes,' Paul Overt presently said.

'Well then give it up.'

Paul stared. 'Give up my "love"?'

'Bless me, no. Your idea.' And then as our hero but still gazed: 'The one you talked with her about. The idea of a decent perfection.'

'She'd help it – she'd help it!' the young man cried.

'For about a year – the first year, yes. After that she'd be as a millstone round its neck.'

Paul frankly wondered. 'Why she has a passion for the real thing, for good work – for everything you and I care for most.'

'"You and I" is charming, my dear fellow!' his friend laughed. 'She has it indeed, but she'd have a still greater passion for her children – and very proper too. She'd insist on everything's being made comfortable, advantageous, propitious for them. That isn't the artist's business.'

'The artist – the artist! Isn't he a man all the same?'

St George had a grand grimace. 'I mostly think not. You know as well as I what he has to do: the concentration, the finish, the independence he must strive for from the moment he begins to wish his work really decent. Ah my young friend, his relation to women, and especially to the one he's most intimately concerned with, is at the mercy of the damning face that whereas he can in the nature of things have but one standard, they have about fifty. That's what makes them so superior,' St George amusingly added. 'Fancy an artist with a change of standards as you'd have a change of shirts or of dinner-plates. To *do* it – to do it and make it divine – is the only thing he has to think about. "Is it done or not?" is his only question. Not "Is it done as well as a proper solicitude for my dear little family will allow?" He has nothing to do with the relative – he has only to do with the absolute; and a dear little family may represent a dozen relatives.'

'Then you don't allow him the common passions and affections of men?' Paul asked.

'Hasn't he a passion, an affection, which includes all the rest? Besides, let him have all the passions he likes – if he only keeps his independence. He must be able to be poor.'

Paul slowly got up. 'Why then did you advise me to make up to her?'

St George laid a hand on his shoulder. 'Because she'd make a splendid wife! And I hadn't read you then.'

The young man had a strained smile. 'I wish you had left me alone!'

'I didn't know that that wasn't good enough for you,' his host returned.

'What a false position, what a condemnation of the artist, that he's a mere disfranchised monk and can produce his effect only by giving up personal happiness. What an arraignment of art!' Paul went on with a trembling voice.

'Ah you don't imagine by chance that I'm defending art? "Arraignment" – I should think so! Happy the societies in which it hasn't made its appearance, for from the moment it comes they have a consuming ache, they have an incurable corruption, in their breast. Most assuredly is the artist in a false position! But I thought we were taking him for granted. Pardon me,' St George continued: '"Ginistrella" made me!'

Paul stood looking at the floor – one o'clock struck, in the stillness, from a neighbouring church-tower. 'Do you think she'd ever look at me?' he put to his friend at last.

'Miss Fancourt – as a suitor? Why shouldn't I think it? That's why I've tried to favour you – I've had a little chance or two of bettering your opportunity.'

'Forgive my asking you, but do you mean by keeping away yourself?' Paul said with a blush.

'I'm an old idiot – my place isn't there,' St George stated gravely.

'I'm nothing yet, I've no fortune; and there must be so many others,' his companion pursued.

The Master took this considerably in, but made little of it. 'You're a gentleman and a man of genius. I think you might do something.'

'But if I must give that up – the genius?'

'Lots of people, you know, think I've kept mine,' St George wonderfully grinned.

'You've a genius for mystification!' Paul declared, but grasping his hand gratefully in attenuation of this judgement.

'Poor dear boy, I do worry you! But try, try, all the same. I think your chances are good and you'll win a great prize.'

Paul held fast the other's hand a minute; he looked into the strange deep face. 'No, I *am* an artist – I can't help it!'

'Ah show it then!' St George pleadingly broke out. 'Let me see before I die the thing I most want, the thing I yearn for: a life in which the passion – ours – is really intense. If you can be rare don't fail of it! Think what it is – how it counts – how it lives!'

They had moved to the door and he had closed both his hands over his companion's. Here they paused again and our hero breathed deep. 'I want to live!'

'In what sense?'

'In the greatest.'

'Well then stick to it – see it through.'

'With your sympathy – your help?'

'Count on that – you'll be a great figure to me. Count on my highest appreciation, my devotion. You'll give me satisfaction – if that has any weight with you!' After which, as Paul appeared still to waver, his host added: 'Do you remember what you said to me at Summersoft?'

'Something infatuated, no doubt!'

' "I'll do anything in the world you tell me." You said that.'

'And you hold me to it?'

'Ah what am I?' the Master expressively sighed.

'Lord, what things I shall have to do!' Paul almost moaned as he departed.

VI

'It goes on too much abroad – hang abroad!' These or something like them had been the Master's remarkable words in relation to the action of 'Ginistrella'; and yet, though they had made a sharp impression on the author of that work, like almost all spoken words from the same source, he a week after the conversation I have noted left England for a long absence and full of brave intentions. It is not a perversion of the truth to pronounce that encounter the direct cause of his departure. If the oral utterance of the eminent writer had the privilege of moving him deeply it was especially on his turning it over at leisure, hours and days later, that it appeared to yield him its full meaning and exhibit its extreme importance. He spent the summer in Switzerland and, having in September begun a new task, determined not to cross the Alps till he should have made a good start. To this end he returned to a quiet corner he knew well, on the edge of the Lake of Geneva and within sight of the towers of Chillon:[51] a region and a view for which he had an affection that sprang from old associations and was capable of mysterious revivals and refreshments. Here he lingered late, till the snow was on the nearer hills, almost down to the limit to which he could climb when his stint, on the shortening afternoons, was performed. The autumn was fine, the lake was blue and his book took form and direction. These felicities, for the time, embroidered his life, which he suffered to cover him with its mantle. At the end of six weeks he felt he had learnt St George's lesson by heart, had tested and proved its doctrine. Nevertheless he did a very inconsistent thing: before crossing the Alps he wrote to Marian Fancourt. He was aware of the perversity of this act, and it was only as a luxury, an amusement, the reward of a strenuous autumn, that he justified it. She had asked of him no such favour when, shortly before he left London, three days after their dinner in Ennismore Gardens, he went to take leave of her. It was true she had had no ground – he hadn't named his intention of absence. He had kept his counsel for want of due assurance: it was that particular visit that was, the next thing, to settle the matter. He had paid the visit to see how much he really cared for her, and quick departure, without so much as an explicit farewell, was the sequel to this enquiry, the answer to which had created within him a deep yearning. When he wrote her from Clarens[52] he noted that he owed her an explanation (more than three months after!) for not having told her what he was doing.

She replied now briefly but promptly, and gave him a striking piece of news: that of the death, a week before, of Mrs St George. This exemplary woman had succumbed, in the country, to a violent attack of inflammation of the lungs – he would remember that for a long time she had been delicate. Miss Fancourt added that she believed her husband overwhelmed by the blow; he would miss her too terribly – she had been everything in life to him. Paul Overt, on this, immediately wrote to St George. He would from the day of their parting have been glad to remain in communication with him, but had hitherto lacked the right excuse for troubling so busy a man. Their long nocturnal talk came back to him in every detail, but this was no bar to an expression of proper sympathy with the head of the profession, for hadn't that very talk made it clear that the late accomplished lady was the influence that ruled his life? What catastrophe could be more cruel than the extinction of such an influence? This was to be exactly the tone taken by St George in answering his young friend upwards of a month later. He made no allusion of course to their important discussion. He spoke of his wife as frankly and generously as if he had quite forgotten that occasion, and the feeling of deep bereavement was visible in his words. 'She took everything off my hands – off my mind. She carried on our life with the greatest art, the rarest devotion, and I was free, as few men can have been, to drive my pen, to shut myself up with my trade. This was a rare service – the highest she could have rendered me. Would I could have acknowledged it more fitly!'

A certain bewilderment, for our hero, disengaged itself from these remarks: they struck him as a contradiction, a retractation, strange on the part of a man who hadn't the excuse of witlessness. He had certainly not expected his correspondent to rejoice in the death of his wife, and it was perfectly in order that the rupture of a tie of more than twenty years should have left him sore. But if she had been so clear a blessing what in the name of consistency had the dear man meant by turning *him* upside down that night – by dosing him to that degree, at the most sensitive hour of his life, with the doctrine of renunciation? If Mrs St George was an irreparable loss, then her husband's inspired advice had been a bad joke and renunciation was a mistake. Overt was on the point of rushing back to London to show that, for his part, he was perfectly willing to consider it so, and he went so far as to take the manuscript of the first chapters of his new book out of his table-drawer and insert it into a pocket of his portmanteau. This led to his catching a glimpse of certain pages he hadn't looked at for months, and that accident, in turn, to his being struck with the high promise they revealed – a rare result of such retrospections, which it was his habit to avoid as much as possible: they usually brought home to him that the glow of composition might be a purely subjective and misleading emotion. On this occasion a certain belief in himself disengaged itself whimsically from the serried erasures of his first draft, making him think it best after all to pursue his present trial to the end. If he could write so well under the rigour of privation it might be a mistake to change the conditions before that spell had spent itself. He would go back to London of course, but he would go back only when he should have finished his book. This was the vow he privately made, restoring his manuscript to the table-drawer. It may be added that it took him a long time to finish his book, for the subject was as difficult as it was fine, and he was literally embarrassed by the fulness of his notes. Something within him warned him he must make it supremely good – otherwise he should lack, as regards his private behaviour, a handsome excuse. He had a horror of this deficiency and found himself as firm as need be on the question of the lamp and the file. He crossed the Alps at last and spent the winter, the spring, the ensuing summer, in Italy, where still, at the end of a twelvemonth, his task was unachieved. 'Stick to it – see it through': this general injunction of St George's was good also for the particular case. He applied it to the utmost, with the result that when in its slow order the summer had come round again he felt he had given all that was in him. This time he put his papers into his portmanteau, with the address of his publisher attached, and took his way northward.

He had been absent from London for two years; two years which, seeming to count as more, had made such a difference in his own life – through the production of a novel far stronger, he believed, than 'Ginistrella' – that he turned out into Piccadilly, the morning after his arrival, with a vague expectation of changes, of finding great things had happened. But there were few transformations in Piccadilly – only three or four big red houses where there had been low black ones – and the brightness of the end of June peeped through the rusty railings of the Green Park and glittered in the varnish of the rolling carriages as he had seen it in other, more cursory Junes. It was a greeting he appreciated; it seemed friendly and pointed, added to the exhilaration of his finished book, of his having his own country and the huge oppressive amusing city that suggested everything, that contained everything, under his hand again. 'Stay at home and do things here – do subjects we can measure,' St George had said; and now it struck him he should ask nothing better than to stay at home for ever. Late in the afternoon he took his way to Manchester Square, looking out for a number he hadn't forgotten. Miss Fancourt, however, was not at home, so that he turned rather dejectedly from the door. His movement brought him face to face with a gentleman just approaching it and recognized on another glance as Miss Fancourt's father. Paul saluted this personage, and the General returned the greeting with his customary good manner – a manner so good, however, that you could never tell whether it meant he placed you. The disappointed caller felt the impulse to address him; then, hesitating, became both aware of having no particular remark to make, and convinced that though the old soldier remembered him he remembered him wrong. He therefore went his way without computing the irresistible effect his own evident recognition would have on the General, who never neglected a chance to gossip. Our young man's face was expressive, and observation seldom let it pass. He hadn't taken ten steps before he heard himself called after with a friendly semi-articulate 'Er – I beg your pardon!' He turned round and the General, smiling at him from the porch, said: 'Won't you come in? I won't leave you the advantage of me!' Paul declined to come in, and then felt regret, for Miss Fancourt, so late in the afternoon, might return at any moment. But her father gave him no second chance; he appeared mainly to wish not to have struck him as ungracious. A further look at the visitor had recalled something, enough at least to enable him to say: 'You've come back, you've come back?' Paul was on the point of replying that he had come back the night before, but he suppressed, the next instant, this strong light on the immediacy of his visit and, giving merely a general assent, alluded to the young lady he deplored not having found. He had come late in the hope she would be in. 'I'll tell her – I'll tell her,' said the old man; and then he added quickly, gallantly: 'You'll be giving us something new? It's a long time, isn't it?' Now he remembered him right.

'Rather long. I'm very slow,' Paul explained. 'I met you at Summersoft a long time ago.'

'Oh yes – with Henry St George. I remember very well. Before his poor wife –' General Fancourt paused a moment, smiling a little less. 'I dare say you know.'

'About Mrs St George's death? Certainly – I heard at the time.'

'Oh no, I mean – I mean he's to be married.'

'Ah I've not heard that!' But just as Paul was about to add 'To whom?' the General crossed his intention.

'When did you come back? I know you've been away – by my daughter. She was very sorry. You ought to give her something new.'

'I came back last night,' said our young man, to whom something had occurred which made his speech for the moment a little thick.

'Ah most kind of you to come so soon. Couldn't you turn up at dinner?'

'At dinner?' Paul just mechanically repeated, not liking to ask whom St George was going to marry, but thinking only of that.

'There are several people, I believe. Certainly St George. Or afterwards if you like better. I believe my daughter expects – ' He appeared to notice something in the visitor's raised face (on his steps he stood higher) which led him to interrupt himself, and the interruption gave him a momentary sense of awkwardness, from which he sought a quick issue. 'Perhaps then you haven't heard she's to be married.'

Paul gaped again. 'To be married?'

'To Mr St George – it has just been settled. Odd marriage, isn't it?' Our listener uttered no opinion on this point: he only continued to stare.

'But I dare say it will do – she's so awfully literary!' said the General.

Paul had turned very red. 'Oh it's a surprise – very interesting, very charming! I'm afraid I can't dine – so many thanks!'

'Well, you must come to the wedding!' cried the General. 'Oh I remember that day at Summersoft. He's a great man, you know.'

'Charming – charming!' Paul stammered for retreat. He shook hands with the General and got off. His face was red and he had the sense of its growing more and more crimson. All the evening at home – he went straight to his rooms and remained there dinnerless – his cheek burned at intervals as if it had been smitten. He didn't understand what had happened to him, what trick had been played him, what treachery practised. 'None, none,' he said to himself. 'I've nothing to do with it. I'm out of it – it's none of my business.' But that bewildered murmur was followed again and again by the incongruous ejaculation: 'Was it a plan – was it a plan?' Sometimes he cried to himself, breathless, 'Have I been duped, sold, swindled?' If at all, he was an absurd, an abject victim. It was as if he hadn't lost her till now. He had renounced her, yes; but that was another affair – that was a closed but not a locked door. Now he seemed to see the door quite slammed in his face. Did he expect her to wait – was she to give him his time like that: two years at a stretch? He didn't know what he had expected – he only knew what he hadn't. It wasn't this – it wasn't this. Mystification bitterness and wrath rose and boiled in him when he thought of the deference, the devotion, the credulity with which he had listened to St George. The evening wore on and the light was long; but even when it had darkened he remained without a lamp. He had flung himself on the sofa, where he lay through the hours with his eyes either closed or gazing at the gloom, in the attitude of a man teaching himself to bear something, to bear having been made a fool of. He had made it too easy – that idea passed over him like a hot wave. Suddenly, as he heard eleven o'clock strike, he jumped up, remembering what General Fancourt had said about his coming after dinner. He'd go – he'd see her at least; perhaps he should see what it meant.

He felt as if some of the elements of a hard sum had been given him and the others were wanting: he couldn't do his sum till he had got all his figures.

He dressed and drove quickly, so that by half-past eleven he was at Manchester Square. There were a good many carriages at the door – a party was going on; a circumstance which at the last gave him a slight relief, for now he would rather see her in a crowd. People passed him on the staircase; they were going away, going 'on' with the hunted herdlike movement of London society at night. But sundry groups remained in the drawing-room, and it was some minutes, as she didn't hear him announced, before he discovered and spoke to her. In this short interval he had seen St George talking to a lady before the fireplace; but he at once looked away, feeling unready for an encounter, and therefore couldn't be sure the author of 'Shadowmere' noticed him. At all events he didn't come over; though Miss Fancourt did as soon as she saw him – she almost rushed at him, smiling rustling radiant beautiful. He had forgotten what her head, what her face offered to the sight; she was in white, there were gold figures on her dress and her hair was a casque of gold. He saw in a single moment that she was happy, happy with an aggressive splendour. But she wouldn't speak to him of that, she would speak only of himself.

'I'm so delighted; my father told me. How kind of you to come!' She struck him as so fresh and brave, while his eyes moved over her, that he said to himself irresistibly: 'Why to *him*, why not to youth, to strength, to ambition, to a future? Why, in her rich young force, to failure, to abdication, to superannuation?' In his thought at that sharp moment he blasphemed even against all that had been left of his faith in the peccable master. 'I'm so sorry I missed you,' she went on. 'My father told me. How charming of you to have come so soon!'

'Does that surprise you?' Paul Overt asked.

'The first day? No, from you – nothing that's nice.' She was interrupted by a lady who bade her good-night, and he seemed to read that it cost her nothing to speak to him in that tone; it was her old liberal lavish way, with a certain added amplitude that time had brought; and if this manner began to operate on the spot, at such a juncture in her history, perhaps in the other days too it had meant just as little or as much – a mere mechanical charity, with the difference now that she was satisfied, ready to give but in want of nothing. Oh she was satisfied – and why shouldn't she be? Why shouldn't she have been surprised at his coming the first day – for all the good she had ever got from him? As the lady continued to hold her attention Paul turned from her with a strange irritation in his complicated artistic soul and a sort of disinterested disappointment. She was so happy that it was almost stupid – a disproof of the extraordinary intelligence he had formerly found in her. Didn't she know how bad St George could be, hadn't she recognised the awful thinness –? If she didn't she was nothing, and if she did why such an insolence of serenity? This question expired as our young man's eyes settled at last on the genius who had advised him in a great crisis. St George was still before the chimney-piece, but now he was alone – fixed, waiting, as if he meant to stop after every one – and he met the clouded gaze of the young friend so troubled as to the degree of his right (the right his resentment would have enjoyed) to regard himself as a victim. Somehow the ravage of the question was checked by the Master's radiance. It was as fine in its way as Marian Fancourt's, it denoted the happy human being; but also it represented to Paul Overt that the author of 'Shadowmere' had now definitely ceased to count – ceased to count as a writer. As he smiled a welcome across the place he was almost *banal*, was almost smug. Paul fancied that for a moment he hesitated to make a movement, as if, for all the world, he *had* his bad conscience; then they had already met in the middle of the room and had shaken hands – expressively, cordially on St George's part. With which they had passed back together to where the elder man had been standing, while St George said: 'I hope you're never going away again. I've been dining here; the General told me.' He was handsome, he was young, he looked as if he had still a great fund of life. He bent the friendliest, most unconfessing eyes on his disciple of a couple of years before; asked him about everything, his health, his plans, his late occupations, the new book. 'When will it be out – soon, soon, I hope? Splendid, eh? That's right; you're a comfort, you're a luxury! I've read you all over again these last six months.' Paul waited to see if he'd tell him what the General had told him in the afternoon and what Miss Fancourt, verbally at least, of course hadn't. But as it didn't come out he at last put the question 'Is it true, the great news I hear – that you're to be married?'

'Ah you *have* heard it then?'

'Didn't the General tell you?' Paul asked.

The Master's face was wonderful. 'Tell me what?'

'That he mentioned it to me this afternoon?'

'My dear fellow, I don't remember. We've been in the midst of people. I'm sorry, in that case, that I lose the pleasure, myself, of announcing to you a fact that touches me so nearly. It *is* a fact, strange as it may appear. It has only just become one. Isn't it ridiculous?' St George made this speech without confusion, but on the other hand, so far as our friend could judge, without latent impudence. It struck his interlocutor that, to talk so comfortably and coolly, he must simply have forgotten what had passed between them. His next words, however, showed he hadn't, and they produced, as an appeal to Paul's own memory, an effect which would have been ludicrous if it hadn't been cruel. 'Do you recall the talk we had at my house that night, into which Miss Fancourt's name entered? I've often thought of it since.'

'Yes; no wonder you said what you did' – Paul was careful to meet his eyes.

'In the light of the present occasion? Ah but there was no light then. How could I have foreseen this hour?'

'Didn't you think it probable?'

'Upon my honour, no,' said Henry St George. 'Certainly I owe you that assurance. Think how my situation has changed.'

'I see – I see,' our young man murmured.

His companion went on as if, now that the subject had been broached, he was, as a person of imagination and tact, quite ready to give every satisfaction – being both by his genius and his method so able to enter into everything another might feel. 'But it's not only that; for honestly, at my age, I never dreamed – a widower with big boys and with so little else! It has turned out differently from anything one could have dreamed, and I'm fortunate beyond all measure. She has been so free, and yet she consents. Better than any one else perhaps – for I remember how you liked her before you went away, and how she liked you – you can intelligently congratulate me.'

'She has been so free!' Those words made a great impression on Paul Overt, and he almost writhed under that irony in them as to which it so little mattered whether it was designed or casual. Of course she had been free, and appreciably perhaps by his own act; for wasn't the Master's allusion to her having liked him a part of the irony too? 'I thought that by your theory you disapproved of a writer's marrying.'

'Surely – surely. But you don't call me a writer?'

'You ought to be ashamed,' said Paul.

'Ashamed of marrying again?'

'I won't say that – but ashamed of your reasons.'

The elder man beautifully smiled. 'You must let me judge of them, my good friend.'

'Yes; why not? For you judged wonderfully of mine.'

The tone of these words appeared suddenly, for St George, to suggest the unsuspected. He stared as if divining a bitterness. 'Don't you think I've been straight?'

'You might have told me at the time perhaps.'

'My dear fellow, when I say I couldn't pierce futurity –!'

'I mean afterwards.'

The Master wondered. 'After my wife's death?'

'When this idea came to you.'

'Ah never, never! I wanted to save you, rare and precious as you are.'

Poor Overt looked hard at him. 'Are you marrying Miss Fancourt to save me?'

'Not absolutely, but it adds to the pleasure. I shall be the making of you,' St George smiled. 'I was greatly struck, after our talk, with the brave devoted way you quitted the country, and still more perhaps with your force of character in remaining abroad. You're very strong – you're wonderfully strong.'

Paul tried to sound his shining eyes; the strange thing was that he seemed sincere – not a mocking fiend. He turned away, and as he did so heard the Master say something about his giving them all the proof, being the joy of his old age. He faced him again, taking another look. 'Do you mean to say you've stopped writing?'

'My dear fellow, of course I have. It's too late. Didn't I tell you?'

'I can't believe it!'

'Of course you can't – with your own talent! No, no; for the rest of my life I shall only read *you*.'

'Does she know that – Miss Fancourt?'

'She will – she will.' Did he mean this, our young man wondered, as a covert intimation that the assistance he should derive from that young lady's fortune, moderate as it was, would make the difference of putting it in his power to cease to work ungratefully an exhausted vein? Somehow, standing there in the ripeness of his successful manhood, he didn't suggest that any of his veins were exhausted. 'Don't you remember the moral I offered myself to you that night as pointing?' St George continued. 'Consider at any rate the warning I am at present.'

This was too much – he *was* the mocking fiend. Paul turned from him with a mere nod for good-night and the sense in a sore heart that he might come back to him and his easy grace, his fine way of arranging things, some time in the far future, but couldn't fraternise with him now. It was necessary to his soreness to believe for the hour in the intensity of his grievance – all the more cruel for its not being a legal one. It was doubtless in the attitude of hugging this wrong that he descended the stairs without taking leave of Miss Fancourt, who hadn't been in view at the moment he quitted the room. He was glad to get out into the honest dusky unsophisticating night, to move fast, to take his way home on foot. He walked a long time, going astray, paying no attention. He was thinking of too many other things. His steps recovered their direction, however, and at the end of an hour he found himself before his door in the small inexpensive empty street. He lingered, questioning himself still before going in, with nothing around and above him but moonless blackness, a bad lamp or two and a few far-away dim stars. To these last faint features he raised his eyes; he had been saying to himself that he should have been 'sold' indeed, diabolically sold, if now, on his new foundation, at the end of a year, St George were to put forth something of his prime quality – something of the type of 'Shadowmere' and finer than his finest. Greatly as he admired his talent Paul literally hoped such an incident wouldn't occur; it seemed to him just then that he shouldn't be able to bear it. His late adviser's words were still in his ears – 'You're very strong, wonderfully strong.'

Was he really? Certainly he would have to be, and it might a little serve for revenge. *Is* he? the reader may ask in turn, if his interest has followed the perplexed young man so far. The best answer to that perhaps is that he's doing his best, but that it's too soon to say. When the new book came out in the autumn Mr and Mrs St George found it really magnificent. The former still has published nothing, but Paul doesn't even yet feel safe. I may say for him, however, that if this event were to occur he would really be the very first to appreciate it: which is perhaps a proof that the Master was essentially right and that Nature had dedicated him to intellectual, not to personal passion.

The Pupil

The poor young man hesitated and procrastinated: it cost him such an effort to broach the subject of terms, to speak of money to a person who spoke only of feelings and, as it were, of the aristocracy. Yet he was unwilling to take leave, treating his engagement as settled, without some more conventional glance in that direction than he could find an opening for in the manner of the large affable lady who sat there drawing a pair of soiled *gants de Suède*[1] through a fat jewelled hand and, at once pressing and gliding, repeated over and over everything but the thing he would have liked to hear. He would have liked to hear the figure of his salary; but just as he was nervously about to sound that note the little boy came back – the little boy Mrs Moreen had sent out of the room to fetch her fan. He came back without the fan, only with the casual observation that he couldn't find it. As he dropped this cynical confession he looked straight and hard at the candidate for the honour of taking his education in hand. This personage reflected somewhat grimly that the first thing he should have to teach his little charge would be to appear to address himself to his mother when he spoke to her – especially not to make her such an improper answer as that.

When Mrs Moreen bethought herself of this pretext for getting rid of their companion Pemberton supposed it was precisely to approach the delicate subject of his remuneration. But it had been only to say some things about her son that it was better a boy of eleven shouldn't catch. They were extravagantly to his advantage save when she lowered her voice to sigh, tapping her left side familiarly, 'And all over-clouded by *this*, you know; all at the mercy of a weakness –!' Pemberton gathered that the weakness was in the region of the heart. He had known the poor child was not robust: this was the basis on which he had been invited to treat, through an English lady, an Oxford acquaintance, then at Nice, who happened to know both his needs and those of the amiable American family looking out for something really superior in the way of a resident tutor.

The young man's impression of his prospective pupil, who had come into the room as if to see for himself the moment Pemberton was admitted, was not quite the soft solicitation the visitor had taken for granted. Morgan Moreen was somehow sickly without being 'delicate,' and that he looked intelligent – it is true Pemberton wouldn't have enjoyed his being stupid – only added to the suggestion that, as with his big mouth and big ears he really couldn't be called pretty, he might too utterly fail to please. Pemberton was modest, was even timid; and the chance that his small scholar would prove cleverer than himself had quite figured, to his anxiety, among the dangers of an untried experiment. He reflected, however, that these were risks one had to run when one accepted a position, as it was called, in a private family; when as yet one's university honours had, pecuniarily speaking, remained barren. At any rate when Mrs Moreen got up as to intimate that, since it was understood he would enter upon his duties within the week she would let him off now, he succeeded, in spite of the presence of the child, in squeezing out a phrase about the rate of payment. It was not the fault of the conscious smile which seemed a reference to the lady's expensive identity, it was not the fault of this demonstration, which had, in a sort, both vagueness and point, if the allusion didn't sound rather vulgar. This was exactly because she became still more gracious to reply: 'Oh I can assure you that all that will be quite regular.'

Pemberton only wondered, while he took up his hat, what 'all that' was to amount to – people had such different ideas. Mrs Moreen's words, however, seemed to commit the family to a pledge definite enough to elicit from the child a strange little comment in the shape of the mocking foreign ejaculation 'Oh la-la!'

Pemberton, in some confusion, glanced at him as he walked slowly to the window with his back turned, his hands in his pockets and the air in his elderly shoulders of a boy who didn't play. The young man wondered if he should be able to teach him to play, though his mother had said it would never do and that this was why school was impossible. Mrs Moreen exhibited no discomfiture; she only continued blandly: 'Mr Moreen will be delighted to meet your wishes. As I told you, he has been called to London for a week. As soon as he comes back you shall have it out with him.'

This was so frank and friendly that the young man could only reply, laughing as his hostess laughed: 'Oh I don't imagine we shall have much of a battle.'

'They'll give you anything you like,' the boy remarked unexpectedly, returning from the window. 'We don't mind what anything costs – we live awfully well.'

'My darling, you're too quaint!' his mother exclaimed, putting out to caress him a practised but ineffectual hand. He slipped out of it, but looked with intelligent innocent eyes at Pemberton, who had already had time to notice that from one moment to the other his small satiric face seemed to change its time of life. At this moment it was infantine, yet it appeared also to be under the influence of curious intuitions and knowledges. Pemberton rather disliked precocity and was disappointed to find gleams of it in a disciple not yet in his teens. Nevertheless he divined on the spot that Morgan wouldn't prove a bore. He would prove on the contrary a source of agitation. This idea held the young man, in spite of a certain repulsion.

'You pompous little person! We're not extravagant!' Mrs Moreen gaily protested, making another unsuccessful attempt to draw the boy to her side. 'You must know what to expect,' she went on to Pemberton.

'The less you expect the better!' her companion interposed. 'But we *are* people of fashion.'

'Only so far as *you* make us so!' Mrs Moreen tenderly mocked. 'Well then, on Friday – don't tell me you're superstitious[2] – and mind you don't fail us. Then you'll see us all. I'm so sorry the girls are out. I guess you'll like the girls. And, you know, I've another son, quite different from this one.'

'He tries to imitate me,' Morgan said to their friend.

'He tries? Why he's twenty years old!' cried Mrs Moreen.

'You're very witty,' Pemberton remarked to the child – a proposition his mother echoed with enthusiasm, declaring Morgan's sallies to be the delight of the house.

The boy paid no heed to this; he only enquired abruptly of the visitor, who was surprised afterwards that he hadn't struck him as offensively forward: 'Do you *want* very much to come?'

'Can you doubt it after such a description of what I shall hear?' Pemberton replied. Yet he didn't want to come at all; he was coming because he had to go somewhere, thanks to the collapse of his fortune at the end of a year abroad spent on the system of putting his scant patrimony into a single full wave of experience. He had had his full wave but couldn't pay the score at his inn. Moreover he had caught in the boy's eyes the glimpse of a far-off appeal.

'Well, I'll do the best I can for you,' said Morgan; with which he turned away again. He passed out of one of the long windows; Pemberton saw him go and lean on the parapet of the terrace. He remained there while the young man took leave of his mother, who, on Pemberton's looking as if he expected a farewell from him, interposed with: 'Leave him, leave him; he's so strange!' Pemberton supposed her to fear something he might say. 'He's a genius – you'll love him,' she added. 'He's much the most interesting person in the family.' And before he could invent some civility to oppose to this she wound up with: 'But we're all good, you know!'

'He's a genius – you'll love him!' were words that recurred to our aspirant before the Friday, suggesting among many things that geniuses were not invariably loveable. However, it was all the better if there was an element that would make tutorship absorbing: he had perhaps taken too much for granted it would only disgust him. As he left the villa after his interview he looked up at the balcony and saw the child leaning over it. 'We shall have great larks!' he called up.

Morgan hung fire a moment and then gaily returned: 'By the time you come back I shall have thought of something witty!'

This made Pemberton say to himself 'After all he's rather nice.'

II

On the Friday he saw them all, as Mrs Moreen had promised, for her husband had come back and the girls and the other son were at home. Mr Moreen had a white moustache, a confiding manner and, in his buttonhole, the ribbon of a foreign order – bestowed, as Pemberton eventually learned, for services. For what services he never clearly ascertained: this was a point – one of a large number – that Mr Moreen's manner never confided. What it emphatically did confide was that he was even more a man of the world than you might first make out. Ulick, the firstborn, was in visible training for the same profession – under the disadvantage as yet, however, of a buttonhole but feebly floral and a moustache with no pretensions to type. The girls had hair and figures and manners and small fat feet, but had never been out alone. As for Mrs Moreen Pemberton saw on a nearer view that her elegance was intermittent and her parts didn't always match. Her husband, as she had promised, met with enthusiasm Pemberton's ideas in regard to a salary. The young man had endeavoured to keep these stammerings modest, and Mr Moreen made it no secret that *he* found them wanting in 'style.' He further mentioned that he aspired to be intimate with his children, to be their best friend, and that he was always looking out for them. That was what he went off for, to London and other places – to look out; and this vigilance was the theory of life, as well as the real occupation, of the whole family. They all looked out, for they were very frank on the subject of its being necessary. They desired it to be understood that they were earnest people, and also that their fortune, though quite adequate for earnest people, required the most careful administration. Mr Moreen, as the parent bird, sought sustenance for the nest. Ulick invoked support mainly at the club, where Pemberton guessed that it was usually served on green cloth.[3] The girls used to do up their hair and their frocks themselves, and our young man felt appealed to to be glad, in regard to Morgan's education, that, though it must naturally be of the best, it didn't cost too much. After a little he *was* glad, forgetting at times his own needs in the interest inspired by the child's character and culture and the pleasure of making easy terms for him.

During the first weeks of their acquaintance Morgan had been as puzzling as a page in an unknown language – altogether different from the obvious little Anglo-Saxons who had misrepresented childhood to Pemberton. Indeed the whole mystic volume in which the boy had been amateurishly bound demanded some practice in translation. To-day, after a considerable interval, there is something phantasmagoric, like a prismatic reflexion or a serial novel, in Pemberton's memory of the queerness of the Moreens. If it were not for a few tangible tokens – a lock of Morgan's hair cut by his own hand, and the half-dozen letters received from him when they were disjoined – the whole episode and the figures peopling it would seem too inconsequent for anything but dreamland. Their supreme quaintness was their success – as it appeared to him for a while at the time; since he had never seen a family so brilliantly equipped for failure. Wasn't it success to have kept him so hatefully long? Wasn't it success to have drawn him in that first morning at déjeuner,[4] the Friday he came – it was enough to *make* one superstitious – so that he utterly committed himself, and this not by calculation or on a signal, but from a happy instinct which made them, like a band of gipsies, work so neatly together? They amused him as much as if they had really been a band of gipsies. He was still young and had not seen much of the world – his English years had been properly arid; therefore the reversed conventions of the Moreens – for they had *their* desperate proprieties – struck him as topsy-turvy. He had encountered nothing like them at Oxford; still less had any such note been struck to his younger American ear during the four years at Yale in which he had richly supposed himself to be reacting against a Puritan strain. The reaction of the Moreens, at any rate, went ever so much further. He had thought himself very sharp that first day in hitting them all off in his mind with the 'cosmopolite' label. Later it seemed feeble and colourless – confessedly helplessly provisional.

He yet when he first applied it felt a glow of joy – for an instructor he was still empirical – rise from the apprehension that living with them would really be to see life. Their sociable strangeness was an intimation of that – their chatter of tongues, their gaiety and good humour, their infinite dawdling (they were always getting themselves up, but it took for ever, and Pemberton had once found Mr Moreen shaving in the drawing-room), their French, their Italian and, cropping up in the foreign fluencies, their cold tough slices of American. They lived on maccaroni[5] and coffee – they had these articles prepared in perfection – but they knew recipes for a hundred other dishes. They overflowed with music and song, were always humming and catching each other up, and had a sort of professional acquaintance with Continental cities. They talked of 'good places' as if they had been pickpockets or strolling players. They had at Nice a villa, a carriage, a piano and a banjo, and they went to official parties. They were a perfect calendar of the 'days' of their friends, which Pemberton knew them, when they were indisposed, to get out of bed to go to, and which made the week larger than life when Mrs Moreen talked of them with Paula and Amy. Their initiations gave their new inmate at first an almost dazzling sense of culture. Mrs Moreen had translated something at some former period – an author whom it made Pemberton feel *borné*[6] never to have heard of. They could imitate Venetian and sing Neapolitan, and when they wanted to say something very particular communicated with each other in an ingenious dialect of their own, an elastic spoken cipher which Pemberton at first took for some *patois* of one of their countries, but which he 'caught on to' as he would not have grasped provincial development of Spanish or German.

'It's the family language – Ultramoreen,' Morgan explained to him drolly enough; but the boy rarely condescended to use it himself, though he dealt in colloquial Latin as if he had been a little prelate.

Among all the 'days' with which Mrs Moreen's memory was taxed she managed to squeeze in one of her own, which her friends sometimes forgot. But the house drew a frequented air from the number of fine people who were freely named there and from several mysterious men with foreign titles and English clothes whom Morgan called the Princes and who, on sofas with the girls, talked French very loud – though sometimes with some oddity of accent – as if to show they were saying nothing improper. Pemberton wondered how the Princes could ever propose in that tone and so publicly: he took for granted cynically that this was what was desired of them. Then he recognised that even for the chance of such an advantage Mrs Moreen would never allow Paula and Amy to receive alone. These young ladies were not at all timid, but it was just the safeguards that made them so candidly free. It was a houseful of Bohemians who wanted tremendously to be Philistines.

In one respect, however, certainly, they achieved no rigour – they were wonderfully amiable and ecstatic about Morgan. It was a genuine tenderness, an artless admiration, equally strong in each. They even praised his beauty, which was small, and were as afraid of him as if they felt him of finer clay. They spoke of him as a little angel and a prodigy – they touched on his want of health with long, vague faces. Pemberton feared at first an extravagance that might make him hate the boy, but before this happened he had become extravagant himself. Later, when he had grown rather to hate the others, it was a bribe to patience for him that they were at any rate nice about Morgan, going on tiptoe if they fancied he was showing symptoms, and even giving up somebody's 'day' to procure him a pleasure. Mixed with this too was the oddest wish to make him independent, as if they had felt themselves not good enough for him. They passed him over to the new members of their circle very much as if wishing to force some charity of adoption on so free an agent and get rid of their own charge. They were delighted when they saw Morgan take so to his kind playfellow, and could think of no higher praise for the young man. It was strange how they contrived to reconcile the appearance, and indeed the essential fact, of adoring the child with their eagerness to wash their hands of him. Did they want to get rid of him before he should find them out? Pemberton was finding them out month by month. The boy's fond family, however this might be, turned their backs with exaggerated delicacy, as if to avoid the reproach of interfering. Seeing in time how little he had in common with them — it was by *them* he first observed it; they proclaimed it with complete humility — his companion was moved to speculate on the mysteries of transmission, the far jumps of heredity. Where his detachment from most of the things they represented had come from was more than an observer could say — it certainly had burrowed under two or three generations.

As for Pemberton's own estimate of his pupil, it was a good while before he got the point of view, so little had he been prepared for it by the smug young barbarians to whom the tradition of tutorship, as hitherto revealed to him, had been adjusted. Morgan was scrappy and surprising, deficient in many properties supposed common to the *genus* and abounding in others that were the portion only of the supernaturally clever. One day his friend made a great stride: it cleared up the question to perceive that Morgan *was* supernaturally clever and that, though the formula was temporarily meagre, this would be the only assumption on which one could successfully deal with him. He had the general quality of a child for whom life had not been simplified by school, a kind of home-bred sensibility which might have been bad for himself but was charming for others, and a whole range of refinement and perception — little musical vibrations as taking as picked-up airs — begotten by wandering about Europe at the tail of his migratory tribe. This might not have been an education to recommend in advance, but its results with so special a subject were as appreciable as the marks on a piece of fine porcelain. There was at the same time in him a small strain of stoicism, doubtless the fruit of having had to begin early to bear pain, which counted for pluck and made it of less consequence that he might have been thought at school rather a polyglot little beast. Pemberton indeed quickly found himself rejoicing that school was out of the question: in any million of boys it was probably good for all but one, and Morgan was that millionth. It would have made him comparative and superior — it might have made him really require kicking. Pemberton would try to be school himself — a bigger seminary than five hundred grazing donkeys, so that, winning no prizes, the boy would remain unconscious and irresponsible and amusing — amusing, because, though life was already intense in his childish nature, freshness still made there a strong draught for jokes. It turned out that even in the still air of Morgan's various disabilities jokes flourished greatly. He was a pale lean acute undeveloped little cosmopolite, who liked intellectual gymnastics and who also, as regards the behaviour of mankind, had noticed more things than you might suppose, but who nevertheless had his proper playroom of superstitions, where he smashed a dozen toys a day.

III

At Nice once, toward evening, as the pair rested in the open air after a walk, and looked over the sea at the pink western lights, he said suddenly to his comrade: 'Do you like it, you know – being with us all in this intimate way?'

'My dear fellow, why should I stay if I didn't?'

'How do I know you'll stay? I'm almost sure you won't, very long.'

'I hope you don't mean to dismiss me,' said Pemberton.

Morgan debated, looking at the sunset. 'I think if I did right I ought to.'

'Well, I know I'm supposed to instruct you in virtue; but in that case don't do right.'

'You're very young – fortunately,' Morgan went on, turning to him again.

'Oh yes, compared with you!'

'Therefore it won't matter so much if you do lose a lot of time.'

'That's the way to look at it,' said Pemberton accommodatingly.

They were silent a minute; after which the boy asked: 'Do you like my father and my mother very much?'

'Dear me, yes. Charming people.'

Morgan received this with another silence; then unexpectedly, familiarly, but at the same time affectionately, he remarked: 'You're a jolly old humbug!'

For a particular reason the words made our young man change colour. The boy noticed in an instant that he had turned red, whereupon he turned red himself and pupil and master exchanged a longish glance in which there was a consciousness of many more things than are usually touched upon, even tacitly, in such a relation. It produced for Pemberton an embarrassment; it raised in a shadowy form a question – this was the first glimpse of it – destined to play a singular and, as he imagined, owing to the altogether peculiar conditions, an unprecedented part in his intercourse with his little companion. Later, when he found himself talking with the youngster in a way in which few youngsters could ever have been talked with, he thought of that clumsy moment on the bench at Nice as the dawn of an understanding that had broadened. What had added to the clumsiness then was that he thought it his duty to declare to Morgan that he might abuse him, Pemberton, as much as he liked, but must never abuse his parents. To this Morgan had the easy retort that he hadn't dreamed of abusing them; which appeared to be true: it put Pemberton in the wrong.

'Then why am I a humbug for saying *I* think them charming?' the young man asked, conscious of a certain rashness.

'Well — they're not your parents.'

'They love you better than anything in the world — never forget that,' said Pemberton.

'Is that why you like them so much?'

'They're very kind to me,' Pemberton replied evasively.

'You *are* a humbug!' laughed Morgan, passing an arm into his tutor's. He leaned against him looking off at the sea again and swinging his long thin legs.

'Don't kick my shins,' said Pemberton while he reflected 'Hang it, I can't complain of them to the child!'

'There's another reason too,' Morgan went on, keeping his legs still.

'Another reason for what?'

'Besides their not being your parents.'

'I don't understand you,' said Pemberton.

'Well, you will before long. All right!'

He did understand fully before long, but he made a fight even with himself before he confessed it. He thought it the oddest thing to have a struggle with the child about. He wondered he didn't hate the hope of the Moreens for bringing the struggle on. But by the time it began any such sentiment for that scion was closed to him. Morgan was a special case, and to know him was to accept him on his own odd terms. Pemberton had spent his aversion to special cases before arriving at knowledge. When at last he did arrive his quandary was great. Against every interest he had attached himself. They would have to meet things together. Before they went home that evening at Nice the boy had said, clinging to his arm:

'Well, at any rate you'll hang on to the last.'

'To the last?'

'Till you're fairly beaten.'

'*You* ought to be fairly beaten!' cried the young man, drawing him closer.

IV

A year after he had come to live with them Mr and Mrs Moreen suddenly gave up the villa at Nice. Pemberton had got used to suddenness, having seen it practised on a considerable scale during two jerky little tours — one in Switzerland the first summer, and the other late in the winter, when they all ran down to

Florence and then, at the end of ten days, liking it much less than they had intended, straggled back in mysterious depression. They had returned to Nice 'for ever,' as they said; but this didn't prevent their squeezing, one rainy muggy May night, into a second-class railway-carriage – you could never tell by which class they would travel – where Pemberton helped them to stow away a wonderful collection of bundles and bags. The explanation of this manoeuvre was that they had determined to spend the summer 'in some bracing place'; but in Paris they dropped into a small furnished apartment – a fourth floor in a third-rate avenue, where there was a smell on the staircase and the *portier*[7] was hateful – and passed the next four months in blank indigence.

The better part of this baffled sojourn was for the preceptor and his pupil, who, visiting the Invalides and Notre Dame, the Conciergerie[8] and all the museums, took a hundred remunerative rambles. They learned to know their Paris, which was useful, for they came back another year for a longer stay, the general character of which in Pemberton's memory to-day mixes pitiably and confusedly with that of the first. He sees Morgan's shabby knickerbockers – the everlasting pair that didn't match his blouse and that as he grew longer could only grow faded. He remembers the particular holes in his three or four pair of coloured stockings.

Morgan was dear to his mother, but he never was better dressed than was absolutely necessary – partly, no doubt, by his own fault, for he was as indifferent to his appearance as a German philosopher.[9] 'My dear fellow, you *are* coming to pieces,' Pemberton would say to him in sceptical remonstrance; to which the child would reply, looking at him serenely up and down: 'My dear fellow, so are you! I don't want to cast you in the shade.' Pemberton could have no rejoinder for this – the assertion so closely represented the fact. If however the deficiencies of his own wardrobe were a chapter by themselves he didn't like his little charge to look too poor. Later he used to say 'Well, if we're poor, why, after all, shouldn't we look it?' and he consoled himself with thinking there was something rather elderly and gentlemanly in Morgan's disrepair – it differed from the untidiness of the urchin who plays and spoils his things. He could trace perfectly the degrees by which, in proportion as her little son confined himself to his tutor for society, Mrs Moreen shrewdly forbore to renew his garments. She did nothing that didn't show, neglected him because he escaped notice, and then, as she illustrated this clever policy, discouraged at home his public appearances. Her position was logical enough – those members of her family who did show had to be showy.

During this period and several others Pemberton was quite aware of how he and his comrade might strike people; wandering languidly through the Jardin des Plantes as if they had nowhere to go, sitting on the winter days in the galleries of the Louvre,[10] so splendidly ironical to the homeless, as if for the advantage of the *calorifere*.[11] They joked about it sometimes: it was the sort of joke that was perfectly within the boy's compass. They figured themselves as part of the vast vague hand-to-mouth multitude of the enormous city and pretended they were proud of their position in it – it showed them 'such a lot of life' and made them conscious of a democratic brotherhood. If Pemberton couldn't feel a sympathy in destitution with his small companion – for after all Morgan's fond parents would never have let him really suffer – the boy would at least feel it with him, so it came to the same thing. He used sometimes to wonder what people would think they were – to fancy they were looked askance at, as if it might be a suspected case of kidnapping. Morgan wouldn't be taken for a young patrician with a preceptor – he wasn't smart enough; though he might pass for his companion's sickly little brother. Now and then he had a five-franc piece, and except once, when they bought a couple of lovely neckties, one of which he made Pemberton accept, they laid it out scientifically in old books. This was sure to be a great day, always spent on the quays,[12] in a rummage of the dusty boxes that garnish the parapets. Such occasions helped them to live, for their books ran low very soon after the beginning of their acquaintance. Pemberton had a good many in England, but he was obliged to write to a friend and ask him kindly to get some fellow to give him something for them.

If they had to relinquish that summer the advantage of the bracing climate the young man couldn't but suspect this failure of the cup when at their very lips to have been the effect of a rude jostle of his own. This had represented his first blow-out, as he called it, with his patrons; his first successful attempt – though there was little other success about it – to bring them to a consideration of his impossible position. As the ostensible eve of a costly journey the moment had struck him as favourable to an earnest protest, the presentation of an ultimatum. Ridiculous as it sounded, he had never yet been able to compass an uninterrupted private interview with the elder pair or with either of them singly. They were always flanked by their elder children, and poor Pemberton usually had his own little charge at his side. He was conscious of its being a house in which the surface of one's delicacy got rather smudged; nevertheless he had preserved the bloom of his scruple against announcing to Mr and Mrs Moreen with publicity that he shouldn't be able to go on longer without a little money. He was still simple enough to suppose Ulick and Paula and Amy might not know that since his arrival he had only had a hundred and forty francs; and he was magnanimous enough to wish not to compromise their parents in their eyes. Mr Moreen now listened to him, as he listened to every one and to every thing, like a man of the world, and seemed to appeal to him – though not of course too grossly – to try and be a little more of one himself. Pemberton recognised in fact the importance of the character – from the advantage it gave Mr Moreen. He was not even confused or embarrassed, whereas the young man in his service was more so than there was any reason for. Neither was he surprised – at least any more than a gentleman had to be who freely confessed himself a little shocked – though not perhaps strictly at Pemberton.

'We must go into this, mustn't we, dear?' he said to his wife. He assured his young friend that the matter should have his very best attention; and he melted into space as elusively as if, at the door, he were taking an inevitable but deprecatory precedence. When, the next moment, Pemberton found himself alone with Mrs Moreen it was to hear her say 'I see, I see' – stroking the roundness of her chin and looking as if she were only hesitating between a dozen easy remedies. If they didn't make their push Mr Moreen could at least disappear for several days. During his absence his wife took up the subject again spontaneously, but her contribution to it was merely that she had thought all the while they were getting on so beautifully. Pemberton's reply to this revelation was that unless they immediately put down something on account he would leave them on the spot and for ever. He knew she would wonder how he would get away, and for a moment expected her to enquire. She didn't, for which he was almost grateful to her, so little was he in a position to tell.

'You won't, you *know* you won't – you're too interested,' she said. 'You *are* interested, you know you are, you dear kind man!' She laughed with almost condemnatory archness, as if it were a reproach – though she wouldn't insist; and flirted a soiled pocket-handkerchief at him.

Pemberton's mind was fully made up to take his step the following week. This would give him time to get an answer to a letter he had dispatched to England. If he did in the event nothing of the sort – that is if he stayed another year and then went away only for three months – it was not merely because before the answer to his letter came (most unsatisfactory when it did arrive) Mr Moreen generously counted out to him, and again with the sacrifice to 'form' of a marked man of the world, three hundred francs in elegant ringing gold. He was irritated to find that Mrs Moreen was right, that he couldn't at the pinch bear to leave the child. This stood out clearer for the very reason that, the night of his desperate appeal to his patrons, he had seen fully for the first time where he was. Wasn't it another proof of the success with which those patrons practised their arts that they had managed to avert for so long the illuminating flash? It descended on our friend with a breadth of effect which perhaps would have struck a spectator as comical, after he had returned to his little servile room, which looked into a close court where a bare dirty opposite wall took, with the sound of shrill clatter, the reflexion of lighted back windows. He had simply given himself away to a band of adventurers. The idea, the word itself, wore a romantic horror for him – he had always lived on such safe lines. Later it assumed a more interesting, almost a soothing, sense:

it pointed a moral, and Pemberton could enjoy a moral. The Moreens were adventurers not merely because they didn't pay their debts, because they lived on society, but because their whole view of life, dim and confused and instinctive, like that of clever colour-blind animals, was speculative and rapacious and mean. Oh they were 'respectable,' and that only made them more *immondes*![13] The young man's analysis, while he brooded, put it at last very simply – they were adventurers because they were toadies and snobs. That was the completest account of them – it was the law of their being. Even when this truth became vivid to their ingenious inmate he remained unconscious of how much his mind had been prepared for it by the extraordinary little boy who had now become such a complication in his life. Much less could he then calculate on the information he was still to owe the extraordinary little boy.

V

But it was during the ensuing time that the real problem came up – the problem of how far it was excusable to discuss the turpitude of parents with a child of twelve, of thirteen, of fourteen. Absolutely inexcusable and quite impossible it of course at first appeared; and indeed the question didn't press for some time after Pemberton had received his three hundred francs. They produced a temporary lull, a relief from the sharpest pressure. The young man frugally amended his wardrobe and even had a few francs in his pocket. He thought the Moreens looked at him as if he were almost too smart, as if they ought to take care not to spoil him. If Mr Moreen hadn't been such a man of the world he would perhaps have spoken of the freedom of such neckties on the part of a subordinate. But Mr Moreen was always enough a man of the world to let things pass – he had certainly shown that. It was singular how Pemberton guessed that Morgan, though saying nothing about it, knew something had happened. But three hundred francs, especially when one owed money, couldn't last for ever; and when the treasure was gone – the boy knew when it had failed – Morgan did break ground. The party had returned to Nice at the beginning of the winter, but not to the charming villa. They went to an hotel, where they stayed three months, and then moved to another establishment, explaining that they had left the first because, after waiting and waiting, they couldn't get the rooms they wanted. These apartments, the rooms they wanted, were generally very splendid; but fortunately they never *could* get them – fortunately, I mean, for Pemberton, who reflected always that if they had got them there would have been a still scanter educational fund. What Morgan said at last was said suddenly, irrelevantly, when the moment came, in the middle of a lesson, and consisted of the apparently unfeeling words: 'You ought to *filer*, you know – you really ought.'

Pemberton stared. He had learnt enough French slang from Morgan to know that to *filer* meant to cut sticks.[14] 'Ah my dear fellow, don't turn me off!'

Morgan pulled a Greek lexicon toward him – he used a Greek-German – to look out a word, instead of asking it of Pemberton. 'You can't go on like this, you know.'

'Like what, my boy?'

'You know they don't pay you up,' said Morgan, blushing and turning his leaves.

'Don't pay me?' Pemberton stared again and feigned amazement. 'What on earth put that into your head?'

'It has been there a long time,' the boy replied rummaging his book.

Pemberton was silent, then he went on: 'I say, what are you hunting for? They pay me beautifully.'

'I'm hunting for the Greek for awful whopper,' Morgan dropped.

'Find that rather for gross impertinence and disabuse your mind. What do I want of money?'

'Oh that's another question!'

Pemberton wavered – he was drawn in different ways. The severely correct thing would have been to tell the boy that such a matter was none of his business and bid him go on with his lines. But they were really too intimate for that; it was not the way he was in the habit of treating him; there had been no reason it should be. On the other hand Morgan had quite lighted on the truth – he really shouldn't be able to keep it up much longer; therefore why not let him know one's real motive for forsaking him? At the same time it wasn't decent to abuse to one's pupil the family of one's pupil; it was better to misrepresent than to do that. So in reply to his comrade's last exclamation he just declared, to dismiss the subject, that he had received several payments.

'I say – I say!' the boy ejaculated, laughing.

'That's all right,' Pemberton insisted. 'Give me your written rendering.'

Morgan pushed a copybook across the table, and he began to read the page, but with something running in his head that made it no sense. Looking up after a minute or two he found the child's eyes fixed on him and felt in them something strange. Then Morgan said: 'I'm not afraid of the stern reality.'

'I haven't yet seen the thing you *are* afraid of – I'll do you that justice!'

This came out with a jump – it was perfectly true – and evidently gave Morgan pleasure. 'I've thought of it a long time,' he presently resumed.

'Well, don't think of it any more.'

The boy appeared to comply, and they had a comfortable and even an amusing hour. They had a theory that they were very thorough, and yet they seemed always to be in the amusing part of lessons, the intervals between the dull dark tunnels, where there were waysides and jolly views. Yet the morning was brought to a violent end by Morgan's suddenly leaning his arms on the table, burying his head in them and bursting into tears: at which Pemberton was the more startled that, as it then came over him, it was the first time he had ever seen the boy cry and that the impression was consequently quite awful.

The next day, after much thought, he took a decision and, believing it to be just, immediately acted on it. He cornered Mr and Mrs Moreen again and let them know that if on the spot they didn't pay him all they owed him he wouldn't only leave their house but would tell Morgan exactly what had brought him to it.

'Oh you *haven't* told him?' cried Mrs Moreen with a pacifying hand on her well-dressed bosom.

'Without warning you? For what do you take me?' the young man returned.

Mr and Mrs Moreen looked at each other; he could see that they appreciated, as tending to their security, his superstition of delicacy, and yet that there was a certain alarm in their relief. 'My dear fellow,' Mr Moreen demanded, 'what use *can* you have, leading the quiet life we all do, for such a lot of money?' – a question to which Pemberton made no answer, occupied as he was in noting that what passed in the mind of his patrons was something like: 'Oh then, if we've felt that the child, dear little angel, has judged us and how he regards us, and we haven't been betrayed, he must have guessed – and in short it's *general*!' an inference that rather stirred up Mr and Mrs Moreen, as Pemberton had desired it should. At the same time, if he had supposed his threat would do something towards bringing them round, he was disappointed to find them taking for granted – how vulgar their perception *had* been! – that he had already given them away. There was a mystic uneasiness in their parental breasts, and that had been the inferior sense of it. None the less, however, his threat did touch them; for if they had escaped it was only to meet a new danger. Mr Moreen appealed to him, on every precedent, as a man of the world; but his wife had recourse, for the first time since his domestication with them, to a fine *hauteur*,[15] reminding him that a devoted mother, with her child, had arts that protected her against gross misrepresentation.

'I should misrepresent you grossly if I accused you of common honesty!' our friend replied; but as he closed the door behind him sharply, thinking he had not done himself much good, while Mr Moreen lighted another cigarette, he heard his hostess shout after him more touchingly:

'Oh you do, you *do*, put the knife to one's throat!'

The next morning, very early, she came to his room. He recognised her knock, but had no hope she brought him money; as to which he was wrong, for she had fifty francs in her hand. She squeezed forward in her dressing-gown, and he received her in his own, between his bath-tub and his bed. He had been tolerably schooled by this time to the 'foreign ways' of his hosts. Mrs Moreen was ardent, and when she was ardent she didn't care what she did; so she now sat down on his bed, his clothes being on the chairs, and, in her preoccupation, forgot, as she glanced round, to be ashamed of giving him such a horrid room. What Mrs Moreen's ardour now bore upon was the design of persuading him that in the first place she was very good-natured to bring him fifty francs, and that in the second, if he would only see it, he was really too absurd to expect to be *paid*. Wasn't he paid enough without perpetual money – wasn't he paid by the comfortable luxurious home he enjoyed with them all, without a care, an anxiety, a solitary want? Wasn't he sure of his position, and wasn't that everything to a young man like him, quite unknown, with singularly little to show, the ground of whose exorbitant pretensions it had never been easy to discover? Wasn't he paid above all by the sweet relation he had established with Morgan – quite ideal as from master to pupil – and by the simple privilege of knowing and living with so amazingly gifted a child; than whom really (and she meant literally what she said) there was no better company in Europe? Mrs Moreen herself took to appealing to him as a man of the world; she said 'Voyons, mon cher,' and 'My dear man, look here now'; and urged him to be reasonable, putting it before him that it was truly a chance for him. She spoke as if, according as he *should* be reasonable, he would prove himself worthy to be her son's tutor and of the extraordinary confidence they had placed in him.

After all, Pemberton reflected, it was only a difference of theory and the theory didn't matter much. They had hitherto gone on that of remunerated, as now they would go on that of gratuitous, service; but why should they have so many words about it? Mrs Moreen at all events continued to be convincing; sitting there with her fifty fancs she talked and reiterated, as women reiterate, and bored and irritated him, while he leaned against the wall with his hands in the pockets of his wrapper, drawing it together round his legs and looking over the head of his visitor at the grey negations of his window. She wound up with saying: 'You see I bring you a definite proposal.'

'A definite proposal?'

'To make our relations regular, as it were – to put them on a comfortable footing.'

'I see – it's a system,' said Pemberton. 'A kind of organised blackmail.'

Mrs Moreen bounded up, which was exactly what he wanted. 'What do you mean by that?'

'You practise on one's fears – one's fears about the child if one should go away.'

'And pray what would happen to him in that event?' she demanded with majesty.

'Why he'd be alone with *you*.'

'And pray with whom *should* a child be but with those whom he loves most?'

'If you think that, why don't you dismiss me?'

'Do you pretend he loves you more than he loves *us*?' cried Mrs Moreen.

'I think he ought to. I make sacrifices for him. Though I've heard of those *you* make I don't see them.'

Mrs Moreen stared a moment; then with emotion she grasped her inmate's hand. '*Will* you make it – the sacrifice?'

He burst out laughing. 'I'll see. I'll do what I can. I'll stay a little longer. Your calculation's just – I *do* hate intensely to give him up; I'm fond of him and he thoroughly interests me, in spite of the inconvenience I suffer. You know my situation perfectly. I haven't a penny in the world and, occupied as you see me with Morgan, am unable to earn money.'

Mrs Moreen tapped her undressed arm with her folded bank-note. 'Can't you write articles? Can't you translate as *I* do?'

'I don't know about translating; it's wretchedly paid.'

'I'm glad to earn what I can,' said Mrs Moreen with prodigious virtue.

'You ought to tell me who you do it for.' Pemberton paused a moment, and she said nothing; so he added; 'I've tried to turn off some little sketches, but the magazines won't have them – they're declined with thanks.'

'You see then you're not such a phoenix,'[16] his visitor pointedly smiled – 'to pretend to abilities you're sacrificing for our sake.'

'I haven't time to do things properly,' he ruefully went on. Then as it came over him that he was almost abjectly good-natured to give these explanations he added: 'If I stay on longer it must be on one condition – that Morgan shall know distinctly on what footing I am.'

Mrs Moreen demurred. 'Surely you don't want to show off to a child?'

'To show *you* off, do you mean?'

Again she cast about, but this time it was to produce a still finer flower. 'And *you* talk of blackmail!'

'You can easily prevent it,' said Pemberton.

'And *you* talk of practising on fears!' she bravely pushed on.

'Yes, there's no doubt I'm a great scoundrel.'

His patroness met his eyes – it was clear she was in straits. Then she thrust out her money at him. 'Mr Moreen desired me to give you this on account.'

'I'm much obliged to Mr Moreen, but we *have* no account.'

'You won't take it?'

'That leaves me more free,' said Pemberton.

'To poison my darling's mind?' groaned Mrs Moreen.

'Oh your darling's mind —!' the young man laughed.

She fixed him a moment, and he thought she was going to break out tormentedly, pleadingly: 'For God's sake, tell me what *is* in it!' But she checked this impulse — another was stronger. She pocketed the money — the crudity of the alternative was comical — and swept out of the room with the desperate concession: 'You may tell him any horror you like!'

VI

A couple of days after this, during which he had failed to profit by so free a permission, he had been for a quarter of an hour walking with his charge in silence when the boy became sociable again with the remark: 'I'll tell you how I know it; I know it through Zénobie.'

'Zénobie? Who in the world is *she*?'

'A nurse I used to have — ever so many years ago. A charming woman. I liked her awfully, and she liked me.'

'There's no accounting for tastes. What is it you know through her?'

'Why what their idea is. She went away because they didn't fork out. She did like me awfully, and she stayed two years. She told me all about it — that at last she could never get her wages. As soon as they saw how much she liked me they stopped giving her anything. They thought she'd stay for nothing — just *because*, don't you know?' And Morgan had a queer little conscious lucid look. 'She did stay ever so long as long as she could. She was only a poor girl. She used to send money to her mother. At last she couldn't afford it any longer, and went away in a fearful rage one night — I mean of course in a rage against *them*. She cried over me tremendously, she hugged me nearly to death. She told me all about it,' the boy repeated. 'She told me it was their idea. So I guessed, ever so long ago, that they have had the same idea with you.'

'Zénobie was very sharp,' said Pemberton. 'And she made you so.'

'Oh that wasn't Zénobie; that was nature. And experience!' Morgan laughed.

'Well, Zénobie was a part of your experience.'

'Certainly I was a part of hers, poor dear!' the boy wisely sighed. 'And I'm part of yours.'

'A very important part. But I don't see how you know I've been treated like Zénobie.'

'Do you take me for the biggest dunce you've known?' Morgan asked. 'Haven't I been conscious of what we've been through together?'

'What we've been through?'

'Our privations – our dark days.'

'Oh our days have been bright enough.'

Morgan went on in silence for a moment. Then he said: 'My dear chap, you're a hero!'

'Well, you're another!' Pemberton retorted.

'No I'm not, but I ain't a baby. I won't stand it any longer. You must get some occupation that pays. I'm ashamed, I'm ashamed!' quavered the boy with a ring of passion, like some high silver note from a small cathedral chorister, that deeply touched his friend.

'We ought to go off and live somewhere together,' the young man said.

'I'll go like a shot if you'll take me.'

'I'd get some work that would keep us both afloat,' Pemberton continued.

'So would I. Why shouldn't *I* work? I ain't such a beastly little muff as *that* comes to.'

'The difficulty is that your parents wouldn't hear of it. They'd never part with you; they worship the ground you tread on. Don't you see the proof of it?' Pemberton developed. 'They don't dislike me; they wish me no harm; they're very amiable people; but they're perfectly ready to expose me to any awkwardness in life for your sake.'

The silence in which Morgan received his fond sophistry struck Pemberton somehow as expressive. After a moment the child repeated: 'You *are* a hero!' Then he added: 'They leave me with you altogether. You've all the responsibility. They put me off on you from morning till night. Why then should they object to my taking up with you completely? I'd help you.'

'They're not particularly keen about my being helped, and they delight in thinking of you as *theirs*. They're tremendously proud of you.'

'I'm not proud of *them*. But you know that,' Morgan returned.

'Except for the little matter we speak of they're charming people,' said Pemberton, not taking up the point made for his intelligence, but wondering greatly at the boy's own, and especially at this fresh reminder of something he had been conscious of from the first – the strangest thing in his friend's large little composition, a temper, a sensibility, even a private ideal, which made him as privately disown the stuff his people were made of. Morgan had in secret a small loftiness which made him acute about betrayed meanness; as well as a critical sense for the manners immediately surrounding him that was quite without precedent in a juvenile nature, especially when one noted that it had not made this nature 'old-fashioned,' as the word is of children – quaint or wizened or offensive. It was as if he had been a little gentleman and had paid the penalty by discovering that he was the only such person in his family. This comparison didn't make him vain, but it could make him melancholy and a trifle austere. While Pemberton guessed at these dim young things, shadows of shadows, he was partly drawn on and partly checked, as for a scruple, by the charm of attempting to sound the little cool shallows that were so quickly growing deeper. When he tried to figure to himself the morning twilight of childhood, so as to deal with it safely, he saw it was never fixed, never arrested, that ignorance, at the instant he touched it, was already flushing faintly into knowledge, that there was nothing that at a given moment you could say an intelligent child didn't know. It seemed to him that he himself knew too much to imagine Morgan's simplicity and too little to disembroil his tangle.

The boy paid no heed to his last remark; he only went on: 'I'd have spoken to them about their idea, as I call it, long ago, if I hadn't been sure what they'd say.'

'And what would they say?'

'Just what they said about what poor Zénobie told me – that it was a horrid dreadful story, that they had paid her every penny they owed her.'

'Well, perhaps they had,' said Pemberton.

'Perhaps they've paid you!'

'Let us pretend they have, and *n'en parlons plus*.'[17]

'They accused her of lying and cheating' – Morgan stuck to historic truth. 'That's why I don't want to speak to them.'

'Lest they should accuse me too?' To this Morgan made no answer, and his companion, looking down at him – the boy turned away his eyes, which had filled – saw that he couldn't have trusted himself to utter. 'You're right. Don't worry them,' Pemberton pursued. 'Except for that, they *are* charming people.'

'Except for *their* lying and *their* cheating?'

'I say – I say!' cried Pemberton, imitating a little tone of the lad's which was itself an imitation.

'We must be frank, at the last; we *must* come to an understanding,' said Morgan with the importance of the small boy who lets himself think he is arranging great affairs – almost playing at shipwreck or at Indians. 'I know all about everything.'

'I dare say your father has his reasons,' Pemberton replied, but too vaguely, as he was aware.

'For lying and cheating?'

'For saving and managing and turning his means to the best account. He has plenty to do with his money. You're an expensive family.'

'Yes, I'm very expensive,' Morgan concurred in a manner that made his preceptor burst out laughing.

'He's saving for *you*,' said Pemberton. 'They think of you in everything they do.'

'He might, while he's about it, save a little — ' The boy paused, and his friend waited to hear what. Then Morgan brought out oddly: 'A little reputation.'

'Oh there's plenty of that. That's all right!'

'Enough of it for the people they know, no doubt. The people they know are awful.'

'Do you mean the princes? We mustn't abuse the princes.'

'Why not? They haven't married Paula — they haven't married Amy. They only clean out Ulick.'

'You *do* know everything!' Pemberton declared.

'No I don't after all. I don't know what they live on, or how they live, or *why* they live! What have they got and how did they get it? Are they rich, are they poor, or have they a *modeste aisance?*[18] Why are they always chiveying me about — living one year like ambassadors and the next like paupers? Who are they, anyway, and what are they? I've thought of all that — I've thought of a lot of things. They're so beastly worldly. That's what I hate most — oh I've *seen* it! All they care about is to make an appearance and to pass for something or other. What the dickens do they want to pass for? What *do* they, Mr Pemberton?'

'You pause for a reply,' said Pemberton, treating the question as a joke, yet wondering too and greatly struck with his mate's intense if imperfect vision. 'I haven't the least idea.'

'And what good does it do? Haven't I seen the way people treat them — the "nice" people, the ones they want to know? They'll take anything from them — they'll lie down and be trampled on. The nice ones hate that — they just sicken them. You're the only really nice person we know.'

'Are you sure? They don't lie down for me!'

'Well, you shan't lie down for them. You've got to go — that's what you've got to do,' said Morgan.

'And what will become of you?'

'Oh I'm growing up. I shall get off before long. I'll see you later.'

'You had better let me finish you,' Pemberton urged, lending himself to the child's strange superiority.

Morgan stopped in their walk, looking up at him. He had to look up much less than a couple of years before — he had grown, in his loose leanness, so long and high. 'Finish me?' he echoed.

'There are such a lot of jolly things we can do together yet. I want to turn you out — I want you to do me credit.'

Morgan continued to look at him. 'To give you credit — do you mean?'

'My dear fellow, you're too clever to live.'

'That's just what I'm afraid you think. No, no; it isn't fair — I can't endure it. We'll separate next week. The sooner it's over the sooner to sleep.'

'If I hear of anything — any other chance — I promise to go,' Pemberton said.

Morgan consented to consider this. 'But you'll be honest,' he demanded; 'you won't pretend you haven't heard?'

'I'm much more likely to pretend I have.'

'But what can you hear of, this way, stuck in a hole with us? You ought to be on the spot, to go to England — you ought to go to America.'

'One would think you were *my* tutor!' said Pemberton.

Morgan walked on and after a little had begun again: 'Well, now that you know I know and that we look at the facts and keep nothing back — it's much more comfortable, isn't it?'

'My dear boy, it's so amusing, so interesting, that it will surely be quite impossible for me to forego such hours as these.'

This made Morgan stop once more. 'You *do* keep something back. Oh you're not straight — *I* am!'

'How am I not straight?'

'Oh you've got your idea!'

'My idea?'

'Why that I probably shan't make old — make older — bones, and that you can stick it out till I'm removed.'

'You *are* too clever to live!' Pemberton repeated.

'I call it a mean idea,' Morgan pursued. 'But I shall punish you by the way I hang on.'

'Look out or I'll poison you!' Pemberton laughed.

'I'm stronger and better every year. Haven't you noticed that there hasn't been a doctor near me since you came?'

'*I'm* your doctor,' said the young man, taking his arm and drawing him tenderly on again.

Morgan proceeded and after a few steps gave a sigh of mingled weariness and relief. 'Ah now that we look at the facts it's all right!'

VII

They looked at the facts a good deal after this; and one of the first consequences of their doing so was that Pemberton stuck it out, in his friend's parlance, for the purpose. Morgan made the facts so vivid and so droll, and at the same time so bald and so ugly, that there was fascination in talking them over with him, just as there would have been heartlessness in leaving him alone with them. Now that the pair had such perceptions in common it was useless for them to pretend they didn't judge such people; but the very judgement and the exchange of perceptions created another tie. Morgan had never been so interesting as now that he himself was made plainer by the sidelight of these confidences. What came out in it most was the small fine passion of his pride. He had plenty of that, Pemberton felt — so much that one might perhaps wisely wish for it some early bruises. He would have liked his people to have a spirit and had waked up to the sense of their perpetually eating humble-pie. His mother would consume any amount, and his father would consume even more than his mother. He had a theory that Ulick had wriggled out of an 'affair' at Nice: there had once been a flurry at home, a regular panic, after which they all went to bed and took medicine, not to be accounted for on any other supposition. Morgan had a romantic imagination, fed by poetry and history, and he would have liked those who 'bore his name' — as he used to say to Pemberton with the humour that made his queer delicacies manly — to carry themselves with an air. But their one idea was to get in with people who didn't want them and to take snubs as if they were honourable scars. Why people didn't want them more he didn't know — that was people's own affair; after all they weren't superficially repulsive, they were a hundred times cleverer than most of the dreary grandees, the 'poor swells' they rushed about Europe to catch up with. 'After all they *are* amusing — they are!' he used to pronounce with the wisdom of the ages. To which Pemberton always replied: 'Amusing — the great Moreen troupe? Why they're altogether delightful; and if it weren't for the hitch that you and I (feeble performers!) make in the *ensemble* they'd carry everything before them.'

What the boy couldn't get over was the fact that this particular blight seemed, in a tradition of self-respect, so undeserved and so arbitrary. No doubt people had a right to take the line they liked; but why should *his* people have liked the line of pushing and toadying and lying and cheating? What had their forefathers — all decent folk, so far as he knew — done to them, or what had *he* done to them? Who had poisoned their blood with the fifth-rate social ideal, the fixed idea of making smart acquaintances and getting into the *monde chic*,[19] especially when it was foredoomed to failure and exposure? They showed so what they were after; that was what made the people they wanted not want *them*. And never a wince for dignity, never a throb of shame at looking each other in the face, never any independence or resentment or disgust. If his father or his brother would only knock some one down once or twice a year! Clever as they were they never guessed the impression they made. They were good-natured, yes — as good-natured as Jews at the doors of clothing-shops![20] But was that the model one wanted one's family to follow? Morgan had dim memories of an old grandfather, the maternal, in New York, whom he had been taken across the ocean at the age of five to see:

a gentleman with a high neck-cloth and a good deal of pronunciation, who wore a dress-coat in the morning, which made one wonder what he wore in the evening, and had, or was supposed to have, 'property' and something to do with the Bible Society.[21] It couldn't have been but that *he* was a good type. Pemberton himself remembered Mrs Clancy, a widowed sister of Mr Moreen's, who was as irritating as a moral tale and had paid a fortnight's visit to the family at Nice shortly after he came to live with them. She was 'pure and refined,' as Amy said over the banjo, and had the air of not knowing what they meant when they talked, and of keeping something rather important back. Pemberton judged that what she kept back was an approval of many of their ways; therefore it was to be supposed that she too was of a good type, and that Mr and Mrs Moreen and Ulick and Paula and Amy might easily have been of a better one if they would.

But that they wouldn't was more and more perceptible from day to day. They continued to 'chivey,' as Morgan called it, and in due time became aware of a variety of reasons for proceeding to Venice. They mentioned a great many of them – they were always strikingly frank and had the brightest friendly chatter, at the late foreign breakfast in especial, before the ladies had made up their faces, when they leaned their arms on the table, had something to follow the *demi-tasse*, and, in the heat of familiar discussion as to what they 'really ought' to do, fell inevitably into the languages in which they could *tutoyer*.[22] Even Pemberton liked them then; he could endure even Ulick when he heard him give his little flat voice for the 'sweet sea-city.'[23] That was what made him have a sneaking kindness for them – that they were so out of the workaday world,[24] and kept him so out of it. The summer had waned when, with cries of ecstasy, they all passed out on the balcony that overhung the Grand Canal.[25] The sunsets then were splendid and the Dorringtons had arrived. The Dorringtons were the only reason they hadn't talked of at breakfast; but the reasons they didn't talk of at breakfast always came out in the end. The Dorringtons on the other hand came out very little; or else when they did they stayed – as was natural – for hours, during which periods Mrs Moreen and the girls sometimes called at their hotel (to see if they had returned) as many as three times running. The gondola was for the ladies, as in Venice too there were 'days,' which Mrs Moreen knew in their order an hour after she arrived. She immediately took one herself, to which the Dorringtons never came, though on a certain occasion when Pemberton and his pupil were together at Saint Mark's[26] – where, taking the best walks they had ever had and haunting a hundred churches, they spent a great deal of time – they saw the old lord turn up with Mr Moreen and Ulick, who showed him the dim basilica as if it belonged to them. Pemberton noted how much less, among its curiosities, Lord Dorrington carried himself as a man of the world; wondering too whether, for such services, his companions took a fee from him. The autumn at any rate waned, the

Dorringtons departed, and Lord Verschoyle, the eldest son, had proposed neither for Amy nor for Paula.

One sad November day, while the wind roared round the old palace and the rain lashed the lagoon, Pemberton, for exercise and even somewhat for warmth – the Moreens were horribly frugal about fires; it was a cause of suffering to their inmate – walked up and down the big bare sala with his pupil. The scagliola floor[27] was cold, the high battered casements shook in the storm, and the stately decay of the place was unrelieved by a particle of furniture. Pemberton's spirits were low, and it came over him that the fortune of the Moreens was now even lower. A blast of desolation, a portent of disgrace and disaster, seemed to draw through the comfortless hall. Mr Moreen and Ulick were in the Piazza,[28] looking out for something, strolling drearily, in mackintoshes, under the arcades; but still, in spite of mackintoshes, unmistakeable men of the world. Paula and Amy were in bed – it might have been thought they were staying there to keep warm. Pemberton looked askance at the boy at his side, to see to what extent he was conscious of these dark omens. But Morgan, luckily for him, was now mainly conscious of growing taller and stronger and indeed of being in his fifteenth year. This fact was intensely interesting to him and the basis of a private theory – which, however, he had imparted to his tutor – that in a little while he should stand on his own feet. He considered that the situation would change – that in short he should be 'finished,' grown up, producible in the world of affairs and ready to prove himself of sterling ability. Sharply as he was capable at times of analysing, as he called it, his life, there were happy hours when he remained, as he also called it – and as the name, really, of their right ideal – 'jolly' superficial; the proof of which was his fundamental assumption that he should presently go to Oxford, to Pemberton's college, and aided and abetted by Pemberton, do the most wonderful things. It depressed the young man to see how little in such a project he took account of ways and means: in other connexions he mostly kept to the measure. Pemberton tried to imagine the Moreens at Oxford and fortunately failed; yet unless they were to adopt it as a residence there would be no *modus vivendi* for Morgan. How could he live without an allowance, and where was the allowance to come from? He, Pemberton, might live on Morgan; but how could Morgan live on *him*? What was to become of him anyhow? Somehow the fact that he was a big boy now, with better prospects of health, made the question of his future more difficult. So long as he was markedly frail the great consideration he inspired seemed enough of an answer to it. But at the bottom of Pemberton's heart was the recognition of his probably being strong enough to live and not yet strong enough to struggle or to thrive. Morgan himself at any rate was in the first flush of the rosiest consciousness of adolescence, so that the beating of the tempest seemed to him after all but the voice of life and the challenge of fate. He had on his shabby little overcoat, with the collar up, but was enjoying his walk.

It was interrupted at last by the appearance of his mother at the end of the sala. She beckoned him to come to her, and while Pemberton saw him, complaisant, pass down the long vista and over the damp false marble, he wondered what was in the air. Mrs Moreen said a word to the boy and made him go into the room she had quitted. Then, having closed the door after him, she directed her steps swiftly to Pemberton. There *was* something in the air, but his wildest flight of fancy wouldn't have suggested what it proved to be. She signified that she had made a pretext to get Morgan out of the way, and then she enquired – without hesitation – if the young man could favour her with the loan of three louis.[29] While, before bursting into a laugh, he stared at her with surprise, she declared that she was awfully pressed for the money; she was desperate for it – it would save her life.

'Dear lady, *c'est trop fort!*'[30] Pemberton laughed in the manner and with the borrowed grace of idiom that marked the best colloquial, the best anecdotic, moments of his friends themselves. 'Where in the world do you suppose I should get three louis, *du train dont vous allez?*'[31]

'I thought you worked – wrote things. Don't they pay you?'

'Not a penny.'

'Are you such a fool as to work for nothing?'

'You ought surely to know that.'

Mrs Moreen stared, then she coloured a little. Pemberton saw she had quite forgotten the terms – if 'terms' they could be called – that he had ended by accepting from herself; they had burdened her memory as little as her conscience. 'Oh yes, I see what you mean – you've been very nice about that; but why drag it in so often?' She had been perfectly urbane with him ever since the rough scene of explanation in his room the morning he made her accept *his* 'terms' – the necessity of his making his case known to Morgan. She had felt no resentment after seeing there was no danger Morgan would take the matter up with her. Indeed, attributing this immunity to the good taste of his influence with the boy, she had once said to Pemberton 'My dear fellow, it's an immense comfort you're a gentleman.' She repeated this in substance now. 'Of course you're a gentleman – that's a bother the less!' Pemberton reminded her that he had not 'dragged in' anything that wasn't already in as much as his foot was in his shoe; and she also repeated her prayer that, somewhere and somehow, he would find her sixty francs. He took the liberty of hinting that if he could find them it wouldn't be to lend them to *her* – as to which he consciously did himself injustice, knowing that if he had them he would certainly put them at her disposal. He accused himself, at bottom and not unveraciously, of a fantastic, a demoralised sympathy with her. If misery made strange bedfellows it also made strange sympathies. It was moreover a part of the abasement of living with such people that one had to make vulgar retorts, quite out of one's own tradition of good manners. 'Morgan, Morgan, to what pass have I come for you?' he groaned while Mrs Moreen floated voluminously down the sala again to liberate the boy, wailing as she went that everything was too odious.

Before their young friend was liberated there came a thump at the door communicating with their staircase, followed by the apparition of a dripping youth who poked in his head. Pemberton recognised him as the bearer of a telegram and recognised the telegram as addressed to himself. Morgan came back as, after glancing at the signature – that of a relative in London – he was reading the words: 'Found jolly job for you, engagement to coach opulent youth on own terms. Come at once.' The answer happily was paid and the messenger waited. Morgan, who had drawn near, waited too and looked hard at Pemberton; and Pemberton, after a moment, having met his look, handed him the telegram. It was really by wise looks – they knew each other so well now – that, while the telegraph-boy, in his waterproof cape, made a great puddle on the floor, the thing was settled between them. Pemberton wrote the answer with a pencil against the frescoed wall, and the messenger departed. When he had gone the young man explained himself.

'I'll make a tremendous charge; I'll earn a lot of money in a short time, and we'll live on it.'

'Well, I hope the opulent youth will be a dismal dunce – he probably will,' Morgan parenthesised – 'and keep you a long time a-hammering of it in.'

'Of course the longer he keeps me the more we shall have for our old age.'

'But suppose *they* don't pay you!' Morgan awfully suggested.

'Oh there are not two such –!' But Pemberton pulled up; he had been on the point of using too invidious a term. Instead of this he said 'Two such fatalities.'

Morgan flushed – the tears came to his eyes. '*Dites toujours*[32] two such rascally crews!' Then in a different tone he added: 'Happy opulent youth!'

'Not if he's a dismal dunce.'

'Oh they're happier then. But you can't have everything, can you?' the boy smiled.

Pemberton held him fast, hands on his shoulders – he had never loved him so. 'What will become of *you*, what will you do?' He thought of Mrs Moreen, desperate for sixty francs.

'I shall become an *homme fait*.'[33] And then as if he recognised all the bearings of Pemberton's allusion: 'I shall get on with them better when you're not here.'

'Ah don't say that – it sounds as if I set you against them!'

'You do – the sight of you. It's all right; you know what I mean. I shall be beautiful. I'll take their affairs in hand; I'll marry my sisters.'

'You'll marry yourself!' joked Pemberton; as high, rather tense pleasantry would evidently be the right, or the safest, tone for their separation.

It was, however, not purely in this strain that Morgan suddenly asked: 'But I say – how will you get to your jolly job? You'll have to telegraph to the opulent youth for money to come on.'

Pemberton bethought himself. 'They won't like that, will they?'

'Oh look out for them!'

Then Pemberton brought out his remedy. 'I'll go to the American Consul; I'll borrow some money of him – just for the few days, on the strength of the telegram.'

Morgan was hilarious. 'Show him the telegram – then collar the money and stay!'

Pemberton entered into the joke sufficiently to reply that for Morgan he was really capable of that; but the boy, growing more serious, and to prove he hadn't meant what he said, not only hurried him off to the Consulate – since he was to start that evening, as he had wired to his friend – but made sure of their affair by going with him. They splashed through the tortuous perforations and over the humpbacked bridges, and they passed through the Piazza, where they saw Mr Moreen and Ulick go into a jeweller's shop. The Consul proved accommodating – Pemberton said it wasn't the letter, but Morgan's grand air – and on their way back they went into Saint Mark's for a hushed ten minutes. Later they took up and kept up the fun of it to the very end; and it seemed to Pemberton a part of that fun that Mrs Moreen, who was very angry when he had announced her his intention, should charge him, grotesquely and vulgarly and in reference to the loan she had vainly endeavoured to effect, with bolting lest they should 'get something out' of him. On the other hand he had to do Mr Moreen and Ulick the justice to recognise that when on coming in *they* heard the cruel news they took it like perfect men of the world.

VIII

When he got at work with the opulent youth, who was to be taken in hand for Balliol,[34] he found himself unable to say if this aspirant had really such poor parts or if the appearance were only begotten of his own long association with an intensely living little mind. From Morgan he heard half a dozen times: the boy wrote charming young letters, a patchwork of tongues, with indulgent postscripts in the family Volapuk[35] and, in little squares and rounds and crannies of the text, the drollest illustrations – letters that he was divided between the impulse to show his present charge as a vain, a wasted incentive, and the sense of something in them that publicity would profane. The opulent youth went up in due course and failed to pass; but it seemed to add to the presumption that brilliancy was not expected of him all at once that his parents, condoning the lapse, which they good-naturedly treated as little as possible as if it were Pemberton's, should have sounded the rally again, begged the young coach to renew the siege.

The young coach was now in a position to lend Mrs Moreen three louis, and he sent her a post-office order even for a larger amount. In return for this favour he received a frantic scribbled line from her: 'Implore you to come back instantly – Morgan dreadfully ill.' They were on the rebound, once more in Paris – often as Pemberton had seen them depressed he had never seen them crushed – and communication was therefore rapid. He wrote to the boy to ascertain the state of his health, but awaited the answer in vain. He accordingly, after three days, took an abrupt leave of the opulent youth and, crossing the Channel, alighted at the small hotel, in the quarter of the Champs Elysees,[36] of which Mrs Moreen had given him the address. A deep if dumb dissatisfaction with this lady and her companions bore him company; they couldn't be vulgarly honest, but they could live at hotels, in velvety *entresols*, amid a smell of burnt pastilles,[37] surrounded by the most expensive city in Europe. When he had left them in Venice it was with an irrepressible suspicion that something was going to happen; but the only thing that could have taken place was again their masterly retreat. 'How is he? where is he?' he asked of Mrs Moreen; but before she could speak these questions were answered by the pressure round his neck of a pair of arms, in shrunken sleeves, which still were perfectly capable of an effusive young foreign squeeze.

'Dreadfully ill – I don't see it!' the young man cried. And then to Morgan: 'Why on earth didn't you relieve me? Why didn't you answer my letter?'

Mrs Moreen declared that when she wrote he was very bad, and Pemberton learned at the same time from the boy that he had answered every letter he had received. This led to the clear inference that Pemberton's note had been kept from him so that the game to be practised should not be interfered with. Mrs Moreen was prepared to see the fact exposed, as Pemberton saw the moment he faced her that she was prepared for a good many other things. She was prepared above all to maintain that she had acted from a sense of duty, that she was enchanted she had got him over, whatever they might say, and that it was useless of him to pretend he didn't know in all his bones that his place at such a time was with Morgan. He had taken the boy away from them and now had no right to abandon him. He had created for himself the gravest responsibilities and must at least abide by what he had done.

'Taken him away from you?' Pemberton exclaimed indignantly.

'Do it – do it for pity's sake; that's just what I want. I can't stand *this* – and such scenes. They're awful frauds – poor dears!' These words broke from Morgan, who had intermitted his embrace, in a key which made Pemberton turn quickly to him and see that he had suddenly seated himself, was breathing in great pain and was very pale.

'*Now* do you say he's not in a state, my precious pet?' shouted his mother, dropping on her knees before him with clasped hands, but touching him no more than if he had been a gilded idol. 'It will pass – it's only for an instant; but don't say such dreadful things!'

'I'm all right – all right,' Morgan panted to Pemberton, whom he sat looking up at with a strange smile, his hands resting on either side on the sofa.

'Now do you pretend I've been dishonest, that I've deceived?' Mrs Moreen flashed at Pemberton as she got up.

'It isn't *he* says it, it's I!' the boy returned, apparently easier but sinking back against the wall; while his restored friend, who had sat down beside him, took his hand and bent over him.

'Darling child, one does what one can; there are so many things to consider,' urged Mrs Moreen. 'It's his *place* – his only place. You see *you* think it is now.'

'Take me away – take me away,' Morgan went on, smiling to Pemberton with his white face.

'Where shall I take you, and how – oh *how*, my boy?' the young man stammered, thinking of the rude way in which his friends in London held that, for his convenience, with no assurance of prompt return, he had thrown them over; of the just resentment with which they would already have called in a successor, and of the scant help to finding fresh employment that resided for him in the grossness of his having failed to pass his pupil.

'Oh we'll settle that. You used to talk about it,' said Morgan. 'If we can only go all the rest's a detail.'

'Talk about it as much as you like, but don't think you can attempt it. Mr Moreen would never consent – it would be so *very* hand-to-mouth,' Pemberton's hostess beautifully explained to him. Then to Morgan she made it clearer: 'It would destroy our peace, it would break our hearts. Now that he's back it will be all the same again. You'll have your life, your work and your freedom, and we'll all be happy as we used to be. You'll bloom and grow perfectly well, and we won't have any more silly experiments, will we? They're too absurd. It's Mr Pemberton's place – every one in his place. You in yours, your papa in his, me in mine – *n'est-ce pas, chéri?*[38] We'll all forget how foolish we've been and have lovely times.'

She continued to talk and to surge vaguely about the little draped stuffy salon while Pemberton sat with the boy, whose colour gradually came back; and she mixed up her reasons, hinting that there were going to be changes, that the other children might scatter (who knew? – Paula had her ideas) and that then it might be fancied how much the poor old parent-birds would want the little nestling. Morgan looked at Pemberton, who wouldn't let him move; and Pemberton knew exactly how he felt at hearing himself called a little nestling. He admitted that he had had one or two bad days, but he protested afresh against the wrong of his mother's having made them the ground of an appeal to poor Pemberton. Poor Pemberton could laugh now, apart from the comicality of Mrs Moreen's mustering so much philosophy for her defence – she seemed to shake it out of her agitated petticoats, which knocked over the light gilt chairs – so little did their young companion, *marked*, unmistakeably marked at the best, strike him as qualified to repudiate any advantage.

He himself was in for it at any rate. He should have Morgan on his hands again indefinitely; though indeed he saw the lad had a private theory to produce which would be intended to smooth this down. He was obliged to him for it in advance; but the suggested amendment didn't keep his heart rather from sinking, any more than it prevented him from accepting the prospect on the spot, with some confidence moreover that he should do so even better if he could have a little supper. Mrs Moreen threw out more hints about the changes that were to be looked for, but she was such a mixture of smiles and shudders – she confessed she was very nervous – that he couldn't tell if she were in high feather[39] or only in hysterics. If the family was really at last going to pieces why shouldn't she recognise the necessity of pitching Morgan into some sort of lifeboat? This presumption was fostered by the fact that they were established in luxurious quarters in the capital of pleasure; that was exactly where they naturally *would* be established in view of going to pieces. Moreover didn't she mention that Mr Moreen and the others were enjoying themselves at the opera with Mr Granger, and wasn't *that* also precisely where one would look for them on the eve of a smash? Pemberton gathered that Mr Granger was a rich vacant American – a big bill with a flourishy heading and no items; so that one of Paula's 'ideas' was probably that this time she hadn't missed fire – by which straight shot indeed she would have shattered the general cohesion. And if the cohesion was to crumble what would become of poor Pemberton? He felt quite enough bound up with them to figure to his alarm as a dislodged block in the edifice.

It was Morgan who eventually asked if no supper had been ordered for him; sitting with him below, later, at the dim delayed meal, in the presence of a great deal of corded green plush, a plate of ornamental biscuit and an aloofness marked on the part of the waiter. Mrs Moreen had explained that they had been obliged to secure a room for the visitor out of the house; and Morgan's consolation – he offered it while Pemberton reflected on the nastiness of lukewarm sauces – proved to be, largely, that this circumstance would facilitate their escape. He talked of their escape – recurring to it often afterwards – as if they were making up a 'boy's book'[40] together. But he likewise expressed his sense that there was something in the air, that the Moreens couldn't keep it up much longer. In point of fact, as Pemberton was to see, they kept it up for five or six months. All the while, however, Morgan's contention was designed to cheer him. Mr Moreen and Ulick, whom he had met the day after his return, accepted that return like perfect men of the world. If Paula and Amy treated it even with less formality an allowance was to be made for them, inasmuch as Mr Granger hadn't come to the opera after all. He had only placed his box at their service, with a bouquet for each of the party; there was even one apiece, embittering the thought of his profusion, for Mr Moreen and Ulick. 'They're all like that,' was Morgan's comment; 'at the very last, just when we think we've landed them they're back in the deep sea!'

Morgan's comments in these days were more and more free; they even included a large recognition of the extraordinary tenderness with which he had been treated while Pemberton was away. Oh yes, they couldn't do enough to be nice to him, to show him they had him on their mind and make up for his loss. That was just what made the whole thing so sad and caused him to rejoice after all in Pemberton's return – he had to keep thinking of their affection less, had less sense of obligation. Pemberton laughed out at this last reason, and Morgan blushed and said 'Well, dash it, you know what I mean.' Pemberton knew perfectly what he meant; but there were a good many things that – dash it too! – it didn't make any clearer. This episode of his second sojourn in Paris stretched itself out wearily, with their resumed readings and wanderings and maunderings, their potterings on the quays, their hauntings of the museums, their occasional lingerings in the Palais Royal when the first sharp weather came on and there was a comfort in warm emanations, before Chevet's wonderful succulent window.[41] Morgan wanted to hear all about the opulent youth – he took an immense interest in him. Some of the details of his opulence – Pemberton could spare him none of them – evidently fed the boy's appreciation of all his friend had given up to come back to him; but in addition to the greater reciprocity established by that heroism he had always his little brooding theory, in which there was a frivolous gaiety too, that their long probation was drawing to a close. Morgan's conviction that the Moreens couldn't go on much longer kept pace with the unexpended impetus with which, from month to month, they did go on. Three weeks after Pemberton had rejoined them they went on to another hotel, a dingier one than the first; but Morgan rejoiced that his tutor had at least still not sacrificed the advantage of a room outside. He clung to the romantic utility of this when the day, or rather the night, should arrive for their escape.

For the first time, in this complicated connexion, our friend felt his collar gall him. It was, as he had said to Mrs Moreen in Venice, *trop fort* – everything was *trop fort*. He could neither really throw off his blighting burden nor find in it the benefit of a pacified conscience or of a rewarded affection. He had spent all the money accruing to him in England, and he saw his youth going and that he was getting nothing back for it. It was all very well of Morgan to count it for reparation that he should now settle on him permanently – there was an irritating flaw in such a view. He saw what the boy had in his mind; the conception that as his friend had had the generosity to come back he must show his gratitude by giving him his life. But the poor friend didn't desire the gift – what could he do with Morgan's dreadful little life? Of course at the same time that Pemberton was irritated he remembered the reason, which was very honourable to Morgan and which dwelt simply in his making one so forget that he was no more than a patched urchin. If one dealt with him on a different basis one's misadventures were one's own fault. So Pemberton waited in a queer confusion of yearning and alarm for the catastrophe which was held to hang over the house of Moreen, of which he certainly at moments felt the symptoms brush his cheek and as to which he wondered much in what form it would find its liveliest effect.

Perhaps it would take the form of sudden dispersal – a frightened *sauve qui peut*,[42] a scuttling into selfish corners. Certainly they were less elastic than of yore; they were evidently looking for something they didn't find. The Dorringtons hadn't re-appeared, the princes had scattered; wasn't that the beginning of the end? Mrs Moreen had lost her reckoning of the famous 'days'; her social calendar was blurred – it had turned its face to the wall. Pemberton suspected that the great, the cruel discomfiture had been the unspeakable behaviour of Mr Granger, who seemed not to know what he wanted, or, what was much worse, what *they* wanted. He kept sending flowers, as if to bestrew the path of his retreat, which was never the path of a return. Flowers were all very well, but – Pemberton could complete the proposition. It was now positively conspicuous that in the long run the Moreens were a social failure; so that the young man was almost grateful the run had not been short. Mr Moreen indeed was still occasionally able to get away on business and, what was more surprising, was likewise able to get back. Ulick had no club, but you couldn't have discovered it from his appearance, which was as much as ever that of a person looking at life from the window of such an institution; therefore Pemberton was doubly surprised at an answer he once heard him make his mother in the desperate tone of a man familiar with the worst privations. Her question Pemberton had not quite caught; it appeared to be an appeal for a suggestion as to whom they might get to take Amy. 'Let the Devil take her!' Ulick snapped; so that Pemberton could see that they had not only lost their amiability but had ceased to believe in themselves. He could also see that if

Mrs Moreen was trying to get people to take her children she might be regarded as closing the hatches for the storm. But Morgan would be the last she would part with.

One winter afternoon – it was a Sunday – he and the boy walked far together in the Bois de Boulogne.[43] The evening was so splendid, the cold lemon-coloured sunset so clear, the stream of carriages and pedestrians so amusing and the fascination of Paris so great, that they stayed out later than usual and became aware that they should have to hurry home to arrive in time for dinner. They hurried accordingly, arm-in-arm, good-humoured and hungry, agreeing that there was nothing like Paris after all and that after everything too that had come and gone they were not yet sated with innocent pleasures. When they reached the hotel they found that, though scandalously late, they were in time for all the dinner they were likely to sit down to. Confusion reigned in the apartments of the Moreens – very shabby ones this time, but the best in the house – and before the interrupted service of the table, with objects displaced almost as if there had been a scuffle and a great wine-stain from an overturned bottle, Pemberton couldn't blink the fact that there had been a scene of the last proprietary firmness. The storm had come – they were all seeking refuge. The hatches were down, Paula and Amy were invisible – they had never tried the most casual art upon Pemberton, but he felt they had enough of an eye to him not to wish to meet him as young ladies whose frocks had been confiscated – and Ulick appeared to have jumped overboard. The host and his staff, in a word, had ceased to 'go on' at the pace of their guests, and the air of embarrassed detention, thanks to a pile of gaping trunks in the passage, was strangely commingled with the air of indignant withdrawal.

When Morgan took all this in – and he took it in very quickly – he coloured to the roots of his hair. He had walked from his infancy among difficulties and dangers, but he had never seen a public exposure. Pemberton noticed in a second glance at him that the tears had rushed into his eyes and that they were tears of a new and untasted bitterness. He wondered an instant, for the boy's sake, whether he might successfully pretend not to understand. Not successfully, he felt, as Mr and Mrs Moreen, dinnerless by their extinguished hearth, rose before him in their little dishonoured salon, casting about with glassy eyes for the nearest port in such a storm. They were not prostrate but were horribly white, and Mrs Moreen had evidently been crying. Pemberton quickly learned however that her grief was not for the loss of her dinner, much as she usually enjoyed it, but the fruit of a blow that struck even deeper, as she made all haste to explain. He would see for himself, so far as that went, how the great change had come, the dreadful bolt had fallen, and how they would now all have to turn themselves about. Therefore cruel as it was to them to part with their darling she must look to him to carry a little further the influence he had so fortunately acquired with the boy – to induce his young charge to follow him into some modest retreat. They depended on him – that was the fact – to take their delightful child temporarily under his protection: it would leave Mr Moreen and herself so much more free to give the proper attention (too little, alas! had been given) to the readjustment of their affairs.

'We trust you – we feel we *can*,' said Mrs Moreen, slowly rubbing her plump white hands and looking with compunction hard at Morgan, whose chin, not to take liberties, her husband stroked with a tentative paternal forefinger.

'Oh yes – we feel that we *can*. We trust Mr Pemberton fully, Morgan,' Mr Moreen pursued.

Pemberton wondered again if he might pretend not to understand; but everything good gave way to the intensity of Morgan's understanding. 'Do you mean he may take me to live with him for ever and ever?' cried the boy. 'May take me away, away, anywhere he likes?'

'For ever and ever? *Comme vous-y-allez!*'[44] Mr Moreen laughed indulgently. 'For as long as Mr Pemberton may be so good.'

'We've struggled, we've suffered,' his wife went on; 'but you've made him so your own that we've already been through the worst of the sacrifice.'

Morgan had turned away from his father – he stood looking at Pemberton with a light in his face. His sense of shame for their common humiliated state had dropped; the case had another side – the thing was to clutch at *that*. He had a moment of boyish joy, scarcely mitigated by the reflexion that with this unexpected consecration of his hope – too sudden and too violent; the turn taken was away from a *good* boy's book – the 'escape' was left on their hands. The boyish joy was there an instant, and Pemberton was almost scared at the rush of gratitude and affection that broke through his first abasement. When he stammered 'My dear fellow, what do you say to *that*?' how could one not say something enthusiastic? But there was more need for courage at something else that immediately followed and that made the lad sit down quickly on the nearest chair. He had turned quite livid and had raised his hand to his left side. They were all three looking at him, but Mrs Moreen suddenly bounded forward. 'Ah his darling little heart!' she broke out; and this time, on her knees before him and without respect for the idol, she caught him ardently in her arms. 'You walked him too far, you hurried him too fast!' she hurled over her shoulder at Pemberton. Her son made no protest, and the next instant, still holding him, she sprang up with her face convulsed and with the terrified cry 'Help, help! he's going, he's gone!' Pemberton saw with equal horror, by Morgan's own stricken face, that he was beyond their wildest recall. He pulled him half out of his mother's hands, and for a moment, while they held him together, they looked all their dismay into each other's eyes.

'He couldn't stand it with his weak organ,' said Pemberton – 'the shock, the whole scene, the violent emotion.'

'But I thought he *wanted* to go to you!' wailed Mrs Moreen.

'I *told* you he didn't, my dear,' her husband made answer. Mr Moreen was trembling all over and was in his way as deeply affected as his wife. But after the very first he took his bereavement as a man of the world.

The Real Thing

When the porter's wife, who used to answer the house-bell, announced 'A gentleman and a lady, sir,' I had, as I often had in those days – the wish being father to the thought – an immediate vision of sitters. Sitters my visitors in this case proved to be; but not in the sense I should have preferred. There was nothing at first however to indicate that they mightn't have come for a portrait. The gentleman, a man of fifty, very high and very straight, with a moustache slightly grizzled and a dark grey walking-coat admirably fitted, both of which I noted professionally – I don't mean as a barber or yet as a tailor – would have struck me as a celebrity if celebrities often were striking. It was a truth of which I had for some time been conscious that a figure with a good deal of frontage was, as one might say, almost never a public institution. A glance at the lady helped to remind me of this paradoxical law: she also looked too distinguished to be a 'personality.' Moreover one would scarcely come across two variations together.

Neither of the pair immediately spoke – they only prolonged the preliminary gaze suggesting that each wished to give the other a chance. They were visibly shy; they stood there letting me take them in – which, as I afterwards perceived, was the most practical thing they could have done. In this way their embarrassment served their cause. I had seen people painfully reluctant to mention that they desired anything so gross as to be represented on canvas; but the scruples of my new friends appeared almost insurmountable. Yet the gentleman might have said 'I should like a portrait of my wife,' and the lady might have said 'I should like a portrait of my husband.' Perhaps they weren't husband and wife – this naturally would make the matter more delicate. Perhaps they wished to be done together – in which case they ought to have brought a third person to break the news.

'We come from Mr Rivet,' the lady finally said with a dim smile that had the effect of a moist sponge passed over a 'sunk' piece of painting,[1] as well as of a vague allusion to vanished beauty. She was as tall and straight, in her degree, as her companion, and with ten years less to carry. She looked as sad as a woman could look whose face was not charged with expression; that is her tinted oval mask showed waste as an exposed surface shows friction. The hand of time had played over her freely, but to an effect of elimination. She was slim and stiff, and so well-dressed, in dark blue cloth, with lappets[2] and pockets and buttons, that it was clear she employed the same tailor as her husband. The couple had an indefinable air of prosperous thrift – they evidently got a good deal of luxury for their money. If I was to be one of their luxuries it would behove me to consider my terms.

'Ah Claude Rivet recommended me?' I echoed; and I added that it was very kind of him, though I could reflect that, as he only painted landscape, this wasn't a sacrifice.

The lady looked very hard at the gentleman, and the gentleman looked round the room. Then staring at the floor a moment and stroking his moustache, he rested his pleasant eyes on me with the remark: 'He said you were the right one.'

'I try to be, when people want to sit.'

'Yes, we should like to,' said the lady anxiously.

'Do you mean together?'

My visitors exchanged a glance. 'If you could do anything with *me* I suppose it would be double,' the gentleman stammered.

'Oh yes, there's naturally a higher charge for two figures than for one.'

'We should like to make it pay,' the husband confessed.

'That's very good of you,' I returned, appreciating so unwonted a sympathy – for I supposed he meant pay the artist.

A sense of strangeness seemed to dawn on the lady. 'We mean for the illustrations – Mr Rivet said you might put one in.'

'Put in – an illustration?' I was equally confused.

'Sketch her off, you know,' said the gentleman, colouring.

It was only then that I understood the service Claude Rivet had rendered me; he had told them how I worked in black-and-white, for magazines, for story-books, for sketches of contemporary life, and consequently had copious employment for models. These things were true, but it was not less true – I may confess it now; whether because the aspiration was to lead to everything or to nothing I leave the reader to guess – that I couldn't get the honours, to say nothing of the emoluments, of a great painter of portraits out of my head. My 'illustrations' were my pot-boilers; I looked to a different branch of art – far and away the most interesting it had always seemed to me – to perpetuate my fame. There was no shame in looking to it also to make my fortune; but that fortune was by so much further from being made from the moment my visitors wished to be 'done' for nothing. I was disappointed; for in the pictorial sense I had immediately *seen* them. I had seized their type – I had already settled what I would do with it. Something that wouldn't absolutely have pleased them, I afterwards reflected.

'Ah you're — you're — a —?' I began as soon as I had mastered my surprise. I couldn't bring out the dingy word 'models': it seemed so little to fit the case.

'We haven't had much practice,' said the lady.

'We've got to *do* something, and we've thought that an artist in your line might perhaps make something of us,' her husband threw off. He further mentioned that they didn't know many artists and that they had gone first, on the off-chance — he painted views of course, but sometimes put in figures; perhaps I remembered — to Mr Rivet, whom they had met a few years before at a place in Norfolk where he was sketching.

'We used to sketch a little ourselves,' the lady hinted.

'It's very awkward, but we absolutely *must* do something,' her husband went on.

'Of course we're not so *very* young,' she admitted with a wan smile.

With the remark that I might as well know something more about them the husband had handed me a card extracted from a neat new pocket-book — their appurtenances were all of the freshest — and inscribed with the words 'Major Monarch.' Impressive as these words were they didn't carry my knowledge much further; but my visitor presently added: 'I've left the army and we've had the misfortune to lose our money. In fact our means are dreadfully small.'

'It's awfully trying — a regular strain,' said Mrs Monarch.

They evidently wished to be discreet — to take care not to swagger because they were gentlefolk. I felt them willing to recognise this as something of a drawback, at the same time that I guessed at an underlying sense — their consolation in adversity — that they *had* their points. They certainly had; but these advantages struck me as preponderantly social; such for instance as would help to make a drawing-room look well. However, a drawing-room was always, or ought to be, a picture.

In consequence of his wife's allusion to their age Major Monarch observed: 'Naturally it's more for the figure that we thought of going in. We can still hold ourselves up.' On the instant I saw that the figure was indeed their strong point. His 'naturally' didn't sound vain, but it lighted up the question. '*She* has the best one,' he continued, nodding at his wife with a pleasant after-dinner absence of circumlocution. I could only reply, as if we were in fact sitting over our wine, that this didn't prevent his own from being very good; which led him in turn to make answer: 'We thought that if you ever have to do people like us we might be something like it. *She* particularly — for a lady in a book, you know.'

I was so amused by them that, to get more of it, I did my best to take their point of view; and though it was an embarrassment to find myself appraising physically, as if they were animals on hire or useful blacks, a pair whom I should have expected to meet only in one of the relations in which criticism is tacit, I looked at Mrs Monarch judicially enough to be able to exclaim after a moment with conviction: 'Oh yes, a lady in a book!' She was singularly like a bad illustration.

'We'll stand up, if you like,' said the Major; and he raised himself before me with a really grand air.

I could take his measure at a glance — he was six feet two and a perfect gentleman. It would have paid any club in process of formation and in want of a stamp to engage him at a salary to stand in the principal window. What struck me at once was that in coming to me they had rather missed their vocation; they could surely have been turned to better account for advertising purposes. I couldn't of course see the thing in detail, but I could see them make somebody's fortune — I don't mean their own. There was something in them for a waistcoat-maker, an hotel-keeper or a soap-vendor. I could imagine 'We always use it' pinned on their bosoms with the greatest effect; I had a vision of the brilliancy with which they would launch a table d'hôte.

Mrs Monarch sat still, not from pride but from shyness, and presently her husband said to her: 'Get up, my dear, and show how smart you are.' She obeyed, but she had no need to get up to show it. She walked to the end of the studio and then came back blushing, her fluttered eyes on the partner of her appeal. I was reminded of an incident I had accidentally had a glimpse of in Paris — being with a friend there, a dramatist about to produce a play, when an actress came to him to ask to be entrusted with a part. She went through her paces before him, walked up and down as Mrs Monarch was doing. Mrs Monarch did it quite as well, but I abstained from applauding. It was very odd to see such people apply for such poor pay. She looked as if she had ten thousand a year. Her husband had used the word that described her: she was in the London current jargon essentially and typically 'smart.' Her figure was, in the same order of ideas, conspicuously and irreproachably 'good.' For a woman of her age her waist was surprisingly small; her elbow moreover had the orthodox crook. She held her head at the conventional angle, but why did she come to *me*? She ought to have tried on jackets at a big shop. I feared my visitors were not only destitute but 'artistic' — which would be a great complication. When she sat down again I thanked her, observing that what a draughtsman most valued in his model was the faculty of keeping quiet.

'Oh *she* can keep quiet,' said Major Monarch. Then he added jocosely: 'I've always kept her quiet.'

'I'm not a nasty fidget, am I?' It was going to wring tears from me, I felt, the way she hid her head, ostrich-like, in the other broad bosom.

The owner of this expanse addressed his answer to me. 'Perhaps it isn't out of place to mention — because we ought to be quite business-like, oughtn't we? — that when I married her she was known as the Beautiful Statue.'

'Oh dear!' said Mrs Monarch ruefully.

'Of course I should want a certain amount of expression,' I rejoined.

'Of *course*!' – and I had never heard such unanimity.

'And then I suppose you know that you'll get awfully tired.'

'Oh we *never* get tired!' they eagerly cried.

'Have you had any kind of practice?'

They hesitated – they looked at each other. 'We've been photographed – *immensely*,' said Mrs Monarch.

'She means the fellows have asked us themselves,' added the Major.

'I see – because you're so good-looking.'

'I don't know what they thought, but they were always after us.'

'We always got our photographs for nothing,' smiled Mrs Monarch.

'We might have brought some, my dear,' her husband remarked.

'I'm not sure we have any left. We've given quantities away,' she explained to me.

'With our autographs and that sort of thing,' said the Major.

'Are they to be got in the shops?' I enquired as a harmless pleasantry.

'Oh yes, *hers* – they used to be.'

'Not now,' said Mrs Monarch with her eyes on the floor.

II

I could fancy the 'sort of thing' they put on the presentation copies of their photographs, and I was sure they wrote a beautiful hand. It was odd how quickly I was sure of everything that concerned them. If they were now so poor as to have to earn shillings and pence they could never have had much of a margin. Their good looks had been their capital, and they had good-humouredly made the most of the career that this resource marked out for them. It was in their faces, the blankness, the deep intellectual repose of the twenty years of country-house visiting that had given them pleasant intonations. I could see the sunny drawing-rooms, sprinkled with periodicals she didn't read, in which Mrs Monarch had continuously sat; I could see the wet shrubberies in which she had walked, equipped to admiration for either exercise. I could see the rich covers[3] the Major had helped to shoot and the wonderful garments in which, late at night, he repaired to the smoking-room to talk about them. I could imagine their leggings and waterproofs, their knowing tweeds and rugs, their rolls of sticks and cases of tackle and neat umbrellas; and I could evoke the exact appearance of their servants and the compact variety of their luggage on the platforms of country stations.

They gave small tips, but they were liked; they didn't do anything themselves, but they were welcome. They looked so well everywhere; they gratified the general relish for stature, complexion and 'form.' They knew it without fatuity or vulgarity, and they respected themselves in consequence. They weren't superficial; they were thorough and kept themselves up – it had been their line. People with such a taste for activity had to have some line. I could feel how even in a dull house they could have been counted on for the joy of life. At present something had happened – it didn't matter what, their little income had grown less, it had grown least – and they had to do something for pocket-money. Their friends could like them, I made out, without liking to support them. There was something about them that represented credit – their clothes, their manners, their type; but if credit is a large empty pocket in which an occasional chink reverberates, the chink at least must be audible. What they wanted of me was to help to make it so. Fortunately they had no children – I soon divined that. They would also perhaps wish our relations to be kept secret: this was why it was 'for the figure' – the reproduction of the face would betray them.

I liked them – I felt, quite as their friends must have done – they were so simple; and I had no objection to them if they would suit. But somehow with all their perfections I didn't easily believe in them. After all they were amateurs, and the ruling passion of my life was the detestation of the amateur. Combined with this was another perversity – an innate preference for the represented subject over the real one: the defect of the real one was so apt to be a lack of representation. I liked things that appeared; then one was sure. Whether they *were* or not was a subordinate and almost always a profitless question. There were other consider-ations, the first of which was that I already had two or three recruits in use, notably a young person with big feet, in alpaca, from Kilburn,[4] who for a couple of years had come to me regularly for my illustrations and with whom I was still – perhaps ignobly – satisfied. I frankly explained to my visitors how the case stood, but they had taken more precautions than I supposed. They had reasoned out their opportunity, for Claude Rivet had told them of the projected *édition de luxe* of one of the writers of our day – the rarest of the novelists – who, long neglected by the multitudinous vulgar and dearly prized by the attentive (need I mention Philip Vincent?) had had the happy fortune of seeing, late in life, the dawn and then the full light of a higher criticism; an estimate in which on the part of the public there was something really of expiation. The edition preparing, planned by a publisher of taste, was practically an act of high reparation; the wood-cuts with which it was to be enriched were the homage of English art to one of the most independent representatives of English letters. Major and Mrs Monarch confessed to me they had hoped I might be able to work *them* into my branch of the enterprise. They knew I was to do the first of the books, 'Rutland

Ramsay,'[5] but I had to make clear to them that my participation in the rest of the affair – this first book was to be a test – must depend on the satisfaction I should give. If this should be limited my employers would drop me with scarce common forms. It was therefore a crisis for me, and naturally I was making special preparations, looking about for new people, should they be necessary, and securing the best types. I admitted however that I should like to settle down to two or three good models who would do for everything.

'Should we have often to – a – put on special clothes?' Mrs Monarch timidly demanded.

'Dear yes – that's half the business.'

'And should we be expected to supply our own costumes?'

'Oh no; I've got a lot of things. A painter's models put on – or put off – anything he likes.'

'And you mean – a – the same?'

'The same?'

Mrs Monarch looked at her husband again.

'Oh she was just wondering,' he explained, 'if the costumes are in *general* use.' I had to confess that they were, and I mentioned further that some of them – I had a lot of genuine greasy last-century things – had served their time, a hundred years ago, on living world-stained men and women; on figures not perhaps so far removed, in that vanished world, from *their* type, the Monarchs', *quoi!*[6] of a breeched and bewigged age. 'We'll put on anything that *fits*,' said the Major.

'Oh I arrange that – they fit in the pictures.'

'I'm afraid I should do better for the modern books. I'd come as you like,' said Mrs Monarch.

'She has got a lot of clothes at home: they might do for contemporary life,' her husband continued.

'Oh I can fancy scenes in which you'd be quite natural.' And indeed I could see the slipshod rearrangements of stale properties – the stories I tried to produce pictures for without the exasperation of reading them – whose sandy tracts the good lady might help to people. But I had to return to the fact that for this sort of work – the daily mechanical grind – I was already equipped: the people I was working with were fully adequate.

'We only thought we might be more like *some* characters,' said Mrs Monarch mildly, getting up.

Her husband also rose; he stood looking at me with a dim wistfulness that was touching in so fine a man. 'Wouldn't it be rather a pull sometimes to have – a – to have –?' He hung fire; he wanted me to help him by phrasing what he meant. But I couldn't – I didn't know. So he brought it out awkwardly: 'The *real* thing;

a gentleman, you know, or a lady.' I was quite ready to give a general assent – I admitted that there was a great deal in that. This encouraged Major Monarch to say, following up his appeal with an unacted gulp: 'It's awfully hard – we've tried everything.' The gulp was communicative; it proved too much for his wife. Before I knew it Mrs Monarch had dropped again upon a divan and burst into tears. Her husband sat down beside her, holding one of her hands; whereupon she quickly dried her eyes with the other, while I felt embarrassed as she looked up at me. 'There isn't a confounded job I haven't applied for – waited for – prayed for. You can fancy we'd be pretty bad first. Secretaryships and that sort of thing? You might as well ask for a peerage. I'd be *anything* – I'm strong; a messenger or a coalheaver. I'd put on a gold-laced cap and open carriage-doors in front of the haberdasher's; I'd hang about a station to carry portmanteaux; I'd be a postman. But they won't *look* at you; there are thousands as good as yourself already on the ground. *Gentlemen*, poor beggars, who've drunk their wine, who've kept their hunters!'

I was as reassuring as I knew how to be, and my visitors were presently on their feet again while, for the experiment, we agreed on an hour. We were discussing it when the door opened and Miss Churm came in with a wet umbrella. Miss Churm had to take the omnibus to Maida Vale[7] and then walk half a mile. She looked a trifle blowsy and slightly splashed. I scarcely ever saw her come in without thinking afresh how odd it was that, being so little in herself, she should yet be so much in others. She was a meagre little Miss Churm, but was such an ample heroine of romance. She was only a freckled cockney, but she could represent everything, from a fine lady to a shepherdess; she had the faculty as she might have had a fine voice or long hair. She couldn't spell and she loved beer, but she had two or three 'points,' and practice, and a knack, and mother-wit, and a whimsical sensibility, and a love of the theatre, and seven sisters, and not an ounce of respect, especially for the h.[8] The first thing my visitors saw was that her umbrella was wet, and in their spotless perfection they visibly winced at it. The rain had come on since their arrival.

'I'm all in a soak; there *was* a mess of people in the 'bus. I wish you lived near a stytion,' said Miss Churm. I requested her to get ready as quickly as possible, and she passed into the room in which she always changed her dress. But before going out she asked me what she was to get into this time.

'It's the Russian princess, don't you know?' I answered; 'the one with the "golden eyes," in black velvet, for the long thing in the *Cheapside*.'[9]

'Golden eyes? I *say*!' cried Miss Churm, while my companions watched her with intensity as she withdrew. She always arranged herself, when she was late, before I could turn round; and I kept my visitors a little on purpose, so that they might get an idea, from seeing her, what would be expected of themselves. I mentioned that she was quite my notion of an excellent model — she was really very clever.

'Do you think she looks like a Russian princess?' Major Monarch asked with lurking alarm.

'When I make her, yes.'

'Oh if you have to *make* her —!' he reasoned, not without point.

'That's the most you can ask. There are so many who are not makeable.'

'Well now, *here's* a lady' — and with a persuasive smile he passed his arm into his wife's — 'who's already made!'

'Oh I'm not a Russian princess,' Mrs Monarch protested a little coldly. I could see she had known some and didn't like them. There at once was a complication of a kind I never had to fear with Miss Churm.

This young lady came back in black velvet — the gown was rather rusty and very low on her lean shoulders — and with a Japanese fan in her red hands. I reminded her that in the scene I was doing she had to look over some one's head. 'I forget whose it is; but it doesn't matter. Just look over a head.'

'I'd rather look over a stove,' said Miss Churm; and she took her station near the fire. She fell into position, settled herself into a tall attitude, gave a certain backward inclination to her head and a certain forward droop to her fan, and looked, at least to my prejudiced sense, distinguished and charming, foreign and dangerous. We left her looking so while I went downstairs with Major and Mrs Monarch.

'I believe I could come about as near it as that,' said Mrs Monarch.

'Oh you think she's shabby, but you must allow for the alchemy of art.'

However, they went off with an evident increase of comfort founded on their demonstrable advantage in being the real thing. I could fancy them shuddering over Miss Churm. She was very droll about them when I went back, for I told her what they wanted.

'Well, if *she* can sit I'll tyke to bookkeeping,' said my model.

'She's very ladylike,' I replied as an innocent form of aggravation.

'So much the worse for *you*. That means she can't turn round.'

'She'll do for the fashionable novels.'

'Oh yes, she'll *do* for them!' my model humorously declared. 'Ain't they bad enough without her?' I had often sociably denounced them to Miss Churm.

III

It was for the elucidation of a mystery in one of these works that I first tried Mrs Monarch. Her husband came with her, to be useful if necessary – it was sufficiently clear that as a general thing he would prefer to come with her. At first I wondered if this were for 'propriety's' sake – if he were going to be jealous and meddling. The idea was too tiresome, and if it had been confirmed it would speedily have brought our acquaintance to a close. But I soon saw there was nothing in it and that if he accompanied Mrs Monarch it was – in addition to the chance of being wanted – simply because he had nothing else to do. When they were separate his occupation was gone[10] and they never *had* been separate. I judged rightly that in their awkward situation their close union was their main comfort and that this union had no weak spot. It was a real marriage, an encouragement to the hesitating, a nut for pessimists to crack. Their address was humble – I remember afterwards thinking it had been the only thing about them that was really professional – and I could fancy the lamentable lodgings in which the Major would have been left alone. He could sit there more or less grimly with his wife – he couldn't sit there anyhow without her.

He had too much tact to try and make himself agreeable when he couldn't be useful; so when I was too absorbed in my work to talk he simply sat and waited. But I liked to hear him talk – it made my work, when not interrupting it, less mechanical, less special. To listen to him was to combine the excitement of going out with the economy of staying at home. There was only one hindrance – that I seemed not to know any of the people this brilliant couple had known. I think he wondered extremely, during the term of our intercourse, whom the deuce I *did* know. He hadn't a stray sixpence of an idea to fumble for, so we didn't spin it very fine; we confined ourselves to questions of leather and even of liquor – saddlers and breeches-makers and how to get excellent claret cheap – and matters like 'good trains' and the habits of small game. His lore on these last subjects was astonishing – he managed to interweave the station-master with the ornithologist. When he couldn't talk about greater things he could talk cheerfully about smaller, and since I couldn't accompany him into reminiscences of the fashionable world he could lower the conversation without a visible effort to my level.

So earnest a desire to please was touching in a man who could so easily have knocked one down. He looked after the fire and had an opinion on the draught of the stove without my asking him, and I could see that he thought many of my arrangements not half knowing. I remember telling him that if I were only rich I'd offer him a salary to come and teach me how to live. Sometimes he gave a random sigh of which the essence might have been: 'Give me even such a bare old barrack as *this*, and I'd do something with it!' When I wanted to use him he came alone; which was an illustration of the superior courage of women. His wife could bear her solitary second floor, and she was in general more discreet; showing by various small reserves that she was alive to the propriety of keeping our relations markedly professional – not letting them slide into sociability. She wished it to remain clear that she and the Major were employed, not cultivated, and if she approved of me as a superior, who could be kept in his place, she never thought me quite good enough for an equal.

She sat with great intensity, giving the whole of her mind to it, and was capable of remaining for an hour almost as motionless as before a photographer's lens. I could see she had been photographed often, but somehow the very habit that made her good for that purpose unfitted her for mine. At first I was extremely pleased with her ladylike air, and it was a satisfaction, on coming to follow her lines, to see how good they were and how far they could lead the pencil. But after a little skirmishing I began to find her too insurmountably stiff; do what I would with it my drawing looked like a photograph or a copy of a photograph. Her figure had no variety of expression – she herself had no sense of variety. You may say that this was my business and was only a question of placing her. Yet I placed her in every conceivable position and she managed to obliterate their differences. She was always a lady certainly, and into the bargain was always the same lady. She was the real thing, but always the same thing. There were moments when I rather writhed under the serenity of her confidence that she *was* the real thing. All her dealings with me and all her husband's were an implication that this was lucky for *me*. Meanwhile I found myself trying to invent types that approached her own, instead of making her own transform itself – in the clever way that was not impossible for instance to poor Miss Churm. Arrange as I would and take the precautions I would, she always came out, in my pictures, too tall – landing me in the dilemma of having represented a fascinating woman as seven feet high, which (out of respect perhaps to my own very much scantier inches) was far from my idea of such a personage.

The case was worse with the Major – nothing I could do would keep *him* down, so that he became useful only for the representation of brawny giants. I adored variety and range, I cherished human accidents, the illustrative note; I wanted to characterise closely, and the thing in the world I most hated was the danger of being ridden by a type. I had quarrelled with some of my friends about it; I had parted company with them for maintaining that one *had* to be, and that if the type was beautiful – witness Raphael and Leonardo[11] – the servitude was only a gain. I was neither Leonardo nor Raphael – I might only be a presumptuous young modern searcher; but I held that everything was to be sacrificed sooner than character. When they claimed that the obsessional form could easily *be* character I retorted, perhaps superficially, 'Whose?' It couldn't be everybody's — it might end in being nobody's.

After I had drawn Mrs Monarch a dozen times I felt surer even than before that the value of such a model as Miss Churm resided precisely in the fact that she had no positive stamp, combined of course with the other fact that what she did have was a curious and inexplicable talent for imitation. Her usual appearance was like a curtain which she could draw up at request for a capital performance. This performance was simply suggestive; but it was a word to the wise — it was vivid and pretty. Sometimes even I thought it, though she was plain herself, too insipidly pretty; I made it a reproach to her that the figures drawn from her were monotonously (*bêtement*,[12] as we used to say) graceful. Nothing made her more angry: it was so much her pride to feel she could sit for characters that had nothing in common with each other. She would accuse me at such moments of taking away her 'reputytion.'

It suffered a certain shrinkage, this queer quantity, from the repeated visits of my new friends. Miss Churm was greatly in demand, never in want of employment, so I had no scruple in putting her off occasionally, to try them more at my ease. It was certainly amusing at first to do the real thing — it was amusing to do Major Monarch's trousers. They *were* the real thing, even if he did come out colossal. It was amusing to do his wife's back hair — it was so mathematically neat — and the particular 'smart' tension of her tight stays. She lent herself especially to positions in which the face was somewhat averted or blurred; she abounded in ladylike back views and *profils perdus*.[13] When she stood erect she took naturally one of the attitudes in which court-painters represent queens and princesses; so that I found myself wondering whether, to draw out this accomplishment, I couldn't get the editor of the *Cheapside* to publish a really royal romance, 'A Tale of Buckingham Palace.' Sometimes however the real thing and the make-believe came into contact; by which I mean that Miss Churm, keeping an appointment or coming to make one on days when I had much work in hand, encountered her invidious rivals. The encounter was not on their part, for they noticed her no more than if she had been the housemaid; not from intentional loftiness, but simply because as yet, professionally, they didn't know how to fraternise, as I could imagine they would have liked — or at least that the Major would. They couldn't talk about the omnibus — they always walked; and they didn't know what else to try — she wasn't interested in good trains or cheap claret. Besides, they must have felt — in the air — that she was amused at them, secretly derisive of their ever knowing how. She wasn't a person to conceal the limits of her faith if she had had a chance to show them. On the other hand Mrs Monarch didn't think her tidy; for why else did she take pains to say to me — it was going out of the way, for Mrs Monarch — that she didn't like dirty women?

One day when my young lady happened to be present with my other sitters — she even dropped in, when it was convenient, for a chat — I asked her to be so good as to lend a hand in getting tea, a service with which she was familiar and which was one of a class that, living as I did in a small way, with slender domestic resources, I often appealed to my models to render. They liked to lay hands on my property, to break the sitting, and sometimes the china — it made them feel Bohemian. The next time I saw Miss Churm after this incident she surprised me greatly by making a scene about it — she accused me of having wished to humiliate her. She hadn't resented the outrage at the time, but had seemed obliging and amused, enjoying the comedy of asking Mrs Monarch, who sat vague and silent, whether she would have cream and sugar, and putting an exaggerated simper into the question. She had tried intonations — as if she too wished to pass for the real thing — till I was afraid my other visitors would take offence.

Oh they were determined not to do this, and their touching patience was the measure of their great need. They would sit by the hour, uncomplaining, till I was ready to use them; they would come back on the chance of being wanted and would walk away cheerfully if it failed. I used to go to the door with them to see in what magnificent order they retreated. I tried to find other employment for them — I introduced them to several artists. But they didn't 'take,' for reasons I could appreciate, and I became rather anxiously aware that after such disappointments they fell back upon me with a heavier weight. They did me the honour to think me most *their* form. They weren't romantic enough for the painters, and in those days there were few serious workers in black-and-white. Besides, they had an eye to the great job I had mentioned to them — they had secretly set their hearts on supplying the right essence for my pictorial vindication of our fine novelist. They knew that for this undertaking I should want no costume-effects, none of the frippery of past ages — that it was a case in which everything would be contemporary and satirical and presumably genteel. If I could work them into it their future would be assured, for the labour would of course be long and the occupation steady.

One day Mrs Monarch came without her husband — she explained his absence by his having had to go to the City.[14] While she sat there in her usual relaxed majesty there came at the door a knock which I immediately recognised as the subdued appeal of a model out of work. It was followed by the entrance of a young man whom I at once saw to be a foreigner and who proved in fact an Italian acquainted with no English word but my name, which he uttered in a way that made it seem to include all others. I hadn't then visited his country, nor was I proficient in his tongue; but as he was not so meanly constituted — what Italian is? — as to depend only on that member for expression he conveyed to me, in familiar but graceful mimicry, that he was in search of exactly the employment in which the lady before me was engaged. I was not struck with him at first, and while I continued to draw I dropped few signs of interest or encouragement. He stood his ground however – not importunately, but with a dumb dog-like fidelity in his eyes that amounted to innocent impudence, the manner of a devoted servant – he might have been in the house for years – unjustly suspected. Suddenly it struck me that this very attitude and expression made a picture; whereupon I told him to sit down and wait till I should be free. There was another picture in the way he obeyed me, and I observed as I worked that there were others still in the way he looked wonderingly, with his head thrown back, about the high studio. He might have been crossing himself in Saint Peter's.[15] Before I finished I said to myself 'The fellow's a bankrupt orange-monger, but a treasure.'

When Mrs Monarch withdrew he passed across the room like a flash to open the door for her, standing there with the rapt pure gaze of the young Dante spellbound by the young Beatrice.[16] As I never insisted, in such situations, on the blankness of the British domestic, I reflected that he had the making of a servant – and I needed one, but couldn't pay him to be only that – as well as of a model; in short I resolved to adopt my bright adventurer if he would agree to officiate in the double capacity. He jumped at my offer, and in the event my rashness – for I had really known nothing about him – wasn't brought home to me. He proved a sympathetic though a desultory ministrant, and had in a wonderful degree the *sentiment de la pose*.[17] It was uncultivated, instinctive, a part of the happy instinct that had guided him to my door and helped him to spell out my name on the card nailed to it. He had had no other introduction to me than a guess, from the shape of my high north window, seen outside, that my place was a studio and that as a studio it would contain an artist. He had wandered to England in search of fortune, like other itinerants, and had embarked, with a partner and a small green hand-cart, on the sale of penny ices. The ices had melted away and the partner had dissolved in their train. My young man wore tight yellow trousers with reddish stripes and his name was Oronte. He was sallow but fair, and when I put him into some old clothes of my own he looked like an Englishman. He was as good as Miss Churm, who could look, when requested, like an Italian.

IV

I thought Mrs Monarch's face slightly convulsed when, on her coming back with her husband, she found Oronte installed. It was strange to have to recognise in a scrap of a lazzarone[18] a competitor to her magnificent Major. It was she who scented danger first, for the Major was anecdotically unconscious. But Oronte gave us tea, with a hundred eager confusions — he had never been concerned in so queer a process — and I think she thought better of me for having at last an 'establishment.' They saw a couple of drawings that I had made of the establishment, and Mrs Monarch hinted that it never would have struck her he had sat for them. 'Now the drawings you make from *us*, they look exactly like us,' she reminded me, smiling in triumph; and I recognised that this was indeed just their defect. When I drew the Monarchs I couldn't anyhow get away from them — get into the character I wanted to represent; and I hadn't the least desire my model should be discoverable in my picture. Miss Churm never was, and Mrs Monarch thought I hid her, very properly, because she was vulgar; whereas if she was lost it was only as the dead who go to heaven are lost — in the gain of an angel more.

By this time I had got a certain start with 'Rutland Ramsay,' the first novel in the great projected series; that is I had produced a dozen drawings, several with the help of the Major and his wife, and I had sent them in for approval. My understanding with the publishers, as I have already hinted, had been that I was to be left to do my work, in this particular case, as I liked, with the whole book committed to me; but my connexion with the rest of the series was only contingent. There were moments when, frankly, it *was* a comfort to have the real thing under one's hand; for there were characters in 'Rutland Ramsay' that were very much like it. There were people presumably as erect as the Major and women of as good a fashion as Mrs Monarch. There was a great deal of country-house life — treated, it is true, in a fine fanciful ironical generalised way — and there was a considerable implication of knickerbockers and kilts. There were certain things I had to settle at the outset; such things for instance as the exact appearance of the hero and the particular bloom and figure of the heroine. The author of course gave me a lead, but there was a margin for interpretation. I took the Monarchs into my confidence, I told them frankly what I was about, I mentioned my embarrassments and alternatives. 'Oh take *him*!' Mrs Monarch murmured sweetly, looking at her husband; and 'What could you want better than my wife?' the Major enquired with the comfortable candour that now prevailed between us.

I wasn't obliged to answer these remarks — I was only obliged to place my sitters. I wasn't easy in mind, and I postponed a little timidly perhaps the solving of my question. The book was a large canvas, the other figures were numerous, and I worked off at first some of the episodes in which the hero and the heroine were not concerned. When once I had set *them* up I should have to stick to them — I couldn't make my young man seven feet high in one place and five feet nine in another. I inclined on the whole to the latter measurement, though the Major more than once reminded me that *he* looked about as young as any one. It was indeed quite possible to arrange him, for the figure, so that it would have been difficult to detect his age. After the spontaneous Oronte had been with me a month, and after I had given him to understand several times over that his native exuberance would presently constitute an insurmountable barrier to our further intercourse, I waked to a sense of his heroic capacity. He was only five feet seven, but the remaining inches were latent. I tried him almost secretly at first, for I was really rather afraid of the judgement my other models would pass on such a choice. If they regarded Miss Churm as little better than a snare what would they think of the representation by a person so little the real thing as an Italian street-vendor of a protagonist formed by a public school?[19]

If I went a little in fear of them it wasn't because they bullied me, because they had got an oppressive foothold, but because in their really pathetic decorum and mysteriously permanent newness they counted on me so intensely. I was therefore very glad when Jack Hawley came home: he was always of such good counsel. He painted badly himself, but there was no one like him for putting his finger on the place. He had been absent from England for a year; he had been somewhere – I don't remember where – to get a fresh eye. I was in a good deal of dread of any such organ, but we were old friends; he had been away for months and a sense of emptiness was creeping into my life. I hadn't dodged a missile for a year.

He came back with a fresh eye, but with the same old black velvet blouse, and the first evening he spent in my studio we smoked cigarettes till the small hours. He had done no work himself, he had only got the eye; so the field was clear for the production of my little things. He wanted to see what I had produced for the *Cheapside*, but he was disappointed in the exhibition. That at least seemed the meaning of two or three comprehensive groans which, as he lounged on my big divan, his leg folded under him, looking at my latest drawings, issued from his lips with the smoke of the cigarette.

'What's the matter with you?' I asked.

'What's the matter with *you*?'

'Nothing save that I'm mystified.'

'You are indeed. You're quite off the hinge. What's the meaning of this new fad?' And he tossed me, with visible irreverence, a drawing in which I happened to have depicted both my elegant models. I asked if he didn't think it good, and he replied that it struck him as execrable, given the sort of thing I had always represented myself to him as wishing to arrive at; but I let that pass – I was so anxious to see exactly what he meant. The two figures in the picture looked colossal, but I supposed this was *not* what he meant, inasmuch as, for aught he knew to the contrary, I might have been trying for some such effect. I maintained that I was working exactly in the same way as when he last had done me the honour to tell me I might do something some day. 'Well, there's a screw loose somewhere,' he answered; 'wait a bit and I'll discover it.' I depended upon him to do so: where else was the fresh eye? But he produced at last nothing more luminous than 'I don't know – I don't like your types.' This was lame for a critic who had never consented to discuss with me anything but the question of execution, the direction of strokes and the mystery of values.

'In the drawings you've been looking at I think my types are very handsome.'

'Oh they won't do!'

'I've been working with new models.'

'I see you have. *They* won't do.'

'Are you very sure of that?'

'Absolutely – they're stupid.'

'You mean *I* am – for I ought to get round that.'

'You *can't* – with such people. Who are they?'

I told him, so far as was necessary, and he concluded heartlessly: 'Ce sont des gens qu'il faut mettre à la porte.'[20]

'You've never seen them; they're awfully good' – I flew to their defence.

'Not seen them? Why all this recent work of yours drops to pieces with them. It's all I want to see of them.'

'No one else has said anything against it – the *Cheapside* people are pleased.'

'Every one else is an ass, and the *Cheapside* people the biggest asses of all. Come, don't pretend at this time of day to have pretty illusions about the public, especially about publishers and editors. It's not for *such* animals you work – it's for those who know, *coloro che sanno;*[21] so keep straight for *me* if you can't keep straight for yourself. There was a certain sort of thing you used to try for – and a very good thing it was. But this twaddle isn't *in* it.' When I talked with Hawley later about 'Rutland Ramsay' and its possible successors he declared that I must get back into my boat again or I should go to the bottom. His voice in short was the voice of warning.

I noted the warning, but I didn't turn my friends out of doors. They bored me a good deal; but the very fact that they bored me admonished me not to sacrifice them – if there was anything to be done with them – simply to irritation. As I look back at this phase they seem to me to have pervaded my life not a little. I have a vision of them as most of the time in my studio, seated against the wall on an old velvet bench to be out of the way, and resembling the while a pair of patient courtiers in a royal ante-chamber. I'm convinced that during the coldest weeks of the winter they held their ground because it saved them fire. Their newness was losing its gloss, and it was impossible not to feel them objects of charity. Whenever Miss Churm arrived they went away, and after I was fairly launched in 'Rutland Ramsay' Miss Churm arrived pretty often. They managed to express to me tacitly that they supposed I wanted her for the low life of the book, and I let them suppose it, since they had attempted to study the work – it was lying about the studio – without discovering that it dealt only with the highest circles. They had dipped into the most brilliant of our novelists without deciphering many passages. I still took an hour from them, now and again, in spite of Jack Hawley's warning: it would be time enough to dismiss them, if dismissal should be necessary, when the rigour of the season was over. Hawley had made their acquaintance – he had met them at my fireside – and thought them a ridiculous pair. Learning that he was a painter they tried to approach him, to show him too that they were the real thing; but he looked at them, across the big room, as if they were miles away: they were a compendium of everything he most objected to in the social system of his country. Such people as that, all convention and patent-leather, with ejaculations that stopped conversation, had no business in a studio. A studio was a place to learn to see, and how could you see through a pair of feather-beds?

The main inconvenience I suffered at their hands was that at first I was shy of letting it break upon them that my artful little servant had begun to sit to me for 'Rutland Ramsay.' They knew I had been odd enough – they were prepared by this time to allow oddity to artists – to pick a foreign vagabond out of the streets when I might have had a person with whiskers and credentials; but it was some time before they learned how high I rated his accomplishments. They found him in an attitude more than once, but they never doubted I was doing him as an organ-grinder. There were several things they never guessed, and one of them was that for a striking scene in the novel, in which a footman briefly figured, it occurred to me to make use of Major Monarch as the menial. I kept putting this off, I didn't like to ask him to don the livery – besides the difficulty of finding a livery to fit him. At last, one day late in the winter, when I was at work on the despised Oronte, who caught one's idea on the wing, and was in the glow of feeling myself go very straight, they came in, the Major and his wife, with their society laugh about nothing (there was less and less to laugh at); came in like country-callers – they always reminded me of that – who have walked across the park after church and are presently persuaded to stay to luncheon. Luncheon was over, but they could stay to tea – I knew they wanted it. The fit was on me, however, and I couldn't let my ardour cool and my work wait, with the fading daylight, while my model prepared it. So I asked Mrs Monarch if she would mind laying it out – a request which for an instant brought all the blood to her face. Her eyes were on her husband's for a second, and some mute telegraphy passed between them. Their folly was over the next instant; his cheerful shrewdness put an end to it. So far from pitying their wounded pride, I must add, I was moved to give it as complete a lesson as I could. They bustled about together and got out the cups and saucers and made the kettle boil. I know they felt as if they were waiting on my servant, and when the tea was prepared I said: 'He'll have a cup, please – he's tired.' Mrs Monarch brought him one where he stood, and he took it from her as if he had been a gentleman at a party squeezing a crush-hat[22] with an elbow.

Then it came over me that she had made a great effort for me – made it with a kind of nobleness – and that I owed her a compensation. Each time I saw her after this I wondered what the compensation could be. I couldn't go on doing the wrong thing to oblige them. Oh it *was* the wrong thing, the stamp of the work for which they sat – Hawley was not the only person to say it now. I sent in a large number of the drawings I had made for 'Rutland Ramsay,' and I received a warning that was more to the point than Hawley's. The artistic adviser of the house for which I was working was of opinion that many of my illustrations were not what had been looked for. Most of these illustrations were the subjects in which the Monarchs had figured. Without going into the question of what *had* been looked for, I had to face the fact that at this rate I shouldn't get the other books to do. I hurled myself in despair on Miss Churm – I put her through all her paces. I not only adopted Oronte publicly as my hero, but one morning when the Major looked in to see if I didn't require him to finish a *Cheapside* figure for which he had begun to sit the week before, I told him I had changed my mind – I'd do the drawing from my man. At this my visitor turned pale and stood looking at me. 'Is *he* your idea of an English gentleman?' he asked.

I was disappointed, I was nervous, I wanted to get on with my work; so I replied with irritation: 'Oh my dear Major – I can't be ruined for *you*!'

It was a horrid speech, but he stood another moment – after which, without a word, he quitted the studio. I drew a long breath, for I said to myself that I shouldn't see him again. I hadn't told him definitely that I was in danger of having my work rejected, but I was vexed at his not having felt the catastrophe in the air, read with me the moral of our fruitless collaboration, the lesson that in the deceptive atmosphere of art even the highest respectability may fail of being plastic.

I didn't owe my friends money, but I did see them again. They reappeared together three days later, and, given all the other facts, there was something tragic in that one. It was a clear proof they could find nothing else in life to do. They had threshed the matter out in a dismal conference – they had digested the bad news that they were not in for the series. If they weren't useful to me even for the *Cheapside* their function seemed difficult to determine, and I could only judge at first that they had come, forgivingly, decorously, to take a last leave. This made me rejoice in secret that I had little leisure for a scene; for I had placed both my other models in position together and I was pegging away at a drawing from which I hoped to derive glory. It had been suggested by the passage in which Rutland Ramsay, drawing up a chair to Artemisia's piano-stool, says extraordinary things to her while she ostensibly fingers out a difficult piece of music. I had done Miss Churm at the piano before – it was an attitude in which she knew how to take on an absolutely poetic grace. I wished the two figures to 'compose' together with intensity, and my little Italian had entered perfectly into my conception. The pair were vividly before me, the piano had been pulled out; it was a charming show of blended youth and murmured love, which I had only to catch and keep. My visitors stood and looked at it, and I was friendly to them over my shoulder.

They made no response, but I was used to silent company and went on with my work, only a little disconcerted – even though exhilarated by the sense that *this* was at least the ideal thing – at not having got rid of them after all. Presently I heard Mrs Monarch's sweet voice beside or rather above me: 'I wish her hair were a little better done.' I looked up and she was staring with a strange fixedness at Miss Churm, whose back was turned to her. 'Do you mind my just touching it?' she went on – a question which made me spring up for an instant as with the instinctive fear that she might do the young lady a harm. But she quieted me with a glance I shall never forget – I confess I should like to have been able to paint *that* – and went for a moment to my model. She spoke to her softly, laying a hand on her shoulder and bending over her; and as the girl, understanding, gratefully assented, she disposed her rough curls, with a few quick passes, in such a way as to make Miss Churm's head twice as charming. It was one of the most heroic personal services I've ever seen rendered. Then Mrs Monarch turned away with a low sigh and, looking about her as if for something to do, stooped to the floor with a noble humility and picked up a dirty rag that had dropped out of my paint-box.

The Major meanwhile had also been looking for something to do, and, wandering to the other end of the studio, saw before him my breakfast-things neglected, unremoved. 'I say, can't I be useful *here*?' he called out to me with an irrepressible quaver. I assented with a laugh that I fear was awkward, and for the next ten minutes, while I worked, I heard the light clatter of china and the tinkle of spoons and glass. Mrs Monarch assisted her husband – they washed up my crockery, they put it away. They wandered off into my little scullery, and I afterwards found that they had cleaned my knives and that my slender stock of plate had an unprecedented surface. When it came over me, the latent eloquence of what they were doing, I confess that my drawing was blurred for a moment – the picture swam. They had accepted their failure, but they couldn't accept their fate. They had bowed their heads in bewilderment to the perverse and cruel law in virtue of which the real thing could be so much less precious than the unreal; but they didn't want to starve. If my servants were my models, then my models might be my servants. They would reverse the parts – the others would sit for the ladies and gentlemen and *they* would do the work. They would still be in the studio – it was an intense dumb appeal to me not to turn them out. 'Take us on,' they wanted to say – 'we'll do *anything*.'

My pencil dropped from my hand; my sitting was spoiled and I got rid of my sitters, who were also evidently rather mystified and awestruck. Then, alone with the Major and his wife I had a most uncomfortable moment. He put their prayer into a single sentence: 'I say, you know – just let *us* do for you, can't you?' I couldn't – it was dreadful to see them emptying my slops; but I pretended I could, to oblige them, for about a week. Then I gave them a sum of money to go away, and I never saw them again. I obtained the remaining books, but my friend Hawley repeats that Major and Mrs Monarch did me a permanent harm, got me into false ways. If it be true I'm content to have paid the price – for the memory.

Greville Fane

Coming in to dress for dinner I found a telegram: 'Mrs Stormer dying; can you give us half a column for to-morrow evening? Let her down easily, but not too easily.' I was late; I was in a hurry; I had very little time to think; but at a venture I dispatched a reply: 'Will do what I can.' It was not till I had dressed and was rolling away to dinner that, in the hansom,[1] I bethought myself of the difficulty of the condition attached. The difficulty was not of course in letting her down easily but in qualifying that indulgence. 'So I simply won't qualify it,' I said. I didn't admire but liked her, and had known her so long that I almost felt heartless in sitting down at such an hour to a feast of indifference. I must have seemed abstracted, for the early years of my acquaintance with her came back to me. I spoke of her to the lady I had taken down,[2] but the lady I had taken down had never heard of Greville Fane. I tried my other neighbour, who pronounced her books 'too vile.' I had never thought them very good, but I should let her down more easily than that.

I came away early, for the express purpose of driving to ask about her. The journey took time, for she lived in the northwest district, in the neighbourhood of Primrose Hill.[3] My apprehension that I should be too late was justified in a fuller sense than I had attached to it – I had only feared that the house would be shut up. There were lights in the windows, and the temperate tinkle of my bell brought a servant immediately to the door; but poor Mrs Stormer had passed into a state in which the resonance of no earthly knocker was to be feared. A lady hovering behind the servant came forward into the hall when she heard my voice. I recognised Lady Luard, but she had mistaken me for the doctor.

'Pardon my appearing at such an hour,' I said; 'it was the first possible moment after I heard.'

'It's all over,' Lady Luard replied. 'Dearest mamma!'

She stood there under the lamp with her eyes on me; she was very tall, very stiff, very cold, and always looked as if these things, and some others beside, in her dress, in her manner and even in her name, were an implication that she was very admirable. I had never been able to follow the argument, but that's a detail.

I expressed briefly and frankly what I felt, while the little mottled maidservant flattened herself against the wall of the narrow passage and tried to look detached without looking indifferent. It was not a moment to make a visit, and I was on the point of retreating when Lady Luard arrested me with a queer casual drawling 'Would you – a – would you perhaps be *writing* something?' I felt for the instant like an infamous interviewer, which I wasn't. But I pleaded guilty to this intention, on which she returned: 'I'm so very glad – but I think my brother would like to see you.' I detested her brother, but it wasn't an occasion to act this out; so I suffered myself to be inducted, to my surprise, into a small back room which I immediately recognised as the scene, during the later years, of Mrs Stormer's imperturbable industry. Her table was there, the battered and blotted accessory to innumerable literary lapses, with its contracted space for the arms (she wrote only from the elbow down) and the confusion of scrappy scribbled sheets which had already become literary remains. Leolin was also there, smoking a cigarette before the fire and looking impudent even in his grief, sincere as it well might have been.

To meet him, to greet him, I had to make a sharp effort; for the air he wore to me as he stood before me was quite that of his mother's murderer. She lay silent for ever upstairs – as dead as an unsuccessful book, and his swaggering erectness was a kind of symbol of his having killed her. I wondered if he had already, with his sister, been calculating what they could get for the poor papers on the table; but I hadn't long to wait to learn, since in reply to the few words of sympathy I addressed him he puffed out: 'It's miserable, miserable, yes; but she has left three books complete.' His words had the oddest effect; they converted the cramped little room into a seat of trade and made the 'book' wonderfully feasible. He would certainly get all that could be got for the three. Lady Luard explained to me that her husband had been with them, but had had to go down to the House.[4] To her brother she mentioned that I was going to write something, and to me again made it clear that she hoped I would 'do mamma justice.' She added that she didn't think this had ever been done. She said to her brother: 'Don't you think there are some things he ought thoroughly to understand?' and on his instantly exclaiming 'Oh thoroughly, thoroughly!' went on rather austerely: 'I mean about mamma's birth.'

'Yes and her connexions,' Leolin added.

I professed every willingness, and for five minutes I listened; but it would be too much to say I clearly understood. I don't even now, but it's not important. My vision was of other matters than those they put before me, and while they desired there should be no mistake about their ancestors I became keener and keener about themselves. I got away as soon as possible and walked home through the great dusky empty London – the best of all conditions for thought. By the time I reached my door my little article was practically composed – ready to be transferred on the morrow from the polished plate of fancy. I believe it attracted some notice, was thought 'graceful' and was said to be by some one else. I had to be pointed without being lively, and it took some doing. But what I said was much less interesting than what I thought – especially during the half-hour I spent in my armchair by the fire, smoking the cigar I always light before going to bed. I went to sleep there, I believe; but I continued to moralise about Greville Fane. I'm reluctant to lose that retrospect altogether, and this is a dim little memory of it, a document not to 'serve.'[5] The dear woman had written a hundred stories, but none so curious as her own.

When first I knew her she had published half a dozen fictions, and I believe I had also perpetrated a novel. She was more than a dozen years my elder, but a person who always acknowledged her comparative state. It wasn't so very long ago, but in London, amid the big waves of the present, even a near horizon gets hidden. I met her at some dinner and took her down, rather flattered at offering my arm to a celebrity. She didn't look like one, with her matronly mild inanimate face, but I supposed her greatness would come out in her conversation. I gave it all the opportunities I could, but was nevertheless not disappointed when I found her only a dull kind woman. This was why I liked her – she rested me so from literature. To myself literature was an irritation, a torment; but Greville Fane slumbered in the intellectual part of it even as a cat on a hearthrug or a Creole in a hammock. She wasn't a woman of genius, but her faculty was so special, so much a gift out of hand, that I've often wondered why she fell below that distinction. This was doubtless because the transaction, in her case, had remained incomplete; genius always pays for the gift, feels the debt, and she was placidly unconscious of a call. She could invent stories by the yard, but couldn't write a page of English. She went down to her grave without suspecting that though she had contributed volumes to the diversion of her contemporaries she hadn't contributed a sentence to the language. This hadn't prevented bushels of criticism from being heaped on her head; she was worth a couple of columns any day to the weekly papers, in which it was shown that her pictures of life were dreadful but her style superior. She asked me to come and see her and I complied. She lived then in Montpellier Square;[6] which helped me to see how dissociated her imagination was from her character.

An industrious widow, devoted to her daily stint, to meeting the butcher and baker and making a home for her son and daughter, from the moment she took her pen in her hand she became a creature of passion. She thought the English novel deplorably wanting in that element, and the task she had cut out for herself was to supply the deficiency. Passion in high life was the general formula of this work, for her imagination was at home only in the most exalted circles. She adored in truth the aristocracy, and they constituted for her the romance of the world or, what is more to the point, the prime material of fiction. Their beauty and luxury, their loves and revenges, their temptations and surrenders, their immoralities and diamonds were as familiar to her as the blots on her writing-table. She was not a belated producer of the old fashionable novel, but, with a cleverness and a modernness of her own, had freshened up the fly-blown tinsel. She turned off plots by the hundred and – so far as her flying quill could convey her – was perpetually going abroad. Her types, her illustrations, her tone were nothing if not cosmopolitan. She recognised nothing less provincial than European society, and her fine folk knew each other and made love to each other from Doncaster to Bucharest.[7] She had an idea that she resembled Balzac, and her favourite historical characters were Lucien de Rubempré and the Vidame de Pamiers.[8] I must add that when I once asked her who the latter personage was she was unable to tell me. She was very brave and healthy and cheerful, very abundant and innocent and wicked. She was expert and vulgar and snobbish, and never so intensely British as when she was particularly foreign.

This combination of qualities had brought her early success, and I remember having heard with wonder and envy of what she 'got,' in those days, for a novel. The revelation gave me a pang: it was such a proof that, practising a totally different style, I should never make my fortune. And yet when, as I knew her better she told me her real tariff and I saw how rumour had quadrupled it, I liked her enough to be sorry. After a while I discovered too that if she got less it was not that *I* was to get any more. My failure never had what Mrs Stormer would have called the banality of being relative – it was always admirably absolute. She lived at ease however in those days – ease is exactly the word, though she produced three novels a year. She scorned me when I spoke of difficulty – it was the only thing that made her angry. If I hinted at the grand licking into shape that a work of art required she thought it a pretension and a *pose*. She never recognised the 'torment of form'; the furthest she went was to introduce into one of her books (in satire her hand was heavy) a young poet who was always talking about it. I couldn't quite understand her irritation on this score, for she had nothing at stake in the matter. She had a shrewd perception that form, in prose at least, never recommended any one to the public we were condemned to address; according to which she lost nothing (her private humiliation not counted) by having none to show. She made no pretence of producing works of art, but had comfortable tea-drinking hours in which she freely confessed herself a common pastrycook, dealing in such tarts and puddings as would bring customers to the shop. She put in plenty of sugar and of cochineal, or whatever it is that gives these articles a rich and attractive colour. She had a calm independence of observation and opportunity which constituted an inexpugnable strength and would enable her to go on indefinitely. It's only real success that wanes, it's only solid things that melt. Greville Fane's ignorance of life was a resource still more unfailing than the most approved receipt. On her saying once that the day would come when she should have written herself out I answered: 'Ah you open straight into fairyland, and the fairies love you and *they* never change. Fairyland's always there; it always was from the beginning of time and always will be to the end. They've given you the key and you can always open the door. With me it's different; I try, in my clumsy way, to be in some direct relation to life.' 'Oh bother your direct relation to life!' she used to reply, for she was always annoyed by the phrase – which wouldn't in the least prevent her using it as a note of elegance. With no more prejudices than an old sausage-mill, she would give forth again with patient punctuality any poor verbal scrap that had been dropped into her. I cheered her with saying that the dark day, at the end, would be for the 'likes' of *me*; since, proceeding in our small way by experience and study – priggish we! – we depended not on a revelation but on a little tiresome process. Attention depended on occasion, and where should we be when occasion failed?

One day she told me that as the novelist's life was so delightful and, during the good years at least, such a comfortable support – she had these staggering optimisms – she meant to train up her boy to follow it.[9] She took the ingenious view that it was a profession like another and that therefore everything was to be gained by beginning young and serving an apprenticeship. Moreover the education would be less expensive than any other special course, inasmuch as she could herself administer it. She didn't profess to keep a school, but she could at least teach her own child. It wasn't that she had such a gift, but – she confessed to me as if she were afraid I should laugh at her – that *he* had. I didn't laugh at her for that, because I thought the boy sharp – I had seen him sundry times. He was well-grown and good-looking and unabashed, and both he and his sister made me wonder about their defunct papa, concerning whom the little I knew was that he had been a country vicar and brother to a small squire. I explained them to myself by suppositions and imputations possibly unjust to the departed; so little were they – superficially at least – the children of their mother. There used to be on an easel in her drawing-room an enlarged photograph of her husband, done by some horrible posthumous 'process' and draped, as to its florid frame, with a silken scarf which testified to the candour of Greville Fane's bad taste. It made him look like an unsuccessful tragedian, but it wasn't a thing to trust. He may have been a successful comedian. Of the two children the girl was the elder, and struck me in all her younger years as singularly colourless. She was only long, very long, like an undecipherable letter. It wasn't till Mrs Stormer came back from a protracted residence abroad that Ethel (which was this young lady's name) began to produce the effect, large and stiff and afterwards eminent in her, of a certain kind of resolution, something as public and important as if a meeting and a chairman had passed it. She gave one to understand she meant to do all she could for herself. She was long-necked and near-sighted and striking, and I thought I had never seen sweet seventeen in a form so hard and high and dry. She was cold and affected and ambitious, and she carried an eyeglass with a long handle, which she put up whenever she wanted not to see. She had come out,[10] as the phrase is, immensely; and yet I felt as if she were surrounded with a spiked iron railing. What she meant to do for herself was to marry, and it was the only thing, I think, that she meant to do for any one else; yet who would be inspired to clamber over that bristling barrier? What flower of tenderness or of intimacy would such an adventurer conceive as his reward?

This was for Sir Baldwin Luard to say; but he naturally never confided me the secret. He was a joyless jokeless young man, with the air of having other secrets as well, and a determination to get on politically that was indicated by his never having been known to commit himself – as regards any proposition whatever – beyond an unchallengeable 'Oh!' His wife and he must have conversed mainly in prim ejaculations, but they understood sufficiently that they were kindred spirits. I remember being angry with Greville Fane when she announced these nuptials to me as magnificent; I remember asking her what splendour there was in the union of the daughter of a woman of genius with an irredeemable mediocrity. 'Oh he has immense ability,' she said; but she blushed for the maternal fib. What she meant was that though Sir Baldwin's estates were not vast – he had a dreary house in South Kensington and a still drearier 'Hall' somewhere in Essex,[11] which was let – the connexion was a 'smarter' one than a child of hers could have aspired to form. In spite of the social bravery of her novels she took a very humble and dingy view of herself, so that of all her productions 'my daughter Lady Luard' was quite the one she was proudest of. That personage thought our authoress vulgar and was distressed and perplexed by the frequent freedoms of her pen, but had a complicated attitude for this indirect connexion with literature. So far as it was lucrative her ladyship approved of it and could compound with the inferiority of the pursuit by practical justice to some of its advantages. I had reason to know – my reason was simply that poor Mrs Stormer told me – how she suffered the inky fingers to press an occasional banknote into her palm. On the other hand she deplored the 'peculiar style' to which Greville Fane had devoted herself, and wondered where a spectator with the advantage of so ladylike a daughter could have picked up such views about the best society. 'She might know better, with Leolin and me,' Lady Luard had been heard to remark; but it appeared that some of Greville Fane's superstitions were incurable. She didn't live in Lady Luard's society, and the best wasn't good enough for her – she must improve on it so prodigiously.

I could see this necessity increase in her during the years she spent abroad, when I had glimpses of her in the shifting sojourns that lay in the path of my annual ramble. She betook herself from Germany to Switzerland and from Switzerland to Italy; she favoured cheap places and set up her desk in the smaller capitals. I took a look at her whenever I could, and I always asked how Leolin was getting on. She gave me beautiful accounts of him, and, occasion favouring, the boy was produced for my advantage. I had entered from the first into the joke of his career — I pretended to regard him as a consecrated child. It had been a joke for Mrs Stormer at first, but the youth himself had been shrewd enough to make the matter serious. If his parent accepted the principle that the intending novelist can't begin too early to see life, Leolin wasn't interested in hanging back from the application of it. He was eager to qualify himself and took to cigarettes at ten on the highest literary grounds. His fond mother gazed at him with extravagant envy and, like Desdemona, wished heaven had made *her* such a man.[12] She explained to me more than once that in her profession she had found her sex a dreadful drawback. She loved the story of Madame George Sand's early rebellion[13] against this hindrance, and believed that if she had worn trousers she could have written as well as that lady. Leolin had for the career at least the qualification of trousers, and as he grew older he recognised its importance by laying in ever so many pair. He grew up thus in gorgeous apparel, which was his way of interpreting his mother's system. Whenever I met her, accordingly, I found her still under the impression that she was carrying this system out and that the sacrifices made him were bearing heavy fruit. She was giving him experience, she was giving him impressions, she was putting a *gagne-pain*[14] into his hand. It was another name for spoiling him with the best conscience in the world. The queerest pictures come back to me of this period of the good lady's life and of the extraordinarily virtuous muddled bewildering tenor of it. She had an idea she was seeing foreign manners as well as her petticoats would allow; but in reality she wasn't seeing anything, least of all, fortunately, how much she was laughed at. She drove her whimsical pen at Dresden and at Florence — she produced in all places and at all times the same romantic and ridiculous fictions. She carried about her box of properties, tumbling out promptly the familiar tarnished old puppets. She believed in them when others couldn't, and as they were like nothing that was to be seen under the sun it was impossible to prove by comparison that they were wrong. You can't compare birds and fishes; you could only feel that, as Greville Fane's characters had the fine plumage of the former species, human beings must be of the latter.

It would have been droll if it hadn't been so exemplary to see her tracing the loves of the duchesses beside the innocent cribs of her children. The immoral and the maternal lived together, in her diligent days, on the most comfortable terms, and she stopped curling the moustaches of her Guardsmen to pat the heads of her babes. She was haunted by solemn spinsters who came to tea from Continental pensions, and by unsophisticated Americans who told her she was just loved in *their* country. 'I had rather be just paid there,' she usually replied; for this tribute of transatlantic opinion was the only thing that galled her. The Americans went away thinking her coarse; though as the author of so many beautiful love-stories she was disappointing to most of these pilgrims, who hadn't expected to find a shy stout ruddy lady in a cap like a crumbled pyramid. She wrote about the affections and the impossibility of controlling them, but she talked of the price of pension[15] and the convenience of an English chemist. She devoted much thought and many thousands of francs to the education of her daughter, who spent three years at a very superior school at Dresden, receiving wonderful instruction in sciences, arts and tongues, and who, taking a different line from Leolin, was to be brought up wholly as a *femme du monde*.[16] The girl was musical and philological; she went in for several languages and learned enough about them to be inspired with a great contempt for her mother's artless accents. Greville Fane's French and Italian were droll; the imitative faculty had been denied her, and she had an unequalled gift, especially pen in hand, of squeezing big mistakes into small opportunities. She knew it but didn't care; correctness was the virtue in the world that, like her heroes and heroines, she valued least. Ethel, who had noted in her pages some remarkable lapses, undertook at one time to revise her proofs; but I remember her telling me a year after the girl had left school that this function had been very briefly exercised. 'She can't read me,' said Mrs Stormer; 'I offend her taste. She tells me that at Dresden – at school – I was never allowed.' The good lady seemed surprised at this, having the best conscience in the world about her lucubrations. She had never meant to fly in the face of anything, and considered that she grovelled before the Rhadamanthus[17] of the English literary tribunal, the celebrated and awful Young Person. I assured her, as a joke, that she was frightfully indecent – she had in fact that element of truth as little as any other – my purpose being solely to prevent her guessing that her daughter had dropped her not because she was immoral but because she was vulgar. I used to figure her children closeted together and putting it to each other with a gaze of dismay: 'Why should she *be* so – and so *fearfully* so – when she has the advantage of our society? Shouldn't *we* have taught her better?' Then I imagined their recognising with a blush and a shrug that she was unteachable, irreformable. Indeed she was, poor lady, but it's never fair to read by the light of taste things essentially not written in it. Greville Fane kept through all her riot of absurdity a witless confidence that should have been as safe from criticism as a stutter or a squint.

She didn't make her son ashamed of the profession to which he was destined, however; she only made him ashamed of the way she herself exercised it. But he bore his humiliation much better than his sister, being ready to assume he should one day restore the balance. A canny and far-seeing youth, with appetites and aspirations, he hadn't a scruple in his composition. His mother's theory of the happy knack he could pick up deprived him of the wholesome discipline required to prevent young idlers from becoming cads. He enjoyed on foreign soil a casual tutor and the common snatch or two of a Swiss school, but addressed himself to no consecutive study nor to any prospect of a university or a degree. It may be imagined with what zeal, as the years went on, he entered into the pleasantry of there being no manual so important to him as the massive book of life. It was an expensive volume to peruse, but Mrs Stormer was willing to lay out a sum in what she would have called her *premiers frais*.[18] Ethel disapproved – she found this education irregular for an English gentleman. Her voice was for Eton and Oxford[19] or for any public school – she would have resigned herself to one of the scrubbier – with the army to follow. But Leolin never was afraid of his sister, and they visibly disliked, though they sometimes agreed to assist, each other. They could combine to work the oracle – to keep their mother at her desk.

When she reappeared in England, telling me she had 'secured' all the Continent could give her, Leolin was a broad-shouldered red-faced young man with an immense wardrobe and an extraordinary assurance of manner. She was fondly, quite aggressively certain she had taken the right course with him, and addicted to boasting of all he knew and had seen. He was now quite ready to embark on the family profession, to commence author, as they used to say, and a little while later she told me he had started. He had written something tremendously clever which was coming out in the *Cheapside*.[20] I believe it came out; I had no time to look for it; I never heard anything about it. I took for granted that if this contribution had passed through his mother's hands it would virtually rather illustrate *her* fine facility, and it was interesting to consider the poor lady's future in the light of her having to write her son's novels as well as her own. This wasn't the way she looked at it herself – she took the charming ground that he'd help her to write hers. She used to assure me he supplied passages of the greatest value to these last – all sorts of telling technical things, happy touches about hunting and yachting and cigars and wine, about City[21] slang and the way men talk at clubs – that she couldn't be expected to get very straight. It was all so much practice for him and so much alleviation for herself. I was unable to identify such pages, for I had long since ceased to 'keep up' with Greville Fane; but I could quite believe at least that the wine-question had been put by Leolin's good offices on a better footing, for the dear woman used to mix her drinks – she was perpetually serving the most splendid suppers – in the queerest fashion. I could see him quite ripe to embrace regularly that care. It occurred to me indeed, when she settled in England again, that she might by a shrewd use of both her children be able to rejuvenate her style. Ethel had come back to wreak her native, her social yearning, and if she couldn't take her mother into company would at least go into it herself. Silently, stiffly, almost grimly, this young lady reared her head, clenched her long teeth, squared her lean elbows and found her way up the staircases she had marked. The only communication she ever made, the only effusion of confidence with which she ever honoured me, was when she said 'I don't want to know the people mamma knows, I mean to know others.' I took due note of the remark, for I wasn't one of the 'others.' I couldn't trace therefore the steps and stages of her climb; I could only admire it at a distance and congratulate her mother in due course on the results. The results, the gradual, the final, the wonderful, were that Ethel went to 'big' parties and got people to take her. Some of them were people she had met abroad, and others people the people she had met abroad had met. They ministered alike to Miss Ethel's convenience, and I wondered how she extracted so many favours without the expenditure of a smile. Her smile was the dimmest thing in nature, diluted, unsweetened, inexpensive lemonade, and she had arrived precociously at social wisdom, recognising that if she was neither pretty enough nor rich enough nor clever enough, she could at least, in her muscular youth, be rude enough. Therefore, so placed to give her parent tips, to let her know what really occurred in the mansions of the great, to supply her with local colour, with *data* to work from, she promoted the driving of the well-worn quill, over the brave old battered blotting book, to a still lustier measure and precisely at the moment when most was to depend on this labour. But if she became a great critic it appeared that the labourer herself was constitutionally inapt for the lesson. It was late in the day for Greville Fane to learn, and I heard nothing of her having developed a new manner. She was to have had only one manner, as Leolin would have said, from start to finish.

She was weary and spent at last, but confided to me that she couldn't afford to pause. She continued to speak of her son's work as the great hope of their future — she had saved no money — though the young man wore to my sense an air more and more professional if you like, but less and less literary. There was at the end of a couple of years something rare in the impudence of his playing of his part in the comedy. When I wondered how she could play hers it was to feel afresh the fatuity of her fondness, which was proof, I believed — I indeed saw to the end — against any interference of reason. She loved the young impostor with a simple blind benighted love, and of all the heroes of romance who had passed before her eyes he was by far the brightest. He was at any rate the most real — she could touch him, pay for him, suffer for him, worship him. He made her think of her princes and dukes, and when she wished to fix these figures in her mind's eye she thought of her boy. She had often told me she was herself carried away by her creations, and she was certainly carried away by Leolin. He vivified — by what romantically might have been at least – the whole question of youth and passion. She held, not unjustly, that the sincere novelist should feel the whole flood of life; she acknowledged with regret that she hadn't had time to feel it herself, and the lapse in her history was in a manner made up by the sight of its rush through this magnificent young man. She exhorted him, I suppose, to encourage the rush; she wrung her own flaccid little sponge into the torrent. What passed between them in her pedagogic hours was naturally a blank to me, but I gathered that she mainly impressed on him that the great thing was to live, because that gave you material. He asked nothing better; he collected material, and the recipe served as a universal pretext. You had only to look at him to see that, with his rings and breastpins, his cross-barred jackets, his early *embon-point*,[22] his eyes that looked like imitation jewels, his various indications of a dense full-blown temperament, his idea of life was singularly vulgar; but he was so far auspicious as that his response to his mother's expectations was in a high degree practical. If she had imposed a profession on him from his tenderest years it was exactly a profession that he followed. The two were not quite the same, inasmuch as the one he had adopted was simply to live at her expense; but at least she couldn't say he hadn't taken a line. If she insisted on believing in him he offered himself to the sacrifice. My impression is that her secret dream was that he should have a *liaison* with a countess, and he persuaded her without difficulty that he had one. I don't know what countesses are capable of, but I've a clear notion of what Leolin was.

He didn't persuade his sister, who despised him – she wished to work her mother in her own way; so that I asked myself why the girl's judgement of him didn't make me like her better. It was because it didn't save her after all from the mute agreement with him to go halves. There were moments when I couldn't help looking hard into his atrocious young eyes, challenging him to confess his fantastic fraud and give it up. Not a little tacit conversation passed between us in this way, but he had always the best of the business. If I said: 'Oh come now, with *me* you needn't keep it up; plead guilty and I'll let you off,' he wore the most ingenuous, the most candid expression, in the depths of which I could read: 'Ah yes, I know it exasperates you – that's just why I do it.' He took the line of earnest enquiry, talked about Balzac and Flaubert, asked me if I thought Dickens *did* exaggerate and Thackeray[23] *ought* to be called a pessimist. Once he came to see me, at his mother's suggestion he declared, on purpose to ask me how far, in my opinion, in the English novel, one really might venture to 'go.' He wasn't resigned to the usual pruderies, the worship of childish twaddle; he suffered already from too much bread and butter. He struck out the brilliant idea that nobody knew how far we might go, since nobody had ever tried. Did I think *he* might safely try – would it injure his mother if he did? He would rather disgrace himself by his timidities than injure his mother, but certainly some one ought to try. Wouldn't *I* try – couldn't I be prevailed upon to look at it as a duty? Surely the ultimate point ought to be fixed – he was worried, haunted by the question. He patronised me unblushingly, made me feel a foolish amateur, a helpless novice, enquired into my habits of work and conveyed to me that I was utterly *vieux jeu*[24] and hadn't had the advantage of an early training. I hadn't been brought up from the egg, I knew nothing of life – didn't go at it on *his* system. He had dipped into French feuilletons[25] and picked up plenty of phrases, and he made a much better show in talk than his poor mother, who never had time to read anything and could only be showy with her pen. If I didn't kick him downstairs it was because he would have landed on her at the bottom.

When she went to live at Primrose Hill I called there and found her wasted and wan. It had visibly dropped, the elation caused the year before by Ethel's marriage; the foam on the cup had subsided and there was bitterness in the draught. She had had to take a cheaper house – and now had to work still harder to pay even for that. Sir Baldwin was obliged to be close; his charges were fearful, and the dream of her living with her daughter – a vision she had never mentioned to me – must be renounced. 'I'd have helped them with things, and could have lived perfectly in one room,' she said; 'I'd have paid for everything, and – after all – I'm some one, ain't I? But I don't fit in, and Ethel tells me there are tiresome people she *must* receive. I can help them from here, no doubt, better than from there. She told me once, you know, what she thinks of my picture of life. "Mamma, your picture of life's preposterous!" No doubt it is, but she's vexed with me for letting my prices go down; and I had to write three novels to pay for all her marriage cost me. I did it very well – I mean the outfit and the wedding; but that's why I'm here. At any rate she doesn't want a dingy old woman at Blicket. I should give the place an atmosphere of literary prestige, but literary prestige is only the eminence of nobodies. Besides, she knows what to think of my glory – she knows I'm glorious only at Peckham and Hackney.[26] She doesn't want her friends to ask if I've never known nice people. She can't tell them I've never been in society. She tried to teach me better once, but I couldn't catch on. It would seem too as if Peckham and Hackney had had enough of me; for (don't tell any one!) I've had to take less for my last than I ever took for anything.' I asked her how little this had been, not from curiosity, but in order to upbraid her, more disinterestedly than Lady Luard had done, for such concessions. She answered 'I'm ashamed to tell you' and then began to cry.

I had never seen her break down and I was proportionately moved; she sobbed like a frightened child over the extinction of her vogue and the exhaustion of her vein. Her little workroom seemed indeed a barren place to grow flowers for the market, and I wondered in the after years (for she continued to produce and publish) by what desperate and heroic process she dragged them out of the soil. I remember asking her on that occasion what had become of Leolin and how much longer she intended to allow him to amuse himself at her cost. She retorted with spirit, wiping her eyes, that he was down at Brighton[27] hard at work – he was in the midst of a novel – and that he *felt* life so, in all its misery and mystery, that it was cruel to speak of such experiences as a pleasure. 'He goes beneath the surface,' she said, 'and he *forces* himself to look at things from which he'd rather turn away. Do you call that amusing yourself? You should see his face sometimes! And he does it for me as much as for himself. He tells me everything – he comes home to me with his *trouvailles*.[28] We're artists together, and to the artist all things are pure. I've often heard you say so yourself.' The novel Leolin was engaged in at Brighton never saw the light, but a friend of mine and of Mrs Stormer's who was staying there happened to mention to me later that he had seen the young apprentice to fiction driving, in a dog-cart,[29] a young lady with a very pink face. When I suggested that she was perhaps a woman of title with whom he was conscientiously flirting my informant replied: 'She is indeed, but do you know what her title is?' He pronounced it – it was familiar and descriptive – but I won't reproduce it here. I don't know whether Leolin mentioned it to his mother: she would have needed all the purity of the artist to forgive him. I hated so to come across him that in the very last years I went rarely to see her, though I knew she had come pretty well to the end of her rope. I didn't want her to tell me she had fairly to give her books away; I didn't want to see her old and abandoned and derided; I didn't want, in a word, to see her terribly cry. She still, however, kept it up amazingly, and every few months, at my club, I saw three new volumes,[30] in green, in crimson, in blue, on the book-table that groaned with light literature. Once I met her at the Academy soirée,[31] where you meet people you thought were dead, and she vouchsafed the information, as if she owed it to me in candour, that Leolin had been obliged to recognize the insuperable difficulties of the question of *form* – he was so fastidious; but that she had now arrived at a definite understanding with him (it was such a comfort!) that *she* would do the form if he would bring home the substance. That was now his employ – he foraged for her in the great world at a salary. 'He's my "devil,"[32] don't you see? as if I were a great lawyer: he gets up the case and I argue it.' She mentioned further that in addition to his salary he was paid by the piece: he got so much for a striking character, so much for a pretty name, so much for a plot, so much for an incident, and had so much promised him if he would invent a new crime.

'He *has* invented one,' I said, 'and he's paid every day of his life.'

'What is it?' she asked, looking hard at the picture of the year, 'Baby's Tub,'[33] near which we happened to be standing.

I hesitated a moment. 'I myself will write a little story about it, and then you'll see.'

But she never saw; she had never seen anything, and she passed away with her fine blindness unimpaired. Her son published every scrap of scribbled paper that could be extracted from her table-drawers, and his sister quarrelled with him mortally about the proceeds, which showed her only to have wanted a pretext, for they can't have been great. I don't know what Leolin lives on unless on a queer lady many years older than himself, whom he lately married. The last time I met him he said to me with his infuriating smile: 'Don't you think we can go a little further still – just a little?' *He* really – with me at least – goes too far.

The Middle Years

The April day was soft and bright, and poor Dencombe, happy in the conceit of reasserted strength, stood in the garden of the hotel, comparing, with a deliberation in which however there was still something of languor, the attractions of easy strolls. He liked the feeling of the south so far as you could have it in the north, he liked the sandy cliffs and the clustered pines, he liked even the colourless sea. 'Bournemouth[1] as a health-resort' had sounded like a mere advertisement, but he was thankful now for the commonest conveniences. The sociable country postman, passing through the garden, had just given him a small parcel which he took out with him, leaving the hotel to the right and creeping to a bench he had already haunted, a safe recess in the cliff. It looked to the south, to the tinted walls of the Island,[2] and was protected behind by the sloping shoulder of the down. He was tired enough when he reached it, and for a moment was disappointed; he was better of course, but better, after all, than what? He should never again, as at one or two great moments of the past, be better than himself. The infinite of life was gone, and what remained of the dose a small glass scored like a thermometer by the apothecary. He sat and stared at the sea, which appeared all surface and twinkle, far shallower than the spirit of man. It was the abyss of human illusion that was the real, the tide-less deep. He held his packet, which had come by book-post, unopened on his knee, liking, in the lapse of so many joys – his illness had made him feel his age – to know it was there, but taking for granted there could be no complete renewal of the pleasure, dear to young experience, of seeing one's self 'just out.'[3] Dencombe, who had a reputation, had come out too often and knew too well in advance how he should look.

His postponement associated itself vaguely, after a little, with a group of three persons, two ladies and a young man, whom, beneath him, straggling and seemingly silent, he could see move slowly together along the sands. The gentleman had his head bent over a book and was occasionally brought to a stop by the charm of this volume, which, as Dencombe could perceive even at a distance, had a cover alluringly red. Then his companions, going a little further, waited for him to come up, poking their parasols into the beach, looking around them at the sea and sky and clearly sensible of the beauty of the day. To these things the young man with the book was still more clearly indifferent; lingering, credulous, absorbed, he was an object of envy to an observer from whose connexion with literature all such artlessness had faded. One of the ladies was large and mature; the other had the spareness of comparative youth and of a social situation possibly inferior. The large lady carried back Dencombe's imagination to the age of crinoline; she wore a hat of the shape of a mushroom, decorated with a blue veil, and had the air, in her aggressive amplitude, of clinging to a vanished fashion or even a lost cause. Presently her companion produced from under the folds of a mantle a limp portable chair which she stiffened out and of which the large lady took possession. This act, and something in the movement of either party, at once characterised the performers – they performed for Dencombe's recreation – as opulent matron and humble dependent. Where moreover was the virtue of an approved novelist if one couldn't establish a relation between such figures? the clever theory for instance that the young man was the son of the opulent matron and that the humble dependent, the daughter of a clergyman or an officer, nourished a secret passion for him. Was that not visible from the way she stole behind her protectress to look back at him? – back to where he had let himself come to a full stop when his mother sat down to rest. His book was a novel, it had the catchpenny binding; so that while the romance of life stood neglected at his side he lost himself in that of the circulating library.[4] He moved mechanically to where the sand was softer and ended by plumping down in it to finish his chapter at his ease. The humble dependent, discouraged by his remoteness, wandered with a martyred droop of the head in another direction, and the exorbitant lady, watching the waves, offered a confused resemblance to a flying-machine that had broken down.

When his drama began to fail Dencombe remembered that he had after all another pastime. Though such promptitude on the part of the publisher was rare he was already able to draw from its wrapper his 'latest,' perhaps his last. The cover of 'The Middle Years'[5] was duly meretricious, the smell of the fresh pages the very odour of sanctity; but for the moment he went no further – he had become conscious of a strange alienation. He had forgotten what his book was about. Had the assault of his old ailment, which he had so fallaciously come to Bournemouth to ward off, interposed utter blankness as to what had preceded it? He had finished the revision of proof before quitting London, but his subsequent fortnight in bed had passed the sponge over colour.[6] He couldn't have chanted to himself a single sentence, couldn't have turned with curiosity or confidence to any particular page. His subject had already gone from him, leaving scarce a superstition behind. He uttered a low moan as he breathed the chill of this dark void, so desperately it seemed to represent the completion of a sinister process.

The tears filled his mild eyes; something precious had passed away. This was the pang that had been sharpest during the last few years – the sense of ebbing time, of shrinking opportunity; and now he felt not so much that his last chance was going as that it was gone indeed. He had done all he should ever do, and yet hadn't done what he wanted. This was the laceration – that practically his career was over: it was as violent as a grip at his throat. He rose from his seat nervously – a creature hunted by a dread; then he fell back in his weakness and nervously opened his book. It was a single volume; he preferred single volumes and aimed at a rare compression. He began to read and, little by little, in this occupation, was pacified and reassured. Everything came back to him, but came back with a wonder, came back above all with a high and magnificent beauty. He read his own prose, he turned his own leaves, and had as he sat there with the spring sunshine on the page an emotion peculiar and intense. His career was over, no doubt, but it was over, when all was said, with *that*.

He had forgotten during his illness the work of the previous year; but what he had chiefly forgotten was that it was extraordinarily good. He dived once more into his story and was drawn down, as by a siren's hand, to where, in the dim underworld of fiction, the great glazed tank of art, strange silent subjects float. He recognised his motive and surrendered to his talent. Never probably had that talent, such as it was, been so fine. His difficulties were still there, but what was also there, to his perception, though probably, alas! to nobody's else, was the art that in most cases had surmounted them. In his surprised enjoyment of this ability he had a glimpse of a possible reprieve. Surely its force wasn't spent – there was life and service in it yet. It hadn't come to him easily, it had been backward and roundabout. It was the child of time, the nursling of delay; he had struggled and suffered for it, making sacrifices not to be counted, and now that it was really mature was it to cease to yield, to confess itself brutally beaten? There was an infinite charm for Dencombe in feeling as he had never felt before that diligence *vincit omnia*.[7] The result produced in his little book was somehow a result beyond his conscious intention: it was as if he had planted his genius, had trusted his method, and they had grown up and flowered with this sweetness. If the achievement had been real, however, the process had been painful enough. What he saw so intensely to-day, what he felt as a nail driven in, was that only now, at the very last, had he come into possession. His development had been abnormally slow, almost grotesquely gradual. He had been hindered and retarded by experience, he had for long periods only groped his way. It had taken too much of his life to produce too little of his art. The art had come, but it had come after everything else. At such a rate a first existence was too short – long enough only to collect material; so that to fructify, to use the material, one should have a second age, an extension. This extension was what poor Dencombe sighed for.

As he turned the last leaves of his volume he murmured 'Ah for another go, ah for a better chance!'

The three persons drawing his attention to the sands had vanished and then reappeared; they had now wandered up a path, an artificial and easy ascent, which led to the top of the cliff. Dencombe's bench was halfway down, on a sheltered ledge, and the large lady, a massive heterogeneous person with bold black eyes and kind red cheeks, now took a few moments to rest. She wore dirty gauntlets and immense diamond ear-rings; at first she looked vulgar, but she contradicted this announcement in an agreeable off-hand tone. While her companions stood waiting for her she spread her skirts on the end of Dencombe's seat. The young man had gold spectacles, through which, with his finger still in his red-covered book, he glanced at the volume, bound in the same shade of the same colour, lying on the lap of the original occupant of the bench. After an instant Dencombe felt him struck with a resemblance; he had recognised the gilt stamp on the crimson cloth, was reading 'The Middle Years' and now noted that somebody else had kept pace with him. The stranger was startled, possibly even a little ruffled, to find himself not the only person favoured with an early copy. The eyes of the two proprietors met a moment, and Dencombe borrowed amusement from the expression of those of his competitor, those, it might even be inferred, of his admirer. They confessed to some resentment – they seemed to say: 'Hang it, has he got it *already*? Of course he's a brute of a reviewer!' Dencombe shuffled his copy out of sight while the opulent matron, rising from her repose, broke out: 'I feel already the good of this air!'

'I can't say I do,' said the angular lady. 'I find myself quite let down.'

'I find myself horribly hungry. At what time did you order luncheon?' her protectress pursued.

The young person put the question by. 'Doctor Hugh always orders it.'

'I ordered nothing to-day – I'm going to make you diet,' said their comrade.

'Then I shall go home and sleep. *Qui dort dîne!*'[8]

'Can I trust you to Miss Vernham?' asked Doctor Hugh of his elder companion.

'Don't I trust *you*?' she archly enquired.

'Not too much!' Miss Vernham, with her eyes on the ground, permitted herself to declare. 'You must come with us at least to the house,' she went on while the personage on whom they appeared to be in attendance began to mount higher. She had got a little out of ear-shot; nevertheless Miss Vernham became, so far as Dencombe was concerned, less distinctly audible to murmur to the young man: 'I don't think you realise all you owe the Countess!'

Absently, a moment, Doctor Hugh caused his gold-rimmed spectacles to shine at her. 'Is that the way I strike you? I see – I see!'

'She's awfully good to us,' continued Miss Vernham, compelled by the lapse of the other's motion to stand there in spite of his discussion of private matters. Of what use would it have been that Dencombe should be sensitive to shades hadn't he detected in that arrest a strange influence from the quiet old convalescent in the great tweed cape? Miss Vernham appeared suddenly to become aware of some such connexion, for she added in a moment: 'If you want to sun yourself here you can come back after you've seen us home.'

Doctor Hugh, at this, hesitated, and Dencombe, in spite of a desire to pass for unconscious, risked a covert glance at him. What his eyes met this time, as happened, was, on the part of the young lady, a queer stare, naturally vitreous, which made her remind him of some figure – he couldn't name it – in a play or a novel, some sinister governess or tragic old maid. She seemed to scan him, to challenge him, to say out of general spite: 'What have you got to do with us?' At the same instant the rich humour of the Countess reached them from above: 'Come, come, my little lambs; you should follow your old *bergère*!'[9] Miss Vernham turned away for it, pursuing the ascent, and Doctor Hugh, after another mute appeal to Dencombe and a minute's evident demur, deposited his book on the bench as if to keep his place, or even as a gage of earnest return, and bounded without difficulty up the rougher part of the cliff.

Equally innocent and infinite are the pleasures of observation and the resources engendered by the trick of analysing life. It amused poor Dencombe, as he dawdled in his tepid air-bath, to believe himself awaiting a revelation of something at the back of a fine young mind. He looked hard at the book on the end of the bench, but wouldn't have touched it for the world. It served his purpose to have a theory that shouldn't be exposed to refutation. He already felt better of his melancholy; he had, according to his old formula, put his head at the window. A passing Countess could draw off the fancy when, like the elder of the ladies who had just retreated, she was as obvious as the giantess of a caravan. It was indeed general views that were terrible; short ones, contrary to an opinion sometimes expressed, were the refuge, were the remedy. Doctor Hugh couldn't possibly be anything but a reviewer who had understandings for early copies with publishers or with newspapers. He reappeared in a quarter of an hour with visible relief at finding Dencombe on the spot and the gleam of white teeth in an embarrassed but generous smile. He was perceptibly disappointed at the eclipse of the other copy of the book; it made a pretext the less for speaking to the quiet gentleman. But he spoke notwithstanding; he held up his own copy and broke out pleadingly: '*Do* say, if you have occasion to speak of it, that it's the best thing he has done yet!'

Dencombe responded with a laugh: 'Done yet' was so amusing to him, made such a grand avenue of the future. Better still, the young man took *him* for a reviewer. He pulled out 'The Middle Years' from under his cape, but instinctively concealed any telltale look of fatherhood. This was partly because a person was always a fool for insisting to others on his work. 'Is that what you're going to say yourself?' he put to his visitor.

'I'm not quite sure I shall write anything. I don't, as a regular thing – I enjoy in peace. But it's awfully fine.'

Dencombe just debated. If the young man had begun to abuse him he would have confessed on the spot to his identity, but there was no harm in drawing out any impulse to praise. He drew it out with such success that in a few moments his new acquaintance, seated by his side, was confessing candidly that the works of the author of the volumes before them were the only ones he could read a second time. He had come the day before from London, where a friend of his, a journalist, had lent him his copy of the last, the copy sent to the office of the journal and already the subject of a 'notice' which, as was pretended there – but one had to allow for 'swagger' – it had taken a full quarter of an hour to prepare. He intimated that he was ashamed for his friend, and in the case of a work demanding and repaying study, of such inferior manners; and, with his fresh appreciation and his so irregular wish to express it, he speedily became for poor Dencombe a remarkable, a delightful apparition. Chance had brought the weary man of letters face to face with the greatest admirer in the new generation of whom it was supposable he might boast. The admirer in truth was mystifying, so rare a case was it to find a bristling young doctor – he looked like a German physiologist – enamoured of literary form. It was an accident, but happier than most accidents, so that Dencombe, exhilarated as well as confounded, spent half an hour in making his visitor talk while he kept himself quiet. He explained his premature possession of 'The Middle Years' by an allusion to the friendship of the publisher, who, knowing he was at Bournemouth for his health, had paid him this graceful attention. He allowed he had been ill, for Doctor Hugh would infallibly have guessed it; he even went so far as to wonder if he mightn't look for some hygienic 'tip' from a personage combining so bright an enthusiasm with a presumable knowledge of the remedies now in vogue. It would shake his faith a little perhaps to have to take a doctor seriously who could take *him* so seriously, but he enjoyed this gushing modern youth and felt with an acute pang that there would still be work to do in a world in which such odd combinations were presented. It wasn't true, what he had tried for renunciation's sake to believe, that all the combinations were exhausted. They weren't by any means – they were infinite: the exhaustion was in the miserable artist.

Doctor Hugh, an ardent physiologist, was saturated with the spirit of the age – in other words he had just taken his degree; but he was independent and various, he talked like a man who would have preferred to love literature best. He would fain have made fine phrases, but nature had denied him the trick. Some of the finest in 'The Middle Years' had struck him inordinately, and he took the liberty of reading them to Dencombe in support of his plea. He grew vivid, in the balmy air, to his companion, for whose deep refreshment he seemed to have been sent; and was particularly ingenuous in describing how recently he had become acquainted, and how instantly infatuated, with the only man who had put flesh between the ribs of an art that was starving on superstitions. He hadn't yet written to him – he was deterred by a strain of respect. Dencombe at this moment rejoiced more inwardly than ever that he had never answered the photographers. His visitor's attitude promised him a luxury of intercourse, though he was sure a due freedom for Doctor Hugh would depend not a little on the Countess. He learned without delay what type of Countess was involved, mastering as well the nature of the tie that united the curious trio. The large lady, an Englishwoman by birth and the daughter of a celebrated baritone, whose taste *minus* his talent she had inherited, was the widow of a French nobleman and mistress of all that remained of the handsome fortune, the fruit of her father's earnings, that had constituted her dower. Miss Vernham, an odd creature but an accomplished pianist, was attached to her person at a salary. The Countess was generous, independent, eccentric; she travelled with her minstrel and her medical man. Ignorant and passionate she had nevertheless moments in which she was almost irresistible. Dencombe saw her sit for her portrait in Doctor Hugh's free sketch, and felt the picture of his young friend's relation to her frame itself in his mind. This young friend, for a representative of the new psychology,[10] was himself easily hypnotised, and if he became abnormally communicative it was only a sign of his real subjection. Dencombe did accordingly what he wanted with him, even without being known as Dencombe.

Taken ill on a journey in Switzerland the Countess had picked him up at an hotel, and the accident of his happening to please her had made her offer him, with her imperious liberality, terms that couldn't fail to dazzle a practitioner without patients and whose resources had been drained dry by his studies. It wasn't the way he would have proposed to spend his time, but it was time that would pass quickly, and meanwhile she was wonderfully kind. She exacted perpetual attention, but it was impossible not to like her. He gave details about his queer patient, a 'type'[11] if there ever was one, who had in connexion with her flushed obesity, and in addition to the morbid strain of a violent and aimless will, a grave organic disorder; but he came back to his loved novelist, whom he was so good as to pronounce more essentially a poet than many of those who went in for verse, with a zeal excited, as all his indiscretion had been excited, by the happy chance of Dencombe's sympathy and the coincidence of their occupation. Dencombe had confessed to a slight personal acquaintance with the author of 'The Middle Years,' but had not felt himself as ready as he could have wished when his companion, who had never yet encountered a being so privileged, began to be eager for particulars. He even divined in Doctor Hugh's eye at that moment a glimmer of suspicion. But the young man was too inflamed to be shrewd and repeatedly caught up the book to exclaim: 'Did you notice this?' or 'Weren't you immensely struck with that?' 'There's a beautiful passage toward the end,' he broke out; and again he laid his hand on the volume. As he turned the pages he came upon something else, while Dencombe saw him suddenly change colour. He had taken up as it lay on the bench Dencombe's copy instead of his own, and his neighbour at once guessed the reason of his start. Doctor Hugh looked grave an instant; then he said: 'I see you've been altering the text!' Dencombe was a passionate corrector, a fingerer of style; the last thing he ever arrived at was a form final for himself. His ideal would have been to publish secretly, and then, on the published text, treat himself to the terrified revise, sacrificing always a first edition and beginning for posterity and even for the collectors, poor dears, with a second. This morning, in 'The Middle Years,' his pencil had pricked a dozen lights. He was amused at the effect of the young man's reproach; for an instant it made him change colour. He stammered at any rate ambiguously, then through a blur of ebbing consciousness saw Doctor Hugh's mystified eyes. He only had time to feel he was about to be ill again – that emotion, excitement, fatigue, the heat of the sun, the solicitation of the air, had combined to play him a trick, before, stretching out a hand to his visitor with a plaintive cry, he lost his senses altogether.

Later he knew he had fainted and that Doctor Hugh had got him home in a Bath-chair,[12] the conductor of which, prowling within hail for custom, had happened to remember seeing him in the garden of the hotel. He had recovered his perception on the way, and had, in bed that afternoon, a vague recollection of Doctor Hugh's young face, as they went together, bent over him in a comforting laugh and expressive of something more than a suspicion of his identity. That identity was ineffaceable now, and all the more that he was rueful and sore. He had been rash, been stupid, had gone out too soon, stayed out too long. He oughtn't to have exposed himself to strangers, he ought to have taken his servant. He felt as if he had fallen into a hole too deep to descry any little patch of heaven. He was confused about the time that had passed – he pieced the fragments together. He had seen his doctor, the real one, the one who had treated him from the first and who had again been very kind. His servant was in and out on tiptoe, looking very wise after the fact. He said more than once something about the sharp young gentleman. The rest was vagueness in so far as it wasn't despair. The vagueness, however, justified itself by dreams, dozing anxieties from which he finally emerged to the consciousness of a dark room and a shaded candle.

'You'll be all right again – I know all about you now,' said a voice near him that he felt to be young. Then his meeting with Doctor Hugh came back. He was too discouraged to joke about it yet, but made out after a little that the interest was intense for his visitor. 'Of course I can't attend you professionally – you've got your own man, with whom I've talked and who's excellent,' Doctor Hugh went on. 'But you must let me come to see you as a good friend. I've just looked in before going to bed. You're doing beautifully, but it's a good job I was with you on the cliff. I shall come in early to-morrow. I want to do something for you. I want to do everything. You've done a tremendous lot for me.' The young man held his hand, hanging over him, and poor Dencombe, weakly aware of this living pressure, simply lay there and accepted his devotion. He couldn't do anything less – he needed help too much.

The idea of the help he needed was very present to him that night, which he spent in a lucid stillness, an intensity of thought that constituted a reaction from his hours of stupor. He was lost, he was lost – he was lost if he couldn't be saved. He wasn't afraid of suffering, of death, wasn't even in love with life; but he had had a deep demonstration of desire. It came over him in the long quiet hours that only with 'The Middle Years' had he taken his flight; only on that day, visited by soundless processions, had he recognised his kingdom. He had had a revelation of his range. What he dreaded was the idea that his reputation should stand on the unfinished. It wasn't with his past but with his future that it should properly be concerned. Illness and age rose before him like spectres with pitiless eyes: how was he to bribe such fates to give him the second chance? He had had the one chance that all men have – he had had the chance of life. He went to sleep again very late, and when he awoke Doctor Hugh was sitting at hand. There was already by this time something beautifully familiar in him.

'Don't think I've turned out your physician,' he said; 'I'm acting with his consent. He has been here and seen you. Somehow he seems to trust me. I told him how we happened to come together yesterday, and he recognises that I've a peculiar right.'

Dencombe felt his own face pressing. 'How have you squared the Countess?'

The young man blushed a little, but turned it off. 'Oh never mind the Countess!'

'You told me she was very exacting.'

Doctor Hugh had a wait. 'So she is.'

'And Miss Vernham's an *intrigante*.'[13]

'How do you know that?'

'I know everything. One *has* to, to write decently!'

'I think she's mad,' said limpid Doctor Hugh.

'Well, don't quarrel with the Countess – she's a present help to you.'

'I don't quarrel,' Doctor Hugh returned. 'But I don't get on with silly women.' Presently he added: 'You seem very much alone.'

'That often happens at my age. I've outlived, I've lost by the way.'

Doctor Hugh faltered; then surmounting a soft scruple: 'Whom have you lost?'

'Every one.'

'Ah no,' the young man breathed, laying a hand on his arm.

'I once had a wife – I once had a son. My wife died when my child was born, and my boy, at school, was carried off by typhoid.'

'I wish I'd been there!' cried Doctor Hugh.

'Well – if you're here!' Dencombe answered with a smile that, in spite of dimness, showed how he valued being sure of his companions's whereabouts.

'You talk strangely of your age. You're not old.'

'Hypocrite – so early!'

'I speak physiologically.'

'That's the way I've been speaking for the last five years, and it's exactly what I've been saying to myself. It isn't till we *are* old that we begin to tell ourselves we're not.'

'Yet I know I myself am young,' Doctor Hugh returned.

'Not so well as I!' laughed his patient, whose visitor indeed would have established the truth in question by the honesty with which he changed the point of view, remarking that it must be one of the charms of age – at any rate in the case of high distinction – to feel that one has laboured and achieved. Doctor Hugh employed the common phrase about earning one's rest, and it made poor Dencombe for an instant almost angry. He recovered himself, however, to explain, lucidly enough, that if, ungraciously, he knew nothing of such a balm, it was doubtless because he had wasted inestimable years. He had followed literature from the first, but he had taken a lifetime to get abreast of her. Only to-day at last had he begun to *see*, so that all he had hitherto shown was a movement without a direction. He had ripened too late and was so clumsily constituted that he had had to teach himself by mistakes.

'I prefer your flowers then to other people's fruit, and your mistakes to other people's successes,' said gallant Doctor Hugh. 'It's for your mistakes I admire you.'

'You're happy – you don't know,' Dencombe answered.

Looking at his watch the young man had got up; he named the hour of the afternoon at which he would return. Dencombe warned him against committing himself too deeply, and expressed again all his dread of making him neglect the Countess – perhaps incur her displeasure.

'I want to be like you – I want to learn by mistakes!' Doctor Hugh laughed.

'Take care you don't make too grave a one! But do come back,' Dencombe added with the glimmer of a new idea.

'You should have had more vanity!' His friend spoke as if he knew the exact amount required to make a man of letters normal.

'No, no – I only should have had more time. I want another go.'

'Another go?'

'I want an extension.'

'An extension?' Again Doctor Hugh repeated Dencombe's words, with which he seemed to have been struck.

'Don't you know? – I want to what they call "live." '

The young man, for good-bye, had taken his hand, which closed with a certain force. They looked at each other hard. 'You *will* live,' said Doctor Hugh.

'Don't be superficial. It's too serious!'

'You *shall* live!' Dencombe's visitor declared, turning pale.

'Ah that's better!' And as he retired the invalid, with a troubled laugh, sank gratefully back.

All that day and all the following night he wondered if it mightn't be arranged. His doctor came again, his servant was attentive, but it was to his confident young friend that he felt himself mentally appeal. His collapse on the cliff was plausibly explained and his liberation, on a better basis, promised for the morrow; meanwhile, however, the intensity of his meditations kept him tranquil and made him indifferent. The idea that occupied him was none the less absorbing because it was a morbid fancy. Here was a clever son of the age, ingenious and ardent, who happened to have set him up for connoisseurs to worship. This servant of his altar had all the new learning in science and all the old reverence in faith; wouldn't he therefore put his knowledge at the disposal of his sympathy, his craft at the disposal of his love? Couldn't he be trusted to invent a remedy for a poor artist to whose art he had paid a tribute? If he couldn't the alternative was hard: Dencombe would have to surrender to silence unvindicated and undivined. The rest of the day and all the next he toyed in secret with this sweet futility. Who would work the miracle for him but the young man who could combine such lucidity with such passion? He thought of the fairy-tales of science and charmed himself into forgetting that he looked for a magic that was not of this world. Doctor Hugh was an apparition, and that placed him above the law. He came and went while his patient, who now sat up, followed him with supplicating eyes. The interest of knowing the great author had made the young man begin 'The Middle Years' afresh and would help him to find a richer sense between its covers. Dencombe had told him what he 'tried for'; with all his intelligence, on a first perusal, Doctor Hugh had failed to guess it. The baffled celebrity wondered then who in the world *would* guess it: he was amused once more at the diffused massive weight that could be thrown into the missing of an intention. Yet he wouldn't rail at the general mind to-day – consoling as that ever had been: the revelation of his own slowness had seemed to make all stupidity sacred.

Doctor Hugh, after a little, was visibly worried, confessing, on enquiry, to a source of embarrassment at home. 'Stick to the Countess – don't mind me,' Dencombe said repeatedly; for his companion was frank enough about the large lady's attitude. She was so jealous that she had fallen ill – she resented such a breach of allegiance. She paid so much for his fidelity that she must have it all: she refused him the right to other sympathies, charged him with scheming to make her die alone, for it was needless to point out how little Miss Vernham was a resource in trouble. When Doctor Hugh mentioned that the Countess would already have left Bournemouth if he hadn't kept her in bed, poor Dencombe held his arm tighter and said with decision: 'Take her straight away.' They had gone out together, walking back to the sheltered nook in which, the other day, they had met. The young man, who had given his companion a personal support, declared with emphasis that his conscience was clear – he could ride two horses at once. Didn't he dream for his future of a time when he should have to ride five hundred? Longing equally for virtue, Dencombe replied that in that golden age no patient would pretend to have contracted with him for his whole attention. On the part of the Countess wasn't such an avidity lawful? Doctor Hugh denied it, said there was no contract, but only a free understanding, and that a sordid servitude was impossible to a generous spirit; he liked moreover to talk about art, and that was the subject on which, this time, as they sat together on the sunny bench, he tried most to engage the author of 'The Middle Years.' Dencombe, soaring again a little on the weak wings of convalescence and still haunted by that happy notion of an organised rescue, found another strain of eloquence to plead the cause of a certain splendid 'last manner,' the very citadel, as it would prove, of his reputation, the stronghold into which his real treasure would be gathered. While his listener gave up the morning and the great still sea ostensibly waited he had a wondrous explanatory hour. Even for himself he was inspired as he told what his treasure would consist of; the precious metals he would dig from the mine, the jewels rare, strings of pearls, he would hang between the columns of his temple. He was wondrous for himself, so thick his convictions crowded, but still more wondrous for Doctor Hugh, who assured him none the less that the very pages he had just published were already encrusted with gems. This admirer, however, panted for the combinations to come and, before the face of the beautiful day, renewed to Dencombe his guarantee that his profession would hold itself responsible for such a life. Then he suddenly clapped his hand upon his watch-pocket and asked leave to absent himself for half an hour. Dencombe waited there for his return, but was at last recalled to the actual by the fall of a shadow across the ground. The shadow darkened into that of Miss Vernham, the young lady in attendance on the Countess; whom Dencombe, recognising her, perceived so clearly to have come to speak to him that he rose from his bench to acknowledge the civility. Miss Vernham indeed proved not particularly civil; she looked strangely agitated, and her type was now unmistakeable.

'Excuse me if I do ask,' she said, 'whether it's too much to hope that you may be induced to leave Doctor Hugh alone.' Then before our poor friend, greatly disconcerted, could protest: 'You ought to be informed that you stand in his light – that you may do him a terrible injury.'

'Do you mean by causing the Countess to dispense with his services?'

'By causing her to disinherit him.' Dencombe stared at this, and Miss Vernham pursued, in the gratification of seeing she could produce an impression: 'It has depended on himself to come into something very handsome. He has had a grand prospect, but I think you've succeeded in spoiling it.'

'Not intentionally, I assure you. Is there no hope the accident may be repaired?' Dencombe asked.

'She was ready to do anything for him. She takes great fancies, she lets herself go – it's her way. She has no relations, she's free to dispose of her money, and she's very ill,' said Miss Vernham for a climax.

'I'm very sorry to hear it,' Dencombe stammered.

'Wouldn't it be possible for you to leave Bournemouth? That's what I've come to see about.'

He sank to his bench. 'I'm very ill myself, but I'll try!'

Miss Vernham still stood there with her colourless eyes and the brutality of her good conscience. 'Before it's too late, please!' she said; and with this she turned her back, in order, quickly, as if it had been a business to which she could spare but a precious moment, to pass out of his sight.

Oh yes, after this Dencombe was certainly very ill. Miss Vernham had upset him with her rough fierce news; it was the sharpest shock to him to discover what was at stake for a penniless young man of fine parts. He sat trembling on his bench, staring at the waste of waters, feeling sick with the directness of the blow. He was indeed too weak, too unsteady, too alarmed; but he would make the effort to get away, for he couldn't accept the guilt of interference and his honour was really involved. He would hobble home, at any rate, and then think what was to be done. He made his way back to the hotel and, as he went, had a characteristic vision of Miss Vernham's great motive. The Countess hated women of course – Dencombe was lucid about that; so the hungry pianist had no personal hopes and could only console herself with the bold conception of helping Doctor Hugh in order to marry him after he should get his money or else induce him to recognise her claim for compensation and buy her off. If she had befriended him at a fruitful crisis he would really, as a man of delicacy – and she knew what to think of that point – have to reckon with her.

At the hotel Dencombe's servant insisted on his going back to bed. The invalid had talked about catching a train and had begun with orders to pack; after which his racked nerves had yielded to a sense of sickness. He consented to see his physician, who immediately was sent for, but he wished it to be understood that his door was irrevocably closed to Doctor Hugh. He had his plan, which was so fine that he rejoiced in it after getting back to bed. Doctor Hugh, suddenly finding himself snubbed without mercy, would, in natural disgust and to the joy of Miss Vernham, renew his allegiance to the Countess. When his physician arrived Dencombe learned that he was feverish and that this was very wrong: he was to cultivate calmness and try, if possible, not to think. For the rest of the day he wooed stupidity; but there was an ache that kept him sentient, the probable sacrifice of his 'extension,' the limit of his course. His medical adviser was anything but pleased; his successive relapses were ominous. He charged this personage to put out a strong hand and take Doctor Hugh off his mind — it would contribute so much to his being quiet. The agitating name, in his room, was not mentioned again, but his security was a smothered fear, and it was not confirmed by the receipt, at ten o'clock that evening, of a telegram which his servant opened and read him and to which, with an address in London, the signature of Miss Vernham was attached. 'Beseech you to use all influence to make our friend join us here in the morning. Countess much the worse for dreadful journey, but everything may still be saved.' The two ladies had gathered themselves up and had been capable in the afternoon of a spiteful revolution. They had started for the capital, and if the elder one, as Miss Vernham had announced, was very ill, she had wished to make it clear that she was proportionately reckless. Poor Dencombe, who was not reckless and who only desired that everything should indeed be 'saved,' sent this missive straight off to the young man's lodging and had on the morrow the pleasure of knowing that he had quitted Bournemouth by an early train.

Two days later he pressed in with a copy of a literary journal in his hand. He had returned because he was anxious and for the pleasure of flourishing the great review of 'The Middle Years.' Here at least was something adequate — it rose to the occasion; it was an acclamation, a reparation, a critical attempt to place the author in the niche he had fairly won. Dencombe accepted and submitted; he made neither objection nor enquiry, for old complications had returned and he had had two dismal days. He was convinced not only that he should never again leave his bed, so that his young friend might pardonably remain, but that the demand he should make on the patience of beholders would be of the most moderate. Doctor Hugh had been to town, and he tried to find in his eyes some confession that the Countess was pacified and his legacy clinched; but all he could see there was the light of his juvenile joy in two or three of the phrases of the newspaper. Dencombe couldn't read them, but when his visitor had insisted on repeating them more than once he was able to shake an unintoxicated head. 'Ah no – but they would have been true of what I *could* have done!'

'What people "could have done" is mainly what they've in fact done,' Doctor Hugh contended.

'Mainly, yes; but I've been an idiot!' Dencombe said.

Doctor Hugh did remain; the end was coming fast. Two days later his patient observed to him, by way of the feeblest of jokes, that there would now be no question whatever of a second chance. At this the young man stared; then he exclaimed: 'Why it has come to pass – it has come to pass! The second chance has been the public's – the chance to find the point of view, to pick up the pearl!'

'Oh the pearl!' poor Dencombe uneasily sighed. A smile as cold as a winter sunset flickered on his drawn lips as he added: 'The pearl is the unwritten – the pearl is the unalloyed, the *rest*, the lost!'

From that hour he was less and less present, heedless to all appearance of what went on round him. His disease was definitely mortal, of an action as relentless, after the short arrest that had enabled him to fall in with Doctor Hugh, as a leak in a great ship. Sinking steadily, though this visitor, a man of rare resources, now cordially approved by his physician, showed endless art in guarding him from pain, poor Dencombe kept no reckoning of favour or neglect, betrayed no symptom of regret or speculation. Yet toward the last he gave a sign of having noticed how for two days Doctor Hugh hadn't been in his room, a sign that consisted of his suddenly opening his eyes to put a question. Had he spent those days with the Countess?

'The Countess is dead,' said Doctor Hugh. 'I knew that in a particular contingency she wouldn't resist. I went to her grave.'

Dencombe's eyes opened wider. 'She left you "something handsome"?'

The young man gave a laugh almost too light for a chamber of woe. 'Never a penny. She roundly cursed me.'

'Cursed you?' Dencombe wailed.

'For giving her up. I gave her up for *you*. I had to choose,' his companion explained.

'You chose to let a fortune go?'

'I chose to accept, whatever they might be, the consequences of my infatuation,' smiled Doctor Hugh. Then as a larger pleasantry: 'The fortune be hanged! It's your own fault if I can't get your things out of my head.'

The immediate tribute to his humour was a long bewildered moan; after which, for many hours, many days, Dencombe lay motionless and absent. A response so absolute, such a glimpse of a definite result and such a sense of credit, worked together in his mind and, producing a strange commotion, slowly altered and transfigured his despair. The sense of cold submersion left him – he seemed to float without an effort. The incident was extraordinary as evidence, and it shed an intenser light. At the last he signed to Doctor Hugh to listen and, when he was down on his knees by the pillow, brought him very near. 'You've made me think it all a delusion.'

'Not your glory, my dear friend,' stammered the young man.

'Not my glory – what there is of it! It *is* glory – to have been tested, to have had our little quality and cast our little spell. The thing is to have made somebody care. You happen to be crazy of course, but that doesn't affect the law.'

'You're a great success!' said Doctor Hugh, putting into his young voice the ring of a marriage-bell.

Dencombe lay taking this in; then he gathered strength to speak once more. 'A second chance – *that's* the delusion. There never was to be but one. We work in the dark – we do what we can – we give what we have. Our doubt is our passion and our passion is our task. The rest is the madness of art.'

'If you've doubted, if you've despaired, you've always "done" it,' his visitor subtly argued.

'We've done something or other,' Dencombe conceded.

'Something or other is everything. It's the feasible. It's *you*!'

'Comforter!' poor Dencombe ironically sighed.

'But it's true,' insisted his friend.

'It's true. It's frustration that doesn't count.'

'Frustration's only life,' said Doctor Hugh.

'Yes, it's what passes.' Poor Dencombe was barely audible, but he had marked with the words the virtual end of his first and only chance.

The Death of the Lion

I

I had simply, I suppose, a change of heart, and it must have begun when I received my manuscript back from Mr Pinhorn. Mr Pinhorn was my 'chief,' as he was called in the office: he had accepted the high mission of bringing the paper up. This was a weekly periodical, which had been supposed to be almost past redemption when he took hold of it. It was Mr Deedy who had let the thing down so dreadfully: he was never mentioned in the office now save in connexion with that misdemeanour. Young as I was I had been in a manner taken over from Mr Deedy, who had been owner as well as editor; forming part of a promiscuous lot, mainly plant and office-furniture, which poor Mrs Deedy, in her bereavement and depression, parted with at a rough valuation. I could account for my continuity but on the supposition that I had been cheap. I rather resented the practice of fathering all flatness on my late protector, who was in his unhonoured grave; but as I had my way to make I found matter enough for complacency in being on a 'staff.'[1] At the same time I was aware of my exposure to suspicion as a product of the old lowering system. This made me feel I was doubly bound to have ideas, and had doubtless been at the bottom of my proposing to Mr Pinhorn that I should lay my lean hands on Neil Paraday. I remember how he looked at me – quite, to begin with, as if he had never heard of this celebrity, who indeed at that moment was by no means in the centre of the heavens; and even when I had knowingly explained he expressed but little confidence in the demand for any such stuff. When I had reminded him that the great principle on which we were supposed to work was just to create the demand we required, he considered a moment and then returned: 'I see – you want to write him up.'

'Call it that if you like.'

'And what's your inducement?'

'Bless my soul – my admiration!'

Mr Pinhorn pursed up his mouth. 'Is there much to be done with him?'

'Whatever there is we should have it all to ourselves, for he hasn't been touched.'

This argument was effective and Mr Pinhorn responded. 'Very well, touch him.' Then he added: 'But where can you do it?'

'Under the fifth rib!'

Mr Pinhorn stared. 'Where's that?'

'You want me to go down and see him?' I asked when I had enjoyed his visible search for the obscure suburb I seemed to have named.

'I don't "want" anything – the proposal's your own. But you must remember that that's the way we do things now,' said Mr Pinhorn with another dig at Mr Deedy.

Unregenerate as I was I could read the queer implications of this speech. The present owner's superior virtue as well as his deeper craft spoke in his reference to the late editor as one of that baser sort who deal in false representations. Mr Deedy would as soon have sent me to call on Neil Paraday as he would have published a 'holiday-number';[2] but such scruples presented themselves as mere ignoble thrift to his successor, whose own sincerity took the form of ringing door-bells and whose definition of genius was the art of finding people at home. It was as if Mr Deedy had published reports without his young men's having, as Pinhorn would have said, really been there. I was unregenerate, as I have hinted, and couldn't be concerned to straighten out the journalistic morals of my chief, feeling them indeed to be an abyss over the edge of which it was better not to peer. Really to be there this time moreover was a vision that made the idea of writing something subtle about Neil Paraday only the more inspiring. I would be as considerate as even Mr Deedy could have wished, and yet I should be as present as only Mr Pinhorn could conceive. My allusion to the sequestered manner in which Mr Paraday lived – it had formed part of my explanation, though I knew of it only by hearsay – was, I could divine, very much what had made Mr Pinhorn nibble. It struck him as inconsistent with the success of his paper that any one should be so sequestered as that. And then wasn't an immediate exposure of everything just what the public wanted? Mr Pinhorn effectually called me to order by reminding me of the promptness with which I had met Miss Braby at Liverpool on her return from her fiasco in the States. Hadn't we published, while its freshness and flavour were unimpaired, Miss Braby's own version of that great international episode? I felt somewhat uneasy at this lumping of the actress and the author, and I confess that after having enlisted Mr Pinhorn's sympathies I procrastinated a little. I had succeeded better than I wished, and I had, as it happened, work nearer at hand. A few days later I called on Lord Crouchley and carried off in triumph the most unintelligible statement that had yet appeared of his lordship's reasons for his change of front. I thus set in motion in the daily papers columns of virtuous verbiage. The following week I ran down to Brighton for a chat, as Mr Pinhorn called it, with Mrs Bounder,[3] who gave me, on the subject of her divorce, many curious particulars that had not been articulated in court. If ever an article flowed from the primal fount it was that article on Mrs Bounder. By this time, however, I became aware that Neil Paraday's new book was on the point of appearing and that its approach had been the ground of my original appeal to Mr Pinhorn, who was now annoyed with me for having lost so many days. He bundled me off — we would at least not lose another. I've always thought his sudden alertness a remarkable example of the journalistic instinct. Nothing had occurred, since I first spoke to him, to create a visible urgency, and no enlightenment could possibly have reached him. It was a pure case of professional *flair* — he had smelt the coming glory as an animal smells its distant prey.

II

I may as well say at once that this little record pretends in no degree to be a picture either of my introduction to Mr Paraday or of certain proximate steps and stages. The scheme of my narrative allows no space for these things, and in any case a prohibitory sentiment would hang about my recollection of so rare an hour. These meagre notes are essentially private, so that if they see the light the insidious forces that, as my story itself shows, make at present for publicity will simply have overmastered my precautions. The curtain fell lately enough on the lamentable drama. My memory of the day I alighted at Mr Paraday's door is a fresh memory of kindness, hospitality, compassion, and of the wonderful illuminating talk in which the welcome was conveyed. Some voice of the air had taught me the right moment, the moment of his life at which an act of unexpected young allegiance might most come home to him. He had recently recovered from a long, grave illness. I had gone to the neighbouring inn for the night, but I spent the evening in his company, and he insisted the next day on my sleeping under his roof. I hadn't an indefinite leave: Mr Pinhorn supposed us to put our victims through on the gallop. It was later, in the office, that the rude motions of the jig were set to music. I fortified myself, however, as my training had taught me to do, by the conviction that nothing could be more advantageous for my article than to be written in the very atmosphere. I said nothing to Mr Paraday about it, but in the morning, after my removal from the inn, while he was occupied in his study, as he had notified me he should need to be, I committed to paper the main heads of my impression. Then thinking to commend myself to Mr Pinhorn by my celerity, I walked out and posted my little packet before luncheon. Once my paper was written I was free to stay on, and if it was calculated to divert attention from my levity in so doing I could reflect with satisfaction that I had never been so clever. I don't mean to deny of course that I was aware it was much too good for Mr Pinhorn; but I was equally conscious that Mr Pinhorn had the supreme shrewdness of recognising from time to time the cases in which an article was not too bad only because it was too good. There was nothing he loved so much as to print on the right occasion a thing he hated. I had begun my visit to the great man on a Monday, and on the Wednesday his book came out. A copy of it arrived by the first post, and he let me go out into the garden with it immediately after breakfast. I read it from beginning to end that day, and in the evening he asked me to remain with him the rest of the week and over the Sunday.

That night my manuscript came back from Mr Pinhorn, accompanied with a letter the gist of which was the desire to know what I meant by trying to fob off on him such stuff. That was the meaning of the question, if not exactly its form, and it made my mistake immense to me. Such as this mistake was I could now only look it in the face and accept it. I knew where I had failed, but it was exactly where I couldn't have succeeded. I had been sent down to be personal and then in point of fact hadn't been personal at all: what I had dispatched to London was just a little finicking feverish study of my author's talent. Anything less relevant to Mr Pinhorn's purpose couldn't well be imagined, and he was visibly angry at my having (at his expense, with a second-class ticket) approached the subject of our enterprise only to stand off so helplessly. For myself, I knew but too well what had happened, and how a miracle – as pretty as some old miracle of legend – had been wrought on the spot to save me. There had been a big brush of wings, the flash of an opaline robe, and then, with a great cool stir of the air, the sense of an angel's having swooped down and caught me to his bosom. He held me only till the danger was over, and it all took place in a minute. With my manuscript back on my hands I understood the phenomenon better, and the reflexions I made on it are what I meant, at the beginning of this anecdote, by my change of heart. Mr Pinhorn's note was not only a rebuke decidedly stern, but an invitation immediately to send him – it was the case to say so – the genuine article, the revealing and reverberating sketch to the promise of which, and of which alone, I owed my squandered privilege. A week or two later I recast my peccant paper and, giving it a particular application to Mr Paraday's new book, obtained for it the hospitality of another journal, where, I must admit, Mr Pinhorn was so far vindicated as that it attracted not the least attention.

III

I was frankly, at the end of three days, a very prejudiced critic, so that one morning when, in the garden, my great man had offered to read me something I quite held my breath as I listened. It was the written scheme of another book – something put aside long ago, before his illness, but that he had lately taken out again to reconsider. He had been turning it round when I came down on him, and it had grown magnificently under this second hand. Loose liberal confident, it might have passed for a great gossiping eloquent letter – the overflow into talk of an artist's amorous plan. The theme I thought singularly rich, quite the strongest he had yet treated; and this familiar statement of it, full too of fine maturities, was really, in summarised splendour, a mine of gold, a precious independent work. I remember rather profanely wondering whether the ultimate production could possibly keep at the pitch. His reading of the fond epistle, at any rate, made me feel as if I were, for the advantage of posterity, in close correspondence with him – were the distinguished person to whom it had been affectionately addressed. It was a high distinction simply to be told such things. The idea he now communicated had all the freshness, the flushed fairness, of the conception untouched and untried: it was Venus rising from the sea[4] and before the airs had blown upon her. I had never been so throbbingly present at such an unveiling. But when he had tossed the last bright word after the others, as I had seen cashiers in banks, weighing mounds of coin, drop a final sovereign into the tray, I knew a sudden prudent alarm.

'My dear master, how, after all, are you going to do it? It's infinitely noble, but what time it will take, what patience and independence, what assured, what perfect conditions! Oh for a lone isle in a tepid sea!'

'Isn't this practically a lone isle, and aren't you, as an encircling medium, tepid enough?' he asked, alluding with a laugh to the wonder of my young admiration and the narrow limits of his little provincial home. 'Time isn't what I've lacked hitherto: the question hasn't been to find it, but to use it. Of course my illness made, while it lasted, a great hole – but I dare say there would have been a hole at any rate. The earth we tread has more pockets than a billiard-table. The great thing is now to keep on my feet.'

'That's exactly what I mean.'

Neil Paraday looked at me with eyes – such pleasant eyes as he had – in which, as I now recall their expression, I seem to have seen a dim imagination of his fate. He was fifty years old, and his illness had been cruel, his convalescence slow. 'It isn't as if I weren't all right.'

'Oh if you weren't all right I wouldn't look at you!' I tenderly said.

We had both got up, quickened as by this clearer air, and he had lighted a cigarette. I had taken a fresh one, which with an intenser smile, by way of answer to my exclamation, he applied to the flame of his match. 'If I weren't better I shouldn't have thought of *that*!' He flourished his script in his hand.

'I don't want to be discouraging, but that's not true,' I returned. 'I'm sure that during the months you lay here in pain you had visitations sublime. You thought of a thousand things. You think of more and more all the while. That's what makes you, if you'll pardon my familiarity, so respectable. At a time when so many people are spent you come into your second wind. But, thank God, all the same, you're better! Thank God too you're not, as you were telling me yesterday, "successful." If *you* weren't a failure what would be the use of trying? That's my one reserve on the subject of your recovery – that it makes you "score," as the newspapers say. It looks well in the newspapers, and almost anything that does that's horrible. "We are happy to announce that Mr Paraday, the celebrated author, is again in the enjoyment of excellent health." Somehow I shouldn't like to see it.'

'You won't see it; I'm not in the least celebrated – my obscurity protects me. But couldn't you bear even to see I was dying or dead?' my host enquired.

'Dead – *passe encore;*⁵ there's nothing so safe. One never knows what a living artist may do – one has mourned so many. However, one must make the worst of it. You must be as dead as you can.'

'Don't I meet that condition in having just published a book?'

'Adequately, let us hope; for the book's verily a masterpiece.'

At this moment the parlour-maid appeared in the door that opened from the garden: Paraday lived at no great cost, and the frisk of petticoats, with a timorous 'Sherry, sir?' was about his modest mahogany. He allowed half his income to his wife, from whom he had succeeded in separating without redundancy of legend. I had a general faith in his having behaved well, and I had once, in London, taken Mrs Paraday down to dinner. He now turned to speak to the maid, who offered him, on a tray, some card or note, while, agitated, excited, I wandered to the end of the precinct. The idea of his security became supremely dear to me, and I asked myself if I were the same young man who had come down a few days before to scatter him to the four winds. When I retraced my steps he had gone into the house, and the woman – the second London post had come in – had placed my letters and a newspaper on a bench. I sat down there to the letters, which were a brief business, and then, without heeding the address, took the paper from its envelope. It was the journal of highest renown, *The Empire* of that morning. It regularly came to Paraday, but I remembered that neither of us had yet looked at the copy already delivered. This one had a great mark on the 'editorial' page, and, uncrumpling the wrapper, I saw it to be directed to my host and stamped with the name of his publishers. I instantly divined that *The Empire* had spoken of him, and I've not forgotten the odd little shock of the circumstance. It checked all eagerness and made me drop the paper a moment. As I sat there conscious of a palpitation I think I had a vision of what was to be. I had also a vision of the letter I would presently address to Mr Pinhorn, breaking, as it were, with Mr Pinhorn. Of course, however, the next minute the voice of *The Empire* was in my ears.

The article wasn't, I thanked heaven, a review; it was a 'leader,' the last of three, presenting Neil Paraday to the human race. His new book, the fifth from his hand, had been but a day or two out, and *The Empire*, already aware of it, fired, as if on the birth of a prince, a salute of a whole column. The guns had been booming these three hours in the house without our suspecting them. The big blundering newspaper had discovered him, and now he was proclaimed and anointed and crowned. His place was assigned him as publicly as if a fat usher with a wand had pointed to the topmost chair; he was to pass up and still up, higher and higher, between the watching faces and the envious sounds — away up to the dais and the throne. The article was 'epoch-making,' a landmark in his life; he had taken rank at a bound, waked up a national glory. A national glory was needed, and it was an immense convenience he was there. What all this meant rolled over me, and I fear I grew a little faint — it meant so much more than I could say 'yea' to on the spot. In a flash, somehow, all was different; the tremendous wave I speak of had swept something away. It had knocked down, I suppose, my little customary altar, my twinkling tapers and my flowers, and had reared itself into the likeness of a temple vast and bare. When Neil Paraday should come out of the house he would come out a contemporary. That was what had happened: the poor man was to be squeezed into his horrible age. I felt as if he had been overtaken on the crest of the hill and brought back to the city. A little more and he would have dipped down the short cut to posterity and escaped.

IV

When he came out it was exactly as if he had been in custody, for beside him walked a stout man with a big black beard, who, save that he wore spectacles, might have been a policeman, and in whom at a second glance I recognised the highest contemporary enterprise.

'This is Mr Morrow,' said Paraday, looking, I thought, rather white: 'he wants to publish heaven knows what about me.'

I winced as I remembered that this was exactly what I myself had wanted.

'Already?' I cried with a sort of sense that my friend had fled to me for protection.

Mr Morrow glared, agreeably, through his glasses: they suggested the electric headlights of some monstrous modern ship, and I felt as if Paraday and I were tossing terrified under his bows. I saw his momentum was irresistible. 'I was confident that I should be the first in the field. A great interest is naturally felt in Mr Paraday's surroundings,' he heavily observed.

'I hadn't the least idea of it,' said Paraday, as if he had been told he had been snoring.

'I find he hasn't read the article in *The Empire*,' Mr Morrow remarked to me. 'That's so very interesting – it's something to start with,' he smiled. He had begun to pull off his gloves, which were violently new, and to look encouragingly round the little garden. As a 'surrounding' I felt how I myself had already been taken in; I was a little fish in the stomach of a bigger one. 'I represent,' our visitor continued, 'a syndicate of influential journals, no less than thirty-seven, whose public – whose publics, I may say – are in peculiar sympathy with Mr Paraday's line of thought. They would greatly appreciate any expression of his views on the subject of the art he so nobly exemplifies. In addition to my connexion with the syndicate just mentioned I hold a particular commission from *The Tatler*,[6] whose most prominent department, "Smatter and Chatter" – I dare say you've often enjoyed it – attracts such attention. I was honoured only last week, as a representative of *The Tatler*, with the confidence of Guy Walsingham, the brilliant author of "Obsessions." She pronounced herself thoroughly pleased with my sketch of her method; she went so far as to say that I had made her genius more comprehensible even to herself.'

Neil Paraday had dropped on the garden-bench and sat there at once detached and confounded; he looked hard at a bare spot in the lawn, as if with an anxiety that had suddenly made him grave. His movement had been interpreted by his visitor as an invitation to sink sympathetically into a wicker chair that stood hard by, and while Mr Morrow so settled himself I felt he had taken official possession and that there was no undoing it. One had heard of unfortunate people's having 'a man in the house,'[7] and this was just what *we* had. There was a silence of a moment, during which we seemed to acknowledge in the only way that was possible the presence of universal fate; the sunny stillness took no pity, and my thought, as I was sure Paraday's was doing, performed within the minute a great distant revolution. I saw just how emphatic I should make my rejoinder to Mr Pinhorn, and that having come, like Mr Morrow, to betray, I must remain as long as possible to save. Not because I had brought my mind back, but because our visitor's last words were in my ear, I presently enquired with gloomy irrelevance if Guy Walsingham were a woman.

'Oh yes, a mere pseudonym – rather pretty, isn't it? – and convenient, you know, for a lady who goes in for the larger latitude.[8] "Obsessions, by Miss So-and-so," would look a little odd, but men are more naturally indelicate. Have you peeped into "Obsessions"?' Mr Morrow continued sociably to our companion.

Paraday, still absent, remote, made no answer, as if he hadn't heard the question: a form of intercourse that appeared to suit the cheerful Mr Morrow as well as any other. Imperturbably bland, he was a man of resources – he only needed to be on the spot. He had pocketed the whole poor place while Paraday and I were wool-gathering, and I could imagine that he had already got his 'heads.'[9] His system, at any rate, was justified by the inevitability with which I replied, to save my friend the trouble: 'Dear no – he hasn't read it. He doesn't read such things!' I unwarily added.

'Things that are *too* far over the fence, eh?' I was indeed a godsend to Mr Morrow. It was the psychological moment; it determined the appearance of his note-book, which, however, he at first kept slightly behind him, even as the dentist approaching his victim keeps the horrible forceps. 'Mr Paraday holds with the good old proprieties – I see!' And thinking of the thirty-seven influential journals, I found myself, as I found poor Paraday, helplessly assisting at the promulgation of this ineptitude. 'There's no point on which distinguished views are so acceptable as on this question – raised perhaps more strikingly than ever by Guy Walsingham – of the permissibility of the larger latitude. I've an appointment, precisely in connexion with it, next week, with Dora Forbes, author of "The Other Way Round," which everybody's talking about. Has Mr Paraday glanced at "The Other Way Round"?' Mr Morrow now frankly appealed to me. I took on myself to repudiate the supposition, while our companion, still silent, got up nervously and walked away. His visitor paid no heed to his withdrawal, but opened out the note-book with a more fatherly pat. 'Dora Forbes, I gather, takes the ground, the same as Guy Walsingham's, that the larger latitude has simply got to come. He holds that it has got to be squarely faced. Of course his sex makes him a less prejudiced witness. But an authoritative word from Mr Paraday – from the point of view of *his* sex, you know – would go right round the globe. He takes the line that we *haven't* got to face it?'

I was bewildered: it sounded somehow as if there were three sexes. My interlocutor's pencil was poised, my private responsibility great. I simply sat staring, none the less, and only found presence of mind to say: 'Is this Miss Forbes a gentleman?'

Mr Morrow had a subtle smile. 'It wouldn't be "Miss" – there's a wife!'

'I mean is she a man?'

'The wife?' – Mr Morrow was for a moment as confused as myself. But when I explained that I alluded to Dora Forbes in person he informed me, with visible amusement at my being so out of it, that this was the 'pen-name' of an indubitable male – he had a big red moustache. 'He goes in for the slight mystification because the ladies are such popular favourites. A great deal of interest is felt in his acting on that idea – which *is* clever, isn't it? – and there's every prospect of its being widely imitated.' Our host at this moment joined us again, and Mr Morrow remarked invitingly that he should be happy to make a note of any observation the movement in question, the bid for success under a lady's name, might suggest to Mr Paraday. But the poor man, without catching the allusion, excused himself, pleading that, though greatly honoured by his visitor's interest, he suddenly felt unwell and should have to take leave of him – have to go and lie down and keep quiet. His young friend might be trusted to answer for him, but he hoped Mr Morrow didn't expect great things even of his young friend. His young friend, at this moment, looked at Neil Paraday with an anxious eye, greatly wondering if he were doomed to be ill again; but Paraday's own kind face met his question reassuringly, seemed to say in a glance intelligible enough: 'Oh I'm not ill, but I'm scared; get him out of the house as quietly as possible.' Getting newspaper-men out of the house was odd business for an emissary of Mr Pinhorn, and I was so exhilarated by the idea of it that I called after him as he left us: 'Read the article in *The Empire* and you'll soon be all right!'

V

'Delicious my having come down to tell him of it!' Mr Morrow ejaculated. 'My cab was at the door twenty minutes after *The Empire* had been laid on my breakfast-table. Now what have you got for me?' he continued, dropping again into his chair, from which, however, he the next moment eagerly rose. 'I was shown into the drawing-room, but there must be more to see – his study, his literary sanctum, the little things he has about, or other domestic objects and features. He wouldn't be lying down on his study-table? There's a great interest always felt in the scene of an author's labours. Sometimes we're favoured with very delightful peeps. Dora Forbes showed me all his table-drawers, and almost jammed my hand into one into which I made a dash! I don't ask that of you, but if we could talk things over right there where he sits I feel as if I should get the keynote.'

I had no wish whatever to be rude to Mr Morrow, I was much too initiated not to tend to more diplomacy; but I had a quick inspiration, and I entertained an insurmountable, an almost superstitious objection to his crossing the threshold of my friend's little lonely shabby consecrated workshop. 'No, no – we shan't get at his life that way,' I said. 'The way to get at his life is to – But wait a moment!'

I broke off and went quickly into the house, whence I in three minutes reappeared before Mr Morrow with the two volumes of Paraday's new book. 'His life's here,' I went on, 'and I'm so full of this admirable thing that I can't talk of anything else. The artist's life's his work, and this is the place to observe him. What he has to tell us he tells us with *this* perfection. My dear sir, the best interviewer's the best reader.'

Mr Morrow good-humouredly protested. 'Do you mean to say that no other source of information should be open to us?'

'None other till this particular one – by far the most copious – has been quite exhausted. Have you exhausted it, my dear sir? Had you exhausted it when you came down here? It seems to me in our time almost wholly neglected, and something should surely be done to restore its ruined credit. It's the course to which the artist himself at every step, and with such pathetic confidence, refers us. This last book of Mr Paraday's is full of revelations.'

'Revelations?' panted Mr Morrow, whom I had forced again into his chair.

'The only kind that count. It tells you with a perfection that seems to me quite final all the author thinks, for instance, about the advent of the "larger latitude."'

'Where does it do that?' asked Mr Morrow, who had picked up the second volume and was insincerely thumbing it.

'Everywhere – in the whole treatment of his case. Extract the opinion, disengage the answer – those are the real acts of homage.'

Mr Morrow, after a minute, tossed the book away. 'Ah but you mustn't take me for a reviewer.'

'Heaven forbid I should take you for anything so dreadful! You came down to perform a little act of sympathy, and so, I may confide to you, did I. Let us perform our little act together. These pages overflow with the testimony we want: let us read them and taste them and interpret them. You'll of course have perceived for yourself that one scarcely does read Neil Paraday till one reads him aloud; he gives out to the ear an extraordinary full tone, and it's only when you expose it confidently to that test that you really get near his style. Take up your book again and let me listen, while you pay it out, to that wonderful fifteenth chapter. If you feel you can't do it justice, compose yourself to attention while I produce for you – I think I can! – this scarcely less admirable ninth.'

Mr Morrow gave me a straight look which was as hard as a blow between the eyes; he had turned rather red, and a question had formed itself in his mind which reached my sense as distinctly as if he had uttered it: 'What sort of a damned fool are *you*?' Then he got up, gathering together his hat and gloves, buttoning his coat, projecting hungrily all over the place the big transparency of his mask. It seemed to flare over Fleet Street[10] and somehow made the actual spot distressingly humble: there was so little for it to feed on unless he counted the blisters of our stucco or saw his way to do something with the roses. Even the poor roses were common kinds. Presently his eyes fell on the manuscript from which Paraday had been reading to me and which still lay on the bench. As my own followed them I saw it looked promising, looked pregnant, as if it gently throbbed with the life the reader had given it. Mr Morrow indulged in a nod at it and a vague thrust of his umbrella. 'What's that?'

'Oh it's a plan – a secret.'

'A secret!' There was an instant's silence, and then Mr Morrow made another movement. I may have been mistaken, but it affected me as the translated impulse of the desire to lay hands on the manuscript, and this led me to indulge in a quick anticipatory grab which may very well have seemed ungraceful, or even impertinent, and which at any rate left Mr Paraday's two admirers very erect, glaring at each other while one of them held a bundle of papers well behind him. An instant later Mr Morrow quitted me abruptly, as if he had really carried something off with him. To reassure myself, watching his broad back recede, I only grasped my manuscript the tighter. He went to the back door of the house, the one he had come out from, but on trying the handle he appeared to find it fastened. So he passed round into the front garden, and by listening intently enough I could presently hear the outer gate close behind him with a bang. I thought again of the thirty-seven influential journals and wondered what would be his revenge. I hasten to add that he was magnanimous: which was just the most dreadful thing he could have been. *The Tatler* published a charming chatty familiar account of Mr Paraday's 'Home-life,' and on the wings of the thirty-seven influential journals it went, to use Mr Morrow's own expression, right round the globe.

VI

A week later, early in May, my glorified friend came up to town, where, it may be veraciously recorded, he was the king of the beasts[11] of the year. No advancement was ever more rapid, no exaltation more complete, no bewilderment more teachable. His book sold but moderately, though the article in *The Empire* had done unwonted wonders for it; but he circulated in person to a measure that the libraries might well have envied.[12] His formula had been found – he was a 'revelation.' His momentary terror had been real, just as mine had been – the overclouding of his passionate desire to be left to finish his work. He was far from unsociable, but he had the finest conception of being let alone that I've ever met. For the time, none the less, he took his profit where it seemed most to crowd on him, having in his pocket the portable sophistries about the nature of the artist's task. Observation too was a kind of work and experience a kind of success; London dinners were all material and London ladies were fruitful toil. 'No one has the faintest conception of what I'm trying for,' he said to me, 'and not many have read three pages that I've written; but I must dine with them first – they'll find out why when they've time.' It was rather rude justice perhaps; but the fatigue had the merit of being a new sort, while the phantasmagoric town was probably after all less of a battlefield than the haunted study. He once told me that he had had no personal life to speak of since his fortieth year, but had had more than was good for him before. London closed the parenthesis and exhibited him in relations; one of the most inevitable of these being that in which he found himself to Mrs Weeks Wimbush, wife of the boundless brewer and proprietress of the universal menagerie. In this establishment, as everybody knows, on occasions when the crush is great, the animals rub shoulders freely with the spectators and the lions sit down for whole evenings with the lambs.[13]

It had been ominously clear to me from the first that in Neil Paraday this lady, who, as all the world agreed, was tremendous fun, considered that she had secured a prime attraction, a creature of almost heraldic oddity. Nothing could exceed her enthusiasm over her capture, and nothing could exceed the confused apprehensions it excited in me. I had an instinctive fear of her which I tried without effect to conceal from her victim, but which I let her notice with perfect impunity. Paraday heeded it, but she never did, for her conscience was that of a romping child. She was a blind violent force to which I could attach no more idea of responsibility than to the creaking of a sign in the wind. It was difficult to say what she conduced to but circulation. She was constructed of steel and leather, and all I asked of her for our tractable friend was not to do him to death. He had consented for a time to be of india-rubber, but my thoughts were fixed on the day he should resume his shape or at least get back into his box. It was evidently all right, but I should be glad when it was well over. I had a special fear – the impression was ineffaceable of the hour when, after Mr Morrow's departure, I had found him on the sofa in his study. That pretext of indisposition had not in the least been meant as a snub to the envoy of *The Tatler* – he had gone to lie down in very truth. He had felt a pang of his old pain, the result of the agitation wrought in him by this forcing open of a new period. His old programme, his old ideal even had to be changed. Say what one would, success was a complication and recognition had to be reciprocal. The monastic life, the pious illumination of the missal in the convent-cell were things of the gathered past. It didn't engender despair, but at least it required adjustment. Before I left him on that occasion we had passed a bargain, my part of which was that I should make it my business to take care of him. Let whoever would represent the interest in his presence (I must have had a mystical prevision of Mrs Weeks Wimbush) I should represent the interest in his work – or otherwise expressed in his absence. These two interests were in their essence opposed; and I doubt, as youth is fleeting, if I shall ever again know the intensity of joy with which I felt that in so good cause I was willing to make myself odious.

One day in Sloane Street[14] I found myself questioning Paraday's landlord, who had come to the door in answer to my knock. Two vehicles, a barouche and a smart hansom,[15] were drawn up before the house.

'In the drawing-room, sir? Mrs Weeks Wimbush.'

'And in the dining-room?'

'A young lady, sir – waiting: I think a foreigner.'

It was three o'clock, and on days when Paraday didn't lunch out he attached a value to these appropriated hours. On which days, however, didn't the dear man lunch out? Mrs Wimbush, at such a crisis, would have rushed round immediately after her own repast. I went into the dining-room first, postponing the pleasure of seeing how, upstairs, the lady of the barouche would, on my arrival, point the moral of my sweet solicitude. No one took such an interest as herself in his doing only what was good for him, and she was always on the spot to see that he did it. She made appointments with him to discuss the best means of economising his time and protecting his privacy. She further made his health her special business, and had so much sympathy with my own zeal for it that she was the author of pleasing fictions on the subject of what my devotion had led me to give up. I gave up nothing (I don't count Mr Pinhorn) because I had nothing, and all I had as yet achieved was to find myself also in the menagerie. I had dashed in to save my friend, but I had only got domesticated and wedged; so that I could do little more for him than exchange with him over people's heads looks of intense but futile intelligence.

VII

The young lady in the dining-room had a brave face, black hair, blue eyes, and in her lap a big volume. 'I've come for his autograph,' she said when I had explained to her that I was under bonds to see people for him when he was occupied. 'I've been waiting half an hour, but I'm prepared to wait all day.' I don't know whether it was this that told me she was American, for the propensity to wait all day is not in general characteristic of her race. I was enlightened probably not so much by the spirit of the utterance as by some quality of its sound. At any rate I saw she had an individual patience and a lovely frock, together with an expression that played among her pretty features like a breeze among flowers. Putting her book on the table she showed me a massive album, showily bound and full of autographs of price. The collection of faded notes, of still more faded 'thoughts,' of quotations, platitudes, signatures, represented a formidable purpose.

I could only disclose my dread of it. 'Most people apply to Mr Paraday by letter, you know.'

'Yes, but he doesn't answer. I've written three times.'

'Very true,' I reflected; 'the sort of letter you mean goes straight into the fire.'

'How do you know the sort I mean?' My interlocutress had blushed and smiled, and in a moment she added: 'I don't believe he gets many like them!'

'I'm sure they're beautiful, but he burns without reading.' I didn't add that I had convinced him he ought to.

'Isn't he then in danger of burning things of importance?'

'He would perhaps be so if distinguished men hadn't an infallible nose for nonsense.'

She looked at me a moment — her face was sweet and gay. 'Do you burn without reading too?' — in answer to which I assured her that if she'd trust me with her repository I'd see that Mr Paraday should write his name in it.

She considered a little. 'That's very well, but it wouldn't make me see him.'

'Do you want very much to see him?' It seemed ungracious to catechise so charming a creature, but somehow I had never yet taken my duty to the great author so seriously.

'Enough to have come from America for the purpose.'

I stared. 'All alone?'

'I don't see that that's exactly your business, but if it will make me more seductive I'll confess that I'm quite by myself. I had to come alone or not come at all.'

She was interesting; I could imagine she had lost parents, natural protectors — could conceive even she had inherited money. I was at a pass of my own fortunes when keeping hansoms at doors seemed to me pure swagger. As a trick of this bold and sensitive girl, however, it became romantic — a part of the general romance of her freedom, her errand, her innocence. The confidence of young Americans was notorious, and I speedily arrived at a conviction that no impulse could have been more generous than the impulse that had operated here. I foresaw at that moment that it would make her my peculiar charge, just as circumstances had made Neil Paraday. She would be another person to look after, so that one's honour would be concerned in guiding her straight. These things became clearer to me later on; at the instant I had scepticism enough to observe to her, as I turned the pages of her volume, that her net had all the same caught many a big fish.

She appeared to have had fruitful access to the great ones of the earth; there were people moreover whose signatures she had presumably secured without a personal interview. She couldn't have worried George Washington and Friedrich Schiller and Hannah More.[16] She met this argument, to my surprise, by throwing up the album without a pang. It wasn't even her own; she was responsible for none of its treasures. It belonged to a girl-friend in America, a young lady in a western city. This young lady had insisted on her bringing it, to pick up more autographs: she thought they might like to see, in Europe, in what company they would be. The 'girl-friend,' the western city, the immortal names, the curious errand, the idyllic faith, all made a story as strange to me, and as beguiling, as some tale in the Arabian Nights.[17] Thus it was that my informant had encumbered herself with the ponderous tome; but she hastened to assure me that this was the first time she had brought it out. For her visit to Mr Paraday it had simply been a pretext. She didn't really care a straw that he should write his name; what she did want was to look straight into his face.

I demurred a little. 'And why do you require to do that?'

'Because I just love him!' Before I could recover from the agitating effect of this crystal ring my companion had continued: 'Hasn't there ever been any face that *you've* wanted to look into?'

How could I tell her so soon how much I appreciated the opportunity of looking into hers? I could only assent in general to the proposition that there were certainly for every one such yearnings, and even such faces; and I felt the crisis demand all my lucidity, all my wisdom. 'Oh yes, I'm a student of physiognomy. Do you mean,' I pursued, 'that you've a passion for Mr Paraday's books?'

'They've been everything to me and a little more beside — I know them by heart. They've completely taken hold of me. There's no author about whom I'm in such a state as I'm in about Neil Paraday.'

'Permit me to remark then,' I presently returned, 'that you're one of the right sort.'

'One of the enthusiasts? Of course I am!'

'Oh there are enthusiasts who are quite of the wrong. I mean you're one of those to whom an appeal can be made.'

'An appeal?' Her face lighted as if with the chance of some great sacrifice.

If she was ready for one it was only waiting for her, and in a moment I mentioned it. 'Give up this crude purpose of seeing him. Go away without it. That will be far better.'

She looked mystified, then turned visibly pale. 'Why, hasn't he any personal charm?' The girl was terrible and laughable in her bright directness.

'Ah that dreadful word "personal"!' I wailed; 'we're dying of it, for you women bring it out with murderous effect. When you meet with a genius as fine as this idol of ours let him off the dreary duty of being a personality as well. Know him only by what's best in him and spare him for the same sweet sake.'

My young lady continued to look at me in confusion and mistrust, and the result of her reflexion on what I had just said was to make her suddenly break out: 'Look here, sir – what's the matter with him?'

'The matter with him is that if he doesn't look out people will eat a great hole in his life.'

She turned it over. 'He hasn't any disfigurement?'

'Nothing to speak of!'

'Do you mean that social engagements interfere with his occupations?'

'That but feebly expresses it.'

'So that he can't give himself up to his beautiful imagination?'

'He's beset, badgered, bothered – he's pulled to pieces on the pretext of being applauded. People expect him to give them his time, his golden time, who wouldn't themselves give five shillings for one of his books.'

'Five? I'd give five thousand!'

'Give your sympathy – give your forbearance. Two thirds of those who approach him only do it to advertise themselves.'

'Why it's too bad!' the girl exclaimed with the face of an angel. 'It's the first time I was ever called crude!' she laughed.

I followed up my advantage. 'There's a lady with him now who's a terrible complication, and who yet hasn't read, I'm sure, ten pages he ever wrote.'

My visitor's wide eyes grew tenderer. 'Then how does she talk –?'

'Without ceasing. I only mention her as a single case. Do you want to know how to show a superlative consideration? Simply avoid him.'

'Avoid him?' she despairingly breathed.

'Don't force him to have to take account of you; admire him in silence, cultivate him at a distance and secretly appropriate his message. Do you want to know,' I continued, warming to my idea, 'how to perform an act of homage really sublime?' Then as she hung on my words: 'Succeed in never seeing him at all!'

'Never at all?' – she suppressed a shriek for it.

'The more you get into his writings the less you'll want to, and you'll be immensely sustained by the thought of the good you're doing him.'

She looked at me without resentment or spite, and at the truth I had put before her with candour, credulity, pity. I was afterwards happy to remember that she must have gathered from my face the liveliness of my interest in herself. 'I think I see what you mean.'

'Oh I express it badly, but I should be delighted if you'd let me come to see you – to explain it better.'

She made no response to this, and her thoughtful eyes fell on the big album, on which she presently laid her hands as if to take it away. 'I did use to say out West that they might write a little less for autographs – to all the great poets, you know – and study the thoughts and style a little more.'

'What do they care for the thoughts and style? They didn't even understand you. I'm not sure,' I added, 'that I do myself, and I dare say that you by no means make me out.'

She had got up to go, and though I wanted her to succeed in not seeing Neil Paraday I wanted her also, inconsequently, to remain in the house. I was at any rate far from desiring to hustle her off. As Mrs Weeks Wimbush, upstairs, was still saving our friend in her own way, I asked my young lady to let me briefly relate, in illustration of my point, the little incident of my having gone down into the country for a profane purpose and been converted on the spot to holiness. Sinking again into her chair to listen she showed a deep interest in the anecdote. Then thinking it over gravely she returned with her odd intonation: 'Yes, but you do see him!' I had to admit that this was the case; and I wasn't so prepared with an effective attenuation as I could have wished. She eased the situation off, however, by the charming quaintness with which she finally said: 'Well, I wouldn't want him to be lonely!' This time she rose in earnest, but I persuaded her to let me keep the album to show Mr Paraday. I assured her I'd bring it back to her myself. 'Well, you'll find my address somewhere in it on a paper!' she sighed all resignedly at the door.

VIII

I blush to confess it, but I invited Mr Paraday that very day to transcribe into the album one of his most characteristic passages. I told him how I had got rid of the strange girl who had brought it – her ominous name was Miss Hurter and she lived at an hotel; quite agreeing with him moreover as to the wisdom of getting rid with equal promptitude of the book itself. This was why I carried it to Albemarle Street[18] no later than on the morrow. I failed to find her at home, but she wrote to me and I went again: she wanted so much to hear more about Neil Paraday. I returned repeatedly, I may briefly declare, to supply her with this information. She had been immensely taken, the more she thought of it, with that idea of mine about the act of homage: it had ended by filling her with a generous rapture. She positively desired to do something sublime for him, though indeed I could see that, as this particular flight was difficult, she appreciated the fact that my visits kept her up. I had it on my conscience to keep her up; I neglected nothing that would contribute to it, and her conception of our cherished author's independence became at last as fine as his very own. 'Read him, read him – *that* will be an education in decency,' I constantly repeated; while, seeking him in his works even as God in nature,[19] she represented herself as convinced that, according to my assurance, this was the system that had, as she expressed it, weaned her. We read him together when I could find time, and the generous creature's sacrifice was fed by our communion. There were twenty selfish women about whom I told her and who stirred her to a beautiful rage. Immediately after my first visit her sister, Mrs Milsom, came over from Paris, and the two ladies began to present, as they called it, their letters. I thanked our stars that none had been presented to Mr Paraday. They received invitations and dined out, and some of these occasions enabled Fanny Hurter to perform, for consistency's sake, touching feats of submission. Nothing indeed would now have induced her even to look at the object of her admiration. Once, hearing his name announced at a party, she instantly left the room by another door and then straightway quitted the house. At another time when I was at the opera with them – Mrs Milsom had invited me to their box – I attempted to point Mr Paraday out to her in the stalls. On this she asked her sister to change places with her and, while that lady devoured the great man through a powerful glass, presented, all the rest of the evening, her inspired back to the house. To torment her tenderly I pressed the glass upon her, telling her how wonderfully near it brought our friend's handsome head. By way of answer she simply looked at me in charged silence, letting me see that tears had gathered in her eyes. These tears, I may remark, produced an effect on me of which the end is not yet. There was a moment when I felt it my duty to mention them to Neil Paraday, but I was deterred by the reflexion that there were questions more relevant to his happiness.

These questions indeed, by the end of the season, were reduced to a single one – the question of reconstituting so far as might be possible the conditions under which he had produced his best work. Such conditions could never all come back, for there was a new one that took up too much place; but some perhaps were not beyond recall. I wanted above all things to see him sit down to the subject he had, on my making his acquaintance, read me that admirable sketch of. Something told me there was no security but in his doing so before the new factor, as we used to say at Mr Pinhorn's, should render the problem incalculable. It only half-reassured me that the sketch itself was so copious and so eloquent that even at the worst there would be the making of a small but complete book, a tiny volume which, for the faithful, might well become an object of adoration. There would even not be wanting critics to declare, I foresaw, that the plan was a thing to be more thankful for than the structure to have been reared on it. My impatience for the structure, none the less, grew and grew with the interruptions. He had on coming up to town begun to sit for his portrait to a young painter, Mr Rumble, whose little game, as we also used to say at Mr Pinhorn's, was to be the first to perch on the shoulders of renown. Mr Rumble's studio was a circus in which the man of the hour, and still more the woman, leaped through the hoops of his showy frames almost as electrically as they burst into telegrams and 'specials.'[20] He pranced into the exhibitions on their back; he was the reporter on canvas, the Vandyke[21] up to date, and there was one roaring year in which Mrs Bounder and Miss Braby, Guy Walsingham and Dora Forbes proclaimed in chorus from the same pictured walls that no one had yet got ahead of him.

Paraday had been promptly caught and saddled, accepting with characteristic good humour his confidential hint that to figure in his show was not so much a consequence as a cause of immortality. From Mrs Wimbush to the last 'representative' who called to ascertain his twelve favourite dishes, it was the same ingenuous assumption that he would rejoice in the repercussion. There were moments when I fancied I might have had more patience with them if they hadn't been so fatally benevolent. I hated at all events Mr Rumble's picture, and had my bottled resentment ready when, later on, I found my distracted friend had been stuffed by Mrs Wimbush into the mouth of another cannon. A young artist in whom she was intensely interested, and who had no connexion with Mr Rumble, was to show how far *he* could make him go. Poor Paraday, in return, was naturally to write something somewhere about the young artist. She played her victims against each other with admirable ingenuity, and her establishment was a huge machine in which the tiniest and the biggest wheels went round to the same treadle. I had a scene with her in which I tried to express that the function of such a man was to exercise his genius – not to serve as a hoarding for pictorial posters. The people I was perhaps angriest with were the editors of magazines who had introduced what they called new features, so aware were they that the newest feature of all would be to make him grind their axes by contributing his views on vital topics and taking part in the periodical prattle about the future of fiction. I made sure that before I should have done with him there would scarcely be a current form of words left me to be sick of; but meanwhile I could make surer still of my animosity to bustling ladies for whom he drew the water that irrigated their social flower-beds.

I had a battle with Mrs Wimbush over the artist she protected, and another over the question of a certain week, at the end of July, that Mr Paraday appeared to have contracted to spend with her in the country. I protested against this visit; I intimated that he was too unwell for hospitality without a *nuance*, for caresses without imagination; I begged he might rather take the time in some restorative way. A sultry air of promises, of ponderous parties, hung over his August, and he would greatly profit by the interval of rest. He hadn't told me he was ill again – that he had had a warning; but I hadn't needed this, for I found his reticence his worst symptom. The only thing he said to me was that he believed a comfortable attack of something or other would set him up: it would put out of the question everything but the exemptions he prized. I'm afraid I shall have presented him as a martyr in a very small cause if I fail to explain that he surrendered himself much more liberally than I surrendered him. He filled his lungs, for the most part, with the comedy of his queer fate: the tragedy was in the spectacles through which I chose to look. He was conscious of inconvenience, and above all of a great renouncement; but how could he have heard a mere dirge in the bells of his accession? The sagacity and the jealousy were mine, and his the impressions and the harvest. Of course, as regards Mrs Wimbush, I was worsted in my encounters, for wasn't the state of his health the very reason for his coming to her at Prestidge? Wasn't it precisely at Prestidge that he was to be coddled, and wasn't the dear Princess coming to help her to coddle him? The dear Princess, now on a visit to England, was of a famous foreign house, and, in her gilded cage, with her retinue of keepers and feeders, was the most expensive specimen in the good lady's collection. I don't think her august presence had had to do with Paraday's consenting to go, but it's not impossible he had operated as a bait to the illustrious stranger. The party had been made up for him, Mrs Wimbush averred, and every one was counting on it, the dear Princess most of all. If he was well enough he was to read them something absolutely fresh, and it was on that particular prospect the Princess had set her heart. She was so fond of genius in *any* walk of life, and was so used to it and understood it so well: she was the greatest of Mr Paraday's admirers, she devoured everything he wrote. And then he read like an angel. Mrs Wimbush reminded me that he had again and again given her, Mrs Wimbush, the privilege of listening to him.

I looked at her a moment. 'What has he read to you?' I crudely enquired.

For a moment too she met my eyes, and for the fraction of a moment she hesitated and coloured. 'Oh all sorts of things!'

I wondered if this were an imperfect recollection or only a perfect fib, and she quite understood my unuttered comment on her measure of such things. But if she could forget Neil Paraday's beauties she could of course forget my rudeness, and three days later she invited me, by telegraph, to join the party at Prestidge. This time she might indeed have had a story about what I had given up to be near the master. I addressed from that fine residence several communications to a young lady in London, a young lady whom, I confess, I quitted with reluctance and whom the reminder of what she herself could give up was required to make me quit at all. It adds to the gratitude I owe her on other grounds that she kindly allows me to transcribe from my letters a few of the passages in which that hateful sojourn is candidly commemorated.

IX

'I suppose I ought to enjoy the joke of what's going on here,' I wrote, 'but somehow it doesn't amuse me. Pessimism on the contrary possesses me and cynicism deeply engages. I positively feel my own flesh sore from the brass nails in Neil Paraday's social harness. The house is full of people who like him, as they mention, awfully, and with whom his talent for talking nonsense has prodigious success. I delight in his nonsense myself; why is it therefore that I grudge these happy folk their artless satisfaction? Mystery of the human heart — abyss of the critical spirit! Mrs Wimbush thinks she can answer that question, and as my want of gaiety has at last worn out her patience she has given me a glimpse of her shrewd guess. I'm made restless by the selfishness of the insincere friend — I want to monopolise Paraday in order that he may push me on. To be intimate with him's a feather in my cap; it gives me an importance that I couldn't naturally pretend to, and I seek to deprive him of social refreshment because I fear that meeting more disinterested people may enlighten him as to my real motive. All the disinterested people here are his particular admirers and have been carefully selected as such. There's supposed to be a copy of his last book in the house, and in the hall I come upon ladies, in attitudes, bending gracefully over the first volume. I discreetly avert my eyes, and when I next look round the precarious joy has been superseded by the book of life. There's a sociable circle or a confidential couple, and the relinquished volume lies open on its face and as dropped under extreme coercion. Somebody else presently finds it and transfers it, with its air of momentary desolation, to another piece of furniture. Every one's asking every one about it all day, and every one's telling every one where they put it last. I'm sure it's rather smudgy about the twentieth page. I've a strong impression too that the second volume is lost — has been packed in the bag of some departing guest; and yet everybody has the impression that somebody else has read to the end. You see therefore that the beautiful book plays a great part in our existence. Why should I take the occasion of such distinguished honours to say that I begin to see deeper into Gustave Flaubert's doleful refrain about the hatred of literature?[22] I refer you again to the perverse constitution of man.

'The Princess is a massive lady with the organisation of an athlete and the confusion of tongues of a *valet de place*.[23] She contrives to commit herself extraordinarily little in a great many languages, and is entertained and conversed with in detachments and relays, like an institution which goes on from generation to generation or a big building contracted for under a forfeit.[24] She can't have a personal taste any more than, when her husband succeeds, she can have a personal crown, and her opinion on any matter is rusty and heavy and plain — made, in the night of ages, to last and be transmitted. I feel as if I ought to "tip" some *custode*[25] for my glimpse of it. She has been told everything in the world and has never perceived anything, and the echoes of her education respond awfully to the rash footfall – I mean the casual remark – in the cold Valhalla of her memory.[26] Mrs Wimbush delights in her wit and says there's nothing so charming as to hear Mr Paraday draw it out. He's perpetually detailed for this job, and he tells me it has a peculiarly exhausting effect. Every one's beginning – at the end of two days – to sidle obsequiously away from her, and Mrs Wimbush pushes him again and again into the breach. None of the uses I have yet seen him put to infuriate me quite so much. He looks very fagged and has at last confessed to me that his condition makes him uneasy – has even promised me he'll go straight home instead of returning to his final engagements in town. Last night I had some talk with him about going to-day, cutting his visit short; so sure am I that he'll be better as soon as he's shut up in his lighthouse. He told me that this is what he would like to do; reminding me, however, that the first lesson of his greatness has been precisely that he can't do what he likes. Mrs Wimbush would never forgive him if he should leave her before the Princess has received the last hand. When I hint that a violent rupture with our hostess would be the best thing in the world for him he gives me to understand that if his reason assents to the proposition his courage hangs woefully back. He makes no secret of being mortally afraid of her, and when I ask what harm she can do him that she hasn't already done he simply repeats: "I'm afraid, I'm afraid! Don't enquire too closely," he said last night; "only believe that I feel a sort of terror. It's strange, when she's so kind! At any rate, I'd as soon overturn that piece of priceless Sèvres[27] as tell her I must go before my date." It sounds dreadfully weak, but he has some reason, and he pays for his imagination, which puts him (I should hate it) in the place of others and makes him feel, even against himself, their feelings, their appetites, their motives. It's indeed inveterately against himself that he makes his imagination act. What a pity he has such a lot of it! He's too beastly intelligent. Besides, the famous reading's still to come off, and it has been postponed a day to allow Guy Walsingham to arrive. It appears this eminent lady's staying at a house a few miles off, which means of course that Mrs Wimbush has forcibly annexed her. She's to come over in a day or two – Mrs Wimbush wants her to hear Mr Paraday.

'To-day's wet and cold, and several of the company, at the invitation of the Duke, have driven over to luncheon at Bigwood. I saw poor Paraday wedge himself, by command, into the little supplementary seat of a brougham[28] in which the Princess and our hostess were already ensconced. If the front glass isn't open on his dear old back perhaps he'll survive. Bigwood, I believe, is very grand and frigid, all marble and precedence, and I wish him well out of the adventure. I can't tell you how much more and more *your* attitude to him, in the midst of all this, shines out by contrast. I never willingly talk to these people about him, but see what a comfort I find it to scribble to you! I appreciate it — it keeps me warm; there are no fires in the house. Mrs Wimbush goes by the calendar, the temperature goes by the weather, the weather goes by God knows what, and the Princess is easily heated. I've nothing but my acrimony to warm me, and have been out under an umbrella to restore my circulation. Coming in an hour ago I found Lady Augusta Minch rummaging about the hall. When I asked her what she was looking for she said she had mislaid something that Mr Paraday had lent her. I ascertained in a moment that the article in question is a manuscript, and I've a foreboding that it's the noble morsel he read me six weeks ago. When I expressed my surprise that he should have bandied about anything so precious (I happen to know it's his only copy — in the most beautiful hand in all the world) Lady Augusta confessed to me that she hadn't had it from himself, but from Mrs Wimbush, who had wished to give her a glimpse of it as a salve for her not being able to stay and hear it read.

'"Is that the piece he's to read," I asked, "when Guy Walsingham arrives?"

'"It's not for Guy Walsingham they're waiting now, it's for Dora Forbes," Lady Augusta said. "She's coming, I believe, early to-morrow. Meanwhile Mrs Wimbush has found out about *him*, and is actively wiring to him. She says he also must hear him."

'"You bewilder me a little," I replied; "in the age we live in one gets lost among the genders and the pronouns. The clear thing is that Mrs Wimbush doesn't guard such a treasure so jealously as she might."

'"Poor dear, she has the Princess to guard! Mr Paraday lent her the manuscript to look over."

'"She spoke, you mean, as if it were the morning paper?"

'Lady Augusta stared — my irony was lost on her. "She didn't have time, so she gave me a chance first; because unfortunately I go to-morrow to Bigwood."

'"And your chance has only proved a chance to lose it?"

'"I haven't lost it. I remember now — it was very stupid of me to have forgotten. I told my maid to give it to Lord Dorimont — or at least to his man."

'"And Lord Dorimont went away directly after luncheon."

'"Of course he gave it back to my maid — or else his man did," said Lady Augusta. "I dare say it's all right."

'The conscience of these people is like a summer sea. They haven't time to "look over" a priceless composition; they've only time to kick it about the house. I suggested that the "man," fired with a noble emulation, had perhaps kept the work for his own perusal; and her ladyship wanted to know whether, if the thing shouldn't reappear for the grand occasion appointed by our hostess, the author wouldn't have something else to read that would do just as well. Their questions are too delightful! I declared to Lady Augusta briefly that nothing in the world can ever do so well as the thing that does best; and at this she looked a little disconcerted. But I added that if the manuscript had gone astray our little circle would have the less of an effort of attention to make. The piece in question was very long – it would keep them three hours.

'"Three hours! Oh the Princess will get up!" said Lady Augusta.

'"I thought she was Mr Paraday's greatest admirer."

'"I dare say she is – she's so awfully clever. But what's the use of being a Princess –"

'"If you can't dissemble your love?" I asked as Lady Augusta was vague. She said at any rate that she'd question her maid; and I'm hoping that when I go down to dinner I shall find the manuscript has been recovered.'

X

'It has *not* been recovered,' I wrote early the next day, 'and I'm moreover much troubled about our friend. He came back from Bigwood with a chill and, being allowed to have a fire in his room, lay down a while before dinner. I tried to send him to bed and indeed thought I had put him in the way of it; but after I had gone to dress Mrs Wimbush came up to see him, with the inevitable result that when I returned I found him under arms and flushed and feverish, though decorated with the rare flower she had brought him for his button-hole. He came down to dinner, but Lady Augusta Minch was very shy of him. To-day he's in great pain, and the advent of *ces dames* – I mean of Guy Walsingham and Dora Forbes – doesn't at all console me. It does Mrs Wimbush, however, for she has consented to his remaining in bed so that he may be all right tomorrow for the listening circle. Guy Walsingham's already on the scene, and the doctor for Paraday also arrived early. I haven't yet seen the author of "Obsessions," but of course I've had a moment by myself with the Doctor. I tried to get him to say that our invalid must go straight home – I mean to-morrow or next day; but he quite refuses to talk about the future. Absolute quiet and warmth and the regular administration of an important remedy are the points he mainly insists on. He returns this afternoon, and I'm to go back to see the patient at one o'clock, when he next takes his medicine. It consoles me a little that he certainly won't be able to read – an exertion he was already more than unfit for. Lady Augusta went off after breakfast, assuring me her first care would be to follow up the lost manuscript. I can see she thinks me a shocking busybody and doesn't understand my alarm, but she'll do what she can, for she's a good-natured woman. "So are they all honourable men."[29] That was precisely what made her give the thing to Lord Dorimont and made Lord Dorimont bag it. What use *he* has for it God only knows. I've the worst forebodings, but somehow I'm strangely without passion – desperately calm. As I consider the unconscious, the well-meaning ravages of our appreciative circle I bow my head in submission to some great natural, some universal accident; I'm rendered almost indifferent, in fact quite gay (ha-ha!) by the sense of immitigable fate. Lady Augusta promises me to trace the precious object and let me have it through the post by the time Paraday's well enough to play his part with it. The last evidence is that her maid did give it to his lordship's valet. One would suppose it some thrilling number of *The Family Budget*.[30] Mrs Wimbush, who's aware of the accident, is much less agitated by it than she would doubtless be were she not for the hour inevitably engrossed with Guy Walsingham.'

Later in the day I informed my correspondent, for whom indeed I kept a loose diary of the situation, that I had made the acquaintance of this celebrity and that she was a pretty little girl who wore her hair in what used to be called a crop. She looked so juvenile and so innocent that if, as Mr Morrow had announced, she was resigned to the larger latitude, her superiority to prejudice must have come to her early. I spent most of the day hovering about Neil Paraday's room, but it was communicated to me from below that Guy Walsingham, at Prestidge, was a success. Toward evening I became conscious somehow that her superiority was contagious, and by the time the company separated for the night I was sure the larger latitude had been generally accepted. I thought of Dora Forbes and felt that he had no time to lose. Before dinner I received a telegram from Lady Augusta Minch. 'Lord Dorimont thinks he must have left bundle in train – enquire.' How could I enquire – if I was to take the word as a command? I was too worried and now too alarmed about Neil Paraday. The Doctor came back, and it was an immense satisfaction to me to be sure he was wise and interested. He was proud of being called to so distinguished a patient, but he admitted to me that night that my friend was gravely ill. It was really a relapse, a recrudescence of his old malady. There could be no question of moving him: we must at any rate see first, on the spot, what turn his condition would take. Meanwhile, on the morrow, he was to have a nurse. On the morrow the dear man was easier, and my spirits rose to such cheerfulness that I could almost laugh over Lady Augusta's second telegram: 'Lord Dorimont's servant been to station – nothing found. Push enquiries.' I did laugh, I'm sure, as I remembered this to be the mystic scroll I had scarcely allowed poor Mr Morrow to point his umbrella at. Fool that I had been: the thirty-seven influential journals wouldn't have destroyed it, they'd only have printed it. Of course I said nothing to Paraday.

When the nurse arrived she turned me out of the room, on which I went downstairs. I should premise that at breakfast the news that our brilliant friend was doing well excited universal complacency, and the Princess graciously remarked that he was only to be commiserated for missing the society of Miss Collop. Mrs Wimbush, whose social gift never shone brighter than in the dry decorum with which she accepted this fizzle in her fireworks, mentioned to me that Guy Walsingham had made a very favourable impression on her Imperial Highness. Indeed I think every one did so, and that, like the money-market or the national honour, her Imperial Highness was constitutionally sensitive. There was a certain gladness, a perceptible bustle in the air, however, which I thought slightly anomalous in a house where a great author lay critically ill. 'Le roy est mort – vive le roy':[31] I was reminded that another great author had already stepped into his shoes. When I came down again after the nurse had taken possession I found a strange gentleman hanging about the hall and pacing to and fro by the closed door of the drawing-room. This personage was florid and bald; he had a big red moustache and wore showy knickerbockers – characteristics all that fitted to my conception of the identity of Dora Forbes. In a moment I saw what had happened: the author of 'The Other Way Round' had just alighted at the portals of Prestidge, but had suffered a scruple to restrain him from penetrating further. I recognised his scruple when, pausing to listen at his gesture of caution, I heard a shrill voice lifted in a sort of rhythmic uncanny chant. The famous reading had begun, only it was the author of 'Obsessions' who now furnished the sacrifice. The new visitor whispered to me that he judged something was going on he oughtn't to interrupt.

'Miss Collop arrived last night,' I smiled, 'and the Princess has a thirst for the *inédit*.'[32]

Dora Forbes raised his bushy brows. 'Miss Collop?'

'Guy Walsingham, your distinguished confrère[33] – or shall I say your formidable rival?'

'Oh!' growled Dora Forbes. Then he added: 'Shall I spoil it if I go in?'

'I should think nothing could spoil it!' I ambiguously laughed.

Dora Forbes evidently felt the dilemma; he gave an irritated crook to his moustache. '*Shall* I go in?' he presently asked.

We looked at each other hard a moment; then I expressed something bitter that was in me, expressed it in an infernal 'Do!' After this I got out into the air, but not so fast as not to hear, when the door of the drawing-room opened, the disconcerted drop of Miss Collop's public manner: she must have been in the midst of the larger latitude. Producing with extreme rapidity, Guy Walsingham has just published a work in which amiable people who are not initiated have been pained to see the genius of a sister-novelist held up to unmistakeable ridicule; so fresh an exhibition does it seem to them of the dreadful way men have always treated women. Dora Forbes, it's true, at the present hour, is immensely pushed by Mrs Wimbush and has sat for his portrait to the young artists she protects, sat for it not only in oils but in monumental alabaster.

What happened at Prestidge later in the day is of course contemporary history. If the interruption I had whimsically sanctioned was almost a scandal, what is to be said of that general scatter of the company which, under the Doctor's rule, began to take place in the evening? His rule was soothing to behold, small comfort as I was to have at the end. He decreed in the interest of his patient an absolutely soundless house and a consequent break-up of the party. Little country practitioner as he was, he literally packed off the Princess. She departed as promptly as if a revolution had broken out, and Guy Walsingham emigrated with her. I was kindly permitted to remain, and this was not denied even to Mrs Wimbush. The privilege was withheld indeed from Dora Forbes; so Mrs Wimbush kept her latest capture temporarily concealed. This was so little, however, her usual way of dealing with her eminent friends that a couple of days of it exhausted her patience and she went up to town with him in great publicity. The sudden turn for the worse her afflicted guest had, after a brief improvement, taken on the third night raised an obstacle to her seeing him before her retreat; a fortunate circumstance doubtless, for she was fundamentally disappointed in him. This was not the kind of performance for which she had invited him to Prestidge, let alone invited the Princess. I must add that none of the generous acts marking her patronage of intellectual and other merit have done so much for her reputation as her lending Neil Paraday the most beautiful of her numerous homes to die in. He took advantage to the utmost of the singular favour. Day by day I saw him sink, and I roamed alone about the empty terraces and gardens. His wife never came near him, but I scarcely noticed it: as I paced there with rage in my heart I was too full of another wrong. In the event of his death it would fall to me perhaps to bring out in some charming form, with notes, with the tenderest editorial care, that precious heritage of his written project. But where *was* that precious heritage, and were both the author and the book to have been snatched from us? Lady Augusta wrote me she had done all she could and that poor Lord Dorimont, who had really been worried to death, was extremely sorry. I couldn't have the matter out with Mrs Wimbush, for I didn't want to be taunted by her with desiring to aggrandise myself by a public connexion with Mr Paraday's sweepings. She had signified her willingness to meet the expense of all advertising, as indeed she was always ready to do. The last night of the horrible series, the night before he died, I put my ear closer to his pillow.

'That thing I read you that morning, you know.'

'In your garden that dreadful day? Yes!'

'Won't it do as it is?'

'It would have been a glorious book.'

'It *is* a glorious book,' Neil Paraday murmured. 'Print it as it stands — beautifully.'

'Beautifully!' I passionately promised.

It may be imagined whether, now that he's gone, the promise seems to me less sacred. I'm convinced that if such pages had appeared in his lifetime the Abbey[34] would hold him to-day. I've kept the advertising in my own hands, but the manuscript has not been recovered. It's impossible, and at any rate intolerable, to suppose it can have been wantonly destroyed. Perhaps some hazard of a blind hand, some brutal fatal ignorance has lighted kitchen-fires with it. Every stupid and hideous accident haunts my meditations. My undiscourageable search for the lost treasure would make a long chapter. Fortunately I've a devoted associate in the person of a young lady who has every day a fresh indignation and a fresh idea, and who maintains with intensity that the prize will still turn up. Sometimes I believe her, but I've quite ceased to believe myself. The only thing for us at all events is to go on seeking and hoping together, and we should be closely united by this firm tie even were we not at present by another.

The Figure in the Carpet

I had done a few things and earned a few pence – I had perhaps even had time to begin to think I was finer than was perceived by the patronising; but when I take the little measure of my course (a fidgety habit, for it's none of the longest yet) I count my real start from the evening George Corvick, breathless and worried, came in to ask me a service. He had done more things than I, and earned more pence, though there were chances for cleverness I thought he sometimes missed. I could only however that evening declare to him that he never missed one for kindness. There was almost rapture in hearing it proposed to me to prepare for *The Middle*, the organ of our lucubrations, so called from the position in the week of its day of appearance, an article for which he had made himself responsible and of which, tied up with a stout string, he laid on my table the subject. I pounced upon my opportunity – that is on the first volume of it – and paid scant attention to my friend's explanation of his appeal. What explanation could be more to the point than my obvious fitness for the task? I had written on Hugh Vereker, but never a word in *The Middle*, where my dealings were mainly with the ladies and the minor poets. This was his new novel, an advance copy, and whatever much or little it should do for his reputation I was clear on the spot as to what it should do for mine. Moreover if I always read him as soon as I could get hold of him I had a particular reason for wishing to read him now: I had accepted an invitation to Bridges for the following Sunday, and it had been mentioned in Lady Jane's note that Mr Vereker was to be there. I was young enough for a flutter at meeting a man of his renown, and innocent enough to believe the occasion would demand the display of an acquaintance with his 'last.'

Corvick, who had promised a review of it, had not even had time to read it; he had gone to pieces in consequence of news requiring – as on precipitate reflexion he judged – that he should catch the night-mail[1] to Paris. He had had a telegram from Gwendolen Erme in answer to his letter offering to fly to her aid. I knew already about Gwendolen Erme; I had never seen her, but I had my ideas, which were mainly to the effect that Corvick would marry her if her mother would only die. That lady seemed now in a fair way to oblige him; after some dreadful mistake about a climate or a 'cure' she had suddenly collapsed on the return from abroad. Her daughter, unsupported and alarmed, desiring to make a rush for home but hesitating at the risk, had accepted our friend's assistance, and it was my secret belief that at sight of him Mrs Erme would pull round. His own belief was scarcely to be called secret; it discernibly at any rate differed from mine. He had showed me Gwendolen's photograph with the remark that she wasn't pretty but was awfully interesting; she had published at the age of nineteen a novel in three volumes, 'Deep Down,' about which, in *The Middle*, he had been really splendid. He appreciated my present eagerness and undertook that the periodical in question should do no less; then at the last, with his hand on the door, he said to me: 'Of course you'll be all right, you know.' Seeing I was a trifle vague he added: 'I mean you won't be silly.'

'Silly – about Vereker! Why what do I ever find him but awfully clever?'

'Well, what's that but silly? What on earth does "awfully clever" mean? For God's sake try to get *at* him. Don't let him suffer by our arrangement. Speak of him, you know, if you can, as *I* should have spoken of him.'

I wondered an instant. 'You mean as far and away the biggest of the lot – that sort of thing?'

Corvick almost groaned. 'Oh you know, I don't put them back to back that way; it's the infancy of art! But he gives me a pleasure so rare; the sense of' – he mused a little – 'something or other.'

I wondered again. 'The sense, pray, of what?'

'My dear man, that's just what I want *you* to say!'

Even before he had banged the door I had begun, book in hand, to prepare myself to say it. I sat up with Vereker half the night; Corvick couldn't have done more than that. He was awfully clever – I stuck to that, but he wasn't a bit the biggest of the lot. I didn't allude to the lot, however; I flattered myself that I emerged on this occasion from the infancy of art. 'It's all right,' they declared vividly at the office; and when the number appeared I felt there was a basis on which I could meet the great man. It gave me confidence for a day or two – then that confidence dropped. I had fancied him reading it with relish, but if Corvick wasn't satisfied how could Vereker himself be? I reflected indeed that the heat of the admirer was sometimes grosser even than the appetite of the scribe. Corvick at all events wrote me from Paris a little ill-humouredly. Mrs Erme was pulling round, and I hadn't at all said what Vereker gave him the sense of.

II

The effect of my visit to Bridges was to turn me out for more profundity. Hugh Vereker, as I saw him there, was of a contact so void of angles that I blushed for the poverty of imagination involved in my small precautions. If he was in spirits it wasn't because he had read my review; in fact on the Sunday morning I felt sure he hadn't read it, though *The Middle* had been out three days and bloomed, I assured myself, in the stiff garden of periodicals which gave one of the ormolu tables the air of a stand at a station. The impression he made on me personally was such that I wished him to read it, and I corrected to this end with a surreptitious hand what might be wanting in the careless conspicuity of the sheet. I'm afraid I even watched the result of my manoeuvre, but up to luncheon I watched in vain.

When afterwards, in the course of our gregarious walk, I found myself for half an hour, not perhaps without another manoeuvre, at the great man's side, the result of his affability was a still livelier desire that he shouldn't remain in ignorance of the peculiar justice I had done him. It wasn't that he seemed to thirst for justice; on the contrary I hadn't yet caught in his talk the faintest grunt of a grudge — a note for which my young experience had already given me an ear. Of late he had had more recognition, and it was pleasant, as we used to say in *The Middle*, to see how it drew him out. He wasn't of course popular, but I judged one of the sources of his good humour to be precisely that his success was independent of that. He had none the less become in a manner the fashion; the critics at least had put on a spurt and caught up with him. We had found out at last how clever he was, and he had had to make the best of the loss of his mystery. I was strongly tempted, as I walked beside him, to let him know how much of that unveiling was my act; and there was a moment when I probably should have done so had not one of the ladies of our party, snatching a place at his other elbow, just then appealed to him in a spirit comparatively selfish. It was very discouraging: I almost felt the liberty had been taken with myself.

I had had on my tongue's end, for my own part, a phrase or two about the right word at the right time; but later on I was glad not to have spoken, for when on our return we clustered at tea I perceived Lady Jane, who had not been out with us, brandishing *The Middle* with her longest arm. She had taken it up at her leisure; she was delighted with what she had found, and I saw that, as a mistake in a man may often be a felicity in a woman, she would practically do for me what I hadn't been able to do for myself. 'Some sweet little truths that needed to be spoken,' I heard her declare, thrusting the paper at rather a bewildered couple by the fireplace. She grabbed it away from them again on the reappearance of Hugh Vereker, who after our walk had been upstairs to change something. 'I know you don't in general look at this kind of thing, but it's an occasion really for doing so. You *haven't* seen it? Then you must. The man has actually got *at* you, at what *I* always feel, you know.' Lady Jane threw into her eyes a look evidently intended to give an idea of what she always felt; but she added that she couldn't have expressed it. The man in the paper expressed it in a striking manner. 'Just see there, and there, where I've dashed it, how he brings it out.' She had literally marked for him the brightest patches of my prose, and if I was a little amused Vereker himself may well have been. He showed how much he was when before us all Lady Jane wanted to read something aloud. I liked at any rate the way he defeated her purpose by jerking the paper affectionately out of her clutch. He'd take it upstairs with him and look at it on going to dress. He did this half an hour later – I saw it in his hand when he repaired to his room. That was the moment at which, thinking to give her pleasure, I mentioned to Lady Jane that I was the author of the review. I did give her pleasure, I judged, but perhaps not quite so much as I had expected. If the author was 'only me' the thing didn't seem quite so remarkable. Hadn't I had the effect rather of diminishing the lustre of the article than of adding to my own? Her ladyship was subject to the most extraordinary drops. It didn't matter; the only effect I cared about was the one it would have on Vereker up there by his bedroom fire.

At dinner I watched for the signs of this impression, tried to fancy some happier light in his eyes; but to my disappointment Lady Jane gave me no chance to make sure. I had hoped she'd call triumphantly down the table, publicly demand if she hadn't been right. The party was large – there were people from outside as well, but I had never seen a table long enough to deprive Lady Jane of a triumph. I was just reflecting in truth that this interminable board would deprive *me* of one when the guest next me, dear woman – she was Miss Poyle, the vicar's sister, a robust unmodulated person – had the happy inspiration and the unusual courage to address herself across it to Vereker, who was opposite, but not directly, so that when he replied they were both leaning forward. She enquired, artless body, what he thought of Lady Jane's 'panegyric,' which she had read – not connecting it however with her right-hand neighbour; and while I strained my ear for his reply I heard him, to my stupefaction, call back gaily, his mouth full of bread: 'Oh it's all right – the usual twaddle!'

I had caught Vereker's glance as he spoke, but Miss Poyle's surprise was a fortunate cover for my own.

'You mean he doesn't do you justice?' said the excellent woman.

Vereker laughed out, and I was happy to be able to do the same. 'It's a charming article,' he tossed us.

Miss Poyle thrust her chin half across the cloth. 'Oh you're so deep!' she drove home.

'As deep as the ocean! All I pretend is that the author doesn't see – ' But a dish was at this point passed over his shoulder, and we had to wait while he helped himself.

'Doesn't see what?' my neighbour continued.

'Doesn't see anything.'

'Dear me – how very stupid!'

'Not a bit,' Vereker laughed again. 'Nobody does.'

The lady on his further side appealed to him and Miss Poyle sank back to myself. 'Nobody sees anything!' she cheerfully announced; to which I replied that I had often thought so too, but had somehow taken the thought for a proof on my own part of a tremendous eye. I didn't tell her the article was mine; and I observed that Lady Jane, occupied at the end of the table, had not caught Vereker's words.

I rather avoided him after dinner, for I confess he struck me as cruelly conceited, and the revelation was a pain. 'The usual twaddle' – my acute little study! That one's admiration should have had a reserve or two could gall him to that point? I had thought him placid, and he was placid enough; such a surface was the hard polished glass that encased the bauble of his vanity. I was really ruffled, and the only comfort was that if nobody saw anything George Corvick was quite as much out of it as I. This comfort however was not sufficient, after the ladies had dispersed, to carry me in the proper manner – I mean in a spotted jacket and humming an air – into the smoking-room. I took my way in some dejection to bed; but in the passage I encountered Mr Vereker, who had been up once more to change, coming out of his room. *He* was humming an air and had on a spotted jacket, and as soon as he saw me his gaiety gave a start.

'My dear young man,' he exclaimed, 'I'm so glad to lay hands on you! I'm afraid I most unwittingly wounded you by those words of mine at dinner to Miss Poyle. I learned but half an hour ago from Lady Jane that you're the author of the little notice in *The Middle*.'

I protested that no bones were broken; but he moved with me to my own door, his hand, on my shoulder, kindly feeling for a fracture; and on hearing that I had come up to bed he asked leave to cross my threshold and just tell me in three words what his qualification of my remarks had represented. It was plain he really feared I was hurt, and the sense of his solicitude suddenly made all the difference to me. My cheap review fluttered off into space, and the best things I had said in it became flat enough beside the brilliancy of his being there. I can see him there still, on my rug, in the firelight and his spotted jacket, his fine clear face all bright with the desire to be tender to my youth. I don't know what he had at first meant to say, but I think the sight of my relief touched him, excited him, brought up words to his lips from far within. It was so these words presently conveyed to me something that, as I afterwards knew, he had never uttered to any one. I've always done justice to the generous impulse that made him speak; it was simply compunction for a snub unconsciously administered to a man of letters in a position inferior to his own, a man of letters moreover in the very act of praising him. To make the thing right he talked to me exactly as an equal and on the ground of what we both loved best. The hour, the place, the unexpectedness deepened the impression: he couldn't have done anything more intensely effective.

III

'I don't quite know how to explain it to you,' he said, 'but it was the very fact that your notice of my book had a spice of intelligence, it was just your exceptional sharpness, that produced the feeling – a very old story with me, I beg you to believe – under the momentary influence of which I used in speaking to that good lady the words you so naturally resent. I don't read the things in the newspapers unless they're thrust upon me as that one was – it's always one's best friend who does it! But I used to read them sometimes – ten years ago. I dare say they were in general rather stupider then; at any rate it always struck me they missed my little point with a perfection exactly as admirable when they patted me on the back as when they kicked me in the shins. Whenever since I've happened to have a glimpse of them they were still blazing away – still missing it, I mean, deliciously. *You* miss it, my dear fellow, with inimitable assurance; the fact of your being awfully clever and your article's being awfully nice doesn't make a hair's breadth of difference. It's quite with you rising young men,' Vereker laughed, 'that I feel most what a failure I am!'

I listened with keen interest; it grew keener as he talked. '*You* a failure – heavens! What then may your "little point" happen to be?'

'Have I got to *tell* you, after all these years and labours?' There was something in the friendly reproach of this – jocosely exaggerated – that made me, as an ardent young seeker for truth, blush to the roots of my hair. I'm as much in the dark as ever, though I've grown used in a sense to my obtuseness; at that moment, however, Vereker's happy accent made me appear to myself, and probably to him, a rare dunce. I was on the point of exclaiming 'Ah yes, don't tell me: for my honour, for that of the craft, don't!' when he went on in a manner that showed he had read my thought and had his own idea of the probability of our some day redeeming ourselves. 'By my little point I mean – what shall I call it? – the particular thing I've written my books most *for*. Isn't there for every writer a particular thing of that sort, the thing that most makes him apply himself, the thing without the effort to achieve which he wouldn't write at all, the very passion of his passion, the part of the business in which, for him, the flame of art burns most intensely? Well, it's *that*!'

I considered a moment — that is I followed at a respectful distance, rather gasping. I was fascinated — easily, you'll say; but I wasn't going after all to be put off my guard. 'Your description's certainly beautiful, but it doesn't make what you describe very distinct.'

'I promise you it would be distinct if it should dawn on you at all.' I saw that the charm of our topic overflowed for my companion into an emotion as lively as my own. 'At any rate,' he went on, 'I can speak for myself: there's an idea in my work without which I wouldn't have given a straw for the whole job. It's the finest fullest intention of the lot, and the application of it has been, I think, a triumph of patience, of ingenuity. I ought to leave that to somebody else to say; but that nobody does say it is precisely what we're talking about. It stretches, this little trick of mine, from book to book, and everything else, comparatively, plays over the surface of it. The order, the form, the texture of my books will perhaps some day constitute for the initiated a complete representation of it. So it's naturally the thing for the critic to look for. It strikes me,' my visitor added, smiling, 'even as the thing for the critic to find.'

This seemed a responsibility indeed. 'You call it a little trick?'

'That's only my little modesty. It's really an exquisite scheme.'

'And you hold that you've carried the scheme out?'

'The way I've carried it out is the thing in life I think a bit well of myself for.'

I had a pause. 'Don't you think you ought — just a trifle — to assist the critic?'

'Assist him? What else have I done with every stroke of my pen? I've shouted my intention in his great blank face!' At this, laughing out again, Vereker laid his hand on my shoulder to show the allusion wasn't to my personal appearance.

'But you talk about the initiated. There must therefore, you see, *be* initiation.'

'What else in heaven's name is criticism supposed to be?' I'm afraid I coloured at this too; but I took refuge in repeating that his account of his silver lining was poor in something or other that a plain man knows things by. 'That's only because you've never had a glimpse of it,' he returned. 'If you had had one the element in question would soon have become practically all you'd see. To me it's exactly as palpable as the marble of this chimney. Besides, the critic just *isn't* a plain man: if he were, pray, what would he be doing in his neighbour's garden? You're anything but a plain man yourself, and the very *raison d'être* of you all is that you're little demons of subtlety. If my great affair's a secret, that's only because it's a secret in spite of itself — the amazing event has made it one. I not only never took the smallest precaution to keep it so, but never dreamed of any such accident. If I had I shouldn't in advance have had the heart to go on. As it was, I only became aware little by little, and meanwhile I had done my work.'

'And now you quite like it?' I risked.

'My work?'

'Your secret. It's the same thing.'

'Your guessing that,' Vereker replied, 'is a proof that you're as clever as I say!' I was encouraged by this to remark that he would clearly be pained to part with it, and he confessed that it was indeed with him now the great amusement of life. 'I live almost to see if it will ever be detected.' He looked at me for a jesting challenge; something far within his eyes seemed to peep out. 'But I needn't worry – it won't!'

'You fire me as I've never been fired,' I declared; 'you make me determined to do or die.' Then I asked: 'Is it a kind of esoteric message?'

His countenance fell at this – he put out his hand as if to bid me good-night. 'Ah my dear fellow, it can't be described in cheap journalese!'

I knew of course he'd be awfully fastidious, but our talk had made me feel how much his nerves were exposed. I was unsatisfied – I kept hold of his hand. 'I won't make use of the expression then,' I said, 'in the article in which I shall eventually announce my discovery, though I dare say I shall have hard work to do without it. But meanwhile, just to hasten that difficult birth, can't you give a fellow a clue?' I felt much more at my ease.

'My whole lucid effort gives him the clue – every page and line and letter. The thing's as concrete there as a bird in a cage, a bait on a hook, a piece of cheese in a mouse-trap. It's stuck into every volume as your foot is stuck into your shoe. It governs every line, it chooses every word, it dots every i, it places every comma.'

I scratched my head. 'Is it something in the style or something in the thought? An element of form or an element of feeling?'

He indulgently shook my hand again, and I felt my questions to be crude and my distinctions pitiful. 'Good-night, my dear boy – don't bother about it. After all, you do like a fellow.'

'And a little intelligence might spoil it?' I still detained him.

He hesitated. 'Well, you've got a heart in your body. Is that an element of form or an element of feeling? What I contend that nobody has ever mentioned in my work is the organ of life.'

'I see – it's some idea *about* life, some sort of philosophy. Unless it be,' I added with the eagerness of a thought perhaps still happier, 'some kind of game you're up to with your style, something you're after in the language. Perhaps it's a preference for the letter P!' I ventured profanely to break out. 'Papa, potatoes, prunes – that sort of thing?' He was suitably indulgent: he only said I hadn't got the right letter. But his amusement was over; I could see he was bored. There was nevertheless something else I had absolutely to learn. 'Should you be able, pen in hand, to state it clearly yourself – to name it, phrase it, formulate it?'

'Oh,' he almost passionately sighed, 'if I were only, pen in hand, one of *you* chaps!'

'That would be a great chance for you of course. But why should you despise us chaps for not doing what you can't do yourself?'

'Can't do?' He opened his eyes. 'Haven't I done it in twenty volumes? I do it in my way,' he continued. 'Go *you* and don't do it in yours.'

'Ours is so devilish difficult,' I weakly observed.

'So's mine! We each choose our own. There's no compulsion. You won't come down and smoke?'

'No. I want to think this thing out.'

'You'll tell me then in the morning that you've laid me bare?'

'I'll see what I can do; I'll sleep on it. But just one word more,' I added. We had left the room − I walked again with him a few steps along the passage. 'This extraordinary "general intention," as you call it − for that's the most vivid description I can induce you to make of it − is then, generally, a sort of buried treasure?'

His face lighted. 'Yes, call it that, though it's perhaps not for me to do so.'

'Nonsense!' I laughed. 'You know you're hugely proud of it.'

'Well, I didn't propose to tell you so; but it *is* the joy of my soul!'

'You mean it's a beauty so rare, so great?'

He waited a little again. 'The loveliest thing in the world!' We had stopped, and on these words he left me; but at the end of the corridor, while I looked after him rather yearningly, he turned and caught sight of my puzzled face. It made him earnestly, indeed I thought quite anxiously, shake his head and wave his finger. 'Give it up − give it up!'

This wasn't a challenge − it was fatherly advice. If I had had one of his books at hand I'd have repeated my recent act of faith − I'd have spent half the night with him. At three o'clock in the morning, not sleeping, remembering moreover how indispensable he was to Lady Jane, I stole down to the library with a candle. There wasn't, so far as I could discover, a line of his writing in the house.

IV

Returning to town I feverishly collected them all; I picked out each in its order and held it up to the light. This gave me a maddening month, in the course of which several things took place. One of these, the last, I may as well immediately mention, was that I acted on Vereker's advice: I renounced my ridiculous attempt.

I could really make nothing of the business; it proved a dead loss. After all I had always, as he had himself noted, liked him; and what now occurred was simply that my new intelligence and vain preoccupation damaged my liking. I not only failed to run a general intention to earth, I found myself missing the subordinate intentions I had formerly enjoyed. His books didn't even remain the charming things they had been for me; the exasperation of my search put me out of conceit of them. Instead of being a pleasure the more they became a resource the less; for from the moment I was unable to follow up the author's hint I of course felt it a point of honour not to make use professionally of my knowledge of them. I *had* no knowledge – nobody had any. It was humiliating, but I could bear it – they only annoyed me now. At last they even bored me, and I accounted for my confusion – perversely, I allow – by the idea that Vereker had made a fool of me. The buried treasure was a bad joke, the general intention a monstrous *pose*.

The great point of it all is, however, that I told George Corvick what had befallen me and that my information had an immense effect on him. He had at last come back, but so, unfortunately, had Mrs Erme, and there was as yet, I could see, no question of his nuptials. He was immensely stirred up by the anecdote I had brought from Bridges; it fell in so completely with the sense he had had from the first that there was more in Vereker than met the eye. When I remarked that the eye seemed what the printed page had been expressly invented to meet he immediately accused me of being spiteful because I had been foiled. Our commerce had always that pleasant latitude. The thing Vereker had mentioned to me was exactly the thing he, Corvick, had wanted me to speak of in my review. On my suggesting at last that with the assistance I had now given him he would doubtless be prepared to speak of it himself he admitted freely that before doing this there was more he must understand. What he would have said, had he reviewed the new book, was that there was evidently in the writer's inmost art something to *be* understood. I hadn't so much as hinted at that: no wonder the writer hadn't been flattered! I asked Corvick what he really considered he meant by his own supersubtlety, and, unmistakeably kindled, he replied: 'It isn't for the vulgar – it isn't for the vulgar!' He had hold of the tail of something: he would pull hard, pull it right out. He pumped me dry on Vereker's strange confidence and, pronouncing me the luckiest of mortals, mentioned half a dozen questions he wished to goodness I had had the gumption to put. Yet on the other hand he didn't want to be told too much – it would spoil the fun of seeing what would come. The failure of *my* fun was at the moment of our meeting not complete, but I saw it ahead, and Corvick saw that I saw it. I, on my side, saw likewise that one of the first things he would do would be to rush off with my story to Gwendolen.

On the very day after my talk with him I was surprised by the receipt of a note from Hugh Vereker, to whom our encounter at Bridges had been recalled, as he mentioned, by his falling, in a magazine, on some article to which my signature was attached. 'I read it with great pleasure,' he wrote, 'and remembered under its influence our lively conversation by your bedroom fire. The consequence of this has been that I begin to measure the temerity of my having saddled you with a knowledge that you may find something of a burden. Now that the fit's over I can't imagine how I came to be moved so much beyond my wont. I had never before mentioned, no matter in what state of expansion, the fact of my little secret, and I shall never speak of that mystery again. I was accidentally so much more explicit with you than it had ever entered into my game to be, that I find this game – I mean the pleasure of playing it – suffers considerably. In short, if you can understand it, I've rather spoiled my sport. I really don't want to give anybody what I believe you clever young men call the tip. That's of course a selfish solicitude, and I name it to you for what it may be worth to you. If you're disposed to humour me don't repeat my revelation. Think me demented – it's your right; but don't tell anybody why.'

The sequel to this communication was that as early on the morrow as I dared I drove straight to Mr Vereker's door. He occupied in those years one of the honest old houses in Kensington Square.[2] He received me immediately, and as soon as I came in I saw I hadn't lost my power to minister to his mirth. He laughed out at sight of my face, which doubtless expressed my perturbation. I had been indiscreet – my compunction was great. 'I *have* told somebody,' I panted, 'and I'm sure that person will by this time have told somebody else! It's a woman, into the bargain.'

'The person you've told?'

'No, the other person. I'm quite sure he must have told her.'

'For all the good it will do her – or do *me*! A woman will never find out.'

'No, but she'll talk all over the place: she'll do just what you don't want.'

Vereker thought a moment, but wasn't so disconcerted as I had feared: he felt that if the harm was done it only served him right. 'It doesn't matter – don't worry.'

'I'll do my best, I promise you, that your talk with me shall go no further.'

'Very good; do what you can.'

'In the meantime,' I pursued, 'George Corvick's possession of the tip may, on his part, really lead to something.'

'That will be a brave day.'

I told him about Corvick's cleverness, his admiration, the intensity of his interest in my anecdote; and without making too much of the divergence of our respective estimates mentioned that my friend was already of opinion that he saw much further into a certain affair than most people. He was quite as fired as I had been at Bridges. He was moreover in love with the young lady: perhaps the two together would puzzle something out.

Vereker seemed struck with this. 'Do you mean they're to be married?'

'I dare say that's what it will come to.'

'That may help them,' he conceded, 'but we must give them time!'

I spoke of my own renewed assault and confessed my difficulties; whereupon he repeated his former advice: 'Give it up, give it up!' He evidently didn't think me intellectually equipped for the adventure. I stayed half an hour, and he was most good-natured, but I couldn't help pronouncing him a man of unstable moods. He had been free with me in a mood, he had repented in a mood, and now in a mood he had turned indifferent. This general levity helped me to believe that, so far as the subject of the tip went, there wasn't much in it. I contrived however to make him answer a few more questions about it, though he did so with visible impatience. For himself, beyond doubt, the thing we were all so blank about was vividly there. It was something, I guessed, in the primal plan; something like a complex figure in a Persian carpet. He highly approved of this image when I used it, and he used another himself.

'It's the very string,' he said, 'that my pearls are strung on!' The reason of his note to me had been that he really didn't want to give us a grain of succour – our density was a thing too perfect in its way to touch. He had formed the habit of depending on it, and if the spell was to break it must break by some force of its own. He comes back to me from that last occasion – for I was never to speak to him again – as a man with some safe preserve for sport. I wondered as I walked away where he had got *his* tip.

V

When I spoke to George Corvick of the caution I had received he made me feel that any doubt of his delicacy would be almost an insult. He had instantly told Gwendolen, but Gwendolen's ardent response was in itself a pledge of discretion. The question would now absorb them and would offer them a pastime too precious to be shared with the crowd. They appeared to have caught instinctively at Vereker's high idea of enjoyment. Their intellectual pride, however, was not such as to make them indifferent to any further light I might throw on the affair they had in hand. They were indeed of the 'artistic temperament,' and I was freshly struck with my colleague's power to excite himself over a question of art. He'd call it letters, he'd call it life, but it was all one thing. In what he said I now seemed to understand that he spoke equally for Gwendolen, to whom, as soon as Mrs Erme was sufficiently better to allow her a little leisure, he made a point of introducing me. I remember our going together one Sunday in August to a huddled house in Chelsea,[3] and my renewed envy of Corvick's possession of a friend who had some light to mingle with his own. He could say things to her that I could never say to him. She had indeed no sense of humour and, with her pretty way of holding her head on one side, was one of those persons whom you want, as the phrase is, to shake, but who have learnt Hungarian by themselves. She conversed perhaps in Hungarian with Corvick; she had remarkably little English for his friend. Corvick afterwards told me that I had chilled her by my apparent indisposition to oblige them with the detail of what Vereker had said to me. I allowed that I felt I had given thought enough to that indication: hadn't I even made up my mind that it was vain and would lead nowhere? The importance they attached to it was irritating and quite envenomed my doubts.

That statement looks unamiable, and what probably happened was that I felt humiliated at seeing other persons deeply beguiled by an experiment that had brought me only chagrin. I was out in the cold while, by the evening fire, under the lamp, they followed the chase for which I myself had sounded the horn. They did as I had done, only more deliberately and sociably – they went over their author from the beginning. There was no hurry, Corvick said – the future was before them and the fascination could only grow; they would take him page by page, as they would take one of the classics, inhale him in slow draughts and let him sink all the way in. They would scarce have got so wound up, I think, if they hadn't been in love: poor Vereker's inner meaning gave them endless occasion to put and to keep their young heads together. None the less it represented the kind of problem for which Corvick had a special aptitude, drew out the particular pointed patience of which, had he lived, he would have given more striking and, it is to be hoped, more fruitful examples. He at least was, in Vereker's words, a little demon of subtlety. We had begun by disputing, but I soon saw that without my stirring a finger his infatuation would have its bad hours. He would bound off on false scents as I had done – he would clap his hands over new lights and see them blown out by the wind of the turned page. He was like nothing, I told him, but the maniacs who embrace some bedlamitical theory of the cryptic character of Shakespeare.[4] To this he replied that if we had had Shakespeare's own word for his being cryptic he would at once have accepted it. The case there was altogether different – we had nothing but the word of Mr Snooks.[5] I returned that I was stupefied to see him attach such importance even to the word of Mr Vereker. He wanted thereupon to know if I treated Mr Vereker's word as a lie. I wasn't perhaps prepared, in my unhappy rebound, to go so far as that, but I insisted that till the contrary was proved I should view it as too fond an imagination. I didn't, I confess, say – I didn't at that time quite know – all I felt. Deep down, as Miss Erme would have said, I was uneasy, I was expectant. At the core of my disconcerted state – for my wonted curiosity lived in its ashes – was the sharpness of a sense that Corvick would at last probably come out somewhere. He made, in defence of his credulity, a great point of the fact that from of old, in his study of this genius, he had caught whiffs and hints of he didn't know what, faint wandering notes of a hidden music. That was just the rarity, that was the charm: it fitted so perfectly into what I reported.

If I returned on several occasions to the little house in Chelsea I dare say it was as much for news of Vereker as for news of Miss Erme's ailing parent. The hours spent there by Corvick were present to my fancy as those of a chessplayer bent with a silent scowl, all the lamplit winter, over his board and his moves. As my imagination filled it out the picture held me fast. On the other side of the table was a ghostlier form, the faint figure of an antagonist good-humouredly but a little wearily secure – an antagonist who leaned back in his chair with his hands in his pockets and a smile on his fine clear face. Close to Corvick, behind him, was a girl who had begun to strike me as pale and wasted and even, on more familiar view, as rather handsome, and who rested on his shoulder and hung on his moves. He would take up a chessman and hold it poised a while over one of the little squares, and then would put it back in its place with a long sigh of disappointment. The young lady, at this, would slightly but uneasily shift her position and look across, very hard, very long, very strangely, at their dim participant. I had asked them at an early stage of the business if it mightn't contribute to their success to have some closer communication with him. The special circumstances would surely be held to have given me a right to introduce them. Corvick immediately replied that he had no wish to approach the altar before he had prepared the sacrifice. He quite agreed with our friend both as to the delight and as to the honour of the chase – he would bring down the animal with his own rifle. When I asked him if Miss Erme were as keen a shot he said after thinking: 'No, I'm ashamed to say she wants to set a trap. She'd give anything to see him; she says she requires another tip. She's really quite morbid about it. But she must play fair – she *shan't* see him!' he emphatically added. I wondered if they hadn't even quarrelled a little on the subject – a suspicion not corrected by the way he more than once exclaimed to me: 'She's quite incredibly literary, you know – quite fantastically!' I remember his saying of her that she felt in italics and thought in capitals. 'Oh when I've run him to earth,' he also said, 'then, you know, I shall knock at his door. Rather – I beg you to believe. I'll have it from his own lips: "Right you are, my boy; you've done it this time!" He shall crown me victor – with the critical laurel.'[6]

Meanwhile he really avoided the chances London life might have given him of meeting the distinguished novelist; a danger, however, that disappeared with Vereker's leaving England for an indefinite absence, as the newspapers announced – going to the south for motives connected with the health of his wife, which had long kept her in retirement. A year – more than a year – had elapsed since the incident at Bridges, but I had had no further sight of him. I think I was at bottom rather ashamed – I hated to remind him that, though I had irremediably missed his point, a reputation for acuteness was rapidly overtaking me. This scruple led me a dance; kept me out of Lady Jane's house, made me even decline, when in spite of my bad manners she was a second time so good as to make me a sign, an invitation to her beautiful seat. I once became aware of her under Vereker's escort at a concert, and was sure I was seen by them, but I slipped out without being caught. I felt, as on that occasion I splashed along in the rain, that I couldn't have done anything else; and yet I remember saying to myself that it was hard, was even cruel. Not only had I lost the books, but I had lost the man himself: they and their author had been alike spoiled for me. I knew too which was the loss I most regretted. I had taken to the man still more than I had ever taken to the books.

VI

Six months after our friend had left England George Corvick, who made his living by his pen, contracted for a piece of work which imposed on him an absence of some length and a journey of some difficulty, and his undertaking of which was much of a surprise to me. His brother-in-law had become editor of a great provincial paper, and the great provincial paper, in a fine flight of fancy, had conceived the idea of sending a 'special commissioner' to India. Special commissioners had begun, in the 'metropolitan press,' to be the fashion, and the journal in question must have felt it had passed too long for a mere country cousin. Corvick had no hand, I knew, for the big brush of the correspondent, but that was his brother-in-law's affair, and the fact that a particular task was not in his line was apt to be with himself exactly a reason for accepting it. He was prepared to out-Herod[7] the metropolitan press; he took solemn precautions against priggishness, he exquisitely outraged taste. Nobody ever knew it – that offended principle was all his own. In addition to his expenses he was to be conveniently paid, and I found myself able to help him, for the usual fat book, to a plausible arrangement with the usual fat publisher. I naturally inferred that his obvious desire to make a little money was not unconnected with the prospect of a union with Gwendolen Erme. I was aware that her mother's opposition was largely addressed to his want of means and of lucrative abilities, but it so happened that, on my saying the last time I saw him something that bore on the question of his separation from our young lady, he brought out with an emphasis that startled me: 'Ah I'm not a bit engaged to her, you know!'

'Not overtly,' I answered, 'because her mother doesn't like you. But I've always taken for granted a private understanding.'

'Well, there *was* one. But there isn't now.' That was all he said save something about Mrs Erme's having got on her feet again in the most extraordinary way – a remark pointing, as I supposed, the moral that private understandings were of little use when the doctor didn't share them. What I took the liberty of more closely inferring was that the girl might in some way have estranged him. Well, if he had taken the turn of jealousy for instance it could scarcely be jealousy of me. In that case – over and above the absurdity of it – he wouldn't have gone away just to leave us together. For some time before his going we had indulged in no allusion to the buried treasure, and from his silence, which my reserve simply emulated, I had drawn a sharp conclusion. His courage had dropped, his ardour had gone the way of mine – this appearance at least he left me to scan. More than that he couldn't do; he couldn't face the triumph with which I might have greeted an explicit admission. He needn't have been afraid, poor dear, for I had by this time lost all need to triumph. In fact I considered I showed magnanimity in not reproaching him with his collapse, for the sense of his having thrown up the game made me feel more than ever how much I at last depended on him. If Corvick had broken down I should never know; no one would be of any use if *he* wasn't. It wasn't a bit true I had ceased to care for knowledge; little by little my curiosity not only had begun to ache again, but had become the familiar torment of my days and my nights. There are doubtless people to whom torments of such an order appear hardly more natural than the contortions of disease; but I don't after all know why I should in this connexion so much as mention them. For the few persons, at any rate, abnormal or not, with whom my anecdote is concerned, literature was a game of skill, and skill meant courage, and courage meant honour, and honour meant passion, meant life. The stake on the table was of a special substance and our roulette the revolving mind, but we sat round the green board as intently as the grim gamblers at Monte Carlo.[8] Gwendolen Erme, for that matter, with her white face and her fixed eyes, was of the very type of the lean ladies one had met in the temples of chance. I recognised in Corvick's absence that she made this analogy vivid. It was extravagant, I admit, the way she lived for the art of the pen. Her passion visibly preyed on her, and in her presence I felt almost tepid. I got hold of 'Deep Down' again: it was a desert in which she had lost herself, but in which too she had dug a wonderful hole in the sand – a cavity out of which Corvick had still more remarkably pulled her.

Early in March I had a telegram from her, in consequence of which I repaired immediately to Chelsea, where the first thing she said to me was: 'He has got it, he has got it!'

She was moved, as I could see, to such depths that she must mean the great thing. 'Vereker's idea?'

'His general intention. George has cabled from Bombay.'

She had the missive open there; it was emphatic though concise. 'Eureka. Immense.' That was all — he had saved the cost of the signature. I shared her emotion, but I was disappointed. 'He doesn't say what it is.'

'How could he — in a telegram? He'll write it.'

'But how does he know?'

'Know it's the real thing? Oh I'm sure that when you see it you do know. *Vera incessu patuit dea!*'[9]

'It's you, Miss Erme, who are a "dear" for bringing me such news!' — I went all lengths in my high spirits. 'But fancy finding our goddess in the temple of Vishnu![10] How strange of George to have been able to go into the thing again in the midst of such different and such powerful solicitations!'

'He hasn't gone into it, I know; it's the thing itself, let severely alone for six months, that has simply sprung out at him like a tigress out of the jungle. He didn't take a book with him — on purpose; indeed he wouldn't have needed to — he knows every page, as I do, by heart. They all worked in him together, and some day somewhere, when he wasn't thinking, they fell, in all their superb intricacy, into the one right combination. The figure in the carpet came out. That's the way he knew it would come and the real reason — you didn't in the least understand, but I suppose I may tell you now — why he went and why I consented to his going. We knew the change would do it — that the difference of thought, of scene, would give the needed touch, the magic shake. We had perfectly, we had admirably calculated. The elements were all in his mind, and in the *secousse*[11] of a new and intense experience they just struck light.' She positively struck light herself — she was literally, facially luminous. I stammered something about unconscious cerebration, and she continued: 'He'll come right home — this will bring him.'

'To see Vereker, you mean?'

'To see Vereker — and to see *me*. Think what he'll have to tell me!'

I hesitated. 'About India?'

'About fiddlesticks! About Vereker — about the figure in the carpet.'

'But, as you say, we shall surely have that in a letter.'

She thought like one inspired, and I remembered how Corvick had told me long before that her face was interesting. 'Perhaps it can't be got into a letter if it's "immense."'

'Perhaps not if it's immense bosh. If he has hold of something that can't be got into a letter he hasn't hold of *the* thing. Vereker's own statement to me was exactly that the "figure" *would* fit into a letter.'

'Well, I cabled to George an hour ago – two words,' said Gwendolen.

'Is it indiscreet of me to ask what they were?'

She hung fire, but at last brought them out. ' "Angel, write." '

'Good!' I cried. 'I'll make it sure – I'll send him the same.'

VII

My words however were not absolutely the same – I put something instead of 'angel'; and in the sequel my epithet seemed the more apt, for when eventually we heard from our traveller it was merely, it was thoroughly to be tantalised. He was magnificent in his triumph, he described his discovery as stupendous; but his ecstasy only obscured it – there were to be no particulars till he should have submitted his conception to the supreme authority. He had thrown up his commission, he had thrown up his book, he had thrown up everything but the instant need to hurry to Rapallo, on the Genoese shore,[12] where Vereker was making a stay. I wrote him a letter which was to await him at Aden[13] – I besought him to relieve my suspense. That he had found my letter was indicated by a telegram which, reaching me after weary days and in the absence of any answer to my laconic dispatch to him at Bombay, was evidently intended as a reply to both communications. Those few words were in familiar French, the French of the day, which Corvick often made use of to show he wasn't a prig. It had for some persons the opposite effect, but his message may fairly be paraphrased. 'Have patience; I want to see, as it breaks on you, the face you'll make!' 'Tellement envie de voir ta tête!'[14] – that was what I had to sit down with. I can certainly not be said to have sat down, for I seem to remember myself at this time as rattling constantly between the little house in Chelsea and my own. Our impatience, Gwendolen's and mine, was equal, but I kept hoping her light would be greater. We all spent during this episode, for people of our means, a great deal of money in telegrams and cabs, and I counted on the receipt of news from Rapallo immediately after the junction of the discoverer with the discovered. The interval seemed an age, but late one day I heard a hansom[15] precipitated to my door with the crash engendered by a hint of liberality. I lived with my heart in my mouth and accordingly bounded to the window – a movement which gave me a view of a young lady erect on the footboard of the vehicle and eagerly looking up at my house. At sight of me she flourished a paper with a movement that brought me straight down, the movement with which, in melodramas, handkerchiefs and reprieves are flourished at the foot of the scaffold.

'Just seen Vereker — not a note wrong. Pressed me to bosom — keeps me a month.' So much I read on her paper while the cabby dropped a grin from his perch. In my excitement I paid him profusely and in hers she suffered it; then as he drove away we started to walk about and talk. We had talked, heaven knows, enough before, but this was a wondrous lift. We pictured the whole scene at Rapallo, where he would have written, mentioning my name, for permission to call; that is *I* pictured it, having more material than my companion, whom I felt hang on my lips as we stopped on purpose before shop-windows we didn't look into. About one thing we were clear: if he was staying on for fuller communication we should at least have a letter from him that would help us through the dregs of delay. We understood his staying on, and yet each of us saw, I think, that the other hated it. The letter we were clear about arrived; it was for Gwendolen, and I called on her in time to save her the trouble of bringing it to me. She didn't read it out, as was natural enough; but she repeated to me what it chiefly embodied. This consisted of the remarkable statement that he'd tell her after they were married exactly what she wanted to know.

'Only *then*, when I'm his wife — not before,' she explained. 'It's tantamount to saying — isn't it? — that I must marry him straight off!' She smiled at me while I flushed with disappointment, a vision of fresh delay that made me at first unconscious of my surprise. It seemed more than a hint that on me as well he would impose some tiresome condition. Suddenly, while she reported several more things from his letter, I remembered what he had told me before going away. He had found Mr Vereker deliriously interesting and his own possession of the secret a real intoxication. The buried treasure was all gold and gems. Now that it was there it seemed to grow and grow before him; it would have been, through all time and taking all tongues, one of the most wonderful flowers of literary art. Nothing, in especial, once you were face to face with it, could show for more consummately *done*. When once it came out it came out, was there with a splendour that made you ashamed; and there hadn't been, save in the bottomless vulgarity of the age, with every one tasteless and tainted, every sense stopped, the smallest reason why it should have been overlooked. It was great, yet so simple, was simple, yet so great, and the final knowledge of it was an experience quite apart. He intimated that the charm of such an experience, the desire to drain it, in its freshness, to the last drop, was what kept him there close to the source. Gwendolen, frankly radiant as she tossed me these fragments, showed the elation of a prospect more assured than my own. That brought me back to the question of her marriage, prompted me to ask if what she meant by what she had just surprised me with was that she was under an engagement.

'Of course I am!' she answered. 'Didn't you know it?' She seemed astonished, but I was still more so, for Corvick had told me the exact contrary. I didn't mention this, however; I only reminded her how little I had been on that score in her confidence, or even in Corvick's, and that moreover I wasn't in ignorance of her mother's interdict. At bottom I was troubled by the disparity of the two accounts; but after a little I felt Corvick's to be the one I least doubted. This simply reduced me to asking myself if the girl had on the spot improvised an engagement – vamped up an old one or dashed off a new – in order to arrive at the satisfaction she desired. She must have had resources of which I was destitute, but she made her case slightly more intelligible by returning presently: 'What the state of things has been is that we felt of course bound to do nothing in mamma's lifetime.'

'But now you think you'll just dispense with mamma's consent?'

'Ah it mayn't come to that!' I wondered what it might come to, and she went on: 'Poor dear, she may swallow the dose. In fact, you know,' she added with a laugh, 'she really *must*!' – a proposition of which, on behalf of every one concerned, I fully acknowledged the force.

VIII

Nothing more vexatious had ever happened to me than to become aware before Corvick's arrival in England that I shouldn't be there to put him through. I found myself abruptly called to Germany by the alarming illness of my younger brother, who, against my advice, had gone to Munich to study, at the feet indeed of a great master, the art of portraiture in oils. The near relative who made him an allowance had threatened to withdraw it if he should, under specious pretexts, turn for superior truth to Paris – Paris being somehow, for a Cheltenham aunt,[16] the school of evil, the abyss. I deplored this prejudice at the time, and the deep injury of it was now visible – first in the fact that it hadn't saved the poor boy, who was clever frail and foolish, from congestion of the lungs, and second in the greater break with London to which the event condemned me. I'm afraid that what was uppermost in my mind during several anxious weeks was the sense that if we had only been in Paris I might have run over to see Corvick. This was actually out of the question from every point of view: my brother, whose recovery gave us both plenty to do, was ill for three months, during which I never left him and at the end of which we had to face the absolute prohibition of a return to England. The consideration of climate imposed itself, and he was in no state to meet it alone. I took him to Meran[17] and there spent the summer with him, trying to show him by example how to get back to work and nursing a rage of another sort that I tried *not* to show him.

The whole business proved the first of a series of phenomena so strangely interlaced that, taken all together – which was how I had to take them – they form as good an illustration as I can recall of the manner in which, for the good of his soul doubtless, fate sometimes deals with a man's avidity. These incidents certainly had larger bearings than the comparatively meagre consequence we are here concerned with – though I feel that consequence also a thing to speak of with some respect. It's mainly in such a light, I confess, at any rate, that the ugly fruit of my exile is at this hour present to me. Even at first indeed the spirit in which my avidity, as I have called it, made me regard that term owed no element of ease to the fact that before coming back from Rapallo George Corvick addressed me in a way I objected to. His letter had none of the sedative action I must today profess myself sure he had wished to give it, and the march of occurrences was not so ordered as to make up for what it lacked. He had begun on the spot, for one of the quarterlies, a great last word on Vereker's writings, and this exhaustive study, the only one that would have counted, have existed, was to turn on the new light, to utter – oh so quietly! – the unimagined truth. It was in other words to trace the figure in the carpet through every convolution, to reproduce it in every tint. The result, according to my friend, would be the greatest literary portrait ever painted, and what he asked of me was just to be so good as not to trouble him with questions till he should hang up his masterpiece before me. He did me the honour to declare that, putting aside the great sitter himself, all aloft in his indifference, I was individually the connoisseur he was most working for. I was therefore to be a good boy and not try to peep under the curtain before the show was ready: I should enjoy it all the more if I sat very still.

I did my best to sit very still, but I couldn't help giving a jump on seeing in *The Times*, after I had been a week or two in Munich and before, as I knew, Corvick had reached London, the announcement of the sudden death of poor Mrs Erme. I instantly, by letter, appealed to Gwendolen for particulars, and she wrote me that her mother had yielded to long-threatened failure of the heart. She didn't say, but I took the liberty of reading into her words, that from the point of view of her marriage and also of her eagerness, which was quite a match for mine, this was a solution more prompt than could have been expected and more radical than waiting for the old lady to swallow the dose. I candidly admit indeed that at the time – for I heard from her repeatedly – I read some singular things into Gwendolen's words and some still more extraordinary ones into her silences. Pen in hand, this way, I live the time over, and it brings back the oddest sense of my having been, both for months and in spite of myself, a kind of coerced spectator. All my life had taken refuge in my eyes, which the procession of events appeared to have committed itself to keep astare. There were days when I thought of writing to Hugh Vereker and simply throwing myself on his charity. But I felt more deeply that I hadn't fallen quite so low – besides which, quite properly, he would send me about my business. Mrs Erme's death brought Corvick straight home, and within the month he was united 'very quietly' – as quietly, I seemed to make out, as he meant in his article to bring out his *trouvaille*[18] – to the young lady he had loved and quitted. I use this last term, I may parenthetically say, because I subsequently grew sure that at the time he went to India, at the time of his great news from Bombay, there had been no positive pledge between them whatever. There had been none at the moment she was affirming to me the very opposite. On the other hand he had certainly become engaged the day he returned. The happy pair went down to Torquay[19] for their honeymoon, and there, in a reckless hour, it occurred to poor Corvick to take his young bride a drive. He had no command of that business: this had been brought home to me of old in a little tour we had once made together in a dog-cart.[20] In a dog-cart he perched his companion for a rattle over Devonshire hills, on one of the likeliest of which he brought his horse, who, it was true, had bolted, down with such violence that the occupants of the cart were hurled forward and that he fell horribly on his head. He was killed on the spot; Gwendolen escaped unhurt.

I pass rapidly over the question of this unmitigated tragedy, of what the loss of my best friend meant for me, and I complete my little history of my patience and my pain by the frank statement of my having, in a postscript to my very first letter to her after the receipt of the hideous news, asked Mrs Corvick whether her husband mightn't at least have finished the great article on Vereker. Her answer was as prompt as my question: the article, which had been barely begun, was a mere heartbreaking scrap. She explained that our friend, abroad, had just settled down to it when interrupted by her mother's death, and that then, on his return, he had been kept from work by the engrossments into which that calamity was to plunge them. The opening pages were all that existed; they were striking, they were promising, but they didn't unveil the idol. That great intellectual feat was obviously to have formed his climax. She said nothing more, nothing to enlighten me as to the state of her own knowledge – the knowledge for the acquisition of which I had fancied her prodigiously acting. This was above all what I wanted to know: had *she* seen the idol unveiled? Had there been a private ceremony for a palpitating audience of one? For what else but that ceremony had the nuptials taken place? I didn't like as yet to press her, though when I thought of what had passed between us on the subject in Corvick's absence her reticence surprised me. It was therefore not till much later, from Meran, that I risked another appeal, risked it in some trepidation, for she continued to tell me nothing. 'Did you hear in those few days of your blighted bliss,' I wrote, 'what we desired so to hear?' I said 'we' as a little hint; and she showed me she could take a little hint. 'I heard everything,' she replied, 'and I mean to keep it to myself!'

IX

It was impossible not to be moved with the strongest sympathy for her, and on my return to England I showed her every kindness in my power. Her mother's death had made her means sufficient, and she had gone to live in a more convenient quarter. But her loss had been great and her visitation cruel; it never would have occurred to me moreover to suppose she could come to feel the possession of a technical tip, of a piece of literary experience, a counterpoise to her grief. Strange to say, none the less, I couldn't help believing after I had seen her a few times that I caught a glimpse of some such oddity. I hasten to add that there had been other things I couldn't help believing, or at least imagining; and as I never felt I was really clear about these, so, as to the point I here touch on, I give her memory the benefit of the doubt. Stricken and solitary, highly accomplished and now, in her deep mourning, her maturer grace and her uncomplaining sorrow, incontestably handsome, she presented herself as leading a life of singular dignity and beauty. I had at first found a way to persuade myself that I should soon get the better of the reserve formulated, the week after the catastrophe, in her reply to an appeal as to which I was not unconscious that it might strike her as mistimed. Certainly that reserve was something of a shock to me – certainly it puzzled me the more I thought of it and even though I tried to explain it (with moments of success) by an imputation of exalted sentiments, of superstitious scruples, of a refinement of loyalty. Certainly it added at the same time hugely to the price of Vereker's secret, precious as this mystery already appeared. I may as well confess abjectly that Mrs Corvick's unexpected attitude was the final tap on the nail that was to fix fast my luckless idea, convert it into the obsession of which I'm for ever conscious.

But this only helped me the more to be artful, to be adroit, to allow time to elapse before renewing my suit. There were plenty of speculations for the interval, and one of them was deeply absorbing. Corvick had kept his information from his young friend till after the removal of the last barrier to their intimacy – then only had he let the cat out of the bag. Was it Gwendolen's idea, taking a hint from him, to liberate this animal only on the basis of the renewal of such a relation? Was the figure in the carpet traceable or describable only for husbands and wives – for lovers supremely united? It came back to me in a mystifying manner that in Kensington Square, when I mentioned that Corvick would have told the girl he loved, some word had dropped from Vereker that gave colour to this possibility. There might be little in it, but there was enough to make me wonder if I should have to marry Mrs Corvick to get what I wanted. Was I prepared to offer her this price for the blessing of her knowledge? Ah that way madness lay![21] – so I at least said to myself in bewildered hours. I could see meanwhile the torch she refused to pass on flame away in her chamber of memory – pour through her eyes a light that shone in her lonely house. At the end of six months I was fully sure of what this warm presence made up to her for. We had talked again and again of the man who had brought us together – of his talent, his character, his personal charm, his certain career, his dreadful doom, and even of his clear purpose in that great study which was to have been a supreme literary portrait, a kind of critical Vandyke or Velasquez.[22] She had conveyed to me in abundance that she was tongue-tied by her perversity, by her piety, that she would never break the silence it had not been given to the 'right person,' as she said, to break. The hour however finally arrived. One evening when I had been sitting with her longer than usual I laid my hand firmly on her arm. 'Now at last what *is* it?'

She had been expecting me and was ready. She gave a long slow soundless headshake, merciful only in being inarticulate. This mercy didn't prevent its hurling at me the largest finest coldest 'Never!' I had yet, in the course of a life that had known denials, had to take full in the face. I took it and was aware that with the hard blow the tears had come into my eyes. So for a while we sat and looked at each other; after which I slowly rose. I was wondering if some day she would accept me; but this was not what I brought out. I said as I smoothed down my hat: 'I know what to think then. It's nothing!'

A remote disdainful pity for me gathered in her dim smile; then she spoke in a voice that I hear at this hour. 'It's my *life*!' As I stood at the door she added: 'You've insulted him!'

'Do you mean Vereker?'

'I mean the Dead!'

I recognised when I reached the street the justice of her charge. Yes, it was her life – I recognised that too; but her life none the less made room with the lapse of time for another interest. A year and a half after Corvick's death she published in a single volume her second novel, 'Overmastered,' which I pounced on in the hope of finding in it some tell-tale echo or some peeping face. All I found was a much better book than her younger performance, showing I thought the better company she had kept. As a tissue tolerably intricate it was a carpet with a figure of its own; but the figure was not the figure I was looking for. On sending a review of it to *The Middle* I was surprised to learn from the office that a notice was already in type. When the paper came out I had no hesitation in attributing this article, which I thought rather vulgarly overdone, to Drayton Deane, who in the old days had been something of a friend of Corvick's, yet had only within a few weeks made the acquaintance of his widow. I had had an early copy of the book, but Deane had evidently had an earlier. He lacked all the same the light hand with which Corvick had gilded the gingerbread – he laid on the tinsel in splotches.

X

Six months later appeared 'The Right of Way,' the last chance, though we didn't know it, that we were to have to redeem ourselves. Written wholly during Vereker's sojourn abroad, the book had been heralded, in a hundred paragraphs, by the usual ineptitudes. I carried it, as early a copy as any, I this time flattered myself, straightway to Mrs Corvick. This was the only use I had for it; I left the inevitable tribute of *The Middle* to some more ingenious mind and some less irritated temper. 'But I already have it,' Gwendolen said. 'Drayton Deane was so good as to bring it to me yesterday, and I've just finished it.'

'Yesterday? How did he get it so soon?'

'He gets everything so soon! He's to review it in *The Middle*.'

'He – Drayton Deane – review Vereker?' I couldn't believe my ears.

'Why not? One fine ignorance is as good as another.'

I winced but I presently said: 'You ought to review him yourself!'

'I don't "review,"' she laughed. 'I'm reviewed!'

Just then the door was thrown open. 'Ah yes, here's your reviewer!' Drayton Deane was there with his long legs and his tall forehead: he had come to see what she thought of 'The Right of Way,' and to bring news that was singularly relevant. The evening papers were just out with a telegram on the author of that work, who, in Rome, had been ill for some days with an attack of malarial fever. It had at first not been thought grave, but had taken, in consequence of complications, a turn that might give rise to anxiety. Anxiety had indeed at the latest hour begun to be felt.

I was struck in the presence of these tidings with the fundamental detachment that Mrs Corvick's overt concern quite failed to hide: it gave me the measure of her consummate independence. That independence rested on her knowledge, the knowledge which nothing now could destroy and which nothing could make different. The figure in the carpet might take on another twist or two, but the sentence had virtually been written. The writer might go down to his grave: she was the person in the world to whom – as if she had been his favoured heir – his continued existence was least of a need. This reminded me how I had observed at a particular moment – after Corvick's death – the drop of her desire to see him face to face. She had got what she wanted without that. I had been sure that if she hadn't got it she wouldn't have been restrained from the endeavour to sound him personally by those superior reflexions, more conceivable on a man's part than on a woman's, which in my case had served as a deterrent. It wasn't however, I hasten to add, that my case, in spite of this invidious comparison, wasn't ambiguous enough. At the thought that Vereker was perhaps at that moment dying there rolled over me a wave of anguish – a poignant sense of how inconsistently I still depended on him. A delicacy that it was my one compensation to suffer to rule me had left the Alps and the Apennines between us, but the sense of the waning occasion suggested that I might in my despair at last have gone to him. Of course I should really have done nothing of the sort. I remained five minutes, while my companions talked of the new book, and when Drayton Deane appealed to me for my opinion of it I made answer, getting up, that I detested Hugh Vereker and simply couldn't read him. I departed with the moral certainty that as the door closed behind me Deane would brand me for awfully superficial. His hostess wouldn't contradict *that* at least.

I continue to trace with a briefer touch our intensely odd successions. Three weeks after this came Vereker's death, and before the year was out the death of his wife. That poor lady I had never seen, but I had had a futile theory that, should she survive him long enough to be decorously accessible, I might approach her with the feeble flicker of my plea. Did she know and if she knew would she speak? It was much to be presumed that for more reasons than one she would have nothing to say; but when she passed out of all reach I felt renouncement indeed my appointed lot. I was shut up in my obsession for ever – my gaolers had gone off with the key. I find myself quite as vague as a captive in a dungeon about the time that further elapsed before Mrs Corvick became the wife of Drayton Deane. I had foreseen, through my bars, this end of the business, though there was no indecent haste and our friendship had rather fallen off. They were both so 'awfully intellectual' that it struck people as a suitable match, but I had measured better than any one the wealth of understanding the bride would contribute to the union. Never, for a marriage in literary circles – so the newspapers described the alliance – had a lady been so bravely dowered. I began with due promptness to look for the fruit of the affair – that fruit, I mean, of which the premonitory symptoms would be peculiarly visible in the husband. Taking for granted the splendour of the other party's nuptial gift, I expected to see him make a show commensurate with his increase of means. I knew what his means had been – his article on 'The Right of Way' had distinctly given one the figure. As he was now exactly in the position in which still more exactly I was not I watched from month to month, in the likely periodicals, for the heavy message poor

Corvick had been unable to deliver and the responsibility of which would have fallen on his successor. The widow and wife would have broken by the rekindled hearth the silence that only a widow and wife might break, and Deane would be as aflame with the knowledge as Corvick in his own hour, as Gwendolen in hers, had been. Well, he was aflame doubtless, but the fire was apparently not to become a public blaze. I scanned the periodicals in vain: Drayton Deane filled them with exuberant pages, but he withheld the page I most feverishly sought. He wrote on a thousand subjects, but never on the subject of Vereker. His special line was to tell truths that other people either 'funked,' as he said, or overlooked, but he never told the only truth that seemed to me in these days to signify. I met the couple in those literary circles referred to in the papers: I have sufficiently intimated that it was only in such circles we were all constructed to revolve. Gwendolen was more than ever committed to them by the publication of her third novel, and I myself definitely classed by holding the opinion that this work was inferior to its immediate predecessor. Was it worse because she had been keeping worse company? If her secret was, as she had told me, her life – a fact discernible in her increasing bloom, an air of conscious privilege that, cleverly corrected by pretty charities, gave distinction to her appearance – it had yet not a direct influence on her work. That only made one – everything only made one – yearn the more for it; only rounded it off with a mystery finer and subtler.

XI

It was therefore from her husband I could never remove my eyes: I beset him in a manner that might have made him uneasy. I went even so far as to engage him in conversation. *Didn't* he know, hadn't he come into it as a matter of course? – that question hummed in my brain. Of course he knew; otherwise he wouldn't return my stare so queerly. His wife had told him what I wanted and he was amiably amused at my impotence. He didn't laugh – he wasn't a laugher: his system was to present to my irritation, so that I should crudely expose myself, a conversational blank as vast as his big bare brow. It always happened that I turned away with a settled conviction from these unpeopled expanses, which seemed to complete each other geographically and to symbolise together Drayton Deane's want of voice, want of form. He simply hadn't the art to use what he knew; he literally was incompetent to take up the duty where Corvick had left it. I went still further – it was the only glimpse of happiness I had. I made up my mind that the duty didn't appeal to him. He wasn't interested, he didn't care. Yes, it quite comforted me to believe him too stupid to have joy of the thing I lacked.

He was as stupid after as he had been before, and that deepened for me the golden glory in which the mystery was wrapped. I had of course none the less to recollect that his wife might have imposed her conditions and exactions. I had above all to remind myself that with Vereker's death the major incentive dropped. He was still there to be honoured by what might be done – he was no longer there to give it his sanction. Who alas but he had the authority?

Two children were born to the pair, but the second cost the mother her life. After this stroke I seemed to see another ghost of a chance. I jumped at it in thought, but I waited a certain time for manners, and at last my opportunity arrived in a remunerative way. His wife had been dead a year when I met Drayton Deane in the smoking-room of a small club of which we both were members, but where for months – perhaps because I rarely entered it – I hadn't seen him. The room was empty and the occasion propitious. I deliberately offered him, to have done with the matter for ever, that advantage for which I felt he had long been looking.

'As an older acquaintance of your late wife's than even you were,' I began, 'you must let me say to you something I have on my mind. I shall be glad to make any terms with you that you see fit to name for the information she must have had from George Corvick – the information, you know, that had come to *him*, poor chap, in one of the happiest hours of his life, straight from Hugh Vereker.'

He looked at me like a dim phrenological bust.[23] 'The information –?'

'Vereker's secret, my dear man – the general intention of his books: the string the pearls were strung on, the buried treasure, the figure in the carpet.'

He began to flush – the numbers on his bumps[24] to come out. 'Vereker's books had a general intention?'

I stared in my turn. 'You don't mean to say you don't know it?' I thought for a moment he was playing with me. 'Mrs Deane knew it; she had it, as I say, straight from Corvick, who had, after infinite search and to Vereker's own delight, found the very mouth of the cave. Where *is* the mouth? He told after their marriage – and told alone – the person who, when the circumstances were reproduced, must have told *you*. Have I been wrong in taking for granted that she admitted you, as one of the highest privileges of the relation in which you stood to her, to the knowledge of which she was after Corvick's death the sole depositary? All *I* know is that that knowledge is infinitely precious, and what I want you to understand is that if you'll in your turn admit me to it you'll do me a kindness for which I shall be lastingly grateful.'

He had turned at last very red; I dare say he had begun by thinking I had lost my wits. Little by little he followed me; on my own side I stared with a livelier surprise. Then he spoke. 'I don't know what you're talking about.'

He wasn't acting – it was the absurd truth. 'She *didn't* tell you –?'

'Nothing about Hugh Vereker.'

I was stupefied; the room went round. It had been too good even for that! 'Upon your honour?'

'Upon my honour. What the devil's the matter with you?' he growled.

'I'm astounded – I'm disappointed. I wanted to get it out of you.'

'It isn't *in* me!' he awkwardly laughed. 'And even if it were –'

'If it were you'd let me have it – oh yes, in common humanity. But I believe you. I see – I see!' I went on, conscious, with the full turn of the wheel, of my great delusion, my false view of the poor man's attitude. What I saw, though I couldn't say it, was that his wife hadn't thought him worth enlightening. This struck me as strange for a woman who had thought him worth marrying. At last I explained it by the reflexion that she couldn't possibly have married him for his understanding. She had married him for something else.

He was to some extent enlightened now, but he was even more astonished, more disconcerted: he took a moment to compare my story with his quickened memories. The result of his meditation was his presently saying with a good deal of rather feeble form: 'This is the first I hear of what you allude to. I think you must be mistaken as to Mrs Drayton Deane's having had any unmentioned, and still less any unmentionable, knowledge of Hugh Vereker. She'd certainly have wished it – should it have borne on his literary character – to be used.'

'It *was* used. She used it herself. She told me with her own lips that she "lived" on it.'

I had no sooner spoken than I repented of my words; he grew so pale that I felt as if I had struck him. 'Ah "lived" –!' he murmured, turning short away from me.

My compunction was real; I laid my hand on his shoulder. 'I beg you to forgive me – I've made a mistake. You *don't* know what I thought you knew. You could, if I had been right, have rendered me a service; and I had my reasons for assuming that you'd be in a position to meet me.'

'Your reasons?' he echoed. 'What were your reasons?'

I looked at him well; I hesitated; I considered. 'Come and sit down with me here and I'll tell you.' I drew him to a sofa, I lighted another cigar and, beginning with the anecdote of Vereker's one descent from the clouds, I recited to him the extraordinary chain of accidents that had, in spite of the original gleam, kept me till that hour in the dark. I told him in a word just what I've written out here. He listened with deepening attention, and I became aware, to my surprise, by his ejaculations, by his questions, that he would have been after all not unworthy to be trusted by his wife. So abrupt an experience of her want of trust had now a disturbing effect on him; but I saw the immediate shock throb away little by little and then gather again into waves of wonder and curiosity – waves that promised, I could perfectly judge, to break in the end with the fury of my own highest tides. I may say that to-day as victims of unappeased desire there isn't a pin to choose between us. The poor man's state is almost my consolation; there are really moments when I feel it to be quite my revenge.

In the Cage

I

It had occurred to her early that in her position – that of a young person spending, in framed and wired confinement, the life of a guinea-pig or a magpie – she should know a great many persons without their recognising the acquaintance. That made it an emotion the more lively – though singularly rare and always, even then, with opportunity still very much smothered – to see any one come in whom she knew outside, as she called it, any one who could add anything to the meanness of her function. Her function was to sit there with two young men – the other telegraphist and the counter-clerk; to mind the 'sounder,'[1] which was always going, to dole out stamps and postal-orders, weigh letters, answer stupid questions, give difficult change and, more than anything else, count words as numberless as the sands of the sea, the words of the telegrams thrust, from morning to night, through the gap left in the high lattice, across the encumbered shelf that her forearm ached with rubbing. This transparent screen fenced out or fenced in, according to the side of the narrow counter on which the human lot was cast, the duskiest corner of a shop pervaded not a little, in winter, by the poison of perpetual gas,[2] and at all times by the presence of hams, cheese, dried fish, soap, varnish, paraffin and other solids and fluids that she came to know perfectly by their smells without consenting to know them by their names.

The barrier that divided the little post-and-telegraph-office from the grocery was a frail structure of wood and wire; but the social, the professional separation was a gulf that fortune, by a stroke quite remarkable, had spared her the necessity of contributing at all publicly to bridge. When Mr Cocker's young men stepped over from behind the other counter to change a five-pound note – and Mr Cocker's situation, with the cream of the 'Court Guide'[3] and the dearest furnished apartments, Simpkin's, Ladle's, Thrupp's, just round the corner, was so select that his place was quite pervaded by the crisp rustle of these emblems – she pushed out the sovereigns as if the applicant were no more to her than one of the momentary, the practically featureless, appearances in the great procession; and this perhaps all the more from the very fact of the connexion (only recognised outside indeed) to which she had lent herself with ridiculous inconsequence. She recognised the others the less because she had at last so unreservedly, so irredeemably, recognised Mr Mudge. However that might be, she was a little ashamed of having to admit to herself that Mr Mudge's removal to a higher sphere – to a more commanding position, that is, though to a much lower neighbourhood – would have been described still better as a luxury than as the mere simplification, the corrected awkwardness, that she contented herself with calling it. He had at any rate ceased to be all day long in her eyes, and this left something a little fresh for them to rest on of a Sunday. During the three months of his happy survival at Cocker's after her consent to their engagement she had often asked herself what it was marriage would be able to add to a familiarity that seemed already to have scraped the platter so clean. Opposite there, behind the counter of which his superior stature, his whiter apron, his more clustering curls and more present, too present, h's[4] had been for a couple of years the principal ornament, he had moved to and fro before her as on the small sanded floor of their contracted future. She was conscious now of the improvement of not having to take her present and her future at once. They were about as much as she could manage when taken separate.

She had, none the less, to give her mind steadily to what Mr Mudge had again written her about, the idea of her applying for a transfer to an office quite similar – she couldn't yet hope for a place in a bigger – under the very roof where he was foreman, so that, dangled before her every minute of the day, he should see her, as he called it, 'hourly,' and in a part, the far N. W. district,[5] where, with her mother, she would save on their two rooms alone nearly three shillings. It would be far from dazzling to exchange Mayfair for Chalk Farm, and it wore upon her much that he could never drop a subject; still, it didn't wear as things *had* worn, the worries of the early times of their great misery, her own, her mother's and her elder sister's – the last of whom had succumbed to all but absolute want when, as conscious and incredulous ladies, suddenly bereft, betrayed, overwhelmed, they had slipped faster and faster down the steep slope at the bottom of which she alone had rebounded. Her mother had never rebounded any more at the bottom than on the way; had only rumbled and grumbled down and down, making, in respect of caps, topics and 'habits,' no effort whatever – which simply meant smelling much of the time of whiskey.

II

It was always rather quiet at Cocker's while the contingent from Ladle's and Thrupp's and all the other great places were at luncheon, or, as the young men used vulgarly to say, while the animals were feeding. She had forty minutes in advance of this to go home for her own dinner; and when she came back and one of the young men took his turn there was often half an hour during which she could pull out a bit of work or a book – a book from the place where she borrowed novels, very greasy, in fine print and all about fine folks, at a ha'penny a day.[6] This sacred pause was one of the numerous ways in which the establishment kept its finger on the pulse of fashion and fell into the rhythm of the larger life. It had something to do, one day, with the particular flare of importance of an arriving customer, a lady whose meals were apparently irregular, yet whom she was destined, she afterwards found, not to forget. The girl was *blasée*; nothing could belong more, as she perfectly knew, to the intense publicity of her profession; but she had a whimsical mind and wonderful nerves; she was subject, in short, to sudden flickers of antipathy and sympathy, red gleams in the grey, fitful needs to notice and to 'care,' odd caprices of curiosity. She had a friend who had invented a new career for women – that of being in and out of people's houses to look after the flowers. Mrs Jordan had a manner of her own of sounding this allusion; 'the flowers,' on her lips, were, in fantastic places, in happy homes, as usual as the coals or the daily papers. She took charge of them, at any rate, in all the rooms, at so much a month, and people were quickly finding out what it was to make over this strange burden of the pampered to the widow of a clergyman. The widow, on her side, dilating on the initiations thus opened up to her, had been splendid to her young friend over the way she was made free of the greatest houses – the way, especially when she did the dinner-tables, set out so often for twenty, she felt that a single step more would transform her whole social position. On its being asked of her then if she circulated only in a sort of tropical solitude, with the upper servants for picturesque natives, and on her having to assent to this glance at her limitations, she had found a reply to the girl's invidious question. 'You've no imagination, my dear!' – that was because a door more than half open to the higher life couldn't be called anything but a thin partition. Mrs Jordan's imagination quite did away with the thickness.

Our young lady had not taken up the charge, had dealt with it good-humouredly, just because she knew so well what to think of it. It was at once one of her most cherished complaints and most secret supports that people didn't understand her, and it was accordingly a matter of indifference to her that Mrs Jordan shouldn't; even though Mrs Jordan, handed down from their early twilight of gentility and also the victim of reverses, was the only member of her circle in whom she recognised an equal. She was perfectly aware that her imaginative life was the life in which she spent most of her time; and she would have been ready, had it been at all worth while, to contend that, since her outward occupation didn't kill it, it must be strong indeed. Combinations of flowers and green-stuff forsooth! What *she* could handle freely, she said to herself, was combinations of men and women. The only weakness in her faculty came from the positive abundance of her contact with the human herd; this was so constant, it had so the effect of cheapening her privilege, that there were long stretches in which inspiration, divination and interest quite dropped. The great thing was the flashes, the quick revivals, absolute accidents all, and neither to be counted on nor to be resisted. Some one had only sometimes to put in a penny for a stamp and the whole thing was upon her. She was so absurdly constructed that these were literally the moments that made up – made up for the long stiffness of sitting there in the stocks,[7] made up for the cunning hostility of Mr Buckton and the importunate sympathy of the counter-clerk, made up for the daily deadly flourishy letter from Mr Mudge, made up even for the most haunting of her worries, the rage at moments of not knowing how her mother did 'get it.'

She had surrendered herself moreover of late to a certain expansion of her consciousness; something that seemed perhaps vulgarly accounted for by the fact that, as the blast of the season[8] roared louder and the waves of fashion tossed their spray further over the counter, there were more impressions to be gathered and really – for it came to that – more life to be led. Definite at any rate it was that by the time May was well started the kind of company she kept at Cocker's had begun to strike her as a reason – a reason she might almost put forward for a policy of procrastination. It sounded silly, of course, as yet, to plead such a motive, especially as the fascination of the place was after all a sort of torment. But she liked her torment; it was a torment she should miss at Chalk Farm. She was ingenious and uncandid, therefore, about leaving the breadth of London a little longer between herself and that austerity. If she hadn't quite the courage in short to say to Mr Mudge that her actual chance for a play of mind was worth any week the three shillings he desired to help her to save, she yet saw something happen in the course of the month that in her heart of hearts at least answered the subtle question. This was connected precisely with the appearance of the memorable lady.

III

She pushed in three bescribbled forms which the girl's hand was quick to appropriate, Mr Buckton having so frequent a perverse instinct for catching first any eye that promised the sort of entertainment with which she had her peculiar affinity. The amusements of captives are full of a desperate contrivance, and one of our young friend's ha'pennyworths had been the charming tale of 'Picciola.'[9] It was of course the law of the place that they were never to take no notice, as Mr Buckton said, whom they served; but this also never prevented, certainly on the same gentleman's own part, what he was fond of describing as the underhand game. Both her companions, for that matter, made no secret of the number of favourites they had among the ladies; sweet familiarities in spite of which she had repeatedly caught each of them in stupidities and mistakes, confusions of identity and lapses of observation that never failed to remind her how the cleverness of men ends where the cleverness of women begins. 'Marguerite, Regent Street. Try on at six. All Spanish lace. Pearls. The full length.' That was the first; it had no signature. 'Lady Agnes Orme, Hyde Park Place. Impossible to-night, dining Haddon. Opera to-morrow, promised Fritz, but could do play Wednesday. Will try Haddon for Savoy, and anything in the world you like, if you can get Gussy. Sunday Montenero. Sit Mason Monday, Tuesday. Marguerite awful. Cissy.' That was the second. The third, the girl noted when she took it, was on a foreign form: 'Everard, Hôtel Brighton, Paris. Only understand and believe. 22d to 26th, and certainly 8th and 9th. Perhaps others. Come. Mary.'

Mary was very handsome, the handsomest woman, she felt in a moment, she had ever seen – or perhaps it was only Cissy. Perhaps it was both, for she had seen stranger things than that – ladies wiring to different persons under different names. She had seen all sorts of things and pieced together all sorts of mysteries. There had once been one – not long before – who, without winking, sent off five over five different signatures. Perhaps these represented five different friends who had asked her – all women, just as perhaps now Mary and Cissy, or one or other of them, were wiring by deputy. Sometimes she put in too much – too much of her own sense; sometimes she put in too little; and in either case this often came round to her afterwards, for she had an extraordinary way of keeping clues. When she noticed she noticed; that was what it came to. There were days and days, there were weeks sometimes, of vacancy. This arose often from Mr Buckton's devilish and successful subterfuges for keeping her at the sounder whenever it looked as if anything might amuse; the sounder, which it was equally his business to mind, being the innermost cell of captivity, a cage within the cage, fenced off from the rest by a frame of ground glass. The counter-clerk would have played into her hands; but the counter-clerk was really reduced to idiocy by the effect of his passion for her. She flattered herself moreover, nobly, that with the unpleasant conspicuity of this passion she would never have consented to be obliged to him. The most she would ever do would be always to shove off on him whenever she could the registration of letters, a job she happened particularly to loathe. After the long stupors, at all events, there almost always suddenly would come a sharp taste of something; it was in her mouth before she knew it; it was in her mouth now.

To Cissy, to Mary, whichever it was, she found her curiosity going out with a rush, a mute effusion that floated back to her, like a returning tide, the living colour and splendour of the beautiful head, the light of eyes that seemed to reflect such utterly other things than the mean things actually before them; and, above all, the high curt consideration of a manner that even at bad moments was a magnificent habit and of the very essence of the innumerable things — her beauty, her birth, her father and mother, her cousins and all her ancestors — that its possessor couldn't have got rid of even had she wished. How did our obscure little public servant know that for the lady of the telegrams this was a bad moment? How did she guess all sorts of impossible things, such as, almost on the very spot, the presence of drama at a critical stage and the nature of the tie with the gentleman at the Hôtel Brighton? More than ever before it floated to her through the bars of the cage that this at last was the high reality, the bristling truth that she had hitherto only patched up and eked out — one of the creatures, in fine, in whom all the conditions for happiness actually met, and who, in the air they made, bloomed with an unwitting insolence. What came home to the girl was the way the insolence was tempered by something that was equally a part of the distinguished life, the custom of a flower-like bend to the less fortunate — a dropped fragrance, a mere quick breath, but which in fact pervaded and lingered. The apparition was very young, but certainly married, and our fatigued friend had a sufficient store of mythological comparison to recognise the port of Juno.[10] Marguerite might be 'awful,' but she knew how to dress a goddess.

Pearls and Spanish lace — she herself, with assurance, could see them, and the 'full length' too, and also red velvet bows, which, disposed on the lace in a particular manner (she could have placed them with the turn of a hand) were of course to adorn the front of a black brocade that would be like a dress in a picture. However, neither Marguerite nor Lady Agnes nor Haddon nor Fritz nor Gussy was what the wearer of this garment had really come in for. She had come in for Everard — and that was doubtless not *his* true name either. If our young lady had never taken such jumps before it was simply that she had never before been so affected. She went all the way. Mary and Cissy had been round together, in their single superb person, to see him — he must live round the corner; they had found that, in consequence of something they had come, precisely, to make up for or to have another scene about, he had gone off – gone off just on purpose to make them feel it: on which they had come together to Cocker's as to the nearest place; where they had put in the three forms partly in order not to put in the one alone. The two others in a manner covered it, muffled it, passed it off. Oh yes, she went all the way, and this was a specimen of how she often went. She would know the hand again any time. It was as handsome and as everything else as the woman herself. The woman herself had, on learning his flight, pushed past Everard's servant and into his room; she had written her missive at his table and with his pen. All this, every inch of it, came in the waft that she blew through and left behind her, the influence that, as I have said, lingered. And among the things the girl was sure of, happily, was that she should see her again.

IV

She saw her in fact, and only ten days later; but this time not alone, and that was exactly a part of the luck of it. Not unaware – as how could her observation have left her so? – of the possibilities through which it could range, our young lady had ever since had in her mind a dozen conflicting theories about Everard's type; as to which, the instant they came into the place, she felt the point settled with a thump that seemed somehow addressed straight to her heart. That organ literally beat faster at the approach of the gentleman who was this time with Cissy, and who, as seen from within the cage, became on the spot the happiest of the happy circumstances with which her mind had invested the friend of Fritz and Gussy. He was a very happy circumstance indeed as, with his cigarette in his lips and his broken familiar talk caught by his companion, he put down the half-dozen telegrams it would take them together several minutes to dispatch. And here it occurred, oddly enough, that if, shortly before, the girl's interest in his companion had sharpened her sense for the messages then transmitted, her immediate vision of himself had the effect, while she counted his seventy words, of preventing intelligibility. *His* words were mere numbers, they told her nothing whatever; and after he had gone she was in possession of no name, of no address, of no meaning, of nothing but a vague sweet sound and an immense impression. He had been there but five minutes, he had smoked in her face, and, busy with his telegrams, with the tapping pencil and the conscious danger, the odious betrayal that would come from a mistake, she had had no wandering glances nor roundabout arts to spare. Yet she had taken him in; she knew everything; she had made up her mind.

He had come back from Paris; everything was rearranged; the pair were again shoulder to shoulder in their high encounter with life, their large and complicated game. The fine soundless pulse of this game was in the air for our young woman while they remained in the shop. While they remained? They remained all day; their presence continued and abode with her, was in everything she did till nightfall, in the thousands of other words she counted, she transmitted, in all the stamps she detached and the letters she weighed and the change she gave, equally unconscious and unerring in each of these particulars, and not, as the run on the little office thickened with the afternoon hours, looking up at a single ugly face in the long sequence, nor really hearing the stupid questions that she patiently and perfectly answered. All patience was possible now, all questions were stupid after his, all faces were ugly. She had been sure she should see the lady again; and even now she should perhaps, she should probably, see her often. But for him it was totally different; she should never never see him. She wanted it too much. There was a kind of wanting that helped – she had arrived, with her rich experience, at that generalization; and there was another kind that was fatal. It was this time the fatal kind; it would prevent.

Well, she saw him the very next day, and on this second occasion it was quite different; the sense of every syllable he paid for was fiercely distinct; she indeed felt her progressive pencil, dabbing as if with a quick caress the marks of his own, put life into every stroke. He was there a long time – had not brought his forms filled out but worked them off in a nook on the counter; and there were other people as well – a changing pushing cluster, with every one to mind at once and endless right change to make and information to produce. But she kept hold of him throughout; she continued, for herself, in a relation with him as close as that in which, behind the hated ground glass, Mr Buckton luckily continued with the sounder. This morning everything changed, but rather to dreariness; she had to swallow the rebuff to her theory about fatal desires, which she did without confusion and indeed with absolute levity; yet if it was now flagrant that he did live close at hand – at Park Chambers[11] – and belonged supremely to the class that wired everything, even their expensive feelings (so that, as he evidently never wrote, his correspondence cost him weekly pounds and pounds and he might be in and out five times a day) there was, all the same, involved in the prospect, and by reason of its positive excess of light, a perverse melancholy, a gratuitous misery. This was at once to give it a place in order of feelings on which I shall presently touch.

Meanwhile, for a month, he was very constant. Cissy, Mary, never re-appeared with him; he was always either alone or accompanied only by some gentleman who was lost in the blaze of his glory. There was another sense, however – and indeed there was more than one – in which she mostly found herself counting in the splendid creature with whom she had originally connected him. He addressed this correspondent neither as Mary nor as Cissy; but the girl was sure of whom it was, in Eaton Square,[12] that he was perpetually wiring to – and all so irreproachably! – as Lady Bradeen. Lady Bradeen was Cissy, Lady Bradeen was Mary, Lady Bradeen was the friend of Fritz and of Gussy, the customer of Marguerite and the close ally in short (as was ideally right, only the girl had not yet found a descriptive term that was) of the most magnificent of men. Nothing could equal the frequency and variety of his communications to her ladyship but their extraordinary, their abysmal propriety. It was just the talk – so profuse sometimes that she wondered what was left for their real meetings – of the very happiest people. Their real meetings must have been constant, for half of it was appointments and allusions, all swimming in a sea of other allusions still, tangled in a complexity of questions that gave a wondrous image of their life. If Lady Bradeen was Juno it was all certainly Olympian.[13] If the girl, missing the answers, her ladyship's own outpourings, vainly reflected that Cocker's should have been one of the bigger offices where telegrams arrived as well as departed, there were yet ways in which, on the whole, she pressed the romance closer by reason of the very quantity of imagination it demanded and consumed. The days and hours of this new friend, as she came to account him, were at all events unrolled, and however much more she might have known she would still have wished to go beyond. In fact she did go beyond; she went quite far enough.

But she could none the less, even after a month, scarce have told if the gentlemen who came in with him recurred or changed; and this in spite of the fact that they too were always posting and wiring, smoking in her face and signing or not signing. The gentlemen who came in with him were nothing when he was there. They turned up alone at other times – then only perhaps with a dim richness of reference. He himself, absent as well as present, was all. He was very tall, very fair, and had, in spite of his thick preoccupations, a good humour that was exquisite, particularly as it so often had the effect of keeping him on. He could have reached over anybody, and anybody – no matter who – would have let him; but he was so extraordinarily kind that he quite pathetically waited, never waggling things at her out of his turn nor saying 'Here!' with horrid sharpness. He waited for pottering old ladies, for gaping slaveys, for the perpetual Buttonses[14] from Thrupp's; and the thing in all this that she would have liked most unspeakably to put to the test was the possibility of her having for him a personal identity that might in a particular way appeal. There were moments when he actually struck her as on her side, as arranging to help, to support, to spare her.

But such was the singular spirit of our young friend that she could remind herself with a pang that when people had awfully good manners – people of that class – you couldn't tell. These manners were for everybody, and it might be drearily unavailing for any poor particular body to be overworked and unusual.

What he did take for granted was all sorts of facility; and his high pleasantness, his relighting of cigarettes while he waited, his unconscious bestowal of opportunities, of boons, of blessings, were all a part of his splendid security, the instinct that told him there was nothing such an existence as his could ever lose by. He was somehow all at once very bright and very grave, very young and immensely complete; and whatever he was at any moment it was always as much as all the rest the mere bloom of his beatitude. He was sometimes Everard, as he had been at the Hôtel Brighton, and he was sometimes Captain Everard. He was sometimes Philip with his surname and sometimes Philip without it. In some directions he was merely Phil, in others he was merely Captain. There were relations in which he was none of these things, but a quite different person — 'the Count.' There were several friends for whom he was William. There were several for whom, in allusion perhaps to his complexion, he was 'the Pink 'Un.'[15] Once, once only by good luck, he had, coinciding comically, quite miraculously, with another person also near to her, been 'Mudge.' Yes, whatever he was, it was a part of his happiness — whatever he was and probably whatever he wasn't. And his happiness was a part — it became so little by little — of something that, almost from the first of her being at Cocker's, had been deeply with the girl.

V

This was neither more nor less than the queer extension of her experience, the double life that, in the cage, she grew at last to lead. As the weeks went on there she lived more and more into the world of whiffs and glimpses, she found her divinations work faster and stretch further. It was a prodigious view as the pressure heightened, a panorama fed with facts and figures, flushed with a torrent of colour and accompanied with wondrous world-music. What it mainly came to at this period was a picture of how London could amuse itself; and that, with the running commentary of a witness so exclusively a witness, turned for the most part to a hardening of the heart. The nose of this observer was brushed by the bouquet, yet she could never really pluck even a daisy. What could still remain fresh in her daily grind was the immense disparity, the difference and contrast, from class to class, of every instant and every motion. There were times when all the wires in the country seemed to start from the little hole-and-corner where she plied for a livelihood, and where, in the shuffle of feet, the flutter of 'forms,' the straying of stamps and the ring of change over the counter, the people she had fallen into the habit of remembering and fitting together with others, and of having her theories and interpretations of, kept up before her their long procession and rotation. What twisted the knife in her vitals was the way the profligate rich scattered about them, in extravagant chatter over their extravagant pleasures and sins, an amount of money that would have held the stricken household of her frightened childhood, her poor pinched mother and tormented father and lost brother and starved sister, together for a lifetime. During her first weeks she had often gasped at the sums people were willing to pay for the stuff they transmitted – the 'much love's, the 'awful' regrets, the compliments and wonderments and vain vague gestures that cost the price of a new pair of boots. She had had a way then of glancing at the people's faces, but she had early learnt that if you became a telegraphist you soon ceased to be astonished. Her eye for types amounted nevertheless to genius, and there were those she liked and those she hated, her feeling for the latter of which grew to a positive possession, an instinct of observation and detection. There were the brazen women, as she called them, of the higher and the lower fashion, whose squanderings and graspings, whose struggles and secrets and love-affairs and lies, she tracked and stored up against them till she had at moments, in private, a triumphant vicious feeling of mastery and ease, a sense of carrying their silly guilty secrets in her pocket, her small retentive brain, and thereby knowing so much more about them than they suspected or would care to think. There were those she would have liked to betray, to trip up, to bring down with words altered and fatal; and all through a personal hostility provoked by the lightest signs, by their accidents of tone and manner, by the particular kind of relation she always happened instantly to feel.

There were impulses of various kinds, alternately soft and severe, to which she was constitutionally accessible and which were determined by the smallest accidents. She was rigid in general on the article of making the public itself affix its stamps, and found a special enjoyment in dealing to that end with some of the ladies who were too grand to touch them. She had thus a play of refinement and subtlety greater, she flattered herself, than any of which she could be made the subject; and though most people were too stupid to be conscious of this it brought her endless small consolations and revenges. She recognised quite as much those of her sex whom she would have liked to help, to warn, to rescue, to see more of; and that alternative as well operated exactly through the hazard of personal sympathy, her vision for silver threads and moonbeams and her gift for keeping the clues and finding her way in the tangle. The moonbeams and silver threads presented at moments all the vision of what poor *she* might have made of happiness. Blurred and blank as the whole thing often inevitably, or mercifully, became, she could still, through crevices and crannies, be stupefied, especially by what, in spite of all seasoning, touched the sorest place in her consciousness, the revelation of the golden shower flying about without a gleam of gold for herself. It remained prodigious to the end, the money her fine friends were able to spend to get still more, or even to complain to fine friends of their own that they were in want. The pleasures they proposed were equalled only by those they declined, and they made their appointments often so expensively that she was left wondering at the nature of the delights to which the mere approaches were so paved with shillings. She quivered on occasion into the perception of this and that one whom she would on the chance have just simply liked to *be*. Her conceit, her baffled vanity, was possibly monstrous; she certainly often threw herself into a defiant conviction that she would have done the whole thing much better. But her greatest comfort, mostly, was her comparative vision of the men; by whom I mean the unmistakeable gentlemen, for she had no interest in the spurious or the shabby and no mercy at all for the poor. She could have found a sixpence, outside, for an appearance of want; but her fancy, in some directions so alert, had never a throb of response for any sign of the sordid. The men she did track, moreover, she tracked mainly in one relation, the relation as to which the cage convinced her, she believed, more than anything else could have done, that it was quite the most diffused.

She found her ladies, in short, almost always in communication with her gentlemen, and her gentlemen with her ladies, and she read into the immensity of their intercourse stories and meanings without end. Incontestably she grew to think that the men cut the best figure; and in this particular, as in many others, she arrived at a philosophy of her own, all made up of her private notations and cynicisms. It was a striking part of the business, for example, that it was much more the women, on the whole, who were after the men than the men who were after the women: it was literally visible that the general attitude of the one sex was that of the object pursued and defensive, apologetic and attenuating, while the light of her own nature helped her more or less to conclude as to the attitude of the other. Perhaps she herself a little even fell into the custom of pursuit in occasionally deviating only for gentlemen from her high rigour about the stamps. She had early in the day made up her mind, in fine, that they had the best manners; and if there were none of them she noticed when Captain Everard was there, there were plenty she could place and trace and name at other times, plenty who, with their way of being 'nice' to her and of handling, as if their pockets were private tills, loose mixed masses of silver and gold, were such pleasant appearances that she could envy them without dislike. *They* never had to give change — they only had to get it. They ranged through every suggestion, every shade of fortune, which evidently included indeed lots of bad luck as well as of good, declining even toward Mr Mudge and his bland firm thrift, and ascending, in wild signals and rocket-flights, almost to within hail of her highest standard. So from month to month she went on with them all, through a thousand ups and downs and a thousand pangs and indifferences. What virtually happened was that in the shuffling herd that passed before her by far the greater part only passed – a proportion but just appreciable stayed. Most of the elements swam straight away, lost themselves in the bottomless common, and by so doing really kept the page clear. On the clearness therefore what she did retain stood sharply out; she nipped and caught it, turned it over and interwove it.

VI

She met Mrs Jordan when she could, and learned from her more and more how the great people, under her gentle shake and after going through everything with the mere shops, were waking up to the gain of putting into the hands of a person of real refinement the question that the shop-people spoke of so vulgarly as that of the floral decorations. The regular dealers in these decorations were all very well; but there was a peculiar magic in the play of taste of a lady who had only to remember, through whatever intervening dusk, all her own little tables, little bowls and little jars and little other arrangements, and the wonderful thing she had made of the garden of the vicarage. This small domain, which her young friend had never seen, bloomed in Mrs Jordan's discourse like a new Eden,[16] and she converted the past into a bank of violets by the tone in which she said 'Of course you always knew my one passion!' She obviously met now, at any rate, a big contemporary need, measured what it was rapidly becoming for people to feel they could trust her without a tremor. It brought them a peace that – during the quarter of an hour before dinner in especial – was worth more to them than mere payment could express. Mere payment, none the less, was tolerably prompt; she engaged by the month, taking over the whole thing; and there was an evening on which, in respect to our heroine, she at last returned to the charge. 'It's growing and growing, and I see that I must really divide the work. One wants an associate – of one's own kind, don't you know? You know the look they want it all to have? – of having come, not from a florist, but from one of themselves. Well, I'm sure *you* could give it – because you *are* one. Then we *should* win. Therefore just come in with me.'

'And leave the P.O.?'

'Let the P.O. simply bring you your letters. It would bring you lots, you'd see: orders, after a bit, by the score.' It was on this, in due course, that the great advantage again came up: 'One seems to live again with one's own people.' It had taken some little time (after their having parted company in the tempest of their troubles and then, in the glimmering dawn, finally sighted each other again) for each to admit that the other was, in her private circle, her only equal; but the admission came, when it did come, with an honest groan; and since equality *was* named, each found much personal profit in exaggerating the other's original grandeur. Mrs Jordan was ten years the older, but her young friend was struck with the smaller difference this now made: it had counted otherwise at the time when, much more as a friend of her mother's, the bereaved lady, without a penny of provision and with stopgaps, like their own, all gone, had, across the sordid landing on which the opposite doors of the pair of scared miseries opened and to which they were bewilderedly bolted, borrowed coals and umbrellas that were repaid in potatoes and postage-stamps. It had been a questionable help, at that time, to ladies submerged, floundering, panting, swimming for their lives, that they *were* ladies; but such an advantage could come up again in proportion as others vanished, and it had grown very great by the time it was the only ghost of one they possessed. They had literally watched it take to itself a portion of the substance of each that had departed; and it became prodigious now, when they could talk of it together, when they could look back at it across a desert of accepted derogation, and when, above all, they could together work up a credulity about it that neither could otherwise work up. Nothing was really so marked as that they felt the need to cultivate this legend much more after having found their feet and stayed their stomachs in the ultimate obscure than they had done in the upper air of mere frequent shocks. The thing they could now oftenest say to each other was that they knew what they meant; and the sentiment with which, all round, they knew it was known had well-nigh amounted to a promise not again to fall apart.

Mrs Jordan was at present fairly dazzling on the subject of the way that, in the practice of her fairy art, as she called it, she more than peeped in – she penetrated. There was not a house of the great kind – and it was of course only a question of those, real homes of luxury – in which she was not, at the rate such people now had things, all over the place. The girl felt before the picture the cold breath of disinheritance as much as she had ever felt it in the cage; she knew moreover how much she betrayed this, for the experience of poverty had begun, in her life, too early, and her ignorance of the requirements of homes of luxury had grown, with other active knowledge, a depth of simplification. She had accordingly at first often found that in these colloquies she could only pretend she understood. Educated as she had rapidly been by her chances at Cocker's, there were still strange gaps in her learning – she could never, like Mrs Jordan, have found her way about one of the 'homes.' Little by little, however, she had caught on, above all in the light of what Mrs Jordan's redemption had materially made of that lady, giving her, though the years and the struggles had naturally not straightened a feature, an almost super-eminent air. There were women in and out of Cocker's who were quite nice and who yet didn't look well; whereas Mrs

Jordan looked well and yet, with her extraordinarily protrusive teeth, was by no means quite nice. It would seem, mystifyingly, that it might really come from all the greatness she could live with. It was fine to hear her talk so often of dinners of twenty and of her doing, as she said, exactly as she liked with them. She spoke as if, for that matter, she invited the company. 'They simply *give* me the table – all the rest, all the other effects, come afterwards.'

VII

'Then you *do* see them?' the girl again asked.

Mrs Jordan hesitated, and indeed the point had been ambiguous before. 'Do you mean the guests?'

Her young friend, cautious about an undue exposure of innocence, was not quite sure. 'Well – the people who live there.'

'Lady Ventnor? Mrs Bubb? Lord Rye? Dear, yes. Why they *like* one.'

'But does one personally *know* them?' our young lady went on, since that was the way to speak. 'I mean socially, don't you know? – as you know *me*.'

'They're not so nice as you!' Mrs Jordan charmingly cried. 'But I *shall* see more and more of them.'

Ah this was the old story. 'But how soon?'

'Why almost any day. Of course,' Mrs Jordan honestly added, 'they're nearly always out.'

'Then why do they want flowers all over?'

'Oh that doesn't make any difference.' Mrs Jordan was not philosophic; she was just evidently determined it *shouldn't* make any. 'They're awfully interested in my ideas, and it's inevitable they should meet me over them.'

Her interlocutress was sturdy enough. 'What do you call your ideas?'

Mrs Jordan's reply was fine. 'If you were to see me some day with a thousand tulips you'd discover.'

'A thousand?' – the girl gaped at such a revelation of the scale of it; she felt for the instant fairly planted out. 'Well, but if in fact they never do meet you?' she none the less pessimistically insisted.

'Never? They *often* do – and evidently quite on purpose. We have grand long talks.'

There was something in our young lady that could still stay her from asking for a personal description of these apparitions; that showed too starved a state. But while she considered she took in afresh the whole of the clergyman's widow. Mrs Jordan couldn't help her teeth, and her sleeves were a distinct rise in the world. A thousand tulips at a shilling clearly took one further than a thousand words at a penny; and the betrothed of Mr Mudge, in whom the sense of the race for life was always acute, found herself wondering, with a twinge of her easy jealousy, if it mightn't after all then, for *her* also, be better – better than where she was – to follow some such scent. Where she was was where Mr Buckton's elbow could freely enter her right side and the counter-clerk's breathing – he had something the matter with his nose – pervade her left ear. It was something to fill an office under Government, and she knew but too well there were places commoner still than Cocker's; but it needed no great range of taste to bring home to her the picture of servitude and promiscuity she couldn't but offer to the eye of comparative freedom. She was so boxed up with her young men, and anything like a margin so absent, that it needed more art than she should ever possess to pretend in the least to compass, with any one in the nature of an acquaintance – say with Mrs Jordan herself, flying in, as it might happen, to wire sympathetically to Mrs Bubb – an approach to a relation of elegant privacy. She remembered the day when Mrs Jordan *had*, in fact, by the greatest chance, come in with fifty-three words for Lord Rye and a five-pound note to change. This had been the dramatic manner of their reunion – their mutual recognition was so great an event. The girl could at first only see her from the waist up, besides making but little of her long telegram to his lordship. It was a strange whirligig that had converted the clergyman's widow into such a specimen of the class that went beyond the sixpence.

Nothing of the occasion, all the more, had ever become dim; least of all the way that, as her recovered friend looked up from counting, Mrs Jordan had just blown, in explanation, through her teeth and through the bars of the cage: 'I *do* flowers, you know.' Our young woman had always, with her little finger crooked out, a pretty movement for counting; and she had not forgotten the small secret advantage, a sharpness of triumph it might even have been called, that fell upon her at this moment and avenged her for the incoherence of the message, an unintelligible enumeration of numbers, colours, days, hours. The correspondence of people she didn't know was one thing; but the correspondence of people she did had an aspect of its own for her even when she couldn't understand it. The speech in which Mrs Jordan had defined a position and announced a profession was like a tinkle of bluebells; but for herself her one idea about flowers was that people had them at funerals, and her present sole gleam of light was that lords probably had them most. When she watched, a minute later, through the cage, the swing of her visitor's departing petticoats, she saw the sight from the waist down; and when the counter-clerk, after a mere male glance, remarked, with an intention unmistakeably low, 'Handsome woman!' she had for him the finest of her chills: 'She's the widow of a bishop.' She always felt, with the counter-clerk, that it was impossible sufficiently to put it on; for what she wished to express to him was the maximum of her contempt, and that element in her nature was confusedly stored. 'A bishop' *was* putting it on, but the counter-clerk's approaches were vile. The night, after this, when, in the fulness of time, Mrs Jordan mentioned the grand long talks, the girl at last brought out: 'Should *I* see them? — I mean if I *were* to give up everything for you.'

Mrs Jordan at this became most arch. 'I'd send you to all the bachelors!'

Our young lady could be reminded by such a remark that she usually struck her friend as pretty. 'Do *they* have their flowers?'

'Oceans. And they're the most particular.' Oh it was a wonderful world. 'You should see Lord Rye's.'

'His flowers?'

'Yes, and his letters. He writes me pages on pages — with the most adorable little drawings and plans. You should see his diagrams!'

VIII

The girl had in course of time every opportunity to inspect these documents, and they a little disappointed her; but in the mean while there had been more talk, and it had led to her saying, as if her friend's guarantee of a life of elegance were not quite definite: 'Well, I see every one at *my* place.'

'Every one?'

'Lots of swells. They flock. They live, you know, all round, and the place is filled with all the smart people, all the fast people, those whose names are in the papers — mamma has still the *Morning Post*[17] — and who come up for the season.'

Mrs Jordan took this in with complete intelligence. 'Yes, and I dare say it's some of your people that *I* do.'

Her companion assented, but discriminated. 'I doubt if you "do" them as much as I! Their affairs, their appointments and arrangements, their little games and secrets and vices — those things all pass before me.'

This was a picture that could make a clergyman's widow not imperceptibly gasp; it was in intention moreover something of a retort to the thousand tulips. 'Their vices? Have they got vices?'

Our young critic even more overtly stared; then with a touch of contempt in her amusement: 'Haven't you found *that* out?' The homes of luxury then hadn't so much to give. '*I* find out everything.'

Mrs Jordan, at bottom a very meek person, was visibly struck. 'I see. You do "have" them.'

'Oh I don't care! Much good it does me!'

Mrs Jordan after an instant recovered her superiority. 'No – it doesn't lead to much.' Her own initiations so clearly did. Still – after all; and she was not jealous: 'There must be a charm.'

'In seeing them?' At this the girl suddenly let herself go. 'I hate them. There's that charm!'

Mrs Jordan gaped again. 'The *real* "smarts"?'

'Is that what you call Mrs Bubb? Yes – it comes to me; I've had Mrs Bubb. I don't think she has been in herself, but there are things her maid has brought. Well, my dear!' – and the young person from Cocker's, recalling these things and summing them up, seemed suddenly to have much to say. She didn't say it, however; she checked it; she only brought out: 'Her maid, who's horrid – *she* must have her!' Then she went on with indifference: 'They're *too* real! They're selfish brutes.'

Mrs Jordan, turning it over, adopted at last the plan of treating it with a smile. She wished to be liberal. 'Well, of course, they do lay it out.'

'They bore me to death,' her companion pursued with slightly more temperance.

But this was going too far. 'Ah that's because you've no sympathy!'

The girl gave an ironic laugh, only retorting that nobody could have any who had to count all day all the words in the dictionary; a contention Mrs Jordan quite granted, the more that she shuddered at the notion of ever failing of the very gift to which she owed the vogue – the rage she might call it – that had caught her up. Without sympathy – or without imagination, for it came back again to that – how should she get, for big dinners, down the middle and toward the far corners at all? It wasn't the combinations, which were easily managed: the strain was over the ineffable simplicities, those that the bachelors above all, and Lord Rye perhaps most of any, threw off – just blew off like cigarette-puffs – such sketches of. The betrothed of Mr Mudge at all events accepted the explanation, which had the effect, as almost any turn of their talk was now apt to have, of bringing her round to the terrific question of that gentleman. She was tormented with the desire to get out of Mrs Jordan, on this subject, what she was sure was at the back of Mrs Jordan's head; and to get it out of her, queerly enough, if only to vent a certain irritation at it. She knew that what her friend would already have risked if she hadn't been timid and tortuous was: 'Give him up – yes, give him up: you'll see that with your sure chances you'll be able to do much better.'

Our young woman had a sense that if that view could only be put before her with a particular sniff for poor Mr Mudge she should hate it as much as she morally ought. She was conscious of not, as yet, hating it quite so much as that. But she saw that Mrs Jordan was conscious of something too, and that there was a degree of confidence she was waiting little by little to arrive at. The day came when the girl caught a glimpse of what was still wanting to make her friend feel strong; which was nothing less than the prospect of being able to announce the climax of sundry private dreams. The associate of the aristocracy had personal calculations — matter for brooding and dreaming, even for peeping out not quite hopelessly from behind the window-curtains of lonely lodgings. If she did the flowers for the bachelors, in short, didn't she expect that to have consequences very different from such an outlook at Cocker's as she had pronounced wholly desperate? There seemed in very truth something auspicious in the mixture of bachelors and flowers, though, when looked hard in the eye, Mrs Jordan was not quite prepared to say she had expected a positive proposal from Lord Rye to pop out of it. Our young woman arrived at last, none the less, at a definite vision of what was in her mind. This was a vivid foreknowledge that the betrothed of Mr Mudge would, unless conciliated in advance by a successful rescue, almost hate her on the day she should break a particular piece of news. How could that unfortunate otherwise endure to hear of what, under the protection of Lady Ventnor, was after all so possible?

IX

Meanwhile, since irritation sometimes relieved her, the betrothed of Mr Mudge found herself indebted to that admirer for amounts of it perfectly proportioned to her fidelity. She always walked with him on Sundays, usually in the Regent's Park,[18] and quite often, once or twice a month, he took her, in the Strand or thereabouts,[19] to see a piece that was having a run. The productions he always preferred were the really good ones — Shakespeare, Thompson or some funny American thing;[20] which, as it also happened that she hated vulgar plays, gave him ground for what was almost the fondest of his approaches, the theory that their tastes were, blissfully, just the same. He was for ever reminding her of that, rejoicing over it and being affectionate and wise about it. There were times when she wondered how in the world she could 'put up with' him, how she could put up with any man so smugly unconscious of the immensity of her difference. It was just for this difference that, if she was to be liked at all, she wanted to be liked, and if that was not the source of Mr Mudge's admiration, she asked herself, what on earth *could* be? She was not different only at one point, she was different all round; unless perhaps indeed in being practically human, which her mind just barely recognised that he also was. She would have made tremendous concessions in other quarters: there was no limit for instance to those she would have made to Captain Everard; but what I have named was the most she was prepared to do for Mr Mudge. It was because *he* was different that, in the oddest way, she liked as well as deplored him; which was after all a proof that the disparity, should they frankly recognise it, wouldn't necessarily be fatal. She felt that, oleaginous – too oleaginous – as he was, he was somehow comparatively primitive: she had once, during the portion of his time at Cocker's that had overlapped her own, seen him collar a drunken soldier, a big violent man who, having come in with a mate to get a postal-order cashed, had made a grab at the money before his friend could reach it and had so determined, among the hams and cheeses and the lodgers from Thrupp's, immediate and alarming reprisals, a scene of scandal and consternation. Mr Buckton and the counter-clerk had crouched within the cage, but Mr Mudge had, with a very quiet but very quick step round the counter, an air of masterful authority she shouldn't soon forget, triumphantly interposed in the scrimmage, parted the combatants and shaken the delinquent in his skin. She had been proud of him at that moment, and had felt that if their affair had not already been settled the neatness of his execution would have left her without resistance.

Their affair had been settled by other things: by the evident sincerity of his passion and by the sense that his high white apron resembled a front of many floors. It had gone a great way with her that he would build up a business to his chin, which he carried quite in the air. This could only be a question of time; he would have all Piccadilly[21] in the pen behind his ear. That was a merit in itself for a girl who had known what she had known. There were hours at which she even found him good-looking, though frankly there could be no crown for her effort to imagine on the part of the tailor or the barber some such treatment of his appearance as would make him resemble even remotely a man of the world. His very beauty was the beauty of a grocer, and the finest future would offer it none too much room consistently to develop. She had engaged herself in short to the perfection of a type, and almost anything square and smooth and whole had its weight for a person still conscious herself of being a mere bruised fragment of wreckage. But it contributed hugely at present to carry on the two parallel lines of her experience in the cage and her experience out of it. After keeping quiet for some time about this opposition she suddenly – one Sunday afternoon on a penny chair in the Regent's Park – broke, for him, capriciously, bewilderingly, into an intimation of what it came to. He had naturally pressed more and more on the point of her again placing herself where he could see her hourly, and for her to recognise that she had as yet given him no sane reason for delay he had small need to describe himself as unable to make out what she was up to. As if, with her absurd bad reasons, she could have begun to tell him! Sometimes she thought it would be amusing to let him have them full in the face, for she felt she should die of him unless she once in a while stupefied him; and sometimes she thought it would be disgusting and perhaps even fatal. She liked him, however, to think her silly, for that gave her the margin which at the best she would always require; and the only difficulty about this was that he hadn't enough imagination to oblige her. It produced none the less something of the desired effect — to leave him simply wondering why, over the matter of their reunion, she didn't yield to his arguments. Then at last, simply as if by accident and out of mere boredom on a day that was rather flat, she preposterously produced her own. 'Well, wait a bit. Where I am I still see things.' And she talked to him even worse, if possible, than she had talked to Mrs Jordan.

Little by little, to her own stupefaction, she caught that he was trying to take it as she meant it and that he was neither astonished nor angry. Oh the British tradesman — this gave her an idea of his resources! Mr Mudge would be angry only with a person who, like the drunken soldier in the shop, should have an unfavourable effect on business. He seemed positively to enter, for the time and without the faintest flash of irony or ripple of laughter, into the whimsical grounds of her enjoyment of Cocker's custom, and instantly to be casting up whatever it might, as Mrs Jordan had said, lead to. What he had in mind was not of course what Mrs Jordan had had: it was obviously not a source of speculation with him that his sweetheart might pick up a husband. She could see perfectly that this was not for a moment even what he supposed she herself dreamed of. What she had done was simply to give his sensibility another push into the dim vast of trade. In that direction it was all alert and she had whisked before it the mild fragrance of a 'connexion.' That was the most he could see in any account of her keeping in, on whatever roundabout lines, with the gentry; and when, getting to the bottom of this, she quickly proceeded to show him the kind of eye she turned on such people and to give him a sketch of what that eye discovered, she reduced him to the particular prostration in which he could still be amusing to her.

X

'They're the most awful wretches, I assure you — the lot all about there.'

'Then why do you want to stay among them?'

'My dear man, just because they *are*. It makes me hate them so.'

'Hate them? I thought you liked them.'

'Don't be stupid. What I "like" is just to loathe them. You wouldn't believe what passes before my eyes.'

'Then why have you never told me? You didn't mention anything before I left.'

'Oh I hadn't got round to it then. It's the sort of thing you don't believe at first;

you have to look round you a bit and then you understand. You work into it more and more. Besides,' the girl went on, 'this is the time of the year when the worst lot come up. They're simply packed together in those smart streets. Talk of the numbers of the poor! What *I* can vouch for is the numbers of the rich! There are new ones every day and they seem to get richer and richer. Oh they do come up!' she cried, imitating for her private recreation – she was sure it wouldn't reach Mr Mudge – the low intonation of the counter-clerk.

'And where do they come from?' her companion candidly enquired.

She had to think a moment; then she found something. 'From the "spring meetings."[22] They bet tremendously.'

'Well, they bet enough at Chalk Farm, if that's all.'

'It *isn't* all. It isn't a millionth part!' she replied with some sharpness. 'It's immense fun' – she *had* to tantalise him. Then as she had heard Mrs Jordan say, and as the ladies at Cocker's even sometimes wired, 'It's quite too dreadful!' She could fully feel how it was Mr Mudge's propriety, which was extreme – he had a horror of coarseness and attended a Wesleyan chapel[23] – that prevented his asking for details. But she gave him some of the more innocuous in spite of himself, especially putting before him how, at Simpkin's and Ladle's, they all made the money fly. That was indeed what he liked to hear: the connexion was not direct, but one was somehow more in the right place where the money was flying than where it was simply and meagrely nesting. The air felt that stir, he had to acknowledge, much less at Chalk Farm than in the district in which his beloved so oddly enjoyed her footing. She gave him, she could see, a restless sense that these might be familiarities not to be sacrificed; germs, possibilities, faint foreshowings – heaven knew what – of the initiation it would prove profitable to have arrived at when in the fulness of time he should have his own shop in some such paradise. What really touched him – that was discernible – was that she could feed him with so much mere vividness of reminder, keep before him, as by the play of a fan, the very wind of the swift banknotes and the charm of the existence of a class that Providence had raised up to be the blessing of grocers. He liked to think that the class was there, that it was always there, and that she contributed in her slight but appreciable degree to keep it up to the mark. He couldn't have formulated his theory of the matter, but the exuberance of the aristocracy was the advantage of trade, and everything was knit together in a richness of pattern that it was good to follow with one's finger-tips. It was a comfort to him to be thus assured that there were no symptoms of a drop. What did the sounder, as she called it, nimbly worked, do but keep the ball going?

What it came to therefore for Mr Mudge was that all enjoyments were, as might be said, inter-related, and that the more people had the more they wanted to have. The more flirtations, as he might roughly express it, the more cheese and pickles. He had even in his own small way been dimly struck with the linked sweetness connecting the tender passion with cheap champagne, or perhaps the other way round. What he would have liked to say had he been able to work out his thought to the end was: 'I see, I see. Lash them up then, lead them on, keep them going: some of it can't help, some time, coming *our* way.' Yet he was troubled by the suspicion of subtleties on his companion's part that spoiled the straight view. He couldn't understand people's hating what they liked or liking what they hated; above all it hurt him somewhere – for he had his private delicacies – to see anything *but* money made out of his betters. To be too enquiring, or in any other way too free, at the expense of the gentry was vaguely wrong; the only thing that was distinctly right was to be prosperous at any price. Wasn't it just because they were up there aloft that they were lucrative? He concluded at any rate by saying to his young friend: 'If it's improper for you to remain at Cocker's, then that falls in exactly with the other reasons I've put before you for your removal.'

'Improper?' – her smile became a prolonged boldness. 'My dear boy, there's no one like you!'

'I dare say,' he laughed; 'but that doesn't help the question.'

'Well,' she returned, 'I can't give up my friends. I'm making even more than Mrs Jordan.'

Mr Mudge considered. 'How much is *she* making?'

'Oh you dear donkey!' – and, regardless of all the Regent's Park, she patted his cheek. This was the sort of moment at which she was absolutely tempted to tell him that she liked to be near Park Chambers. There was a fascination in the idea of seeing if, on a mention of Captain Everard, he wouldn't do what she thought he might; wouldn't weigh against the obvious objection the still more obvious advantage. The advantage of course could only strike him at the best as rather fantastic; but it was always to the good to keep hold when you *had* hold, and such an attitude would also after all involve a high tribute to her fidelity. Of one thing she absolutely never doubted: Mr Mudge believed in her with a belief –! She believed in herself too, for that matter: if there was a thing in the world no one could charge her with it was being the kind of low barmaid person who rinsed tumblers and bandied slang. But she forbore as yet to speak; she had not spoken even to Mrs Jordan; and the hush that on her lips surrounded the Captain's name maintained itself as a kind of symbol of the success that, up to this time, had attended something or other – she couldn't have said what – that she humoured herself with calling, without words, her relation with him.

XI

She would have admitted indeed that it consisted of little more than the fact that his absences, however frequent and however long, always ended with his turning up again. It was nobody's business in the world but her own if that fact continued to be enough for her. It was of course not enough just in itself; what it had taken on to make it so was the extraordinary possession of the elements of his life that memory and attention had at last given her. There came a day when this possession on the girl's part actually seemed to enjoy between them, while their eyes met, a tacit recognition that was half a joke and half a deep solemnity. He bade her good-morning always now; he often quite raised his hat to her. He passed a remark when there was time or room, and once she went so far as to say to him that she hadn't seen him for 'ages.' 'Ages' was the word she consciously and carefully, though a trifle tremulously, used; 'ages' was exactly what she meant. To this he replied in terms doubtless less anxiously selected, but perhaps on that account not the less remarkable, 'Oh yes, hasn't it been awfully wet?' That was a specimen of their give and take; it fed her fancy that no form of intercourse so transcendent and distilled had ever been established on earth. Everything, so far as they chose to consider it so, might mean almost anything. The want of margin in the cage, when he peeped through the bars, wholly ceased to be appreciable. It was a drawback only in superficial commerce. With Captain Everard she had simply the margin of the universe. It may be imagined therefore how their unuttered reference to all she knew about him could in this immensity play at its ease. Every time he handed in a telegram it was an addition to her knowledge: what did his constant smile mean to mark if it didn't mean to mark that? He never came into the place without saying to her in this manner: 'Oh yes, you have me by this time so completely at your mercy that it doesn't in the least matter what I give you now. You've become a comfort, I assure you!'

She had only two torments; the greatest of which was that she couldn't, not even once or twice, touch with him on any individual fact. She would have given anything to have been able to allude to one of his friends by name, to one of his engagements by date, to one of his difficulties by the solution. She would have given almost as much for just the right chance – it would have to be tremendously right – to show him in some sharp sweet way that she had perfectly penetrated the greatest of these last and now lived with it in a kind of heroism of sympathy. He was in love with a woman to whom, and to any view of whom, a lady-telegraphist, and especially one who passed a life among hams and cheeses, was as the sand on the floor; and what her dreams desired was the possibility of its somehow coming to him that her own interest in him could take a pure and noble account of such an infatuation and even of such an impropriety. As yet, however, she could only rub along with the hope that an accident, sooner or later, might give her a lift toward popping out with something that would surprise and perhaps even, some fine day, assist him. What could people mean moreover – cheaply sarcastic people – by not feeling all that could be got out of the weather? *She* felt it all, and seemed literally to feel it most when she went quite wrong, speaking of the stuffy days as cold, of the cold ones as stuffy, and betraying how little she knew, in her cage, of whether it was foul or fair. It was for that matter always stuffy at Cocker's, and she finally settled down to the safe proposition that the outside element was 'changeable.' Anything seemed true that made him so radiantly assent.

This indeed is a small specimen of her cultivation of insidious ways of making things easy for him – ways to which of course she couldn't be at all sure he did real justice. Real justice was not of this world: she had had too often to come back to that; yet, strangely, happiness was, and her traps had to be set for it in a manner to keep them unperceived by Mr Buckton and the counter-clerk. The most she could hope for apart from the question, which constantly flickered up and died down, of the divine chance of his consciously liking her, would be that, without analysing it, he should arrive at a vague sense that Cocker's was – well, attractive: easier, smoother, sociably brighter, slightly more picturesque, in short more propitious in general to his little affairs, than any other establishment just thereabouts. She was quite aware that they couldn't be, in so huddled a hole, particularly quick; but she found her account in the slowness – she certainly could bear it if *he* could. The great pang was that just thereabouts post-offices were so awfully thick. She was always seeing him in imagination at other places and with other girls. But she would defy any other girl to follow him as she followed. And though they weren't, for so many reasons, quick at Cocker's, she could hurry for him when, through an intimation light as air, she gathered that he was pressed.

When hurry was, better still, impossible, it was because of the pleasantest thing of all, the particular element of their contact – she would have called it their friendship – that consisted of an almost humorous treatment of the look of some of his words. They would never perhaps have grown half so intimate if he had not, by the blessing of heaven, formed some of his letters with a queerness –! It was positive that the queerness could scarce have been greater if he had practised it for the very purpose of bringing their heads together over it as far as was possible to heads on different sides of a wire fence. It had taken her truly but once or twice to master these tricks, but, at the cost of striking him perhaps as stupid, she could still challenge them when circumstances favoured. The great circumstance that favoured was that she sometimes actually believed he knew she only feigned perplexity. If he knew it therefore he tolerated it; if he tolerated it he came back; and if he came back he liked her. This was her seventh heaven; and she didn't ask much of his liking – she only asked of it to reach the point of his not going away because of her own. He had at times to be away for weeks; he had to lead his life; he had to travel – there were places to which he was constantly wiring for 'rooms': all this she granted him, forgave him; in fact, in the long run, literally blessed and thanked him for. If he had to lead his life, that precisely fostered his leading it so much by telegraph: therefore the benediction was to come in when he could. That was all she asked – that he shouldn't wholly deprive her.

Sometimes she almost felt that he couldn't have deprived her even had he been minded, by reason of the web of revelation that was woven between them. She quite thrilled herself with thinking what, with such a lot of material, a bad girl would do. It would be a scene better than many in her ha'penny novels, this going to him in the dusk of evening at Park Chambers and letting him at last have it. 'I know too much about a certain person now not to put it to you – excuse my being so lurid – that it's quite worth your while to buy me off. Come therefore: buy me!' There was a point indeed at which such flights had to drop again – the point of an unreadiness to name, when it came to that, the purchasing medium. It wouldn't certainly be anything so gross as money, and the matter accordingly remained rather vague, all the more that *she* was not a bad girl. It wasn't for any such reason as might have aggravated a mere minx that she often hoped he would again bring Cissy. The difficulty of this, however, was constantly present to her, for the kind of communion to which Cocker's so richly ministered rested on the fact that Cissy and he were so often in different places. She knew by this time all the places – Suchbury, Monkhouse, Whiteroy, Finches – and even how the parties on these occasions were composed; but her subtlety found ways to make her knowledge fairly protect and promote their keeping, as she had heard Mrs Jordan say, in touch. So, when he actually sometimes smiled as if he really felt the awkwardness of giving her again one of the same old addresses, all her being went out in the desire – which her face must have expressed – that he should recognise her forbearance to criticise as one of the finest tenderest sacrifices a woman had ever made for love.

XII

She was occasionally worried, however this might be, by the impression that these sacrifices, great as they were, were nothing to those that his own passion had imposed; if indeed it was not rather the passion of his confederate, which had caught him up and was whirling him round like a great steam-wheel. He was at any rate in the strong grip of a splendid dizzy fate; the wild wind of his life blew him straight before it. Didn't she catch in his face at times, even through his smile and his happy habit, the gleam of that pale glare with which a bewildered victim appeals, as he passes, to some pair of pitying eyes? He perhaps didn't even himself know how scared he was; but *she* knew. They were in danger, they were in danger, Captain Everard and Lady Bradeen: it beat every novel in the shop. She thought of Mr Mudge and his safe sentiment; she thought of herself and blushed even more for her tepid response to it. It was a comfort to her at such moments to feel that in another relation – a relation supplying that affinity with her nature that Mr Mudge, deluded creature, would never supply – she should have been no more tepid than her ladyship. Her deepest soundings were on two or three occasions of finding herself almost sure that, if she dared, her ladyship's lover would have gathered relief from 'speaking' to her. She literally fancied once or twice that, projected as he was toward his doom, her own eyes struck him, while the air roared in his ears, as the one pitying pair in the crowd. But how could he speak to her while she sat sandwiched there between the counter-clerk and the sounder?

She had long ago, in her comings and goings, made acquaintance with Park Chambers and reflected as she looked up at their luxurious front that *they* of course would supply the ideal setting for the ideal speech. There was not an object in London that, before the season was over, was more stamped upon her brain. She went roundabout to pass it, for it was not on the short way; she passed on the opposite side of the street and always looked up, though it had taken her a long time to be sure of the particular set of windows. She had made that out finally by an act of audacity that at the time had almost stopped her heart-beats and that in retrospect greatly quickened her blushes. One evening she had lingered late and watched – watched for some moment when the porter, who was in uniform and often on the steps, had gone in with a visitor. Then she followed boldly, on the calculation that he would have taken the visitor up and that the hall would be free. The hall *was* free, and the electric light played over the gilded and lettered board that showed the names and numbers of the occupants of the different floors. What she wanted looked straight at her – Captain Everard was on the third. It was as if, in the immense intimacy of this, they were, for the instant and the first time, face to face outside the cage. Alas! they were face to face but a second or two: she was whirled out on the wings of a panic fear that he might just then be entering or issuing. This fear was indeed, in her shameless deflexions, never very far from her, and was mixed in the oddest way with depressions and disappointments. It was dreadful, as she trembled by, to run the risk of looking to him as if she basely hung about; and yet it was dreadful to be obliged to pass only at such moments as put an encounter out of the question.

At the horrible hour of her first coming to Cocker's he was always – it was to be hoped – snug in bed; and at the hour of her final departure he was of course – she had such things all on her fingers'-ends – dressing for dinner. We may let it pass that if she couldn't bring herself to hover till he was dressed, this was simply because such a process for such a person could only be terribly prolonged. When she went in the middle of the day to her own dinner[24] she had too little time to do anything but go straight, though it must be added that for a real certainty she would joyously have omitted the repast. She had made up her mind as to there being on the whole no decent pretext to justify her flitting casually past at three o'clock in the morning. That was the hour at which, if the ha'penny novels were not all wrong, he probably came home for the night. She was therefore reduced to the vainest figuration of the miraculous meeting toward which a hundred impossibilities would have to conspire. But if nothing was more impossible than the fact, nothing was more intense than the vision. What may not, we can only moralise, take place in the quickened muffled perception of a young person with an ardent soul? All our humble friend's native distinction, her refinement of personal grain, of heredity, of pride, took refuge in this small throbbing spot; for when she was most conscious of the abjection of her vanity and the pitifulness of her little flutters and manoeuvres, then the consolation and the redemption were most sure to glow before her in some just discernible sign. He did like her!

XIII

He never brought Cissy back, but Cissy came one day without him, as fresh as before from the hands of Marguerite, or only, at the season's end, a trifle less fresh. She was, however, distinctly less serene. She had brought nothing with her and looked about with impatience for the forms and the place to write. The latter convenience, at Cocker's, was obscure and barely adequate, and her clear voice had the light note of disgust which her lover's never showed as she responded with a 'There?' of surprise to the gesture made by the counter-clerk in answer to her sharp question. Our young friend was busy with half a dozen people, but she had dispatched them in her most business-like manner by the time her ladyship flung through the bars this light of re-appearance. Then the directness with which the girl managed to receive the accompanying missive was the result of the concentration that had caused her to make the stamps fly during the few minutes occupied by the production of it. This concentration, in turn, may be described as the effect of the apprehension of imminent relief. It was nineteen days, counted and checked off, since she had seen the object of her homage; and as, had he been in London, she should, with his habits, have been sure to see him often, she was now about to learn what other spot his presence might just then happen to sanctify. For she thought of them, the other spots, as ecstatically conscious of it, expressively happy in it.

But, gracious, how handsome *was* her ladyship, and what an added price it gave him that the air of intimacy he threw out should have flowed originally from such a source! The girl looked straight through the cage at the eyes and lips that must so often have been so near his own — looked at them with a strange passion that for an instant had the result of filling out some of the gaps, supplying the missing answers, in his correspondence. Then as she made out that the features she thus scanned and associated were totally unaware of it, that they glowed only with the colour of quite other and not at all guessable thoughts, this directly added to their splendour, gave the girl the sharpest impression she had yet received of the uplifted, the unattainable plains of heaven, and yet at the same time caused her to thrill with a sense of the high company she did somehow keep. She was with the absent through her ladyship and with her ladyship through the absent. The only pang — but it didn't matter — was the proof in the admirable face, in the sightless preoccupation of its possessor, that the latter hadn't a notion of her. Her folly had gone to the point of half-believing that the other party to the affair must sometimes mention in Eaton Square the extraordinary little person at the place from which he so often wired. Yet the perception of her visitor's blankness actually helped this extraordinary little person, the next instant, to take refuge in a reflexion that could be as proud as it liked. 'How little she knows, how little she knows!' the girl cried to herself; for what did that show after all but that Captain Everard's telegraphic confidant was Captain Everard's charming secret? Our young friend's perusal of her ladyship's telegram was literally prolonged by a momentary daze: what swam between her and the words, making her see them as through rippled shallow sunshot water, was the great, the perpetual flood of 'How much *I* know — how much *I* know!' This produced a delay in her catching that, on the face, these words didn't give her what she wanted, though she was prompt enough with her remembrance that her grasp was, half the time, just of what was *not* on the face. 'Miss Dolman, Parade Lodge, Parade Terrace, Dover. Let him instantly know right one, Hôtel de France, Ostend. Make it seven nine four nine six one.[25] Wire me alternative Burfield's.'

The girl slowly counted. Then he was at Ostend. This hooked on with so sharp a click that, not to feel she was as quickly letting it all slip from her, she had absolutely to hold it a minute longer and to do something to that end. Thus it was that she did on this occasion what she never did – threw off a 'Reply paid?' that sounded officious, but that she partly made up for by deliberately affixing the stamps and by waiting till she had done so to give change. She had, for so much coolness, the strength that she considered she knew all about Miss Dolman.

'Yes – paid.' She saw all sorts of things in this reply, even to a small suppressed start of surprise at so correct an assumption; even to an attempt the next minute at a fresh air of detachment. 'How much, with the answer?' The calculation was not abstruse, but our intense observer required a moment more to make it, and this gave her ladyship time for a second thought. 'Oh just wait!' The white begemmed hand bared to write rose in sudden nervousness to the side of the wonderful face which, with eyes of anxiety for the paper on the counter, she brought closer to the bars of the cage. 'I think I must alter a word!' On this she recovered her telegram and looked over it again; but she had a new, an obvious trouble, and studied it without deciding and with much of the effect of making our young woman watch her.

This personage meanwhile, at the sight of her expression, had decided on the spot. If she had always been sure they were in danger her ladyship's expression was the best possible sign of it. There was a word wrong, but she had lost the right one, and much clearly depended on her finding it again. The girl therefore, sufficiently estimating the affluence of customers and the distraction of Mr Buckton and the counter-clerk, took the jump and gave it. 'Isn't it Cooper's?'

It was as if she had bodily leaped – cleared the top of the cage and alighted on her interlocutress. 'Cooper's?' – the stare was heightened by a blush. Yes, she had made Juno blush.

This was all the greater reason for going on. 'I mean instead of Burfield's.'

Our young friend fairly pitied her; she had made her in an instant so helpless, and yet not a bit haughty nor outraged. She was only mystified and scared. 'Oh you know –?'

'Yes, I know!' Our young friend smiled, meeting the other's eyes, and, having made Juno blush, proceeded to patronise her. 'I'll do it' – she put out a competent hand. Her ladyship only submitted, confused and bewildered, all presence of mind quite gone; and the next moment the telegram was in the cage again and its author out of the shop. Then quickly, boldly, under all the eyes that might have witnessed her tampering, the extraordinary little person at Cocker's made the proper change. People were really too giddy, and if they *were*, in a certain case, to be caught, it shouldn't be the fault of her own grand memory. Hadn't it been settled weeks before? – for Miss Dolman it was always to be 'Cooper's.'

XIV

But the summer 'holidays' brought a marked difference; they were holidays for almost every one but the animals in the cage. The August days were flat and dry, and, with so little to feed it, she was conscious of the ebb of her interest in the secrets of the refined. She was in a position to follow the refined to the extent of knowing – they had made so many of their arrangements with her aid – exactly where they were; yet she felt quite as if the panorama had ceased unrolling and the band stopped playing. A stray member of the latter occasionally turned up, but the communications that passed before her bore now largely on rooms at hotels, prices of furnished houses, hours of trains, dates of sailings and arrangements for being 'met': she found them for the most part prosaic and coarse. The only thing was that they brought into her stuffy corner as straight a whiff of Alpine meadows and Scotch moors[26] as she might hope ever to inhale; there were moreover in especial fat hot dull ladies who had out with her, to exasperation, the terms for seaside lodgings, which struck her as huge, and the matter of the number of beds required, which was not less portentous: this in reference to places of which the names – Eastbourne, Folkestone, Cromer, Scarborough, Whitby[27] – tormented her with something of the sound of the plash of water that haunts the traveller in the desert. She had not been out of London for a dozen years, and the only thing to give a taste to the present dead weeks was the spice of a chronic resentment. The sparse customers, the people she did see, were the people who were 'just off' – off on the decks of fluttered yachts, off to the uttermost point of rocky headlands where the very breeze was then playing for the want of which she said to herself that she sickened.

There was accordingly a sense in which, at such a period, the great differences of the human condition could press upon her more than ever; a circumstance drawing fresh force in truth from the very fact of the chance that at last, for a change, did squarely meet her – the chance to be 'off,' for a bit, almost as far as anybody. They took their turns in the cage as they took them both in the shop and at Chalk Farm; she had known these two months that time was to be allowed in September – no less than eleven days – for her personal private holiday. Much of her recent intercourse with Mr Mudge had consisted of the hopes and fears, expressed mainly by himself, involved in the question of their getting the same dates – a question that, in proportion as the delight seemed assured, spread into a sea of speculation over the choice of where and how. All through July, on the Sunday evenings and at such other odd times as he could seize, he had flooded their talk with wild waves of calculation. It was practically settled that, with her mother, somewhere 'on the south coast' (a phrase of which she liked the sound) they should put in their allowance together; but she already felt the prospect quite weary and worn with the way he went round and round on it. It had become his sole topic, the theme alike of his most solemn prudences and most placid jests, to which every opening led for return and revision and in which every little flower of a foretaste was pulled up as soon as planted. He had announced at the earliest day – characterising the whole business, from that moment, as their 'plans,' under which name he handled it as a Syndicate handles a Chinese or other Loan[28] – he had promptly declared that the question must be thoroughly studied, and he produced, on the whole subject, from day to day, an amount of information that excited her wonder and even, not a little, as she frankly let him know, her disdain. When she thought of the danger in which another pair of lovers rapturously lived she enquired of him anew why he could leave nothing to chance. Then she got for answer that this profundity was just his pride, and he pitted Ramsgate against Bournemouth and even Boulogne against Jersey[29] – for he had great ideas – with all the mastery of detail that was some day, professionally, to carry him far.

The longer the time since she had seen Captain Everard the more she was booked, as she called it, to pass Park Chambers; and this was the sole amusement that in the lingering August days and the twilights sadly drawn out it was left her to cultivate. She had long since learned to know it for a feeble one, though its feebleness was perhaps scarce the reason for her saying to herself each evening as her time for departure approached: 'No, no – not to-night.' She never failed of that silent remark, any more than she failed of feeling, in some deeper place than she had even yet fully sounded, that one's remarks were as weak as straws and that, however one might indulge in them at eight o'clock, one's fate infallibly declared itself in absolute indifference to them at about eight-fifteen. Remarks were remarks, and very well for that; but fate was fate, and this young lady's was to pass Park Chambers every night in the working week. Out of the immensity of her knowledge of the life of the world there bloomed on these occasions a specific remembrance that it was regarded in that region, in August and September, as rather pleasant just to be caught for something or other in passing through town. Somebody was always passing and somebody might catch somebody else. It was in full cognisance of this subtle law that she adhered to the most ridiculous circuit she could have made to get home. One warm dull featureless Friday, when an accident had made her start from Cocker's a little later than usual, she became aware that something of which the infinite possibilities had for so long peopled her dreams was at last prodigiously upon her, though the perfection in which the conditions happened to present it was almost rich enough to be but the positive creation of a dream. She saw, straight before her, like a vista painted in a picture, the empty street and the lamps that burned pale in the dusk not yet established. It was into the convenience of this quiet twilight that a gentleman on the doorstep of the Chambers gazed with a vagueness that our young lady's little figure violently trembled, in the approach, with the measure of its power to dissipate. Everything indeed grew in a flash terrific and distinct; her old uncertainties fell away from her, and, since she was so familiar with fate, she felt as if the very nail that fixed it were driven in by the hard look with which, for a moment, Captain Everard awaited her.

The vestibule was open behind him and the porter as absent as on the day she had peeped in; he had just come out — was in town, in a tweed suit and a pot-hat,[30] but between two journeys — duly bored over his evening and at a loss what to do with it. Then it was that she was glad she had never met him in that way before: she reaped with such ecstasy the benefit of his not being able to think she passed often. She jumped in two seconds to the determination that he should even suppose it to be the very first time and the very oddest chance: this was while she still wondered if he would identify or notice her. His original attention had not, she instinctively knew, been for the young woman at Cocker's; it had only been for any young woman who might advance to the tune of her not troubling the quiet air, and in fact the poetic hour, with ugliness. Ah but then, and just as she had reached the door, came his second observation, a long light reach with which, visibly and quite amusedly, he recalled and placed her. They were on different sides, but the street, narrow and still, had only made more of a stage for the small momentary drama. It was not over, besides, it was far from over, even on his sending across the way, with the pleasantest laugh she had ever heard, a little lift of his hat and an 'Oh good-evening!' It was still less over on their meeting, the next minute, though rather indirectly and awkwardly, in the middle of the road — a situation to which three or four steps of her own had unmistakeably contributed — and then passing not again to the side on which she had arrived, but back toward the portal of Park Chambers.

'I didn't know you at first. Are you taking a walk?'

'Ah I don't take walks at night! I'm going home after my work.'

'Oh!'

That was practically what they had meanwhile smiled out, and his exclamation to which for a minute he appeared to have nothing to add, left them face to face and in just such an attitude as, for his part, he might have worn had he been wondering if he could properly ask her to come in. During this interval in fact she really felt his question to be just 'How properly —?' It was simply a question of the degree of properness.

XV

She never knew afterwards quite what she had done to settle it, and at the time she only knew that they presently moved, with vagueness, yet with continuity, away from the picture of the lighted vestibule and the quiet stairs and well up the street together. This also must have been in the absence of a definite permission, of anything vulgarly articulate, for that matter, on the part of either; and it was to be, later on, a thing of remembrance and reflexion for her that the limit of what just here for a longish minute passed between them was his taking in her thoroughly successful deprecation, though conveyed without pride or sound or touch, of the idea that she might be, out of the cage, the very shopgirl at large that she hugged the theory she wasn't. Yes, it was strange, she afterwards thought, that so much could have come and gone and yet not disfigured the dear little intense crisis either with impertinence or with resentment, with any of the horrid notes of that kind of acquaintance. He had taken no liberty, as she would have called it; and, through not having to betray the sense of one, she herself had, still more charmingly, taken none. On the spot, nevertheless, she could speculate as to what it meant that, if his relation with Lady Bradeen continued to be what her mind had built it up to, he should feel free to proceed with marked indepen-dence. This was one of the questions he was to leave her to deal with – the question whether people of his sort still asked girls up to their rooms when they were so awfully in love with other women. Could people of his sort do that without what people of *her* sort would call being 'false to their love'? She had already a vision of how the true answer was that people of her sort didn't, in such cases, matter – didn't count as infidelity, counted only as something else: she might have been curious, since it came to that, to see exactly as what.

Strolling together slowly in their summer twilight and their empty corner of Mayfair, they found themselves emerge at last opposite to one of the smaller gates of the Park;[31] upon which, without any particular word about it – they were talking so of other things – they crossed the street and went in and sat down on a bench. She had gathered by this time one magnificent hope about him – the hope he would say nothing vulgar. She knew thoroughly what she meant by that; she meant something quite apart from any matter of his being 'false.' Their bench was not far within; it was near the Park Lane paling and the patchy lamplight and the rumbling cabs and 'buses. A strange emotion had come to her, and she felt indeed excitement within excitement; above all a conscious joy in testing him with chances he didn't take. She had an intense desire he should know the type she really conformed to without her doing anything so low as tell him, and he had surely begun to know it from the moment he didn't seize the opportunities into which a common man would promptly have blundered. These were on the mere awkward surface, and *their* relation was beautiful behind and below them. She had questioned so little on the way what they might be doing that as soon as they were seated she took straight hold of it. Her hours, her confinement, the many conditions of service in the post-office, had – with a glance at his own postal resources and alternatives – formed, up to this stage, the subject of their talk. 'Well, here we are, and it may be right enough; but this isn't the least, you know, where I was going.'

'You were going home?'

'Yes, and I was already rather late. I was going to my supper.'

'You haven't had it?'

'No indeed!'

'Then you haven't eaten –?'

He looked of a sudden so extravagantly concerned that she laughed out. 'All day? Yes, we do feed once. But that was long ago. So I must presently say good-bye.'

'Oh deary *me*!' he exclaimed with an intonation so droll and yet a touch so light and a distress so marked – a confession of helplessness for such a case, in short, so unrelieved – that she at once felt sure she had made the great difference plain. He looked at her with the kindest eyes and still without saying what she had known he wouldn't. She had known he wouldn't say 'Then sup with *me*!' but the proof of it made her feel as if she had feasted.

'I'm not a bit hungry,' she went on.

'Ah you *must* be, awfully!' he made answer, but settling himself on the bench as if, after all, that needn't interfere with his spending his evening. 'I've always quite wanted the chance to thank you for the trouble you so often take for me.'

'Yes, I know,' she replied; uttering the words with a sense of the situation far deeper than any pretence of not fitting his allusion. She immediately felt him surprised and even a little puzzled at her frank assent; but for herself the trouble she had taken could only, in these fleeting minutes – they would probably never come back – be all there like a little hoard of gold in her lap. Certainly he might look at it, handle it, take up the pieces. Yet if he understood anything he must understand all. 'I consider you've already immensely thanked me.' The horror was back upon her of having seemed to hang about for some reward. 'It's awfully odd you should have been there just the one time –!'

'The one time you've passed my place?'

'Yes; you can fancy I haven't many minutes to waste. There was a place to-night I had to stop at.'

'I see, I see' – he knew already so much about her work. 'It must be an awful grind – for a lady.'

348

'It is, but I don't think I groan over it any more than my companions — and you've seen *they're* not ladies!' She mildly jested, but with an intention. 'One gets used to things, and there are employments I should have hated much more.' She had the finest conception of the beauty of not at least boring him. To whine, to count up her wrongs, was what a barmaid or a shopgirl would do, and it was quite enough to sit there like one of these.

'If you had had another employment,' he remarked after a moment, 'we might never have become acquainted.'

'It's highly probable — and certainly not in the same way.' Then, still with her heap of gold in her lap and something of the pride of it in her manner of holding her head, she continued not to move — she only smiled at him. The evening had thickened now; the scattered lamps were red; the Park, all before them, was full of obscure and ambiguous life; there were other couples on other benches whom it was impossible not to see, yet at whom it was impossible to look. 'But I've walked so much out of my way with you only just to show you that — that' — with this she paused; it was not after all so easy to express — 'that anything you may have thought is perfectly true.'

'Oh I've thought a tremendous lot!' her companion laughed. 'Do you mind my smoking?'

'Why should I? You always smoke *there*.'

'At your place? Oh yes, but here it's different.'

'No,' she said as he lighted a cigarette, 'that's just what it isn't. It's quite the same.'

'Well then, that's because "there" it's so wonderful!'

'Then you're conscious of how wonderful it is?' she returned.

He jerked his handsome head in literal protest at a doubt. 'Why that's exactly what I mean by my gratitude for all your trouble. It has been just as if you took a particular interest.' She only looked at him by way of answer in such sudden headlong embarrassment, as she was quite aware, that while she remained silent he showed himself checked by her expression. 'You *have* — haven't you? — taken a particular interest?'

'Oh a particular interest!' she quavered out, feeling the whole thing — her headlong embarrassment — get terribly the better of her, and wishing, with a sudden scare, all the more to keep her emotion down. She maintained her fixed smile a moment and turned her eyes over the peopled darkness, unconfused now, because there was something much more confusing. This, with a fatal great rush, was simply the fact that they were thus together. They were near, near, and all she had imagined of that had only become more true, more dreadful and overwhelming. She stared straight away in silence till she felt she looked an idiot; then, to say something, to say nothing, she attempted a sound which ended in a flood of tears.

Her tears helped her really to dissimulate, for she had instantly, in so public a situation, to recover herself. They had come and gone in half a minute, and she immediately explained them. 'It's only because I'm tired. It's that — it's that!' Then she added a trifle incoherently: 'I shall never see you again.'

'Ah but why not?' The mere tone in which her companion asked this satisfied her once for all as to the amount of imagination for which she could count on him. It was naturally not large: it had exhausted itself in having arrived at what he had already touched upon — the sense of an intention in her poor zeal at Cocker's. But any deficiency of this kind was no fault in him: *he* wasn't obliged to have an inferior cleverness — to have second-rate resources and virtues. It had been as if he almost really believed she had simply cried for fatigue, and he had accordingly put in some kind confused plea — 'You ought really to take something: won't you have something or other *somewhere?*' — to which she had made no response but a headshake of a sharpness that settled it. 'Why shan't we all the more keep meeting?'

'I mean meeting this way — only this way. At my place there — *that* I've nothing to do with, and I hope of course you'll turn up, with your correspondence, when it suits you. Whether I stay or not, I mean; for I shall probably not stay.'

'You're going somewhere else?' — he put it with positive anxiety.

'Yes, ever so far away — to the other end of London. There are all sorts of reasons I can't tell you, and it's practically settled. It's better for me, much; and I've only kept on at Cocker's for *you.*'

'For me?'

Making out in the dusk that he fairly blushed, she now measured how far he had been from knowing too much. Too much, she called it at present; and that was easy, since it proved so abundantly enough for her that he should simply be where he was. 'As we shall never talk this way but to-night — never, never again! — here it all is. I'll say it; I don't care what you think; it doesn't matter; I only want to help you. Besides, you're kind — you're kind. I've been thinking then of leaving for ever so long. But you've come so often — at times — and you've had so much to do, and it has been so pleasant and interesting, that I've remained, I've kept putting off my change. More than once, when I had nearly decided, you've turned up again and I've thought "Oh no!" That's the simple fact!' She had by this time got her confusion down so completely that she could laugh. 'This's what I meant when I said to you just now that I "knew." I've known perfectly that you knew I took trouble for you; and that knowledge has been for me, and I seemed to see it was for you, as if there were something — I don't know what to call it! – between us. I mean something unusual and good and awfully nice – something not a bit horrid or vulgar.'

She had by this time, she could see, produced a great effect on him; but she would have spoken the truth to herself had she at the same moment declared that she didn't in the least care: all the more that the effect must be one of extreme perplexity. What, in it all, was visibly clear for him, none the less, was that he was tremendously glad he had met her. She held him, and he was astonished at the force of it; he was intent, immensely considerate. His elbow was on the back of the seat, and his head, with the pot-hat pushed quite back, in a boyish way, so that she really saw almost for the first time his forehead and hair, rested on the hand into which he had crumpled his gloves. 'Yes,' he assented, 'it's not a bit horrid or vulgar.'

She just hung fire a moment, then she brought out the whole truth. 'I'd do anything for you. I'd do anything for you.' Never in her life had she known anything so high and fine as this, just letting him have it and bravely and magnificently leaving it. Didn't the place, the associations and circumstances, perfectly make it sound what it wasn't? and wasn't that exactly the beauty?

So she bravely and magnificently left it, and little by little she felt him take it up, take it down, as if they had been on a satin sofa in a boudoir. She had never seen a boudoir, but there had been lots of boudoirs in the telegrams. What she had said at all events sank into him, so that after a minute he simply made a movement that had the result of placing his hand on her own – presently indeed that of her feeling herself firmly enough grasped. There was no pressure she need return, there was none she need decline; she just sat admirably still, satisfied for the time with the surprise and bewilderment of the impression she made on him. His agitation was even greater on the whole than she had at first allowed for. 'I say, you know, you mustn't think of leaving!' he at last broke out.

'Of leaving Cocker's, you mean?'

'Yes, you must stay on there, whatever happens, and help a fellow.'

She was silent a little, partly because it was so strange and exquisite to feel him watch her as if it really mattered to him and he were almost in suspense. 'Then you *have* quite recognised what I've tried to do?' she asked.

'Why, wasn't that exactly what I dashed over from my door just now to thank you for?'

'Yes; so you said.'

'And don't you believe it?'

She looked down a moment at his hand, which continued to cover her own; whereupon he presently drew it back, rather restlessly folding his arms. Without answering his question she went on: 'Have you ever spoken of me?'

'Spoken of you?'

'Of my being there – of my knowing, and that sort of thing.'

'Oh never to a human creature!' he eagerly declared.

She had a small drop at this, which was expressed in another pause, and she then returned to what he had just asked her. 'Oh yes, I quite believe you like it – my always being there and our taking things up so familiarly and successfully: if not exactly where we left them,' she laughed, 'almost always at least at an interesting point!' He was about to say something in reply to this, but her friendly gaiety was quicker. 'You want a great many things in life, a great many comforts and helps and luxuries – you want everything as pleasant as possible. Therefore so far as it's in the power of any particular person to contribute to all that –' She had turned her face to him smiling, just thinking.

'Oh see here!' But he was highly amused. 'Well, what then?' he enquired as if to humour her.

'Why the particular person must never fail. We must manage it for you somehow.'

He threw back his head, laughing out; he was really exhilarated. 'Oh yes, somehow!'

'Well, I think we each do – don't we? – in one little way and another and according to our limited lights. I'm pleased at any rate, for myself, that you are; for I assure you I've done my best.'

'You do better than any one!' He had struck a match for another cigarette, and the flame lighted an instant his responsive finished face, magnifying into a pleasant grimace the kindness with which he paid her this tribute. 'You're awfully clever, you know; cleverer, cleverer, cleverer –!' He had appeared on the point of making some tremendous statement; then suddenly, puffing his cigarette and shifting almost with violence on his seat, he let it altogether fall.

XVII

In spite of this drop, if not just by reason of it, she felt as if Lady Bradeen, all but named out, had popped straight up; and she practically betrayed her consciousness by waiting a little before she rejoined: 'Cleverer than who?'

'Well, if I wasn't afraid you'd think I swagger I should say – than anybody! If you leave your place there, where shall you go?' he more gravely asked.

'Oh too far for you ever to find me!'

'I'd find you anywhere.'

The tone of this was so still more serious that she had but her one acknowledgement. 'I'd do anything for you – I'd do anything for you,' she repeated. She had already, she felt, said it all; so what did anything more, anything less, matter? That was the very reason indeed why she could, with a lighter note, ease him generously of any awkwardness produced by solemnity, either his own or hers. 'Of course it must be nice for you to be able to think there are people all about who feel in such a way.'

In immediate appreciation of this, however, he only smoked without looking at her. 'But you don't want to give up your present work?' he at last threw out. 'I mean you *will* stay in the post-office?'

'Oh yes; I think I've a genius for that.'

'Rather! No one can touch you.' With this he turned more to her again. 'But you can get, with a move, greater advantages?'

'I can get in the suburbs cheaper lodgings. I live with my mother. We need some space. There's a particular place that has other inducements.'

He just hesitated. 'Where is it?'

'Oh quite out of *your* way. You'd never have time.'

'But I tell you I'd go anywhere. Don't you believe it?'

'Yes, for once or twice. But you'd soon see it wouldn't do for you.'

He smoked and considered; seemed to stretch himself a little and, with his legs out, surrender himself comfortably. 'Well, well, well — I believe everything you say. I take it from you — anything you like — in the most extraordinary way.' It struck her certainly — and almost without bitterness — that the way in which she was already, as if she had been an old friend, arranging for him and preparing the only magnificence she could muster, was quite the most extraordinary. 'Don't, *don't* go!' he presently went on. 'I shall miss you too horribly!'

'So that you just put it to me as a definite request?' — oh how she tried to divest this of all sound of the hardness of bargaining! That ought to have been easy enough, for what was she arranging to get? Before he could answer she had continued: 'To be perfectly fair I should tell you I recognise at Cocker's certain strong attractions. All you people come. I like all the horrors.'

'The horrors?'

'Those you all — you know the set I mean, *your* set — show me with as good a conscience as if I had no more feeling than a letter-box.'

He looked quite excited at the way she put it. 'Oh they don't know!'

'Don't know I'm not stupid? No, how should they?'

'Yes, how should they?' said the Captain sympathetically. 'But isn't "horrors" rather strong?'

'What you *do* is rather strong!' the girl promptly returned.

'What *I* do?'

'Your extravagance, your selfishness, your immorality, your crimes,' she pursued without heeding his expression.

'I *say*!' – her companion showed the queerest stare.

'I like them, as I tell you – I revel in them. But we needn't go into that,' she quietly went on; 'for all I get out of it is the harmless pleasure of knowing. I know, I know, I know!' – she breathed it ever so gently.

'Yes; that's what has been between us,' he answered much more simply.

She could enjoy his simplicity in silence, and for a moment she did so. 'If I do stay because you want it – and I'm rather capable of that – there are two or three things I think you ought to remember. One is, you know, that I'm there sometimes for days and weeks together without your ever coming.'

'Oh I'll come every day!' he honestly cried.

She was on the point, at this, of imitating with her hand his movement of shortly before; but she checked herself, and there was no want of effect in her soothing substitute. 'How can you? How can you?' He had, too manifestly, only to look at it there, in the vulgarly animated gloom, to see that he couldn't; and at this point, by the mere action of his silence, everything they had so definitely not named, the whole presence round which they had been circling, became part of their reference, settled in solidly between them. It was as if then for a minute they sat and saw it all in each other's eyes, saw so much that there was no need of a pretext for sounding it at last. 'Your danger, your danger –!' Her voice indeed trembled with it, and she could only for the moment again leave it so.

During this moment he leaned back on the bench, meeting her in silence and with a face that grew more strange. It grew so strange that after a further instant she got straight up. She stood there as if their talk were now over, and he just sat and watched her. It was as if now – owing to the third person they had brought in – they must be more careful; so that the most he could finally say was: 'That's where it is!'

'That's where it is!' the girl as guardedly replied. He sat still, and she added: 'I won't give you up. Good-bye.'

'Good-bye?' – he appealed, but without moving.

'I don't quite see my way, but I won't give you up,' she repeated. 'There. Good-bye.'

It brought him with a jerk to his feet, tossing away his cigarette. His poor face was flushed. 'See here – see here!'

'No, I won't; but I must leave you now,' she went on as if not hearing him.

'See here – see here!' He tried, from the bench, to take her hand again.

But that definitely settled it for her: this would, after all, be as bad as his asking her to supper. 'You mustn't come with me – no, no!'

He sank back, quite blank, as if she had pushed him. 'I mayn't see you home?'

'No, no; let me go.' He looked almost as if she had struck him, but she didn't care; and the manner in which she spoke – it was literally as if she were angry – had the force of a command. 'Stay where you are!'

'See here – see here!' he nevertheless pleaded.

'I won't give you up!' she cried once more – this time quite with passion; on which she got away from him as fast as she could and left him staring after her.

XVIII

Mr Mudge had lately been so occupied with their famous 'plans' that he had neglected for a while the question of her transfer; but down at Bournemouth, which had found itself selected as the field of their recreation by a process consisting, it seemed, exclusively of innumerable pages of the neatest arithmetic in a very greasy but most orderly little pocket-book, the distracting possible melted away – the fleeting absolute ruled the scene. The plans, hour by hour, were simply superseded, and it was much of a rest to the girl, as she sat on the pier and overlooked the sea and the company, to see them evaporate in rosy fumes and to feel that from moment to moment there was less left to cipher about. The week proved blissfully fine, and her mother, at their lodgings – partly to her embarrassment and partly to her relief – struck up with the landlady an alliance that left the younger couple a great deal of freedom. This relative took her pleasure of a week at Bournemouth in a stuffy back kitchen and endless talks; to that degree even that Mr Mudge himself – habitually inclined indeed to a scrutiny of all mysteries and to seeing, as he sometimes admitted, too much in things – made remarks on it as he sat on the cliff with his betrothed, or on the decks of steamers that conveyed them, close-packed items in terrific totals of enjoyment, to the Isle of Wight and the Dorset coast.

He had a lodging in another house, where he had speedily learned the importance of keeping his eyes open, and he made no secret of his suspecting that sinister mutual connivances might spring, under the roof of his companions, from unnatural sociabilities. At the same time he fully recognised that as a source of anxiety, not to say of expense, his future mother-in-law would have weighted them more by accompanying their steps than by giving her hostess, in the interest of the tendency they considered that they never mentioned, equivalent pledges as to the tea-caddy and the jam-pot. These were the questions – these indeed the familiar commodities – that he had now to put into the scales; and his betrothed had in consequence, during her holiday, the odd and yet pleasant and almost languid sense of an anticlimax. She had become conscious of an extraordinary collapse, a surrender to stillness and to retrospect. She cared neither to walk nor to sail; it was enough for her to sit on benches and wonder at the sea and taste the air and not be at Cocker's and not see the counter-clerk. She still seemed to wait for something – something in the key of the immense discussions that had mapped out their little week of idleness on the scale of a world-atlas. Something came at last, but without perhaps appearing quite adequately to crown the monument.

Preparation and precaution were, however, the natural flowers of Mr Mudge's mind, and in proportion as these things declined in one quarter they inevitably bloomed elsewhere. He could always, at the worst, have on Tuesday the project of their taking the Swanage boat[32] on Thursday, and on Thursday that of their ordering minced kidneys on Saturday. He had moreover a constant gift of inexorable enquiry as to where and what they should have gone and have done if they hadn't been exactly as they were. He had in short his resources, and his mistress had never been so conscious of them; on the other hand they had never interfered so little with her own. She liked to be as she was – if it could only have lasted. She could accept even without bitterness a rigour of economy so great that the little fee they paid for admission to the pier had to be balanced against other delights. The people at Ladle's and at Thrupp's had *their* ways of amusing themselves, whereas she had to sit and hear Mr Mudge talk of what he might do if he didn't take a bath, or of the bath he might take if he only hadn't taken something else. He was always with her now, of course, always beside her; she saw him more than 'hourly,' more than ever yet, more even than he had planned she should do at Chalk Farm. She preferred to sit at the far end, away from the band and the crowd; as to which she had frequent differences with her friend, who reminded her often that they could have only in the thick of it the sense of the money they were getting back. That had little effect on her, for she got back her money by seeing many things, the things of the past year, fall together and connect themselves, undergo the happy relegation that transforms melancholy and misery, passion and effort, into experience and knowledge.

She liked having done with them, as she assured herself she had practically done, and the strange thing was that she neither missed the procession now nor wished to keep her place for it. It had become there, in the sun and the breeze and the sea-smell, a far-away story, a picture of another life. If Mr Mudge himself liked processions, liked them at Bournemouth and on the pier quite as much as at Chalk Farm or anywhere, she learned after a little not to be worried by his perpetual counting of the figures that made them up. They were dreadful women in particular, usually fat and in men's caps and white shoes, whom he could never let alone – not that *she* cared; it was not the great world, the world of Cocker's and Ladle's and Thrupp's, but it offered an endless field to his faculties of memory, philosophy and frolic. She had never accepted him so much, never arranged so successfully for making him chatter while she carried on secret conversations. This separate commerce was with herself; and if they both practised a great thrift she had quite mastered that of merely spending words enough to keep him imperturbably and continuously going.

He was charmed with the panorama, not knowing – or at any rate not at all showing that he knew – what far other images peopled her mind than the women in the navy caps and the shopboys in the blazers. His observations on these types, his general interpretation of the show, brought home to her the prospect of Chalk Farm. She wondered sometimes that he should have derived so little illumination, during his period, from the society at Cocker's. But one evening while their holiday cloudlessly waned he gave her such a proof of his quality as might have made her ashamed of her many suppressions. He brought out something that, in all his overflow, he had been able to keep back till other matters were disposed of. It was the announcement that he was at last ready to marry – that he saw his way. A rise at Chalk Farm had been offered him; he was to be taken into the business, bringing with him a capital the estimation of which by other parties constituted the handsomest recognition yet made of the head on his shoulders. Therefore their waiting was over – it could be a question of a near date. They would settle this date before going back, and he meanwhile had his eye on a sweet little home. He would take her to see it on their first Sunday.

XIX

His having kept this great news for the last, having had such a card up his sleeve and not floated it out in the current of his chatter and the luxury of their leisure, was one of those incalculable strokes by which he could still affect her; the kind of thing that reminded her of the latent force that had ejected the drunken soldier – an example of the profundity of which his promotion was the proof. She listened a while in silence, on this occasion, to the wafted strains of the music; she took it in as she had not quite done before that her future was now constituted. Mr Mudge was distinctly her fate; yet at this moment she turned her face quite away from him, showing him so long a mere quarter of her cheek that she at last again heard his voice. He couldn't see a pair of tears that were partly the reason of her delay to give him the assurance he required; but he expressed at a venture the hope that she had had her fill of Cocker's.

She was finally able to turn back. 'Oh quite. There's nothing going on. No one comes but the Americans at Thrupp's, and *they* don't do much. They don't seem to have a secret in the world.'

'Then the extraordinary reason you've been giving me for holding on there has ceased to work?'

She thought a moment. 'Yes, that one. I've seen the thing through – I've got them all in my pocket.'

'So you're ready to come?'

For a little again she made no answer. 'No, not yet, all the same. I've still got a reason – a different one.'

He looked her all over as if it might have been something she kept in her mouth or her glove or under her jacket – something she was even sitting upon. 'Well I'll have it, please.'

'I went out the other night and sat in the Park with a gentleman,' she said at last.

Nothing was ever seen like his confidence in her; and she wondered a little now why it didn't irritate her. It only gave her ease and space, as she felt, for telling him the whole truth that no one knew. It had arrived at present at her really wanting to do that, and yet to do it not in the least for Mr Mudge, but altogether and only for herself. This truth filled out for her there the whole experience she was about to relinquish, suffused and coloured it as a picture that she should keep and that, describe it as she might, no one but herself would ever really see. Moreover she had no desire whatever to make Mr Mudge jealous; there would be no amusement in it, for the amusement she had lately known had spoiled her for lower pleasures. There were even no materials for it. The odd thing was how she never doubted that, properly handled, his passion was poisonable; what had happened was that he had cannily selected a partner with no poison to distil. She read then and there that she should never interest herself in anybody as to whom some other sentiment, some superior view, wouldn't be sure to interfere for him with jealousy. 'And what did you get out of that?' he asked with a concern that was not in the least for his honour.

'Nothing but a good chance to promise him I wouldn't forsake him. He's one of my customers.'

'Then it's for him not to forsake *you*.'

'Well, he won't. It's all right. But I must just keep on as long as he may want me.'

'Want you to sit with him in the Park?'

'He may want me for that – but I shan't. I rather liked it, but once, under the circumstances, is enough. I can do better for him in another manner.'

'And what manner, pray?'

'Well, elsewhere.'

'Elsewhere? – I *say*!'

This was an ejaculation used also by Captain Everard, but oh with what a different sound! 'You needn't "say" – there's nothing to be said. And yet you ought perhaps to know.'

'Certainly I ought. But *what* – up to now?'

'Why exactly what I told him. That I'd do anything for him.'

'What do you mean by "anything"?'

'Everything.'

Mr Mudge's immediate comment on this statement was to draw from his pocket a crumpled paper containing the remains of half a pound of 'sundries.' These sundries had figured conspicuously in his prospective sketch of their tour, but it was only at the end of three days that they had defined themselves unmistakeably as chocolate-creams. 'Have another? – *that* one,' he said. She had another, but not the one he indicated, and then he continued: 'What took place afterwards?'

'Afterwards?'

'What did you do when you had told him you'd do everything?'

'I simply came away.'

'Out of the Park?'

'Yes, leaving him there. I didn't let him follow me.'

'Then what did you let him do?'

'I didn't let him do anything.'

Mr Mudge considered an instant. 'Then what did you go there for?' His tone was even slightly critical.

'I didn't quite know at the time. It was simply to be with him, I suppose – just once. He's in danger, and I wanted him to know I know it. It makes meeting him – at Cocker's, since it's that I want to stay on for – more interesting.'

'It makes it mighty interesting for *me*!' Mr Mudge freely declared. 'Yet he didn't follow you?' he asked. '*I* would!'

'Yes, of course. That was the way you began, you know. You're awfully inferior to him.'

'Well, my dear, you're not inferior to anybody. You've got a cheek! What's he in danger of?'

'Of being found out. He's in love with a lady – and it isn't right – and I've found him out.'

'That'll be a lookout for *me*!' Mr Mudge joked. 'You mean she has a husband?'

'Never mind what she has! They're in awful danger, but his is the worst, because he's in danger from her too.'

'Like me from you – the woman *I* love? If he's in the same funk as me –'

'He's in a worse one. He's not only afraid of the lady – he's afraid of other things.'

Mr Mudge selected another chocolate-cream. 'Well, I'm only afraid of one! But how in the world can you help this party?'

'I don't know – perhaps not at all. But so long as there's a chance –!'

'You won't come away?'

'No, you've got to wait for me.'

Mr Mudge enjoyed what was in his mouth. 'And what will he give you?'

'Give me?'

'If you do help him.'

'Nothing. Nothing in all the wide world.'

'Then what will he give *me*?' Mr Mudge enquired. 'I mean for waiting.'

The girl thought a moment, then she got up to walk. 'He never heard of you,' she replied.

'You haven't mentioned me?'

'We never mention anything. What I've told you is just what I've found out.'

Mr Mudge, who had remained on the bench, looked up at her; she often preferred to be quiet when he proposed to walk, but now that he seemed to wish to sit she had a desire to move. 'But you haven't told me what *he* has found out.'

She considered her lover. 'He'd never find *you*, my dear!'

Her lover, still on his seat, appealed to her in something of the attitude in which she had last left Captain Everard, but the impression was not the same. 'Then where do I come in?'

'You don't come in at all. That's just the beauty of it!' – and with this she turned to mingle with the multitude collected round the band. Mr Mudge presently overtook her and drew her arm into his own with a quiet force that expressed the serenity of possession; in consonance with which it was only when they parted for the night at her door that he referred again to what she had told him.

'Have you seen him, since?'

'Since the night in the Park? No, not once.'

'Oh what a cad!' said Mr Mudge.

XX

It was not till the end of October that she saw Captain Everard again, and on that occasion – the only one of all the series on which hindrance had been so utter – no communication with him proved possible. She had made out even from the cage that it was a charming golden day: a patch of hazy autumn sunlight lay across the sanded floor and also, higher up, quickened into brightness a row of ruddy bottled syrups. Work was slack and the place in general empty; the town, as they said in the cage, had not waked up, and the feeling of the day likened itself to something that in happier conditions she would have thought of romantically as

Saint Martin's summer.[33] The counter-clerk had gone to his dinner; she herself was busy with arrears of postal jobs, in the midst of which she became aware that Captain Everard had apparently been in the shop a minute and that Mr Buckton had already seized him.

He had as usual half a dozen telegrams; and when he saw that she saw him and their eyes met he gave, on bowing to her, an exaggerated laugh in which she read a new consciousness. It was a confession of awkwardness; it seemed to tell her that of course he knew he ought better to have kept his head, ought to have been clever enough to wait, on some pretext, till he should have found her free. Mr Buckton was a long time with him, and her attention was soon demanded by other visitors; so that nothing passed between them but the fulness of their silence. The look she took from him was his greeting, and the other one a simple sign of the eyes sent her before going out. The only token they exchanged therefore was his tacit assent to her wish that since they couldn't attempt a certain frankness they should attempt nothing at all. This was her intense preference; she could be as still and cold as any one when that was the sole solution.

Yet more than any contact hitherto achieved these counted instants struck her as marking a step: they were built so — just in the mere flash — on the recognition of his now definitely knowing what it was she would do for him. The 'anything, anything' she had uttered in the Park went to and fro between them and under the poked-out chins that interposed. It had all at last even put on the air of their not needing now clumsily to manoeuvre to converse: their former little postal make-believes, the intense implications of questions and answers and change, had become in the light of the personal fact, of their having had their moment, a possibility comparatively poor. It was as if they had met for all time — it exerted on their being in presence again an influence so prodigious. When she watched herself, in the memory of that night, walk away from him as if she were making an end, she found something too pitiful in the primness of such a gait. Hadn't she precisely established on the part of each a consciousness that could end only with death?

It must be admitted that in spite of this brave margin an irritation, after he had gone, remained with her; a sense that presently became one with a still sharper hatred of Mr Buckton, who, on her friend's withdrawal, had retired with the telegrams to the sounder and left her the other work. She knew indeed she should have a chance to see them, when she would, on file; and she was divided, as the day went on, between the two impressions of all that was lost and all that was re-asserted. What beset her above all, and as she had almost never known it before, was the desire to bound straight out, to overtake the autumn afternoon before it passed away for ever and hurry off to the Park and perhaps be with him there again on a bench. It became for an hour a fantastic vision with her that he might just have gone to sit and wait for her. She could almost hear him, through the tick of the sounder, scatter with his stick, in his impatience, the fallen leaves of October. Why should such a vision seize her at this particular moment with such a shake? There was a time – from four to five – when she could have cried with happiness and rage.

Business quickened, it seemed, toward five, as if the town did wake up; she had therefore more to do, and she went through it with little sharp stampings and jerkings: she made the crisp postal-orders fairly snap while she breathed to herself 'It's the last day – the last day!' The last day of what? She couldn't have told. All she knew now was that if she *were* out of the cage she wouldn't in the least have minded, this time, its not yet being dark. She would have gone straight toward Park Chambers and have hung about there till no matter when. She would have waited, stayed, rung, asked, have gone in, sat on the stairs. What the day was the last of was probably, to her strained inner sense, the group of golden ones, of any occasion for seeing the hazy sunshine slant at that angle into the smelly shop, of any range of chances for his wishing still to repeat to her the two words she had in the Park scarcely let him bring out. 'See here – see here!' – the sound of these two words had been with her perpetually; but it was in her ears today without mercy, with a loudness that grew and grew. What was it they then expressed? what was it he had wanted her to see? She seemed, whatever it was, perfectly to see it now – to see that if she should just chuck the whole thing, should have a great and beautiful courage, he would somehow make everything up to her. When the clock struck five she was on the very point of saying to Mr Buckton that she was deadly ill and rapidly getting worse. This announcement was on her lips and she had quite composed the pale hard face she would offer him: 'I can't stop – I must go home. If I feel better, later on, I'll come back. I'm very sorry, but I *must* go.' At that instant Captain Everard once more stood there, producing in her agitated spirit, by his real presence, the strangest, quickest revolution. He stopped her off without knowing it, and by the time he had been a minute in the shop she felt herself saved.

That was from the first minute how she thought of it. There were again other persons with whom she was occupied, and again the situation could only be expressed by their silence. It was expressed, of a truth, in a larger phrase than ever yet, for her eyes now spoke to him with a kind of supplication. 'Be quiet, be quiet!' they pleaded; and they saw his own reply: 'I'll do whatever you say; I won't even look at you – see, see!' They kept conveying thus, with the friendliest liberality, that they wouldn't look, quite positively wouldn't. What she was to see was that he hovered at the other end of the counter, Mr Buckton's end, and surrendered himself again to that frustration. It quickly proved so great indeed that what she was to see further was how he turned away before he was attended to, and hung off, waiting, smoking, looking about the shop; how he went over to Mr Cocker's own counter and appeared to price things, gave in fact presently two or three orders and put down money, stood there a long time with his back to her, considerately abstaining from any glance round to see if she were free. It at last came to pass in this way that he had remained in the shop longer than she had ever yet known him to do, and that, nevertheless, when he did turn about she could see him time himself — she was freshly taken up — and cross straight to her postal subordinate, whom some one else had released. He had in his hand all this while neither letters nor telegrams, and now that he was close to her — for she was close to the counter-clerk — it brought her heart into her mouth merely to see him look at her neighbour and open his lips. She was too nervous to bear it. He asked for a Post-Office Guide,[34] and the young man whipped out a new one; whereupon he said he wished not to purchase, but only to consult one a moment; with which, the copy kept on loan being produced, he once more wandered off.

What was he doing to her? What did he want of her? Well, it was just the aggravation of his 'See here!' She felt at this moment strangely and portentously afraid of him — had in her ears the hum of a sense that, should it come to that kind of tension, she must fly on the spot to Chalk Farm. Mixed with her dread and with her reflexion was the idea that, if he wanted her so much as he seemed to show, it might be after all simply to do for him the 'anything' she had promised, the 'everything' she had thought it so fine to bring out to Mr Mudge. He might want her to help him, might have some particular appeal; though indeed his manner didn't denote that — denoted on the contrary an embarrassment, an indecision, something of a desire not so much to be helped as to be treated rather more nicely than she had treated him the other time. Yes, he considered quite probably that he had help rather to offer than to ask for. Still, none the less, when he again saw her free he continued to keep away from her; when he came back with his thumbed 'Guide' it was Mr Buckton he caught — it was from Mr Buckton he obtained half-a-crown's-worth of stamps.

After asking for the stamps he asked, quite as a second thought, for a postal-order for ten shillings. What did he want with so many stamps when he wrote so few letters? How could he enclose a postal-order in a telegram? She expected him, the next thing, to go into the corner and make up one of his telegrams — half a dozen of them — on purpose to prolong his presence. She had so completely stopped looking at him that she could only guess his movements — guess even where his eyes rested. Finally she saw him make a dash that might have been toward the nook where the forms were hung; and at this she suddenly felt that she couldn't keep it up. The counter-clerk had just taken a telegram from a slavey, and, to give herself something to cover her, she snatched it out of his hand. The gesture was so violent that he gave her in return an odd look, and she also perceived that Mr Buckton noticed it. The latter personage, with a quick stare at her, appeared for an instant to wonder whether his snatching it in *his* turn mightn't be the thing she would least like, and she anticipated this practical criticism by the frankest glare she had ever given him. It sufficed: this time it paralysed him, and she sought with her trophy the refuge of the sounder.

XXI

It was repeated the next day; it went on for three days; and at the end of that time she knew what to think. When, at the beginning, she had emerged from her temporary shelter Captain Everard had quitted the shop; and he had not come again that evening, as it had struck her he possibly might – might all the more easily that there were numberless persons who came, morning and afternoon, numberless times, so that he wouldn't necessarily have attracted attention. The second day it was different and yet on the whole worse. His access to her had become possible – she felt herself even reaping the fruit of her yesterday's glare at Mr Buckton; but transacting his business with him didn't simplify – it could, in spite of the rigour of circumstance, feed so her new conviction. The rigour was tremendous, and his telegrams – not now mere pretexts for getting at her – were apparently genuine; yet the conviction had taken but a night to develop. It could be simply enough expressed; she had had the glimmer of it the day before in her idea that he needed no more help than she had already given; that it was help he himself was prepared to render. He had come up to town but for three or four days; he had been absolutely obliged to be absent after the other time; yet he would, now that he was face to face with her, stay on as much longer as she liked. Little by little it was thus clarified, though from the first flash of his re-appearance she had read into it the real essence.

That was what the night before, at eight o'clock, her hour to go, had made her hang back and dawdle. She did last things or pretended to do them; to be in the cage had suddenly become her safety, and she was literally afraid of the alternate self who might be waiting outside. *He* might be waiting; it was he who was her alternate self, and of him she was afraid. The most extraordinary change had taken place in her from the moment of her catching the impression he seemed to have returned on purpose to give her. Just before she had done so, on that bewitched afternoon, she had seen herself approach without a scruple the porter at Park Chambers; then as the effect of the rush of a consciousness quite altered she had, on at last quitting Cocker's, gone straight home for the first time since her return from Bournemouth. She had passed his door every night for weeks, but nothing would have induced her to pass it now. This change was the tribute of her fear – the result of a change in himself as to which she needed no more explanation than his mere face vividly gave her; strange though it was to find an element of deterrence in the object that she regarded as the most beautiful in the world. He had taken it from her in the Park that night that she wanted him not to propose to her to sup; but he had put away the lesson by this time – he practically proposed supper every time he looked at her. This was what, for that matter, mainly filled the three days. He came in twice on each of these, and it was as if he came in to give her a chance to relent. That was after all, she said to herself in the intervals, the most that he did. There were ways, she fully recognised, in which he spared her, and other particular ways as to which she meant that her silence should be full to him of exquisite pleading. The most particular of all was his not being outside, at the corner, when she quitted the place for the night. This he might so easily have been – so easily if he hadn't been so nice. She continued to recognise in his forbearance the fruit of her dumb supplication, and the only compensation he found for it was the harmless freedom of being able to appear to say: 'Yes, I'm in town only for three or four days, but, you know, I *would* stay on.' He struck her as calling attention each day, each hour, to the rapid ebb of time; he exaggerated to the point of putting it that there were only two days more, that there was at last, dreadfully, only one.

There were other things still that he struck her as doing with a special intention; as to the most marked of which – unless indeed it were the most obscure – she might well have marvelled that it didn't seem to her more horrid. It was either the frenzy of her imagination or the disorder of his baffled passion that gave her once or twice the vision of his putting down redundant money – sovereigns not concerned with the little payments he was perpetually making – so that she might give him some sign of helping him to slip them over to her. What was most extraordinary in this impression was the amount of excuse that, with some incoherence, she found for him. He wanted to pay her because there was nothing to pay her for. He wanted to offer her things he knew she wouldn't take. He wanted to show her how much he respected her by giving her the supreme chance to show *him* she was respectable. Over the dryest transactions, at any rate, their eyes had out these questions. On the third day he put in a telegram that had evidently something of the same point as the stray sovereigns – a message that was in the first place concocted and that on a second thought he took back from her before she had stamped it. He had given her time to read it and had only then bethought himself that he had better not send it. If it was not to Lady Bradeen at Twindle – where she knew her ladyship then to be – this was because an address to Doctor Buzzard at Brickwood was just as good, with the added merit of its not giving away quite so much a person whom he had still, after all, in a manner to consider. It was of course most complicated, only half-lighted; but there was, discernibly enough, a scheme of communication in which Lady Bradeen at Twindle and Dr Buzzard at Brickwood were, within limits, one and the same person. The words he had shown her and then taken back consisted, at all events, of the brief but vivid phrase. 'Absolutely impossible.' The point was not that she should transmit it; the point was just that she should see it. What was absolutely impossible was that before he had settled something at Cocker's he should go either to Twindle or to Brickwood.

The logic of this, in turn, for herself, was that she could lend herself to no settlement so long as she so intensely knew. What she knew was that he was, almost under peril of life, clenched in a situation: therefore how could she also know where a poor girl in the P.O. might really stand? It was more and more between them that if he might convey to her he was free, with all the impossible locked away into a closed chapter, her own case might become different for her, she might understand and meet him and listen. But he could convey nothing of the sort, and he only fidgeted and floundered in his want of power. The chapter wasn't in the least closed, not for the other party; and the other party had a pull, somehow and somewhere: this his whole attitude and expression confessed, at the same time that they entreated her not to remember and not to mind. So long as she did remember and did mind he could only circle about and go and come, doing futile things of which he was ashamed. He was ashamed of his two words to Dr Buzzard; he went out of the shop as soon as he had crumpled up the paper again and thrust it into his pocket. It had been an abject little exposure of dreadful impossible passion. He appeared in fact to be too ashamed to come back. He had once more left town, and a first week elapsed, and a second. He had had naturally to return to the real mistress of his fate; she had insisted — she knew how to insist, and he couldn't put in another hour. There was always a day when she called time. It was known to our young friend moreover that he had now been dispatching telegrams from other offices. She knew at last so much that she had quite lost her earlier sense of merely guessing. There were no different shades of distinctness — it all bounced out.

XXII

Eighteen days elapsed, and she had begun to think it probable she should never see him again. He too then understood now: he had made out that she had secrets and reasons and impediments, that even a poor girl at the P.O. might have her complications. With the charm she had cast on him lightened by distance he had suffered a final delicacy to speak to him, had made up his mind that it would be only decent to let her alone. Never so much as during these latter days had she felt the precariousness of their relation – the happy beautiful untroubled original one, if it could only have been restored – in which the public servant and the casual public only were concerned. It hung at the best by the merest silken thread, which was at the mercy of any accident and might snap at any minute. She arrived by the end of the fortnight at the highest sense of actual fitness, never doubting that her decision was now complete. She would just give him a few days more to come back to her on a proper impersonal basis – for even to an embarrassing representative of the casual public a public servant with a conscience did owe something – and then would signify to Mr Mudge that she was ready for the little home. It had been visited, in the further talk she had had with him at Bournemouth, from garret to cellar, and they had especially lingered, with their respectively darkened brows, before the niche into which it was to be broached to her mother that she must find means to fit.

He had put it to her more definitely than before that his calculations had allowed for that dingy presence, and he had thereby marked the greatest impression he had ever made on her. It was a stroke superior even again to his handling of the drunken soldier. What she considered that in the face of it she hung on at Cocker's for was something she could only have described as the common fairness of a last word. Her actual last word had been, till it should be superseded, that she wouldn't forsake her other friend, and it stuck to her through thick and thin that she was still at her post and on her honour. This other friend had shown so much beauty of conduct already that he would surely after all just re-appear long enough to relieve her, to give her something she could take away. She saw it, caught it, at times, his parting present; and there were moments when she felt herself sitting like a beggar with a hand held out to an almsgiver who only fumbled. She hadn't taken the sovereigns, but she *would* take the penny. She heard, in imagination, on the counter, the ring of the copper. 'Don't put yourself out any longer,' he would say, 'for so bad a case. You've done all there is to be done. I thank and acquit and release you. Our lives take us. I don't know much – though I've really been interested – about yours, but I suppose you've got one. Mine at any rate will take *me* – and where it will. Heigh-ho! Good-bye.' And then once more, for the sweetest faintest flower of all: 'Only I say – see here!' She had framed the whole picture with a squareness that included also the image of how again she would decline to 'see there,' decline, as she might say, to see anywhere, see anything. Yet it befell that just in the fury of this escape she saw more than ever.

He came back one night with a rush, near the moment of their closing, and showed her a face so different and new, so upset and anxious, that almost anything seemed to look out of it but clear recognition. He poked in a telegram very much as if the simple sense of pressure, the distress of extreme haste, had blurred the remembrance of where in particular he was. But as she met his eyes a light came; it broke indeed on the spot into a positive conscious glare. That made up for everything, since it was an instant proclamation of the celebrated 'danger'; it seemed to pour things out in a flood. 'Oh yes, here it is – it's upon me at last! Forget, for God's sake, my having worried or bored you, and just help me, just *save* me, by getting this off without the loss of a second!' Something grave had clearly occurred, a crisis declared itself. She recognised immediately the person to whom the telegram was addressed – the Miss Dolman of Parade Lodge to whom Lady Bradeen had wired, at Dover, on the last occasion, and whom she had then, with her recollection of previous arrangements, fitted into a particular setting. Miss Dolman had figured before and not figured since, but she was now the subject of an imperative appeal. 'Absolutely necessary to see you. Take last train Victoria[35] if you can catch it. If not, earliest morning, and answer me direct either way.'

'Reply paid?' said the girl. Mr Buckton had just departed and the counter-clerk was at the sounder. There was no other representative of the public, and she had never yet, as it seemed to her, not even in the street nor in the Park, been so alone with him.

'Oh yes, reply paid, and as sharp as possible, please.'

She affixed the stamps in a flash. 'She'll catch the train!' she then declared to him breathlessly, as if she could absolutely guarantee it.

'I don't know – I hope so. It's awfully important. So kind of you. Awfully sharp, please.' It was wonderfully innocent now, his oblivion of all but his danger. Anything else that had ever passed between them was utterly out of it. Well, she had wanted him to be impersonal!

There was less of the same need therefore, happily, for herself; yet she only took time, before she flew to the sounder, to gasp at him: 'You're in trouble?'

'Horrid, horrid – there's a row!' But they parted, on it, in the next breath; and as she dashed at the sounder, almost pushing, in her violence, the counter-clerk off the stool, she caught the bang with which, at Cocker's door, in his further precipitation, he closed the apron of the cab into which he had leaped. As he rebounded to some other precaution suggested by his alarm, his appeal to Miss Dolman flashed straight away.

But she had not, on the morrow, been in the place five minutes before he was with her again, still more discomposed and quite, now, as she said to herself, like a frightened child coming to its mother. Her companions were there, and she felt it to be remarkable how, in the presence of his agitation, his mere scared exposed nature, she suddenly ceased to mind. It came to her as it had never come to her before that with absolute directness and assurance they might carry almost anything off. He had nothing to send – she was sure he had been wiring all over – and yet his business was evidently huge. There was nothing but that in his eyes – not a glimmer of reference or memory. He was almost haggard with anxiety and had clearly not slept a wink. Her pity for him would have given her any courage, and she seemed to know at last why she had been such a fool. 'She didn't come?' she panted.

'Oh yes, she came; but there has been some mistake. We want a telegram.'

'A telegram?'

'One that was sent from here ever so long ago. There was something in it that has to be recovered. Something very, *very* important, please – we want it immediately.'

He really spoke to her as if she had been some strange young woman at Knightsbridge or Paddington; but it had no other effect on her than to give her the measure of his tremendous flurry. Then it was that, above all, she felt how much she had missed in the gaps and blanks and absent answers – how much she had had to dispense with: it was now black darkness save for this little wild red flare. So much as that she saw, so much her mind dealt with. One of the lovers was quaking somewhere out of town, and the other was quaking just where he stood. This was vivid enough, and after an instant she knew it was all she wanted. She wanted no detail, no fact – she wanted no nearer vision of discovery or shame. 'When was your telegram? Do you mean you sent it from here?' She tried to do the young woman at Knightsbridge.

'Oh yes, from here – several weeks ago. Five, six, seven' he was confused and impatient – 'don't you remember?'

'Remember?' she could scarcely keep out of her face, at the word, the strangest of smiles.

But the way he didn't catch what it meant was perhaps even stranger still. 'I mean don't you keep the old ones?'

'For a certain time.'

'But how long?'

She thought; she *must* do the young woman, and she knew exactly what the young woman would say and, still more, wouldn't. 'Can you give me the date?'

'Oh God, no! It was some time or other in August – toward the end. It was to the same address as the one I gave you last night.'

'Oh!' said the girl, knowing at this the deepest thrill she had ever felt. It came to her there, with her eyes on his face, that she held the whole thing in her hand, held it as she held her pencil, which might have broken at that instant in her tightened grip. This made her feel like the very fountain of fate, but the emotion was such a flood that she had to press it back with all her force. That was positively the reason, again, of her flute-like Paddington tone. 'You can't give us anything a little nearer?' Her 'little' and her 'us' came straight from Paddington. These things were no false note for him – his difficulty absorbed them all. The eyes with which he pressed her, and in the depths of which she read terror and rage and literal tears, were just the same he would have shown any other prim person.

'I don't know the date. I only know the thing went from here, and just about the time I speak of. It wasn't delivered, you see. We've got to recover it.'

XXIII

She was as struck with the beauty of his plural pronoun as she had judged he might be with that of her own; but she knew now so well what she was about that she could almost play with him and with her new-born joy. 'You say "about the time you speak of." But I don't think you speak of an exact time – *do* you?'

He looked splendidly helpless. 'That's just what I want to find out. Don't you keep the old ones? – can't you look it up?'

Our young lady – still at Paddington – turned the question over. 'It wasn't delivered?'

'Yes, it *was*; yet, at the same time, don't you know? it wasn't.' He just hung back, but he brought it out. 'I mean it was intercepted, don't you know? and there was something in it.' He paused again and, as if to further his quest and woo and supplicate success and recovery, even smiled with an effort at the agreeable that was almost ghastly and that turned the knife in her tenderness. What must be the pain of it all, of the open gulf and the throbbing fever, when this was the mere hot breath? 'We want to get what was in it – to know what it was.'

'I see – I see.' She managed just the accent they had at Paddington when they stared like dead fish. 'And you have no clue?'

'Not at all – I've the clue I've just given you.'

'Oh the last of August?' If she kept it up long enough she would make him really angry.

'Yes, and the address, as I've said.'

'Oh the same as last night?'

He visibly quivered, as with a gleam of hope; but it only poured oil on her quietude, and she was still deliberate. She ranged some papers. 'Won't you look?' he went on.

'I remember your coming,' she replied.

He blinked with a new uneasiness; it might have begun to come to him, through her difference, that he was somehow different himself. 'You were much quicker then, you know!'

'So were you – you must do me that justice,' she answered with a smile. 'But let me see. Wasn't it Dover?'

'Yes, Miss Dolman –'

'Parade Lodge, Parade Terrace?'

'Exactly – thank you so awfully much!' He began to hope again. 'Then you *have* it – the other one?'

She hesitated afresh; she quite dangled him. 'It was brought by a lady?'

'Yes; and she put in by mistake something wrong. That's what we've got to get hold of!'

Heavens, what was he going to say? – flooding poor Paddington with wild betrayals! She couldn't too much, for her joy, dangle him, yet she couldn't either, for his dignity, warn or control or check him. What she found herself doing was just to treat herself to the middle way. 'It was intercepted?'

'It fell into the wrong hands. But there's something in it,' he continued to blurt out, 'that *may* be all right. That is if it's wrong, don't you know? It's all right if it's wrong,' he remarkably explained.

What *was* he, on earth, going to say? Mr Buckton and the counter-clerk were already interested; no one *would* have the decency to come in; and she was divided between her particular terror for him and her general curiosity. Yet she already saw with what brilliancy she could add, to carry the thing off, a little false knowledge to all her real. 'I quite understand,' she said with benevolent, with almost patronising quickness. 'The lady has forgotten what she did put.'

'Forgotten most wretchedly, and it's an immense inconvenience. It has only just been found that it didn't get there; so that if we could immediately have it –'

'Immediately?'

'Every minute counts. You *have*,' he pleaded, 'surely got them on file?'

'So that you can see it on the spot?'

'Yes, please – this very minute.' The counter rang with his knuckles, with the knob of his stick, with his panic of alarm. 'Do, do hunt it up!' he repeated.

'I dare say we could get it for you,' the girl sweetly returned.

'Get it?' he looked aghast. 'When?'

'Probably by to-morrow.'

'Then it isn't here?' – his face was pitiful.

She caught only the uncovered gleams that peeped out of the blackness, and she wondered what complication, even among the most supposable, the very worst, could be bad enough to account for the degree of his terror. There were twists and turns, there were places where the screw drew blood, that she couldn't guess. She was more and more glad she didn't want to. 'It has been sent on.'

'But how do you know if you don't look?'

She gave him a smile that was meant to be, in the absolute irony of its propriety, quite divine. 'It was August 23d, and we've nothing later here than August 27th.'

Something leaped into his face. '27th – 23d? Then you're sure? You know?'

She felt she scarce knew what – as if she might soon be pounced upon for some lurid connexion with a scandal. It was the queerest of all sensations, for she had heard, she had read, of these things, and the wealth of her intimacy with them at Cocker's might be supposed to have schooled and seasoned her. This particular one that she had really quite lived with was, after all, an old story; yet what it had been before was dim and distant beside the touch under which she now winced. Scandal? – it had never been but a silly word. Now it was a great tense surface, and the surface was somehow Captain Everard's wonderful face. Deep down in his eyes was a picture, a scene – a great place like a chamber of justice, where, before a watching crowd, a poor girl, exposed but heroic, swore with a quavering voice to a document, proved an *alibi*, supplied a link. In this picture she bravely took her place. 'It was the twenty-third.'

'Then can't you get it this morning – or some time to-day?'

She considered, still holding him with her look, which she then turned on her two companions, who were by this time unreservedly enlisted. She didn't care – not a scrap, and she glanced about for a piece of paper. With this she had to recognise the rigour of official thrift – a morsel of blackened blotter was the only loose paper to be seen. 'Have you got a card?' she said to her visitor. He was quite away from Paddington now, and the next instant, pocket-book in hand, he had whipped a card out. She gave no glance at the name on it – only turned it to the other side. She continued to hold him, she felt at present, as she had never held him; and her command of her colleagues was for the moment not less marked. She wrote something on the back of the card and pushed it across to him.

He fairly glared at it. 'Seven, nine, four –'

'Nine, six, one' – she obligingly completed the number. 'Is it right?' she smiled.

He took the whole thing in with a flushed intensity; then there broke out in him a visibility of relief that was simply a tremendous exposure. He shone at them all like a tall lighthouse, embracing even, for sympathy, the blinking young men. 'By all the powers – it's wrong!' And without another look, without a word of thanks, without time for anything or anybody, he turned on them the broad back of his great stature, straightened his triumphant shoulders and strode out of the place.

She was left confronted with her habitual critics.

' "If it's wrong it's all right!" ' she extravagantly quoted to them.

The counter-clerk was really awestricken. 'But how did you know, dear?'

'I remembered, love!'

Mr Buckton, on the contrary, was rude. 'And what game is that, miss?'

No happiness she had ever known came within miles of it, and some minutes elapsed before she could recall herself sufficiently to reply that it was none of his business.

XXIV

If life at Cocker's, with the dreadful drop of August, had lost something of its savour, she had not been slow to infer that a heavier blight had fallen on the graceful industry of Mrs Jordan. With Lord Rye and Lady Ventnor and Mrs Bubb all out of town, with the blinds down on all the homes of luxury, this ingenious woman might well have found her wonderful taste left quite on her hands. She bore up, however, in a way that began by exciting much of her young friend's esteem; they perhaps even more frequently met as the wine of life flowed less free from other sources, and each, in the lack of better diversion, carried on with more mystification for the other an intercourse that consisted not a little in peeping out and drawing back. Each waited for the other to commit herself, each profusely curtained for the other the limits of low horizons. Mrs Jordan was indeed probably the more reckless skirmisher; nothing could exceed her frequent incoherence unless it was indeed her occasional bursts of confidence. Her account of her private affairs rose and fell like a flame in the wind – sometimes the bravest bonfire and sometimes a handful of ashes. This our young woman took to be an effect of the position, at one moment and another, of the famous door of the great world. She had been struck in one of her ha'penny volumes with the translation of a French proverb according to which such a door, any door, had to be either open or shut;[36] and it seemed part of the precariousness of Mrs Jordan's life that hers mostly managed to be neither. There had been occasions when it appeared to gape wide – fairly to woo her across its threshold; there had been others, of an order distinctly disconcerting, when it was all but banged in her face. On the whole, however, she had evidently not lost heart; these still belonged to the class of things in spite of which she looked well. She intimated that the profits of her trade had swollen so as to float her through any state of the tide, and she had, besides this, a hundred profundities and explanations.

She rose superior, above all, on the happy fact that there were always gentlemen in town and that gentlemen were her greatest admirers; gentlemen from the City[37] in especial – as to whom she was full of information about the passion and pride excited in such breasts by the elements of her charming commerce. The City men *did* in short go in for flowers. There was a certain type of awfully smart stockbroker – Lord Rye called them Jews and bounders, but she didn't care – whose extravagance, she more than once threw out, had really, if one had any conscience, to be forcibly restrained. It was not perhaps a pure love of beauty; it was a matter of vanity and a sign of business; they wished to crush their rivals, and that was one of their weapons. Mrs Jordan's shrewdness was extreme; she knew in any case her customer – she dealt, as she said, with all sorts; and it was at the worst a race for her – a race even in the dull months – from one set of chambers to another. And then, after all, there were also still the ladies; the ladies of stockbroking circles were perpetually up and down. They were not quite perhaps Mrs Bubb or Lady Ventnor; but you couldn't tell the difference unless you quarrelled with them, and then you knew it only by their making-up sooner. These ladies formed the branch of her subject on which she most swayed in the breeze; to that degree that her confidant had ended with an inference or two tending to banish regret for opportunities not embraced. There were indeed tea-gowns that Mrs Jordan described – but tea-gowns were not the whole of respectability, and it was odd that a clergyman's widow should sometimes speak as if she almost thought so. She came back, it was true, unfailingly to Lord Rye, never, evidently, quite losing sight of him even on the longest excursions. That he was kindness itself had become in fact the very moral it all pointed – pointed in strange flashes of the poor woman's nearsighted eyes. She launched at her young friend portentous looks, solemn heralds of some extraordinary communication. The communication itself, from week to week, hung fire; but it was to the facts over which it hovered that she owed her power of going on. 'They *are*, in one way *and* another,' she often emphasised, 'a tower of strength'; and as the allusion was to the aristocracy the girl could quite wonder why, if they were so in 'one way,' they should require to be so in two. She thoroughly knew, however, how many ways Mrs Jordan counted in. It all meant simply that her fate was pressing her close. If that fate was to be sealed at the matrimonial altar it was perhaps not remarkable that she shouldn't come all at once to the scratch of overwhelming a mere telegraphist. It would necessarily present to such a person a prospect of regretful sacrifice. Lord Rye – if it *was* Lord Rye – wouldn't be 'kind' to a nonentity of that sort, even though people quite as good had been.

One Sunday afternoon in November they went, by arrangement, to church together; after which – on the inspiration of the moment; the arrangement had not included it – they proceeded to Mrs Jordan's lodging in the region of Maida Vale.[38] She had raved to her friend about her service of predilection; she was excessively 'high'[39] and had more than once wished to introduce the girl to the same comfort and privilege. There was a thick brown fog[40] and Maida Vale tasted of acrid smoke; but they had been sitting among chants and incense and wonderful music, during which, though the effect of such things on her mind was great, our young lady had indulged in a series of reflexions but indirectly related to them. One of these was the result of Mrs Jordan's having said to her on the way, and with a certain fine significance, that Lord Rye had been for some time in town. She had spoken as if it were a circumstance to which little required to be added – as if the bearing of such an item on her life might easily be grasped. Perhaps it was the wonder of whether Lord Rye wished to marry her that made her guest, with thoughts straying to that quarter, quite determine that some other nuptials also should take place at Saint Julian's.[41] Mr Mudge was still an attendant at his Wesleyan chapel, but this was the least of her worries – it had never even vexed her enough for her to so much as name it to Mrs Jordan. Mr Mudge's form of worship was one of several things – they made up in superiority and beauty for what they wanted in number – that she had long ago settled he should take from her, and she had now moreover for the first time definitely established her own. Its principal feature was that it was to be the same as that of Mrs Jordan and Lord Rye; which was indeed very much what she said to her hostess as they sat together later on. The brown fog was in this hostess's little parlour, where it acted as a postponement of the question of there being, besides, anything else than the teacups and a pewter pot and a very black little fire and a paraffin lamp without a shade. There was at any rate no sign of a flower; it was not for herself Mrs Jordan gathered sweets. The girl waited till they had had a cup of tea – waited for the announcement that she fairly believed her friend had, this time, possessed herself of her formally at last to make; but nothing came, after the interval, save a little poke at the fire, which was like the clearing of a throat for a speech.

XXV

'I think you must have heard me speak of Mr Drake?' Mrs Jordan had never looked so queer, nor her smile so suggestive of a large benevolent bite.

'Mr Drake? Oh yes; isn't he a friend of Lord Rye?'

'A great and trusted friend. Almost – I may say – a loved friend.'

Mrs Jordan's 'almost' had such an oddity that her companion was moved, rather flippantly perhaps, to take it up. 'Don't people as good as love their friends when they "trust" them?'

It pulled up a little the eulogist of Mr Drake. 'Well, my dear, I love you –'

'But you don't trust me?' the girl unmercifully asked.

Again Mrs Jordan paused – still she looked queer. 'Yes,' she replied with a certain austerity; 'that's exactly what I'm about to give you rather a remarkable proof of.' The sense of its being remarkable was already so strong that, while she bridled a little, this held her auditor in a momentary muteness of submission. 'Mr Drake has rendered his lordship for several years services that his lordship has highly appreciated and that make it all the more – a – unexpected that they should, perhaps a little suddenly, separate.'

'Separate?' Our young lady was mystified, but she tried to be interested; and she already saw that she had put the saddle on the wrong horse. She had heard something of Mr Drake, who was a member of his lordship's circle – the member with whom, apparently, Mrs Jordan's avocations had most happened to throw her. She was only a little puzzled at the 'separation.' 'Well, at any rate,' she smiled, 'if they separate as friends –!'

'Oh his lordship takes the greatest interest in Mr Drake's future. He'll do anything for him; he has in fact just done a great deal. There *must*, you know, be changes –!'

'No one knows it better than I,' the girl said. She wished to draw her interlocutress out. 'There will be changes enough for me.'

'You're leaving Cocker's?'

The ornament of that establishment waited a moment to answer, and then it was indirect. 'Tell me what *you're* doing.'

'Well, what will you think of it?'

'Why that you've found the opening you were always so sure of.'

Mrs Jordan, on this, appeared to muse with embarrassed intensity. 'I was always sure, yes – and yet I often wasn't!'

'Well, I hope you're sure now. Sure, I mean, of Mr Drake.'

'Yes, my dear, I think I may say I *am*. I kept him going till I was.'

'Then he's yours?'

'My very own.'

'How nice! And awfully rich?' our young woman went on.

Mrs Jordan showed promptly enough that she loved for higher things. 'Awfully handsome – six foot two. And he *has* put by.'

'Quite like Mr Mudge then!' that gentleman's friend rather desperately exclaimed.

'Oh not *quite*!' Mr Drake's was ambiguous about it, but the name of Mr Mudge had evidently given her some sort of stimulus. 'He'll have more opportunity now, at any rate. He's going to Lady Bradeen.'

'To Lady Bradeen?' This was bewilderment. '"Going" –?'

The girl had seen, from the way Mrs Jordan looked at her, that the effect of the name had been to make her let something out. 'Do you know her?'

She floundered, but she found her feet. 'Well, you'll remember I've often told you that if you've grand clients I have them too.'

'Yes,' said Mrs Jordan; 'but the great difference is that you hate yours, whereas I really love mine. *Do* you know Lady Bradeen?' she pursued.

'Down to the ground! She's always in and out.'

Mrs Jordan's foolish eyes confessed, in fixing themselves on this sketch, to a degree of wonder and even of envy. But she bore up and, with a certain gaiety, 'Do you hate *her*?' she demanded.

Her visitor's reply was prompt. 'Dear no! – not nearly so much as some of them. She's too outrageously beautiful.'

Mrs Jordan continued to gaze. 'Outrageously?'

'Well, yes; deliciously.' What was really delicious was Mrs Jordan's vagueness. 'You don't know her? you've not seen her?' her guest lightly continued.

'No, but I've heard a great deal about her.'

'So have I!' our young lady exclaimed.

Mrs Jordan looked an instant as if she suspected her good faith, or at least her seriousness. 'You know some friend –?'

'Of Lady Bradeen's? Oh yes – I know one.'

'Only one?'

The girl laughed out. 'Only one – but he's so intimate.'

Mrs Jordan just hesitated. 'He's a gentleman?'

'Yes, he's not a lady.'

Her interlocutress appeared to muse. 'She's immensely surrounded.'

'She *will* be – with Mr Drake!'

Mrs Jordan's gaze became strangely fixed. 'Is she *very* good-looking?'

'The handsomest person I know.'

Mrs Jordan continued to brood. 'Well, *I* know some beauties.' Then with her odd jerkiness: 'Do you think she looks *good*?'

'Because that's not always the case with the good-looking?' – the other took it up. 'No indeed, it isn't: that's one thing Cocker's has taught me. Still, there are some people who have everything. Lady Bradeen, at any rate, has enough: eyes and a nose and a mouth, a complexion, a figure –'

'A figure?' Mrs Jordan almost broke in.

'A figure, a head of hair!' The girl made a little conscious motion that seemed to let the hair all down, and her companion watched the wonderful show. 'But Mr Drake *is* another –?'

'Another?' – Mrs Jordan's thoughts had to come back from a distance.

'Of her ladyship's admirers. He's "going," you say, to her?'

At this Mrs Jordan really faltered. 'She has engaged him.'

'Engaged him?' – our young woman was quite at sea.

'In the same capacity as Lord Rye.'

'And was Lord Rye engaged?'

XXVI

Mrs Jordan looked away from her now – looked, she thought, rather injured and, as if trifled with, even a little angry. The mention of Lady Bradeen had frustrated for a while the convergence of our heroine's thoughts; but with this impression of her old friend's combined impatience and diffidence they began again to whirl round her, and continued it till one of them appeared to dart at her, out of the dance, as if with a sharp peck. It came to her with a lively shock, with a positive sting, that Mr Drake was – could it be possible? With the idea she found herself afresh on the edge of laughter, of a sudden and strange perversity of mirth. Mr Drake loomed, in a swift image, before her; such a figure as she had seen in open doorways of houses in Cocker's quarter – majestic, middle-aged, erect, flanked on either side by a footman and taking the name of a visitor. Mr Drake then verily *was* a person who opened the door! Before she had time, however, to recover from the effect of her evocation, she was offered a vision which quite engulfed it. It was communicated to her somehow that the face with which she had seen it rise prompted Mrs Jordan to dash, a bit wildly, at something, at anything, that might attenuate criticism. 'Lady Bradeen's re-arranging – she's going to be married.'

'Married?' The girl echoed it ever so softly, but there it was at last.

'Didn't you know it?'

She summoned all her sturdiness. 'No, she hasn't told me.'

'And her friends – haven't they?'

'I haven't seen any of them lately. I'm not so fortunate as *you*.'

Mrs Jordan gathered herself. 'Then you haven't even heard of Lord Bradeen's death?'

Her comrade, unable for a moment to speak, gave a slow headshake. 'You know it from Mr Drake?' It was better surely not to learn things at all than to learn them by the butler.

'She tells him everything.'

'And he tells *you* – I see.' Our young lady got up; recovering her muff and her gloves she smiled. 'Well, I haven't unfortunately any Mr Drake. I congratulate you with all my heart. Even without your sort of assistance, however, there's a trifle here and there that I do pick up. I gather that if she's to marry any one it must quite necessarily be my friend.'

Mrs Jordan was now also on her feet. 'Is Captain Everard your friend?'

The girl considered, drawing on a glove. 'I saw, at one time, an immense deal of him.'

Mrs Jordan looked hard at the glove, but she hadn't after all waited for that to be sorry it wasn't cleaner. 'What time was that?'

'It must have been the time you were seeing so much of Mr Drake.' She had now fairly taken it in: the distinguished person Mrs Jordan was to marry would answer bells and put on coals and superintend, at least, the cleaning of boots for the other distinguished person whom *she* might – well, whom she might have had, if she had wished, so much more to say to. 'Good-bye,' she added; 'good-bye.'

Mrs Jordan, however, again taking her muff from her, turned it over, brushed it off and thoughtfully peeped into it. 'Tell me this before you go. You spoke just now of your own changes. Do you mean that Mr Mudge –?'

'Mr Mudge has had great patience with me – he has brought me at last to the point. We're to be married next month and have a nice little home. But he's only a grocer, you know' – the girl met her friend's intent eyes – 'so that I'm afraid that, with the set you've got into, you won't see your way to keep up our friendship.'

Mrs Jordan for a moment made no answer to this; she only held the muff up to her face, after which she gave it back. 'You don't like it. I see, I see.'

To her guest's astonishment there were tears now in her eyes. 'I don't like what?' the girl asked.

'Why my engagement. Only, with your great cleverness,' the poor lady quavered out, 'you put it in your own way. I mean that you'll cool off. You already *have* –!' And on this, the next instant, her tears began to flow. She succumbed to them and collapsed; she sank down again, burying her face and trying to smother her sobs.

Her young friend stood there, still in some rigour, but taken much by surprise even if not yet fully moved to pity. 'I don't put anything in any "way", and I'm very glad you're suited. Only, you know, you did put to me so splendidly what, even for me, if I had listened to you, it might lead to.'

Mrs Jordan kept up a mild thin weak wail; then, drying her eyes, as feebly considered this reminder. 'It has led to my not starving!' she faintly gasped.

Our young lady, at this, dropped into the place beside her, and now, in a rush, the small silly misery was clear. She took her hand as a sign of pitying it, then, after another instant, confirmed this expression with a consoling kiss. They sat there together; they looked out, hand in hand, into the damp dusky shabby little room and into the future, of no such very different complexion, at last accepted by each. There was no definite utterance, on either side, of Mr Drake's position in the great world, but the temporary collapse of his prospective bride threw all further necessary light; and what our heroine saw and felt for in the whole business was the vivid reflexion of her own dreams and delusions and her own return to reality. Reality, for the poor things they both were, could only be ugliness and obscurity, could never be the escape, the rise. She pressed her friend – she had tact enough for that – with no other personal question, brought on no need of further revelations, only just continued to hold and comfort her and to acknowledge by stiff little forbearances the common element in their fate. She felt indeed magnanimous in such matters; since if it was very well, for condolence or reassurance, to suppress just then invidious shrinkings, she yet by no means saw herself sitting down, as she might say, to the same table with Mr Drake. There would luckily, to all appearance, be little question of tables; and the circumstance that, on their peculiar lines, her friend's interests would still attach themselves to Mayfair flung over Chalk Farm the first radiance it had shown. Where was one's pride and one's passion when the real way to judge of one's luck was by making not the wrong but the right comparison? Before she had again gathered herself to go she felt very small and cautious and thankful. 'We shall have our own house,' she said, 'and you must come very soon and let me show it you.'

'*We* shall have our own too,' Mrs Jordan replied; 'for, don't you know? he makes it a condition that he sleeps out.'

'A condition?' – the girl felt out of it.

'For any new position. It was on that he parted with Lord Rye. His lordship can't meet it. So Mr Drake has given him up.'

'And all for you?' – our young woman put it as cheerfully as possible.

'For me and Lady Bradeen. Her ladyship's too glad to get him at any price. Lord Rye, out of interest in us, had in fact quite *made* her take him. So, as I tell you, he will have his own establishment.'

Mrs Jordan, in the elation of it, had begun to revive; but there was nevertheless between them rather a conscious pause – a pause in which neither visitor nor hostess brought out a hope or an invitation. It expressed in the last resort that, in spite of submission and sympathy, they could now after all only look at each other across the social gulf. They remained together as if it would be indeed their last chance, still sitting, though awkwardly, quite close, and feeling also – and this most unmistakeably – that there was one thing more to go into. By the time it came to the surface, moreover, our young friend had recognised the whole of the main truth, from which she even drew again a slight irritation. It was not the main truth perhaps that most signified; but after her momentary effort, her embarrassment and her tears Mrs Jordan had begun to sound afresh – and even without speaking – the note of a social connexion. She hadn't really let go of it that she was marrying into society. Well, it was a harmless compensation, and it was all the prospective bride of Mr Mudge had to leave with her.

XXVII

This young lady at last rose again, but she lingered before going. 'And has Captain Everard nothing to say to it?'

'To what, dear?'

'Why, to such questions – the domestic arrangements, things in the house.'

'How *can* he, with any authority, when nothing in the house is his?'

'Not his?' The girl wondered, perfectly conscious of the appearance she thus conferred on Mrs Jordan of knowing, in comparison with herself, so tremendously much about it. Well, there were things she wanted so to get at that she was willing at last, though it hurt her, to pay for them with humiliation. 'Why are they not his?'

'Don't you know, dear, that he has nothing?'

'Nothing?' It was hard to see him in such a light, but Mrs Jordan's power to answer for it had a superiority that began, on the spot, to grow. 'Isn't he rich?'

Mrs Jordan looked immensely, looked both generally and particularly, informed. 'It depends upon what you call –! Not at any rate in the least as *she* is. What does he bring? Think what she has. And then, love, his debts.'

'His debts?' His young friend was fairly betrayed into helpless innocence. She could struggle a little, but she had to let herself go; and if she had spoken frankly she would have said: 'Do tell me, for I don't know so much about him as *that*!' As she didn't speak frankly she only said: 'His debts are nothing – when she so adores him.'

Mrs Jordan began to fix her again, and now she saw that she must only take it all. That was what it had come to: his having sat with her there on the bench and under the trees in the summer darkness and put his hand on her, making her know what he would have said if permitted; his having returned to her afterwards, repeatedly, with supplicating eyes and a fever in his blood; and her having on her side, hard and pedantic, helped by some miracle and with her impossible condition, only answered him, yet supplicating back, through the bars of the cage – all simply that she might hear of him, now for ever lost, only through Mrs Jordan, who touched him through Mr Drake, who reached him through Lady Bradeen. 'She adores him – but of course that wasn't all there was about it.'

The girl met her eyes a minute, then quite surrendered. 'What was there else about it?'

'Why, don't you know?' – Mrs Jordan was almost compassionate.

Her interlocutress had, in the cage, sounded depths, but there was a suggestion here somehow of an abyss quite measureless. 'Of course I know she would never let him alone.'

'How *could* she – fancy! – when he had so compromised her?'

The most artless cry they had ever uttered broke, at this, from the younger pair of lips. '*Had* he so –?'

'Why, don't you know the scandal?'

Our heroine thought, recollected; there was something, whatever it was, that she knew after all much more of than Mrs Jordan. She saw him again as she had seen him come that morning to recover the telegram – she saw him as she had seen him leave the shop. She perched herself a moment on this. 'Oh there was nothing public.'

'Not exactly public – no. But there was an awful scare and an awful row. It was all on the very point of coming out. Something was lost – something was found.'

'Ah yes,' the girl replied, smiling as if with the revival of a blurred memory; 'something was found.'

'It all got about – and there was a point at which Lord Bradeen had to act.'

'Had to – yes. But he didn't.'

Mrs Jordan was obliged to admit it. 'No, he didn't. And then, luckily for them, he died.'

'I didn't know about his death,' her companion said.

'It was nine weeks ago, and most sudden. It has given them a prompt chance.'

'To get married' – this was a wonder – 'within nine weeks?'

'Oh not immediately, but – in all the circumstances – very quietly and, I assure you, very soon. Every preparation's made. Above all she holds him.'

'Oh yes, she holds him!' our young friend threw off. She had this before her again a minute; then she continued: 'You mean through his having made her talked about?'

'Yes, but not only that. She has still another pull.'

'Another?'

Mrs Jordan hesitated. 'Why, he was *in* something.'

Her comrade wondered. 'In what?'

'I don't know. Something bad. As I tell you, something was found.'

The girl stared. 'Well?'

'It would have been very bad for him. But she helped him some way – she recovered it, got hold of it. It's even said she stole it!'

Our young woman considered afresh. 'Why it was what was found that precisely saved him.'

Mrs Jordan, however, was positive. 'I beg your pardon. I happen to know.'

Her disciple faltered but an instant. 'Do you mean through Mr Drake? Do they tell *him* these things?'

'A good servant,' said Mrs Jordan, now thoroughly superior and proportionately sententious, 'doesn't need to be told! Her ladyship saved – as a woman so often saves! – the man she loves.'

This time our heroine took longer to recover herself, but she found a voice at last. 'Ah well – of course I don't know! The great thing was that he got off. They seem then, in a manner,' she added, 'to have done a great deal for each other.'

'Well, it's she that has done most. She has him tight.'

'I see, I see. Good-bye.' The women had already embraced, and this was not repeated; but Mrs Jordan went down with her guest to the door of the house. Here again the younger lingered, reverting, though three or four other remarks had on the way passed between them, to Captain Everard and Lady Bradeen. 'Did you mean just now that if she hadn't saved him, as you call it, she wouldn't hold him so tight?'

'Well, I dare say,' Mrs Jordan, on the doorstep, smiled with a reflexion that had come to her; she took one of her big bites of the brown gloom. 'Men always dislike one when they've done one an injury.'

'But what injury had he done her?'

'The one I've mentioned. He *must* marry her, you know.'

'And didn't he want to?'

'Not before.'

'Not before she recovered the telegram?'

Mrs Jordan was pulled up a little. 'Was it a telegram?'

The girl hesitated. 'I thought you said so. I mean whatever it was.'

'Yes, whatever it was, I don't think she saw *that*.'

'So she just nailed him?'

'She just nailed him.' The departing friend was now at the bottom of the little flight of steps; the other was at the top, with a certain thickness of fog. 'And when am I to think of you in your little home? – next month?' asked the voice from the top.

'At the very latest. And when am I to think of you in yours?'

'Oh even sooner. I feel, after so much talk with you about it, as if I were already there!' Then 'Good-bye!' came out of the fog.

'Good-bye!' went into it. Our young lady went into it also, in the opposed quarter, and presently, after a few sightless turns, came out on the Paddington canal. Distinguishing vaguely what the low parapet enclosed she stopped close to it and stood a while very intently, but perhaps still sightlessly, looking down on it. A policeman, while she remained, strolled past her; then, going his way a little further and half lost in the atmosphere, paused and watched her. But she was quite unaware – she was full of her thoughts. They were too numerous to find a place just here, but two of the number may at least be mentioned. One of these was that, decidedly, her little home must be not for next month, but for next week; the other, which came indeed as she resumed her walk and went her way, was that it was strange such a matter should be at last settled for her by Mr Drake.

The Real Right Thing

I

When, after the death of Ashton Doyne – but three months after – George Withermore was approached, as the phrase is, on the subject of a 'volume,' the communication came straight from his publishers, who had been, and indeed much more, Doyne's own; but he was not surprised to learn, on the occurrence of the interview they next suggested, that a certain pressure as to the early issue of a Life had been applied them by their late client's widow. Doyne's relations with his wife had been to Withermore's knowledge a special chapter – which would present itself, by the way, as a delicate one for the biographer; but a sense of what she had lost, and even of what she had lacked, had betrayed itself, on the poor woman's part, from the first days of her bereavement, sufficiently to prepare an observer at all initiated for some attitude of reparation, some espousal even exaggerated of the interests of a distinguished name. George Withermore was, as he felt, initiated; yet what he had not expected was to hear that she had mentioned him as the person in whose hands she would most promptly place the materials for a book.

These materials – diaries, letters, memoranda, notes, documents of many sorts – were her property and wholly in her control, no conditions at all attaching to any portion of her heritage; so that she was free at present to do as she liked – free in particular to do nothing. What Doyne would have arranged had he had time to arrange could be but supposition and guess. Death had taken him too soon and too suddenly, and there was all the pity that the only wishes he was known to have expressed were wishes leaving it positively out. He had broken short off – that was the way of it; and the end was ragged and needed trimming. Withermore was conscious, abundantly, of how close he had stood to him, but also was not less aware of his comparative obscurity. He was young, a journalist, a critic, a hand-to-mouth character, with little, as yet, of any striking sort, to show. His writings were few and small, his relations scant and vague. Doyne, on the other hand, had lived long enough – above all had had talent enough – to become great, and among his many friends gilded also with greatness were several to whom his wife would have affected those who knew her as much more likely to appeal.

385

The preference she had at all events uttered – and uttered in a roundabout considerate way that left him a measure of freedom – made our young man feel that he must at least see her and that there would be in any case a good deal to talk about. He immediately wrote to her, she as promptly named an hour, and they had it out. But he came away with his particular idea immensely strengthened. She was a strange woman, and he had never thought her an agreeable, yet there was something that touched him now in her bustling blundering zeal. She wanted the book to make up, and the individual whom, of her husband's set, she probably believed she might most manipulate was in every way to help it to do so. She hadn't taken Doyne seriously enough in life, but the biography should be a full reply to every imputation on herself. She had scantly known how such books were constructed, but she had been looking and had learned something. It alarmed Withermore a little from the first to see that she'd wish to go in for quantity. She talked of 'volumes,' but he had his notion of that.

'My thought went straight to *you*, as his own would have done,' she had said almost as soon as she rose before him there in her large array of mourning – with her big black eyes, her big black wig, her big black fan and gloves, her general gaunt ugly tragic, but striking and, as might have been thought from a certain point of view, 'elegant' presence. 'You're the one he liked most; oh *much*!' – and it had quite sufficed to turn Withermore's head. It little mattered that he could afterwards wonder if she had known Doyne enough, when it came to that, to be sure. He would have said for himself indeed that her testimony on such a point could scarcely count. Still, there was no smoke without fire;[1] she knew at least what she meant, and he wasn't a person she could have an interest in flattering. They went up together without delay to the great man's vacant study at the back of the house and looking over the large green garden – a beautiful and inspiring scene to poor Withermore's view – common to the expensive row.

'You can perfectly work here, you know,' said Mrs Doyne: 'you shall have the place quite to yourself – I'll give it all up to you; so that in the evenings in particular, don't you see? it will be perfection for quiet and privacy.'

Perfection indeed, the young man felt as he looked about – having explained that, as his actual occupation was an evening paper and his earlier hours, for a long time yet, regularly taken up, he should have to come always at night. The place was full of their lost friend; everything in it had belonged to him; everything they touched had been part of his life. It was all at once too much for Withermore – too great an honour and even too great a care; memories still recent came back to him, so that, while his heart beat faster and his eyes filled with tears, the pressure of his loyalty seemed almost more than he could carry. At the sight of his tears Mrs Doyne's own rose to her lids, and the two for a minute only looked at each other. He half-expected her to break out 'Oh help me to feel as I know you know I want to feel!' And after a little one of them said, with the other's deep assent – it didn't matter which: 'It's here that we're *with* him.' But it was definitely the young man who put it, before they left the room, that it was there he was with themselves.

The young man began to come as soon as he could arrange it, and then it was, on the spot, in the charmed stillness, between the lamp and the fire and with the curtains drawn, that a certain intenser consciousness set in for him. He escaped from the black London November; he passed through the large hushed house and up the red-carpeted staircase where he only found in his path the whisk of a soundless trained maid or the reach, out of an open room, of Mrs Doyne's queenly weeds[2] and approving tragic face; and then, by a mere touch of the well-made door that gave so sharp and pleasant a click, shut himself in for three or four warm hours with the spirit – as he had always distinctly declared it – of his master. He was not a little frightened when, even the first night, it came over him that he had really been most affected, in the whole matter, by the prospect, the privilege and the luxury, of this sensation. He hadn't, he could now reflect, definitely considered the question of the book – as to which there was here even already much to consider: he had simply let his affection and admiration – to say nothing of his gratified pride – meet to the full the temptation Mrs Doyne had offered them.

How did he know without more thought, he might begin to ask himself, that the book was on the whole to be desired? What warrant had he ever received from Ashton Doyne himself for so direct and, as it were, so familiar an approach? Great was the art of biography, but there were lives and lives, there were subjects and subjects. He confusedly recalled, so far as that went, old words dropped by Doyne over contemporary compilations, suggestions of how he himself discriminated as to other heroes and other panoramas. He even remembered how his friend would at moments have shown himself as holding that the 'literary' career might – save in the case of a Johnson and a Scott, with a Boswell and a Lockhart[3] to help – best content itself to be represented. The artist was what he *did* – he was nothing else. Yet how on the other hand wasn't *he*, George Withermore, poor devil, to have jumped at the chance of spending his winter in an intimacy so rich? It had been simply dazzling – that was the fact. It hadn't been the 'terms,' from the publishers – though these were, as they said at the office, all right; it had been Doyne himself, his company and contact and presence, it had been just what it was turning out, the possibility of an intercourse closer than that of life. Strange that death, of the two things, should have the fewer mysteries and secrets! The first night our young man was alone in the room it struck him his master and he were really for the first time together.

II

Mrs Doyne had for the most part let him expressively alone, but she had on two or three occasions looked in to see if his needs had been met, and he had had the opportunity of thanking her on the spot for the judgement and zeal with which she had smoothed his way. She had to some extent herself been looking things over and had been able already to muster several groups of letters; all the keys of drawers and cabinets she had moreover from the first placed in his hands, with helpful information as to the apparent whereabouts of different matters. She had put him, to be brief, in the fullest possible possession, and whether or no her husband had trusted her she at least, it was clear, trusted her husband's friend. There grew upon Withermore nevertheless the impression that in spite of all these offices she wasn't yet at peace and that a certain unassuageable anxiety continued even to keep step with her confidence. Though so full of consideration she was at the same time perceptibly *there*: he felt her, through a supersubtle sixth sense that the whole connexion had already brought into play, hover, in the still hours, at the top of landings and on the other side of doors; he gathered from the soundless brush of her skirts the hint of her watchings and waitings. One evening when, at his friend's table, he had lost himself in the depths of correspondence, he was made to start and turn by the suggestion that some one was behind him. Mrs Doyne had come in without his hearing the door, and she gave a strained smile as he sprang to his feet. 'I hope,' she said, 'I haven't frightened you.'

'Just a little – I was so absorbed. It was as if, for the instant,' the young man explained, 'it had been himself.'

The oddity of her face increased in her wonder. 'Ashton?'

'He does seem so near,' said Withermore.

'To you too?'

This naturally struck him. 'He does then to you?'

She waited, not moving from the spot where she had first stood, but looking round the room as if to penetrate its duskier angles. She had a way of raising to the level of her nose the big black fan which she apparently never laid aside and with which she thus covered the lower half of her face, her rather hard eyes, above it, becoming the more ambiguous. 'Sometimes.'

'Here,' Withermore went on, 'it's as if he might at any moment come in. That's why I jumped just now. The time's so short since he really used to – it only *was* yesterday. I sit in his chair, I turn his books, I use his pens, I stir his fire – all exactly as if, learning he would presently be back from a walk, I had come up here contentedly to wait. It's delightful – but it's strange.'

Mrs Doyne, her fan still up, listened with interest. 'Does it worry you?'

'No – I like it.'

Again she faltered. 'Do you ever feel as if he were – a – quite – a – personally in the room?'

'Well, as I said just now,' her companion laughed, 'on hearing you behind me I seemed to take it so. What do we want, after all,' he asked, 'but that he shall be with us?'

'Yes, as you said he'd be – that first time.' She gazed in full assent. 'He *is* with us.'

She was rather portentous, but Withermore took it smiling. 'Then we must keep him. We must do only what he'd like.'

'Oh only that of course – only. But if he *is* here –?' And her sombre eyes seemed to throw it out in vague distress over her fan.

'It proves he's pleased and wants only to help? Yes, surely; it must prove that.'

She gave a light gasp and looked again round the room. 'Well,' she said as she took leave of him, 'remember that I too want only to help.' On which, when she had gone, he felt sufficiently that she had come in simply to see he was all right.

He was all right more and more, it struck him after this, for as he began to get into his work he moved, as it appeared to him, but the closer to the idea of Doyne's personal presence. When once this fancy had begun to hang about him he welcomed it, persuaded it, encouraged it, quite cherished it, looking forward all day to feeling it renew itself in the evening, and waiting for the growth of dusk very much as one of a pair of lovers might wait for the hour of their appointment. The smallest accidents humoured and confirmed it, and by the end of three or four weeks he had come fully to regard it as the consecration of his enterprise. Didn't it just settle the question of what Doyne would have thought of what they were doing? What they were doing was what he wanted done, and they could go on from step to step without scruple or doubt. Withermore rejoiced indeed at moments to feel this certitude: there were times of dipping deep into some of Doyne's secrets when it was particularly pleasant to be able to hold that Doyne desired him, as it were, to know them. He was learning many things he hadn't suspected – drawing many curtains, forcing many doors, reading many riddles, going, in general, as they said, behind almost everything. It was at an occasional sharp turn of some of the duskier of these wanderings 'behind' that he really, of a sudden, most felt himself, in the intimate sensible way, face to face with his friend; so that he could scarce have told, for the instant, if their meeting occurred in the narrow passage and tight squeeze of the past or at the hour and in the place that actually held him. Was it a matter of '67? – or but of the other side of the table?

Happily, at any rate, even in the vulgarest light publicity could ever shed, there would be the great fact of the way Doyne was 'coming out.' He was coming out too beautifully – better yet than such a partisan as Withermore could have supposed. All the while as well, nevertheless, how would this partisan have represented to any one else the special state of his own consciousness? It wasn't a thing to talk about – it was only a thing to feel. There were moments for instance when, while he bent over his papers, the light breath of his dead host was as distinctly in his hair as his own elbows were on the table before him. There were moments when, had he been able to look up, the other side of the table would have shown him this companion as vividly as the shaded lamplight showed him his page. That he couldn't at such a juncture look up was his own affair, for the situation was ruled – that was but natural – by deep delicacies and fine timidities, the dread of too sudden or too rude an advance. What was intensely in the air was that if Doyne *was* there it wasn't nearly so much for himself as for the young priest of his altar. He hovered and lingered, he came and went, he might almost have been, among the books and the papers, a hushed discreet librarian, doing the particular things, rendering the quiet aid, liked by men of letters.

Withermore himself meanwhile came and went, changed his place, wandered on quests either definite or vague; and more than once when, taking a book down from a shelf and finding in it marks of Doyne's pencil, he got drawn on and lost he had heard documents on the table behind him gently shifted and stirred, had literally, on his return, found some letter mislaid pushed again into view, some thicket cleared by the opening of an old journal at the very date he wanted. How should he have gone so, on occasion, to the special box or drawer, out of fifty receptacles, that would help him, had not his mystic assistant happened, in fine prevision, to tilt its lid or pull it half-open, just in the way that would catch his eye? – in spite, after all, of the fact of lapses and intervals in which, *could* one have really looked, one would have seen somebody standing before the fire a trifle detached and over-erect—somebody fixing one the least bit harder than in life.

III

That this auspicious relation had in fact existed, had continued, for two or three weeks, was sufficiently shown by the dawn of the distress with which our young man found himself aware of having, for some reason, from the close of a certain day, begun to miss it. The sign of that was an abrupt surprised sense – on the occasion of his mislaying a marvellous unpublished page which, hunt where he would, remained stupidly irrecoverably lost – that his protected state was, with all said, exposed to some confusion and even to some depression. If, for the joy of the business, Doyne and he had, from the start, been together, the situation had within a few days of his first suspicion of it suffered the odd change of their ceasing to be so. That was what was the matter, he mused, from the moment an impression of mere mass and quantity struck him as taking, in his happy outlook at his material, the place of the pleasant assumption of a clear course and a quick pace. For five nights he struggled; then, never at his table, wandering about the room, taking up his references only to lay them down, looking out of the window, poking the fire, thinking strange thoughts and listening for signs and sounds not as he suspected or imagined, but as he vainly desired and invoked them, he yielded to the view that he was for the time at least forsaken.

The extraordinary thing thus became that it made him not only sad but in a high degree uneasy not to feel Doyne's presence. It was somehow stranger he shouldn't be there than it had ever been he *was* – so strange indeed at last that Withermore's nerves found themselves quite illogically touched. They had taken kindly enough to what was of an order impossible to explain, perversely reserving their sharpest state for the return to the normal, the supersession of the false. They were remarkably beyond control when finally, one night after his resisting them an hour or two, he simply edged out of the room. It had now but for the first time become impossible to him to stay. Without design, but panting a little and positively as a man scared, he passed along his usual corridor and reached the top of the staircase. From this point he saw Mrs Doyne look up at him from the bottom quite as if she had known he would come; and the most singular thing of all was that, though he had been conscious of no motion to resort to her, had only been prompted to relieve himself by escape, the sight of her position made him recognise it as just, quickly feel it as a part of some monstrous oppression that was closing over them both. It was wonderful how, in the mere modern London hall, between the Tottenham Court Road rugs[4] and the electric light, it came up to him from the tall black lady, and went again from him down to her, that he knew what she meant by looking as if he would know. He descended straight, she turned into her own little lower room, and there, the next thing, with the door shut, they were, still in silence and with queer faces, confronted over confessions that had taken sudden life from these two or three movements. Withermore gasped as it came to him why he had lost his friend. 'He has been with *you*?'

With this it was all out – out so far that neither had to explain and that, when 'What do you suppose is the matter?' quickly passed between them, one appeared to have said it as much as the other. Withermore looked about at the small bright room in which, night after night, she had been living her life as he had been living his own upstairs. It was pretty, cosy, rosy; but she had by turns felt in it what he had felt and heard in it what he had heard. Her effect there – fantastic black, plumed and extravagant, upon deep pink — was that of some 'decadent' coloured print,[5] some poster of the newest school. 'You understood he had left me?' he asked.

She markedly wished to make it clear. 'This evening — yes. I've made things out.'

'You knew — before — that he was with me?'

She hesitated again. 'I felt he wasn't with *me*. But on the stairs —'

'Yes?'

'Well — he passed; more than once. He was in the house. And at your door —'

'Well?' he went on as she once more faltered.

'If I stopped I could sometimes tell. And from your face,' she added, 'to-night, at any rate, I knew your state.'

'And that was why you came out?'

'I thought you'd come to me.'

He put out to her, on this, his hand, and they thus for a minute of silence held each other clasped. There was no peculiar presence for either now — nothing more peculiar than that of each for the other. But the place had suddenly become as if consecrated, and Withermore played over it again his anxiety. 'What *is* then the matter?'

'I only want to do the real right thing,' she returned after her pause.

'And aren't we doing it?'

'I wonder. Aren't *you*?'

He wondered too. 'To the best of my belief. But we must think.'

'We must think,' she echoed. And they did think — thought with intensity the rest of that evening together, and thought independently (Withermore at least could answer for himself) during many days that followed. He intermitted a little his visits and his work, trying, all critically, to catch himself in the act of some mistake that might have accounted for their disturbance. Had he taken, on some important point — or looked as if he might take — some wrong line or wrong view? had he somewhere benightedly falsified or inadequately insisted? He went back at last with the idea of having guessed two or three questions he might have been on the way to muddle; after which he had abovestairs, another period of agitation, presently followed by another interview below with Mrs Doyne, who was still troubled and flushed.

'He's there?'

'He's there.'

'I knew it!' she returned in an odd gloom of triumph. Then as to make it clear: 'He hasn't been again with *me*.'

'Nor with me again to help,' said Withermore.

She considered. 'Not to help?'

'I can't make it out – I'm at sea. Do what I will I feel I'm wrong.'

She covered him a moment with her pompous pain. 'How do you feel it?'

'Why by things that happen. The strangest things. I can't describe them – and you wouldn't believe them.'

'Oh yes I should!' Mrs Doyne cried.

'Well, he intervenes.' Withermore tried to explain. 'However I turn I find him.'

She earnestly followed. '"Find" him?'

'I meet him. He seems to rise there before me.'

Staring, she waited a little. 'Do you mean you see him?'

'I feel as if at any moment I may. I'm baffled. I'm checked.' Then he added: 'I'm afraid.'

'Of *him*?' asked Mrs Doyne.

He thought. 'Well – of what I'm doing.'

'Then what, that's so awful, *are* you doing?'

'What you proposed to me. Going into his life.'

She showed, in her present gravity, a new alarm. 'And don't you *like* that?'

'Doesn't *he*? That's the question. We lay him bare. We serve him up. What is it called? We give him to the world.'

Poor Mrs Doyne, as if on a menace to her hard atonement, glared at this for an instant in deeper gloom. 'And why shouldn't we?'

'Because we don't know. There are natures, there are lives, that shrink. He mayn't wish it,' said Withermore. 'We never asked him.'

'How *could* we?'

He was silent a little. 'Well, we ask him now. That's after all what our start has so far represented. We've put it to him.'

'Then – if he has been with us – we've had his answer.'

Withermore spoke now as if he knew what to believe. 'He hasn't been "with" us – he has been against us.'

'Then why did you think –'

'What I *did* think at first – that what he wishes to make us feel is his sympathy? Because I was in my original simplicity mistaken. I was – I don't know what to call it – so excited and charmed that I didn't understand. But I understand at last. He only wanted to communicate. He strains forward out of his darkness, he reaches toward us out of his mystery, he makes us dim signs out of his horror.'

'"Horror"?' Mrs Doyne gasped with her fan up to her mouth.

'At what we're doing.' He could by this time piece it all together. 'I see now that at first –'

'Well, what?'

'One had simply to feel he was there and therefore not indifferent. And the beauty of that misled me. But he's there as a protest.'

'Against *my* Life?' Mrs Doyne wailed.

'Against *any* Life. He's there to *save* his Life. He's there to be let alone.'

'So you give up?' she almost shrieked.

He could only meet her. 'He's there as a warning.'

For a moment, on this, they looked at each other deep. 'You *are* afraid!' she at last brought out.

It affected him, but he insisted. 'He's there as a curse!'

With that they parted, but only for two or three days; her last word to him continuing to sound so in his ears that, between his need really to satisfy her and another need presently to be noted, he felt he mightn't yet take up his stake. He finally went back at his usual hour and found her in her usual place. 'Yes, I *am* afraid,' he announced as if he had turned that well over and knew now all it meant. 'But I gather you're not.'

She faltered, reserving her word. 'What is it you fear?'

'Well, that if I go on I *shall* see him.'

'And then —?'

'Oh then,' said George Withermore, 'I *should* give up!'

She weighed it with her proud but earnest air. 'I think, you know, we must have a clear sign.'

'You wish me to try again?'

She debated. 'You see what it means — for me — to give up.'

'Ah but *you* needn't,' Withermore said.

She seemed to wonder, but in a moment went on. 'It would mean that he won't take from me —' But she dropped for despair.

'Well, what?'

'Anything,' said poor Mrs Doyne.

He faced her a moment more. 'I've thought myself of the clear sign. I'll try again.'

As he was leaving her however she remembered. 'I'm only afraid that to-night there's nothing ready — no lamp and no fire.'

'Never mind,' he said from the foot of the stairs; 'I'll find things.'

To which she answered that the door of the room would probably at any rate be open; and retired again as to wait for him. She hadn't long to wait; though, with her own door wide and her attention fixed, she may not have taken the time quite as it appeared to her visitor. She heard him, after an interval, on the stair, and he presently stood at her entrance, where, if he hadn't been precipitate, but rather, for step and sound, backward and vague, he showed at least as livid and blank.

'I give up.'

'Then you've seen him?'

'On the threshold – guarding it.'

'Guarding it?' She glowed over her fan. 'Distinct?'

'Immense. But dim. Dark. Dreadful,' said poor George Withermore.

She continued to wonder. 'You didn't go in?'

The young man turned away. 'He forbids!'

'You say *I* needn't,' she went on after a moment. 'Well then need I?'

'See him?' George Withermore asked.

She waited an instant. 'Give up.'

'You must decide.' For himself he could at last but sink to the sofa with his bent face in his hands. He wasn't quite to know afterwards how long he had sat so; it was enough that what he did next know was that he was alone among her favourite objects. Just as he gained his feet however, with this sense and that of the door standing open to the hall, he found himself afresh confronted, in the light, the warmth, the rosy space, with her big black perfumed presence. He saw at a glance, as she offered him a huger bleaker stare over the mask of her fan, that she had been above; and so it was that they for the last time faced together their strange question. 'You've seen him?' Withermore asked.

He was to infer later on from the extraordinary way she closed her eyes and, as if to steady herself, held them tight and long, in silence, that beside the unutterable vision of Ashton Doyne's wife his own might rank as an escape. He knew before she spoke that all was over. 'I give up.'

Broken Wings

Conscious as he was of what was between them, though perhaps less conscious than ever of why there should at that time of day be anything, he would yet scarce have supposed they could be so long in a house together without some word or some look. It had been since the Saturday afternoon, and that made twenty-four hours. The party — five-and-thirty people and some of them great — was one in which words and looks might more or less have gone astray. The effect, none the less, he judged, would have been, for her quite as for himself, that no sound and no sign from the other had been picked up by either. They had happened both at dinner and at luncheon to be so placed as not to have to glare — or to grin — across; and for the rest they could each, in such a crowd, as freely help the general ease to keep them apart as assist it to bring them together. One chance there was, of course, that might be beyond their control. He had been the night before half-surprised at not finding her his 'fate' when the long procession to the dining-room solemnly hooked itself together. He would have said in advance — recognising it as one of the sharp 'notes' of Mundham — that, should the gathering contain a literary lady, the literary lady would, for congruity, be apportioned to the arm, when there was a question of arms, of the gentleman present who represented the nearest thing to literature. Poor Straith represented 'art,' and that, no doubt, would have been near enough had not the party offered for choice a slight excess of men. The representative of art had been of the two or three who went in alone, whereas Mrs Harvey had gone in with one of the representatives of banking.

It was certain, however, that she wouldn't again be consigned to Lord Belgrove, and it was just possible that he himself should not be again alone. She would be on the whole the most probable remedy to that state, on his part, of disgrace; and this precisely was the great interest of their situation — they were the only persons present without some advantage over somebody else. They hadn't a single advantage; they could be named for nothing but their cleverness; they were at the bottom of the social ladder. The social ladder had even at Mundham — as they might properly have been told, as indeed practically they *were* told — to end somewhere; which is no more than to say that as he strolled about and thought of many things Stuart Straith had after all a good deal the sense of helping to hold it up. Another of the things he thought of was the special oddity – for it was nothing else – of his being there at all, being there in particular so out of his order and turn. He couldn't answer for Mrs Harvey's turn and order. It might well be that she was *in* hers; but these Saturday-to-Monday occasions had hitherto mostly struck him as great gilded cages as to which care was taken that the birds should be birds of a feather.

There had been a wonderful walk in the afternoon, within the limits of the place, to a far-away tea-house; and in spite of the combinations and changes of this episode he had still escaped the necessity of putting either his old friend or himself to the test. Also it had been all, he flattered himself, without the pusillanimity of his avoiding her. Life was indeed well understood in these great conditions; the conditions constituted in their greatness a kind of fundamental facility, provided a general exemption, bathed the hour, whatever it was, in a universal blandness, that were all a happy solvent for awkward relations. It was for instance beautiful that if their failure to meet amid so much meeting had been of Mrs Harvey's own contrivance he couldn't be in the least vulgarly sure of it. There were places in which he would have had no doubt, places different enough from Mundham. He felt all the same and without anguish that these were much more *his* places – even if she didn't feel that they were much more hers. The day had been warm and splendid, and this moment of its wane – with dinner in sight, but as across a field of polished pink marble which seemed to say that wherever in such a house there was space there was also, benignantly, time – formed, of the whole procession of the hours, the one dearest to our friend, who on such occasions interposed it, whenever he could, between the set of impressions that ended and the set that began with 'dressing.'[1] The great terraces and gardens were almost void; people had scattered, though not altogether even yet to dress. The air of the place, with the immense house all seated aloft in strength, robed with summer and crowned with success, was such as to contribute something of its own to the poetry of early evening. This visitor at any rate saw and felt it all through one of those fine hazes of August that remind you – at least they reminded *him* – of the artful gauze stretched across the stage of a theatre when an effect of mystery or some particular pantomimic ravishment is desired.

Should he in fact have to pair with Mrs Harvey for dinner it would be a shame to him not to have addressed her sooner; and should she on the contrary be put with some one else the loss of so much of the time would have but the greater ugliness. Didn't he meanwhile make out that there were ladies in the lower garden, from which the sound of voices, faint but, as always in the upper air of Mundham, exceedingly sweet, was just now borne to him? She might be among them, and if he should find her he'd let her know he had sought her. He'd treat it frankly as an occasion for declaring that what had happened between them – or rather what had *not* happened – was too absurd. What at present occurred, however, was that in his quest of her he suddenly, at the turn of an alley, perceived her, not far off, seated in a sort of bower with the Ambassador. With this he pulled up, going another way and pretending not to see them. Three times already that afternoon he had observed her in different situations with the Ambassador. He was the more struck accordingly when, upwards of an hour later, again alone and with his state unremedied, he saw her placed for dinner next his Excellency. It wasn't at all what would have been at Mundham her right seat, so that it could only be explained by his Excellency's direct request. She *was* a success! This time Straith was well in her view and could see that in the candle-light of the wonderful room, where the lustres were, like the table, all crystal and silver, she was as handsome as any one, taking the women of her age, and also as 'smart' as the evening before, and as true as any of the others to the law of a marked difference in her smartness. If the beautiful way she held herself – for decidedly it *was* beautiful – came in a great measure from the good thing she professionally made of it all, our observer could reflect that the poor thing *he* professionally made of it probably affected his attitude in just the opposite way; but they communicated neither in the glare nor in the grin he had dreaded. Still, their eyes did now meet, and then it struck him her own were strange.

II

She, on her side, had her private consciousness, and quite as full a one, doubtless, as he, but with the advantage that when the company separated for the night she was not, like her friend, reduced to a vigil unalloyed. Lady Claude, at the top of the stairs, had said 'May I look in – in five minutes – if you don't mind?' and then had arrived in due course and in a wonderful new beribboned gown, the thing just launched for such occasions. Lady Claude was young and earnest and delightfully bewildered and bewildering, and however interesting she might, through certain elements in her situation, have seemed to a literary lady, her own admirations and curiosities were such as from the first promised to rule the hour. She had already expressed to Mrs Harvey a really informed enthusiasm. She not only delighted in her numerous books, which was a tribute the author had not infrequently met, but she even appeared to have read them – an appearance with which our authoress was much less acquainted. The great thing was that she also yearned to write, and that she had turned up in her fresh furbelows not only to reveal this secret and to ask for direction and comfort, but literally to make a stranger confidence, for which the mystery of midnight seemed propitious. Midnight was indeed, as the situation developed, well over before her confidence was spent, for it had ended by gathering such a current as floated forth, with everything in Lady Claude's own life, many things more in that of her adviser. Mrs Harvey was at all events amused, touched and effectually kept awake; so by the end of half an hour they had quite got what might have been called their second wind of frankness and were using it for a discussion of the people in the house. Their primary communion had been simply on the question of the pecuniary profits of literature as the producer of so many admired volumes was prepared to present them to an aspirant. Lady Claude was in financial difficulties and desired the literary issue. This was the breathless revelation she had rustled over a mile of crimson velvet corridor to make.

'Nothing?' she had three minutes later incredulously gasped. 'I can make nothing at all?' But the gasp was slight compared with the stupefaction communicated by a brief further parley, in the course of which Mrs Harvey had, after an hesitation, taken her own plunge. '*You* make so little – wonderful *you*?' And then as the producer of the admired volumes simply sat there in her dressing-gown, with the saddest of slow headshakes, looking suddenly too wan even to care that it was at last all out: 'What in that case is the use of success and celebrity and genius? You *have* no success?' She had looked almost awestruck at this further confession of her friend. They were face to face in a poor human crudity, which transformed itself quickly into an effusive embrace. 'You've had it and lost it? Then when it has been as great as yours one *can* lose it?'

'More easily than one can get it.'

Lady Claude continued to marvel. 'But you do so much – and it's so beautiful!' On which Mrs Harvey simply smiled again in her handsome despair, and after a moment found herself again in the arms of her visitor. The younger woman had remained for a time a good deal arrested and hushed, and had at any rate, sensitive and charming, immediately dropped, in the presence of this almost august unveiling, the question of her own thin troubles. But there are short cuts at that hour of night that morning scarce knows, and it took but little more of the breath of the real to suggest to Lady Claude more questions in such a connexion than she could answer for herself. 'How then, if you haven't private means, do you get on?'

'Ah I don't get on!'

Lady Claude looked about. There were objects scattered in the fine old French room. 'You've lovely things.'

'Two.'

'Two?'

'Two frocks. I couldn't stay another day.'

'Ah what's *that*? I couldn't either,' said Lady Claude soothingly. 'And you have,' she continued, in the same spirit, 'your nice maid —'

'Who's indeed a charming woman, but my cook in disguise!' Mrs Harvey dropped.

'Ah you *are* clever!' her friend cried with a laugh that was as a climax of reassurance.

'Extraordinarily. But don't think,' Mrs Harvey hastened to add, 'that I mean that that's why I'm here.'

Her companion candidly thought. 'Then why are you?'

'I haven't the least idea. I've been wondering all the while, as I've wondered so often before on such occasions, and without arriving at any other reason than that London's so wild.'

Lady Claude wondered. 'Wild?'

'Wild!' said her friend with some impatience. 'That's the way London strikes.'

'But do you call such an invitation a blow?'

'Yes — crushing. No one else, at all events, either,' Mrs Harvey added, 'could tell you why I'm here.'

Lady Claude's power to drink in (and it was perhaps her most attaching quality) was greater still, when she felt strongly, than her power to reject. 'Why how can you say that when you've only to see how every one likes and admires you? Just look at the Ambassador,' she had earnestly insisted. And this was what had precisely, as I have mentioned, carried the stream of their talk a good deal away from its source. It had therefore not much further to go before setting in motion the name of Stuart Straith, as to whom Lady Claude confessed to an interest — good-looking, distinguished, 'sympathetic' as he was — that she could really almost hate him for having done nothing whatever to encourage. He hadn't spoken to her once.

'But, my dear, if he hasn't spoken to *me* —!'

Lady Claude appeared to regret this not too much for a hint that after all there might be a difference. 'Oh but *could* he?'

'Without my having spoken to him first?' Mrs Harvey turned it over. 'Perhaps not; but I couldn't have done that.' Then to explain, and not only because Lady Claude was naturally vague, but because what was still visibly most vivid to her was her independent right to have been 'made up' to: 'And yet not because we're not acquainted.'

'You know him then?'

'But too well.'

'You mean you don't like him?'

'On the contrary I like him to distraction.'

'Then what's the matter?' Lady Claude asked with some impatience.

Her friend hung fire but a moment. 'Well, he wouldn't have me.'

'"Have" you?'

'Ten years ago, after Mr Harvey's death, when if he had lifted a finger I'd have married him.'

'But he didn't lift it?'

'He was too grand. I was too small – by *his* measure. He wanted to keep himself. He saw his future.'

Lady Claude earnestly followed. 'His present position?'

'Yes – everything that was to come to him; his steady rise in value.'

'Has it been so great?'

'Surely – his situation and name. Don't you know his lovely work and what's thought of it?'

'Oh yes, I know. That's why – ' But Lady Claude stopped. After which: 'But if he's still keeping himself?'

'Oh it's not for me,' said Mrs Harvey.

'And evidently not for *me*. Whom then,' her visitor asked, 'does he think good enough?'

'Oh these great people!' Mrs Harvey smiled.

'But *we're* great people – you and I!' And Lady Claude kissed her good-night.

'You mustn't, all the same,' the elder woman said, 'betray the secret of *my* greatness, which I've told you, please remember, only in the deepest confidence.'

Her tone had a quiet purity of bitterness that for a moment longer held her friend, after which Lady Claude had the happy inspiration of meeting it with graceful gaiety. 'It's quite for the best, I'm sure, that Mr Straith wouldn't have you. You've kept yourself too; you'll marry yet – an ambassador!' And with another good-night she reached the door. 'You say you don't get on, but you do.'

'Ah!' said Mrs Harvey with vague attenuation.

'Oh yes, you do,' Lady Claude insisted, while the door emphasised it with a little clap that sounded through the still house.

III

The first night of 'The New Girl'[2] occurred, as every one remembers, three years ago, and the play is running yet, a fact that may render strange the failure to be deeply conscious of which two persons in the audience were guilty. It was not till afterwards present either to Mrs Harvey or to Stuart Straith that 'The New Girl' was one of the greatest successes of modern times. Indeed if the question had been put to them on the spot they might have appeared much at sea. But this, I may as well immediately say, was the result of their having found themselves side by side in the stalls and thereby given most of their attention to their own predicament. Straith showed he felt the importance of meeting it promptly, for he turned to his neighbour, who was already in her place, as soon as her identity had flushed well through his own arrival and subsidence. 'I don't quite see how you can help speaking to me now.'

Her face could only show him how long she had been aware of his approach. 'The sound of your voice, coming to me straight, makes it indeed as easy for me as I could possibly desire.'

He looked about at the serried rows, the loaded galleries and the stuffed boxes, with recognitions and nods; and this made between them another pause, during which, while the music seemed perfunctory and the bustle that in a London audience represents concentration increased, they felt how effectually, in the thick preoccupied medium, how extraordinarily, they were together.

'Well, that second afternoon at Mundham, just before dinner, I was very near forcing your hand. But something put me off. You're really too grand.'

'Oh!' she murmured.

'Ambassadors,' said Stuart Straith.

'Oh!' she again sounded. And before anything more could pass the curtain was up. It came down in due course and achieved, after various intervals, the rest of its motions without interrupting for our friends the sense of an evening of talk. They said when it was down almost nothing about the play, and when one of them toward the end put to the other, vaguely, 'Is – a – this thing going?' the question had scarce the effect of being even relevant. What was clearest to them was that the people about were somehow enough taken up to leave them at their ease – but what taken up with they but half made out. Mrs Harvey had none the less mentioned early that her presence had a reason and that she ought to attend, and her companion had asked her what she thought of a certain picture made at a given moment by the stage, in the reception of which he was so interested that it was really what had brought him. These were glances, however, that quickly strayed – strayed, for instance (as this could carry them far), in its coming to one of them to say that, whatever the piece might be, the real thing, as they had seen it at Mundham, was more than a match for any piece. For Mundham *was*, theatrically, the real thing; better for scenery, dresses, music, pretty women, bare shoulders, everything – even coherent dialogue; a much bigger and braver show, and got up, as it were, infinitely more 'regardless.' By Mundham they were held long enough to find themselves, though with an equal surprise, quite at one as to the special oddity of their having caught each other in such a plight. Straith said that he supposed what his friend meant was that it was odd *he* should have been there; to which she returned that she had been imputing to him exactly that judgement of her own presence.

'But why shouldn't *you* be?' he asked. 'Isn't that just what you *are*? Aren't you in your way – like those people – a child of fortune and fashion?'

He got no more answer to this for some time than if he had fairly wounded her. He indeed that evening got no answer at all that was direct. But in the next interval she brought out with abruptness, taking no account of some other matter he had just touched: 'Don't you really know –?'

She had paused. 'Know what?'

Again she went on without heeding. 'A place like Mundham is, for me, a survival, though poor Mundham in particular won't, for me, have survived that visit – on which it's to be pitied, isn't it? It was a glittering ghost – since laid! – of my old time.'

Straith, at this, almost gave a start. 'Have *you* got a new time?'

'Do you mean you yourself have?'

'Well,' said Straith, 'mine may now be called middle-aged. It seems so long, I mean, since I set my watch to it.'

'Oh I haven't even a watch!' she returned with a laugh. 'I'm beyond watches.' After which she added: 'We *might* have met more – or, I should say perhaps, have got more out of it when we *have* met.'

'Yes, it has been too little. But I've always explained it by our living in such different worlds.'

Mrs Harvey could risk an abruptness. 'Are you unhappy?'

He gave her a mild glare. 'You said just now that you're beyond watches. I'm beyond unhappiness.'

She turned from him and presently brought out: 'I ought absolutely to take away *something* of the play.'

'By all means. There's certainly something *I* shall take.'

'Ah then you must help me – give it me.'

'With all my heart,' said Straith, 'if it *can* help you. It's my feeling of our renewal.'

She had one of the sad slow headshakes that at Mundham had been impressive to Lady Claude. 'That won't help me.'

'Then you must let me put to you now what I should have tried to get near enough to you there to put if I hadn't been so afraid of the Ambassador. What has it been so long – our impossibility?'

'Well, I can only answer for my own vision of it, which is – which always was – that you were sorry for me, but felt a sort of scruple of showing me you had nothing better than pity to give.'

'May I come to see you?' Straith asked some minutes after this.

Her words, for which he had also a while to wait, had in truth as little as his own the appearance of a reply. '*Are* you unhappy – really? Haven't you everything?'

'You're beautiful!' he said for all answer. 'Mayn't I come?'

She demurred. 'Where's your studio?'

'Oh not too far for me to go to places. Don't be anxious; I can walk, or even take the bus.'

Mrs Harvey once more delayed. Then she said: 'Mayn't I rather come there?'

'I shall be but too delighted.'

It was spoken promptly, even eagerly; yet the understanding appeared shortly after to have left between them a certain awkwardness, and it was almost as if to change the subject and relieve them equally that she suddenly reminded him of something he had spoken earlier. 'You were to tell me why in particular you had to be here.'

'Oh yes. To see my dresses.'

'Yours!' She wondered.

'The second act. I made them out for them – designed them.'

Before she could check it her tone escaped. 'You?'

'I.' He looked straight before him. 'For the fee. And we didn't even notice them.'

'*I* didn't,' she confessed. But it offered the fact as a sign of her kindness for him, and this kindness was traceably what inspired something she said in the draughty porch, after the performance, while the footman of the friend, a fat rich immensely pleased lady who had given her a lift and then rejoined her from a seat in the balcony, went off to make sure of the brougham.[3] 'May I do something about your things?'

' "Do something"?'

'When I've paid you my visit. Write something – about your pictures. I do a correspondence,' said Mrs Harvey.

He wondered as she had done in the stalls. 'For a paper?'

'*The Blackport Banner*. A "London Letter." The new books, the new plays, the new twaddle of any sort – a little music, a little gossip, a little "art." You'll help me – I need it awfully – with the art. I do three a month.'

'*You* – wonderful you?' He spoke as Lady Claude had done, and could no more help it again than Mrs Harvey had been able to help it in the stalls.

'Oh as you say, for the fee!' On which, as the footman signalled, her old lady began to plunge through the crowd.

IV

At the studio, where she came to him within the week, her first movement had been to exclaim on the splendid abundance of his work. She had looked round charmed – so struck as to be, as she called it, crushed. 'You've such a wonderful lot to show.'

'Indeed I have!' said Stuart Straith.

'That's where you beat *us*.'

'I think it may very well be,' he went on, 'where I beat almost every one.'

'And is much of it new?'

He looked about with her. 'Some of it's pretty old. But my things have a way, I admit, of growing old extraordinarily fast. They seem to me in fact nowadays quite "born old." '

She had after a little the manner of coming back to something. 'You *are* unhappy. You're *not* beyond it. You're just nicely, just fairly and squarely, in the middle of it.'

'Well,' said Straith, 'if it surrounds me like a desert, so that I'm lost in it, that comes to the same thing. But I want you to tell me about yourself.'

She had continued at first to move about and had taken out a pocket-book, which she held up at him. 'This time I shall insist on notes. You made my mind a blank about that play, which is the sort of thing we can't afford. If it hadn't been for my fat old lady and the next day's papers!' She kept looking, going up to things, saying 'How wonderful!' and 'Oh your *way*!' and then stopping for a general impression, something in the whole charm. The place, high, handsome, neat, with two or three pale tapestries and several rare old pieces of furniture, showed a perfection of order, an absence of loose objects, as if it had been swept and squared for the occasion and made almost too immaculate. It was polished and cold – rather cold for the season and the weather; and Stuart Straith himself, buttoned and brushed, as fine and as clean as his room, might at her arrival have reminded her of the master of a neat bare ship on his deck and awaiting a cargo. 'May I see everything? May I "use" everything?'

'Oh no; you mayn't by any means use everything. You mayn't use half. *Did* I spoil your "London Letter"?' he continued after a moment.

'No one can spoil them as I spoil them myself. I can't do them – I don't know how, and don't want to. I do them wrong, and the people want such trash. Of course they'll "sack" me.'

She was in the centre, and he had the effect of going round her, restless and vague, in large slow circles. 'Have you done them long?'

'Two or three months – this lot. But I've done others and I know what happens. Oh, my dear, I've done strange things!'

'And is it a good job?'

She hesitated, then puffed prettily enough an indifferent sigh. 'Three and ninepence. Is that good?' He had stopped before her, looking at her up and down. 'What do you get?' she went on, 'for what you do for a play?'

'A little more, it would seem, than you. Four and sixpence. But I've only done as yet that one. Nothing else has offered.'

'I see. But something *will*, eh?'

Poor Straith took a turn again. 'Did you like them – for colour?' But again he pulled up. 'Oh I forgot; we didn't notice them!'

For a moment they could laugh about it. 'I noticed them, I assure you, in the *Banner*. "The costumes in the second act are of the most marvellous beauty." That's what I said.'

'Oh that'll fetch the managers!' But before her again he seemed to take her in from head to foot. 'You speak of "using" things. If you'd only use yourself – for my enlightenment. Tell me all.'

'You look at me,' said Mrs Harvey, 'as with the wonder of who designs *my* costumes. How I dress on it, how I do even what I still do on it – on the three and ninepence – is *that* what you want to know?'

'What has happened to you?' Straith asked.

'How do I keep it up?' she continued as if she hadn't heard him. 'But I *don't* keep it up. *You* do,' she declared as she again looked round her.

Once more it set him off, but for a pause again almost as quick. 'How long have you been –?'

'Been what?' she asked as he faltered.

'Unhappy.'

She smiled at him from a depth of indulgence. 'As long as you've been ignorant – that what I've been *wanting* is your pity. Ah to have to know, as I believed I did, that you supposed it would wound me, and not to have been able to make you see it was the one thing left to me that would help me! Give me your pity now. It's all I want. I don't care for anything else. But give me that.'

He had, as it happened at the moment, to do a smaller and a usual thing before he could do one so great and so strange. The youth whom he kept for service arrived with a tea-tray, in arranging a place for which, with the sequel of serving Mrs Harvey, seating her and seeing the youth again out of the room, some minutes passed. 'What pity could I dream of for you,' he demanded as he at last dropped near her, 'when I was myself so miserably sore?'

'Sore?' she wondered. 'But you were happy – then.'

'Happy not to have struck you as good enough? For I didn't, you know,' he insisted. 'You had your success, which was so immense. You had your high value, your future, your big possibilities; and I perfectly understood that, given those things, and given also my very much smaller situation, you should wish to keep yourself.'

'Oh, oh!' She gasped as if hurt.

'I understand it; but how could it really make me "happy"?' he asked.

She turned at him as with her hand on the old scar she could now carry. 'You mean that all these years you've really not known —?'

'But not known what?'

His voice was so blank that at the sound of it, and at something that looked out from him, she only found another 'Oh, oh!' which became the next instant a burst of tears.

V

She had appeared at first unwilling to receive him at home; but he understood it after she had left him, turning over more and more everything their meeting had shaken to the surface and piecing together memories that at last, however darkly, made a sense. He was to call on her, it was finally agreed, but not till the end of the week, when she should have finished 'moving' — she had but just changed quarters; and meanwhile, as he came and went, mainly in the cold chamber of his own past endeavour, which looked even to himself as studios look when artists are dead and the public, in the arranged place, are admitted to stare, he had plenty to think about. What had come out — he could see it now — was that each, ten years before, had miserably misunderstood and then had turned for relief from pain to a perversity of pride. But it was himself above all he now sharply judged, since women, he felt, have to get on as they can, and for the mistake of this woman there were reasons he had to acknowledge with a sore heart. She had really found in the pomp of his early success, at the time they used to meet, and to care to, exactly the ground for her sense of failure with him that he had found in the vision of her gross popularity for his conviction that she judged him as comparatively small. Each had blundered, as sensitive souls of the 'artistic temperament' blunder, into a conception not only of the other's attitude, but of the other's material situation at the moment, that had thrown them back on stupid secrecy, where their estrangement had grown like an evil plant in the shade. He had positively believed her to have gone on all the while making the five thousand a year that the first eight or ten of her so supremely happy novels had brought her in, just as she on her side had read into the felicity of his first new hits, his pictures 'of the year' at three or four Academies, the absurdest theory of the sort of career that, thanks to big dealers and intelligent buyers, his gains would have built up for him. It looked vulgar enough now, but it had been grave enough then. His long detached delusion about her 'prices,' at any rate, appeared to have been more than matched by the strange stories occasionally floated to her – and all to make her but draw more closely in – on the subject of his own.

It was with each equally that everything had changed – everything but the stiff consciousness in either of the need to conceal changes from the other. If she had cherished for long years the soreness of her not being 'good' enough, so this was what had counted most in her sustained effort to appear at least as good as he. London meanwhile was big, London was blind and benighted; and nothing had ever occurred to undermine for him the fiction of her prosperity. Before his eyes there while she sat with him she had pulled off one by one those vain coverings of her state that she confessed she had hitherto done her best – and so always with an eye on himself – deceptively to draw about it. He had felt frozen, as he listened, by such likenesses to things he knew. He recognised as she talked, he groaned as he understood. He understood – oh at last, whatever he hadn't done before! And yet he could well have smiled, out of their common abyss, at such odd identities and recurrences. Truly the arts were sisters, as was so often said; for what apparently could be more like the experience of one than the experience of another? And she spared him things with it all. He felt this too, just as, even while showing her how he followed, he had bethought himself of closing his lips for the hour, none too soon, on his own stale story. There had been a beautiful intelligence for that matter in her having asked him nothing more. She had overflowed because shaken by not finding him happy, and her surrender had somehow offered itself to him as her way – the first that sprang up – of considering his trouble. She had left him at all events in full possession of all the phases through which in 'literary circles' acclaimed states may pass on their regular march to eclipse and extinction. One had but one's hour, and if one had it soon – it was really almost a case of choice – one didn't have it late. It might also never even remotely have approached, at its best, things ridiculously rumoured. Straith felt on the whole how little he had known of literary circles, or of any mystery but his own indeed; on which, up to actual impending collapse, he had mounted such anxious guard.

It was when he went on the Friday to see her that he took in the latest of the phases in question, which might very well be almost the final one; there was at least that comfort in it. She had just settled in a small flat, where he recognised in the steady disposal, for the best, of various objects she had not yet parted with, her reason for having made him wait. Here they had together – these two worn and baffled workers – a wonderful hour of gladness in their lost battle and of freshness in their lost youth; for it was not till Stuart Straith had also raised the heavy mask and laid it beside her own on the table that they began really to feel themselves recover something of that possibility of each other they had so wearily wasted. Only she couldn't get over it that he was like herself and that what she had shrunken to in her three or four simplified rooms had its perfect image in the specious show of his ordered studio and his accumulated work. He told everything now, kept no more back than she had kept at their previous meeting, while she repeated over and over 'You – wonderful you?' as if the knowledge made a deeper darkness of fate, as if the pain of his having come down at all almost quenched the joy of his having come so much nearer. When she learned that he hadn't for three years sold a picture – 'You, beautiful you?' – it seemed a new cold breath out of the dusk of her own outlook. Disappointment and despair were in such relations contagious, and there was clearly as much less again left to her as the little that was left to him. He showed her, laughing at the long queerness of it, how awfully little, as they called it, this was. He let it all come, but with more mirth than misery, and with a final abandonment of pride that was like changing at the end of a dreadful day from tight shoes to loose ones. There were moments when they might have resembled a couple united by some misdeed and meeting to decide on some desperate course; they gave themselves so to the great irony – the vision of the comic in contrasts – that precedes surrenders and extinctions.

They went over the whole thing, remounted the dwindling stream, reconstructed, explained, understood – recognised in short the particular example they gave and how without mutual suspicion they had been giving it side by side. 'We're simply the case,' Straith familiarly put it, 'of having been had enough of. No case is perhaps more common, save that for you and for me, each in our line, it did look in the good time – didn't it? – as if nobody *could* have enough.' With which they counted backward, gruesome as it was, the symptoms of satiety up to the first dawn, and lived again together the unforgettable hours – distant now – out of which it had begun to glimmer that the truth had to be faced and the right names given to the wrong facts. They laughed at their original explanations and the minor scale even of their early fears; compared notes on the fallibility of remedies and hopes and, more and more united in the identity of their lesson, made out perfectly that, though there appeared to be many kinds of success, there was only one kind of failure. And yet what had been hardest had not been to have to shrink, but in the long game of bluff as Straith called it, to have to keep up. It fairly swept them away at present, however, the hugeness of the relief of no longer keeping up as against each other. This gave them all the measure of the motive their courage, on either side, in silence and gloom, had forced into its service.

'Only what shall we do now for a motive?' Straith went on.

She thought. 'A motive for courage?'

'Yes – to keep up.'

'And go again for instance, do you mean, to Mundham? We shall, thank heaven, never go again to Mundham. The Mundhams are over.'

> 'Nous n'irons plus au bois;
> Les lauriers sont coupés,'[4]

sang Straith. 'It does cost.'

'As everything costs that one does for the rich. It's not our poor relations who make us pay.'

'No; one must have means to acknowledge the others. We can't afford the opulent. But it isn't only the money they take.'

'It's the imagination,' said Mrs Harvey. 'As they have none themselves –'

'It's an article we have to supply? We've certainly to use a lot to protect ourselves,' Straith agreed. 'And the strange thing is they like us.'

She thought again. 'That's what makes it easy to cut them. They forgive.'

'Yes,' her companion laughed; 'once they really don't know you enough –!'

'They treat you as old friends. But what do we want now of courage?' she went on.

He wondered. 'Yes, after all, what?'

'To keep up, I mean. Why *should* we keep up?'

It seemed to strike him. 'I see. After all, why? The courage *not* to keep up –!'

'We have *that* at least,' she declared, 'haven't we?' United there at her little high-perched window overhanging grey house-tops they let the consideration of this pass between them in a deep look as well as in a hush of which the intensity had something commensurate. 'If we're beaten –!' she then continued.

'Let us at least be beaten together!' He took her in his arms, she let herself go, and he held her long and close for the compact. But when they had recovered themselves enough to handle their agreement more responsibly the words in which they confirmed it broke in sweetness as well as sadness from both together: 'And now to work!'

The Abasement of the Northmores

I

When Lord Northmore died public reference to the event took for the most part rather a ponderous and embarrassed form. A great political figure had passed away. A great light of our time had been quenched in mid-career. A great usefulness had somewhat anticipated its term, though a great part, none the less, had been signally played. The note of greatness, all along the line, kept sounding, in short, by a force of its own, and the image of the departed evidently lent itself with ease to figures and flourishes, the poetry of the daily press. The newspapers and their purchasers equally did their duty by it — arranged it neatly and impressively, though perhaps with a hand a little violently expeditious, upon the funeral-car, saw the conveyance properly down the avenue and then, finding the subject suddenly quite exhausted, proceeded to the next item on their list. His lordship had been a person in connexion with whom — that was it — there was almost nothing but the fine monotony of his success to mention. This success had been his profession, his means as well as his end; so that his career admitted of no other description and demanded, indeed suffered, no further analysis. He had made politics, he had made literature, he had made land, he had made a bad manner and a great many mistakes, he had made a gaunt foolish wife, two extravagant sons and four awkward daughters — he had made everything, as he *could* have made almost anything, thoroughly pay. There had been something deep down in him that did it, and his old friend Warren Hope, the person knowing him earliest and probably on the whole best, had never, even to the last, for curiosity, quite made out what it was. The secret was one that this distinctly distanced competitor had in fact mastered as little for intellectual relief as for emulous use; and there was a virtual tribute to it in the way that, the night before the obsequies and addressing himself to his wife, he said after some silent thought: 'Hang it, you know, I must see the old boy through. I must go to the grave.'

Mrs Hope at first looked at her husband but in anxious silence. 'I've no patience with you. You're much more ill than *he* ever was.'

'Ah but if that qualifies me only for the funerals of others —!'

'It qualifies you to break my heart by your exaggerated chivalry, your renewed refusal to consider your interests. You sacrificed them to him, for thirty years, again and again, and from this supreme sacrifice – possibly that of your life – you might, in your condition, I think, be absolved.' She indeed lost patience. 'To the grave – in this weather – after his treatment of you?'

'My dear girl,' Hope replied, 'his treatment of me is a figment of your ingenious mind – your too-passionate, your beautiful loyalty. Loyalty, I mean, to *me*.'

'I certainly leave it to you,' she declared, 'to have any to *him*!'

'Well, he was after all one's oldest, one's earliest friend. I'm not in such bad case – I do go out; and I want to do the decent thing. The fact remains that we never broke – we always kept together.'

'Yes indeed,' she laughed in her bitterness, 'he always took care of that! He never recognised you, but he never let you go. You kept him up, and he kept you down. He used you, to the last drop he could squeeze, and left you the only one to wonder, in your incredible idealism and your incorrigible modesty, how on earth such an idiot made his way. He made his way on your back. You put it candidly to others – "What in the world was his gift?" And others are such gaping idiots that they too haven't the least idea. *You* were his gift!'

'And you're mine, my dear!' her husband, pressing her to him, more gaily and resignedly cried. He went down the next day by 'special'[1] to the interment, which took place on the great man's own property and in the great man's own church. But he went alone – that is in a numerous and distinguished party, the flower of the unanimous gregarious demonstration; his wife had no wish to accompany him, though she was anxious while he travelled. She passed the time uneasily, watching the weather and fearing the cold; she roamed from room to room, pausing vaguely at dull windows, and before he came back she had thought of many things. It was as if, while he saw the great man buried, she also, by herself, in the contracted home of their later years, stood before an open grave. She lowered into it with her weak hands the heavy past and all their common dead dreams and accumulated ashes. The pomp surrounding Lord Northmore's extinction made her feel more than ever that it was not Warren who had made anything pay. He had been always what he was still, the cleverest man and the hardest worker she knew; but what was there, at fifty-seven, as the vulgar said, to 'show' for it all but his wasted genius, his ruined health and his paltry pension? It was the term of comparison conveniently given her by his happy rival's now foreshortened splendour that set these things in her eye. It was as happy rivals to their own flat union that she always had thought of the Northmore pair; the two men at least having started together, after the University, shoulder to shoulder and with – superficially speaking – much the same outfit of preparation, ambition and opportunity. They had begun at the same point and wanting the same things

– only wanting them in such different ways. Well, the dead man had wanted them in the way that got them; but got too, in his peerage for instance, those Warren had never wanted: there was nothing else to be said. There was nothing else, and yet, in her sombre, her strangely apprehensive solitude at this hour, she said much more than I can tell. It all came to this – that there had been somewhere and somehow a wrong. Warren was the one who should have succeeded. But she was the one person who knew it now, the single other person having descended, with *his* knowledge, to the tomb.

She sat there, she roamed there, in the waiting greyness of her small London house, with a deepened sense of the several odd knowledges that had flourished in their company of three. Warren had always known everything and, with his easy power – in nothing so high as for indifference – had never cared. John Northmore had known, for he had, years and years before, told her so; and thus had had a reason the more – in addition to not believing her stupid – for guessing at her view. She lived back; she lived it over; she had it all there in her hand. John Northmore had known her first, and how he had wanted to marry her the fat little bundle of his love-letters still survived to tell. He had introduced Warren Hope to her – quite by accident and because, at the time they had chambers[2] together, he couldn't help it: that was the one thing he *had* done for them. Thinking of it now she perhaps saw how much he might conscientiously have considered that it disburdened him of more. Six months later she had accepted Warren, and just for the reason the absence of which had determined her treatment of his friend. She had believed in his future. She held that John Northmore had never afterwards remitted the effort to ascertain the degree in which she felt herself 'sold.' But, thank God, she had never shown him.

Her husband came home with a chill and she put him straight to bed. For a week, as she hovered near him, they only looked deep things at each other; the point was too quickly passed at which she could bearably have said 'I told you so!' That his late patron should never have had difficulty in making *him* pay was certainly no marvel. But it was indeed a little too much, after all, that he should have made him pay with his life. This was what it had come to – she was now sure from the first. Congestion of the lungs declared itself that night and on the morrow, sickeningly, she was face to face with pneumonia. It was more than – with all that had gone before – they could meet. Ten days later Warren Hope succumbed. Tenderly, divinely as he loved her, she felt his surrender, through all the anguish, as an unspeakable part of the sublimity of indifference into which his hapless history had finally flowered. 'His easy power, his easy power!' – her passion had never yet found such relief in that simple secret phrase for him. He was so proud, so fine and so flexible that to fail a little had been as bad for him as to fail much; therefore he had opened the flood-gates wide – had thrown, as the saying was, the helve after the hatchet.[3] He had amused himself with seeing what the devouring world would take. Well, it had taken all.

II

But it was after he had gone that his name showed as written in water. What had he left? He had only left *her* and her grey desolation, her lonely piety and her sore unresting rebellion. When a man died it sometimes did for him what life hadn't done; people after a little, on one side or the other, discovered and named him, claiming him for their party, annexing him to their flag. But the sense of having lost Warren Hope appeared not in the least to have quickened the world's wit; the sharper pang for his widow indeed sprang just from the commonplace way in which he was spoken of as known. She received letters enough, when it came to that, for personally of course he had been liked; the newspapers were fairly copious and perfectly stupid; the three or four societies, 'learned' and other, to which he had belonged, passed resolutions of regret and condolence, and the three or four colleagues about whom he himself used to be most amusing stammered eulogies; but almost anything really would have been better for her than the general understanding that the occasion had been met. Two or three solemn noodles in 'administrative circles' wrote her that she must have been gratified at the unanimity of regret, the implication being quite that she was else of the last absurdity. Meanwhile what she felt was that she could have borne well enough his not being noticed at all; what she couldn't bear was this treatment of him as a minor celebrity. He was, in economics, in the higher politics, in philosophic history, a splendid unestimated genius or he was nothing. He wasn't at any rate – heaven forbid! – a 'notable figure.' The waters, none the less, closed over him as over Lord Northmore; which was precisely, as time went on, the fact she found it hardest to accept. That personage, the week after his death, without an hour of reprieve, the place swept as clean of him as a hall lent for a charity, of the tables and booths of a three-days' bazaar – that personage had gone straight to the bottom, dropped like a crumpled circular into the waste-basket. Where then was the difference? – if the end *was* the end for each alike? For Warren it should have been properly the beginning.

During the first six months she wondered what she could herself do, and had much of the time the sense of walking by some swift stream on which an object dear to her was floating out to sea. All her instinct was to keep up with it, not to lose sight of it, to hurry along the bank and reach in advance some point from which she could stretch forth and catch and save it. Alas it only floated and floated; she held it in sight, for the stream was long, but no gentle promontory offered itself to the rescue. She ran, she watched, she lived with her great fear; and all the while, as the distance to the sea diminished, the current visibly increased. To do anything at the last she must hurry. She went into his papers, she ransacked his drawers; something of that sort at least she might do. But there were difficulties, the case was special; she lost herself in the labyrinth and her competence was challenged; two or three friends to whose judgement she appealed struck her as tepid, even as cold, and publishers, when sounded – most of all in fact the house through which his three or four important volumes had been given to the world – showed an absence of eagerness for a collection of literary remains. It was only now she fully understood how remarkably little the three or four important volumes had 'done.' He had successfully kept that from her, as he had kept other things she might have ached at: to handle his notes and memoranda was to come at every turn, amid the sands of her bereavement, upon the footsteps of some noble reason. But she had at last to accept the truth that it was only for herself, her own relief, that she must follow him. His work, unencouraged and interrupted, failed of a final form: there would have been nothing to offer but fragments of fragments. She felt, all the same, in recognising this, that she abandoned him: he died for her at that hour over again.

The hour moreover happened to coincide with another hour, so that the two mingled their bitterness. She received from Lady Northmore a note announcing a desire to gather in and publish his late lordship's letters, so numerous and so interesting, and inviting Mrs Hope, as a more than probable depositary, to be so good as to enrich the scheme with those addressed to her husband. This gave her a start of more kinds than one. The long comedy of his late lordship's greatness was *not* then over? The monument was to be built to him that she had but now schooled herself to regard as impossible for his defeated friend? Everything was to break out afresh, the comparisons, the contrasts, the conclusions so invidiously in his favour? – the business all cleverly managed to place him in the light and keep every one else in the shade? Letters? – had John Northmore indited three lines that could at that time of day be of the smallest consequence? Whose inept idea was such a publication, and what infatuated editorial patronage could the family have secured? She of course didn't know, but she should be surprised if there were material. Then it came to her, on reflexion, that editors and publishers must of course have flocked – his star would still rule. Why shouldn't he make his letters pay in death as he had made them pay in life? Such as they were they *had* paid. They would be a tremendous hit. She thought again of her husband's rich confused relics – thought of the loose blocks of marble that could only lie now where they had fallen; after which, with one of her deep and frequent sighs, she took up anew Lady Northmore's communication.

His letters to Warren, kept or not kept, had never so much as occurred to her. Those to herself were buried and safe – she knew where her hand would find them; but those to herself her correspondent had carefully not asked for and was probably unaware of the existence of. They belonged moreover to that phase of the great man's career that was distinctly – as it could only be called – previous: previous to the greatness, to the proper subject of the volume, previous above all to Lady Northmore. The faded fat packet lurked still where it had lurked for years; but she could no more to-day have said why she had kept it than why – though he knew of the early episode – she had never mentioned her preservation of it to Warren. This last maintained reserve certainly absolved her from mentioning it to Lady Northmore, who probably knew of the episode too. The odd part of the matter was at any rate that her retention of these documents had not been an accident. She had obeyed a dim instinct or a vague calculation. A calculation of what? She couldn't have told: it had operated, at the back of her head, simply as a sense that, not destroyed, the complete little collection made for safety. But for whose, just heaven? Perhaps she should still see; though nothing, she trusted, would occur requiring her to touch the things or to read them over. She wouldn't have touched them or read them over for the world.

She had not as yet, in any case, overhauled those receptacles in which the letters Warren kept would have accumulated; and she had her doubts of their containing any of Lord Northmore's. Why should he have kept any? Even she herself had had more reasons. Was his lordship's later epistolary manner supposed to be good, or of the kind that, on any grounds, prohibited the waste-basket or the glowing embers? Warren had lived in a deluge of documents, but these perhaps he might have regarded as contributions to contemporary history. None the less, surely, he wouldn't have stored up many. She began a search in cupboards, boxes, drawers yet unvisited, and she had her surprises both at what he had kept and at what he hadn't. Every word of her own was there – every note that in occasional absence he had ever had from her. Well, that matched happily enough her knowing just where to put her finger on every note that, on such occasions, she herself had received. *Their* correspondence at least was complete. But so, in fine, on one side, it gradually appeared, was Lord Northmore's. The superabundance of these missives hadn't been sacrificed by her husband, evidently, to any passing convenience; she judged more and more that he had preserved every scrap; and she was unable to conceal from herself that she was – she scarce knew why – a trifle disappointed. She hadn't quite unhopefully, even though vaguely, seen herself informing Lady Northmore that, to her great regret and after a general hunt, she could find nothing at all.

She in fact, alas, found everything. She was conscientious and she rummaged to the end, by which time one of the tables quite groaned with the fruits of her quest. The letters appeared moreover to have been cared for and roughly classified – she should be able to consign them to the family in excellent order. She made sure at the last that she had overlooked nothing, and then, fatigued and distinctly irritated, she prepared to answer in a sense so different from the answer she had, as might have been said, planned. Face to face with her note, however, she found she couldn't write it; and, not to be alone longer with the pile on the table, she presently went out of the room. Late in the evening – just before going to bed – she came back almost as if hoping there might have been since the afternoon some pleasant intervention in the interest of her distaste. Mightn't it have magically happened that her discovery was a mistake? – that the letters either weren't there or were after all somebody's else? Ah they *were* there, and as she raised her lighted candle in the dusk the pile on the table squared itself with insolence. On this, poor lady, she had for an hour her temptation.

It was obscure, it was absurd; all that could be said of it was that it was for the moment extreme. She saw herself, as she circled round the table, writing with perfect impunity: 'Dear Lady Northmore, I've hunted high and low and have found nothing whatever. My husband evidently, before his death, destroyed everything. I'm *so* sorry – I should have liked so much to help you. Yours most truly.' She should have only on the morrow privately and resolutely to annihilate the heap, and those words would remain an account of the matter that nobody was in a position to challenge. What good it would do her? – was *that* the question? It would do her the good that it would make poor Warren seem to have been just a little less used and duped. This, in her mood, would ease her off. Well, the temptation was real; but so, she after a while felt, were other things. She sat down at midnight to her note. 'Dear Lady Northmore, I'm happy to say I've found a great deal – my husband appears to have been so careful to keep everything. I've a mass at your disposition if you can conveniently send. So glad to be able to help your work. Yours most truly.' She stepped out as she was and dropped the letter into the nearest pillar-box. By noon the next day the table had, to her relief, been cleared. Her ladyship sent a responsible servant – her butler – in a four-wheeler and with a large japanned box.

III

After this, for a twelvemonth, there were frequent announcements and allusions. They came to her from every side, and there were hours at which the air, to her imagination, contained almost nothing else. There had been, at an early stage, immediately after Lady Northmore's communication to her, an official appeal, a circular *urbi et orbi*,[4] reproduced, applauded, commented in every newspaper, desiring all possessors of letters to remit them without delay to the family. The family, to do it justice, rewarded the sacrifice freely – so far as it was a reward to keep the world informed of the rapid progress of the work. Material had shown itself more copious than was to have been conceived. Interesting as the imminent volumes had naturally been expected to prove, those who had been favoured with a glimpse of their contents already felt warranted in promising the public an unprecedented treat. They would throw upon certain sides of the writer's mind and career lights hitherto unsuspected. Lady Northmore, deeply indebted for favours received, begged to renew her solicitation; gratifying as the response had been it was believed that, particularly in connexion with several dates now specified, a residuum of buried treasure might still be looked for.

Mrs Hope saw, she could but recognise, fewer and fewer people; yet her circle was even now not too narrow for her to hear it blown about that Thompson and Johnson had 'been asked.' Conversation in the London world struck her for a time as almost confined to such questions and answers. 'Have *you* been asked?' 'Oh yes – rather. Months ago. And you?' With the whole place under contribution the striking thing seemed that being asked had been attended in every case by the ability to respond. The spring had but to be touched – millions of letters flew out. Ten volumes at such a rate, Mrs Hope brooded, wouldn't exhaust the supply. She brooded a great deal, did nothing but brood; and, strange as this may at first appear, one of the final results of her brooding was the growth of a germ of doubt. It could only seem possible, in view of such unanimity, that she should have been stupidly mistaken. The great departed's reputation *was* then to the general sense a sound safe thing. Not he, immortal, had been at fault, but just her silly self, still burdened with the fallibility of Being. He had thus been a giant, and the letters would triumphantly show it. She had looked only at the envelopes of those she had surrendered, but she was prepared for anything. There was the fact, not to be blinked, of Warren's own marked testimony. The attitude of others was but *his* attitude; and she sighed as she found him in this case for the only time in his life on the side of the chattering crowd.

She was perfectly aware that her obsession had run away with her, but as Lady Northmore's publication really loomed into view – it was now definitely announced for March, and they were in January – her pulses quickened so that she found herself, in the long nights, mostly lying awake. It was in one of these vigils that suddenly, in the cold darkness, she felt the brush of almost the only thought that for many a month hadn't made her wince; the effect of which was that she bounded out of bed with a new felicity. Her impatience flashed on the spot up to its maximum – she could scarce wait for day to give herself to action. Her idea was neither more nor less than immediately to collect and put forth the letters of *her* hero. She would publish her husband's own – glory be to God! – and she even wasted none of her time in wondering why she had waited. She *had* waited – all too long; yet it was perhaps no more than natural that, for eyes sealed with tears and a heart heavy with injustice, there shouldn't have been an instant vision of where her remedy lay. She thought of it already as her remedy – though she would probably have found an awkwardness in giving a name publicly to her wrong. It was a wrong to feel, but doubtless not to talk about. And lo, straightway, the balm had begun to drop: the balance would so soon be even. She spent all that day in reading over her own old letters, too intimate and too sacred – oh unluckily! – to figure in her project, but pouring wind nevertheless into its sails and adding greatness to her presumption. She had of course, with separation, all their years, never frequent and never prolonged, known her husband as a correspondent much less than others; still, these relics constituted a property – she was surprised at their number – and testified hugely to his inimitable gift.

He was a letter-writer if you liked – natural witty various vivid, playing with the idlest lightest hand up and down the whole scale. His easy power – his easy power: everything that brought him back brought back that. The most numerous were of course the earlier and the series of those during their engagement, witnesses of their long probation, which were rich and unbroken; so full indeed and so wonderful that she fairly groaned at having to defer to the common measure of married modesty. There was discretion, there was usage, there was taste; but she would fain have flown in their face. If many were pages too intimate to publish, most others were too rare to suppress. Perhaps after her death –! It not only pulled her up, the happy thought of that liberation alike for herself and for her treasure, making her promise herself straightway to arrange: it quite re-emphasised her impatience for the term of her mortality, which would leave a free field to the justice she invoked. Her great resource, however, clearly, would be the friends, the colleagues, the private admirers to whom he had written for years, to whom she had known him to write, and many of whose own letters, by no means remarkable, she had come upon in her recent sortings and siftings. She drew up a list of these persons and immediately wrote to them or, in cases in which they had passed away, to their widows, children, representatives; reminding herself in the process not disagreeably, in fact quite inspiringly, of Lady Northmore in person. It had struck her that Lady Northmore in person took somehow a good deal for granted; but this idea failed, oddly enough, to occur to her in regard to Mrs Hope. It was indeed with her ladyship she began, addressing her exactly in the terms of the noble widow's own appeal, every word of which she recalled.

Then she waited, but she had not, in connexion with that quarter, to wait long. 'Dear Mrs Hope, I have hunted high and low and have found nothing whatever.

My husband evidently before his death destroyed everything. I'm so sorry — I should have liked so much to help you. Yours most truly.' This was all Lady Northmore wrote, without the grace of an allusion to the assistance she herself had received; though even in the first flush of amazement and resentment our friend recognised the odd identity of form between her note and another that had never been written. She was answered as she had, in the like case and in her one evil hour,[5] dreamed of answering. But the answer wasn't over with this — it had still to flow in, day after day, from every other source reached by her question. And day after day, while amazement and resentment deepened, it consisted simply of three lines of regret. Everybody had looked, and everybody had looked in vain. Everybody would have been so glad, but everybody was reduced to being, like Lady Northmore, so sorry. Nobody could find anything, and nothing, it was therefore to be gathered, had been kept. Some of these informants were more prompt than others, but all replied in time, and the business went on for a month, at the end of which the poor woman, stricken, chilled to the heart, accepted perforce her situation and turned her face to the wall. In this position, as it were, she remained for days, taking heed of nothing and only feeling and nursing her wound. It was a wound the more cruel for having found her so unguarded. From the moment her remedy had glimmered to her she hadn't had an hour of doubt, and the beautiful side of it had seemed that it was just so easy. The strangeness of the issue was even greater than the pain. Truly it was a world *pour rire*,[6] the world in which John Northmore's letters were classed and labelled for posterity and Warren Hope's helped housemaids to light fires. All sense, all measure of anything, could only leave one — leave one indifferent and dumb. There was nothing to be done — the show was upside-down. John Northmore was immortal and Warren Hope was damned. For herself, therefore, she was finished. She was beaten. She leaned thus, motionless, muffled, for a time of which, as I say, she took no account; then at last she was reached by a great sound that made her turn her veiled head. It was the report of the appearance of Lady Northmore's volumes.

IV

This filled the air indeed, and all the papers that day were particularly loud with it. It met the reader on the threshold and then within, the work everywhere the subject of a 'leader' as well as of a review. The reviews moreover, she saw at a glance, overflowed with quotation; to look at two or three sheets was to judge fairly of the raptures. Mrs Hope looked at the two or three that, for confirmation of the single one she habitually received, she caused, while at breakfast, to be purchased; but her attention failed to penetrate further: she couldn't, she found, face the contrast between the pride of the Northmores on such a morning and her own humiliation. The papers brought it too sharply home; she pushed them away and, to get rid of them, not to feel their presence, left the house early. She found pretexts for remaining out; there had been a cup prescribed for her to drain, yet she could put off the hour of the ordeal. She filled the time as she might; bought things, in shops, for which she had no use, and called on friends for whom she had no taste. Most of her friends at present were reduced to that category, and she had to choose for visits the houses guiltless, as she might have said, of her husband's blood. She couldn't speak to the people who had answered in such dreadful terms her late circular; on the other hand the people out of its range were such as would also be stolidly unconscious of Lady Northmore's publication and from whom the sop of sympathy could be but circuitously extracted. As she had lunched at a pastry-cook's so she stopped out to tea, and the March dusk had fallen when she got home. The first thing she then saw in her lighted hall was a large neat package on the table; whereupon she knew before approaching it that Lady Northmore had sent her the book. It had arrived, she learned, just after her going out; so that, had she not done this, she might have spent the day with it. She now quite understood her prompt instinct of flight. Well, flight had helped her, and the touch of the great indifferent general life. She would at last face the music.

She faced it, after dinner, in her little closed drawing-room, unwrapping the two volumes – *The Public and Private Correspondence of the Right Honourable &c., &c.* – and looking well, first, at the great escutcheon on the purple cover and at the various portraits within, so numerous that wherever she opened she came on one. It hadn't been present to her before that he was so perpetually 'sitting,' but he figured in every phase and in every style, while the gallery was further enriched with views of his successive residences, each one a little grander than the last. She had ever, in general, found that in portraits, whether of the known or the obscure, the eyes seemed to seek and to meet her own; but John Northmore everywhere looked straight away from her, quite as if he had been in the room and were unconscious of acquaintance. The effect of this was, oddly enough, so sharp that at the end of ten minutes she felt herself sink into his text as if she had been a stranger beholden, vulgarly and accidentally, to one of the libraries. She had been afraid to plunge, but from the moment she got in she was – to do every one all round justice – thoroughly held. Sitting there late she made so many reflexions and discoveries that – as the only way to put it – she passed from mystification to stupefaction. Her own offered series figured practically entire; she had counted Warren's letters before sending them and noted now that scarce a dozen were absent – a circumstance explaining to her Lady Northmore's courtesy. It was to these pages she had turned first, and it was as she hung over them that her stupefaction dawned. It took in truth at the outset a particular form – the form of a sharpened wonder at Warren's unnatural piety. Her original surprise had been keen – when she had tried to take reasons for granted; but her original surprise was as nothing to her actual bewilderment. The letters to Warren had been virtually, she judged, for the family, the great card; yet if the great card made only that figure what on earth was one to think of the rest of the pack?

She pressed on at random and with a sense of rising fever; she trembled, almost panting, not to be sure too soon; but wherever she turned she found the prodigy spread. The letters to Warren were an abyss of inanity; the others followed suit as they could; the book was surely then a gaping void, the publication a theme for mirth. She so lost herself in uplifting visions as her perception of the scale of the mistake deepened that toward eleven o'clock, when her parlour-maid opened the door, she almost gave the start of guilt surprised. The girl, withdrawing for the night, had come but to mention that, and her mistress, supremely wide awake and with remembrance kindled, appealed to her, after a blank stare, with intensity. 'What have you done with the papers?'

'The papers, ma'am?'

'All those of this morning – don't tell me you've destroyed them! Quick, quick – bring them back.'

The young woman, by a rare chance, hadn't destroyed the public prints; she presently reappeared with them neatly folded; and Mrs Hope, dismissing her with benedictions, had at last in a few minutes taken the time of day. She saw her impression portentously reflected in the long grey columns. It wasn't then the illusion of her jealousy – it was the triumph, unhoped for, of her justice. The reviewers observed a decorum, but frankly, when one came to look, their stupefaction matched her own. What she had taken in the morning for enthusiasm proved mere perfunctory attention, unwarned in advance and seeking an issue for its mystification. The question was, if one liked, asked civilly, yet asked none the less all round: 'What *could* have made Lord Northmore's family take him for a letter-writer?' Pompous and ponderous and at the same time loose and obscure, he managed by a trick of his own to be both slipshod and stiff. Who in such a case had been primarily responsible and under what strangely belated advice had a group of persons destitute of wit themselves been thus deplorably led astray? With fewer accomplices in the preparation it might almost have been assumed that they had been designedly befooled, been elaborately trapped.

They had at all events committed an error of which the most merciful thing to say was that, as founded on loyalty, it was touching. These things, in the welcome offered, lay perhaps not quite on the face, but they peeped between the lines and would force their way through on the morrow. The long quotations given were quotations marked Why? – 'Why,' in other words, as interpreted by Mrs Hope, 'drag to light such helplessness of expression? why give the text of his dulness and the proof of his fatuity?' The victim of the error had certainly been, in his way and day, a useful and remarkable person, but almost any other evidence of the fact might more happily have been adduced. It rolled over her, as she paced her room in the small hours, that the wheel had come full circle. There was after all a rough justice. The monument that had overdarkened her was reared, but it would be within a week the opportunity of every humourist, the derision of intelligent London. Her husband's strange share in it continued, that night, between dreams and vigils, to puzzle her, but light broke with her final waking, which was comfortably late. She opened her eyes to it and, on its staring straight into them, greeted it with the first laugh that had for a long time passed her lips. How could she idiotically not have guessed? Warren, playing insidiously the part of a guardian, had done what he had done on purpose! He had acted to an end long foretasted, and the end – the full taste – had come.

V

It was after this, none the less – after the other organs of criticism, including the smoking-rooms of the clubs, the lobbies of the House[7] and the dinner-tables of everywhere, had duly embodied their reserves and vented their irreverence, and the unfortunate two volumes had ranged themselves, beyond appeal, as a novelty insufficiently curious and prematurely stale – it was when this had come to pass that she really felt how beautiful her own chance would now have been and how sweet her revenge. The success of *her* volumes, for the inevitability of which nobody had had an instinct, would have been as great as the failure of Lady Northmore's, for the inevitability of which everybody had had one. She read over and over her letters and asked herself afresh if the confidence that had preserved *them* mightn't, at such a crisis, in spite of everything, justify itself. Didn't the discredit to English wit, as it were, proceeding from the uncorrected attribution to an established public character of such mediocrity of thought and form, really demand, for that matter, some such redemptive stroke as the appearance of a collection of masterpieces gathered from a similar walk? To have such a collection under one's hand and yet sit and see one's self not use it was a torment through which she might well have feared to break down.

But there was another thing she might do, not redemptive indeed, but perhaps after all, as matters were going, relevant. She fished out of their nook, after long years, the packet of John Northmore's epistles to herself and, reading them over in the light of his later style, judged them to contain to the full the promise of that inimitability; felt how they would deepen the impression and how, in the way of the *inédit*,[8] they constituted her supreme treasure. There was accordingly a terrible week for her in which she itched to put them forth. She composed mentally the preface, brief, sweet, ironic, presenting her as prompted by an anxious sense of duty to a great reputation and acting upon the sight of laurels[9] so lately gathered. There would naturally be difficulties; the documents were her own, but the family, bewildered, scared, suspicious, figured to her fancy as a dog with a dust-pan tied to its tail and ready for any dash to cover at the sound of the clatter of tin. They would have, she surmised, to be consulted, or, if not consulted, would put in an injunction; yet, of the two courses, that of scandal braved for the man she had rejected drew her on, while the charm of this vision worked, still further than that of delicacy over-ridden for the man she had married.

The vision closed round her and she lingered on the idea – fed, as she handled again her faded fat packet, by re-perusals more richly convinced. She even took opinions as to the interference open to her old friend's relatives; took in fact, from this time on, many opinions; went out anew, picked up old threads, repaired old ruptures, resumed, as it was called, her place in society. She had not been for years so seen of men as during the few weeks that followed the abasement of the Northmores. She called in particular on every one she had cast out after the failure of her appeal. Many of these persons figured as Lady Northmore's contributors, the unwitting agents of the cruel exposure; they having, it was sufficiently clear, acted in dense good faith. Warren, foreseeing and calculating, might have the benefit of such subtlety, but it wasn't for any one else. With every one else – for they did, on facing her, as she said to herself, look like fools – she made inordinately free; putting right and left the question of what in the past years they or their progenitors could have been thinking of. 'What on earth had you in mind and where among you were the rudiments of intelligence when you burnt up my husband's priceless letters and clung as for salvation to Lord Northmore's? You see how you've been saved!' The weak explanations, the imbecility, as she judged it, of the reasons given, were so much balm to her wound. The great balm, however, she kept to the last: she would go to see Lady Northmore only when she had exhausted all other comfort. That resource would be as supreme as the treasure of the fat packet. She finally went and, by a happy chance, if chance could ever be happy in such a house, was received. She remained half an hour – there were other persons present; and on rising to go knew herself satisfied. She had taken in what she desired, had sounded to the bottom what she saw; only, unexpectedly, something had overtaken her more absolute than the hard need she had obeyed or the vindictive advantage she had cherished. She had counted on herself for anything rather than pity of these people, yet it was in pity that at the end of ten minutes she felt everything else dissolve.

They were suddenly, on the spot, transformed for her by the depth of their misfortune, and she saw them, the great Northmores, as – of all things – consciously weak and flat. She neither made nor encountered an allusion to volumes published or frustrated; and so let her arranged enquiry die away that when on separation she kissed her wan sister in widowhood it was not with the kiss of Judas.[10] She had meant to ask lightly if she mightn't have *her* turn at editing; but the renunciation with which she re-entered her house had formed itself before she left the room. When she got home indeed she at first only wept – wept for the commonness of failure and the strangeness of life. Her tears perhaps brought her a sense of philosophy; it was all so as broad as it was long. When they were spent, at all events, she took out for the last time the faded fat packet. Sitting down by a receptacle daily emptied for the benefit of the dustman, she destroyed one by one the gems of the collection in which each piece had been a gem. She tore up to the last scrap Lord Northmore's letters. It would never be known now, as regards this series, either that they had been hoarded or that they had been sacrificed. And she was content so to let it rest. On the following day she began another task. She took out her husband's and attacked the business of transcription. She copied them piously, tenderly, and, for the purpose to which she now found herself settled, judged almost no omissions imperative. By the time they should be published –! She shook her head, both knowingly and resignedly, as to criticism so remote. When her transcript was finished she sent it to a printer to set up, and then, after receiving and correcting proof, and with every precaution for secrecy, had a single copy struck off and the type dispersed under her eyes. Her last act but one – or rather perhaps but two – was to put these sheets, which she was pleased to find, would form a volume of three hundred pages, carefully away. Her next was to add to her testamentary instrument a definite provision for the issue, after her death, of such a volume. Her last was to hope that death would come in time.

The Beast in the Jungle

I

What determined the speech that startled him in the course of their encounter scarcely matters, being probably but some words spoken by himself quite without intention – spoken as they lingered and slowly moved together after their renewal of acquaintance. He had been conveyed by friends an hour or two before to the house at which she was staying; the party of visitors at the other house, of whom he was one, and thanks to whom it was his theory, as always, that he was lost in the crowd, had been invited over to luncheon. There had been after luncheon much dispersal, all in the interest of the original motive, a view of Weatherend itself and the fine things, intrinsic features, pictures, heirlooms, treasures of all the arts, that made the place almost famous; and the great rooms were so numerous that guests could wander at their will, hang back from the principal group and in cases where they took such matters with the last seriousness give themselves up to mysterious appreciations and measurements. There were persons to be observed, singly or in couples, bending toward objects in out-of-the-way corners with their hands on their knees and their heads nodding quite as with the emphasis of an excited sense of smell. When they were two they either mingled their sounds of ecstasy or melted into silences of even deeper import, so that there were aspects of the occasion that gave it for Marcher much the air of the 'look round,' previous to a sale highly advertised, that excites or quenches, as may be, the dream of acquisition. The dream of acquisition at Weatherend would have had to be wild indeed, and John Marcher found himself, among such suggestions, disconcerted almost equally by the presence of those who knew too much and by that of those who knew nothing. The great rooms caused so much poetry and history to press upon him that he needed some straying apart to feel in a proper relation with them, though this impulse was not, as happened, like the gloating of some of his companions, to be compared to the movements of a dog sniffing a cupboard. It had an issue promptly enough in a direction that was not to have been calculated.

It led, briefly, in the course of the October afternoon, to his closer meeting with May Bartram, whose face, a reminder, yet not quite a remembrance, as they sat much separated at a very long table, had begun merely by troubling him rather pleasantly. It affected him as the sequel of something of which he had lost the beginning. He knew it, and for the time quite welcomed it, as a continuation, but didn't know what it continued, which was an interest or an amusement the greater as he was also somehow aware — yet without a direct sign from her — that the young woman herself hadn't lost the thread. She hadn't lost it, but she wouldn't give it back to him, he saw, without some putting forth of his hand for it; and he not only saw that, but saw several things more, things odd enough in the light of the fact that at the moment some accident of grouping brought them face to face he was still merely fumbling with the idea that any contact between them in the past would have had no importance. If it had had no importance he scarcely knew why his actual impression of her should so seem to have so much; the answer to which, however, was that in such a life as they all appeared to be leading for the moment one could but take things as they came. He was satisfied, without in the least being able to say why, that this young lady might roughly have ranked in the house as a poor relation; satisfied also that she was not there on a brief visit, but was more or less a part of the establishment — almost a working, a remunerated part. Didn't she enjoy at periods a protection that she paid for by helping, among other services, to show the place and explain it, deal with the tiresome people, answer questions about the dates of the building, the styles of the furniture, the authorship of the pictures, the favourite haunts of the ghost? It wasn't that she looked as if you could have given her shillings — it was impossible to look less so. Yet when she finally drifted toward him, distinctly handsome, though ever so much older — older than when he had seen her before — it might have been as an effect of her guessing that he had, within the couple of hours, devoted more imagination to her than to all the others put together, and had thereby penetrated to a kind of truth that the others were too stupid for. She *was* there on harder terms than any one; she was there as a consequence of things suffered, one way and another, in the interval of years; and she remembered him very much as she was remembered — only a good deal better.

By the time they at last thus came to speech they were alone in one of the rooms — remarkable for a fine portrait over the chimney-place — out of which their friends had passed, and the charm of it was that even before they had spoken they had practically arranged with each other to stay behind for talk. The charm, happily, was in other things too — partly in there being scarce a spot at Weatherend without something to stay behind for. It was in the way the autumn day looked into the high windows as it waned; the way the red light, breaking at the close from under a low sombre sky, reached out in a long shaft and played over old wainscots, old tapestry, old gold, old colour. It was most of all perhaps in the way she came to him as if, since she had been turned on to deal with the simpler sort, he might, should he choose to keep the whole thing down, just take her mild attention for a part of her general business. As soon as he heard her voice, however, the gap was filled up and the missing link supplied; the slight irony he divined in her attitude lost its advantage. He almost jumped at it to get there before her. 'I met you years and years ago in Rome. I remember all about it.' She confessed to disappointment – she had been so sure he didn't; and to prove how well he did he began to pour forth the particular recollections that popped up as he called for them. Her face and her voice, all at his service now, worked the miracle – the impression operating like the torch of a lamplighter who touches into flame, one by one, a long row of gas-jets. Marcher flattered himself the illumination was brilliant, yet he was really still more pleased on her showing him, with amusement, that in his haste to make everything right he had got most things rather wrong. It hadn't been at Rome – it had been at Naples; and it hadn't been eight years before – it had been more nearly ten. She hadn't been, either, with her uncle and aunt, but with her mother and her brother; in addition to which it was not with the Pembles *he* had been, but with the Boyers, coming down in their company from Rome – a point on which she insisted, a little to his confusion, and as to which she had her evidence in hand. The Boyers she had known, but didn't know the Pembles, though she had heard of them, and it was the people he was with who had made them acquainted. The incident of the thunderstorm that had raged round them with such violence as to drive them for refuge into an excavation – this incident had not occurred at the Palace of the Caesars, but at Pompeii,[1] on an occasion when they had been present there at an important find.

He accepted her amendments, he enjoyed her corrections, though the moral of them was, she pointed out, that he *really* didn't remember the least thing about her; and he only felt it as a drawback that when all was made strictly historic there didn't appear much of anything left. They lingered together still, she neglecting her office – for from the moment he was so clever she had no proper right to him – and both neglecting the house, just waiting as to see if a memory or two more wouldn't again breathe on them. It hadn't taken them many minutes, after all, to put down on the table, like the cards of a pack, those that constituted their respective hands; only what came out was that the pack was unfortunately not perfect – that the past, invoked, invited, encouraged, could give them, naturally, no more than it had. It had made them anciently meet – her at twenty, him at twenty-five; but nothing was so strange, they seemed to say to each other, as that, while so occupied, it hadn't done a little more for them. They looked at each other as with the feeling of an occasion missed; the present would have been so much better if the other, in the far distance, in the foreign land, hadn't been so stupidly meagre. There weren't apparently, all counted, more than a dozen little old things that had succeeded in coming to pass between them; trivialities of youth, simplicities of freshness, stupidities of ignorance, small possible germs, but too deeply buried – too deeply (didn't it seem?) to sprout after so many years. Marcher could only feel he ought to have rendered her some service – saved her from a capsized boat in the Bay or at least recovered her dressing-bag, filched from her cab in the streets of Naples by a lazzarone with a stiletto.[2] Or it would have been nice if he could have been taken with fever[3] all alone at his hotel, and she could have come to look after him, to write to his people, to drive him out in convalescence. *Then* they would be in possession of the something or other that their actual show seemed to lack. It yet somehow presented itself, this show, as too good to be spoiled; so that they were reduced for a few minutes more to wondering a little helplessly why – since they seemed to know a certain number of the same people – their reunion had been so long averted. They didn't use that name for it, but their delay from minute to minute to join the others was a kind of confession that they didn't quite want it to be a failure. Their attempted supposition of reasons for their not having met but showed how little they knew of each other. There came in fact a moment when Marcher felt a positive pang. It was vain to pretend she was an old friend, for all the communities were wanting, in spite of which it was as an old friend that he saw she would have suited him. He had new ones enough – was surrounded with them for instance on the stage of the other house; as a new one he probably wouldn't have so much as noticed her. He would have liked to invent something, get her to make-believe with him that some passage of a romantic or critical kind *had* originally occurred. He was really almost reaching out in imagination – as against time – for something that would do, and saying to himself that if it didn't come this sketch of a fresh start would show for quite awkwardly bungled. They would separate, and now for no second or no third chance. They would have tried and not succeeded. Then it was, just at the turn, as he afterwards made it out to himself, that, everything else failing, she herself decided to take up the case and, as it were, save the situation. He felt as soon as she spoke that she had been consciously keeping back what she said and hoping to get on without it; a scruple in her that immensely touched him when, by the end of three or four minutes more, he was able to measure it. What she brought out, at any rate, quite cleared the air and supplied the link – the link it was so odd he should frivolously have managed to lose.

'You know you told me something I've never forgotten and that again and again has made me think of you since; it was that tremendously hot day when we went to Sorrento, across the bay,[4] for the breeze. What I allude to was what you said to me, on the way back, as we sat under the awning of the boat enjoying the cool. Have you forgotten?'

He had forgotten and was even more surprised than ashamed. But the great thing was that he saw in this no vulgar reminder of any 'sweet' speech. The vanity of women had long memories, but she was making no claim on him of a compliment or a mistake. With another woman, a totally different one, he might have feared the recall possibly even some imbecile 'offer.' So, in having to say that he had indeed forgotten, he was conscious rather of a loss than of a gain; he already saw an interest in the matter of her mention. 'I try to think – but I give it up. Yet I remember the Sorrento day.'

'I'm not very sure you do,' May Bartram after a moment said; 'and I'm not very sure I ought to want you to. It's dreadful to bring a person back at any time to what he was ten years before. If you've lived away from it,' she smiled, 'so much the better.'

'Ah if *you* haven't why should I?' he asked.

'Lived away, you mean, from what I myself was?'

'From what *I* was. I was of course an ass,' Marcher went on; 'but I would rather know from you just the sort of ass I was than – from the moment you have something in your mind – not know anything.'

Still, however, she hesitated. 'But if you've completely ceased to be that sort –?'

'Why I can then all the more bear to know. Besides, perhaps I haven't.'

'Perhaps. Yet if you haven't,' she added, 'I should suppose you'd remember. Not indeed that *I* in the least connect with my impression the invidious name you use. If I had only thought you foolish,' she explained, 'the thing I speak of wouldn't so have remained with me. It was about yourself.' She waited as if it might come to him; but as, only meeting her eyes in wonder, he gave no sign, she burnt her ships. 'Has it ever happened?'

Then it was that, while he continued to stare, a light broke for him and the blood slowly came to his face, which began to burn with recognition. 'Do you mean I told you –?' But he faltered, lest what came to him shouldn't be right, lest he should only give himself away.

'It was something about yourself that it was natural one shouldn't forget – that is if one remembered you at all. That's why I ask you,' she smiled, 'if the thing you then spoke of has ever come to pass?'

Oh then he saw, but he was lost in wonder and found himself embarrassed. This, he also saw, made her sorry for him, as if her allusion had been a mistake. It took him but a moment, however, to feel it hadn't been, much as it had been a surprise. After the first little shock of it her knowledge on the contrary began, even if rather strangely, to taste sweet to him. She was the only other person in the world then who would have it, and she had had it all these years, while the fact of his having so breathed his secret had unaccountably faded from him. No wonder they couldn't have met as if nothing had happened. 'I judge,' he finally said, 'that I know what you mean. Only I had strangely enough lost any sense of having taken you so far into my confidence.'

'Is it because you've taken so many others as well?'

'I've taken nobody. Not a creature since then.'

'So that I'm the only person who knows?'

'The only person in the world.'

'Well,' she quickly replied, 'I myself have never spoken. I've never, never repeated of you what you told me.' She looked at him so that he perfectly believed her. Their eyes met over it in such a way that he was without a doubt. 'And I never will.'

She spoke with an earnestness that, as if almost excessive, put him at ease about her possible derision. Somehow the whole question was a new luxury to him – that is from the moment she was in possession. If she didn't take the sarcastic view she clearly took the sympathetic, and that was what he had had, in all the long time, from no one whomsoever. What he felt was that he couldn't at present have begun to tell her, and yet could profit perhaps exquisitely by the accident of having done so of old. 'Please don't then. We're just right as it is.'

'Oh I am,' she laughed, 'if you are!' To which she added: 'Then you do still feel in the same way?'

It was impossible he shouldn't take to himself that she was really interested, though it all kept coming as perfect surprise. He had thought of himself so long as abominably alone, and lo he wasn't alone a bit. He hadn't been, it appeared, for an hour – since those moments on the Sorrento boat. It was *she* who had been, he seemed to see as he looked at her – she who had been made so by the graceless fact of his lapse of fidelity. To tell her what he had told her – what had it been but to ask something of her? something that she had given, in her charity, without his having, by a remembrance, by a return of the spirit, failing another encounter, so much as thanked her. What he had asked of her had been simply at first not to laugh at him. She had beautifully not done so for ten years, and she was not doing so now. So he had endless gratitude to make up. Only for that he must see just how he had figured to her. 'What, exactly, was the account I gave –?'

'Of the way you did feel? Well, it was very simple. You said you had had from your earliest time, as the deepest thing within you, the sense of being kept for something rare and strange, possibly prodigious and terrible, that was sooner or later to happen to you, that you had in your bones the foreboding and the conviction of, and that would perhaps overwhelm you.'

'Do you call that very simple?' John Marcher asked.

She thought a moment. 'It was perhaps because I seemed, as you spoke, to understand it.'

'You do understand it?' he eagerly asked.

Again she kept her kind eyes on him. 'You still have the belief?'

'Oh!' he exclaimed helplessly. There was too much to say.

'Whatever it's to be,' she clearly made out, 'it hasn't yet come.'

He shook his head in complete surrender now. 'It hasn't yet come. Only, you know, it isn't anything I'm to *do*, to achieve in the world, to be distinguished or admired for. I'm not such an ass as *that*. It would be much better, no doubt, if I were.'

'It's to be something you're merely to suffer?'

'Well, say to wait for – to have to meet, to face, to see suddenly break out in my life; possibly destroying all further consciousness, possibly annihilating me; possibly, on the other hand, only altering everything, striking at the root of all my world and leaving me to the consequences, however they shape themselves.'

She took this in, but the light in her eyes continued for him not to be that of mockery. 'Isn't what you describe perhaps but the expectation – or at any rate the sense of danger, familiar to so many people – of falling in love?'

John Marcher wondered. 'Did you ask me that before?'

'No – I wasn't so free-and-easy then. But it's what strikes me now.'

'Of course,' he said after a moment, 'it strikes you. Of course it strikes *me*. Of course what's in store for me may be no more than that. The only thing is,' he went on, 'that I think if it had been that I should by this time know.'

'Do you mean because you've *been* in love?' And then as he but looked at her in silence: 'You've been in love, and it hasn't meant such a cataclysm, hasn't proved the great affair?'

'Here I am, you see. It hasn't been overwhelming.'

'Then it hasn't been love,' said May Bartram.

'Well, I at least thought it was. I took it for that – I've taken it till now. It was agreeable, it was delightful, it was miserable,' he explained. 'But it wasn't strange. It wasn't what *my* affair's to be.'

'You want something all to yourself – something that nobody else knows or *has* known?'

'It isn't a question of what I "want" – God knows I don't want anything. It's only a question of the apprehension that haunts me – that I live with day by day.'

He said this so lucidly and consistently that he could see it further impose itself. If she hadn't been interested before she'd have been interested now. 'Is it a sense of coming violence?'

Evidently now too again he liked to talk of it. 'I don't think of it as – when it does come – necessarily violent. I only think of it as natural and as of course above all unmistakeable. I think of it simply as *the* thing. *The* thing will of itself appear natural.'

'Then how will it appear strange?'

432

Marcher bethought himself. 'It won't – to *me*.'

'To whom then?'

'Well,' he replied, smiling at last, 'say to you.'

'Oh then I'm to be present?'

'Why you *are* present – since you know.'

'I see.' She turned it over. 'But I mean at the catastrophe.'⁵

At this, for a minute, their lightness gave way to their gravity; it was as if the long look they exchanged held them together. 'It will only depend on yourself – if you'll watch with me.'

'Are you afraid?' she asked.

'Don't leave me *now*,' he went on.

'Are you afraid?' she repeated.

'Do you think me simply out of my mind?' he pursued instead of answering. 'Do I merely strike you as a harmless lunatic?'

'No,' said May Bartram. 'I understand you. I believe you.'

'You mean you feel how my obsession – poor old thing! – may correspond to some possible reality?'

'To some possible reality.'

'Then you *will* watch with me?'

She hesitated, then for the third time put her question. 'Are you afraid?'

'Did I tell you I was – at Naples?'

'No, you said nothing about it.'

'Then I don't know. And I should *like* to know,' said John Marcher. 'You'll tell me yourself whether you think so. If you'll watch with me you'll see.'

'Very good then.' They had been moving by this time across the room, and at the door, before passing out, they paused as for the full wind-up of their understanding. 'I'll watch with you,' said May Bartram.

II

The fact that she 'knew' – knew and yet neither chaffed him nor betrayed him – had in a short time begun to constitute between them a goodly bond, which became more marked when, within the year that followed their afternoon at Weatherend, the opportunities for meeting multiplied. The event that thus promoted these occasions was the death of the ancient lady her great-aunt, under whose wing, since losing her mother, she had to such an extent found shelter, and who, though but the widowed mother of the new successor to the property, had succeeded – thanks to a high tone and a high temper – in not forfeiting the supreme position at the great house. The deposition of this personage arrived but with her death, which, followed by many changes, made in particular a difference for the young woman in whom Marcher's expert attention had recognised from the first a dependent with a pride that might ache though it didn't bristle. Nothing for a long time had made him easier than the thought that the aching must have been much soothed by Miss Bartram's now finding herself able to set up a small home in London. She had acquired property, to an amount that made that luxury just possible, under her aunt's extremely complicated will, and when the whole matter began to be straightened out, which indeed took time, she let him know that the happy issue was at last in view. He had seen her again before that day, both because she had more than once accompanied the ancient lady to town and because he had paid another visit to the friends who so conveniently made of Weatherend one of the charms of their own hospitality. These friends had taken him back there; he had achieved there again with Miss Bartram some quiet detachment; and he had in London succeeded in persuading her to more than one brief absence from her aunt. They went together, on these latter occasions, to the National Gallery and the South Kensington Museum,[6] where, among vivid reminders, they talked of Italy at large – not now attempting to recover, as at first, the taste of their youth and their ignorance. That recovery, the first day at Weatherend, had served its purpose well, had given them quite enough; so that they were, to Marcher's sense, no longer hovering about the headwaters of their stream, but had felt their boat pushed sharply off and down the current.

They were literally afloat together; for our gentleman this was marked, quite as marked as that the fortunate cause of it was just the buried treasure of her knowledge. He had with his own hands dug up this little hoard, brought to light – that is to within reach of the dim day constituted by their discretions and privacies – the object of value the hiding-place of which he had, after putting it into the ground himself, so strangely, so long forgotten. The rare luck of his having again just stumbled on the spot made him indifferent to any other question; he would doubtless have devoted more time to the odd accident of his lapse of memory if he hadn't been moved to devote so much to the sweetness, the comfort, as he felt, for the future, that this accident itself had helped to keep fresh. It had never entered into his plan that any one should 'know,' and mainly for the reason that it wasn't in him to tell any one. That would have been impossible, for nothing but the amusement of a cold world would have waited on it. Since, however, a mysterious fate had opened his mouth betimes, in spite of him, he would count that a compensation and profit by it to the utmost. That the right person *should* know tempered the asperity of his secret more even than his shyness had permitted him to imagine; and May Bartram was clearly right, because – well, because there she was. Her knowledge simply settled it; he would have been sure enough by this time had she been wrong. There was that in his situation, no doubt, that disposed him too much to see her as a mere confidant, taking all her light for him from the fact — the fact only — of her interest in his predicament; from her mercy, sympathy, seriousness, her consent not to regard him as the funniest of the funny. Aware, in fine, that her price for him was just in her giving him this constant sense of his being admirably spared, he was careful to remember that she had also a life of her own, with things that might happen to *her*, things that in friendship one should likewise take account of. Something fairly remarkable came to pass with him, for that matter, in this connexion — something represented by a certain passage of his consciousness, in the suddenest way, from one extreme to the other.

He had thought himself, so long as nobody knew, the most disinterested person in the world, carrying his concentrated burden, his perpetual suspense, ever so quietly, holding his tongue about it, giving others no glimpse of it nor of its effect upon his life, asking of them no allowance and only making on his side all those that were asked. He hadn't disturbed people with the queerness of their having to know a haunted man, though he had had moments of rather special temptation on hearing them say they were forsooth 'unsettled.' If they were as unsettled as he was — he who had never been settled for an hour in his life — they would know what it meant. Yet it wasn't, all the same, for him to make them, and he listened to them civilly enough. This was why he had such good — though possibly such rather colourless — manners; this was why, above all, he could regard himself, in a greedy world, as decently — as in fact perhaps even a little sublimely — unselfish. Our point is accordingly that he valued this character quite sufficiently to measure his present danger of letting it lapse, against which he promised himself to be much on his guard. He was quite ready, none the less, to be selfish just a little, since surely no more charming occasion for it had come to him. 'Just a little,' in a word, was just as much as Miss Bartram, taking one day with another, would let him. He never would be in the least coercive, and would keep well before him the lines on which consideration for her — the very highest — ought to proceed. He would thoroughly establish the heads under which her affairs, her require- ments, her peculiarities — he went so far as to give them the latitude of that name — would come into their intercourse. All this naturally was a sign of how much he took the intercourse itself for granted. There was nothing more to be done about *that*. It simply existed; had sprung into being with her first penetrating question to him in the autumn light there at Weatherend. The real form it should have taken on the basis that stood out large was the form of their marrying. But the devil in this was that the very basis itself put marrying out of the question. His conviction, his apprehension, his obsession, in short, wasn't a privilege he could invite a woman to share; and that consequence of it was precisely what was the matter with him. Something or other lay in wait for him, amid the twists and the turns of the months and the years, like a crouching beast in the jungle. It signified little whether the crouching beast were destined to slay him or to be slain. The definite point was the inevitable spring of the creature; and the definite lesson from that was that a man of feeling didn't cause himself to be accompanied by a lady on a tiger-hunt. Such was the image under which he had ended by figuring his life.

They had at first, none the less, in the scattered hours spent together, made no allusion to that view of it; which was a sign he was handsomely alert to give that he didn't expect, that he in fact didn't care, always to be talking about it. Such a feature in one's outlook was really like a hump on one's back. The difference it made every minute of the day existed quite independently of discussion. One discussed of course *like* a hunchback, for there was always, if nothing else, the hunchback face. That remained, and she was watching him; but people watched best, as a general thing, in silence, so that such would be predominantly the manner of their vigil. Yet he didn't want, at the same time, to be tense and solemn; tense and solemn was what he imagined he too much showed for with other people. The thing to be, with the one person who knew, was easy and natural — to make the reference rather than be seeming to avoid it, to avoid it rather than be seeming to make it, and to keep it, in any case, familiar, facetious even, rather than pedantic and portentous. Some such consideration as the latter was doubtless in his mind for instance when he wrote pleasantly to Miss Bartram that perhaps the great thing he had so long felt as in the lap of the gods was no more than this circumstance, which touched him so nearly, of her acquiring a house in London. It was the first allusion they had yet again made, needing any other hitherto so little; but when she replied, after having given him the news, that she was by no means satisfied with such a trifle as the climax to so special a suspense, she almost set him wondering if she hadn't even a larger conception of singularity for him than he had for himself. He was at all events destined to become aware little by little, as time went by, that she was all the while looking at his life, judging it, measuring it, in the light of the thing she knew, which grew to be at last, with the consecration of the years, never mentioned between them save as 'the real truth' about him. That had always been his own form of reference to it, but she adopted the form so quietly that, looking back at the end of a period, he knew there was no moment at which it was traceable that she had, as he might say, got inside his idea, or exchanged the attitude of beautifully indulging for that of still more beautifully believing him.

It was always open to him to accuse her of seeing him but as the most harmless of maniacs, and this, in the long run — since it covered so much ground — was his easiest description of their friendship. He had a screw loose for her, but she liked him in spite of it and was practically, against the rest of the world, his kind wise keeper, unremunerated but fairly amused and, in the absence of other near ties, not disreputably occupied. The rest of the world of course thought him queer, but she, she only, knew how, and above all why, queer; which was precisely what enabled her to dispose the concealing veil in the right folds. She took his gaiety from him – since it had to pass with them for gaiety – as she took everything else; but she certainly so far justified by her unerring touch his finer sense of the degree to which he had ended by convincing her. *She* at least never spoke of the secret of his life except as 'the real truth about you,' and she had in fact a wonderful way of making it seem, as such, the secret of her own life too. That was in fine how he so constantly felt her as allowing for him; he couldn't on the whole call it anything else. He allowed for himself, but she, exactly, allowed still more; partly because, better placed for a sight of the matter, she traced his unhappy perversion through reaches of its course into which he could scarce follow it. He knew how he felt, but, besides knowing that, she knew how he *looked* as well; he knew each of the things of importance he was insidiously kept from doing, but she could add up the amount they made, understand how much, with a lighter weight on his spirit, he might have done, and thereby establish how, clever as he was, he fell short. Above all she was in the secret of the difference between the forms he went through – those of his little office under Government, those of caring for his modest patrimony, for his library, for his garden in the country, for the people in London whose invitations he accepted and repaid – and the detachment that reigned beneath them and that made of all behaviour, all that could in the least be called behaviour, a long act of dissimulation. What it had come to was that he wore a mask painted with the social simper, out of the eye-holes of which there looked eyes of an expression not in the least matching the other features. This the stupid world, even after years, had never more than half-discovered. It was only May Bartram who had, and she achieved, by an art indescribable, the feat of at once – or perhaps it was only alternately – meeting the eyes from in front and mingling her own vision, as from over his shoulder, with their peep through the apertures.

So while they grew older together she did watch with him, and so she let this association give shape and colour to her own existence. Beneath *her* forms as well detachment had learned to sit, and behaviour had become for her, in the social sense, a false account of herself. There was but one account of her that would have been true all the while and that she could give straight to nobody, least of all to John Marcher. Her whole attitude was a virtual statement, but the perception of that only seemed called to take its place for him as one of the many things necessarily crowded out of his consciousness. If she had moreover, like himself, to make sacrifices to their real truth, it was to be granted that her compensation might have affected her as more prompt and more natural. They had long periods, in this London time, during which, when they were together, a stranger might have listened to them without in the least pricking up his ears; on the other hand the real truth was equally liable at any moment to rise to the surface, and the auditor would then have wondered indeed what they were talking about. They had from an early hour made up their mind that society was, luckily, unintelligent, and the margin allowed them by this had fairly become one of their commonplaces. Yet there were still moments when the situation turned almost fresh – usually under the effect of some expression drawn from herself. Her expressions doubtless repeated themselves, but her intervals were generous. 'What saves us, you know, is that we answer so completely to so usual an appearance: that of the man and woman whose friendship has become such a daily habit – or almost – as to be at last indispensable.' That for instance was a remark she had frequently enough had occasion to make, though she had given it at different times different developments. What we are especially concerned with is the turn it happened to take from her one afternoon when he had come to see her in honour of her birthday. This anniversary had fallen on a Sunday, at a season of thick fog and general outward gloom; but he had brought her his customary offering, having known her now long enough to have established a hundred small traditions. It was one of his proofs to himself, the present he made her on her birthday, that he hadn't sunk into real selfishness. It was mostly nothing more than a small trinket, but it was always fine of its kind, and he was regularly careful to pay for it more than he thought he could afford. 'Our habit saves you at least, don't you see? because it makes you, after all, for the vulgar, indistinguishable from other men. What's the most inveterate mark of men in general? Why the capacity to spend endless time with dull women – to spend it I won't say without being bored, but without minding that they are, without being driven off at a tangent by it; which comes to the same thing. I'm your dull woman, a part of the daily bread for which you pray at church. That covers your tracks more than anything.'

'And what covers yours?' asked Marcher, whom his dull woman could mostly to this extent amuse. 'I see of course what you mean by your saving me, in this way and that, so far as other people are concerned – I've seen it all along. Only what is it that saves *you*? I often think, you know, of that.'

She looked as if she sometimes thought of that too, but rather in a different way. 'Where other people, you mean, are concerned?'

'Well, you're really so in with me, you know – as a sort of result of my being so in with yourself. I mean of my having such an immense regard for you, being so tremendously mindful of all you've done for me. I sometimes ask myself if it's quite fair. Fair I mean to have so involved and – since one may say it – interested you. I almost feel as if you hadn't really had time to do anything else.'

'Anything else but be interested?' she asked. 'Ah what else does one ever want to be? If I've been "watching" with you, as we long ago agreed I was to do, watching's always in itself an absorption.'

'Oh certainly,' John Marcher said, 'if you hadn't had your curiosity –! Only doesn't it sometimes come to you as time goes on that your curiosity isn't being particularly repaid?'

May Bartram had a pause. 'Do you ask that, by any chance, because you feel at all that yours isn't? I mean because you have to wait so long.'

Oh he understood what she meant! 'For the thing to happen that never does happen? For the beast to jump out? No, I'm just where I was about it. It isn't a matter as to which I can *choose*, I can decide for a change. It isn't one as to which there *can* be a change. It's in the lap of the gods. One's in the hands of one's law – there one is. As to the form the law will take, the way it will operate, that's its own affair.'

'Yes,' Miss Bartram replied; 'of course one's fate's coming, of course it *has* come in its own form and its own way, all the while. Only, you know, the form and the way in your case were to have been – well, something so exceptional and, as one may say, so particularly *your* own.'

Something in this made him look at her with suspicion. 'You say "were to *have* been," as if in your heart you had begun to doubt.'

'Oh!' she vaguely protested.

'As if you believed,' he went on, 'that nothing will now take place.'

She shook her head slowly but rather inscrutably. 'You're far from my thought.'

He continued to look at her. 'What then is the matter with you?'

'Well,' she said after another wait, 'the matter with me is simply that I'm more sure than ever my curiosity, as you call it, will be but too well repaid.'

They were frankly grave now; he had got up from his seat, had turned once more about the little drawing-room to which, year after year, he brought his inevitable topic; in which he had, as he might have said, tasted their intimate community with every sauce, where every object was as familiar to him as the things of his own house and the very carpets were worn with his fitful walk very much as the desks in old counting-houses are worn by the elbows of generations of clerks. The generations of his nervous moods had been at work there, and the place was the written history of his whole middle life. Under the impression of what his friend had just said he knew himself, for some reason, more aware of these things; which made him, after a moment, stop again before her. 'Is it possibly that you've grown afraid?'

'Afraid?' He thought, as she repeated the word, that his question had made her, a little, change colour; so that, lest he should have touched on a truth, he explained very kindly: 'You remember that that was what you asked *me* long ago – that first day at Weatherend.'

'Oh yes, and you told me you didn't know — that I was to see for myself. We've said little about it since, even in so long a time.'

'Precisely,' Marcher interposed — 'quite as if it were too delicate a matter for us to make free with. Quite as if we might find, on pressure, that I *am* afraid. For then,' he said, 'we shouldn't, should we? quite know what to do.'

She had for the time no answer to this question. 'There have been days when I thought you were. Only, of course,' she added, 'there have been days when we have thought almost anything.'

'Everything. Oh!' Marcher softly groaned as with a gasp, half-spent, at the face, more uncovered just then than it had been for a long while, of the imagination always with them. It had always had its incalculable moments of glaring out, quite as with the very eyes of the very Beast, and, used as he was to them, they could still draw from him the tribute of a sigh that rose from the depths of his being. All they had thought, first and last, rolled over him; the past seemed to have been reduced to mere barren speculation. This in fact was what the place had just struck him as so full of — the simplification of everything but the state of suspense. That remained only by seeming to hang in the void surrounding it. Even his original fear, if fear it had been, had lost itself in the desert. 'I judge, however,' he continued, 'that you see I'm not afraid now.'

'What I see, as I make it out, is that you've achieved something almost unprecedented in the way of getting used to danger. Living with it so long and so closely you've lost your sense of it; you know it's there, but you're indifferent, and you cease even, as of old, to have to whistle in the dark. Considering what the danger is,' May Bartram wound up, 'I'm bound to say I don't think your attitude could well be surpassed.'

John Marcher faintly smiled. 'It's heroic?'

'Certainly — call it that.'

It was what he would have liked indeed to call it. 'I *am* then a man of courage?'

'That's what you were to show me.'

He still, however, wondered. 'But doesn't the man of courage know what he's afraid of — or not afraid of? I don't know *that*, you see. I don't focus it. I can't name it. I only know I'm exposed.'

'Yes, but exposed — how shall I say? — so directly. So intimately. That's sure enough.'

'Enough to make you feel then — as what we may call the end and the upshot of our watch — that I'm not afraid?'

'You're not afraid. But it isn't,' she said, 'the end of our watch. That is it isn't the end of yours. You've everything still to see.'

'Then why haven't you?' he asked. He had had, all along to-day, the sense of her keeping something back, and he still had it. As this was his first impression of that it quite made a date. The case was the more marked as she didn't at first answer; which in turn made him go on. 'You know something I don't.' Then his voice, for that of a man of courage, trembled a little. 'You know what's to happen.' Her silence, with the face she showed, was almost a confession – it made him sure. 'You know, and you're afraid to tell me. It's so bad that you're afraid I'll find out.'

All this might be true, for she did look as if, unexpectedly to her, he had crossed some mystic line that she had secretly drawn round her. Yet she might, after all, not have worried; and the real climax was that he himself, at all events, needn't. 'You'll never find out.'

III

It was all to have made, none the less, as I have said, a date; which came out in the fact that again and again, even after long intervals, other things that passed between them wore in relation to this hour but the character of recalls and results. Its immediate effect had been indeed rather to lighten insistence – almost to provoke a reaction; as if their topic had dropped by its own weight and as if moreover, for that matter, Marcher had been visited by one of his occasional warnings against egotism. He had kept up, he felt, and very decently on the whole, his consciousness of the importance of not being selfish, and it was true that he had never sinned in that direction without promptly enough trying to press the scales the other way. He often repaired his fault, the season permitting, by inviting his friend to accompany him to the opera; and it not infrequently thus happened that, to show he didn't wish her to have but one sort of food for her mind, he was the cause of her appearing there with him a dozen nights in the month. It even happened that, seeing her home at such times, he occasionally went in with her to finish, as he called it, the evening, and, the better to make his point, sat down to the frugal but always careful little supper that awaited his pleasure. His point was made, he thought, by his not eternally insisting with her on himself; made for instance, at such hours, when it befell that, her piano at hand and each of them familiar with it, they went over passages of the opera together. It chanced to be on one of these occasions, however, that he reminded her of her not having answered a certain question he had put to her during the talk that had taken place between them on her last birthday. 'What is it that saves *you*?' – saved her, he meant, from that appearance of variation from the usual human type. If he had practically escaped remark, as she pretended, by doing, in the most important particular, what most men do – find the answer to life in patching up an alliance of a sort with a woman no better than himself – how had she escaped it, and how could the alliance, such as it was, since they must suppose it had been more or less noticed, have failed to make her rather positively talked about?

'I never said,' May Bartram replied, 'that it hadn't made me a good deal talked about.'

'Ah well then you're not "saved." '

'It hasn't been a question for me. If you've had your woman I've had,' she said, 'my man.'

'And you mean that makes you all right?'

Oh it was always as if there were so much to say! 'I don't know why it shouldn't make me – humanly, which is what we're speaking of – as right as it makes you.'

'I see,' Marcher returned. ' "Humanly," no doubt, as showing that you're living for something. Not, that is, just for me and my secret.'

May Bartram smiled. 'I don't pretend it exactly shows that I'm not living for you. It's my intimacy with you that's in question.'

He laughed as he saw what she meant. 'Yes, but since, as you say, I'm only, so far as people make out, ordinary, you're – aren't you? – no more than ordinary either. You help me to pass for a man like another. So if I *am*, as I understand you, you're not compromised. Is that it?'

She had another of her waits, but she spoke clearly enough. 'That's it. It's all that concerns me – to help you to pass for a man like another.'

He was careful to acknowledge the remark handsomely. 'How kind, how beautiful, you are to me! How shall I ever repay you?'

She had her last grave pause, as if there might be a choice of ways. But she chose. 'By going on as you are.'

It was into this going on as he was that they relapsed, and really for so long a time that the day inevitably came for a further sounding of their depths. These depths, constantly bridged over by a structure firm enough in spite of its lightness and of its occasional oscillation in the somewhat vertiginous air, invited on occasion, in the interest of their nerves, a dropping of the plummet and a measurement of the abyss. A difference had been made moreover, once for all, by the fact that she had all the while not appeared to feel the need of rebutting his charge of an idea within her that she didn't dare to express – a charge uttered just before one of the fullest of their later discussions ended. It had come up for him then that she 'knew' something and that what she knew was bad – too bad to tell him. When he had spoken of it as visibly so bad that she was afraid he might find it out, her reply had left the matter too equivocal to be let alone and yet, for Marcher's special sensibility, almost too formidable again to touch. He circled about it at a distance that alternately narrowed and widened and that still wasn't much affected by the consciousness in him that there was nothing she could 'know,' after all, any better than he did. She had no source of knowledge he hadn't equally – except of course that she might have finer nerves. That was what women had where they were interested; they made out things, where people were concerned, that the people often couldn't have made out for themselves. Their nerves, their sensibility, their imagination, were conductors and revealers, and the beauty of May Bartram was in particular that she had given herself so to his case. He felt in these days what, oddly enough, he had never felt before, the growth of a dread of losing her by some catastrophe – some catastrophe that yet wouldn't at all be *the* catastrophe: partly because she had almost of a sudden begun to strike him as more useful to him than ever yet, and partly by reason of an appearance of uncertainty in her health, coincident and equally new. It was characteristic of the inner detachment he had hitherto so successfully cultivated and to which our whole account of him is a reference, it was characteristic that his complications, such as they were, had never yet seemed so as at this crisis to thicken about him, even to the point of making him ask himself if he were, by any chance, of a truth, within sight or sound, within touch or reach, within the immediate jurisdiction, of the thing that waited.

When the day came, as come it had to, that his friend confessed to him her fear of a deep disorder in her blood, he felt somehow the shadow of a change and the chill of a shock. He immediately began to imagine aggravations and disasters, and above all to think of her peril as the direct menace for himself of personal privation. This indeed gave him one of those partial recoveries of equanimity that were agreeable to him – it showed him that what was still first in his mind was the loss she herself might suffer. 'What if she should have to die before knowing, before seeing –?' It would have been brutal, in the early stages of her trouble, to put that question to her; but it had immediately sounded for him to his own concern, and the possibility was what most made him sorry for her. If she did 'know,' moreover, in the sense of her having had some – what should he think? – mystical irresistible light, this would make the matter not better, but worse, inasmuch as her original adoption of his own curiosity had quite become the basis of her life. She had been living to see what would *be* to be seen, and it would quite lacerate her to have to give up before the accomplishment of the vision. These reflexions, as I say, quickened his generosity; yet, make them as he might, he saw himself, with the lapse of the period, more and more disconcerted. It lapsed for him with a strange steady sweep, and the oddest oddity was that it gave him, independently of the threat of much inconvenience, almost the only positive surprise his career, if career it could be called, had yet offered him. She kept the house as she had never done; he had to go to her to see her – she could meet him nowhere now, though there was scarce a corner of their loved old London in which she hadn't in the past, at one time or another, done so; and he found her always seated by her fire in the deep old-fashioned chair she was less and less able to leave. He had been struck one day, after an absence exceeding his usual measure, with her suddenly looking much older to him than he had ever thought of her being; then he recognised that the suddenness was all on his side — he had just simply and suddenly noticed. She looked older because inevitably, after so many years, she *was* old, or almost; which was of course true in still greater measure of her companion. If she was old, or almost, John Marcher assuredly was, and yet it was her showing of the lesson, not his own, that brought the truth home to him. His surprises began here; when once they had begun they multiplied; they came rather with a rush: it was as if, in the oddest way in the world, they had all been kept back, sown in a thick cluster, for the late afternoon of life, the time at which for people in general the unexpected has died out.

One of them was that he should have caught himself — for he *had* so done — *really* wondering if the great accident would take form now as nothing more than his being condemned to see this charming woman, this admirable friend, pass away from him. He had never so unreservedly qualified her as while confronted in thought with such a possibility; in spite of which there was small doubt for him that as an answer to his long riddle the mere effacement of even so fine a feature of his situation would be an abject anti-climax. It would represent, as connected with his past attitude, a drop of dignity under the shadow of which his existence could only become the most grotesque of failures. He had been far from holding it a failure — long as he had waited for the appearance that was to make it a success. He had waited for quite another thing, not for such a thing as that. The breath of his good faith came short, however, as he recognised how long he had waited, or how long at least his companion had. That she, at all events, might be recorded as having waited in vain — this affected him sharply, and all the more because of his at first having done little more than amuse himself with the idea. It grew more grave as the gravity of her condition grew, and the state of mind it produced in him, which he himself ended by watching as if it had been some definite disfigurement of his outer person, may pass for another of his surprises. This conjoined itself still with another, the really stupefying consciousness of a question that he would have allowed to shape itself had he dared. What did everything mean — what, that is, did *she* mean, she and her vain waiting and her probable death and the soundless admonition of it all — unless that, at this time of day, it was simply, it was overwhelmingly too late? He had never at any stage of his queer consciousness admitted the whisper of such a correction; he had never till within these last few months been so false to his conviction as not to hold that what was to come to him had time, whether *he* struck himself as having it or not.

That at last, at last, he certainly hadn't it, to speak of, or had it but in the scantiest measure – such, soon enough, as things went with him, became the inference with which his old obsession had to reckon: and this it was not helped to do by the more and more confirmed appearance that the great vagueness casting the long shadow in which he had lived had, to attest itself, almost no margin left. Since it was in Time that he was to have met his fate, so it was in Time that his fate was to have acted; and as he waked up to the sense of no longer being young, which was exactly the sense of being stale, just as that, in turn, was the sense of being weak, he waked up to another matter beside. It all hung together; they were subject, he and the great vagueness, to an equal and indivisible law. When the possibilities themselves had accordingly turned stale, when the secret of the gods had grown faint, had perhaps even quite evaporated, that, and that only, was failure. It wouldn't have been failure to be bankrupt, dishonoured, pilloried, hanged; it was failure not to be anything. And so, in the dark valley into which his path had taken its unlooked-for twist, he wondered not a little as he groped. He didn't care what awful crash might overtake him, with what ignominy or what monstrosity he might yet be associated – since he wasn't after all too utterly old to suffer – if it would only be decently proportionate to the posture he had kept, all his life, in the threatened presence of it. He had but one desire left – that he shouldn't have been 'sold.'

IV

Then it was that, one afternoon, while the spring of the year was young and new she met all in her own way his frankest betrayal of these alarms. He had gone in late to see her, but evening hadn't settled and she was presented to him in that long fresh light of waning April days which affects us often with a sadness sharper than the greyest hours of autumn. The week had been warm, the spring was supposed to have begun early, and May Bartram sat, for the first time in the year, without a fire; a fact that, to Marcher's sense, gave the scene of which she formed part a smooth and ultimate look, an air of knowing, in its immaculate order and cold meaningless cheer, that it would never see a fire again. Her own aspect – he could scarce have said why – intensified this note. Almost as white as wax, with the marks and signs in her face as numerous and as fine as if they had been etched by a needle, with soft white draperies relieved by a faded green scarf on the delicate tone of which the years had further refined, she was the picture of a serene and exquisite but impenetrable sphinx, whose head, or indeed all whose person, might have been powdered with silver. She was a sphinx, yet with her white petals and green fronds she might have been a lily too – only an artificial lily, wonderfully imitated and constantly kept, without dust or stain, though not exempt from a slight droop and a complexity of faint creases, under some clear glass bell. The perfection of household care, of high polish and finish, always reigned in her rooms, but they now looked most as if everything had been wound up, tucked in, put away, so that she might sit with folded hands and with nothing more to do. She was 'out of it,' to Marcher's vision; her work was over; she communicated with him as across some gulf or from some island of rest that she had already reached, and it made him feel strangely abandoned. Was it – or rather wasn't it – that if for so long she had been watching with him the answer to their question must have swum into her ken and taken on its name, so that her occupation was verily gone?[27] He had as much as charged her with this in saying to her, many months before, that she even then knew something she was keeping from him. It was a point he had never since ventured to press, vaguely fearing as he did that it might become a difference, perhaps a disagreement, between them. He had in this later time turned nervous, which was what he in all the other years had never been; and the oddity was that his nervousness should have waited till he had begun to doubt, should have held off so long as he was sure. There was something, it seemed to him, that the wrong word would bring down on his head, something that would so at least ease off his tension. But he wanted not to speak the wrong word; that would make everything ugly. He wanted the knowledge he lacked to drop on him, if drop it could, by its own august weight. If she was to forsake him it was surely for her to take leave. This was why he didn't directly ask her again what she knew; but it was also why, approaching the matter from another side, he said to her in the course of his visit: 'What do you regard as the very worst that at this time of day *can* happen to me?'

He had asked her that in the past often enough; they had, with the odd irregular rhythm of their intensities and avoidances, exchanged ideas about it and then had seen the ideas washed away by cool intervals, washed like figures traced in sea-sand. It had ever been the mark of their talk that the oldest allusions in it required but a little dismissal and reaction to come out again, sounding for the hour as new. She could thus at present meet his enquiry quite freshly and patiently. 'Oh yes, I've repeatedly thought, only it always seemed to me of old that I couldn't quite make up my mind. I thought of dreadful things, between which it was difficult to choose; and so must you have done.'

'Rather! I feel now as if I had scarce done anything else. I appear to myself to have spent my life in thinking of nothing *but* dreadful things. A great many of them I've at different times named to you, but there were others I couldn't name.'

'They were too, too dreadful?'

'Too, too dreadful – some of them.'

She looked at him a minute, and there came to him as he met it an inconsequent sense that her eyes, when one got their full clearness, were still as beautiful as they had been in youth, only beautiful with a strange cold light – a light that somehow was a part of the effect, if it wasn't rather a part of the cause, of the pale hard sweetness of the season and the hour. 'And yet,' she said at last, 'there are horrors we've mentioned.'

It deepened the strangeness to see her, as such a figure in such a picture, talk of 'horrors,' but she was to do in a few minutes something stranger yet – though even of this he was to take the full measure but afterwards – and the note of it already trembled. It was, for the matter of that, one of the signs that her eyes were having again the high flicker of their prime. He had to admit, however, what she said. 'Oh yes, there were times when we did go far.' He caught himself in the act of speaking as if it all were over. Well, he wished it were; and the consummation depended for him clearly more and more on his friend.

But she had now a soft smile. 'Oh far –!'

It was oddly ironic. 'Do you mean you're prepared to go further?'

She was frail and ancient and charming as she continued to look at him, yet it was rather as if she had lost the thread. 'Do you consider that we went far?'

'Why I thought it the point you were just making – that we *had* looked most things in the face.'

'Including each other?' She still smiled. 'But you're quite right. We've had together great imaginations, often great fears; but some of them have been unspoken.'

'Then the worst – we haven't faced that. I *could* face it, I believe, if I knew what you think it. I feel,' he explained, 'as if I had lost my power to conceive such things.' And he wondered if he looked as blank as he sounded. 'It's spent.'

'Then why do you assume,' she asked, 'that mine isn't?'

'Because you've given me signs to the contrary. It isn't a question for you of conceiving, imagining, comparing. It isn't a question now of choosing.' At last he came out with it. 'You know something I don't. You've shown me that before.'

These last words had affected her, he made out in a moment, exceedingly, and she spoke with firmness. 'I've shown you, my dear, nothing.'

He shook his head. 'You can't hide it.'

'Oh, oh!' May Bartram sounded over what she couldn't hide. It was almost a smothered groan.

'You admitted it months ago, when I spoke of it to you as of something you were afraid I should find out. Your answer was that I couldn't, that I wouldn't, and I don't pretend I have. But you had something therefore in mind, and I now see how it must have been, how it still is, the possibility that, of all possibilities, has settled itself for you as the worst. This,' he went on, 'is why I appeal to you. I'm only afraid of ignorance to-day – I'm not afraid of knowledge.' And then as for a while she said nothing: 'What makes me sure is that I see in your face and feel here, in this air and amid these appearances, that you're out of it. You've done. You've had your experience. You leave me to my fate.'

Well, she listened, motionless and white in her chair, as on a decision to be made, so that her manner was fairly an avowal, though still, with a small fine inner stiffness, an imperfect surrender. 'It *would* be the worst,' she finally let herself say. 'I mean the thing I've never said.'

It hushed him a moment. 'More monstrous than all the monstrosities we've named?'

'More monstrous. Isn't that what you sufficiently express,' she asked, 'in calling it the worst?'

Marcher thought. 'Assuredly – if you mean, as I do, something that includes all the loss and all the shame that are thinkable.'

'It would if it *should* happen,' said May Bartram. 'What we're speaking of, remember, is only my idea.'

'It's your belief,' Marcher returned. 'That's enough for me. I feel your beliefs are right. Therefore if having this one, you give me no more light on it, you abandon me.'

'No, no!' she repeated. 'I'm with you – don't you see? – still.' And as to make it more vivid to him she rose from her chair – a movement she seldom risked in these days – and showed herself, all draped and all soft, in her fairness and slimness. 'I haven't forsaken you.'

It was really, in its effort against weakness, a generous assurance, and had the success of the impulse not, happily, been great, it would have touched him to pain more than to pleasure. But the cold charm in her eyes had spread, as she hovered before him, to all the rest of her person, so that it was for the minute almost a recovery of youth. He couldn't pity her for that; he could only take her as she showed – as capable even yet of helping him. It was as if, at the same time, her light might at any instant go out; wherefore he must make the most of it. There passed before him with intensity the three or four things he wanted most to know; but the question that came of itself to his lips really covered the others. 'Then tell me if I shall consciously suffer.'

She promptly shook her head. 'Never!'

It confirmed the authority he imputed to her, and it produced on him an extraordinary effect. 'Well, what's better than that? Do you call that the worst?'

'You think nothing is better?' she asked.

She seemed to mean something so special that he again sharply wondered, though still with the dawn of a prospect of relief. 'Why not, if one doesn't *know?*' After which, as their eyes, over his question, met in a silence, the dawn deepened and something to his purpose came prodigiously out of her very face. His own, as he took it in, suddenly flushed to the forehead, and he gasped with the force of a perception to which, on the instant, everything fitted. The sound of his gasp filled the air; then he became articulate. 'I see – if I don't suffer!'

In her own look, however, was doubt. 'You see what?'

'Why what you mean – what you've always meant.'

She again shook her head. 'What I mean isn't what I've always meant. It's different.'

'It's something new?'

She hung back from it a little. 'Something new. It's not what you think. I see what you think.'

His divination drew breath then; only her correction might be wrong. 'It isn't that I *am* a blockhead?' he asked between faintness and grimness. 'It isn't that it's all a mistake?'

'A mistake?' she pityingly echoed. *That* possibility, for her, he saw, would be monstrous; and if she guaranteed him the immunity from pain it would accordingly not be what she had in mind. 'Oh no,' she declared; 'it's nothing of that sort. You've been right.'

Yet he couldn't help asking himself if she weren't, thus pressed, speaking but to save him. It seemed to him he should be most in a hole if his history should prove all a platitude. 'Are you telling me the truth, so that I shan't have been a bigger idiot than I can bear to know? I *haven't* lived with a vain imagination, in the most besotted illusion? I haven't waited but to see the door shut in my face?'

She shook her head again. 'However the case stands *that* isn't the truth. Whatever the reality, it *is* a reality. The door isn't shut. The door's open,' said May Bartram.

'Then something's to come?'

She waited once again, always with her cold sweet eyes on him. 'It's never too late.' She had, with her gliding step, diminished the distance between them, and she stood nearer to him, close to him, a minute, as if still charged with the unspoken. Her movement might have been for some finer emphasis of what she was at once hesitating and deciding to say. He had been standing by the chimney-piece, fireless and sparely adorned, a small perfect old French clock and two morsels of rosy Dresden[8] constituting all its furniture; and her hand grasped the shelf while she kept him waiting, grasped it a little as for support and encouragement. She only kept him waiting, however; that is he only waited. It had become suddenly, from her movement and attitude, beautiful and vivid to him that she had something more to give him; her wasted face delicately shone with it – it glittered almost as with the white lustre of silver in her expression. She was right, incontestably, for what he saw in her face was the truth, and strangely, without consequence, while their talk of it as dreadful was still in the air, she appeared to present it as inordinately soft. This, prompting bewilderment, made him but gape the more gratefully for her revelation, so that they continued for some minutes silent, her face shining at him, her contact imponderably pressing, and his stare all kind but all expectant. The end, none the less, was that what he had expected failed to come to him. Something else took place instead, which seemed to consist at first in the mere closing of her eyes. She gave way at the same instant to a slow fine shudder, and though he remained staring – though he stared in fact but the harder – turned off and regained her chair. It was the end of what she had been intending, but it left him thinking only of that.

'Well, you don't say——?'

She had touched in her passage a bell near the chimney and had sunk back strangely pale. 'I'm afraid I'm too ill.'

'Too ill to tell me?' It sprang up sharp to him, and almost to his lips, the fear she might die without giving him light. He checked himself in time from so expressing his question, but she answered as if she had heard the words.

'Don't you know – now?'

' "Now" –?' She had spoken as if some difference had been made within the moment. But her maid, quickly obedient to her bell, was already with them. 'I know nothing.' And he was afterwards to say to himself that he must have spoken with odious impatience, such an impatience as to show that, supremely disconcerted, he washed his hands of the whole question.

'Oh!' said May Bartram.

'Are you in pain?' he asked as the woman went to her.

'No,' said May Bartram.

Her maid, who had put an arm round her as if to take her to her room, fixed on him eyes that appealingly contradicted her; in spite of which, however, he showed once more his mystification. 'What then has happened?'

She was once more, with her companion's help, on her feet, and, feeling withdrawal imposed on him, he had blankly found his hat and gloves and had reached the door. Yet he waited for her answer. 'What *was* to,' she said.

V

He came back the next day, but she was then unable to see him, and as it was literally the first time this had occurred in the long stretch of their acquaintance he turned away, defeated and sore, almost angry – or feeling at least that such a break in their custom was really the beginning of the end – and wandered alone with his thoughts, especially with the one he was least able to keep down. She was dying and he would lose her; she was dying and his life would end. He stopped in the Park,[9] into which he had passed, and stared before him at his recurrent doubt. Away from her the doubt pressed again; in her presence he had believed her, but as he felt his forlornness he threw himself into the explanation that, nearest at hand, had most of a miserable warmth for him and least of a cold torment. She had deceived him to save him – to put him off with something in which he should be able to rest. What could the thing that was to happen to him be, after all, but just this thing that had begun to happen? Her dying, her death, his consequent solitude – *that* was what he had figured as the Beast in the Jungle, that was what had been in the lap of the gods. He had had her word for it as he left her – what else on earth could she have meant? It wasn't a thing of a monstrous order; not a fate rare and distinguished; not a stroke of fortune that overwhelmed and immortalised; it had only the stamp of the common doom. But poor Marcher at this hour judged the common doom sufficient. It would serve his turn, and even as the consummation of infinite waiting he would bend his pride to accept it. He sat down on a bench in the twilight. He hadn't been a fool. Something had *been*, as she had said, to come. Before he rose indeed it had quite struck him that the final fact really matched with the long avenue through which he had had to reach it. As sharing his suspense and as giving herself all, giving her life, to bring it to an end, she had come with him every step of the way. He had lived by her aid, and to leave her behind would be cruelly, damnably to miss her. What could be more overwhelming than that?

Well, he was to know within the week, for though she kept him a while at bay, left him restless and wretched during a series of days on each of which he asked about her only again to have to turn away, she ended his trial by receiving him where she had always received him. Yet she had been brought out at some hazard into the presence of so many of the things that were, consciously, vainly, half their past, and there was scant service left in the gentleness of her mere desire, all too visible, to check his obsession and wind up his long trouble. That was clearly what she wanted, the one thing more for her own peace while she could still put out her hand. He was so affected by her state that, once seated by her chair, he was moved to let everything go; it was she herself therefore who brought him back, took up again, before she dismissed him, her last word of the other time. She showed how she wished to leave their business in order. 'I'm not sure you understood. You've nothing to wait for more. It *has* come.'

Oh how he looked at her! 'Really?'

'Really.'

'The thing that, as you said, *was* to?'

'The thing that we began in our youth to watch for.'

Face to face with her once more he believed her; it was a claim to which he had so abjectly little to oppose. 'You mean that it has come as a positive definite occurrence, with a name and a date?'

'Positive. Definite. I don't know about the "name," but oh with a date!'

He found himself again too helplessly at sea. 'But come in the night — come and passed me by?'

May Bartram had her strange faint smile. 'Oh no, it hasn't passed you by!'

'But if I haven't been aware of it and it hasn't touched me —?'

'Ah your not being aware of it' — and she seemed to hesitate an instant to deal with this — 'your not being aware of it is the strangeness *in* the strangeness. It's the wonder *of* the wonder.' She spoke as with the softness almost of a sick child, yet now at last, at the end of all, with the perfect straightness of a sibyl. She visibly knew that she knew, and the effect on him was of something co-ordinate, in its high character, with the law that had ruled him. It was the true voice of the law; so on her lips would the law itself have sounded. 'It *has* touched you,' she went on. 'It has done its office. It has made you all its own.'

'So utterly without my knowing it?'

'So utterly without your knowing it.' His hand, as he leaned to her, was on the arm of her chair, and, dimly smiling always now, she placed her own on it. 'It's enough if *I* know it.'

'Oh!' he confusedly breathed, as she herself of late so often had done.

'What I long ago said is true. You'll never know now, and I think you ought to be content. You've *had* it,' said May Bartram.

'But had what?'

'Why what was to have marked you out. The proof of your law. It has acted. I'm too glad,' she then bravely added, 'to have been able to see what it's *not*.'

He continued to attach his eyes to her, and with the sense that it was all beyond him, and that *she* was too, he would still have sharply challenged her hadn't he so felt it an abuse of her weakness to do more than take devoutly what she gave him, take it hushed as to a revelation. If he did speak, it was out of the foreknowledge of his loneliness to come. 'If you're glad of what it's "not" it might then have been worse?'

She turned her eyes away, she looked straight before her; with which after a moment: 'Well, you know our fears.'

He wondered. 'It's something then we never feared?'

On this slowly she turned to him. 'Did we ever dream, with all our dreams, that we should sit and talk of it thus?'

He tried for a little to make out that they had; but it was as if their dreams, numberless enough, were in solution in some thick cold mist through which thought lost itself. 'It might have been that we couldn't talk?'

'Well' – she did her best for him – 'not from this side. This, you see,' she said, 'is the *other* side.'

'I think,' poor Marcher returned, 'that all sides are the same to me.' Then, however, as she gently shook her head in correction: 'We mightn't, as it were, have got across –?'

'To where we are – no. We're *here*' – she made her weak emphasis.

'And much good does it do us!' was her friend's frank comment.

'It does us the good it can. It does us the good that *it* isn't here. It's past. It's behind,' said May Bartram. 'Before –' but her voice dropped.

He had got up, not to tire her, but it was hard to combat his yearning. She after all told him nothing but that his light had failed – which he knew well enough without her. 'Before –?' he blankly echoed.

'Before, you see, it was always to *come*. That kept it present.'

'Oh I don't care what comes now! Besides,' Marcher added, 'it seems to me I liked it better present, as you say, than I can like it absent with *your* absence.'

'Oh mine!' – and her pale hands made light of it.

'With the absence of everything.' He had a dreadful sense of standing there before her for – so far as anything but this proved, this bottomless drop was concerned – the last time of their life. It rested on him with a weight he felt he could scarce bear, and this weight it apparently was that still pressed out what remained in him of speakable protest. 'I believe you; but I can't begin to pretend I understand. *Nothing*, for me, is past; nothing *will* pass till I pass myself, which I pray my stars may be as soon as possible. Say, however,' he added, 'that I've eaten my cake, as you contend, to the last crumb – how can the thing I've never felt at all be the thing I was marked out to feel?'

She met him perhaps less directly, but she met him unperturbed. 'You take your "feelings" for granted. You were to suffer your fate. That was not necessarily to know it.'

'How in the world – when what is such knowledge but suffering?'

She looked up at him a while in silence. 'No – you don't understand.'

'I suffer,' said John Marcher.

'Don't, don't!'

'How can I help at least *that*?'

'*Don't!*' May Bartram repeated.

She spoke it in a tone so special, in spite of her weakness, that he stared an instant – stared as if some light, hitherto hidden, had shimmered across his vision. Darkness again closed over it, but the gleam had already become for him an idea. 'Because I haven't the right –?'

'Don't *know* – when you needn't,' she mercifully urged. 'You needn't – for we shouldn't.'

'Shouldn't?' If he could but know what she meant!

'No – it's too much.'

'Too much?' he still asked but, with a mystification that was the next moment of a sudden to give way. Her words, if they meant something, affected him in this light – the light also of her wasted face – as meaning *all*, and the sense of what knowledge had been for herself came over him with a rush which broke through into a question. 'Is it of that then you're dying?'

She but watched him, gravely at first, as to see, with this, where he was, and she might have seen something or feared something that moved her sympathy. 'I would live for you still – if I could.' Her eyes closed for a little, as if, withdrawn into herself, she were for a last time trying. 'But I can't!' she said as she raised them again to take leave of him.

She couldn't indeed, as but too promptly and sharply appeared, and he had no vision of her after this that was anything but darkness and doom. They had parted for ever in that strange talk; access to her chamber of pain, rigidly guarded, was almost wholly forbidden him; he was feeling now moreover, in the face of doctors, nurses, the two or three relatives attracted doubtless by the presumption of what she had to 'leave,' how few were the rights, as they were called in such cases, that he had to put forward, and how odd it might even seem that their intimacy shouldn't have given him more of them. The stupidest fourth cousin had more, even though she had been nothing in such a person's life. She had been a feature of features in *his*, for what else was it to have been so indispensable? Strange beyond saying were the ways of existence, baffling for him the anomaly of his lack, as he felt it to be, of producible claim. A woman might have been, as it were, everything to him, and it might yet present him in no connexion that any one seemed held to recognise. If this was the case in these closing weeks it was the case more sharply on the occasion of the last offices rendered, in the great grey London cemetery,[10] to what had been mortal, to what had been precious, in his friend. The concourse at her grave was not numerous, but he saw himself treated as scarce more nearly concerned with it than if there had been a thousand others. He was in short from this moment face to face with the fact that he was to profit extraordinarily little by the interest May Bartram had taken in him. He couldn't quite have said what he expected, but he hadn't surely expected this approach to a double privation. Not only had her interest failed him, but he seemed to feel himself unattended — and for a reason he couldn't seize — by the distinction, the dignity, the propriety, if nothing else, of the man markedly bereaved. It was as if in the view of society he had not *been* markedly bereaved, as if there still failed some sign or proof of it, and as if none the less his character could never be affirmed nor the deficiency ever made up. There were moments as the weeks went by when he would have liked, by some almost aggressive act, to take his stand on the intimacy of his loss, in order that it *might* be questioned and his retort, to the relief of his spirit, so recorded; but the moments of an irritation more helpless followed fast on these, the moments during which, turning things over with a good conscience but with a bare horizon, he found himself wondering if he oughtn't to have begun, so to speak, further back.

He found himself wondering indeed at many things, and this last speculation had others to keep it company. What could he have done, after all, in her lifetime, without giving them both, as it were, away? He couldn't have made known she was watching him, for that would have published the superstition of the Beast. This was what closed his mouth now — now that the Jungle had been threshed to vacancy and that the Beast had stolen away. It sounded too foolish and too flat; the difference for him in this particular, the extinction in his life of the element of suspense, was such as in fact to surprise him. He could scarce have said what the effect resembled; the abrupt cessation, the positive prohibition, of music perhaps, more than anything else, in some place all adjusted and all accustomed to sonority and to attention. If he could at any rate have conceived lifting the veil from his image at some moment of the past (what had he done, after all, if not lift it to *her*?) so to do this to-day, to talk to people at large of the Jungle cleared and confide to them that he now felt it as safe, would have been not only to see them listen as to a goodwife's tale, but really to hear himself tell one. What it presently came to in truth was that poor Marcher waded through his beaten grass, where no life stirred, where no breath sounded, where no evil eye seemed to gleam from a possible lair, very much as if vaguely looking for the Beast, and still more as if acutely missing it. He walked about in an existence that had grown strangely more spacious, and, stopping fitfully in places where the undergrowth of life struck him as closer, asked himself yearningly, wondered secretly and sorely, if it would have lurked here or there. It would have at all events *sprung*; what was at least complete was his belief in the truth itself of the assurance given him. The change from his old sense to his new was absolute and final: what was to happen *had* so absolutely and finally happened that he was as little able to know a fear for his future as to know a hope; so absent in short was any question of anything still to come. He was to live entirely with the other question, that of his unidentified past, that of his having to see his fortune impenetrably muffled and masked.

The torment of this vision became then his occupation; he couldn't perhaps have consented to live but for the possibility of guessing. She had told him, his friend, not to guess; she had forbidden him, so far as he might, to know, and she had even in a sort denied the power in him to learn: which were so many things, precisely, to deprive him of rest. It wasn't that he wanted, he argued for fairness, that anything past and done should repeat itself; it was only that he shouldn't, as an anticlimax, have been taken sleeping so sound as not to be able to win back by an effort of thought the lost stuff of consciousness. He declared to himself at moments that he would either win it back or have done with consciousness for ever; he made this idea his one motive in fine, made it so much his passion that none other, to compare with it, seemed ever to have touched him. The lost stuff of consciousness became thus for him as a strayed or stolen child to an unappeasable father; he hunted it up and down very much as if he were knocking at doors and enquiring of the police. This was the spirit in which, inevitably, he set himself to travel; he started on a journey that was to be as long as he could make it; it danced before him that, as the other side of the globe couldn't possibly have less to say to him, it might, by a possibility of suggestion, have more. Before he quitted London, however, he made a pilgrimage to May Bartram's grave, took his way to it through the endless avenues of the grim suburban metropolis, sought it out in the wilderness of tombs, and, though he had come but for the renewal of the act of farewell, found himself, when he had at last stood by it, beguiled into long intensities. He stood for an hour, powerless to turn away and yet powerless to penetrate the darkness of death; fixing with his eyes her inscribed name and date, beating his forehead against the fact of the secret they kept, drawing his breath, while he waited, as if some sense would in pity of him rise from the stones. He kneeled on the stones, however, in vain; they kept what they concealed; and if the face of the tomb did become a face for him it was because her two names became a pair of eyes that didn't know him. He gave them a last long look, but no palest light broke.

VI

He stayed away, after this, for a year; he visited the depths of Asia, spending himself on scenes of romantic interest, of superlative sanctity; but what was present to him everywhere was that for a man who had known what *he* had known the world was vulgar and vain. The state of mind in which he had lived for so many years shone out to him, in reflexion, as a light that coloured and refined, a light beside which the glow of the East was garish, cheap and thin. The terrible truth was that he had lost – with everything else – a distinction as well; the things he saw couldn't help being common when he had become common to look at them. He was simply now one of them himself – he was in the dust, without a peg for the sense of difference; and there were hours when, before the temples of gods and the sepulchres of kings, his spirit turned for nobleness of association to the barely discriminated slab in the London suburb. That had become for him, and more intensely with time and distance, his one witness of a past glory. It was all that was left to him for proof or pride, yet the past glories of Pharaohs were nothing to him as he thought of it. Small wonder then that he came back to it on the morrow of his return. He was drawn there this time as irresistibly as the other, yet with a confidence, almost, that was doubtless the effect of the many months that had elapsed. He had lived, in spite of himself, into his change of feeling, and in wandering over the earth had wandered, as might be said, from the circumference to the centre of his desert. He had settled to his safety and accepted perforce his extinction; figuring to himself, with some colour, in the likeness of certain little old men he remembered to have seen, of whom, all meagre and wizened as they might look, it was related that they had in their time fought twenty duels or been loved by ten princesses. They indeed had been wondrous for others while he was but wondrous for himself; which, however, was exactly the cause of his haste to renew the wonder by getting back, as he might put it, into his own presence. That had quickened his steps and checked his delay. If his visit was prompt it was because he had been separated so long from the part of himself that alone he now valued.

It's accordingly not false to say that he reached his goal with a certain elation and stood there again with a certain assurance. The creature beneath the sod *knew* of his rare experience, so that, strangely now, the place had lost for him its mere blankness of expression. It met him in mildness – not, as before, in mockery; it wore for him the air of conscious greeting that we find, after absence, in things that have closely belonged to us and which seem to confess of themselves to the connexion. The plot of ground, the graven tablet, the tended flowers affected him so as belonging to him that he resembled for the hour a contented landlord reviewing a piece of property. Whatever had happened – well, had happened. He had not come back this time with the vanity of that question, his former worrying 'What, *what*?' now practically so spent. Yet he would none the less never again so cut himself off from the spot; he would come back to it every month, for if he did nothing else by its aid he at least held up his head. It thus grew for him, in the oddest way, a positive resource; he carried out his idea of periodical returns, which took their place at last among the most inveterate of his habits. What it all amounted to, oddly enough, was that in his finally so simplified world this garden of death gave him the few square feet of earth on which he could still most live. It was as if, being nothing anywhere else for anyone, nothing even for himself, he were just everything here, and if not for a crowd of witnesses or indeed for any witness but John Marcher, then by clear right of the register that he could scan like an open page. The open page was the tomb of his friend, and *there* were the facts of the past, there the truth of his life, there the backward reaches in which he could lose himself. He did this from time to time with such effect that he seemed to wander through the old years with his hand in the arm of a companion who was, in the most extraordinary manner, his other, his younger self; and to wander, which was more extraordinary yet, round and round a third presence – not wandering she, but stationary, still, whose eyes, turning with his revolution, never ceased to follow him, and whose seat was his point, so to speak, of orientation. Thus in short he settled to live – feeding all on the sense that he once *had* lived, and dependent on it not alone for a support but for an identity.

It sufficed him in its way for months and the year elapsed; it would doubtless even have carried him further but for an accident, superficially slight, which moved him, quite in another direction, with a force beyond any of his impressions of Egypt or of India. It was a thing of the merest chance – the turn, as he afterwards felt, of a hair, though he was indeed to live to believe that if light hadn't come to him in this particular fashion it would still have come in another. He was to live to believe this, I say, though he was not to live, I may not less definitely mention, to do much else. We allow him at any rate the benefit of the conviction, struggling up for him at the end, that, whatever might have happened or not happened, he would have come round of himself to the light. The incident of an autumn day had put the match to the train laid from of old by his misery. With the light before him he knew that even of late his ache had only been smothered. It was strangely drugged, but it throbbed; at the touch it began to bleed. And the touch, in the event, was the face of a fellow mortal. This face, one grey afternoon when the leaves were thick in the alleys, looked into Marcher's own, at the cemetery, with an expression like the cut of a blade. He felt it, that is, so deep down that he winced at the steady thrust. The person who so mutely assaulted him was a figure he had noticed, on reaching his own goal, absorbed by a grave a short distance away, a grave apparently fresh, so that the emotion of the visitor would probably match it for frankness. This fact alone forbade further attention, though during the time he stayed he remained vaguely conscious of his neighbour, a middle-aged man apparently, in mourning, whose bowed back, among the clustered monuments and mortuary yews, was constantly presented. Marcher's theory that these were elements in contact with which he himself revived, had suffered, on this occasion, it may be granted, a marked, an excessive check. The autumn day was dire for him as none had recently been, and he rested with a heaviness he had not yet known on the low stone table that bore May Bartram's name. He rested without power to move, as if some spring in him, some spell vouchsafed, had suddenly been broken for ever. If he could have done that moment as he wanted he would simply have stretched himself on the slab that was ready to take him, treating it as a place prepared to receive his last sleep. What in all the wide world had he now to keep awake for? He stared before him with the question, and it was then that, as one of the cemetery walks passed near him, he caught the shock of the face.

His neighbour at the other grave had withdrawn, as he himself, with force enough in him, would have done by now, and was advancing along the path on his way to one of the gates. This brought him close, and his pace was slow, so that – and all the more as there was a kind of hunger in his look – the two men were in a minute directly confronted. Marcher knew him at once for one of the deeply stricken – a perception so sharp that nothing else in the picture compara- tively lived, neither his dress, his age, nor his presumable character and class; nothing lived but the deep ravage of the features he showed. He *showed* them – that was the point; he was moved, as he passed, by some impulse that was either a signal for sympathy or, more possibly, a challenge to an opposed sorrow. He might already have been aware of our friend, might at some previous hour have noticed in him the smooth habit of the scene, with which the state of his own senses so scantly consorted, and might thereby have been stirred as by an overt discord. What Marcher was at all events conscious of was in the first place that the image of scarred passion presented to him was conscious too – of something that profaned the air; and in the second that, roused, startled, shocked, he was yet the next moment looking after it, as it went, with envy. The most extraordinary thing that had happened to him – though he had given that name to other matters as well – took place, after his immediate vague stare, as a consequence of this impression. The stranger passed, but the raw glare of his grief remained, making our friend wonder in pity what wrong, what wound it expressed, what injury not to be healed. What had the man *had*, to make him by the loss of it so bleed and yet live?

Something – and this reached him with a pang – that *he*, John Marcher, hadn't; the proof of which was precisely John Marcher's arid end. No passion had ever touched him, for this was what passion meant; he had survived and maundered and pined, but where had been *his* deep ravage? The extraordinary thing we speak of was the sudden rush of the result of this question. The sight that had just met his eyes named to him, as in letters of quick flame, something he had utterly, insanely missed, and what he had missed made these things a train of fire, made them mark themselves in an anguish of inward throbs. He had seen *outside* of his life, not learned it within, the way a woman was mourned when she had been loved for herself: such was the force of his conviction of the meaning of the stranger's face, which still flared for him as a smoky torch. It hadn't come to him, the knowledge, on the wings of experience; it had brushed him, jostled him, upset him, with the disrespect of chance, the insolence of accident. Now that the illumination had begun, however, it blazed to the zenith, and what he presently stood there gazing at was the sounded void of his life. He gazed, he drew breath, in pain; he turned in his dismay, and, turning, he had before him in sharper incision than ever the open page of his story. The name on the table smote him as the passage of his neighbour had done, and what it said to him, full in the face, was that *she* was what he had missed. This was the awful thought, the answer to all the past, the vision at the dread clearness of which he grew as cold as the stone beneath him. Everything fell together, confessed, explained, overwhelmed; leaving him most of all stupefied at the blindness he had cherished. The fate he had been marked for he had met with a vengeance — he had emptied the cup to the lees; he had been the man of his time, *the* man, to whom nothing on earth was to have happened. That was the rare stroke — that was his visitation. So he saw it, as we say, in pale horror, while the pieces fitted and fitted. So *she* had seen it while he didn't, and so she served at this hour to drive the truth home. It was the truth, vivid and monstrous, that all the while he had waited the wait was itself his portion. This the companion of his vigil had at a given moment made out, and she had then offered him the chance to baffle his doom. One's doom, however, was never baffled, and on the day she told him his own had come down she had seen him but stupidly stare at the escape she offered him.

The escape would have been to love her; then, *then* he would have lived. *She* had lived — who could say now with what passion? — since she had loved him for himself; whereas he had never thought of her (ah how it hugely glared at him!) but in the chill of his egotism and the light of her use. Her spoken words came back to him — the chain stretched and stretched. The Beast had lurked indeed, and the Beast, at its hour, had sprung; it had sprung in that twilight of the cold April when, pale, ill, wasted, but all beautiful, and perhaps even then recoverable, she had risen from her chair to stand before him and let him imaginably guess. It had sprung as he didn't guess; it had sprung as she hopelessly turned from him, and the mark, by the time he left her, had fallen where it *was* to fall. He had justified his fear and achieved his fate; he had failed, with the last exactitude, of all he was to fail of; and a moan now rose to his lips as he remembered she had prayed he mightn't know. This horror of waking — *this* was knowledge, knowledge under the breath of which the very tears in his eyes seemed to freeze. Through them, none the less, he tried to fix it and hold it; he kept it there before him so that he might feel the pain. That at least, belated and bitter, had something of the taste of life. But the bitterness suddenly sickened him, and it was as if, horribly, he saw, in the truth, in the cruelty of his image, what had been appointed and done. He saw the Jungle of his life and saw the lurking Beast; then, while he looked, perceived it, as by a stir of the air, rise, huge and hideous, for the leap that was to settle him. His eyes darkened – it was close; and, instinctively turning, in his hallucination, to avoid it, he flung himself, face down, on the tomb.

The Birthplace

I

It seemed to them at first, the offer, too good to be true, and their friend's letter, addressed to them to feel, as he said, the ground, to sound them as to inclinations and possibilities, had almost the effect of a brave joke at their expense. Their friend, Mr Grant-Jackson, a highly preponderant pushing person, great in discussion and arrangement, abrupt in overture, unexpected, if not perverse, in attitude, and almost equally acclaimed and objected to in the wide midland region to which he had taught, as the phrase was, the size of his foot – their friend had launched his bolt quite out of the blue and had thereby so shaken them as to make them fear almost more than hope. The place had fallen vacant by the death of one of the two ladies, mother and daughter, who had discharged its duties for fifteen years; the daughter was staying on alone, to accommodate, but had found, though extremely mature, an opportunity of marriage that involved retirement, and the question of the new incumbents was not a little pressing. The want thus determined was of a united couple of some sort, of the right sort, a pair of educated and competent sisters possibly preferred, but a married pair having its advantages if other qualifications were marked. Applicants, candidates, besiegers of the door of every one supposed to have a voice in the matter, were already beyond counting, and Mr Grant-Jackson, who was in his way diplomatic and whose voice, though not perhaps of the loudest, possessed notes of insistence, had found his preference fixing itself on some person or brace of persons who had been decent and dumb. The Gedges appeared to have struck him as waiting in silence – though absolutely, as happened, no busybody had brought them, far away in the North, a hint either of bliss or of danger; and the happy spell, for the rest, had obviously been wrought in him by a remembrance which, though now scarcely fresh, had never before borne any such fruit.

Morris Gedge had for a few years, as a young man, carried on a small private school of the order known as preparatory, and had happened then to receive under his roof the small son of the great man, who was not at that time so great. The little boy, during an absence of his parents from England, had been dangerously ill, so dangerously that they had been recalled in haste, though with inevitable delays, from a far country — they had gone to America, with the whole continent and the great sea to cross again — and had got back to find the child saved, but saved, as couldn't help coming to light, by the extreme devotion and perfect judgement of Mrs Gedge. Without children of her own she had particularly attached herself to this tiniest and tenderest of her husband's pupils, and they had both dreaded as a dire disaster the injury to their little enterprise that would be caused by their losing him. Nervous anxious sensitive persons, with a pride — as they were for that matter well aware — above their position, never, at the best, to be anything but dingy, they had nursed him in terror and had brought him through in exhaustion. Exhaustion, as befell, had thus overtaken them early and had for one reason and another managed to assert itself as their permanent portion. The little boy's death would, as they said, have done for them, yet his recovery hadn't saved them; with which it was doubtless also part of a shy but stiff candour in them that they didn't regard themselves as having in a more indirect manner laid up treasure. Treasure was not to be, in any form whatever, of their dreams or of their waking sense; and the years that followed had limped under their weight, had now and then rather grievously stumbled, had even barely escaped laying them in the dust. The school hadn't prospered, had but dwindled to a close. Gedge's health had failed and still more every sign in him of a capacity to publish himself as practical. He had tried several things, he had tried many, but the final appearance was of their having tried him not less. They mostly, at the time I speak of, were trying his successors, while he found himself, with an effect of dull felicity that had come in this case from the mere postponement of change, in charge of the grey town-library of Blackport-on-Dwindle, all granite, fog and female fiction. This was a situation in which his general intelligence — admittedly his strong point — was doubtless imaged, around him, as feeling less of a strain than that mastery of particulars in which he was recognised as weak.

It was at Blackport-on-Dwindle that the silver shaft reached and pierced him; it was as an alternative to dispensing dog's-eared volumes the very titles of which, on the lips of innumerable glib girls, were a challenge to his nerves, that the wardenship of so different a temple presented itself. The stipend named exceeded little the slim wage at present paid him, but even had it been less the interest and the honour would have struck him as determinant. The shrine at which he was to preside — though he had always lacked occasion to approach it — figured to him as the most sacred known to the steps of men, the early home of the supreme poet, the Mecca of the English-speaking race.[1] The tears came into his eyes sooner still than into his wife's while he looked about with her at their actual narrow prison, so grim with enlightenment, so ugly with industry, so turned away from any dream, so intolerable to any taste. He felt as if a window had opened into a great green woodland, a woodland that had a name all glorious, immortal, that was peopled with vivid figures, each of them renowned, and that gave out a murmur, deep as the sound of the sea, which was the rustle in forest shade of all the poetry, the beauty, the colour of life. It would be prodigious that of this transfigured world[2] *he* should keep the key. No – he couldn't believe it, not even when Isabel, at sight of his face, came and helpfully kissed him. He shook his head with a strange smile. 'We shan't get it. Why should we? It's perfect.'

'If we don't he'll simply have been cruel; which is impossible when he has waited all this time to be kind.' Mrs Gedge did believe – she *would*: since the wide doors of the world of poetry had suddenly pushed back for them it was in the form of poetic justice that they were first to know it. She had her faith in their patron; it was sudden, but now complete. 'He remembers – that's all; and that's our strength.'

'And what's *his*?' Gedge asked. 'He may want to put us through, but that's a different thing from being able. What are our special advantages?'

'Well, that we're just the thing.' Her knowledge of the needs of the case was as yet, thanks to scant information, of the vaguest, and she had never, more than her husband, stood on the sacred spot; but she saw herself waving a nicely-gloved hand over a collection of remarkable objects and saying to a compact crowd of gaping awestruck persons: 'And now, please, *this* way.' She even heard herself meeting with promptness and decision an occasional enquiry from a visitor in whom audacity had prevailed over awe. She had once been with a cousin, years before, to a great northern castle, and that was the way the housekeeper had taken them round. And it was not moreover, either, that she thought of herself as a housekeeper: she was well above that, and the wave of her hand wouldn't fail to be such as to show it. This and much else she summed up as she answered her mate. 'Our special advantages are that you're a gentleman.'

'Oh!' said Gedge as if he had never thought of it, and yet as if too it were scarce worth thinking of.

'I see it all,' she went on; 'they've *had* the vulgar – they find they don't do. We're poor and we're modest, but any one can see what we are.'

Gedge wondered. 'Do you mean –?' More modest than she, he didn't know quite what she meant.

'We're refined. We know how to speak.'

'Do we?' – he still, suddenly, wondered.

But she was from the first surer of everything than he; so that when a few weeks more had elapsed and the shade of uncertainty – though it was only a shade – had grown almost to sicken him, her triumph was to come with the news that they were fairly named. 'We're on poor pay, though we manage' – she had at the present juncture contended for her point. 'But we're highly cultivated, and for them to get *that*, don't you *see*? without getting too much with it in the way of pretensions and demands, must be precisely their dream. We've no social position, but we don't *mind* that we haven't, do we? a bit; which is because we know the difference between realities and shams. We hold to reality, and that gives us common sense, which the vulgar have less than anything and which yet must be wanted there, after all, as well as anywhere else.'

Her companion followed her, but musingly, as if his horizon had within a few moments grown so great that he was almost lost in it and required a new orientation. The shining spaces surrounded him; the association alone gave a nobler arch to the sky. 'Allow that we hold also a little to the romance. It seems to me that that's the beauty. We've missed it all our life, and now it's come. We shall be at headquarters for it. We shall have our fill of it.'

She looked at his face, at the effect in it of these prospects, and her own lighted as if he had suddenly grown handsome. 'Certainly – we shall live as in a fairy-tale. But what I mean is that we shall give, in a way – and so gladly – quite as much as we get. With all the rest of it we're for instance neat.' Their letter had come to them at breakfast, and she picked a fly out of the butter-dish. 'It's the way we'll *keep* the place' – with which she removed from the sofa to the top of the cottage-piano³ a tin of biscuits that had refused to squeeze into the cupboard. At Blackport they were in lodgings – of the lowest description, she had been known to declare with a freedom felt by Blackport to be slightly invidious. The Birthplace – and that itself, after such a life, was exaltation – wouldn't be lodgings, since a house close beside it was set apart for the warden, a house joining on to it as a sweet old parsonage is often annexed to a quaint old church. It would all together be their home, and such a home as would make a little world that they would never want to leave. She dwelt on the gain, for that matter, to their income; as obviously, though the salary was not a change for the better, the house given them would make all the difference. He assented to this, but absently, and she was almost impatient at the range of his thoughts. It was as if something, for him – the very swarm of them – veiled the view; and he presently of himself showed what it was.

'What I can't get over is its being such a man –!' He almost, from inward emotion, broke down.

'Such, a man –?'

'Him, *him*, HIM –!' It was too much.

'Grant-Jackson? Yes, it's a surprise, but one sees how he has been meaning, all the while, the right thing by us.'

'I mean *Him*,' Gedge returned more coldly; 'our becoming familiar and intimate – for that's what it will come to. We shall just live with Him.'

'Of course – it *is* the beauty.' And she added quite gaily: 'The more we do the more we shall love Him.'

'No doubt – but it's rather awful. The more we *know* Him,' Gedge reflected, 'the more we shall love Him. We don't as yet, you see, know Him so very tremendously.'

'We do so quite as well, I imagine, as the sort of people they've had. And that probably isn't – unless you care, as we do – so awfully necessary. For there are the facts.'

'Yes – there are the facts.'

'I mean the principal ones. They're all that the people – the people who come – want.'

'Yes – they must be all *they* want.'

'So that they're all that those who've been in charge have needed to know.'

'Ah,' he said as if it were a question of honour, '*we* must know everything.'

She cheerfully acceded: she had the merit, he felt, of keeping the case within bounds. 'Everything. But about him personally,' she added, 'there isn't, is there? so very very much.'

'More, I believe, than there used to be. They've made discoveries.'

It was a grand thought. 'Perhaps *we* shall make some!'

'Oh I shall be content to be a little better up in what has been done.' And his eyes rested on a shelf of books, half of which, little worn but much faded, were of the florid 'gift' order and belonged to the house. Of those among them that were his own most were common specimens of the reference sort, not excluding an old Bradshaw[4] and a catalogue of the town-library. 'We've not even a Set of our own. Of the Works,' he explained in quick repudiation of the sense, perhaps more obvious, in which she might have taken it.

As a proof of their scant range of possessions this sounded almost abject, till the painful flush with which they met on the admission melted presently into a different glow. It was just for that kind of poorness that their new situation was, by its intrinsic charm, to console them. And Mrs Gedge had a happy thought. 'Wouldn't the Library more or less have them?'

'Oh no, we've nothing of that sort; for what do you take us?' This, however, was but the play of Gedge's high spirits: the form both depression and exhilaration most frequently took with him being a bitterness on the subject of the literary taste of Blackport. No one was so deeply acquainted with it. It acted with him in fact as so lurid a sign of the future that the charm of the thought of removal was sharply enhanced by the prospect of escape from it. The institution he served didn't of course deserve the particular reproach into which his irony had flowered; and indeed if the several Sets in which the Works were present were a trifle dusty, the dust was a little his own fault. To make up for that now he had the vision of immediately giving his time to the study of them; he saw himself indeed, inflamed with a new passion, earnestly commenting and collating. Mrs Gedge, who had suggested that, till their move should come, they ought to read Him regularly of an evening – certain as they were to do it still more when in closer quarters with Him – Mrs Gedge felt also, in her degree, the spell; so that the very happiest time of their anxious life was perhaps to have been the series of lamplight hours, after supper, in which, alternately taking the book, they declaimed, they almost performed, their beneficent author. He became speedily more than their author – their personal friend, their universal light, their final authority and divinity. Where in the world, they were already asking themselves, would they have been without Him? By the time their appointment arrived in form their relation to Him had immensely developed. It was amusing to Morris Gedge that he had so lately blushed for his ignorance, and he made this remark to his wife during the last hour they were able to give their study before proceeding, across half the country, to the scene of their romantic future. It was as if, in deep close throbs, in cool after-waves that broke of a sudden and bathed his mind, all possession and comprehension and sympathy, all the truth and the life and the story, had come to him, and come, as the newspapers said, to stay. 'It's absurd,' he didn't hesitate to say, 'to talk of our not "knowing." So far as we don't it's because we're dunces. He's *in* the thing, over His ears, and the more we get into it the more we're with Him. I seem to myself at any rate,' he declared, 'to *see* Him in it as if He were painted on the wall.'

'Oh *doesn't* one rather, the dear thing? And don't you feel where it is?' Mrs Gedge finely asked. 'We see Him because we love Him – that's what we do. How can we not, the old darling – with what He's doing for us? There's no light' – she had a sentential turn – 'like true affection.'

'Yes, I suppose that's it. And yet,' her husband mused, 'I see, confound me, the faults.'

'That's because you're so critical. You see them, but you don't mind them. You see them, but you forgive them. You mustn't mention them *there*. We shan't, you know, be there for *that*.'

'Dear no!' he laughed: 'we'll chuck out any one who hints at them.'

II

If the sweetness of the preliminary months had been great, great too, though almost excessive as agitation, was the wonder of fairly being housed with Him, of treading day and night in the footsteps He had worn, of touching the objects, or at all events the surfaces, the substances, over which His hands had played, which His arms, His shoulders had rubbed, of breathing the air – or something not too unlike it — in which His voice had sounded. They had had a little at first their bewilderments, their disconcertedness; the place was both humbler and grander than they had exactly prefigured, more at once of a cottage and of a museum, a little more archaically bare and yet a little more richly official. But the sense was strong with them that the point of view, for the inevitable ease of the connexion, patiently, indulgently awaited them; in addition to which, from the first evening, after closing-hour, when the last blank pilgrim had gone, the mere spell, the mystic presence — as if they had had it quite to themselves — were all they could have desired. They had received, at Grand-Jackson's behest and in addition to a table of instructions and admonitions by the number and in some particulars by the nature of which they found themselves slightly depressed, various little guides, manuals, travellers' tributes, literary memorials and other catch-penny publications;[5] which, however, were to be for the moment swallowed up in the interesting episode of the induction or initiation appointed for them in advance at the hands of several persons whose relation to the establishment was, as superior to their own, still more official, and at those in especial of one of the ladies who had for so many years borne the brunt. About the instructions from above, about the shilling books and the well-known facts and the full-blown legend, the supervision, the subjection, the submission, the view as of a cage in which he should circulate and a groove in which he should slide, Gedge had preserved a certain play of mind; but all power of reaction appeared suddenly to desert him in the presence of his so visibly competent predecessor and as an effect of her good offices. He had not the resource, enjoyed by his wife, of seeing himself, with impatience, attired in black silk of a make characterised by just the right shade of austerity; so that this firm smooth expert and consummately respectable middle-aged person had him somehow, on the whole ground, completely at her mercy.

It was evidently something of a rueful moment when, as a lesson — she being for the day or two still in the field — he accepted Miss Putchin's suggestion of 'going round' with her and with the successive squads of visitors she was there to deal with. He appreciated her method — he saw there had to *be* one; he admired her as succinct and definite; for there were the facts, as his wife had said at Blackport, and they were to be disposed of in the time; yet he felt a very little boy as he dangled, more than once, with Mrs Gedge, at the tail of the human comet. The idea had been that they should by this attendance more fully embrace the possible accidents and incidents, so to put it, of the relation to the great public in which they were to find themselves; and the poor man's excited perception of the great public rapidly became such as to resist any diversion meaner than that of the admirable manner of their guide. It wandered from his gaping companions to that of the priestess in black silk, whom he kept asking himself if either he or

Isabel could hope by any possibility ever remotely to resemble; then it bounded restlessly back to the numerous persons who revealed to him as it had never yet been revealed the happy power of the simple to hang upon the lips of the wise. The great thing seemed to be – and quite surprisingly – that the business was easy and the strain, which as a strain they had feared, moderate; so that he might have been puzzled, had he fairly caught himself in the act, by his recognising as the last effect of the impression an odd absence of the power really to rest in it, an agitation deep within him that vaguely threatened to grow. 'It isn't, you see, so very complicated,' the black silk lady seemed to throw off, with everything else, in her neat crisp cheerful way; in spite of which he already, the very first time – that is after several parties had been in and out and up and down – went so far as to wonder if there weren't more in it than she imagined. She was, so to speak, kindness itself – was all encouragement and reassurance; but it was just her slightly coarse redolence of these very things that, on repetition, before they parted, dimmed a little, as he felt, the light of his acknowledging smile. This again she took for a symptom of some pleading weakness in him – he could never be as brave as she; so that she wound up with a few pleasant words from the very depth of her experience. 'You'll get into it, never fear – it will *come*; and then you'll feel as if you had never done anything else.' He was afterwards to know that, on the spot, at this moment, he must have begun to wince a little at such a menace; that he might come to feel as if he had never done anything but what Miss Putchin did loomed for him, in germ, as a penalty to pay. The support she offered, none the less, continued to strike him; she put the whole thing on so sound a basis when she said: 'You see they're so nice about it – they take such an interest. And they never do a thing they shouldn't. That was always everything to mother and me.' 'They,' Gedge had already noticed, referred constantly and hugely, in the good woman's talk, to the millions who shuffled through the house; the pronoun in question was for ever on her lips, the hordes it represented filled her consciousness, the addition of their numbers ministered to her glory. Mrs Gedge promptly fell in. 'It must be indeed delightful to see the effect on so many and to feel that one may perhaps do something to make it – well, permanent.' But he was kept silent by his becoming more sharply aware that this was a new view, for him, of the reference made, that he had never thought of the quality of the place as derived from Them, but from Somebody Else, and that They, in short, seemed to have got into the way of crowding Him out. He found himself even a little resenting this for Him – which perhaps had something to do with the slightly invidious cast of his next enquiry.

'And are They always, as one might say – a – stupid?'

'Stupid!' She stared, looking as if no one *could* be such a thing in such a connexion. No one had ever been anything but neat and cheerful and fluent, except to be attentive and unobjectionable and, so far as was possible, American.

'What I mean is,' he explained, 'is there any perceptible proportion that take an interest in Him?'

His wife stepped on his toe; she deprecated levity. But his mistake fortunately was lost on their friend. 'That's just why they come, that they take such an interest. I sometimes think they take more than about anything else in the world.' With which Miss Putchin looked about at the place. 'It *is* pretty, don't you think, the way they've got it now?' This, Gedge saw, was a different 'They'; it applied to the powers that were – the people who had appointed him, the governing, visiting Body, in respect to which he was afterwards to remark to Mrs Gedge that a fellow – it was the difficulty – didn't know 'where to have her.' His wife, at a loss, questioned at that moment the necessity of having her anywhere, and he said, good-humouredly 'Of course; it's all right.' He was in fact content enough with the last touches their friend had given the picture. 'There are many who know all about it when they come, and the Americans often are tremendously up. Mother and me really enjoyed' – it was her only slip – 'the interest of the Americans. We've sometimes had ninety a day, and all wanting to see and hear everything. But you'll work them off; you'll see the way – it's all experience.' She came back for his comfort to that. She came back also to other things: she did justice to the considerable class who arrived positive and primed. 'There are those who know more about it than you do. But *that* only comes from their interest.'

'Who know more about what?' Gedge enquired.

'Why about the place. I mean they have their ideas – of what everything is, and *where* it is, and what it isn't and where it *should* be. They do ask questions,' she said, yet not so much in warning as in the complacency of being herself seasoned and sound; 'and they're down on you when they think you go wrong. As if you ever could! You know too much,' she astutely smiled; 'or you *will*.'

'Oh you mustn't know *too* much, must you?' And Gedge now smiled as well. He knew, he thought, what he meant.

'Well, you must know as much as anybody else. I claim at any rate that I do,' Miss Putchin declared. 'They never really caught me out.'

'I'm very certain of *that*' – and Mrs Gedge had an elation almost personal.

'Surely,' he said, 'I don't want to be caught out.' She rejoined that in such a case he would have *Them* down on him, and he saw that this time she meant the powers above. It quickened his sense of all the elements that were to reckon with, yet he felt at the same time that the powers above were not what he should most fear. 'I'm glad,' he observed, 'that they ever ask questions; but I happened to notice, you know, that no one did to-day.'

'Then you missed several – and no loss. There were three or four put to me too silly to remember. But of course they mostly *are* silly.'

'You mean the questions?'

She laughed with all her cheer. 'Yes, sir; I don't mean the answers.'

Whereupon, for a moment snubbed and silent, he felt like one of the crowd. Then it made him slightly vicious. 'I didn't know but you meant the people in general – till I remembered that I'm to understand from you that *they're* wise, only occasionally breaking down.'

It wasn't really till then, he thought, that she lost patience; and he had had, much more than he meant no doubt, a cross-questioning air. 'You'll see for yourself.' Of which he was sure enough. He was in fact so ready to take this that she came round to full accommodation, put it frankly that every now and then they broke out – not the silly, oh no, the intensely enquiring. 'We've had quite lively discussions, don't you know, about well-known points. They want it all *their* way, and I know the sort that are going to as soon as I see them. That's one of the things you do – you get to know the sorts. And if it's what you're afraid of – their taking you up,' she was further gracious enough to say, 'you needn't mind a bit. What *do* they know, after all, when for us it's our life? I've never moved an inch, because, you see, I shouldn't have been here if I didn't know where I was. No more will *you* be a year hence – you know what I mean, putting it impossibly – if *you* don't. I expect you do, in spite of your fancies.' And she dropped once more to bed-rock. 'There are the facts. Otherwise where would any of us be? That's all you've got to go upon. A person, however cheeky, can't have them *his* way just because he takes it into his head. There can only be *one* way, and,' she gaily added as she took leave of them, 'I'm sure it's quite enough!'

III

Gedge not only assented eagerly – one way *was* quite enough if it were the right one – but repeated it, after this conversation, at odd moments, several times over to his wife. 'There can only be one way, one way,' he continued to remark – though indeed much as if it were a joke; till she asked him how many more he supposed she wanted. He failed to answer this question, but resorted to another repetition. 'There are the facts, the facts,' which perhaps, however, he kept a little more to himself, sounding it at intervals in different parts of the house. Mrs Gedge was full of comment on their clever introductress, though not restrictively save in the matter of her speech, 'Me and mother,' and a general tone – which certainly was not their sort of thing. 'I don't know,' he said, 'perhaps it comes with the place, since speaking in immortal verse doesn't seem to come. It must be, one seems to see, one thing or the other. I dare say that in a few months I shall also be at it – "me and the wife."'

'Why not "me and the missus" at once?' Mrs Gedge resentfully enquired. 'I don't think,' she observed at another time, 'that I quite know what's the matter with you.'

'It's only that I'm excited, awfully excited – as I don't see how one can't be. You wouldn't have a fellow drop into this berth as into an appointment at the Post Office. Here on the spot it goes to my head – how can that be helped? But we shall live into it, and perhaps,' he said with an implication of the other possibility that was doubtless but part of his fine ecstasy, 'we shall live through it.' The place acted on his imagination – how, surely, shouldn't it? And his imagination acted on his nerves, and these things together, with the general vividness and the new and complete immersion, made rest for him almost impossible, so that he could scarce go to bed at night and even during the first week more than once rose in the small hours to move about, up and down, with his lamp – standing, sitting, listening, wondering, in the stillness, as if positively to recover some echo, to surprise some secret, of the *genius loci*.[6] He couldn't have explained it – and didn't in fact need to explain it, at least to himself, since the impulse simply held him and shook him; but the time after closing, the time above all after the people – Them, as he felt himself on the way habitually to put it, predominant, insistent, all in the foreground – brought him, or ought to have brought him, he seemed to see, nearer to the enshrined Presence, enlarging the opportunity for communion and intensifying the sense of it. These nightly prowls, as he called them, were disquieting to his wife, who had no disposition to share in them, speaking with decision of the whole place as just the place to be forbidding after dark. She rejoiced in the distinctness, contiguous though it was, of their own little residence, where she trimmed the lamp and stirred the fire and heard the kettle sing, repairing the while the omissions of the small domestic who slept out; she foresaw herself, with some promptness, drawing rather sharply the line between her own precinct and that in which the great spirit might walk. It would be with them, the great spirit, all day – even if indeed on her making that remark, and in just that form, to her husband, he replied with a queer 'But will he though?' And she vaguely imaged the development of a domestic antidote after a while, precisely, in the shape of curtains more markedly drawn and everything most modern and lively, tea, 'patterns,'[7] the newspapers, the female fiction itself that they had reacted against at Blackport, quite defiantly cultivated.

These possibilities, however, were all right, as her companion said it was, all the first autumn – they had arrived at summer's end; and he might have been more than content with a special set of his own that he had access to from behind, passing out of their low door for the few steps between it and the Birthplace.

With his lamp ever so carefully guarded and his nursed keys that made him free of treasures, he crossed the dusky interval so often that she began to qualify it as a habit that 'grew.' She spoke of it almost as if he had taken to drink, and he humoured that view of it by allowing the cup to be strong. This had been in truth altogether his immediate sense of it; strange and deep for him the spell of silent sessions before familiarity and, to some small extent, disappointment had set in. The exhibitional side of the establishment had struck him, even on arrival, as qualifying too much its character; he scarce knew what he might best have looked for, but the three or four rooms bristled overmuch, in the garish light of day, with busts and relics, not even ostensibly always *His*, old prints and old editions, old objects fashioned in His likeness, furniture 'of the time' and autographs of celebrated worshippers. In the quiet hours and the deep dusk, none the less, under the play of the shifted lamp and that of his own emotion, these things too recovered their advantage, ministered to the mystery, or at all events to the impression, seemed consciously to offer themselves as personal to the poet. Not one of them was really or unchallengeably so, but they had somehow, through long association, got, as Gedge always phrased it, into the secret, and it was about the secret he asked them while he restlessly wandered. It wasn't till months had elapsed that he found how little they had to tell him, and he was quite at his ease with them when he knew they were by no means where his sensibility had first placed them. They were as out of it as he; only, to do them justice, they had made him immensely feel. And still, too, it was not they who had done that most, since his sentiment had gradually cleared itself to deep, to deeper refinements.

The Holy of Holies of the Birthplace was the low, the sublime Chamber of Birth, sublime because, as the Americans usually said – unlike the natives they mostly found words – it was so pathetic; and pathetic because it was – well, really nothing else in the world that one could name, number or measure. It was as empty as a shell of which the kernel has withered, and contained neither busts nor prints nor early copies; it contained only the Fact – *the* Fact itself – which, as he stood sentient there at midnight, our friend, holding his breath, allowed to sink into him. He *had* to take it as the place where the spirit would most walk and where He would therefore be most to be met, with possibilities of recognition and reciprocity. He hadn't, most probably – *He* hadn't – much inhabited the room, as men weren't apt, as a rule, to convert to their later use and involve in their wider fortune the scene itself of their nativity. But as there were moments when, in the conflict of theories, the sole certainty surviving for the critic threatened to be that He had not – unlike other successful men – *not* been born, so Gedge, though little of a critic, clung to the square feet of space that connected themselves, however feebly, with the positive appearance. He was little of a critic – he was nothing of one; he hadn't pretended to the character before coming, nor come to pretend to it; also, luckily for him, he was seeing day by day how little use he could possibly have for it. It would be to him, the attitude of a high expert, distinctly a stumbling-block, and that he rejoiced, as the winter waned, in his ignorance, was one of the propositions he betook himself, in his odd manner, to enunciating to his wife. She denied it, for hadn't she in the first place been present, wasn't she still present, at his pious, his tireless study of everything connected with the subject? – so present that she had herself learned more about it than had ever seemed likely. Then in the second place he wasn't to proclaim on the house-tops any point at which he might be weak, for who knew, if it should get abroad that they were ignorant, what effect might be produced –?

'On the attraction' – he took her up – ' of the Show?'

He had fallen into the harmless habit of speaking of the place as the 'Show'; but she didn't mind this so much as to be diverted by it. 'No; on the attitude of the Body. You know they're pleased with us, and I don't see why you should want to spoil it. We got in by a tight squeeze – you know we've had evidence of that, and that it was about as much as our backers could manage. But we're proving a comfort to them, and it's absurd of you to question your suitability to people who were content with the Putchins.'

'I don't, my dear,' he returned, 'question anything; but if I should do so it would be precisely because of the greater advantage constituted for the Putchins by the simplicity of their spirit. They were kept straight by the quality of their ignorance – which was denser even than mine. It was a mistake in us from the first to have attempted to correct or to disguise ours. We should have waited simply to become good parrots, to learn our lesson – all on the spot here, so little of it is wanted – and squawk it off.'

'Ah "squawk," love – what a word to use about Him!'

'It isn't about Him – nothing's about Him. None of Them care tuppence about Him. The only thing They care about is this empty shell – or rather, for it isn't empty, the extraneous preposterous stuffing of it.'

'Preposterous?' – he made her stare with this as he hadn't yet done.

At sight of her look, however – the gleam, as it might have been, of a queer suspicion – he bent to her kindly and tapped her cheek. 'Oh it's all right. We *must* fall back on the Putchins. Do you remember what she said? – "They've made it so pretty now." They *have* made it pretty, and it's a first-rate show. It's a first-rate show and a first-rate billet, and He was a first-rate poet, and you're a first-rate woman – to put up so sweetly, I mean, with my nonsense.'

She appreciated his domestic charm and she justified that part of his tribute which concerned herself. 'I don't care how much of your nonsense you talk to me, so long as you *keep* it all for me and don't treat *Them* to it.'

'The pilgrims? No,' he conceded – 'it isn't fair to Them. They mean well.'

'What complaint have we after all to make of Them so long as They don't break off bits – as They used, Miss Putchin told us, so awfully – in order to conceal them about Their Persons? She broke Them at least of that.'

'Yes,' Gedge mused again; 'I wish awfully she hadn't!'

'You'd like the relics destroyed, removed? That's all that's wanted!'

'There *are* no relics.'

'There won't be any *soon* – unless you take care.' But he was already laughing, and the talk wasn't dropped without his having patted her once more. An impression or two nevertheless remained with her from it, as she saw from a question she asked him on the morrow. 'What did you mean yesterday about Miss Putchin's simplicity – its keeping her "straight"? Do you mean mentally?'

Her 'mentally' was rather portentous, but he practically confessed. 'Well, it kept her up. I mean,' he amended, laughing, 'it kept her down.'

It was really as if she had been a little uneasy. 'You consider there's a danger of your being affected? You know what I mean – of its going to your head. You do know,' she insisted as he said nothing. 'Through your caring for him so. You'd certainly be right in that case about its having been a mistake for you to plunge so deep.' And then as his listening without reply, though with his look a little sad for her, might have denoted that, allowing for extravagance of statement, he saw there was something in it: 'Give up your prowls. Keep it for daylight. Keep it for *Them*.'

'Ah,' he smiled, 'if one could! My prowls,' he added, 'are what I most enjoy. They're the only time, as I've told you before, that I'm really with *Him*. Then I don't see the place. He isn't the place.'

'I don't care for what you "don't see," ' she returned with vivacity; 'the question is of what you do see.'

Well, if it was, he waited before meeting it. 'Do you know what I sometimes do?' And then as she waited too: 'In the Birthroom there, when I look in late, I often put out my light. That makes it better.'

'Makes what –?'

'Everything.'

'What is it then you see in the dark?'

'Nothing!' said Morris Gedge.

'And what's the pleasure of that?'

'Well, what the American ladies say. It's so fascinating!'

IV

The autumn was brisk, as Miss Putchin had told them it would be, but business naturally fell off with the winter months and the short days. There was rarely an hour indeed without a call of some sort, and they were never allowed to forget that they kept the shop in all the world, as they might say, where custom was least fluctuating. The seasons told on it, as they tell on travel, but no other influence, consideration or convulsion to which the population of the globe is exposed. This population, never exactly in simultaneous hordes, but in a full swift and steady stream, passed through the smoothly-working mill and went, in its variety of degrees duly impressed and edified, on its artless way. Gedge gave himself up, with much ingenuity of spirit, to trying to keep in relation with it; having even at moments, in the early time, glimpses of the chance that the impressions gathered from so rare an opportunity for contact with the general mind might prove as interesting as anything else in the connexion. Types, classes, nationalities, manners, diversities of behaviour, modes of seeing, feeling, of expression, would pass before him and become for him, after a fashion, the experience of an untravelled man. His journeys had been short and saving, but poetic justice again seemed inclined to work for him in placing him just at the point in all Europe perhaps where the confluence of races was thickest. The theory at any rate carried him on, operating helpfully for the term of his anxious beginnings and gilding in a manner – it was the way he characterised the case to his wife – the somewhat stodgy gingerbread of their daily routine. They hadn't known many people and their visiting-list was small – which made it again poetic justice that they should be visited on such a scale. They dressed and were at home, they were under arms and received, and except for the offer of refreshment – and Gedge had his view that there would eventually be a *buffet* farmed out to a great firm – their hospitality would have made them princely if mere hospitality ever did. Thus they were launched, and it was interesting; so that from having been ready to drop, originally, with fatigue they emerged as even-winded and strong in the legs as if they had had an Alpine holiday. This experience, Gedge opined, also represented, as a gain, a like seasoning of the spirit – by which he meant a certain command of impenetrable patience.

The patience was needed for the particular feature of the ordeal that, by the time the lively season was with them again, had disengaged itself as the sharpest – the immense assumption of veracities and sanctities, of the general soundness of the legend, with which every one arrived. He was well provided certainly for meeting it, and he gave all he had, yet he had sometimes the sense of a vague resentment on the part of his pilgrims at his not ladling out their fare with a bigger spoon. An irritation had begun to grumble in him during the comparatively idle months of winter when a pilgrim would turn up singly. The pious individual, entertained for the half-hour, had occasionally seemed to offer him the promise of beguilement or the semblance of a personal relation; it came back again to the few pleasant calls he had received in the course of a life almost void of social amenity. Sometimes he liked the person, the face, the speech: an educated man, a gentleman, not one of the herd; a graceful woman, vague, accidental, unconscious of him, but making him wonder, while he hovered, who she was. These chances represented for him light yearnings and faint flutters; they acted indeed within him to a special, an extraordinary tune. He would have liked to talk with such stray companions, to talk with them *really*, to talk with them as he might have talked had he met them where he couldn't meet them – at dinner, in the 'world,' on a visit at a country-house. Then he could have said – and about the shrine and the idol always – things he couldn't say now. The form in which his irritation first came to him was that of his feeling obliged to say to them – to the single visitor, even when sympathetic, quite as to the gaping group – the particular things, a dreadful dozen or so, that they expected. If he had thus arrived at characterising these things as dreadful the reason touched the very point that, for a while turning everything over, he kept dodging, not facing, trying to ignore. The point was that he was on his way to become two quite different persons, the public and the private – as to which it would somehow have to be managed that these persons should live together. He was splitting into halves, unmistakeably – he who, whatever else he had been, had at least always been so entire and in his way so solid. One of the halves, or perhaps even, since the split promised to be rather unequal, one of the quarters, was the keeper, the showman, the priest of the idol; the other piece was the poor unsuccessful honest man he had always been.

There were moments when he recognised this primary character as he had never done before; when he in fact quite shook in his shoes at the idea that it perhaps had in reserve some supreme assertion of its identity. It was honest, verily, just by reason of the possibility. It was poor and unsuccessful because here it was just on the verge of quarrelling with its bread and butter. Salvation would be of course – the salvation of the showman – rigidly to *keep* it on the verge; nor to let it, in other words, overpass by an inch. He might count on this, he said to himself, if there weren't any public – if there weren't thousands of people demanding of him what he was paid for. He saw the approach of the stage at which they would affect him, the thousands of people – and perhaps even more the earnest individual – as coming really to see if he were earning his wage. Wouldn't he soon begin to fancy them in league with the Body, practically deputed by it – given, no doubt, a kindled suspicion – to look in and report observations?

It was the way he broke down with the lonely pilgrim that led to his first heart-searchings – broke down as to the courage required for damping an uncritical faith. What they all most wanted was to feel that everything was 'just as it was'; only the shock of having to part with that vision was greater than any individual could bear unsupported. The bad moments were upstairs in the Birthroom, for here the forces pressing on the very edge assumed a dire intensity. The mere expression of eye, all-credulous, omnivorous and fairly moistening in the act, with which many persons gazed about, might eventually make it difficult for him to remain fairly civil. Often they came in pairs – sometimes one had come before – and then they explained to each other. He in that case never corrected; he listened, for the lesson of listening: after which he would remark to his wife that there was no end to what he was learning. He saw that if he should really ever break down it would be with her he would begin. He had given her hints and digs enough, but she was so inflamed with appreciation that she either didn't feel them or pretended not to understand.

This was the greater complication that, with the return of the spring and the increase of the public, her services were more required. She took the field with him from an early hour; she was present with the party above while he kept an eye, and still more an ear, on the party below; and how could he know, he asked himself, what she might say to them and what she might suffer *Them* to say – or in other words, poor wretches, to believe – while removed from his control? Some day or other, and before too long, he couldn't but think, he must have the matter out with her – the matter, namely, of the *morality* of their position. The morality of women was special – he was getting lights on that. Isabel's conception of her office was to cherish and enrich the legend. It was already, the legend, very taking, but what was she there for but to make it more so? She certainly wasn't there to chill any natural piety. If it was all in the air – all in their 'eye,' as the vulgar might say – that He *had* been born in the Birthroom, where was the value of the sixpences they took? where the equivalent they had engaged to supply? 'Oh dear, yes – just about *here*'; and she must tap the place with her foot. 'Altered? Oh dear, no – save in a few trifling particulars; you see the place – and isn't that just the charm of it? – quite as *He* saw it. Very poor and homely, no doubt; but that's just what's so wonderful.' He didn't want to hear her, and yet he didn't want to give her her head; he didn't want to make difficulties or to snatch the bread from her mouth. But he must none the less give her a warning before they had gone *too* far. That was the way, one evening in June, he put it to her; the affluence, with the finest weather, having lately been of the largest and the crowd all day fairly gorged with the story. 'We mustn't, you know, go *too* far.'

The odd thing was that she had now ceased even to be conscious of what troubled him – she was so launched in her own career. 'Too far for what?'

'To save our immortal souls. We mustn't, love, tell too many lies.'

She looked at him with dire reproach. 'Ah now are you going to begin again?'

'I never *have* begun; I haven't wanted to worry you. But, you know, we don't know anything about it.' And then as she stared, flushing: 'About His having been born up there. About anything really. Not the least little scrap that would weigh in any other connexion as evidence. So don't rub it in so.'

'Rub it in how?'

'That He *was* born – ' But at sight of her face he only sighed. 'Oh dear, oh dear!'

'Don't you think,' she replied cuttingly, 'that He was born anywhere?'

He hesitated – it was such an edifice to shake. 'Well, we don't know. There's very little *to* know. He covered His tracks as no other human being has ever done.'

She was still in her public costume and hadn't taken off the gloves she made a point of wearing as a part of that uniform; she remembered how the rustling housekeeper in the Border castle, on whom she had begun by modelling herself, had worn them. She seemed official and slightly distant. 'To cover His tracks He must have had to exist. Have we got to give *that* up?'

'No, I don't ask you to give it up *yet*. But there's very little to go upon.'

'And is that what I'm to tell Them in return for everything?'

Gedge waited – he walked about. The place was doubly still after the bustle of the day, and the summer evening rested on it as a blessing, making it, in its small state and ancientry, mellow and sweet. It was good to be there and it would be good to stay. At the same time there was something incalculable in the effect on one's nerves of the great gregarious density. This was an attitude that had nothing to do with degrees and shades, the attitude of wanting all or nothing. And you couldn't talk things over with it. You could only do that with friends, and then but in cases where you were sure the friends wouldn't betray you. 'Couldn't you adopt,' he replied at last, 'a slightly more discreet method? What we can say is that things have been *said*; that's all *we* have to do with. "And is this really" – when they jam their umbrellas into the floor – "the very *spot* where He was born?" "So it has, from a long time back, been described as being." Couldn't one meet Them, to be decent a little, in some such way as that?'

She looked at him very hard. 'Is that the way *you* meet them?'

'No; I've kept on lying – without scruple, without shame.'

'Then why do you haul me up?'

'Because it has seemed to me we might, like true companions, work it out a little together.'

This was not strong, he felt, as, pausing with his hands in his pockets, he stood before her; and he knew it as weaker still after she had looked at him a minute. 'Morris Gedge, I propose to be *your* true companion, and I've come here to stay. That's all I've got to say.' It was not, however, for 'You had better try yourself and see,' she presently added. 'Give the place, give the story away, by so much as a look, and – well, I'd allow you about nine days. Then you'd see.'

He feigned, to gain time, an innocence. 'They'd take it so ill?' And then as she said nothing: 'They'd turn and rend me? They'd tear me to pieces?'

But she wouldn't make a joke of it. 'They wouldn't *have* it, simply.'

'No – They wouldn't. That's what I say. They won't.'

'You had better,' she went on, 'begin with Grant-Jackson. But even that isn't necessary. It would get to him, it would get to the Body, like wildfire.'

'I see,' said poor Gedge. And indeed for the moment he did see, while his companion followed up what she believed her advantage.

'Do you consider it's *all* a fraud?'

'Well, I grant you there was somebody. But the details are naught. The links are missing. The evidence – in particular about that room upstairs, in itself our Casa Santa[8] – is *nil*. It was so awfully long ago.' Which he knew again sounded weak.

'Of course it was awfully long ago – that's just the beauty and the interest. Tell Them, *tell* Them,' she continued, 'that the evidence is *nil*, and I'll tell Them something else.' She spoke it with such meaning that his face seemed to show a question, to which she was on the spot of replying 'I'll tell Them you're a –' She stopped, however, changing it. 'I'll tell Them exactly the opposite. And I'll find out what you say – it won't take long – to do it. If we tell different stories *that* possibly may save us.'

'I see what you mean. It would perhaps, as an oddity, have a success of curiosity. It might become a draw. Still, They but want broad masses.' And he looked at her sadly. 'You're no more than one of Them.'

'If it's being no more than one of Them to love it,' she answered, 'then I certainly am. And I'm not ashamed of my company.'

'To love *what*?' said Morris Gedge.

'To love to think He was born there.'

'You think too much. It's bad for you.' He turned away with his chronic moan. But it was without losing what she called after him.

'I decline to let the place down.' And what was there indeed to say? They *were* there to keep it up.

V

He kept it up through the summer, but with the queerest consciousness, at times, of the want of proportion between his secret rage and the spirit of those from whom the friction came. He said to himself — so sore his sensibility had grown — that They were gregariously ferocious at the very time he was seeing Them as individually mild. He said to himself that They were mild only because *he* was — he flattered himself that he was divinely so, considering what he might be; and that he should, as his wife had warned him, soon enough have news of it were he to deflect by a hair's breadth from the line traced for him. *That* was the collective fatuity — that it was capable of turning on the instant both to a general and to a particular resentment. Since the least breath of discrimination would get him the sack without mercy, it was absurd, he reflected, to speak of his discomfort as light. He was gagged, he was goaded, as in omnivorous companies he doubtless sometimes showed by a strange silent glare. They'd get him the sack for that as well, if he didn't look out; therefore wasn't it in effect ferocity when you mightn't even hold your tongue? They wouldn't let you off with silence — They insisted on your committing yourself. It was the pound of flesh[9] — They *would* have it; so under his coat he bled. But a wondrous peace, by exception, dropped on him one afternoon at the end of August. The pressure had, as usual, been high, but it had diminished with the fall of day, and the place was empty before the hour for closing. Then it was that, within a few minutes of this hour, there presented themselves a pair of pilgrims to whom in the ordinary course he would have remarked that they were, to his regret, too late. He was to wonder afterwards why the course had at sight of the visitors — a gentleman and a lady, appealing and fairly young — shown for him as other than ordinary; the consequence sprang doubtless from something rather fine and unnameable, something for example in the tone of the young man or in the light of his eye, after hearing the statement on the subject of the hour. 'Yes, we know it's late; but it's just, I'm afraid, *because* of that. We've had rather a notion of escaping the crowd — as I suppose you mostly have one now; and it was really on the chance of finding you alone — !'

These things the young man said before being quite admitted, and they were words any one might have spoken who hadn't taken the trouble to be punctual or who desired, a little ingratiatingly, to force the door. Gedge even guessed at the sense that might lurk in them, the hint of a special tip if the point were stretched. There were no tips, he had often thanked his stars, at the Birthplace; there was the charged fee and nothing more; everything else was out of order, to the relief of a palm not formed by nature as a scoop. Yet in spite of everything, in spite especially of the almost audible chink of the gentleman's sovereigns, which might in another case exactly have put him out, he presently found himself, in the Birthroom, access to which he had gracefully enough granted, almost treating the visit as personal and private. The reason – well, the reason would have been, if anywhere, in something naturally persuasive on the part of the couple; unless it had been rather again, in the way the young man, once he was in the place, met the caretaker's expression of face, held it a moment and seemed to wish to sound it. That they were Americans was promptly clear, and Gedge could very nearly have told what kind; he had arrived at the point of distinguishing kinds, though the difficulty might have been with him now that the case before him was rare. He saw it suddenly in the light of the golden midland evening which reached them through low old windows, saw it with a rush of feeling, unexpected and smothered, that made him a moment wish to keep it before him as a case of inordinate happiness. It made him feel old shabby poor, but he watched it no less intensely for its doing so. They were children of fortune, of the greatest, as it might seem to Morris Gedge, and they were of course lately married; the husband, smooth-faced and soft, but resolute and fine, several years older than the wife, and the wife vaguely, delicately, irregularly, but mercilessly pretty. Somehow the world was theirs; they gave the person who took the sixpences at the Birthplace such a sense of the high luxury of freedom as he had never had. The thing was that the world was theirs not simply because they had money – he had seen rich people enough – but because they could in a supreme degree think and feel and say what they liked. They had a nature and a culture, a tradition, a facility of some sort – and all producing in them an effect of positive beauty – that gave a light to their liberty and an ease to their tone. These things moreover suffered nothing from the fact that they happened to be in mourning; this was probably worn for some lately-deceased opulent father – if not some delicate mother who would be sure to have been a part of the source of the beauty; and it affected Gedge, in the gathered twilight and at his odd crisis, as the very uniform of their distinction.

He couldn't quite have said afterwards by what steps the point had been reached, but it had become at the end of five minutes a part of their presence in the Birthroom, a part of the young man's look, a part of the charm of the moment, and a part above all of a strange sense within him of 'Now or never!' that Gedge had suddenly, thrillingly, let himself go. He hadn't been definitely conscious of drifting to it; he had been, for that, too conscious merely of thinking how different, in all their range, were such a united couple from another united couple known to him. They were everything he and his wife weren't; this was more than anything else the first lesson of their talk. Thousands of couples of whom the same was true certainly had passed before him, but none of whom it was true with just that engaging intensity. And just *because* of their transcendent freedom;

that was what, at the end of five minutes, he saw it all come back to. The husband, who had been there at some earlier time, had his impression, which he wished now to make his wife share. But he already, Gedge could see, hadn't concealed it from her. A pleasant irony in fine our friend seemed to taste in the air – he who hadn't yet felt free to taste his own.

'I think you weren't here four years ago' – that was what the young man had almost begun by remarking. Gedge liked his remembering it, liked his frankly speaking to him; all the more that he had offered, as it were, no opening. He had let them look about below and then had taken them up, but without words, without the usual showman's song, of which he would have been afraid. The visitors didn't ask for it; the young man had taken the matter out of his hands by himself dropping for the benefit of the young woman a few detached remarks. What Gedge oddly felt was that these remarks were not inconsiderate of him; he had heard others, both of the priggish order and the crude, that might have been called so. And as the young man hadn't been aided to this cognition of him as new, it already began to make for them a certain common ground. The ground became immense when the visitor presently added with a smile: 'There was a good lady, I recollect, who had a great deal to say.'

It was the gentleman's smile that had done it; the irony *was* there. 'Ah there has been a great deal said.' And Gedge's look at his interlocutor doubtless showed his sense of being sounded. It was extraordinary of course that a perfect stranger should have guessed the travail of his spirit, should have caught the gleam of his inner commentary. That probably leaked in spite of him out of his poor old eyes. 'Much of it, in such places as this,' he heard himself adding, 'is of course said very irresponsibly.' *Such places as this*! – he winced at the words as soon as he had uttered them.

There was no wincing, however, on the part of his pleasant companions. 'Exactly so; the whole thing becomes a sort of stiff smug convention – like a dressed-up sacred doll in a Spanish church – which you're a monster if you touch.'

'A monster,' Gedge assented, meeting his eyes.

The young man smiled, but he thought looking at him a little harder. 'A blasphemer.'

'A blasphemer.'

It seemed to do his visitor good – he certainly *was* looking at him harder. Detached as he was he was interested – he was at least amused. 'Then you don't claim or at any rate don't insist –? I mean you personally.'

He had an identity for him, Gedge felt, that he couldn't have had for a Briton, and the impulse was quick in our friend to testify to this perception. 'I don't insist to *you*.'

The young man laughed. 'It really — I assure you if I may — wouldn't do any good. I'm too awfully interested.'

'Do you mean,' his wife lightly enquired, 'in — a — pulling it down? That's rather in what you've said to me.'

'Has he said to you,' Gedge intervened, though quaking a little, 'that he would like to pull it down?'

She met, in her free sweetness, this appeal with such a charm! 'Oh perhaps not quite the *house* — !'

'Good. You see we live on it — I mean *we* people.'

The husband had laughed, but had now so completely ceased to look about him that there seemed nothing left for him but to talk avowedly with the caretaker. 'I'm interested,' he explained, 'in what I think *the* interesting thing — or at all events the eternally tormenting one. The fact of the abysmally little that, in proportion, we know.'

'In proportion to what?' his companion asked.

'Well, to what there must have been — to what in fact there *is* — to wonder about. That's the interest; it's immense. He escapes us like a thief at night,[10] carrying off — well, carrying off everything. And people pretend to catch Him like a flown canary, over whom you can close your hand, and put Him back in the cage. He won't *go* back; he won't *come* back. He's not' — the young man laughed — 'such a fool! It makes Him the happiest of all great men.'

He had begun by speaking to his wife, but had ended, with his friendly, his easy, his indescribable competence, for Gedge — poor Gedge who quite held his breath and who felt, in the most unexpected way, that he had somehow never been in such good society. The young wife, who for herself meanwhile had continued to look about, sighed out, smiled out — Gedge couldn't have told which — her little answer to these remarks. 'It's rather a pity, you know, that He *isn't* here. I mean as Goethe's at Weimar.[11] For Goethe *is* at Weimar.'

'Yes, my dear; that's Goethe's bad luck. There he sticks. *This* man isn't anywhere. I defy you to catch Him.'

'Why not say, beautifully,' the young woman laughed, 'that, like the wind, He's everywhere?'

It wasn't of course the tone of discussion, it was the tone of pleasantry, though of better pleasantry, Gedge seemed to feel, and more within his own appreciation, than he had ever listened to; and this was precisely why the young man could go on without the effect of irritation, answering his wife but still with eyes for their companion. 'I'll be hanged if He's *here*!'

It was almost as if he were taken — that is, struck and rather held — by their companion's unruffled state, which they hadn't meant to ruffle, but which suddenly presented its interest, perhaps even projected its light. The gentleman didn't know, Gedge was afterwards to say to himself, how that hypocrite was inwardly all of a tremble, how it seemed to him his fate was being literally pulled down on his head. He was trembling for the moment certainly too much to speak; abject he might be, but he didn't want his voice to have the absurdity of a quaver. And the young woman – charming creature! – still had another word. It was for the guardian of the spot, and she made it in her way delightful. They had remained in the Holy of Holies, where she had been looking for a minute, with a ruefulness just marked enough to be pretty, at the queer old floor. 'Then if you say it *wasn't* in this room He was born – well, what's the use?'

'What's the use of what?' her husband asked. 'The use, you mean, of our coming here? Why the place is charming in itself. And it's also interesting,' he added to Gedge, 'to know how you get on.'

Gedge looked at him a moment in silence, but answering the young woman first. If poor Isabel, he was thinking, could only have been like that! – not as to youth, beauty, arrangement of hair or picturesque grace of hat – these things he didn't mind; but as to sympathy, facility, light perceptive, and yet not cheap, detachment! 'I don't say it wasn't – but I don't say it *was*.'

'Ah but doesn't that,' she returned, 'come very much to the same thing? And don't They want also to see where He had His dinner and where He had His tea?'

'They want everything,' said Morris Gedge. 'They want to see where He hung up His hat and where He kept His boots and where His mother boiled her pot.'

'But if you don't show them –?'

'They show *me*. It's in all their little books.'

'You mean,' the husband asked, 'that you've only to hold your tongue?'

'I try to,' said Gedge.

'Well,' his visitor smiled, 'I see you *can*.'

Gedge hesitated. 'I can't.'

'Oh well,' said his friend, 'what does it matter?'

'I do speak,' he continued. 'I can't sometimes not.'

'Then how do you get on?'

Gedge looked at him more abjectly, to his own sense, than ever at any one – even at Isabel when she frightened him. 'I don't get on. I speak,' he said – 'since I've spoken to *you*.'

'Oh *we* shan't hurt you!' the young man reassuringly laughed.

The twilight meanwhile had sensibly thickened, the end of the visit was indicated. They turned together out of the upper room and came down the narrow stair. The words just exchanged might have been felt as producing an awkwardness which the young woman gracefully felt the impulse to dissipate. 'You must rather wonder why we've come.' And it was the first note for Gedge of a further awkwardness — as if he had definitely heard it make the husband's hand, in a full pocket, begin to fumble.

It was even a little awkwardly that the husband still held off. 'Oh we like it as it is. There's always *something*.' With which they had approached the door of egress.

'What is there, please?' asked Morris Gedge, not yet opening the door, since he would fain have kept the pair on, and conscious only for a moment after he had spoken that his question was just having for the young man too dreadfully wrong a sound. This personage wondered yet feared, and had evidently for some minutes been putting himself a question; so that, with his preoccupation, the caretaker's words had represented to him inevitably: 'What is there, please, for *me*?' Gedge already knew with it moreover that he wasn't stopping him in time. He had uttered that challenge to show he himself wasn't afraid, and he must have had in consequence, he was subsequently to reflect, a lamentable air of waiting.

The visitor's hand came out. 'I hope I may take the liberty —?' What afterwards happened our friend scarcely knew, for it fell into a slight confusion, the confusion of a queer gleam of gold — a sovereign fairly thrust at him; of a quick, almost violent motion on his own part, which, to make the matter worse, might well have sent the money rolling on the floor; and then of marked blushes all round and a sensible embarrassment; producing indeed in turn rather oddly and ever so quickly an increase of communion. It was as if the young man had offered him money to make up to him for having, as it were, led him on, and then, perceiving the mistake, but liking him the better for his refusal, had wanted to obliterate this aggravation of his original wrong. He had done so, presently, while Gedge got the door open, by saying the best thing he could, and by saying it frankly and gaily. 'Luckily it doesn't at all affect the *work*!'

The small town-street, quiet and empty in the summer eventide, stretched to right and left, with a gabled and timbered house or two, and fairly seemed to have cleared itself to congruity with the historic void over which our friends, lingering an instant to converse, looked at each other. The young wife, rather, looked about a moment at all there wasn't to be seen, and then, before Gedge had found a reply to her husband's remark, uttered, evidently in the interest of conciliation, a little question of her own that she tried to make earnest. 'It's our unfortunate ignorance, you mean, that doesn't?'

'Unfortunate or fortunate. I like it so,' said the husband. '"The play's the thing." Let the author alone.'

Gedge, with his key on his forefinger, leaned against the door-post, took in the stupid little street and was sorry to see them go — they seemed so to abandon him. 'That's just what They won't do — nor let *me* do. It's all I want — to let the author alone. Practically' – he felt himself getting the last of his chance – 'there *is* no author; that is for us to deal with. There are all the immortal people – *in* the work; but there's nobody else.'

'Yes,' said the young man – 'that's what it comes to. There should really, to clear the matter up, be no such Person.'

'As you say,' Gedge returned, 'it's what it comes to. There *is* no such Person.'

The evening air listened, in the warm thick midland stillness, while the wife's little cry rang out. 'But *wasn't* there –?'

'There was somebody,' said Gedge against the door-post. 'But They've killed Him. And, dead as He is, They keep it up, They do it over again, They kill Him every day.'

He was aware of saying this so grimly – more than he wished – that his companions exchanged a glance and even perhaps looked as if they felt him extravagant. That was really the way Isabel had warned him all the others would be looking if he should talk to Them as he talked to *her*. He liked, however, for that matter, to hear how he should sound when pronounced incapable through deterioration of the brain. 'Then if there's no author, if there's nothing to be said but that there isn't anybody,' the young woman smilingly asked, 'why in the world should there be a house?'

'There shouldn't,' said Morris Gedge.

Decidedly, yes, he affected the young man. 'Oh, I don't say, mind you, that you should pull it down!'

'Then where would you *go*?' their companion sweetly enquired.

'That's what my wife asks,' Gedge returned.

'Then keep it up, keep it up!' And the husband held out his hand.

'That's what my wife says,' Gedge went on as he shook it.

The young woman, charming creature, emulated the other visitor; she offered their remarkable friend her handshake. 'Then mind your wife.'

The poor man faced her gravely. 'I would if she were such a wife as you!'

VI

It had made for him, all the same, an immense difference; it had given him an extraordinary lift, so that a certain sweet aftertaste of his freedom might a couple of months later have been suspected of aiding to produce for him another and really a more considerable adventure. It was an absurd way to reason, but he had been, to his imagination, for twenty minutes in good society – that being the term that best described for him the company of people to whom he hadn't to talk, as he phrased it, rot. It was his title to good society that he had, in his doubtless awkward way, affirmed; and the difficulty was just that, having affirmed it, he couldn't take back the affirmation. Few things had happened to him in life, that is few that were agreeable, but at least *this* had, and he wasn't so constructed that he could go on as if it hadn't. It was going on as if it had, however, that landed him, alas! in the situation unmistakeably marked by a visit from Grant-Jackson late one afternoon toward the end of October. This had been the hour of the call of the young Americans. Every day that hour had come round something of the deep throb of it, the successful secret, woke up; but the two occasions were, of a truth, related only by being so intensely opposed. The secret had been successful in that he had said nothing of it to Isabel, who, occupied in their own quarter while the incident lasted, had neither heard the visitors arrive nor seen them depart. It was on the other hand scarcely successful in guarding itself from indirect betrayals. There were two persons in the world at least who felt as he did; they were persons also who had treated him, benignly, as feeling after *their* style; who had been ready in fact to overflow in gifts as a sign of it, and though they were now off in space they were still with him sufficiently in spirit to make him play, as it were, with the sense of their sympathy. This in turn made him, as he was perfectly aware, more than a shade or two reckless, so that, in his reaction from that gluttony of the public for false facts which had from the first tormented him, he fell into the habit of sailing, as he would have said, too near the wind, or in other words – all in presence of the people – of washing his hands of the legend. He had crossed the line – he knew it; he had struck wild – They drove him to it; he had substituted, by a succession of uncontrollable profanities, an attitude that couldn't be understood for an attitude that but too evidently *had* been.

This was of course the franker line, only he hadn't taken it, alas! for frankness – hadn't in the least really adopted it at all, but had been simply himself caught up and disposed of by it, hurled by his fate against the bedizened walls of the temple, quite in the way of a priest possessed to excess of the god, or, more vulgarly, that of a blind bull in a china-shop – an animal to which he often compared himself. He had let himself fatally go, in fine, just for irritation, for rage, having, in his predicament, nothing whatever to do with frankness – a luxury reserved for quite other situations. It had always been his view that one lived to learn; he had learned something every hour of his life, though people mostly never knew what, in spite of its having generally been – hadn't it? – at somebody's expense. What he was at present continually learning was the sense of a form of words heretofore so vain – the famous 'false position' that had so often helped out a phrase. One used names in that way without knowing what they were worth; then of a sudden, one fine day, their meaning grew bitter in the mouth. This was a truth with the relish of which his fireside hours were occupied, and he was aware of how much it exposed a man to look so perpetually as if something had disagreed with him. The look to be worn at the Birthplace was properly the beatific, and when once it had fairly been missed by those who took it for granted, who indeed paid sixpence for it – like the table-wine in provincial France it was *compris*[13] – one would be sure to have news of the remark.

News accordingly was what Gedge had been expecting and what he knew, above all, had been expected by his wife, who had a way of sitting at present as with an ear for a certain knock. She didn't watch him, didn't follow him about the house, at the public hours, to spy upon his treachery; and that could touch him even though her averted eyes went through him more than her fixed. Her mistrust was so perfectly expressed by her manner of showing she trusted that he never felt so nervous, never tried so to keep straight, as when she most let him alone. When the crowd thickened and they had of necessity to receive together he tried himself to get off by allowing her as much as possible the word. When people appealed to him he turned to her – and with more of ceremony than their relation warranted: he couldn't help *this* either, if it seemed ironic – as to the person most concerned or most competent. He flattered himself at these moments that no one would have guessed her being his wife; especially as, to do her justice, she met his manner with a wonderful grim bravado – grim, so to say, for himself, grim by its outrageous cheerfulness for the simple-minded. The lore she *did* produce for them, the associations of the sacred spot she developed, multiplied, embroidered; the things in short she said and the stupendous way she said them! She wasn't a bit ashamed, since why need virtue be ever ashamed? It *was* virtue, for it put bread into his mouth – he meanwhile on his side taking it out of hers. He had seen Grant-Jackson on the October day in the Birthplace itself – the right setting of course for such an interview; and what had occurred was that, precisely, when the scene had ended and he had come back to their own sitting-room, the question she put to him for information was: 'Have you settled it that I'm to starve?'

She had for a long time said nothing to him so straight – which was but a proof of her real anxiety; the straightness of Grant-Jackson's visit, following on the very slight sinuosity of a note shortly before received from him, made tension show for what it was. By this time, really, however, his decision had been taken; the minutes elapsing between his reappearance at the domestic fireside and his having, from the other threshold, seen Grant-Jackson's broad well-fitted back, the back of a banker and a patriot, move away, had, though few, presented themselves to him as supremely critical. They formed, as it were, the hinge of his door, that door actually ajar so as to show him a possible fate beyond it, but which, with his hand, in a spasm, thus tightening on the knob, he might either open wide or close partly or altogether. He stood at autumn dusk in the little museum that constituted the vestibule of the temple, and there, as with a concentrated push at the crank of a windlass, he brought himself round. The portraits on the walls seemed vaguely to watch for it; it was in their august presence – kept dimly august for the moment by Grant-Jackson's impressive check of his application of a match to the vulgar gas – that the great man had uttered, as if it said all, his 'You know, my dear fellow, really –!' He had managed it with the special tact of a fat man, always, when there *was* any, very fine; he had got the most out of the time, the place, the setting, all the little massed admonitions and symbols; confronted there with his victim on the spot that he took occasion to name afresh as, to *his* piety and patriotism, the most sacred on earth, he had given it to be understood that in the first place he was lost in amazement and that in the second he expected a single warning now to suffice. Not to insist too much moreover on the question of gratitude, he would let his remonstrance rest, if need be, solely on the question of taste. As a matter of taste alone –! But he was surely not to be obliged to follow that up. Poor Gedge indeed would have been sorry to oblige him, for he saw it was exactly to the atrocious taste of unthankfulness the allusion was made. When he said he wouldn't dwell on what the fortunate occupant of the post owed him for the stout battle originally fought on his behalf, he simply meant he *would*. That was his tact – which, with everything else that has been mentioned, in the scene, to help, really had the ground to itself. The day *had* been when Gedge couldn't have thanked him enough – though he had thanked him, he considered, almost fulsomely – and nothing, nothing that he could coherently or reputably name, had happened since then. From the moment he was pulled up, in short, he had no case, and if he exhibited, instead of one, only hot tears in his eyes, the mystic gloom of the temple either prevented his friend from seeing them or rendered it possible that they stood for remorse. He had dried them, with the pads formed by the base of his bony thumbs, before he went in to Isabel. This was the more fortunate as, in spite of her enquiry, prompt and pointed, he but moved about the room looking at her hard. Then he stood before the fire a little with his hands behind him and his coat-tails divided, quite as the person in permanent possession. It was an indication his wife appeared to take in; but she put nevertheless presently another question. 'You object to telling me what he said?'

'He said "You know, my dear fellow, really –!"'

'And is that all?'

'Practically. Except that I'm a thankless beast.'

'Well!' she responded, not with dissent.

'You mean that I *am*?'

'Are those the words he used?' she asked with a scruple.

Gedge continued to think. 'The words he used were that I give away the Show and that, from several sources, it has come round to Them.'

'As of course a baby would have known!' And then as her husband said nothing: 'Were *those* the words he used?'

'Absolutely. He couldn't have used better ones.'

'Did he call it,' Mrs Gedge enquired, 'the "Show"?'

'Of course he did. The Biggest on Earth.'

She winced, looking at him hard — she wondered, but only for a moment. 'Well, it *is*.'

'Then it's something,' Gedge went on, 'to have given *that* away. But,' he added, 'I've taken it back.'

'You mean you've been convinced?'

'I mean I've been scared.'

'At last, at last!' she gratefully breathed.

'Oh it was easily done. It was only two words. But here I am.'

Her face was now less hard for him. 'And what two words?'

' "You know, Mr Gedge, that it simply won't do." That was all. But it was the way such a man says them.'

'I'm glad then,' Mrs Gedge frankly averred, 'that he *is* such a man. How did you ever think it *could* do?'

'Well, it was my critical sense. I didn't ever know I had one — till They came and (by putting me here) waked it up in me. Then I had somehow, don't you see? to live with it; and I seemed to feel that, with one thing and another, giving it time and in the long run, it might, it *ought* to, come out on top of the heap. Now that's where, he says, it simply won't "do." So I must put it — I *have* put it — at the bottom.'

'A very good place then for a critical sense!' And Isabel, more placidly now, folded her work. '*If*, that is, you can only keep it there. If it doesn't struggle up again.'

'It can't struggle.' He was still before the fire, looking round at the warm low room, peaceful in the lamplight, with the hum of the kettle for the ear, with the curtain drawn over the leaded casement, a short moreen[14] curtain artfully chosen by Isabel for the effect of the olden time, its virtue of letting the light within show ruddy to the street. 'It's dead,' he went on; 'I killed it just now.'

He really spoke so that she wondered. 'Just now?'

'There in the other place — I strangled it, poor thing, in the dark. If you'll go out and see, there must be blood. Which, indeed,' he added, 'on an altar of sacrifice, is all right. But the place is for ever spattered.'

'I don't want to go out and see.' She locked her hands over the needlework folded on her knee, and he knew, with her eyes on him, that a look he had seen before was in her face. 'You're off your head, you know, my dear, in a way.' Then, however, more cheeringly: 'It's a good job it hasn't been too late.'

'Too late to get it under?'

'Too late for Them to give you the second chance that I thank God you accept.'

'Yes, if it *had* been – !' And he looked away as through the ruddy curtain and into the chill street. Then he faced her again. 'I've scarcely got over my fright yet. I mean,' he went on, 'for you.'

'And I mean for *you*. Suppose what you had come to announce to me now were that we had *got* the sack. How should I enjoy, do you think, seeing you turn out? Yes, out *there*!' she added as his eyes again moved from their little warm circle to the night of early winter on the other side of the pane, to the rare quick footsteps, to the closed doors, to the curtains drawn like their own, behind which the small flat town, intrinsically dull, was sitting down to supper.

He stiffened himself as he warmed his back; he held up his head, shaking himself a little as if to shake the stoop out of his shoulders, but he had to allow she was right. 'What would have become of us?'

'What indeed? We should have begged our bread – or I should be taking in washing.'

He was silent a little. 'I'm too old. I should have begun sooner.'

'Oh God forbid!' she cried.

'The pinch,' he pursued, 'is that I can do nothing else.'

'Nothing whatever!' she agreed with elation.

'Whereas here – if I cultivate it – I perhaps *can* still lie. But I must cultivate it.'

'Oh you old dear!' And she got up to kiss him.

'I'll do my best,' he said.

VII

'Do you remember us?' the gentleman asked and smiled – with the lady beside him smiling too; speaking so much less as an earnest pilgrim or as a tiresome tourist than as an old acquaintance. It was history repeating itself as Gedge had somehow never expected, with almost everything the same except that the evening was now a mild April-end, except that the visitors had put off mourning and showed all their bravery – besides showing, as he doubtless did himself, though so differently, for a little older; except, above all, that – oh seeing them again suddenly affected him not a bit as the thing he'd have supposed it. 'We're in England again and we were near; I've a brother at Oxford[15] with whom we've been spending a day, so that we thought we'd come over.' This the young man pleasantly said while our friend took in the queer fact that he must himself seem to them rather coldly to gape. They had come in the same way at the quiet close; another August had passed, and this was the second spring; the Birthplace, given the hour, was about to suspend operations till the morrow; the last lingerer had gone and the fancy of the visitors was once more for a look round by themselves. This represented surely no greater presumption than the terms on which they had last parted with him seemed to warrant; so that if he did inconsequently stare it was just in fact because he was so supremely far from having forgotten them. But the sight of the pair luckily had a double effect, and the first precipitated the second – the second being really his sudden vision that everything perhaps depended for him on his recognising no complication. He must go straight on, since it was what had for more than a year now so handsomely answered; he must brazen it out consistently, since that only was what his dignity was at last reduced to. He mustn't be afraid in one way any more than he had been in another; besides which it came over him to the point of his flushing for it that their visit, in its essence, must have been for himself. It was good society again, and *they* were the same. It wasn't for him therefore to behave as if he couldn't meet them.

These deep vibrations, on Gedge's part, were as quick as they were deep; they came in fact all at once, so that his response, his declaration that it was all right – 'Oh *rather*; the hour doesn't matter for *you*!' – had hung fire but an instant; and when they were well across the threshold and the door closed behind them, housed in the twilight of the temple, where, as before, the votive offerings glimmered on the walls, he drew the long breath of one who might by a self-betrayal have done something too dreadful. For what had brought them back was indubitably not the glamour of the shrine itself – since he had had a glimpse of their analysis of that quantity; but their critical (not to say their sentimental) interest in the queer case of the priest. Their call was the tribute of curiosity, of sympathy, of a compassion really, as such things went, exquisite – a tribute *to* that queerness which entitled them to the frankest welcome. They had wanted, for the generous wonder of it, to judge how he was getting on, how such a man in such a place *could*; and they had doubtless more than half-expected to see the door opened by somebody who had succeeded him. Well, somebody *had* – only with a strange equivocation; as they would have, poor things, to make out themselves, an embarrassment for which he pitied them. Nothing could have been more odd, but verily it was this troubled vision of their possible bewilderment, and this compunctious view of such a return for their amenity, that practically determined in him his tone. The lapse of the months had but made their name familiar to him; they had on the other occasion inscribed it, among the thousand names, in the current public register, and he had since then, for reasons of his own, reasons of feeling, again and again turned back to it. It was nothing in itself; it told him nothing – 'Mr and Mrs B. D. Hayes, New York' – one of those American labels that were just like every other American label and that were precisely the most remarkable thing about people reduced to achieving an identity in such other ways. They could be Mr and Mrs B. D. Hayes and yet could be, with all presumptions missing – well, what these callers were. It had quickly enough indeed cleared the situation a little further that his friends had absolutely, the other time, as it came back to him, warned him of his original danger, their anxiety about which had been the last note sounded among them. What he was afraid of, with this reminiscence, was that, finding him still safe, they would, the next thing, definitely congratulate him and perhaps even, no less candidly, ask him how he had managed. It was with the sense of nipping some such enquiry in the bud that, losing no time and holding himself with a firm grip, he began on the spot, downstairs, to make plain to them how he had managed. He routed the possibility of the question in short by the assurance of his answer. 'Yes, yes, I'm still here; I suppose it *is* in a manner to one's profit that one does, such as it is, one's best.' He did his best on the present occasion, did it with the gravest face he had ever worn and a soft serenity that was like a large damp sponge passed over their previous meeting – over everything in it, that is, but the fact of its pleasantness.

'We stand here, you see, in the old living-room, happily still to be reconstructed in the mind's eye, in spite of the havoc of time, which we have fortunately of late years been able to arrest. It was of course rude and humble, but it must have been snug and quaint, and we have at least the pleasure of knowing that the tradition in respect to the features that do remain is delightfully uninterrupted. Across that threshold He habitually passed; through those low windows, in childhood, He peered out into the world that He was to make so much happier by the gift to it of His genius; over the boards of this floor – that is over *some* of them, for we mustn't be carried away! – his little feet often pattered; and the beams of this ceiling (we must really in some places take care of *our* heads!) he endeavoured, in boyish strife, to jump up and touch. It's not often that in the early home of genius and renown the whole tenor of existence is laid so bare, not often that we are able to retrace, from point to point and from step to step, its connexion with objects, with influences – to build it round again with the little solid facts out of which it sprang. This therefore, I need scarcely remind you, is what makes the small space between these walls – so modest to measurement, so insignificant of aspect – unique on all the earth. *There's nothing like it*,' Morris Gedge went on, insisting as solemnly and softly, for his bewildered hearers, as over a pulpit-edge; 'there's nothing at all like it anywhere in the world. There's nothing, only reflect, for the combination of greatness and, as we venture to say, of intimacy. You may find elsewhere perhaps absolutely fewer changes, but where shall you find a *Presence* equally diffused, uncontested and undisturbed? Where in particular shall you find, on the part of the abiding spirit, an equally towering eminence? You may find elsewhere eminence of a considerable order, but where shall you find *with* it, don't you see, changes after all so few and the contemporary element caught so, as it were, in the very fact?' His visitors, at first confounded but gradually spellbound, were still gaping with the universal gape – wondering, he judged, into what strange pleasantry he had been suddenly moved to explode, and yet beginning to see in him an intention beyond a joke, so that they started, at this point, they almost jumped, when, by as rapid a transition, he made, toward the old fireplace, a dash that seemed to illustrate precisely the act of eager catching. 'It is in this old chimney-corner, the quaint inglenook of our ancestors – just there in the far angle, where His little stool was placed, and where, I dare say, if we could look close enough, we should find the hearthstone scraped with His little feet – that we see the inconceivable child gazing into the blaze of the old oaken logs and making out there pictures and stories, see Him conning, with curly bent head, His well-worn hornbook,[16] or poring over some scrap of an ancient ballad, some page of some such rudely-bound volume of chronicles as lay, we may be sure, in His father's window-seat.'

It was, he even himself felt at this moment, wonderfully done; no auditors, for all his thousands, had ever yet so inspired him. The odd slightly alarmed shyness in the two faces, as if in a drawing-room, in their 'good society' exactly, some act incongruous, something grazing the indecent, had abruptly been perpetrated, the painful reality of which stayed itself before coming home – the visible effect on his friends in fine wound him up as to the sense that *they* were worth the trick. It came of itself now – he had got it so by heart; but perhaps really it had never come so well, with the staleness so disguised, the interest so renewed and the clerical unction demanded by the priestly character so successfully distilled. Mr Hayes of New York had more than once looked at his wife, and Mrs Hayes of New York had more than once looked at her husband – only, up to now, with a stolen glance, with eyes it hadn't been easy to detach from the remarkable countenance by the aid of which their entertainer held them. At present, however, after an exchange less furtive, they ventured on a sign that they hadn't been appealed to in vain. 'Charming, charming, Mr Gedge!' Mr Hayes broke out. 'We feel that we've caught you in the mood.'

His wife hastened to assent – it eased the tension. 'It *would* be quite the way; except,' she smiled, 'that you'd be too dangerous. You've really a genius!'

Gedge looked at her hard, but yielding no inch, even though she touched him there at a point of consciousness that quivered. This was the prodigy for him, and had been, the year through – that he did it all, he found, easily, did it better than he had done anything else in life; with so high and broad an effect, in truth, an inspiration so rich and free, that his poor wife now, literally, had been moved more than once to fresh fear. She had had her bad moments, he knew, after taking the measure of his new direction – moments of readjusted suspicion in which she wondered if he hadn't simply adopted another, a different perversity. There would be more than one fashion of giving away the Show, and wasn't *this* perhaps a question of giving it away by excess? He could dish them by too much romance as well as by too little; she hadn't hitherto fairly grasped that there might *be* too much. It was a way like another, at any rate, of reducing the place to the absurd; which reduction, if he didn't look out, would reduce *them* again to the prospect of the streets, and this time surely without appeal. It all depended indeed – he knew she knew that – on how much Grant-Jackson and the others, how much the Body, in a word, would take. He knew she knew what he himself held it would take – that he considered no limit could be imputed to the quantity. They simply wanted it piled up, and so did every one else; wherefore if no one reported him as before why were They to be uneasy? It was in consequence of idiots tempted to reason that he had been dealt with before; but as there was now no form of idiocy that he didn't systematically flatter, goading it on really to its *own* private doom, who was ever to pull the string of the guillotine? The axe was in the air – yes; but in a world gorged to satiety there were no revolutions. And it had been vain for Isabel to ask if the other thundergrowl also hadn't come out of the blue. There was actually proof positive that the winds were now at rest. How could they be more so? – he appealed to the receipts. These were golden days – the Show had never so flourished. So he had argued, so he was arguing still – and, it had to be owned, with every appearance in his favour. Yet if he inwardly winced at the tribute to his plausibility rendered by his flushed friends, this was because he felt in it the real ground of his optimism. The charming woman before him acknowledged his 'genius' as he himself had had to do. He had been surprised at his facility until he had grown used to it. Whether or no he had, as a fresh menace to his future, found a new perversity, he had found a vocation much older, evidently, than he had at first been prepared to recognise. He had done himself injustice. He liked to be brave because it came so easy; he could measure it off by the yard. It was in the Birthroom, above all, that he continued to do this, having ushered up his companions without, as he was still more elated to feel, the turn of a hair. She might take it as she liked, but he had had the lucidity – all, that is, for his own safety – to meet without the grace of an answer the homage of her beautiful smile. She took it apparently, and her husband took it, but as a part of his odd humour, and they followed him aloft with faces now a little more responsive to the manner in which on *that* spot he would naturally come out. He came out, according to the word of his assured private receipt, 'strong.' He missed a little, in truth, the usual round-eyed question from them – the inveterate artless cue with which, from moment to moment, clustered troops had for a year obliged him. Mr and Mrs Hayes were from New York, but it was a little like singing, as he had heard one of his Americans once say about something, to a Boston audience.[17] He did none the less what he could, and it was ever his practice to stop still at a certain spot in the room and, after having secured attention by look and gesture, suddenly shoot off: 'Here!'

They always understood, the good people – he could fairly love them now for it; they always said breathlessly and unanimously 'There?' and stared down at the designated point quite as if some trace of the grand event were still to be made out. This movement produced he again looked round. 'Consider it well:[18] *the* spot of earth –!' 'Oh but it isn't *earth*!' the boldest spirit – there was always a boldest – would generally pipe out. Then the guardian of the Birthplace would be truly superior – as if the unfortunate had figured the Immortal coming up, like a potato, through the soil. 'I'm not suggesting that He was born on the bare ground. He was born *here*!' – with an uncompromising dig of his heel. 'There ought to be a brass, with an inscription, let in.' 'Into the floor?' – it always came. 'Birth and burial: seedtime, summer, autumn!' – that always, with its special right cadence, thanks to his unfailing spring, came too. 'Why not as well as into the pavement of the church? – you've *seen* our grand old church?' The former of which questions nobody ever answered – abounding, on the other hand, to make up, in relation to the latter. Mr and Mrs Hayes even were at first left dumb by it – not indeed, to do them justice, having uttered the word that called for it. They had uttered no word while he kept the game up, and (though that made it a little more difficult) he could yet stand triumphant before them after he had finished with his flourish. Only then it was that Mr Hayes of New York broke silence.

'Well, if we wanted to see I think I may say we're quite satisfied. As my wife says, it *would* seem your line.' He spoke now, visibly, with more ease, as if a light had come: though he made no joke of it, for a reason that presently appeared. They were coming down the little stair, and it was on the descent that his companion added her word.

'Do you know what we half *did* think –?' And then to her husband: 'Is it dreadful to tell him?' They were in the room below, and the young woman, also relieved, expressed the feeling with gaiety. She smiled as before at Morris Gedge, treating him as a person with whom relations were possible, yet remaining just uncertain enough to invoke Mr Hayes's opinion. 'We *have* awfully wanted – from what we had heard.' But she met her husband's graver face; he was not quite out of the wood. At this she was slightly flurried – but she cut it short. 'You must know – don't you? – that, with the crowds who listen to you, we'd have heard.'

He looked from one to the other, and once more again, with force, something came over him. They had kept him in mind, they were neither ashamed nor afraid to show it, and it was positively an interest on the part of this charming creature and this keen cautious gentleman, an interest resisting oblivion and surviving separation, that had governed their return. Their other visit had been the brightest thing that had ever happened to him, but this was the gravest; so that at the end of a minute something broke in him and his mask dropped of itself. He chucked, as he would have said, consistency; which, in its extinction, left the tears in his eyes. His smile was therefore queer. 'Heard how I'm going it?'

The young man, though still looking at him hard, felt sure, with this, of his own ground. 'Of course you're tremendously talked about. You've gone round the world.'

'You've heard of me in America?'

'Why almost of nothing else!'

'That was what made us feel –!' Mrs Hayes contributed.

'That you must see for yourselves?' Again he compared, poor Gedge, their faces. 'Do you mean I excite – a – scandal?'

'Dear no! Admiration. You renew so,' the young man observed, 'the interest.'

'Ah there it is!' said Gedge with eyes of adventure that seemed to rest beyond the Atlantic.

'They listen, month after month, when they're out here, as you must have seen; then they go home and talk. But they sing your praise.'

Our friend could scarce take it in. 'Over *there*!'

'Over there. I think you must be even in the papers.'

'Without abuse?'

'Oh we don't abuse every one.'

Mrs Hayes, in her beauty, it was clear, stretched the point. 'They rave about you.'

'Then they *don't* know?'

'Nobody knows,' the young man declared; 'it wasn't any one's knowledge, at any rate, that made us uneasy.'

'It was your own? I mean your own sense?'

'Well, call it that. We remembered, and we wondered what had happened. So,' Mr Hayes now frankly laughed, 'we came to see.'

Gedge stared through his film of tears. 'Came from America to see *me*?'

'Oh a part of the way. But we wouldn't, in England, have missed you.'

'And now we *haven't*!' the young woman soothingly added.

Gedge still could only gape at the candour of the tribute. But he tried to meet them – it was what was least poor for him – in their own key. 'Well, how do you like it?'

Mrs Hayes, he thought – if their answer were important – laughed a little nervously. 'Oh you see.'

Once more he looked from one to the other. 'It's too beastly easy, you know.'

Her husband raised his eyebrows. 'You conceal your art. The emotion – yes; that must be easy; the general tone must flow. But about your facts – you've so many: how do you get *them* through?'

Gedge wondered. 'You think I get too many –?'

At this they were amused together. 'That's just what we came to see!'

'Well, you know, I've felt my way; I've gone step by step; you wouldn't believe how I've tried it on. *This* – where you see me – is where I've come out.' After which, as they said nothing: 'You hadn't thought I *could* come out?'

Again they just waited, but the husband spoke: 'Are you so awfully sure you *are* out?'

Gedge drew himself up in the manner of his moments of emotion, almost conscious even that, with his sloping shoulders, his long lean neck and his nose so prominent in proportion to other matters, he resembled the more a giraffe. It was now at last he really caught on. 'I *may* be in danger again – and the danger is what has moved you? Oh!' the poor man fairly moaned. His appreciation of it quite weakened him, yet he pulled himself together. 'You've your view of my danger?'

It was wonderous how, with that note definitely sounded, the air was cleared. Lucid Mr Hayes, at the end of a minute, had put the thing in a nutshell. 'I don't know what you'll think of us – for being so beastly curious.'

'I think,' poor Gedge grimaced, 'you're only too beastly kind.'

'It's all your own fault,' his friend returned, 'for presenting us (who are not idiots, say) with so striking a picture of a crisis. At our other visit, you remember,' he smiled, 'you created an anxiety for the opposite reason. Therefore if *this* should again be a crisis for you, you'd really give us the case with an ideal completeness.'

'You make me wish,' said Morris Gedge, 'that it might be one.'

'Well, don't try – for our amusement – to bring one on. I don't see, you know, how you can have much margin. Take care – take care.'

Gedge did it pensive justice. 'Yes, that was what you said a year ago. You did me the honour to be uneasy – as my wife was.'

Which determined on the young woman's part an immediate question. 'May I ask then if Mrs Gedge is now at rest?'

'No – since you do ask. *She* fears at least that I go too far; she doesn't believe in my margin. You see we *had* our scare after your visit. They came down.'

His friends were all interest. 'Ah! They came down?'

'Heavy. They brought *me* down. That's *why* –'

'Why you *are* down?' Mrs Hayes sweetly demanded.

'Ah but my dear man,' her husband interposed, 'you're not down; you're *up*! You're only up a different tree, but you're up at the tip-top.'

'You mean I take it too high?'

'That's exactly the question,' the young man answered; 'and the possibility, as matching your first danger, is just what we felt we couldn't, if you didn't mind, miss the measure of.'

Gedge gazed at him. 'I feel that I know what you at bottom *hoped*.'

'We at bottom "hope," surely, that you're all right?'

'In spite of the fool it makes of every one?'

Mr Hayes of New York smiled. 'Say *because* of that. We only ask to believe every one *is* a fool!'

'Only you haven't been, without reassurance, able to imagine fools of the size that my case demands?' And Gedge had a pause while, as if on the chance of some proof, his companion waited. 'Well, I won't pretend to you that your anxiety hasn't made me, doesn't threaten to make me, a bit nervous; though I don't quite understand it if, as you say, people but rave about me.'

'Oh *that* report was from the other side; people in our country so very easily rave. You've seen small children laugh to shrieks when tickled in a new place. So there are amiable millions with us who are but small shrieking children. They perpetually present new places for the tickler. What we've seen in further lights,' Mr Hayes good-humouredly pursued, 'is your people *here* – the Committee, the Board, or whatever the powers to whom you're responsible.'

'Call them my friend Grant-Jackson then – my original backer, though I admit for that reason perhaps my most formidable critic. It's with him practically I deal; or rather it's by him I'm dealt with – *was* dealt with before. I stand or fall by him. But he has given me my head.'

'Mayn't he then want you,' Mrs Hayes enquired, 'just to show as flagrantly running away.'

'Of course – I see what you mean. I'm riding, blindly, for a fall, and They're watching (to be tender of me!) for the smash that may come of itself. It's Machiavellic[19] – but everything's possible. And what did you just now mean,' Gedge asked – 'especially if you've only heard of my prosperity – by your "further lights"?'

His friends for an instant looked embarrassed, but Mr Hayes came to the point. 'We've heard of your prosperity, but we've also, remember, within a few minutes, heard *you*.'

'I was determined you *should*,' said Gedge. 'I'm good then – but I overdo?' His strained grin was still sceptical.

Thus challenged, at any rate, his visitor pronounced. 'Well, if you don't; if at the end of six months more it's clear that you haven't overdone; then, *then* –'

'Then what?'

'Then it's great.'

'But it *is* great – greater than anything of the sort ever was. I overdo, thank goodness, yes; or I would if it were a thing you *could*.'

'Oh well, if there's *proof* that you can't –!' With which and an expressive gesture Mr Hayes threw up his fears.

His wife, however, for a moment seemed unable to let them go. 'Don't They want then *any* truth? – none even for the mere look of it?'

'The look of it,' said Morris Gedge, 'is what I give!'

It made them, the others, exchange a look of their own. Then she smiled. 'Oh, well, if they think so –!'

'You at least don't? You're like my wife – which indeed, I remember,' Gedge added, 'is a similarity I expressed a year ago the wish for! At any rate I frighten *her*.'

The young husband, with an 'Ah wives are terrible!' smoothed it over, and their visit would have failed of further excuse had not at this instant a movement at the other end of the room suddenly engaged them. The evening had so nearly closed in, though Gedge, in the course of their talk, had lighted the lamp nearest them, that they had not distinguished, in connexion with the opening of the door of communication to the warden's lodge, the appearance of another person, an eager woman who in her impatience had barely paused before advancing. Mrs Gedge – her identity took but a few seconds to become vivid – was upon them, and she had not been too late for Mr Hayes's last remark. Gedge saw at once that she had come with news; no need even, for that certitude, of her quick retort to the words in the air – 'You may say as well, sir, that they're often, poor wives, terrified!' She knew nothing of the friends whom, at so unnatural an hour, he was showing about; but there was no livelier sign for him that this didn't matter than the possibility with which she intensely charged her 'Grant-Jackson, to see you at once!' – letting it, so to speak, fly in his face.

'He has been with you?'

'Only a minute – he's there. But it's you he wants to see.'

He looked at the others. 'And what does he want, dear?'

'God knows! There it is. It's his horrid hour – it *was* that other time.'

She had nervously turned to the others, overflowing to them, in her dismay, for all their strangeness – quite, as he said to himself, like a woman of the people. She was the bareheaded goodwife talking in the street about the row in the house, and it was in this character that he instantly introduced her: 'My dear doubting wife, who will do her best to entertain you while I wait upon our friend.' And he explained to her as he could his now protesting companions – 'Mr and Mrs Hayes of New York, who have been here before.' He knew, without knowing why, that her announcement chilled him; he failed at least to see why it should chill him so much. His good friends had themselves been visibly affected by it, and heaven knew that the depths of brooding fancy in him were easily stirred by contact. If they had wanted a crisis they accordingly had found one, albeit they had already asked leave to retire before it. This he wouldn't have. 'Ah no, you must really see!'

'But we shan't be able to bear it, you know,' said the young woman, 'if it *is* to turn you out.'

Her crudity attested her sincerity, and it was the latter, doubtless, that instantly held Mrs Gedge. 'It *is* to turn us out.'

'Has he told you that, madam?' Mr Hayes enquired of her — it being wondrous how the breath of doom had drawn them together.

'No, not told me; but there's something in him there — I mean in his awful manner — that matches too well with other things. We've seen,' said the poor pale lady, 'other things enough.'

The young woman almost clutched her. 'Is his manner very awful?'

'It's simply the manner,' Gedge interposed, 'of a very great man.'

'Well, very great men,' said his wife, 'are very awful things.'

'It's exactly,' he laughed, 'what we're finding out! But I mustn't keep him waiting. Our friends here,' he went on, 'are directly interested. You mustn't, mind you, let them go until we know.'

Mr Hayes, however, held him; he found himself stayed. 'We're so directly interested that I want you to understand this. If anything happens —'

'Yes?' said Gedge, all gentle as he faltered.

'Well, *we* must set you up.'

Mrs Hayes quickly abounded. 'Oh *do* come to us!'

Again he could but take them in. They were really wonderful folk. And with it all but Mr and Mrs Hayes! It affected even Isabel through her alarm; though the balm, in a manner, seemed to foretell the wound. He had reached the threshold of his own quarters; he stood there as at the door of the chamber of judgement. But he laughed; at least he could be gallant in going up for sentence. 'Very good then — I'll come to you!'

This was very well, but it didn't prevent his heart, a minute later, at the end of the passage, from thumping with beats he could count. He had paused again before going in; on the other side of this second door his poor future was to be let loose at him. It was broken, at best, and spiritless, but wasn't Grant-Jackson there like a beast-tamer in a cage, all tights and spangles and circus attitudes, to give it a cut with the smart official whip and make it spring at him? It was during this moment that he fully measured the effect for his nerves of the impression made on his so oddly earnest friends — whose earnestness he verily, in the spasm of this last effort, came within an ace of resenting. They had upset him by contact; he was afraid literally of meeting his doom on his knees; it wouldn't have taken much more, he absolutely felt, to make him approach with his forehead in the dust the great man whose wrath was to be averted. Mr and Mrs Hayes of New York had brought tears to his eyes, but was it to be reserved for Grant-Jackson to make him cry like a baby? He wished, yes, while he palpitated, that Mr and Mrs Hayes of New York hadn't had such an eccentricity of interest, for it seemed somehow to come from *them* that he was going so fast to pieces. Before he turned the knob of the door, however, he had another queer instant; making out that it had been, strictly, his case that was interesting, his funny power, however accidental, to show as in a picture the attitude of others – not his poor pale personality. It was this latter quantity, none the less, that was marching to execution. It is to our friend's credit that he *believed*, as he prepared to turn the knob, that he was going to be hanged; and it's certainly not less to his credit that his wife, on the chance, had his supreme thought. Here it was that – possibly with his last articulate breath – he thanked his stars, such as they were, for Mr and Mrs Hayes of New York. At least they would take care of her.

They were doing that certainly with some success when he returned to them ten minutes later. She sat between them in the beautified Birthplace, and he couldn't have been sure afterwards that each wasn't holding her hand. The three together had at any rate the effect of recalling to him – it was too whimsical – some picture, a sentimental print, seen and admired in his youth, a 'Waiting for the Verdict,' a 'Counting the Hours,' or something of that sort; humble respectability in suspense about humble innocence. He didn't know how he himself looked, and he didn't care; the great thing was that he wasn't crying – though he might have been; the glitter in his eyes was assuredly dry, though that there *was* a glitter, or something slightly to bewilder, the faces of the others as they rose to meet him sufficiently proved. His wife's eyes pierced his own, but it was Mrs Hayes of New York who spoke. '*Was* it then for that –?'

He only looked at them at first – he felt he might now enjoy it. 'Yes, it was for "that." I mean it was about the way I've been going on. He came to speak of it.'

'And he's gone?' Mr Hayes permitted himself to enquire.

'He's gone.'

'It's over?' Isabel hoarsely asked.

'It's over.'

'Then we go?'

This it was that he enjoyed. 'No, my dear; we stay.'

There was fairly a triple gasp; relief took time to operate. 'Then why did he come?'

'In the fulness of his kind heart and of *Their* discussed and decreed satisfaction. To express Their sense —!'

Mr Hayes broke into a laugh, but his wife wanted to know. 'Of the grand work you're doing?'

'Of the way I polish it off. They're most handsome about it. The receipts, it appears, speak —'

He was nursing his effect; Isabel intently watched him and the others hung on his lips. 'Yes, speak —?'

'Well, volumes. They tell the truth.'

At this Mr Hayes laughed again. 'Oh *they* at least do?'

Near him thus once more Gedge knew their intelligence as one — which was so good a consciousness to get back that his tension now relaxed as by the snap of a spring and he felt his old face at ease. 'So you can't say,' he continued, 'that we don't want it.'

'I bow to it,' the young man smiled. 'It's what I said then. It's *great*.'

'It's great,' said Morris Gedge. 'It couldn't be greater.'

His wife still watched him; her irony hung behind. 'Then we're just as we were?'

'No, not as we were.'

She jumped at it. 'Better?'

'Better. They give us a rise.'

'Of income?'

'Of our sweet little stipend — by a vote of the Committee. That's what, as Chairman, he came to announce.'

The very echoes of the Birthplace were themselves, for the instant, hushed; the warden's three companions showed in the conscious air a struggle for their own breath. But Isabel, almost with a shriek, was the first to recover hers. 'They double us?'

'Well — call it that. "In recognition." There you are.' Isabel uttered another sound — but this time inarticulate; partly because Mrs Hayes of New York had already jumped at her to kiss her. Mr Hayes meanwhile, as with too much to say, but put out his hand, which our friend took in silence. So Gedge had the last word. 'And there *you* are!'

Fordham Castle

Sharp little Madame Massin, who carried on the pleasant pension and who had her small hard eyes everywhere at once, came out to him on the terrace and held up a letter addressed in a manner that he recognised even from afar, held it up with a question in her smile, or a smile, rather a pointed one, in her question — he could scarce have said which. She was looking, while so occupied, at the German group engaged in the garden, near by, with aperitive beer and disputation — the noonday luncheon being now imminent; and the way in which she could show prompt lips while her observation searchingly ranged might have reminded him of the object placed by a spectator at the theatre in the seat he desires to keep during the entr'acte.[1] Conscious of the cross-currents of international passion, she tried, so far as possible, not to mix her sheep and her goats. The view of the bluest end of the Lake of Geneva — she insisted in persuasive circulars that it *was* the bluest — had never, on her high-perched terrace, wanted for admirers, though thus early in the season, during the first days of May, they were not so numerous as she was apt to see them at midsummer. This precisely, Abel Taker could infer, was the reason of a remark she had made him before the claims of the letter had been settled. 'I shall put you next the American lady — the one who arrived yesterday. I know you'll be kind to her; she had to go to bed, as soon as she got here, with a sick-headache brought on by her journey. But she's better. Who isn't better as soon as they get here? She's coming down, and I'm sure she'd like to know you.'

Taker had now the letter in his hand — the letter intended for 'Mr C. P. Addard'; which was not the name inscribed in the two or three books he had left out in his room, any more than it matched the initials, 'A. F. T.' attached to the few pieces of his modest total of luggage. Moreover, since Madame Massin's establishment counted, to his still somewhat bewildered mind, so little for an hotel, as hotels were mainly known to him, he had avoided the act of 'registering,' and the missive with which his hostess was practically testing him represented the very first piece of postal matter taken in since his arrival that hadn't been destined to some one else. He had privately blushed for the meagreness of his

505

mail, which made him look unimportant. That however was a detail, an appearance he was used to; indeed the reasons making for such an appearance might never have been so pleasant to him as on this vision of his identity formally and legibly denied. It was denied there in his wife's large straight hand; his eyes, attached to the envelope, took in the failure of any symptom of weakness in her stroke; she at least had the courage of his passing for somebody he wasn't, of his passing rather for nobody at all, and he felt the force of her character more irresistibly than ever as he thus submitted to what she was doing with him. He wasn't used to lying; whatever his faults – and he was used, perfectly, to the idea of his faults – he hadn't made them worse by any perverse theory, any tortuous plea, of innocence; so that probably, with every inch of him giving him away, Madame Massin didn't believe him a bit when he appropriated the letter. He was quite aware he could have made no fight if she had challenged his right to it. That would have come of his making no fight, nowadays, on any ground, with any woman; he had so lost the proper spirit, the necessary confidence. It was true that he had had to do for a long time with no woman in the world but Sue, and of the practice of opposition so far as Sue was concerned the end had been determined early in his career. His hostess fortunately accepted his word, but the way in which her momentary attention bored into his secret like the turn of a gimlet gave him a sense of the quantity of life that passed before her as a dealer with all comers – gave him almost an awe of her power of not wincing. She knew he wasn't, he couldn't be, C. P. Addard, even though she mightn't know, or still less care, who he was; and there was therefore something queer about him if he pretended to be. That was what she didn't mind, there being something queer about him; and what was further present to him was that she would have known when to mind, when really to be on her guard. She attached no importance to his trick; she had doubtless somewhere at the rear, amid the responsive underlings with whom she was sometimes heard volubly, yet so obscurely, to chatter, her clever French amusement about it. He couldn't at all events have said if the whole passage with her most brought home to him the falsity of his position or most glossed it over. On the whole perhaps it rather helped him, since from this moment his masquerade had actively begun.

Taking his place for luncheon, in any case, he found himself next the American lady, as he conceived, spoken of by Madame Massin – in whose appearance he was at first as disappointed as if, a little, though all unconsciously, he had been building on it. Had she loomed into view, on their hostess's hint, as one of the vague alternatives, the possible beguilements, of his leisure – presenting herself solidly where so much else had refused to crystallise? It was certain at least that she presented herself solidly, being a large mild smooth person with a distinct double chin, with grey hair arranged in small flat regular circles, figures of a geometrical perfection; with diamond earrings, with a long-handled eye-glass, with an accumulation of years and of weight and presence, in fine, beyond what his own rather melancholy consciousness acknowledged. He was forty-five, and it took every year of his life, took all he hadn't done with them, to account for his present situation – since you couldn't be, conclusively, of so little use, of so scant an application, to any mortal career, above all to your own, unless you had been given up and cast aside after a long succession of experiments tried with you. But the American lady with the mathematical hair which reminded him in a manner of the old-fashioned 'work,' the weeping willows and mortuary urns represented by the little glazed-over flaxen or auburn or sable or silvered convolutions and tendrils, the capillary flowers, that he had admired in the days of his innocence – the American lady had probably seen her half-century; all the more that before luncheon was done she had begun to strike him as having, like himself, slipped slowly down over its stretched and shiny surface, an expanse as insecure to fumbling feet as a great cold curved ice-field, into the comparatively warm hollow of resignation and obscurity. She gave him from the first – and he was afterwards to see why – an attaching impression of being, like himself, in exile, and of having like himself learned to butter her bread with a certain acceptance of fate. The only thing that puzzled him on this head was that to parallel his own case she would have had openly to consent to be shelved; which made the difficulty, here, that that was exactly what, as between wife and husband, remained unthinkable on the part of the wife. The necessity for the shelving of one or the other was a case that appeared often to arise, but this wasn't the way he had in general seen it settled. She made him in short, through some influence he couldn't immediately reduce to its elements, vaguely think of her as sacrificed – without blood, as it were; as obligingly and persuadedly passive. Yet this effect, a reflexion of his own state, would doubtless have been better produced for him by a mere melancholy man. She testified unmistakeably to the greater energy of women; for he could think of no manifestation of spirit on his own part that might pass for an equivalent, in the way of resistance, of protest, to the rhythmic though rather wiggy water-waves that broke upon her bald-looking brow as upon a beach bared by a low tide. He had cocked up often enough – and as with the intention of doing it still more under Sue's nose than under his own – the two ends of his half-'sandy' half-grizzled moustache, and he had in fact given these ornaments an extra twist just before coming in to luncheon. That however was but a momentary flourish; the most marked ferocity of which hadn't availed not to land him – well, where he was landed now.

His new friend mentioned that she had come up from Rome and that Madame Massin's establishment had been highly spoken of to her there, and this, slight as it was, straightway contributed in its degree for Abel Taker to the idea that they had something in common. He was in a condition in which he could feel the drift of vague currents, and he knew how highly the place had been spoken of to *him*. There was but a shade of difference in his having had his lesson in Florence. He let his companion know, without reserve, that he too had come up from Italy, after spending three or four months there: though he remembered in time that, being now C. P. Addard, it was only as C. P. Addard he could speak. He tried to think, in order to give himself something to say, what C. P. Addard would have done; but he was doomed to feel always, in the whole connexion, his lack of imagination. He had had many days to come to it and nothing else to do; but he hadn't even yet made up his mind who C. P. Addard was or invested him with any distinguishing marks. He felt like a man who, moving in this, that or the other direction, saw each successively lead him to some danger; so that he began to ask himself why he shouldn't just lie outright, boldly and inventively, and see what that could do for him. There was an excitement, the excitement of personal risk, about it — much the same as would belong for an ordinary man to the first trial of a flying-machine; yet it was exactly such a course as Sue had prescribed on his asking her what he should do. 'Anything in the world you like but talk about *me*: think of some other woman, as bad and bold as you please, and say you're married to *her*.' Those had been literally her words, together with others, again and again repeated, on the subject of his being free to 'kill and bury' her as often as he chose. This was the way she had met his objection to his own death and interment; she had asked him, in her bright hard triumphant way, why he couldn't defend himself by shooting back. The real reason was of course that he was nothing without her, whereas she was everything, could be anything in the wide world she liked, without him. That question precisely had been a part of what was before him while he strolled in the projected green gloom of Madame Massin's plane-trees; he wondered what she *was* choosing to be and how good a time it was helping her to have. He could be sure she was rising to it, on some line or other, and that was what secretly made him say: 'Why shouldn't I get something out of it too, just for the harmless fun —?'

It kept coming back to him, naturally, that he hadn't the breadth of fancy, that he knew himself as he knew the taste of ill-made coffee, that he was the same old Abel Taker he had ever been, in whose aggregation of items it was as vain to feel about for latent heroisms as it was useless to rummage one's trunk for presentable clothes that one didn't possess. But did that absolve him (having so definitely Sue's permission) from seeing to what extent he might temporarily make believe? If he were to flap his wings very hard and crow very loud and take as long a jump as possible at the same time — if he were to do all that perhaps he should achieve for half a minute the sensation of soaring. He knew only one thing Sue couldn't do, from the moment she didn't divorce him: she couldn't get rid of his name, unaccountably, after all, as she hated it; she couldn't get rid of it because she would have always sooner or later to come back to it. She might consider that her being a thing so dreadful as Mrs Abel Taker was a stumbling-block in her social path that nothing but his real, his official, his advertised circulated demise (with 'American papers please copy') would avail to dislodge: she would have none the less to reckon with his continued existence as the drop of bitterness in her cup that seasoned undisguiseably each draught. He might make use of his present opportunity to row out into the lake with his pockets full of stones and there quietly slip overboard; but he could think of no shorter cut for her ceasing to be what her marriage and the law of the land had made her. She was not an inch less Mrs Abel Taker for these days of his sequestration, and the only thing she indeed claimed was that the concealment of the source of her shame, the suppression of the person who had divided with her his inherited absurdity, made the difference of a shade or two for getting honourably, as she called it, 'about.' How she had originally come to incur this awful inconvenience – *that* part of the matter, left to herself, she would undertake to keep vague; and she wasn't really left to herself so long as he too flaunted the dreadful flag.

This was why she had provided him with another and placed him out at board, to constitute, as it were, a permanent *alibi*; telling him she should quarrel with no colours under which he might elect to sail, and promising to take him back when she had got where she wanted. She wouldn't mind so much then – she only wanted a fair start. It wasn't a fair start – *was* it? she asked him frankly – so long as he was always there, so terribly cruelly there, to speak of what she *had* been. She had been nothing worse, to his sense, than a very pretty girl of eighteen out in Peoria,[2] who had seen at that time no one else she wanted more to marry, nor even any one who had been so supremely struck by her. That, absolutely, was the worst that could be said of her. It was so bad at any rate in her own view – it had grown so bad in the widening light of life – that it had fairly become more than she could bear and that something, as she said, had to be done about it. She hadn't known herself originally any more than she had known him – hadn't foreseen how much better she was going to come out, nor how, for her individually, as distinguished from him, there might be the possibility of a big future. He couldn't be explained away – he cried out with all his dreadful presence that she *had* been pleased to marry him; and what they therefore had to do must transcend explaining. It was perhaps now helping her, off there in London, and especially at Fordham Castle – she was staying last at Fordham Castle, Wilts[3] – it was perhaps inspiring her even more than she had expected, that they were able to try together this particular substitute: news of her progress in fact – her progress on from Fordham Castle, if anything could be higher – would not improbably be contained in the unopened letter he had lately pocketed.

There was a given moment at luncheon meanwhile, in his talk with his countrywoman, when he did try that flap of the wing – did throw off, for a flight into the blue, the first falsehood he could think of. 'I stopped in Italy, you see, on my way back from the East, where I had gone – to Constantinople' – he rose actually to Constantinople[4] – 'to visit Mrs Addard's grave.' And after they had all come out to coffee in the rustling shade, with the vociferous German tribe at one end of the terrace, the English family keeping silence with an English accent, as it struck him, in the middle, and his direction taken, by his new friend's side, to the other unoccupied corner, he found himself oppressed with what he had on his hands, the burden of keeping up this expensive fiction. He had never been to Constantinople – it could easily be proved against him; he ought to have thought of something better, have got his effect on easier terms. Yet a funnier thing still than this quick repentance was the quite equally fictive ground on which his companion had affected him – when he came to think of it – as meeting him.

'Why you know that's very much the same errand that took me to Rome. I visited the grave of my daughter – whom I lost there some time ago.'

She had turned her face to him after making this statement, looked at him with an odd blink of her round kind plain eyes, as if to see how he took it. He had taken it on the spot, for this was the only thing to do; but he had felt how much deeper down he was himself sinking as he replied: 'Ah it's a sad pleasure, isn't it? But those are places one doesn't want to neglect.'

'Yes – that's what I feel. I go,' his neighbour had solemnly pursued, 'about every two years.'

With which she had looked away again, leaving him really not able to emulate her. 'Well, I hadn't been before. You see it's a long way.'

'Yes – that's the trying part. It makes you feel you'd have done better –'

'To bring them right home and have it done over there?' he had asked as she let the sad subject go a little. He quite agreed. 'Yes – that's what many do.'

'But it gives of course a peculiar interest.' So they had kept it up. 'I mean in places that mightn't have so *very* much.'

'Places like Rome and Constantinople?' he had rejoined while he noticed the cautious anxious sound of her 'very.' The tone was to come back to him, and it had already made him feel sorry for her, with its suggestion of her being at sea like himself. Unmistakeably, poor lady, she too was trying to float – was striking out in timid convulsive movements. Well, he wouldn't make it difficult for her, and immediately, so as not to appear to cast any ridicule, he observed that, wherever great bereavements might have occurred, there was no place so remarkable as not to gain an association. Such memories made at the least another object for coming. It was after this recognition, on either side, that they adjourned to the garden – Taker having in his ears again the good lady's rather troubled or muddled echo: 'Oh yes, when you come to all the *objects* – !' The grave of one's wife or one's daughter was an object quite as much as all those that one looked up in Baedeker[5] – those of the family of the Castle of Chillon and the Dent du Midi,[6] features of the view to be enjoyed from different parts of Madame Massin's premises. It was very soon, none the less, rather as if these latter presences, diffusing their reality and majesty, had taken the colour out of all other evoked romance; and to that degree that when Abel's fellow guest happened to lay down on the parapet of the terrace three or four articles she had brought out with her, her fan, a couple of American newspapers and a letter that had obviously come to her by the same post as his own, he availed himself of the accident to jump at a further conclusion. Their coffee, which was 'extra,' as he knew and as, in the way of benevolence, he boldly warned her, was brought forth to them, and while she was giving her attention to her demi-tasse he let his eyes rest for three seconds on the superscription of her letter. His mind was by this time made up, and the beauty of it was that he couldn't have said why: the letter was from her daughter, whom she had been burying for him in Rome, and it would be addressed in a name that was really no more hers than the name his wife had thrust upon him was his. Her daughter had put *her* out at cheap board, pending higher issues, just as Sue had put him – so that there was a logic not other than fine in his notifying her of what coffee every day might let her in for. She was addressed on her envelope as 'Mrs Vanderplank,' but he had privately arrived, before she so much as put down her cup, at the conviction that this was a borrowed and lawless title, for all the world as if, poor dear innocent woman, she were a bold bad adventuress. He had acquired furthermore the moral certitude that he was on the track, as he would have said, of her true identity, such as it might be. He couldn't think of it as in itself either very mysterious or very impressive; but, whatever it was, her duplicity had as yet mastered no finer art than his own, inasmuch as she had positively not escaped, at table, inadvertently dropping a name which, while it lingered on Abel's ear, gave her quite away. She had spoken, in her solemn sociability and as by the force of old habit, of 'Mr Magaw,' and nothing was more to be presumed than that this gentleman was her defunct husband, not so very long defunct, who had permitted her while in life the privilege of association with him, but whose extinction had left her to be worked upon by different ideas.

These ideas would have germed, infallibly, in the brain of the young woman, her only child, under whose rigid rule she now – it was to be detected – drew her breath in pain. Madame Massin would abysmally know, Abel reflected, for he was at the end of a few minutes more intimately satisfied that Mrs Magaw's American newspapers, coming to her straight from the other side and not yet detached from their wrappers, would not be directed to Mrs Vanderplank, and that, this being the case, the poor lady would have had to invent some pretext for a claim to goods likely still perhaps to be lawfully called for. And she wasn't formed for duplicity, the large simple scared foolish fond woman, the vague anxiety in whose otherwise so uninhabited and unreclaimed countenance, as void of all history as an expanse of Western prairie seen from a car-window,[7] testified to her scant aptitude for her part. He was far from the desire to question their hostess, however — for the study of his companion's face on its mere inferred merits had begun to dawn upon him as the possible resource of his ridiculous leisure. He might verily have some fun with her — or he would so have conceived it had he not become aware before they separated, half an hour later, of a kind of fellow-feeling for her that seemed to plead for her being spared. She *wasn't* being, in some quarter still indistinct to him — and so no more was he, and these things were precisely a reason. Her sacrifice, he divined, was an act of devotion, a state not yet disciplined to the state of confidence. She had presently, as from a return of vigilance, gathered in her postal property, shuffling it together at her further side and covering it with her pocket-handkerchief — though this very betrayal indeed but quickened his temporary impulse to break out to her, sympathetically, with a 'Had you the misfortune to *lose* Magaw?' or with the effective production of his own card and a smiling, an inviting, a consoling 'That's who *I* am if you want to know!' He really made out, with the idle human instinct, the crude sense for other people's pains and pleasures that had, on his showing, to his so great humiliation, been found an inadequate outfit for the successful conduct of the coal, the commission, the insurance and, as a last resort, desperate and disgraceful, the book-agency business[8] — he really made out that she didn't want to know, or wouldn't for some little time; that she was decidedly afraid in short, and covertly agitated, and all just because she too, with him, suspected herself dimly in presence of that mysterious 'more' than, in the classic phrase, met the eye. They parted accordingly, as if to relieve, till they could recover themselves, the conscious tension of their being able neither to hang back with grace nor to advance with glory; but flagrantly full, at the same time, both of the recognition that they couldn't in such a place avoid each other even if they had desired it, and of the suggestion that they wouldn't desire it, after such subtlety of communion, even were it to be thought of.

Abel Taker, till dinner-time, turned over his little adventure and extracted, while he hovered and smoked and mused, some refreshment from the impression the subtlety of communion had left with him. Mrs Vanderplank was his senior by several years, and was neither fair nor slim nor 'bright' nor truly, nor even falsely, elegant, nor anything that Sue had taught him, in her wonderful way, to associate with the American woman at the American woman's best — that best than which there was nothing better, as he had so often heard her say, on God's great earth. Sue would have banished her to the wildest waste of the unknowable, would have looked over her head in the manner he had often seen her use – as if she were in an exhibition of pictures, were in front of something bad and negligible that had got itself placed on the line, but that had the real thing, the thing of interest for those who *knew* (and when didn't Sue know?) hung above it. In Mrs Magaw's presence everything would have been of more interest to Sue than Mrs Magaw; but that consciousness failed to prevent his feeling the appeal of this inmate much rather confirmed than weakened when she reappeared for dinner. It was impressed upon him, after they had again seated themselves side by side, that she was reaching out to him indirectly, guardedly, even as he was to her; so that later on, in the garden, where they once more had their coffee together – it *might* have been so free and easy, so wildly foreign, so almost Bohemian – he lost all doubt of the wisdom of his taking his plunge. This act of resolution was not, like the other he had risked in the morning, an upward flutter into fiction, but a straight and possibly dangerous dive into the very depths of truth. Their instinct was unmistakeably to cling to each other, but it was as if they wouldn't know where to take hold till the air had really been cleared. Actually, in fact, they required a light – the aid prepared by him in the shape of a fresh match for his cigarette after he had extracted, under cover of the scented dusk, one of his cards from his pocket-book.

'There I honestly am, you see – Abel F. Taker; which I think you ought to know.' It was relevant to nothing, relevant only to the grope of their talk, broken with sudden silences where they stopped short for fear of mistakes; but as he put the card before her he held out to it the little momentary flame. And this was the way that, after a while and from one thing to another, he himself, in exchange for what he had to give and what he gave freely, heard all about 'Mattie' – Mattie Magaw, Mrs Vanderplank's beautiful and high-spirited daughter, who, as he learned, found her two names, so dreadful even singly, a combination not to be borne, and carried on a quarrel with them no less desperate than Sue's quarrel with – well, with everything. She had, quite as Sue had done, declared her need of a free hand to fight them, and she was, for all the world like Sue again, now fighting them to the death. This similarity of situation was wondrously completed by the fact that the scene of Miss Magaw's struggle was, as her mother explained, none other than that uppermost walk of 'high' English life which formed the present field of Mrs Taker's operations; a circumstance on which Abel presently produced his comment. 'Why if they're after the same thing in the same place, I wonder if we shan't hear of their meeting.'

Mrs Magaw appeared for a moment to wonder too. 'Well, if they do meet I guess we'll hear. I will say for Mattie that she writes me pretty fully. And I presume,' she went on, 'Mrs Taker keeps *you* posted?'

'No,' he had to confess – 'I don't hear from her in much detail. She knows I
back her,' Abel smiled, 'and that's enough for her. "You be quiet and I'll let you
know when you're wanted" – that's her motto; I'm to wait, wherever I am, till
I'm called for. But I guess she won't be in a hurry to call for me' – this reflexion
he showed he was familiar with. 'I've stood in her light so long – her "social"
light, outside of which everything is for Sue black darkness – that I don't really
see the reason she should ever want me back. That at any rate is what I'm doing
– I'm just waiting. And I didn't expect the luck of being able to wait in your
company. I couldn't suppose – that's the truth,' he added – 'that there was
another, anywhere about, with the same ideas or the same strong character. It
had never seemed to be possible,' he ruminated, 'that there could be any one like
Mrs Taker.'

He was to remember afterwards how his companion had appeared to consider
this approximation. 'Another, you mean, like my Mattie?'

'Yes – like my Sue. Any one that really comes up to her. It will be,' he declared,
'the first one I've struck.'

'Well,' said Mrs Vanderplank, 'my Mattie's remarkably handsome.'

'I'm sure –! But Mrs Taker's remarkably handsome too. Oh,' he added, both
with humour and with earnestness, 'if it wasn't for that I wouldn't trust her so!
Because, for what she wants,' he developed, 'it's a great help to be fine-looking.'

'Ah it's always a help for a lady!' – and Mrs Magaw's sigh fluttered vaguely
between the expert and the rueful. 'But what is it,' she asked, 'that Mrs Taker
wants?'

'Well, she could tell you herself. I don't think she'd trust me to give an account
of it. Still,' he went on, 'she *has* stated it more than once for my benefit, and
perhaps that's what it all finally comes to. She wants to get where she truly
belongs.'

Mrs Magaw had listened with interest. 'That's just where Mattie wants to get!
And she seems to know just where it is.'

'Oh Mrs Taker knows – you can bet your life,' he laughed, 'on that. It seems
to be somewhere in London or in the country round, and I dare say it's the same
place as your daughter's. Once she's there, as I understand it, she'll be all right;
but she has got to get there – that is to be seen there thoroughly fixed and
photographed, and have it in all the papers – first. After she's fixed, she says,
we'll talk. We *have* talked a good deal: when Mrs Taker says "We'll talk" I know
what she means. But this time we'll have it out.'

There were communities in their fate that made his friend turn pale. 'Do you
mean she won't want you to come?'

'Well, for me to "come," don't you see? will be for me to come to life. How can
I come to life when I've been as dead as I am now?'

Mrs Vanderplank looked at him with a dim delicacy. 'But surely, sir, I'm not conversing with the remains –!'

'You're conversing with C. P. Addard. *He* may be alive – but even this I don't know yet; I'm just trying him,' he said: 'I'm trying him, Mrs Magaw, on you. Abel Taker's in his grave, but does it strike you that Mr Addard is at all above ground?'

He had smiled for the slightly gruesome joke of it, but she looked away as if it made her uneasy. Then, however, as she came back to him, 'Are you going to wait here?' she asked.

He held her, with some gallantry, in suspense. 'Are you?'

She postponed her answer, visibly not quite comfortable now; but they were inevitably the next day up to their necks again in the question; and then it was that she expressed more of her sense of her situation. 'Certainly I feel as if I must wait – as long as I *have* to wait. Mattie likes this place – I mean she likes it for *me*. It seems the right *sort* of place,' she opined with her perpetual earnest emphasis.

But it made him sound again the note. 'The right sort to pass for dead in?'

'Oh she doesn't want me to pass for *dead*.'

'Then what does she want you to pass for?'

The poor lady cast about. 'Well, only for Mrs Vanderplank.'

'And who or what is Mrs Vanderplank?'

Mrs Magaw considered this personage, but didn't get far. 'She isn't any one in particular, I guess.'

'That means,' Abel returned, 'that she isn't alive.'

'She isn't more than *half* alive,' Mrs Magaw conceded. 'But it isn't what I *am* – it's what I'm passing for. Or rather' – she worked it out – 'what I'm just not. I'm not passing – I don't, can't here, where it doesn't matter, you see – for her mother.'

Abel quite fell in. 'Certainly – she doesn't want to have any mother.'

'She doesn't want to have *me*. She wants me to lay low. If I lay low, she says –'

'Oh I know what she says' – Abel took it straight up. 'It's the very same as what Mrs Taker says. If you lie low she can fly high.'

It kept disconcerting her in a manner, as well as steadying, his free possession of their case. 'I don't feel as if I *was* lying – I mean as low as she wants – when I talk to you so.' She broke it off thus, and again and again, anxiously, responsibly; her sense of responsibility making Taker feel, with his braver projection of humour, quite ironic and sardonic; but as for a week, for a fortnight, for many days more, they kept frequently and intimately meeting, it was natural that the so extraordinary fact of their being, as he put it, in the same sort of box,[9] and of their boxes having so even more remarkably bumped together under Madame Massin's *tilleuls*,[10] shouldn't only make them reach out to each other across their queer coil of communications, cut so sharp off in other quarters, but should prevent their pretending to any real consciousness but that of their ordeal. It was Abel's idea, promptly enough expressed to Mrs Magaw, that they ought to get something out of it; but when he had said that a few times over (the first time she had met it in silence), she finally replied, and in a manner that he thought quite sublime: 'Well, we *shall* – if they do all they want. We shall feel we've helped. And it isn't so *very* much to do.'

'You think it isn't so very much to do – to lie down and die for them?'

'Well, if I don't hate it any worse when I'm really dead –!' She took herself up, however, as if she had skirted the profane. 'I don't say that if I didn't *believe* in Mat –! But I do believe, you see. That's where she *has* me.'

'Oh I see more or less. That's where Sue has *me*.'

Mrs Magaw fixed him with a milder solemnity. 'But what has Mrs Taker against you?'

'It's sweet of you to ask,' he smiled; while it really came to him that he was living with her under ever so much less strain than what he had been feeling for ever so long before from Sue. Wouldn't he have liked it to go on and on – wouldn't that have suited C. P. Addard? He seemed to be finding out who C. P. Addard was – so that it came back again to the way Sue fixed things. She had fixed them so that C. P. Addard could become quite interested in Mrs Vanderplank and quite soothed by her – and so that Mrs Vanderplank as well, wonderful to say, had lost her impatience for Mattie's summons a good deal more, he was sure, than she confessed. It was from this moment none the less that he began, with a strange but distinct little pang, to see that he couldn't be sure of her. Her question had produced in him a vibration of the sensibility that even the long series of mortifications, of publicly proved inaptitudes, springing originally from his lack of business talent, but owing an aggravation of aspect to an absence of nameable 'type' of which he hadn't been left unaware, wasn't to have wholly toughened. Yet it struck him positively as the prettiest word ever spoken to him, so straight a surprise at his wife's dissatisfaction; and he was verily so unused to tributes to his adequacy that this one lingered in the air a moment and seemed almost to create a possibility. He wondered, honestly, what she could see in him, in whom Sue now at last saw really less than nothing; and his fingers instinctively moved to his moustache, a corner of which he twiddled up again, also wondering if it were perhaps only *that* – though Sue had as good as told him that the undue flourish of this feature but brought out to her view the insignificance of all the rest of him. Just to hang in the iridescent ether with Mrs Vanderplank, to whom he wasn't insignificant, just for them to sit on there together, protected, indeed positively ennobled, by their loss of identity, struck him as the foretaste of a kind of felicity that he hadn't in the past known enough about really to miss it. He appeared to have become aware that he should miss it quite sharply, that he would find how he had already learned to, if she should go; and the very sadness of his apprehension quickened his vision of what would work with her. She would want, with all the roundness of her kind, plain eyes, to see Mattie fixed – whereas he'd be hanged if he wasn't willing, on his side, to take Sue's elevation quite on trust. For the instant, however, he said nothing of that; he only followed up a little his acknowledgement of her having touched him. 'What you ask me, you know, is just what I myself was going to ask. What has Miss Magaw got against *you*?'

'Well, if you were to see her I guess you'd know.'

'Why I should think she'd like to show you,' said Abel Taker.

'She doesn't so much mind their *seeing* me – when once she has had a look at me first. But she doesn't like them to hear me – though I don't talk so very much. Mattie speaks in the real English style,' Mrs Magaw explained.

'But ain't the real English style not to speak at all?'

'Well, she's having the best kind of time, she writes me – so I presume there must be some talk in which she can shine.'

'Oh I've no doubt at all Miss Magaw *talks*!' – and Abel, in his contemplative way, seemed to have it before him.

'Well, don't you go and believe she talks too much,' his companion rejoined with spirit; and this it was that brought to a head his prevision of his own fate.

'I see what's going to happen. You only want to go to her. You want to get your share, after all. You'll leave me without a pang.'

Mrs Magaw stared. 'But won't you be going too? When Mrs Taker sends for you?'

He shook, as by a rare chance, a competent head. 'Mrs Taker won't send for me. I don't make out the use Mrs Taker can ever have for me again.'

Mrs Magaw looked grave. 'But not to enjoy your seeing – ?'

'My seeing where she has come out? Oh that won't be necessary to *her* enjoyment of it. It would be well enough perhaps if I could see without being seen; but the trouble with me – for I'm worse than you,' Abel said – 'is that it doesn't do for me either to be heard *or* seen. I haven't got *any* side – !' But it dropped; it was too old a story.

'Not any possible side at all?' his friend, in her candour, doubtingly echoed. 'Why what do they want over there?'

It made him give a comic pathetic wail. 'Ah to know a person who says such things as that to me, and to have to give her up – !'

She appeared to consider with a certain alarm what this might portend, and she really fell back before it. 'Would you think I'd be able to give up Mattie?'

'Why not – if she's successful? The thing you wouldn't like – *you* wouldn't, I'm sure – would be to give her up if she should find, or if you should find, she wasn't.'

'Well, I guess Mattie will be successful,' said Mrs Magaw.

'Ah you're a worshipper of success!' he groaned. 'I'd give Mrs Taker up, definitely, just to remain C. P. Addard with you.'

She allowed it her thought; but, as he felt, superficially. 'She's your wife, sir, you know, whatever you do.'

' "Mine"? Ah but whose? She isn't C. P. Addard's.'

She rose at this as if they were going too far; yet she showed him, he seemed to see, the first little concession – which was indeed to be the only one – of her inner timidity; something that suggested how she must have preserved as a token, laid away among spotless properties, the visiting-card he had originally handed her. 'Well, I guess the one I feel for is Abel F. Taker!'

This, in the end, however, made no difference; since one of the things that inevitably came up between them was that if Mattie had a quarrel with her name her most workable idea would be to get somebody to give her a better. That, he easily made out, was fundamentally what she was after, and, though, delicately and discreetly, as he felt, he didn't reduce Mrs Vanderplank to so stating the case, he finally found himself believing in Miss Magaw with just as few reserves as those with which he believed in Sue. If it was a question of her 'shining' she would indubitably shine; she was evidently, like the wife by whom he had been, in the early time, too provincially, too primitively accepted, of the great radiating substance, and there were times, here at Madame Massin's, while he strolled to and fro and smoked, when Mrs Taker's distant lustre fairly peeped at him over the opposite mountain-tops, fringing their silhouettes as with the little hard bright rim of a coming day. It was clear that Mattie's mother couldn't be expected not to want to see her married; the shade of doubt bore only on the stage of the business at which Mrs Magaw might safely be let out of the box. Was she to emerge abruptly *as* Mrs Magaw? – or was the lid simply to be tipped back so that, for a good look, she might sit up a little straighter? She had got news at any rate, he inferred, which suggested to her that the term of her suppression was in sight; and she even let it out to him that, yes, certainly, for Mattie to be ready for her – and she did look as if she were going to be ready – she must be right down sure. They had had further lights by this time moreover, lights much more vivid always in Mattie's bulletins than in Sue's; which latter, as Abel insistently imaged it, were really each time, on Mrs Taker's part, as limited as a peep into a death-chamber. The death-chamber was Madame Massin's terrace; and – he completed the image – how could Sue *not* want to know how things were looking for the funeral, which was in any case to be thoroughly 'quiet'? *The* vivid thing seemed to pass before Abel's eyes the day he heard of the bright compatriot, just the person to go round with, a charming handsome witty widow, whom Miss Magaw had met at Fordham Castle, whose ideas were, on all important points, just the same as her own, whose means also (so that they could join forces on an equality) matched beautifully, and whose name in fine was Mrs Sherrington Reeve. 'Mattie has felt the want,' Mrs Magaw explained, 'of some lady, some real lady like that, to go round with: she says she sometimes doesn't find it very pleasant going round alone.'

Abel Taker had listened with interest – this information left him staring. 'By Gosh then, she has struck Sue!'

' "Struck" Mrs Taker –?'

'She isn't Mrs Taker now – she's Mrs Sherrington Reeve.' It had come to him with all its force – as if the glare of her genius were, at a bound, high over the summits. 'Mrs Taker's dead: I thought, you know, all the while, she must be, and this makes me sure. She died at Fordham Castle. So we're both dead.'

His friend, however, with her large blank face, lagged behind. 'At Fordham Castle too – died there?'

'Why she has been as good as *living* there!' Abel Taker emphasised. ' "Address Fordham Castle" – that's about all she has written me. But perhaps she died before she went' – he had it before him, he made it out. 'Yes, she must have gone as Mrs Sherrington Reeve. She had to die to go – as it would be for her like going to heaven. Marriages, sometimes, they say, are made up there; and so, sometimes then, apparently, are friendships – that, you see, for instance, of our two shining ones.'

Mrs Magaw's understanding was still in the shade. 'But are you sure –?'

'Why Fordham Castle settles it. If she wanted to get where she truly belongs she has got *there*. She belongs at Fordham Castle.'

The noble mass of this structure seemed to rise at his words, and his companion's grave eyes, he could see, to rest on its towers. 'But how has she become Mrs Sherrington Reeve?'

'By my death. And also after that by her own. I had to die first, you see, for *her* to be able to – that is for her to be sure. It's what she has been looking for, as I told you – to *be* sure. But oh – she was sure from the first. She knew I'd die off, when she had made it all right for me – so she felt no risk. She simply became, the day I became C. P. Addard, something as different as possible from the thing she had always so hated to be. She's what she always would have liked to be – so why shouldn't we rejoice for her? Her baser part, her vulgar part, has ceased to be, and she lives only as an angel.'

It affected his friend, this elucidation, almost with awe; she took it at least, as she took everything, stolidly. 'Do you call Mrs Taker an angel?'

Abel had turned about, as he rose to the high vision, moving, with his hands in his pockets, to and fro. But at Mrs Magaw's question he stopped short – he considered with his head in the air. 'Yes – now!'

'But do you mean it's her idea to marry?'

He thought again. 'Why for all I know she is married.'

'With you, Abel Taker, living?'

'But I ain't living. That's just the point.'

'Oh you're too dreadful' – and she gathered herself up. 'And I won't,' she said as she broke off, 'help to bury you!'

This office, none the less, as she practically had herself to acknowledge, was in a manner, and before many days, forced upon her by further important information from her daughter, in the light of the true inevitability of which they had, for that matter, been living. She was there before him with her telegram, which she simply held out to him as from a heart too full for words. 'Am engaged to Lord Dunderton, and Sue thinks you can come.'

Deep emotion sometimes confounds the mind – and Mrs Magaw quite flamed with excitement. But on the other hand it sometimes illumines, and she could see, it appeared, what Sue meant. 'It's because he's so much in love.'

'So far gone that she's safe?' Abel frankly asked.

'So far gone that she's safe.'

'Well,' he said, 'if Sue feels it –!' He had so much, he showed, to go by. 'Sue *knows*.'

Mrs Magaw visibly yearned, but she could look at all sides. 'I'm bound to say, since you speak of it, that I've an idea Sue has helped. She'll like to have her there.'

'Mattie will like to have Sue?'

'No, Sue will like to have Mattie.' Elation raised to such a point was in fact already so clarifying that Mrs Magaw could come all the way. 'As Lady Dunderton.'

'Well,' Abel smiled, 'one good turn deserves another!' If he meant it, however, in any such sense as that Mattie might be able in due course to render an equivalent of aid, this notion clearly had to reckon with his companion's sense of its strangeness, exhibited in her now at last upheaved countenance. 'Yes,' he accordingly insisted, 'it will work round to that – you see if it doesn't. If that's where they were to come out, and they *have* come – by which I mean if Sue has realised it for Mattie and acted as she acts when she does realise, then she can't neglect it in her own case: she'll just *have* to realise it for herself. And, for that matter, you'll help her too. You'll be able to tell her, you know, that you've seen the last of me.' And on the morrow, when, starting for London, she had taken her place in the train, to which he had accompanied her, he stood by the door of her compartment and repeated this idea. 'Remember, for Mrs Taker, that you've seen the last –!'

'Oh but I hope I haven't, sir.'

'Then you'll come back to me? If you only will, you know, Sue will be delighted to fix it.'

'To fix it – how?'

'Well, she'll tell you how. You've seen how she can fix things, and that will be the way, as I say, you'll help her.'

She stared at him from her corner, and he could see she was sorry for him; but it was as if she had taken refuge behind her large high-shouldered reticule, which she held in her lap, presenting it almost as a bulwark. 'Mr Taker,' she launched at him over it, 'I'm afraid of you.'

'Because I'm dead?'

'Oh sir!' she pleaded, hugging her morocco defence. But even through this alarm her finer thought came out. 'Do you suppose I shall go to Fordham Castle?'

'Well, I guess that's what they're discussing now. You'll know soon enough.'

'If I write you from there,' she asked, 'won't you come?'

'I'll come as the ghost. Don't old castles always have one?'

She looked at him darkly; the train had begun to move. 'I *shall* fear you!' she said.

'Then there you are.' And he moved an instant beside the door. 'You'll be glad, when you get there, to be able to say –' But she got out of hearing, and, turning away, he felt as abandoned as he had known he should – felt left, in his solitude, to the sense of his extinction. He faced it completely now, and to himself at least could express it without fear of protest. 'Why certainly I'm dead.'

Julia Bride

I

She had walked with her friend to the top of the wide steps of the Museum,[1] those that descend from the galleries of painting, and then, after the young man had left her, smiling, looking back, waving all gaily and expressively his hat and stick, had watched him, smiling too, but with a different intensity – had kept him in sight till he passed out of the great door. She might have been waiting to see if he would turn there for a last demonstration; which was exactly what he did, renewing his cordial gesture and with his look of glad devotion, the radiance of his young face, reaching her across the great space, as she felt, in undiminished truth. Yes, so she could feel, and she remained a minute even after he was gone; she gazed at the empty air as if he had filled it still, asking herself what more she wanted and what, if it didn't signify glad devotion, his whole air could have represented.

She was at present so anxious that she could wonder if he stepped and smiled like that for mere relief at separation; yet if he wanted in such a degree to break the spell and escape the danger why did he keep coming back to her, and why, for that matter, had she felt safe a moment before in letting him go? She felt safe, felt almost reckless – that was the proof – so long as he was with her; but the chill came as soon as he had gone, when she instantly took the measures of all she yet missed. She might have been taking it afresh, by the testimony of her charming clouded eyes and of the rigour that had already replaced her beautiful play of expression. Her radiance, for the minute, had 'carried' as far as his, travelling on the light wings of her brilliant prettiness – he on his side not being facially handsome, but only sensitive, clean and eager. Then with its extinction the sustaining wings dropped and hung.

She wheeled about, however, full of a purpose; she passed back through the pictured rooms, for it pleased her, this idea of a talk with Mr Pitman – as much, that is, as anything could please a young person so troubled. It had happened indeed that when she saw him rise at sight of her from the settee where he had told her five minutes before that she would find him, it was just with her nervousness that his presence seemed, as through an odd suggestion of help, to connect itself. Nothing truly would be quite so odd for her case as aid proceeding from Mr Pitman; unless perhaps the oddity would be even greater for himself – the oddity of her having taken into her head an appeal to him.

She had had to feel alone with a vengeance – inwardly alone and miserably alarmed – to be ready to 'meet,' that way, at the first sign from him, the successor to her dim father in her dim father's lifetime, the second of her mother's two divorced husbands. It made a queer relation for her; a relation that struck her at this moment as less edifying, less natural and graceful, than it would have been even for her remarkable mother – and still in spite of this parent's third marriage, her union with Mr Connery, from whom she was informally separated. It was at the back of Julia's head as she approached Mr Pitman, or it was at least somewhere deep within her soul, that if this last of Mrs Connery's withdrawals from the matrimonial yoke had received the sanction of the Court (Julia had always heard, from far back, so much about the 'Court') she herself, as after a fashion, in that event, a party to it, wouldn't have had the cheek to make up – which was how she inwardly phrased what she was doing – to the long lean loose slightly cadaverous gentleman who was a memory, for her, of the period from her twelfth to her seventeenth year. She had got on with him, perversely, much better than her mother had, and the bulging misfit of his duck[2] waistcoat, with his trick of swinging his eye-glass, at the end of an extraordinarily long string, far over the scene, came back to her as positive features of the image of her remoter youth. Her present age – for her later time had seen so many things happen – gave her a perspective.

Fifty things came up as she stood there before him, some of them floating in from the past, others hovering with freshness: how she used to dodge the rotary movement made by his pince-nez while he always awkwardly, and kindly, and often funnily, talked – it had once hit her rather badly in the eye; how she used to pull down and straighten his waistcoat, making it set a little better, a thing of a sort her mother never did; how friendly and familiar she must have been with him for that, or else a forward little minx; how she felt almost capable of doing it again now, just to sound the right note, and how sure she was of the way he would take it if she did; how much nicer he had clearly been, all the while, poor dear man, than his wife and the Court had made it possible for him publicly to appear; how much younger too he now looked, in spite of his rather melancholy, his mildly-jaundiced, humorously-determined sallowness and his careless assumption, everywhere, from his forehead to his exposed and relaxed blue socks, almost sky-blue, as in past days, of creases and folds and furrows that would have been perhaps tragic if they hadn't seemed rather to show, like his whimsical black eyebrows, the vague interrogative arch.

Of course he wasn't wretched if he wasn't more sure of his wretchedness than that! Julia Bride would have been sure – had she been through what she supposed *he* had! With his thick loose black hair, in any case, untouched by a thread of grey, and his kept gift of a certain big-boyish awkwardness – that of his taking their encounter, for instance, so amusedly, so crudely, though, as she was not unaware, so eagerly too – he could by no means have been so little his wife's junior as it had been that lady's habit, after the divorce, to represent him. Julia had remembered him as old, since she had so constantly thought of her mother as old; which Mrs Connery was indeed now, for her daughter, with her dozen years of actual seniority to Mr Pitman and her exquisite hair, the densest, the finest tangle of arranged silver tendrils that had ever enhanced the effect of a preserved complexion.

Something in the girl's vision of her quondam step-father as still comparatively young – with the confusion, the immense element of rectification, not to say of rank disproof, that it introduced into Mrs Connery's favourite picture of her own injured past – all this worked, even at the moment, to quicken once more the clearness and harshness of judgement, the retrospective disgust, as she might have called it, that had of late grown up in her, the sense of all the folly and vanity and vulgarity, the lies, the perversities, the falsification of all life in the interest of who could say what wretched frivolity, what preposterous policy, amid which she had been condemned so ignorantly, so pitifully to sit, to walk, to grope, to flounder, from the very dawn of her consciousness. Didn't poor Mr Pitman just touch the sensitive nerve of it when, raking her in with his facetious cautious eyes, he spoke to her, right out, of the old, old story, the everlasting little wonder of her beauty?

'Why, you know, you've grown up so lovely – you're the prettiest girl I've ever seen!' Of course she was the prettiest girl he had ever seen; she was the prettiest girl people much more privileged than he had ever seen; since when hadn't she been passing for the prettiest girl any one had ever seen? She had lived in that, from far back, from year to year, from day to day and from hour to hour – she had lived for it and literally *by* it, as who should say; but Mr Pitman was somehow more illuminating than he knew, with the present lurid light that he cast upon old dates, old pleas, old values and old mysteries, not to call them old abysses: it had rolled over her in a swift wave, with the very sight of him, that her mother couldn't possibly have been right about him – as about what in the world had she ever been right? – so that in fact he was simply offered her there as one more of Mrs Connery's lies. She might have thought she knew them all by this time; but he represented for her, coming in just as he did, a fresh discovery, and it was this contribution of freshness that made her somehow feel she liked him. It was she herself who, for so long, with her retained impression, had been right about him; and the rectification he represented had *all* shone out of him, ten minutes before, on his catching her eye while she moved through the room with Mr French. She had never doubted of his probable faults – which her mother had vividly depicted as the basest of vices; since some of them, and the most obvious (not the vices, but the faults) were written on him as he stood there: notably, for instance, the exasperating 'business slackness' of which Mrs Connery had, before the tribunal, made so pathetically much. It might have been, for that matter, the very business slackness that affected Julia as presenting its friendly breast, in the form of a cool loose sociability, to her own actual tension; though it was also true for her, after they had exchanged fifty words, that he had as well his inward fever and that, if he was perhaps wondering what was so particularly the matter with her, she could make out not less that something was the matter with *him*. It had been vague, yet it had been intense, the mute reflexion, 'Yes, I'm going to like him, and he's going somehow to help me!' that had directed her steps so straight to him. She was sure even then of this, that he wouldn't put to her a query about his former wife, that he took to-day no grain of interest in Mrs Connery; that his interest, such as it was – and he couldn't look *quite* like that, to Julia Bride's expert perception, without something in the nature of a new one – would be a thousand times different.

It was as a value of *disproof* that his worth meanwhile so rapidly grew: the good sight of him, the good sound and sense of him, such as they were, demolished at a stroke so blessedly much of the horrid inconvenience of the past that she thought of him, she clutched at him, for a *general* saving use, an application as sanative, as redemptive, as some universal healing wash, precious even to the point of perjury if perjury should be required. That was the terrible thing, that had been the inward pang with which she watched Basil French recede: perjury would have to come in somehow and somewhere – oh so quite certainly! – before the so strange, so rare young man, truly smitten though she believed him, could be made to rise to the occasion, before her measureless prize could be assured. It was present to her, it had been present a hundred times, that if there had only been some one to (as it were) 'deny everything' the situation might yet be saved. She so needed some one to lie for her – ah she so needed some one to lie! Her mother's version of everything, her mother's version of anything, had been at the best, as they said, discounted; and she herself could but show of course for an interested party, however much she might claim to be none the less a decent girl – to whatever point, that is, after all that had both remotely and recently happened, presumptions of anything to be called decency could come in.

After what had recently happened – the two or three indirect but so worrying questions Mr French had put to her – it would only be some thoroughly detached friend or witness who might effectively testify. An odd form of detachment certainly would reside, for Mr Pitman's evidential character, in her mother's having so publicly and so brilliantly – though, thank the powers, all off in North Dakota! – severed their connexion with him; and yet mightn't it do *her* some good, even if the harm it might do her mother were so little ambiguous? The more her mother had got divorced – with her dreadful cheap-and-easy second performance in that line and her present extremity of alienation from Mr Connery, which enfolded beyond doubt the germ of a third petition on one side or the other – the more her mother had distinguished herself in the field of folly the worse for her own prospect with the Frenches, whose minds she had guessed to be accessible, and with such an effect of dissimulated suddenness, to some insidious poison.

It was all unmistakeable, in other words, that the more dismissed and detached Mr Pitman should have come to appear, the more as divorced, or at least as divorcing, his before-time wife would by the same stroke figure – so that it was here poor Julia could but lose herself. The crazy divorces only, or the half-dozen successive and still crazier engagements only – gathered fruit, bitter fruit, of her own incredibly allowed, her own insanely fostered frivolity – either of these two groups of skeletons at the banquet might singly be dealt with; but the combination, the fact of each party's having been so mixed-up with whatever was least presentable for the other, the fact of their having so shockingly amused themselves together, made all present steering resemble the classic middle course between Scylla and Charybdis.[3]

It was not, however, that she felt wholly a fool in having obeyed this impulse to pick up again her kind old friend. *She* at least had never divorced him, and her horrid little filial evidence in Court had been but the chatter of a parrakeet, of precocious plumage and croak, repeating words earnestly taught her and that she could scarce even pronounce. Therefore, as far as steering went, he *must* for the hour take a hand. She might actually have wished in fact that he shouldn't now have seemed so tremendously struck with her; since it was an extraordinary situation for a girl, this crisis of her fortune, this positive wrong that the flagrancy, what she would have been ready to call the very vulgarity, of her good looks might do her at a moment when it was vital she should hang as straight as a picture on the wall. Had it ever yet befallen any young woman in the world to wish with secret intensity that she might have been, for her convenience, a shade less inordinately pretty? She had come to that, to this view of the bane, the primal curse, of their lavishly physical outfit, which had included everything and as to which she lumped herself resentfully with her mother. The only thing was that her mother was, thank goodness, still so much prettier, still so assertively, so publicly, so trashily, so ruinously pretty. Wonderful the small grimness with which Julia Bride put off on this parent the middle-aged maximum of their case and the responsibility of their defect. It cost her so little to recognise in Mrs Connery at forty-seven, and in spite, or perhaps indeed just by reason, of the arranged silver tendrils which were so like some rare bird's-nest in a morning frost, a facile supremacy for the dazzling effect – it cost her so little that her view even rather exaggerated the lustre of the different maternal items. She would have put it *all* off if possible, all off on other shoulders and on other graces and other morals than her own, the burden of physical charm that had made so easy a ground, such a native favouring air, for the aberrations which, apparently inevitable and without far consequences at the time, had yet at this juncture so much better not have been.

She could have worked it out at her leisure, to the last link of the chain, the way their prettiness had set them trap after trap, all along – had foredoomed them to awful ineptitude. When you were as pretty as that you could, by the whole idiotic consensus, be nothing *but* pretty; and when you were nothing 'but' pretty you could get into nothing but tight places, out of which you could then scramble by nothing but masses of fibs. And there was no one, all the while, who wasn't eager to egg you on, eager to make you pay to the last cent the price of your beauty. What creature would ever for a moment help you to behave as if something that dragged in its wake a bit less of a lumbering train would, on the whole, have been better for you? The consequences of being plain were only negative – you failed of this and that; but the consequences of being as *they* were, what were these but endless? though indeed, as far as failing went, your beauty too could let you in for enough of it. Who, at all events, would ever for a moment credit you, in the luxuriance of that beauty, with the study, on your own side, of such truths as these? Julia Bride could, at the point she had reached, positively ask herself this even while lucidly conscious of the inimitable, the triumphant and attested projection, all round her, of her exquisite image. It was only Basil French who had at last, in his doubtless dry but all distinguished way – the way, surely as it was borne in upon her, of all the blood of all the Frenches – stepped out of the vulgar rank. It was only he who, by the trouble she discerned in him, had made her see certain things. It was only for him – and not a bit ridiculously, but just beautifully, almost sublimely – that their being 'nice,' her mother and she between them, had *not* seemed to profit by their being so furiously handsome.

This had, ever so grossly and ever so tiresomely, satisfied every one else; since every one had thrust upon them, had imposed upon them as by a great cruel conspiracy, their silliest possibilities; fencing them in to these, and so not only shutting them out from others, but mounting guard at the fence, walking round and round outside it to see they didn't escape, and admiring them, talking to them, through the rails, in mere terms of chaff, terms of chucked cakes and apples – as if they had been antelopes or zebras, or even some superior sort of performing, of dancing, bear. It had been reserved for Basil French to strike her as willing to let go, so to speak, a pound or two of this fatal treasure if he might only have got in exchange for it an ounce or so more of their so much less obvious and less published personal history. Yes, it described him to say that, in addition to all the rest of him, and of *his* personal history, and of his family, and of theirs, in addition to their social posture, as that of a serried phalanx, and to their notoriously enormous wealth and crushing respectability, she might have been ever so much less lovely for him if she had been only — well, a little prepared to answer questions. And it wasn't as if, quiet, cultivated, earnest, public-spirited, brought up in Germany, infinitely travelled, awfully like a high-caste Englishman, and all the other pleasant things, it wasn't as if he didn't love to be with her, to look at her, just as she was; for he loved it exactly as much, so far as that footing simply went, as any free and foolish youth who had ever made the last demonstration of it. It was that marriage was for him — and for them all, the serried Frenches — a great matter, a goal to which a man of intelligence, a real shy beautiful man of the world, didn't hop on one foot, didn't skip and jump, as if he were playing an urchins' game, but toward which he proceeded with a deep and anxious, a noble and highly just deliberation.

For it was one thing to stare at a girl till she was bored at it, it was one thing to take her to the Horse Show and the Opera, and to send her flowers by the stack, and chocolates by the ton, and 'great' novels, the very latest and greatest, by the dozen; but something quite other to hold open for her, with eyes attached to eyes, the gate, moving on such stiff silver hinges, of the grand square forecourt of the palace of wedlock. The state of being 'engaged' represented to him the introduction to this precinct of some young woman with whom his outside parley would have had the duration, distinctly, of his own convenience. That might be cold-blooded if one choose to think so; but nothing of another sort would equal the high ceremony and dignity and decency, above all the grand gallantry and finality, of their then passing in. Poor Julia could have blushed red, before that view, with the memory of the way the forecourt, as she now imagined it, had been dishonoured by her younger romps. She had tumbled over the wall with this, that and the other raw playmate, and had played 'tag' and leap-frog, as she might say, from corner to corner. That would be the 'history' with which, in case of definite demand, she should be able to supply Mr French: that she had already, again and again, any occasion offering, chattered and scuffled over ground provided, according to his idea, for walking the gravest of minuets. If that then had been all their *kind* of history, hers and her mother's, at least there was plenty of it: it was the superstructure raised on the other group of facts, those of the order of their having been always so perfectly pink and white, so perfectly possessed of clothes, so perfectly splendid, so perfectly idiotic. These things had been the 'points' of antelope and zebra; putting Mrs Connery for the zebra, as the more remarkably striped or spotted. Such were the data Basil French's enquiry

would elicit: her own six engagements and her mother's three nullified marriages
– nine nice distinct little horrors in all. What on earth was to be done about them?

II

It was notable, she was afterwards to recognise, that there had been nothing of
the famous business slackness in the positive pounce with which Mr Pitman put
it to her that, as soon as he had made her out 'for sure,' identified her there as
old Julia grown-up and gallivanting with a new admirer, a smarter young fellow
than ever yet, he had had the inspiration of her being exactly the good girl to help
him. She certainly found him strike the hour again with these vulgarities of tone
– forms of speech that her mother had anciently described as by themselves, once
he had opened the whole battery, sufficient ground for putting him away. Full,
however, of the use she should have for him, she wasn't going to mind trifles.
What she really gasped at was that, so oddly, he was ahead of her at the start.
'Yes, I want something of you, Julia, and I want it right now: you can do me a
turn, and I'm blest if my luck – which has once or twice been pretty good, you
know – hasn't sent you to me.' She knew the luck he meant – that of her mother's
having so enabled him to get rid of her; but it was the nearest allusion of the
merely invidious kind that he would make. It had thus come to our young woman
on the spot and by divination: the service he desired of her matched with
remarkable closeness what she had so promptly taken into her head to name to
himself – to name in her own interest, though deterred as yet from having brought
it right out. She had been prevented by his speaking, the first thing, in that way,
as if he had known Mr French – which surprised her till he explained that every
one in New York knew by appearance a young man of his so quoted wealth
('What did she take them all in New York then *for*?') and of whose marked
attention to her he had moreover, for himself, round at clubs and places, lately
heard. This had accompanied the inevitable free question 'Was she engaged to
him now?' – which she had in fact almost welcomed as holding out to her the
perch of opportunity. She was waiting to deal with it properly, but meanwhile he
had gone on, and to such effect that it took them but three minutes to turn out,
on either side, like a pair of pickpockets comparing, under shelter, their day's
booty, the treasures of design concealed about their persons.

'I want you to tell the truth for me – as you only can. I want you to say that I
was really all right – as right as you know; and that I simply acted like an angel
in a story-book, gave myself away to have it over.'

'Why my dear man,' Julia cried, 'you take the wind straight out of my sails!

What I'm here to ask of *you* is that you'll confess to having been even a worse fiend than you were shown up for; to having made it impossible mother should *not* take proceedings.' There! — she had brought it out, and with the sense of their situation turning to high excitement for her in the teeth of his droll stare, his strange grin, his characteristic 'Lordy, lordy! What good will that do you?' She was prepared with her clear statement of reasons for her appeal, and feared so he might have better ones for his own that all her story came in a flash. 'Well, Mr Pitman, I want to get married this time, by way of a change; but you see we've been such fools that, when something really good at last comes up, it's too dreadfully awkward. The fools we were capable of being — well, you know better than any one; unless perhaps not quite so well as Mr Connery. It has got to be denied,' said Julia ardently — 'it has got to be denied flat. But I can't get hold of Mr Connery — Mr Connery has gone to China. Besides, if he were here,' she had ruefully to confess, 'he'd be no good — on the contrary. He wouldn't deny anything — he'd only tell more. So thank heaven he's away — there's *that* amount of good! I'm not engaged yet,' she went on — but he had already taken her up.

'You're not engaged to Mr French?' It was all, clearly, a wondrous show for him, but his immediate surprise, oddly, might have been greatest for that.

'No, not to any one — for the seventh time!' She spoke as with her head held well up both over the shame and the pride. 'Yes, the next time I'm engaged I want something to happen. But he's afraid; he's afraid of what may be told him. He's dying to find out, and yet he'd die if he did! He wants to be talked to, but he has got to be talked to right. You could talk to him right, Mr Pitman — if you only *would*! He can't get over mother — that I feel: he loathes and scorns divorces, and we've had first and last too many. So if he could hear from you that you just made her life a hell — why,' Julia concluded, 'it would be too lovely. If she *had* to go in for another — after having already, when I was little, divorced father — it would "sort of" make, don't you see? one less. You'd do the high-toned thing by her: you'd say what a wretch you then were, and that she had had to save her life. In that way he mayn't mind it. Don't you see, you sweet man?' poor Julia pleaded. 'Oh,' she wound up as if his fancy lagged or his scruple looked out, 'of course I want you to *lie* for me!'

It did indeed sufficiently stagger him. 'It's a lovely idea for the moment when I was just saying to myself — as soon as I saw you — that you'd speak the truth for *me*!'

'Ah what's the matter with "you"?' Julia sighed with an impatience not sensibly less sharp for her having so quickly scented some lion in her path.

'Why, do you think there's no one in the world but you who has seen the cup of promised affection, of something really to be depended on, only, at the last moment, by the horrid jostle of your elbow, spilled all over you? I want to provide for my future too as it happens; and my good friend who's to help me to that – the most charming of women this time – disapproves of divorce quite as much as Mr French. Don't you see,' Mr Pitman candidly asked, 'what that by itself must have done toward attaching me to her? *She* has got to be talked to – to be told how little I could help it.'

'Oh lordy, lordy!' the girl emulously groaned. It was such a relieving cry. 'Well, *I* won't talk to her!' she declared.

'You *won't*, Julia?' he pitifully echoed. 'And yet you ask of *me* –!'

His pang, she felt, was sincere, and even more than she had guessed, for the previous quarter of an hour, he had been building up his hope, building it with her aid for a foundation. Yet was he going to see how their testimony, on each side, would, if offered, *have* to conflict? If he was to prove himself for her sake – or, more queerly still, for that of Basil French's high conservatism – a person whom there had been but that one way of handling, how could she prove him, in this other and so different interest, a mere gentle sacrifice to his wife's perversity? She had, before him there, on the instant, all acutely, a sense of rising sickness – a wan glimmer of foresight as to the end of the fond dream. Everything else was against her, everything in her dreadful past – just as if she had been a person represented by some 'emotional actress,' some desperate erring lady 'hunted down' in a play; but was that going to be the case too with her own very decency, the fierce little residuum deep within her, for which she was counting, when she came to think, on so little glory or even credit? Was this also going to turn against her and trip her up – just to show she was really, under the touch and the test, as decent as any one; and with no one but herself the wiser for it meanwhile, and no proof to show but that, as a consequence, she should be unmarried to the end? She put it to Mr Pitman quite with resentment: 'Do you mean to say you're going to be married –?'

'Oh my dear, I too must get engaged first!' – he spoke with his inimitable grin. 'But that, you see, is where you come in. I've told her about you. She wants awfully to meet you. The way it happens is too lovely – that I find you just in this place. She's coming,' said Mr Pitman – and as in all the good faith of his eagerness now; 'she's coming in about three minutes.'

'Coming here?'

'Yes, Julia – right here. It's where we usually meet;' and he was wreathed again, this time as if for life, in his large slow smile. 'She loves this place – she's awfully keen on art. Like *you*, Julia, if you haven't changed – I remember how you did love art.' He looked at her quite tenderly, as to keep her up to it. 'You must still of course – from the way you're here. Just let her *feel* that,' the poor man fantastically urged. And then with his kind eyes on her and his good ugly mouth stretched as for delicate emphasis from ear to ear: 'Every little helps!'

He made her wonder for him, ask herself, and with a certain intensity, questions she yet hated the trouble of; as whether he were still as moneyless as in the other time – which was certain indeed, for any fortune he ever would have made. His slackness on that ground stuck out of him almost as much as if he had been of rusty or 'seedy' aspect – which, luckily for him, he wasn't at all: he looked, in his way, like some pleasant eccentric ridiculous but real gentleman, whose taste might be of the queerest, but his credit with his tailor none the less of the best. She wouldn't have been the least ashamed, had their connexion lasted, of going about with him: so that what a fool, again, her mother had been – since Mr Connery, sorry as one might be for him, was irrepressibly vulgar. Julia's quickness was, for the minute, charged with all this; but she had none the less her feeling of the right thing to say and the right way to say it. If he was after a future financially assured, even as she herself so frantically was, she wouldn't cast the stone.[4] But if he had talked about her to strange women she couldn't be less than a little majestic. 'Who then is the person in question for you –?'

'Why such a dear thing, Julia – Mrs David E. Drack. Have you heard of her?' he almost fluted.

New York was vast, and she hadn't had that advantage. 'She's a widow –?'

'Oh yes: she's not –!' He caught himself up in time. 'She's a real one.' It was as near as he came. But it was as if he had been looking at her now so pathetically hard. 'Julia, she has millions.'

Hard, at any rate – whether pathetic or not – was the look she gave him back. 'Well, so has – or so *will* have – Basil French. And more of them than Mrs Drack, I guess,' Julia quavered.

'Oh I know what *they've* got!' He took it from her – with the effect of a vague stir, in his long person, of unwelcome embarrassment. But was she going to give up because he was embarrassed? He should know at least what he was costing her. It came home to her own spirit more than ever; but meanwhile he had found his footing. 'I don't see how your mother matters. It isn't a question of his marrying *her*.'

'No; but, constantly together as we've always been, it's a question of there being so disgustingly much to get over. If we had, for people like them, but the one ugly spot and the one weak side; if we had made, between us, but the one vulgar *kind* of mistake: well, I don't say!' She reflected with a wistfulness of note that was in itself a touching eloquence. 'To have our reward in this world we've had too sweet a time. We've had it all right down here!' said Julia Bride. 'I should have taken the precaution to have about a dozen fewer lovers.'

'Ah my dear, "lovers" –!' He ever so comically attenuated.

'Well they *were*!' She quite flared up. 'When you've had a ring from each (three diamonds, two pearls and a rather bad sapphire: I've kept them all, and they tell my story!) what are you to call them?'

'Oh rings –!' Mr Pitman didn't call rings anything. 'I've given Mrs Drack a ring.'

Julia stared. 'Then aren't you her lover?'

'That, dear child,' he humorously wailed, 'is what I want you to find out! But I'll handle your rings all right,' he more lucidly added.

'You'll "handle" them?'

'I'll fix your lovers. I'll lie about *them*, if that's all you want.'

'Oh about "them" –!' She turned away with a sombre drop, seeing so little in it. 'That wouldn't count – from *you*!' She saw the great shining room, with its mockery of art and 'style' and security, all the things she was vainly after, and its few scattered visitors who had left them, Mr Pitman and herself, in their ample corner, so conveniently at ease. There was only a lady in one of the far doorways, of whom she took vague note and who seemed to be looking at them. 'They'd have to lie for themselves!'

'Do you mean he's capable of putting it to them?'

Mr Pitman's tone threw discredit on that possibility, but she knew perfectly well what she meant. 'Not of getting at them directly, not, as mother says, of nosing round himself; but of listening – and small blame to him! – to the horrible things other people say of me.'

'But what other people?'

'Why Mrs George Maule, to begin with – who intensely loathes us, and who talks to his sisters, so that they may talk to *him*: which they do, all the while, I'm morally sure (hating me as they also must). But it's she who's the real reason – I mean of his holding off. She poisons the air he breathes.'

'Oh well,' said Mr Pitman with easy optimism, 'if Mrs George Maule's a cat –!'

'If she's a cat she has kittens – four little spotlessly white ones, among whom she'd give her head that Mr French should make his pick. He could do it with his eyes shut – you can't tell them apart. But she has every name, every date, as you may say, for my dark "record" – as of course they all call it: she'll be able to give him, if he brings himself to ask her, every fact in its order. And all the while, don't you see? there's no one to speak *for* me.'

It would have touched a harder heart than her loose friend's to note the final flush of clairvoyance witnessing this assertion and under which her eyes shone as with the rush of quick tears. He stared at her, and what this did for the deep charm of her prettiness, as in almost witless admiration. 'But can't you – lovely as you are, you beautiful thing! – speak for yourself?'

'Do you mean can't I tell the lies? No then, I can't – and I wouldn't if I could. I don't lie myself you know – as it happens; and it could represent to him then about the only thing, the only bad one, I don't do. I *did* – "lovely as I am"! –

have my regular time; I wasn't so hideous that I couldn't! Besides, do you imagine he'd come and ask me?'

'Gad, I wish he would, Julia!' said Mr Pitman with his kind eyes on her.

'Well then I'd tell him!' And she held her head again high. 'But he won't.'

It fairly distressed her companion. 'Doesn't he want then to know –?'

'He wants *not* to know. He wants to be told without asking – told, I mean, that each of the stories, those that have come to him, is a fraud and a libel. *Qui s'excuse s'accuse*,[5] don't they say? – so that do you see me breaking out to him, unprovoked, with four or five what-do-you-call-'ems, the things mother used to have to prove in Court, a set of neat little "alibis" in a row? How can I get hold of so *many* precious gentlemen, to turn them on? How can *they* want everything fished up?'

She had paused for her climax, in the intensity of these considerations; which gave Mr Pitman a chance to express his honest faith. 'Why, my sweet child, they'd be just glad –!'

It determined in her loveliness almost a sudden glare. 'Glad to swear they never had anything to do with such a creature? Then I'd be glad to swear they had lots!'

His persuasive smile, though confessing to bewilderment, insisted. 'Why, my love, they've got to swear either one thing or the other.'

'They've got to keep out of the way – that's *their* view of it, I guess,' said Julia. 'Where *are* they, please – now that they *may* be wanted? If you'd like to hunt them up for me you're very welcome.' With which, for the moment, over the difficult case, they faced each other helplessly enough. And she added to it now the sharpest ache of her despair. 'He knows about Murray Brush. The others' – and her pretty white-gloved hands and charming pink shoulders gave them up – 'may go hang!'

'Murray Brush –?' It had opened Mr Pitman's eyes.

'Yes – yes; I do mind *him*.'

'Then what's the matter with his at least rallying –?'

'The matter is that, being ashamed of himself, as he well might, he left the country as soon as he could and has stayed away. The matter is that he's in Paris or somewhere, and that if you expect him to come home for me –!' She had already dropped, however, as at Mr Pitman's look.

'Why, you foolish thing, Murray Brush is in New York!' It had quite brightened him up.

'He has come back –?'

'Why sure! I saw him – when was it? Tuesday! – on the Jersey boat.'[6] Mr Pitman rejoiced in his news. '*He's* your man!'

Julia too had been affected by it; it had brought in a rich wave her hot colour back. But she gave the strangest dim smile. 'He *was*!'

'Then get hold of him, and – if he's a gentleman – he'll prove for you, to the hilt, that he wasn't.'

It lighted in her face, the kindled train of this particular sudden suggestion, a glow, a sharpness of interest, that had deepened the next moment, while she gave a slow and sad headshake, to a greater strangeness yet. 'He isn't a gentleman.'

'Ah lordy, lordy!' Mr Pitman again sighed. He struggled out of it but only into the vague. 'Oh then if he's a pig –!'

'You see there are only a few gentlemen – not enough to go round – and that makes them count so!' It had thrust the girl herself, for that matter, into depths; but whether most of memory or of roused purpose he had no time to judge – aware as he suddenly was of a shadow (since he mightn't perhaps too quickly call it a light) across the heaving surface of their question. It fell upon Julia's face, fell with the sound of the voice he so well knew, but which could only be odd to her for all it immediately assumed.

'There are indeed very few – and one mustn't try *them* too much!' Mrs Drack, who had supervened while they talked, stood, in monstrous magnitude – at least to Julia's reimpressed eyes – between them: she was the lady our young woman had descried across the room, and she had drawn near while the interest of their issue so held them. We have seen the act of observation and that of reflexion alike swift in Julia – once her subject was within range – and she had now, with all her perceptions at the acutest, taken in, by a single stare, the strange presence to a happy connexion with which Mr Pitman aspired and which had thus sailed, with placid majesty, into their troubled waters. She was clearly not shy, Mrs David E. Drack, yet neither was she ominously bold; she was bland and 'good,' Julia made sure at a glance, and of a large complacency, as the good and the bland are apt to be – a large complacency, a large sentimentality, a large innocent elephantine archness: she fairly rioted in that dimension of size. Habited in an extraordinary quantity of stiff and lustrous black brocade, with enhancements, of every description, that twinkled and tinkled, that rustled and rumbled with her least movement, she presented a huge hideous pleasant face, a featureless desert in a remote quarter of which the disproportionately small eyes might have figured a pair of rash adventurers all but buried in the sand. They reduced themselves when she smiled to barely discernible points – a couple of mere tiny emergent heads – though the foreground of the scene, as if to make up for it, gaped with a vast benevolence. In a word Julia saw – and as if she had needed nothing more; saw Mr Pitman's opportunity, saw her own, saw the exact nature both of Mrs Drack's circumspection and of Mrs Drack's sensibility, saw even, glittering there in letters of gold and as a part of the whole metallic coruscation, the large figure of her income, largest of all her attributes, and (though perhaps a little more as a luminous blur beside all this) the mingled ecstasy and agony of Mr Pitman's hope and Mr Pitman's fear.

He was introducing them, with his pathetic belief in the virtue for every occasion, in the solvent for every trouble, of an extravagant genial professional humour; he was naming her to Mrs Drack as the charming young friend he had told her so much about and who had been as an angel to him in a weary time; he was saying that the loveliest chance in the world, this accident of a meeting in those promiscuous halls, had placed within his reach the pleasure of bringing them together. It didn't indeed matter, Julia felt, what he was saying: he conveyed everything, as far as she was concerned, by a moral pressure as unmistakeable as if, for a symbol of it, he had thrown himself on her neck. Above all, meanwhile, this high consciousness prevailed – that the good lady herself, however huge she loomed, had entered, by the end of a minute, into a condition as of suspended weight and arrested mass, stilled to artless awe by the effect of her vision. Julia had practised almost to lassitude the art of tracing in the people who looked at her the impression promptly sequent; but it was a singular fact that if, in irritation, in depression, she felt that the lighted eyes of men, stupid at their clearest, had given her pretty well all she should ever care for, she could still gather a freshness from the tribute of her own sex, still care to see her reflexion in the faces of women. Never, probably, never would that sweet be tasteless – with such a straight grim spoon was it mostly administered, and so flavoured and strengthened by the competence of their eyes. Women knew so much best *how* a woman surpassed – how and where and why, with no touch or torment of it lost on them; so that as it produced mainly and primarily the instinct of aversion, the sense of extracting the recognition, of gouging out the homage, was on the whole the highest crown one's felicity could wear. Once in a way, however, the grimness beautifully dropped, the jealousy failed: the admiration was all there and the poor plain sister handsomely paid it. It had never been so paid, she was presently certain, as by this great generous object of Mr Pitman's flame, who without optical aid, it well might have seemed, nevertheless entirely grasped her – might in fact, all benevolently, have been groping her over as by some huge mild proboscis. She gave Mrs Drack pleasure in short; and who could say of what other pleasures the poor lady hadn't been cheated?

It was somehow a muddled world in which one of her conceivable joys, at this time of day, would be to marry Mr Pitman – to say nothing of a state of things in which this gentleman's own fancy could invest such a union with rapture. That, however, was their own mystery, and Julia, with each instant, was more and more clear about hers: so remarkably primed in fact, at the end of three minutes, that though her friend, and though *his* friend, were both saying things, many things and perhaps quite wonderful things, she had no free attention for them and was only rising and soaring. She was rising to her value, she was soaring *with* it – the value Mr Pitman almost convulsively imputed to her, the value that consisted for her of being so unmistakeably the most dazzling image Mrs Drack had ever beheld. These were the uses, for Julia, in fine, of adversity;[7] the range of Mrs Drack's experience might have been as small as the measure of her presence was large: Julia was at any rate herself in face of the occasion of her life, and, after all her late repudiations and reactions, had perhaps never yet known the quality of this moment's success. She hadn't an idea of what, on either side, had been uttered – beyond Mr Pitman's allusion to her having befriended him of old: she simply held his companion with her radiance and knew she might be, for her effect, as irrelevant as she chose. It was relevant to do what he wanted – it was relevant to dish herself. She did it now with a kind of passion, to say nothing of her knowing, with it, that every word of it added to her beauty. She gave him away in short, up to the hilt, for any use of her own, and should have nothing to clutch at now but the possibility of Murray Brush.

'He says I was good to him, Mrs Drack; and I'm sure I hope I was, since I should be ashamed to be anything else. If I could be good to him now I should be glad – that's just what, a while ago, I rushed up to him here, after so long, to give myself the pleasure of saying. I saw him years ago very particularly, very miserably tried – and I saw the way he took it. I did see it, you dear man,' she sublimely went on – 'I saw it for all you may protest, for all you may hate me to talk about you! I saw you behave like a gentleman – since Mrs Drack agrees with me so charmingly that there are not many to be met. I don't know whether you care, Mrs Drack' – she abounded, she revelled in the name – 'but I've always remembered it of him: that under the most extraordinary provocation he was decent and patient and brave. No appearance of anything different matters, for I speak of what I *know*. Of course I'm nothing and nobody; I'm only a poor frivolous girl, but I was very close to him at the time. That's all my little story – if it *should* interest you at all.' She measured every beat of her wing, she knew how high she was going and paused only when it was quite vertiginous. Here she hung a moment as in the glare of the upper blue; which was but the glare – what else could it be? – of the vast and magnificent attention of both her auditors, hushed, on their side, in the splendour she emitted. She had at last to steady herself, and she scarce knew afterwards at what rate or in what way she had still inimitably come down – her own eyes fixed all the while on the very figure of her achievement. She had sacrificed her mother on the altar – proclaimed her false and cruel; and if that didn't 'fix' Mr Pitman, as he would have said – well, it was all she could do. But the cost of her action already somehow came back to her with increase; the dear gaunt man fairly wavered, to her sight, in the glory of it, as if signalling at her, with wild gleeful arms, from some mount of safety, while the massive lady just spread and spread like a rich fluid a bit helplessly spilt. It was really the outflow of the poor woman's honest response, into which she seemed to melt, and Julia scarce distinguished the two apart even for her taking gracious leave of each. 'Good-bye, Mrs Drack; I'm awfully happy to have met you' – like as not it was for this she had grasped Mr Pitman's hand. And then to him or to her, it didn't matter which, 'Good-bye, dear good Mr Pitman – hasn't it been nice after so long?'

III

Julia floated even to her own sense swanlike away – she left in her wake their fairly stupefied submission: it was as if she had, by an exquisite authority, now *placed* them, each for each, and they would have nothing to do but be happy together. Never had she so exulted as on this ridiculous occasion in the noted items of her beauty. *Le compte y était*,[8] as they used to say in Paris – every one of them, for her immediate employment, was there; and there was something in it after all. It didn't necessarily, this sum of thumping little figures, imply charm – especially for 'refined' people: nobody knew better than Julia that inexpressible charm and quoteable 'charms' (quoteable like prices, rates, shares, or whatever, the things they dealt in downtown)[9] are two distinct categories; the safest thing for the latter being, on the whole, that it might include the former, and the great strength of the former being that it might perfectly dispense with the latter. Mrs Drack wasn't refined, not the least little bit; but what would be the case with Murray Brush now – after his three years of Europe? He had done so what he liked with her – which had seemed so then just the meaning, hadn't it? of their being 'engaged' – that he had made her not see, while the absurdity lasted (the absurdity of their pretending to believe they could marry without a cent) how little he was of metal without alloy: this had come up for her, remarkably, but afterwards – come up for her as she looked back. Then she had drawn her conclusion, which was one of the many that Basil French had made her draw. It was a queer service Basil was going to have rendered her, this having made everything she had ever done impossible, if he wasn't going to give her a new chance. If he was it was doubtless right enough. On the other hand Murray might have improved, if such a quantity of alloy, as she called it, *were*, in any man, reducible, and if Paris were the place all happily to reduce it. She had her doubts – anxious and aching on the spot, and had expressed them to Mr Pitman: certainly, of old, he had been more open to the quoteable than to the inexpressible, to charms than to charm. If she could try the quoteable, however, and with such a grand result, on Mrs Drack, she couldn't now on Murray – in respect to whom everything had changed. So that if he hadn't a sense for the subtler appeal, the appeal appreciable by people *not* vulgar, on which alone she could depend, what on earth would become of her? She could but yearningly hope, at any rate, as she made up her mind to write to him immediately at his club. It was a question of the right sensibility in him. Perhaps he would have acquired it in Europe.

Two days later indeed – for he had promptly and charmingly replied, keeping with alacrity the appointment she had judged best to propose, a morning hour in a sequestered alley of the Park[10] – two days later she was to be struck well-nigh to alarm by everything he had acquired: so much it seemed to make that it threatened somehow a complication, and her plan, so far as she had arrived at one, dwelt in the desire above all to simplify. She wanted no grain more of extravagance or excess in anything – risking as she had done, none the less, a recall of ancient licence in proposing to Murray such a place of meeting. She had her reasons – she wished intensely to discriminate: Basil French had several times waited on her at her mother's habitation, their horrible flat which was so much too far up and too near the East Side;[11] he had dined there and lunched there and gone with her thence to other places, notably to see pictures, and had in particular adjourned with her twice to the Metropolitan Museum, in which he took a great interest, in which she professed a delight, and their second visit to which had wound up in her encounter with Mr Pitman, after her companion had yielded, at her urgent instance, to an exceptional need of keeping a business engagement. She mightn't in delicacy, in decency, entertain Murray Brush where she had entertained Mr French – she was given over now to these exquisite perceptions and proprieties and bent on devoutly observing them; and Mr French, by good luck, had never been with her in the Park: partly because he had never pressed it, and partly because she would have held off if he had, so haunted were those devious paths and favouring shades by the general echo of her untrammelled past. If he had never suggested their taking a turn there this was because, quite divineably, he held it would commit him further than he had yet gone; and if she on her side had practised a like reserve it was because the place reeked for her, as she inwardly said, with old associations. It reeked with nothing so much perhaps as with the memories evoked by the young man who now awaited her in the nook she had been so competent to indicate; but in what corner of the town, should she look for them, wouldn't those footsteps creak back into muffled life, and to what expedient would she be reduced should she attempt to avoid all such tracks? The Museum was full of tracks, tracks by the hundred – the way really she had knocked about! – but she had to see people somewhere, and she couldn't pretend to dodge every ghost.

All she could do was not to make confusion, make mixtures, of the living;

though she asked herself enough what mixture she mightn't find herself to have prepared if Mr French should not so very impossibly for a restless roaming man – *her* effect on him! – happen to pass while she sat there with the moustachioed personage round whose name Mrs Maule would probably have caused detrimental anecdote most thickly to cluster. There existed, she was sure, a mass of luxuriant legend about the 'lengths' her engagement with Murray Brush had gone; she could herself fairly feel them in the air, these streamers of evil, black flags flown as in warning, the vast redundancy of so cheap and so dingy social bunting, in fine, that flapped over the stations she had successively moved away from and which were empty now, for such an ado, even to grotesqueness. The vivacity of that conviction was what had at present determined her, while it was the way he listened after she had quickly broken ground, while it was the special character of the interested look in his handsome face, handsomer than ever yet, that represented for her the civilisation he had somehow taken on. Just so it was the quantity of that gain, in its turn, that had at the end of ten minutes begun to affect her as holding up a light to the wide reach of her step. 'There was never anything the least serious between us, not a sign or a scrap, do you mind? of anything beyond the merest pleasant friendly acquaintance; and if you're not ready to go to the stake on it for me you may as well know in time what it is you'll probably cost me.'

She had immediately plunged, measuring her effect and having thought it well over; and what corresponded to her question of his having become a better person to appeal to was the appearance of interest she had so easily created in him. She felt on the spot the difference that made – it was indeed his form of being more civilised: it was the sense in which Europe in general and Paris in particular had made him develop. By every calculation – and her calculations, based on the intimacy of her knowledge, had been many and deep – he would help her the better the more intelligent he should have become; yet she was to recognise later on that the first chill of foreseen disaster had been caught by her as, at a given moment, this greater refinement of his attention seemed to exhale it. It was just what she had wanted – 'if I can only get him interested –!' so that, this proving quite vividly possible, why did the light it lifted strike her as lurid? Was it partly by reason of his inordinate romantic good looks, those of a gallant genial conqueror, but which, involving so glossy a brownness of eye, so manly a crispness of curl, so red-lipped a radiance of smile, so natural a bravery of port, prescribed to any response he might facially, might expressively make a sort of florid disproportionate amplitude? The explanation, in any case, didn't matter; he was going to mean well' – that she could feel, and also that he had meant better in the past, presumably, than he had managed to convince her of his doing at the time: the oddity she hadn't now reckoned with was this fact that from the moment he did advertise an interest it should show almost as what she would have called weird. It made a change in him that didn't go with the rest — as if he had broken his nose or put on spectacles, lost his handsome hair or sacrificed his splendid moustache: her conception, her necessity, as she saw, had been that something should be added to him for her use, but nothing for his own alteration.

He had affirmed himself, and his character, and his temper, and his health, and his appetite, and his ignorance, and his obstinacy, and his whole charming coarse heartless personality, during their engagement, by twenty forms of natural emphasis, but never by emphasis of interest. How in fact could you feel interest unless you should know, within you, some dim stir of imagination? There was nothing in the world of which Murray Brush was less capable than of such a dim stir, because you only began to imagine when you felt some approach to a need to understand. *He* had never felt it; for hadn't he been born, to his personal vision, with that perfect intuition of everything which reduces all the suggested preliminaries of judgement to the impertinence — when it's a question of your entering your house — of a dumpage of bricks at your door? He had had, in short, neither to imagine nor to perceive, because he had, from the first pulse of his intelligence, simply and supremely known: so that, at this hour, face to face with him, it came over her that she had in their old relation dispensed with any such convenience of comprehension on his part even to a degree she had not measured at the time. What therefore must he not have seemed to her as a form of life, a form of avidity and activity, blatantly successful in its own conceit, that he could have dazzled her so against the interest of her very faculties and functions? Strangely and richly historic all that backward mystery, and only leaving for her mind the wonder of such a mixture of possession and detachment as they would clearly to-day both know. For each to be so little at last to the other when, during months together, the idea of all abundance, all quantity, had been, for each, drawn from the other and addressed to the other — what was it monstrously like but some fantastic act of getting rid of a person by going to lock yourself up in the *sanctum sanctorum*[12] of that person's house, amid every evidence of that person's habits and nature? What was going to happen, at any rate, was that Murray would show himself as beautifully and consciously understanding — and it would be prodigious that Europe should have inoculated him with that delicacy. Yes, he wouldn't claim to know now till she had told him — an aid to performance he had surely never before waited for or been indebted to from any one; and then, so knowing, he would charmingly endeavour to 'meet,' to oblige and to gratify. He would find it, her case, ever so worthy of his benevolence, and would be literally inspired to reflect that he must hear about it first.

She let him hear then everything, in spite of feeling herself slip, while she did so, to some doom as yet incalculable; she went on very much as she had done for

Mr Pitman and Mrs Drack, with the rage of desperation and, as she was afterwards to call it to herself, the fascination of the abyss. She didn't know, couldn't have said at the time, *why* his projected benevolence should have had most so the virtue to scare her: he would patronise her, as an effect of her vividness, if not of her charm, and would do this with all high intention, finding her case, or rather *their* case, their funny old case, taking on of a sudden such refreshing and edifying life, to the last degree curious and even important; but there were gaps of connexion between this and the intensity of the perception here overtaking her that she shouldn't be able to move in *any* direction without dishing herself. That she couldn't afford it where she had got to — couldn't afford the deplorable vulgarity of having been so many times informally affianced and contracted (putting it only at that, at its being by the new lights and fashions so unpardonably vulgar): he took this from her without turning, as she might have said, a hair; except just to indicate, with his new superiority, that he felt the distinguished appeal and notably the pathos of it. He still took it from her that she hoped nothing, as it were, from any other *alibi* — the people to drag into court being too many and too scattered; but that, as it was with him, Murray Brush, she had been *most* vulgar, most everything she had better not have been, so she depended on him for the innocence it was actually vital she should establish. He blushed or frowned or winced no more at that than he did when she once more fairly emptied her satchel and, quite as if they had been Nancy and the Artful Dodger, or some nefarious pair of that sort, talking things over in the manner of 'Oliver Twist,'[13] revealed to him the fondness of her view that, could she but have produced a cleaner slate, she might by this time have pulled it off with Mr French. Yes, he let her in that way sacrifice her honourable connexion with him — all the more honourable for being so completely at an end — to the crudity of her plan for not missing another connexion, so much more brilliant than what he offered, and for bringing another man, with whom she so invidiously and unflatteringly compared him, into her greedy life.

There was only a moment during which, by a particular lustrous look she had never had from him before, he just made her wonder which turn he was going to take; she felt, however, as safe as was consistent with her sense of having probably but added to her danger, when he brought out, the next instant: 'Don't you seem to take the ground that we were guilty — that *you* were ever guilty — of something we shouldn't have been? What did we ever do that was secret, or underhand, or any way not to be acknowledged? What did we do but exchange our young vows with the best faith in the world — publicly, rejoicingly, with the full assent of every one connected with us? I mean of course,' he said with his grave kind smile, 'till we broke off so completely because we found that — practically, financially, on the hard worldly basis — we couldn't work it. What harm, in the sight of God or man, Julia,' he asked in his fine rich way, 'did we ever do?'

She gave him back his look, turning pale. 'Am I talking of *that*? Am I talking of what *we* know? I'm talking of what others feel – of what they *have* to feel; of what it's just enough for them to know not to be able to get over it, once they do really know it. How do they know what *didn't* pass between us, with all the opportunities we had? That's none of their business – if we were idiots enough, on the top of everything! What you may or mayn't have done doesn't count, for *you*; but there are people for whom it's loathsome that a girl should have gone on like that from one person to another and still pretend to be – well, all that a nice girl is supposed to be. It's as if we had but just waked up, mother and I, to such a remarkable prejudice; and now we have it – when we could do so well without it! – staring us in the face. That mother should have insanely *let* me, should so vulgarly have taken it for my natural, my social career – *that's* the disgusting humiliating thing: with the lovely account it gives of both of us! But mother's view of a delicacy in things!' she went on with scathing grimness; 'mother's measure of anything, with her grand "gained cases" (there'll be another yet, she finds them so easy!) of which she's so publicly proud! You see I've no margin,' said Julia; letting him take it from her flushed face as much as he would that her mother hadn't left her an inch. It was that he should make use of the spade with her for the restoration of a bit of a margin just wide enough to perch on till the tide of peril should have ebbed a little, it was that he should give her *that* lift –!

Well, it was all there from him after these last words; it was before her that he really took hold. 'Oh, my dear child, I can see! Of course there are people – ideas change in our society so fast! – who are not in sympathy with the old American freedom[14] and who read, I dare say, all sorts of uncanny things into it. Naturally you must take them as they are – from the moment,' said Murray Brush, who had lighted, by her leave, a cigarette, 'your life-path does, for weal or for woe, cross with theirs.' He had every now and then such an elegant phrase. 'Awfully interesting, certainly, your case. It's enough for me that it *is* yours – I make it my own. I put myself absolutely in your place; you'll understand from me, without professions, won't you? that I do. Command me in every way! What I do like is the sympathy with which you've inspired *him*. I don't, I'm sorry to say, happen to know him personally' – he smoked away, looking off; 'but of course one knows all about him generally, and I'm sure he's right for you, I'm sure it would be charming, if you yourself think so. Therefore trust me and even – what shall I say? – leave it to me a little, won't you?' He had been watching, as in his fumes, the fine growth of his possibilities; and with this he turned on her the large warmth of his charity. It was like a subscription of a half a million. 'I'll take care of you.'

She found herself for a moment looking up at him from as far below as the point from which the school-child, with round eyes raised to the wall, gazes at the particoloured map of the world. Yes, it was a warmth, it was a special benignity, that had never yet dropped on her from any one; and she wouldn't for the first few moments have known how to describe it or even quite what to do with it. Then as it still rested, his fine improved expression aiding, the sense of what had happened came over her with a rush. She was being, yes, patronised; and that was really as new to her – the freeborn American girl who might, if she had wished, have got engaged and disengaged not six times but sixty – as it would have been to be crowned or crucified. The Frenches themselves didn't do it – the Frenches themselves didn't dare it. It was as strange as one would: she recognised it when it came, but anything might have come rather – and it was coming by (of all people in the world) Murray Brush! It overwhelmed her; still she could speak, with however faint a quaver and however sick a smile. 'You'll lie for me like a gentleman?'

'As far as that goes till I'm black in the face!' And then while he glowed at her and she wondered if he would pointedly look his lies that way, and if, in fine, his florid gallant knowing, almost winking intelligence, *common* as she had never seen the common vivified, would represent his notion of 'blackness': 'See here, Julia; I'll do more.'

' "More" –?'

'Everything. I'll take it right in hand. I'll fling over you –'

'Fling over me –?' she continued to echo as he fascinatingly fixed her.

'Well, the biggest *kind* of rose-coloured mantle!' And this time, oh, he did wink: it *would* be the way he was going to wink (and in the grandest good faith in the world) when indignantly denying, under inquisition, that there had been 'a sign or a scrap' between them. But there was more to come; he decided she should have it all. 'Julia, you've got to know now.' He hung fire but an instant more. 'Julia, I'm going to be married.' His 'Julias' were somehow death to her; she could feel that even *through* all the rest. 'Julia, I announce my engagement.'

'Oh lordy, lordy!' she wailed: it might have been addressed to Mr Pitman.

The force of it had brought her to her feet, but he sat there smiling up as at the natural tribute of her interest. 'I tell you before any one else; it's not to be "out" for a day or two yet. But we want you to know; *she* said that as soon as I mentioned to her that I had heard from you. I mention to her everything, you see!' – and he almost simpered while, still in his seat, he held the end of his cigarette, all delicately and as for a form of gentle emphasis, with the tips of his fine fingers. 'You've not met her, Mary Lindeck, I think: she tells me she hasn't the pleasure of knowing you, but she desires it so much – particularly longs for it. She'll take an interest too,' he went on; 'you must let me immediately bring her to you. She has heard so much about you and she really wants to see you.'

'Oh mercy *me*!' poor Julia gasped again – so strangely did history repeat itself and so did this appear the echo, on Murray Brush's lips, and quite to drollery, of that sympathetic curiosity of Mrs Drack's which Mr Pitman, as they said, voiced. Well, there had played before her the vision of a ledge of safety in face of a rising tide; but this deepened quickly to a sense more forlorn, the cold swish of waters already up to her waist and that would soon be up to her chin. It came really but from the air of her friend, from the perfect benevolence and high unconsciousness with which he kept his posture – as if to show he could patronise her from below upward quite as well as from above down. And as she took it all in, as it spread to a flood, with the great lumps and masses of truth it was floating, she knew inevitable submission, not to say submersion, as she had never known it in her life; going down and down before it, not even putting out her hands to resist or cling by the way, only reading into the young man's very face an immense fatality and, for all his bright nobleness, his absence of rancour or of protesting pride, the great grey blankness of her doom. It was as if the earnest Miss Lindeck, tall and mild, high and lean, with eye-glasses and a big nose, but 'marked' in a noticeable way, elegant and distinguished and refined, as you could see from a mile off, and as graceful, for common despair of imitation, as the curves of the 'copy' set of old by one's writing-master – it was as if this stately well-wisher, whom indeed she had never exchanged a word with, but whom she had recognised and placed and winced at as soon as he spoke of her, figured there beside him now as also in portentous charge of her case.

He had ushered her into it in that way, as if his mere right word sufficed; and Julia could see them throned together, beautifully at one in all the interests they now shared, and regard her as an object of almost tender solicitude. It was positively as if they had become engaged for her good – in such a happy light as it shed. That was the way people you had known, known a bit intimately, looked at you as soon as they took on the high matrimonial propriety that sponged over the more or less wild past to which you belonged and of which, all of a sudden, they were aware only through some suggestion it made them for reminding you definitely that you still had a place. On her having had a day or two before to meet Mrs Drack and to rise to her expectation she had seen and felt herself act, had above all admired herself, and had at any rate known what she said, even though losing, at her altitude, any distinctness in the others. She could have repeated afterwards the detail of her performance – if she hadn't preferred to keep it with her as a mere locked-up, a mere unhandled treasure. At present, however, as everything was for her at first deadened and vague, true to the general effect of sounds and motions in water, she couldn't have said afterwards what words she spoke, what face she showed, what impression she made – at least till she had pulled herself round to precautions. She only knew she had turned away, and that this movement must have sooner or later determined his rising to join her, his deciding to accept it, gracefully and condoningly – condoningly in respect to her natural emotion, her inevitable little pang – for an intimation that they would be better on their feet.

They trod then afresh their ancient paths; and though it pressed upon her hatefully that he must have taken her abruptness for a smothered shock, the flare-up of her old feeling at the breath of his news, she had still to see herself condemned to allow him this, condemned really to encourage him in the mistake of believing her suspicious of feminine spite and doubtful of Miss Lindeck's zeal. She was so far from doubtful that she was but too appalled at it and at the officious mass in which it loomed, and this instinct of dread, before their walk was over, before she had guided him round to one of the smaller gates, there to slip off again by herself, was positively to find on the bosom of her flood a plank under aid of which she kept in a manner and for the time afloat. She took ten minutes to pant, to blow gently, to paddle disguisedly, to accommodate herself, in a word, to the elements she had let loose; but as a reward of her effort at least she then saw how her determined vision accounted for everything. Beside her friend on the bench she had truly felt all his cables cut, truly swallowed down the fact that if he still perceived she was pretty – and *how* pretty! – it had ceased appreciably to matter to him. It had lighted the folly of her preliminary fear, the fear of his even yet, to some effect of confusion or other inconvenience for her, proving more alive to the quoteable in her, as she had called it, than to the inexpressible. She had reckoned with the awkwardness of that possible lapse of his measure of her charm, by which his renewed apprehension of her grosser ornaments, those with which he had most affinity, might too much profit; but she need have concerned herself as little for his sensibility on one head as on the other. She had ceased personally, ceased materially – in respect, as who should say, to any optical or tactile advantage – to exist for him, and the whole office of his manner had been the more piously and gallantly to dress the dead presence with flowers. This was all to his credit and his honour, but what it clearly certified was that their case was at last not even one of spirit reaching out to spirit. *He* had plenty of spirit – had all the spirit required for his having engaged himself to Miss Lindeck; into which result, once she had got her head well up again, she read, as they proceeded, one sharp meaning after another. It was therefore toward the subtler essence of that mature young woman alone that he was occupied in stretching; what was definite to him about Julia Bride being merely, being entirely – which was indeed thereby quite enough – that she *might* end by scaling her worldly height. They would push, they would shove, they would 'boost,' they would arch both their straight backs as pedestals for her tiptoe; and at the same time, by some sweet prodigy of mechanics, she would pull them up and up with her.

Wondrous things hovered before her in the course of this walk; her consciousness had become, by an extraordinary turn, a music-box in which, its lid well down, the most remarkable tunes were sounding. It played for her ear alone, and the lid, as she might have figured, was her firm plan of holding out till she got home, of not betraying – to her companion at least – the extent to which she was demoralised. To see him think her demoralised by mistrust of the sincerity of the service to be meddlesomely rendered her by his future wife – she would have hurled herself publicly into the lake there at their side, would have splashed, in her beautiful clothes, among the frightened swans, rather than invite him to that ineptitude. Oh her sincerity, Mary Lindeck's – she would be drenched with her sincerity, and she would be drenched, yes, with *his*; so that, from inward convulsion to convulsion, she had, before they reached their gate, pulled up in the path. There was something her head had been full of these three or four minutes, the intensest little tune of the music-box, and it had made its way to her lips now; belonging – for all the good it could do her! – to the two or three sorts of solicitude she might properly express.

'I hope *she* has a fortune, if you don't mind my speaking of it: I mean some of the money we didn't in *our* time have – and that we missed, after all, in our poor way and for what we then wanted of it, so quite dreadfully.'

She had been able to wreathe it in a grace quite equal to any he himself had employed; and it was to be said for him also that he kept up, on this, the standard. 'Oh she's not, thank goodness, at all badly off, poor dear. We shall do very well. How sweet of you to have thought of it! May I tell her that too?' he splendidly glared. Yes, he glared – how couldn't he, with what his mind was really full of? But, all the same, he came just here, by her vision, nearer than at any other point to being a gentleman. He came quite within an ace of it – with his taking from her thus the prescription of humility of service, his consenting to act in the interest of her avidity, his letting her mount that way, on his bowed shoulders, to the success in which he could suppose she still believed. He couldn't know, he would never know, that she had then and there ceased to believe in it – that she saw as clear as the sun in the sky the exact manner in which, between them, before they had done, the Murray Brushes, all zeal and sincerity, all interest in her interesting case, would dish, would ruin, would utterly destroy her. He wouldn't have needed to go on, for the force and truth of this; but he did go on – he was as crashingly consistent as a motor-car without a brake. He was visibly in love with the idea of what they might do for her and of the rare 'social' opportunity that they would, by the same stroke, embrace. How he had been offhand with it, how he had made it parenthetic, that he didn't happen 'personally' to know Basil French – as if it would have been at all likely he *should* know him, even im*personally*, and as if he could conceal from her the fact that, since she had made him her overture, this gentleman's name supremely baited her hook! Oh they would help Julia Bride if they could – they would do their remarkable best; but they would at any rate have made his acquaintance over it, and she might indeed leave the rest to their thoroughness. He would already have known, he would already have heard; her appeal, she was more and more sure, wouldn't have come to him as a revelation. He had already talked it over with *her*, with Miss Lindeck, to whom the Frenches, in their fortress, had never been accessible, and his whole attitude bristled, to Julia's eyes, with the betrayal of her hand, her voice, her pressure, her calculation. His tone in fact, as he talked, fairly thrust these things into her face. 'But you must see her for yourself. You'll judge her. You'll love her. My dear child' – he brought it all out, and if he spoke of children he might, in his candour, have been himself infantine – 'my dear child, she's the person to do it for you. Make it over to her; but,' he laughed, 'of course see her first! Couldn't you,' he wound up – for they were now near their gate, where she was to leave him – 'couldn't you just simply make us meet him, at tea, say, informally; just *us* alone, as pleasant old friends of whom you'd have so naturally and frankly spoken to him; and then see what we'd *make* of that?'

It was all in his expression; he couldn't keep it undetected, and his shining good looks couldn't: ah he was so fatally much too handsome for her! So the gap showed just there, in his admirable mask and his admirable eagerness; the yawning little chasm showed where the gentleman fell short. But she took this in, she took everything in, she felt herself do it, she heard herself say, while they paused before separation, that she quite saw the point of the meeting, as he suggested, at her tea. She would propose it to Mr French and would let them know; and he must assuredly bring Miss Lindeck, bring her 'right away,' bring her soon, bring *them*, his fiancée and her, together somehow, and as quickly as possible – so that they *should* be old friends before the tea. She would propose it to Mr French, propose it to Mr French: that hummed in her ears as she went – after she had really got away; hummed as if she were repeating it over, giving it out to the passers, to the pavement, to the sky, and all as in wild discord with the intense little concert of her music-box. The extraordinary thing too was that she quite believed she should do it, and fully meant to; desperately, fantastically passive – since she almost reeled with it as she proceeded – she was capable of proposing anything to any one: capable too of thinking it likely Mr French would come, for he had never on her previous proposals declined anything. Yes, she would keep it up to the end, this pretence of owing them salvation, and might even live to take comfort in having done for them what they wanted. What they wanted *couldn't* but be to get at the Frenches, and what Miss Lindeck above all wanted, baffled of it otherwise, with so many others of the baffled, was to get at Mr French – for all Mr French would want of either of them! – still more than

Murray did. It wasn't till after she had got home, got straight into her own room and flung herself on her face, that she yielded to the full taste of the bitterness of missing a connexion, missing the man himself, with power to create such a social appetite, such a grab at what might be gained by them. He could make people, even people like these two and whom there were still other people to envy, he could make them push and snatch and scramble like that – and then remain as incapable of taking her from the hands of such patrons as of receiving her straight, say, from those of Mrs Drack. It was a high note, too, of Julia's wonderful composition that, even in the long lonely moan of her conviction of her now certain ruin, all this grim lucidity, the perfect clearance of passion, but made her supremely proud of him.

The Jolly Corner

I

'Every one asks me what I "think" of everything,' said Spencer Brydon; 'and I make answer as I can — begging or dodging the question, putting them off with any nonsense. It wouldn't matter to any of them really,' he went on, 'for, even were it possible to meet in that stand-and-deliver way so silly a demand on so big a subject, my "thoughts" would still be almost altogether about something that concerns only myself.' He was talking to Miss Staverton, with whom for a couple of months now he had availed himself of every possible occasion to talk; this disposition and this resource, this comfort and support, as the situation in fact presented itself, having promptly enough taken the first place in the considerable array of rather unattenuated surprises attending his so strangely belated return to America. Everything was somehow a surprise; and that might be natural when one had so long and so consistently neglected everything, taken pains to give surprises so much margin for play. He had given them more than thirty years — thirty-three, to be exact; and they now seemed to him to have organised their performance quite on the scale of that licence. He had been twenty-three on leaving New York — he was fifty-six to-day: unless indeed he were to reckon as he had sometimes, since his repatriation, found himself feeling; in which case he would have lived longer than is often allotted to man. It would have taken a century, he repeatedly said to himself, and said also to Alice Staverton, it would have taken a longer absence and a more averted mind than those even of which he had been guilty, to pile up the differences, the newnesses, the queernesses, above all the bignesses, for the better or the worse, that at present assaulted his vision wherever he looked.

The great fact all the while however had been the incalculability; since he *had* supposed himself, from decade to decade, to be allowing, and in the most liberal and intelligent manner, for brilliancy of change. He actually saw that he had allowed for nothing; he missed what he would have been sure of finding, he found what he would never have imagined. Proportions and values were upside-down; the ugly things he had expected, the ugly things of his far-away youth, when he had too promptly waked up to a sense of the ugly — these uncanny phenomena placed him rather, as it happened, under the charm; whereas the 'swagger' things, the modern, the monstrous, the famous things, those he had more particularly, like thousands of ingenuous enquirers every year, come over to see, were exactly his sources of dismay. They were as so many set traps for displeasure, above all for reaction, of which his restless tread was constantly pressing the spring. It was interesting, doubtless, the whole show, but it would have been too disconcerting hadn't a certain finer truth saved the situation. He had distinctly not, in this steadier light, come over *all* for the monstrosities; he had come, not only in the last analysis but quite on the face of the act, under an impulse with which they had nothing to do. He had come – putting the thing pompously – to look at his 'property,' which he had thus for a third of a century not been within four thousand miles of; or, expressing it less sordidly, he had yielded to the humour of seeing again his house on the jolly corner, as he usually, and quite fondly, described it – the one in which he had first seen the light, in which various members of his family had lived and had died, in which the holidays of his overschooled boyhood had been passed and the few social flowers of his chilled adolescence gathered, and which, alienated then for so long a period, had, through the successive deaths of his two brothers and the termination of old arrangements, come wholly into his hands. He was the owner of another, not quite so 'good' – the jolly corner having been, from far back, superlatively extended and conse-crated; and the value of the pair represented his main capital, with an income consisting, in these later years, of their respective rents which (thanks precisely to their original excellent type) had never been depressingly low. He could live in 'Europe,' as he had been in the habit of living, on the product of these flourishing New York leases, and all the better since, that of the second structure, the mere number in its long row, having within a twelvemonth fallen in, renovation at a high advance had proved beautifully possible.

These were items of property indeed, but he had found himself since his arrival distinguishing more than ever between them. The house within the street, two bristling blocks westward, was already in course of reconstruction as a tall mass of flats; he had acceded, some time before, to overtures for this conversion – in which, now that it was going forward, it had been not the least of his astonish-ments to find himself able, on the spot, and though without a previous ounce of such experience, to participate with a certain intelligence, almost with a certain authority. He had lived his life with his back so turned to such concerns and his face addressed to those of so different an order that he scarce knew what to make of this lively stir, in a compartment of his mind never yet penetrated, of a capacity for business and a sense for construction. These virtues, so common all round him now, had been dormant in his own organism – where it might be said of them perhaps that they had slept the sleep of the just. At present, in the splendid autumn weather – the autumn at least was a pure boon in the terrible place – he loafed about his 'work' undeterred, secretly agitated; not in the least 'minding' that the whole proposition, as they said, was vulgar and sordid, and ready to climb ladders, to walk the plank, to handle materials and look wise about them, to ask questions, in fine, and challenge explanations and really 'go into' figures.

It amused, it verily quite charmed him; and, by the same stroke, it amused, and even more, Alice Staverton, though perhaps charming her perceptibly less. She wasn't however going to be better-off for it, as *he* was – and so astonishingly much: nothing was now likely, he knew, ever to make her better-off than she found herself, in the afternoon of life, as the delicately frugal possessor and tenant of the small house in Irving Place[1] to which she had subtly managed to cling through her almost unbroken New York career. If he knew the way to it now better than to any other address among the dreadful multiplied numberings which seemed to him to reduce the whole place to some vast ledger-page, overgrown, fantastic, of ruled and criss-crossed lines and figures – if he had formed, for his consolation, that habit, it was really not a little because of the charm of his having encountered and recognised, in the vast wilderness of the wholesale, breaking through the mere gross generalisation of wealth and force and success, a small still scene where items and shades, all delicate things, kept the sharpness of the notes of a high voice perfectly trained, and where economy hung about like the scent of a garden. His old friend lived with one maid and herself dusted her relics and trimmed her lamps and polished her silver; she stood off, in the awful modern crush, when she could, but she sallied forth and did battle when the challenge was really to 'spirit,' the spirit she after all confessed to, proudly and a little shyly, as to that of the better time, that of *their* common, their quite far-away and antediluvian social period and order. She made use of the street-cars when need be, the terrible things that people scrambled for as the panic-stricken at sea scramble for the boats; she affronted, inscrutably, under stress, all the public concussions and ordeals; and yet, with that slim mystifying grace of her appearance, which defied you to say if she were a fair young woman who looked older through trouble, or a fine smooth older one who looked young through successful indifference; with her precious reference, above all, to memories and histories into which he could enter, she was as exquisite for him as some pale pressed flower (a rarity to begin with), and, failing other sweetnesses, she was a sufficient reward of his effort. They had communities of knowledge, 'their' knowledge (this discriminating possessive was always on her lips) of presences of the other age, presences all overlaid, in his case, by the experience of a man and the freedom of a wanderer, overlaid by pleasure, by infidelity, by passages of life that were strange and dim to her, just by 'Europe' in short, but still unobscured, still exposed and cherished, under that pious visitation of the spirit from which she had never been diverted.

She had come with him one day to see how his 'apartment-house' was rising; he had helped her over gaps and explained to her plans, and while they were there had happened to have, before her, a brief but lively discussion with the man in charge, the representative of the building-firm that had undertaken his work. He had found himself quite 'standing-up' to this personage over a failure on the latter's part to observe some detail of one of their noted conditions, and had so lucidly argued his case that, besides ever so prettily flushing, at the time, for sympathy in his triumph, she had afterwards said to him (though to a slightly greater effect of irony) that he had clearly for too many years neglected a real gift. If he had but stayed at home he would have anticipated the inventor of the sky-scraper.[2] If he had but stayed at home he would have discovered his genius in time really to start some new variety of awful architectural hare and run it till it burrowed in a goldmine. He was to remember these words, while the weeks elapsed, for the small silver ring they had sounded over the queerest and deepest of his own lately most disguised and most muffled vibrations.

It had begun to be present to him after the first fortnight, it had broken out with the oddest abruptness, this particular wanton wonderment: it met him there – and this was the image under which he himself judged the matter, or at least, not a little, thrilled and flushed with it – very much as he might have been met by some strange figure, some unexpected occupant, at a turn of one of the dim passages of an empty house. The quaint analogy quite hauntingly remained with him, when he didn't indeed rather improve it by a still intenser form: that of his opening a door behind which he would have made sure of finding nothing, a door into a room shuttered and void, and yet so coming, with a great suppressed start, on some quite erect confronting presence, something planted in the middle of the place and facing him through the dusk. After that visit to the house in construction he walked with his companion to see the other and always so much the better one, which in the eastward direction formed one of the corners, the 'jolly' one precisely, of the street now so generally dishonoured and disfigured in its westward reaches, and of the comparatively conservative Avenue. The Avenue still had pretensions, as Miss Staverton said, to decency; the old people had mostly gone, the old names were unknown, and here and there an old association seemed to stray, all vaguely, like some very aged person, out too late, whom you might meet and feel the impulse to watch or follow, in kindness, for safe restoration to shelter.

They went in together, our friends; he admitted himself with his key, as he kept no one there, he explained, preferring, for his reasons, to leave the place empty, under a simple arrangement with a good woman living in the neighbourhood and who came for a daily hour to open windows and dust and sweep. Spencer Brydon had his reasons and was growingly aware of them; they seemed to him better each time he was there, though he didn't name them all to his companion, any more than he told her as yet how often, how quite absurdly often, he himself came. He only let her see for the present, while they walked through the great blank rooms, that absolute vacancy reigned and that, from top to bottom, there was nothing but Mrs Muldoon's broomstick, in a corner, to tempt the burglar. Mrs Muldoon was then on the premises, and she loquaciously attended the visitors, preceding them from room to room and pushing back shutters and throwing up sashes — all to show them, as she remarked, how little there was to see. There was little indeed to see in the great gaunt shell where the main dispositions and the general apportionment of space, the style of an age of ampler allowances, had nevertheless for its master their honest pleading message, affecting him as some good old servant's, some lifelong retainer's appeal for a character, or even for a retiring-pension; yet it was also a remark of Mrs Muldoon's that, glad as she was to oblige him by her noonday round, there was a request she greatly hoped he would never make of her. If he should wish her for any reason to come in after dark she would just tell him, if he 'plased,' that he must ask it of somebody else.

The fact that there was nothing to see didn't militate for the worthy woman against what one *might* see, and she put it frankly to Miss Staverton that no lady could be expected to like, could she? 'craping up to thim top storeys in the ayvil hours.' The gas and the electric light were off the house, and she fairly evoked a gruesome vision of her march through the great grey rooms — so many of them as there were too! — with her glimmering taper. Miss Staverton met her honest glare with a smile and the profession that she herself certainly would recoil from such an adventure. Spencer Brydon meanwhile held his peace — for the moment; the question of the 'evil' hours in his old home had already become too grave for him. He had begun some time since to 'crape,' and he knew just why a packet of candles addressed to that pursuit had been stowed by his own hand, three weeks before, at the back of a drawer of the fine old sideboard that occupied, as a 'fixture,' the deep recess in the dining-room. Just now he laughed at his companions — quickly however changing the subject; for the reason that, in the first place, his laugh struck him even at that moment as starting the odd echo, the conscious human resonance (he scarce knew how to qualify it) that sounds made while he was there alone sent back to his ear or his fancy; and that, in the second, he imagined Alice Staverton for the instant on the point of asking him, with a divination, if he ever so prowled. There were divinations he was unprepared for, and he had at all events averted enquiry by the time Mrs Muldoon had left them, passing on to other parts.

There was happily enough to say, on so consecrated a spot, that could be said freely and fairly; so that a whole train of declarations was precipitated by his friend's having herself broken out, after a yearning look round: 'But I hope you don't mean they want you to pull *this* to pieces!' His answer came, promptly, with his re-awakened wrath: it was of course exactly what they wanted, and what they were 'at' him for, daily, with the iteration of people who couldn't for their life understand a man's liability to decent feelings. He had found the place, just as it stood and beyond what he could express, an interest and a joy. There were values other than the beastly rent-values, and in short, in short —! But it was thus Miss Staverton took him up. 'In short you're to make so good a thing of your sky-scraper that, living in luxury on *those* ill-gotten gains, you can afford for a while to be sentimental here!' Her smile had for him, with the words, the particular mild irony with which he found half her talk suffused; an irony without bitterness and that came, exactly, from her having so much imagination — not, like the cheap sarcasms with which one heard most people, about the world of 'society,' bid for the reputation of cleverness, from nobody's really having any. It was agreeable to him at this very moment to be sure that when he had answered, after a brief demur, 'Well yes: so, precisely, you may put it!' her imagination would still do him justice. He explained that even if never a dollar were to come to him from the other house he would nevertheless cherish this one; and he dwelt, further, while they lingered and wandered, on the fact of the stupefaction he was already exciting, the positive mystification he felt himself create.

He spoke of the value of all he read into it, into the mere sight of the walls, mere shapes of the rooms, mere sound of the floors, mere feel, in his hand, of the old silver-plated knobs of the several mahogany doors, which suggested the pressure of the palms of the dead; the seventy years of the past in fine that these things represented, the annals of nearly three generations, counting his grandfather's, the one that had ended there, and the impalpable ashes of his long-extinct youth, afloat in the very air like microscopic motes. She listened to everything; she was a woman who answered intimately but who utterly didn't chatter. She scattered abroad therefore no cloud of words; she could assent, she could agree, above all she could encourage, without doing that. Only at the last she went a little further than he had done himself. 'And then how do you know? You may still, after all, want to live here.' It rather indeed pulled him up, for it wasn't what he had been thinking, at least in her sense of the words. 'You mean I may decide to stay on for the sake of it?'

'Well, *with* such a home —!' But, quite beautifully, she had too much tact to dot so monstrous an *i*, and it was precisely an illustration of the way she didn't rattle. How could any one — of any wit — insist on any one else's 'wanting' to live in New York?

'Oh,' he said, 'I *might* have lived here (since I had my opportunity early in life); I might have put in here all these years. Then everything would have been different enough – and, I dare say, "funny" enough. But that's another matter. And then the beauty of it – I mean of my perversity, of my refusal to agree to a "deal" – is just in the total absence of a reason. Don't you see that if I had a reason about the matter at all it would *have* to be the other way, and would then be inevitably a reason of dollars? There are no reasons here *but* of dollars. Let us therefore have none whatever – not the ghost of one.'

They were back in the hall then for departure, but from where they stood the vista was large, through an open door, into the great square main saloon, with its almost antique felicity of brave spaces between windows. Her eyes came back from that reach and met his own a moment. 'Are you very sure the "ghost" of one doesn't, much rather, serve –?'

He had a positive sense of turning pale. But it was as near as they were then to come. For he made answer, he believed, between a glare and a grin: 'Oh ghosts – of course the place must swarm with them! I should be ashamed of it if it didn't. Poor Mrs Muldoon's right, and it's why I haven't asked her to do more than look in.'

Miss Staverton's gaze again lost itself, and things she didn't utter, it was clear, came and went in her mind. She might even for the minute, off there in the fine room, have imagined some element dimly gathering. Simplified like the death-mask of a handsome face, it perhaps produced for her just then an effect akin to the stir of an expression in the 'set' commemorative plaster. Yet whatever her impression may have been she produced instead a vague platitude. 'Well, if it were only furnished and lived in –!'

She appeared to imply that in case of its being still furnished he might have been a little less opposed to the idea of a return. But she passed straight into the vestibule, as if to leave her words behind her, and the next moment he had opened the house-door and was standing with her on the steps. He closed the door and, while he re-pocketed his key, looking up and down, they took in the comparatively harsh actuality of the Avenue, which reminded him of the assault of the outer light of the Desert on the traveller emerging from an Egyptian tomb. But he risked before they stepped into the street his gathered answer to her speech. 'For me it *is* lived in. For me it *is* furnished.' At which it was easy for her to sigh 'Ah yes –!' all vaguely and discreetly; since his parents and his favourite sister, to say nothing of other kin, in numbers, had run their course and met their end there. That represented, within the walls, ineffaceable life.

It was a few days after this that, during an hour passed with her again, he had expressed his impatience of the too flattering curiosity – among the people he met – about his appreciation of New York. He had arrived at none at all that was socially producible, and as for that matter of his 'thinking' (thinking the better or the worse of anything there) he was wholly taken up with one subject of thought. It was mere vain egoism, and it was moreover, if she liked, a morbid obsession. He found all things come back to the question of what he personally might have been, how he might have led his life and 'turned out,' if he had not so, at the outset, given it up. And confessing for the first time to the intensity within him of this absurd speculation – which but proved also, no doubt, the habit of too selfishly thinking – he affirmed the impotence there of any other source of interest, any other native appeal. 'What would it have made of me, what would it have made of me? I keep for ever wondering, all idiotically; as if I could possibly know! I see what it has made of dozens of others, those I meet, and it positively aches within me, to the point of exasperation, that it would have made something of me as well. Only I can't make out *what*, and the worry of it, the small rage of curiosity never to be satisfied, brings back what I remember to have felt, once or twice, after judging best, for reasons, to burn some important letter unopened. I've been sorry, I've hated it – I've never known what was in the letter. You may of course say it's a trifle –!'

'I don't say it's a trifle,' Miss Staverton gravely interrupted.

She was seated by her fire, and before her, on his feet and restless, he turned to and fro between this intensity of his idea and a fitful and unseeing inspection, through his single eye-glass, of the dear little old objects on her chimney-piece. Her interruption made him for an instant look at her harder. 'I shouldn't care if you did!' he laughed, however; 'and it's only a figure, at any rate, for the way I now feel. *Not* to have followed my perverse young course – and almost in the teeth of my father's curse, as I may say; not to have kept it up, so, "over there," from that day to this, without a doubt or a pang; not, above all, to have liked it, to have loved it, so much, loved it, no doubt, with such an abysmal conceit of my own preference: some variation from *that*, I say, must have produced some different effect for my life and for my "form." I should have stuck here – if it had been possible; and I was too young, at twenty-three, to judge, *pour deux sous*,[3] whether it *were* possible. If I had waited I might have seen it was, and then I might have been, by staying here, something nearer to one of these types who have been hammered so hard and made so keen by their conditions. It isn't that I admire them so much – the question of any charm in them, or of any charm, beyond that of the rank money-passion, exerted by their conditions *for* them, has nothing to do with the matter: it's only a question of what fantastic, yet perfectly possible, development of my own nature I mayn't have missed. It comes over me that I had then a strange *alter ego* deep down somewhere within me, as the full-blown flower is in the small tight bud, and that I just took the course, I just transferred him to the climate, that blighted him for once and for ever.'

'And you wonder about the flower,' Miss Staverton said. 'So do I, if you want to know; and so I've been wondering these several weeks. I believe in the flower,' she continued, 'I feel it would have been quite splendid, quite huge and monstrous.'

'Monstrous above all!' her visitor echoed; 'and I imagine, by the same stroke, quite hideous and offensive.'

'You don't believe that,' she returned; 'if you did you wouldn't wonder. You'd know, and that would be enough for you. What you feel – and what I feel *for* you – is that you'd have had power.'

'You'd have liked me that way?' he asked.

She barely hung fire. 'How should I not have liked you?'

'I see. You'd have liked me, have preferred me, a billionaire!'

'How should I not have liked you?' she simply again asked.

He stood before her still – her question kept him motionless. He took it in, so much there was of it; and indeed his not otherwise meeting it testified to that. 'I know at least what I am,' he simply went on; 'the other side of the medal's clear enough. I've not been edifying – I believe I'm thought in a hundred quarters to have been barely decent. I've followed strange paths and worshipped strange gods; it must have come to you again and again – in fact you've admitted to me as much – that I was leading, at any time these thirty years, a selfish frivolous scandalous life. And you see what it has made of me.'

She just waited, smiling at him. 'You see what it has made of *me*.'

'Oh you're a person whom nothing can have altered. You were born to be what you are, anywhere, anyway: you've the perfection nothing else could have blighted. And don't you see how, without my exile, I shouldn't have been waiting till now –?' But he pulled up for the strange pang.

'The great thing to see,' she presently said, 'seems to me to be that it has spoiled nothing. It hasn't spoiled your being here at last. It hasn't spoiled this. It hasn't spoiled your speaking – ' She also however faltered.

He wondered at everything her controlled emotion might mean. 'Do you believe then – too dreadfully! – that I *am* as good as I might ever have been?'

'Oh no! Far from it!' With which she got up from her chair and was nearer to him. 'But I don't care,' she smiled.

'You mean I'm good enough?'

She considered a little. 'Will you believe it if I say so? I mean will you let that settle your question for you?' And then as if making out in his face that he drew back from this, that he had some idea which, however absurd, he couldn't yet bargain away: 'Oh you don't care either – but very differently: you don't care for anything but yourself.'

Spencer Brydon recognised it – it was in fact what he had absolutely professed.

Yet he importantly qualified. '*He* isn't myself. He's the just so totally other person. But I do want to see him,' he added. 'And I can. And I shall.'

Their eyes met for a minute while he guessed from something in hers that she divined his strange sense. But neither of them otherwise expressed it, and her apparent understanding, with no protesting shock, no easy derision, touched him more deeply than anything yet, constituting for his stifled perversity, on the spot, an element that was like breathable air. What she said however was unexpected. 'Well, *I've* seen him.'

'You −?'

'I've seen him in a dream.'

'Oh a "dream" −!' It let him down.

'But twice over,' she continued. 'I saw him as I see you now.'

'You've dreamed the same dream −?'

'Twice over,' she repeated. 'The very same.'

This did somehow a little speak to him, as it also gratified him. 'You dream about me at that rate?'

'Ah about *him*!' she smiled.

His eyes again sounded her. 'Then you know all about him.' And as she said nothing more: 'What's the wretch like?'

She hesitated, and it was as if he were pressing her so hard that, resisting for reasons of her own, she had to turn away. 'I'll tell you some other time!'

II

It was after this that there was most of a virtue for him, most of a cultivated charm, most of a preposterous secret thrill, in the particular form of surrender to his obsession and of address to what he more and more believed to be his privilege. It was what in these weeks he was living for − since he really felt life to begin but after Mrs Muldoon had retired from the scene and, visiting the ample house from attic to cellar, making sure he was alone, he knew himself in safe possession and, as he tacitly expressed it, let himself go. He sometimes came twice in the twenty-four hours; the moments he liked best were those of gathering dusk, of the short autumn twilight; this was the time of which, again and again, he found himself hoping most. Then he could, as seemed to him, most intimately wander and wait, linger and listen, feel his fine attention, never in his life before so fine, on the pulse of the great vague place: he preferred the lampless hour and only wished he might have prolonged each day the deep crepuscular spell. Later − rarely much before midnight, but then for a considerable vigil − he watched with his glimmering light; moving slowly, holding it high, playing it far, rejoicing above all, as much as he might, in open vistas, reaches of communication between rooms and by passages; the long straight chance or show, as he would have called it, for the revelation he pretended to invite. It was a practice he found he could perfectly 'work' without exciting remark; no one was in the least the wiser for it; even Alice Staverton, who was moreover a well of discretion, didn't quite fully imagine.

He let himself in and let himself out with the assurance of calm proprietorship; and accident so far favoured him that, if a fat Avenue 'officer' had happened on occasion to see him entering at eleven-thirty, he had never yet, to the best of his belief, been noticed as emerging at two. He walked there on the crisp November nights, arrived regularly at the evening's end; it was as easy to do this after dining out as to take his way to a club or to his hotel. When he left his club, if he hadn't been dining out, it was ostensibly to go to his hotel; and when he left his hotel, if he had spent a part of the evening there, it was ostensibly to go to his club. Everything was easy in fine; everything conspired and promoted: there was truly even in the strain of his experience something that glossed over, something that salved and simplified, all the rest of consciousness. He circulated, talked, renewed, loosely and pleasantly, old relations – met indeed, so far as he could, new expectations and seemed to make out on the whole that in spite of the career, of such different contacts, which he had spoken of to Miss Staverton as ministering so little, for those who might have watched it, to edification, he was positively rather liked than not. He was a dim secondary social success – and all with people who had truly not an idea of him. It was all mere surface sound, this murmur of their welcome, this popping of their corks – just as his gestures of response were the extravagant shadows, emphatic in proportion as they meant little, of some game of *ombres chinoises*.[4] He projected himself all day, in thought, straight over the bristling line of hard unconscious heads and into the other, the real, the waiting life; the life that, as soon as he had heard behind him the click of his great house-door, began for him, on the jolly corner, as beguilingly as the slow opening bars of some rich music follows the tap of the conductor's wand.

He always caught the first effect of the steel point of his stick on the old marble of the hall pavement, large black-and-white squares that he remembered as the admiration of his childhood and that had then made in him, as he now saw, for the growth of an early conception of style. This effect was the dim reverberating tinkle as of some far-off bell hung who should say where? – in the depths of the house, of the past, of that mystical other world that might have flourished for him had he not, for weal or woe, abandoned it. On this impression he did ever the same thing; he put his stick noiselessly away in a corner – feeling the place once more in the likeness of some great glass bowl, all precious concave crystal, set delicately humming by the play of a moist finger round its edge. The concave crystal held, as it were, this mystical other world, and the indescribably fine murmur of its rim was the sigh there, the scarce audible pathetic wail to his strained ear, of all the old baffled forsworn possibilities. What he did therefore by this appeal of his hushed presence was to wake them into such measure of ghostly life as they might still enjoy. They were shy, all but unappeasably shy, but they weren't really sinister; at least they weren't as he had hitherto felt them – before they had taken the Form he so yearned to make them take, the Form he at moments saw himself in the light of fairly hunting on tiptoe, the points of his evening-shoes, from room to room and from storey to storey.

That was the essence of his vision – which was all rank folly, if one would, while he was out of the house and otherwise occupied, but which took on the last verisimilitude as soon as he was placed and posted. He knew what he meant and what he wanted; it was as clear as the figure on a cheque presented in demand for cash. His *alter ego* 'walked' – that was the note of his image of him, while his image of his motive for his own odd pastime was the desire to waylay him and meet him. He roamed, slowly, warily, but all restlessly, he himself did – Mrs Muldoon had been right, absolutely, with her figure of their 'craping'; and the presence he watched for would roam restlessly too. But it would be as cautious and as shifty; the conviction of its probable, in fact its already quite sensible, quite audible evasion of pursuit grew for him from night to night, laying on him finally a rigour to which nothing in his life had been comparable. It had been the theory of many superficially-judging persons, he knew, that he was wasting that life in a surrender to sensations, but he had tasted of no pleasure so fine as his actual tension, had been introduced to no sport that demanded at once the patience and the nerve of this stalking of a creature more subtle, yet at bay perhaps more formidable, than any beast of the forest. The terms, the comparisons, the very practices of the chase positively came again into play; there were even moments when passages of his occasional experience as a sportsman, stirred memories, from his younger time, of moor and mountain and desert, revived for him – and to the increase of his keenness – by the tremendous force of analogy. He found himself at moments – once he had placed his single light on some mantel-shelf or in some recess – stepping back into shelter or shade, effacing himself behind a door or in an embrasure, as he had sought of old the vantage of rock and tree; he found himself holding his breath and living in the joy of the instant, the supreme suspense created by big game alone.

He wasn't afraid (though putting himself the question as he believed gentlemen on Bengal tiger-shoots or in close quarters with the great bear of the Rockies had been known to confess to having put it); and this indeed – since here at least he might be frank! – because of the impression, so intimate and so strange, that he himself produced as yet a dread, produced certainly a strain, beyond the liveliest he was likely to feel. They fell for him into categories, they fairly became familiar, the signs, for his own perception, of the alarm his presence and his vigilance created; though leaving him always to remark, portentously, on his probably having formed a relation, his probably enjoying a consciousness, unique in the experience of man. People enough, first and last, had been in terror of apparitions, but who had ever before so turned the tables and become himself, in the apparitional world, an incalculable terror? He might have found this sublime had he quite dared to think of it; but he didn't too much insist, truly, on that side of his privilege. With habit and repetition he gained to an extraordinary degree the power to penetrate the dusk of distances and the darkness of corners, to resolve back into their innocence the treacheries of uncertain light, the evil-looking forms taken in the gloom by mere shadows, by accidents of the air, by shifting effects of perspective; putting down his dim luminary he could still wander on without it, pass into other rooms and, only knowing it was there behind him in case of need, see his way about, visually project for his purpose a comparative clearness. It made him feel, this acquired faculty, like some monstrous stealthy cat; he wondered if he would have glared at these moments with large shining yellow eyes, and what it mightn't verily be, for the poor hard-pressed *alter ego*, to be confronted with such a type.

He liked however the open shutters; he opened everywhere those Mrs Muldoon had closed, closing them as carefully afterwards, so that she shouldn't notice: he liked – oh this he did like, and above all in the upper rooms! – the sense of the hard silver of the autumn stars through the window-panes, and scarcely less the flare of the street-lamps below, the white electric lustre which it would have taken curtains to keep out. This was human actual social; this was of the world he had lived in, and he was more at his ease certainly for the countenance, coldly general and impersonal, that all the while and in spite of his detachment it seemed to give him. He had support of course mostly in the rooms at the wide front and the prolonged side; it failed him considerably in the central shades and the parts at the back. But if he sometimes, on his rounds, was glad of his optical reach, so none the less often the rear of the house affected him as the very jungle of his prey. The place was there more subdivided; a large 'extension' in particular, where small rooms for servants had been multiplied, abounded in nooks and corners, in closets and passages, in the ramifications especially of an ample back staircase over which he leaned, many a time, to look far down – not deterred from his gravity even while aware that he might, for a spectator, have figured some solemn simpleton playing at hide-and-seek. Outside in fact he might himself make that ironic *rapprochement*; but within the walls, and in spite of the clear windows, his consistency was proof against the cynical light of New York.

It had belonged to that idea of the exasperated consciousness of his victim to become a real test for him; since he had quite put it to himself from the first that, oh distinctly! he could 'cultivate' his whole perception. He had felt it as above all open to cultivation — which indeed was but another name for his manner of spending his time. He was bringing it on, bringing it to perfection, by practice; in consequence of which it had grown so fine that he was now aware of impressions, attestations of his general postulate, that couldn't have broken upon him at once. This was the case more specifically with a phenomenon at last quite frequent for him in the upper rooms, the recognition — absolutely unmistakeable, and by a turn dating from a particular hour, his resumption of his campaign after a diplomatic drop, a calculated absence of three nights — of his being definitely followed, tracked at a distance carefully taken and to the express end that he should the less confidently, less arrogantly, appear to himself merely to pursue. It worried, it finally quite broke him up, for it proved, of all the conceivable impressions, the one least suited to his book. He was kept in sight while remaining himself — as regards the essence of his position — sightless, and his only recourse then was in abrupt turns, rapid recoveries of ground. He wheeled about, retracing his steps, as if he might so catch in his face at least the stirred air of some other quick revolution. It was indeed true that his fully dislocalised thought of these manoeuvres recalled to him Pantaloon, at the Christmas farce, buffeted and tricked from behind by ubiquitous Harlequin;[5] but it left intact the influence of the conditions themselves each time he was re-exposed to them, so that in fact this association, had he suffered it to become constant, would on a certain side have but ministered to his intenser gravity. He had made, as I have said, to create on the premises the baseless sense of a reprieve, his three absences; and the result of the third was to confirm the after-effect of the second.

On his return, that night — the night succeeding his last intermission — he stood in the hall and looked up the staircase with a certainty more intimate than any he had yet known. 'He's *there*, at the top, and waiting — not, as in general, falling back for disappearance. He's holding his ground, and it's the first time — which is a proof, isn't it? that something has happened for him.' So Brydon argued with his hand on the banister and his foot on the lowest stair; in which position he felt as never before the air chilled by his logic. He himself turned cold in it, for he seemed of a sudden to know what now was involved. 'Harder pressed? — yes, he takes it in, with its thus making clear to him that I've come, as they say, "to stay." He finally doesn't like and can't bear it, in the sense, I mean, that his wrath, his menaced interest, now balances with his dread. I've hunted him till he has "turned": that, up there, is what has happened — he's the fanged or the antlered animal brought at last to bay.' There came to him, as I say — but determined by an influence beyond my notation! — the acuteness of this certainty;

under which however the next moment he had broken into a sweat that he would as little have consented to attribute to fear as he would have dared immediately to act upon it for enterprise. It marked none the less a prodigious thrill, a thrill that represented sudden dismay, no doubt, but also represented, and with the selfsame throb, the strangest, the most joyous, possibly the next minute almost the proudest, duplication of consciousness.

'He has been dodging, retreating, hiding, but now, worked up to anger, he'll fight!' – this intense impression made a single mouthful, as it were, of terror and applause. But what was wondrous was that the applause, for the felt fact, was so eager, since, if it was his other self he was running to earth, this ineffable identity was thus in the last resort not unworthy of him. It bristled there – somewhere near at hand, however unseen still – as the hunted thing, even as the trodden worm of the adage[6] *must* at last bristle; and Brydon at this instant tasted probably of a sensation more complex than had ever before found itself consistent with sanity. It was as if it would have shamed him that a character so associated with his own should triumphantly succeed in just skulking, should to the end not risk the open; so that the drop of this danger was, on the spot, a great lift of the whole situation. Yet with another rare shift of the same subtlety he was already trying to measure by how much more he himself might now be in peril of fear; so rejoicing that he could, in another form, actively inspire that fear, and simultaneously quaking for the form in which he might passively know it.

The apprehension of knowing it must after a little have grown in him, and the strangest moment of his adventure perhaps, the most memorable or really most interesting, afterwards, of his crisis, was the lapse of certain instants of concentrated conscious *combat*, the sense of a need to hold on to something, even after the manner of a man slipping and slipping on some awful incline; the vivid impulse, above all, to move, to act, to charge, somehow and upon something – to show himself, in a word, that he wasn't afraid. The state of 'holding-on' was thus the state to which he was momentarily reduced; if there had been anything, in the great vacancy, to seize, he would presently have been aware of having clutched it as he might under a shock at home have clutched the nearest chair-back. He had been surprised at any rate – of this he *was* aware – into something unprecedented since his original appropriation of the place; he had closed his eyes, held them tight, for a long minute, as with that instinct of dismay and that terror of vision. When he opened them the room, the other contiguous rooms, extraordinarily, seemed lighter – so light, almost, that at first he took the change for day. He stood firm, however that might be, just where he had paused; his resistance had helped him – it was as if there were something he had tided over. He knew after a little what this was – it had been in the imminent danger of flight. He had stiffened his will against going; without this he would have made for the stairs, and it seemed to him that, still with his eyes closed, he would have descended them, would have known how, straight and swiftly, to the bottom.

Well, as he had held out, here he was – still at the top, among the more intricate upper rooms and with the gauntlet of the others, of all the rest of the house, still to run when it should be his time to go. He would go at his time – only at his time: didn't he go every night very much at the same hour? He took out his watch – there was light for that: it was scarcely a quarter past one, and he had never withdrawn so soon. He reached his lodgings for the most part at two – with his walk of a quarter of an hour. He would wait for the last quarter – he wouldn't stir till then; and he kept his watch there with his eyes on it, reflecting while he held it that this deliberate wait, a wait with an effort, which he recognised, would serve perfectly for the attestation he desired to make. It would prove his courage – unless indeed the latter might most be proved by his budging at last from his place. What he mainly felt now was that, since he hadn't originally scuttled, he had his dignities – which had never in his life seemed so many – all to preserve and to carry aloft. This was before him in truth as a physical image, an image almost worthy of an age of greater romance. That remark indeed glimmered for him only to glow the next instant with a finer light; since what age of romance, after all, could have matched either the state of his mind or, 'objectively,' as they said, the wonder of his situation? The only difference would have been that, brandishing his dignities over his head as in a parchment scroll, he might then – that is in the heroic time – have proceeded downstairs with a drawn sword in his other grasp.

At present, really, the light he had set down on the mantel of the next room would have to figure his sword; which utensil, in the course of a minute, he had taken the requisite number of steps to possess himself of. The door between the rooms was open, and from the second another door opened to a third. These rooms, as he remembered, gave all three upon a common corridor as well, but there was a fourth, beyond them, without issue save through the preceding. To have moved, to have heard his step again, was appreciably a help; though even in recognising this he lingered once more a little by the chimney-piece on which his light had rested. When he next moved, just hesitating where to turn, he found himself considering a circumstance that, after his first and comparatively vague apprehension of it, produced in him the start that often attends some pang of recollection, the violent shock of having ceased happily to forget. He had come into sight of the door in which the brief chain of communication ended and which he now surveyed from the nearer threshold, the one not directly facing it. Placed at some distance to the left of this point, it would have admitted him to the last room of the four, the room without other approach or egress, had it not, to his intimate conviction, been closed *since* his former visitation, the matter probably of a quarter of an hour before. He stared with all his eyes at the wonder of the fact, arrested again where he stood and again holding his breath while he sounded its sense. Surely it had been *subsequently* closed – that is it had been on his previous passage indubitably open!

He took it full in the face that something had happened between – that he couldn't not have noticed before (by which he meant on his original tour of all the rooms that evening) that such a barrier had exceptionally presented itself. He had indeed since that moment undergone an agitation so extraordinary that it might have muddled for him any earlier view; and he tried to convince himself that he might perhaps then have gone into the room and, inadvertently, automatically, on coming out, have drawn the door after him. The difficulty was that this exactly was what he never did; it was against his whole policy, as he might have said, the essence of which was to keep vistas clear. He had them from the first, as he was well aware, quite on the brain: the strange apparition, at the far end of one of them, of his baffled 'prey' (which had become by so sharp an irony so little the term now to apply!) was the form of success his imagination had most cherished, projecting into it always a refinement of beauty. He had known fifty times the start of perception that had afterwards dropped; had fifty times gasped to himself 'There!' under some fond brief hallucination. The house, as the case stood, admirably lent itself; he might wonder at the taste, the native architecture of the particular time, which could rejoice so in the multiplication of doors – the opposite extreme to the modern, the actual almost complete proscription of them; but it had fairly contributed to provoke this obsession of the presence encountered telescopically, as he might say, focussed and studied in diminishing perspective and as by a rest for the elbow.

It was with these considerations that his present attention was charged – they perfectly availed to make what he saw portentous. He *couldn't*, by any lapse, have blocked that aperture; and if he hadn't, if it was unthinkable, why what else was clear but that there had been another agent? Another agent? – he had been catching, as he felt, a moment back, the very breath of him; but when had he been so close as in this simple, this logical, this completely personal act? It was so logical, that is, that one might have *taken* it for personal; yet for what did Brydon take it, he asked himself, while, softly panting, he felt his eyes almost leave their sockets. Ah this time at last they *were*, the two, the opposed projections of him, in presence; and this time, as much as one would, the question of danger loomed. With it rose, as not before, the question of courage – for what he knew the blank face of the door to say to him was 'Show us how much you have!' It stared, it glared back at him with that challenge; it put to him the two alternatives: should he just push it open or not? Oh to have this consciousness was to *think* – and to think, Brydon knew, as he stood there, was, with the lapsing moments, not to have acted! Not to have acted – that was the misery and the pang – was even still not to act; was in fact *all* to feel the thing in another, in a new and terrible way. How long did he pause and how long did he debate? There was presently nothing to measure it; for his vibration had already changed – as just by the effect of its intensity. Shut up there, at bay, defiant, and with the prodigy of the thing palpably proveably *done*, thus giving notice like some stark signboard – under that accession of accent the situation itself had turned; and Brydon at last remarkably made up his mind on what it had turned to.

It had turned altogether to a different admonition; to a supreme hint, for him, of the value of Discretion! This slowly dawned, no doubt – for it could take its time; so perfectly, on his threshold, had he been stayed, so little as yet had he either advanced or retreated. It was the strangest of all things that now when, by his taking ten steps and applying his hand to a latch, or even his shoulder and his knee, if necessary, to a panel, all the hunger of his prime need might have been met, his high curiosity crowned, his unrest assuaged – it was amazing, but it was also exquisite and rare, that insistence should have, at a touch, quite dropped from him. Discretion – he jumped at that; and yet not, verily, at such a pitch, because it saved his nerves or his skin, but because, much more valuably, it saved the situation. When I say he 'jumped' at it I feel the consonance of this term with the fact that – at the end indeed of I know not how long – he did move again, he crossed straight to the door. He wouldn't touch it – it seemed now that he might *if* he would: he would only just wait there a little, to show, to prove, that he wouldn't. He had thus another station, close to the thin partition by which revelation was denied him; but with his eyes bent and his hands held off in a mere intensity of stillness. He listened as if there had been something to hear, but this attitude, while it lasted, was his own communication. 'If you won't then – good: I spare you and I give up. You affect me as by the appeal positively for pity: you convince me that for reasons rigid and sublime – what do I know? – we both of us should have suffered. I respect them then, and, though moved and privileged as, I believe, it has never been given to man, I retire, I renounce – never, on my honour, to try again. So rest for ever – and let *me*!'

That, for Brydon was the deep sense of this last demonstration – solemn, measured, directed, as he felt it to be. He brought it to a close, he turned away; and now verily he knew how deeply he had been stirred. He retraced his steps, taking up his candle, burnt, he observed, well-nigh to the socket, and marking again, lighten it as he would, the distinctness of his footfall; after which, in a moment, he knew himself at the other side of the house. He did here what he had not yet done at these hours – he opened half a casement, one of those in the front, and let in the air of the night; a thing he would have taken at any time previous for a sharp rupture of his spell. His spell was broken now, and it didn't matter –

broken by his concession and his surrender, which made it idle henceforth that he should ever come back. The empty street – its other life so marked even by the great lamplit vacancy – was within call, within touch; he stayed there as to be in it again, high above it though he was still perched; he watched as for some comforting common fact, some vulgar human note, the passage of a scavenger or a thief, some night-bird however base. He would have blessed that sign of life; he would have welcomed positively the slow approach of his friend the policeman, whom he had hitherto only sought to avoid, and was not sure that if the patrol had come into sight he mightn't have felt the impulse to get into relation with it, to hail it, on some pretext, from his fourth floor.

The pretext that wouldn't have been too silly or too compromising, the explanation that would have saved his dignity and kept his name, in such a case, out of the papers, was not definite to him: he was so occupied with the thought of recording his Discretion – as an effect of the vow he had just uttered to his intimate adversary – that the importance of this loomed large and something had overtaken all ironically his sense of proportion. If there had been a ladder applied to the front of the house, even one of the vertiginous perpendiculars employed by painters and roofers and sometimes left standing overnight, he would have managed somehow, astride of the window-sill, to compass by outstretched leg and arm that mode of descent. If there had been some such uncanny thing as he had found in his room at hotels, a workable fire-escape in the form of notched cable or a canvas shoot, he would have availed himself of it as a proof – well, of his present delicacy. He nursed that sentiment, as the question stood, a little in vain, and even – at the end of he scarce knew, once more, how long – found it, as by the action on his mind of the failure of response of the outer world, sinking back to vague anguish. It seemed to him he had waited an age for some stir of the great grim hush; the life of the town was itself under a spell – so unnaturally, up and down the whole prospect of known and rather ugly objects, the blankness and the silence lasted. Had they ever, he asked himself, the hard-faced houses, which had begun to look livid in the dim dawn, had they ever spoken so little to any need of his spirit? Great builded voids, great crowded stillnesses put on, often, in the heart of cities, for the small hours, a sort of sinister mask, and it was of this large collective negation that Brydon presently became conscious – all the more that the break of day was, almost incredibly, now at hand, proving to him what a night he had made of it.

He looked again at his watch, saw what had become of his time-values (he had taken hours for minutes – not, as in other tense situations, minutes for hours) and the strange air of the streets was but the weak, the sullen flush of a dawn in which everything was still locked up. His choked appeal from his own open window had been the sole note of life, and he could but break off at last as for a worse despair. Yet while so deeply demoralised he was capable again of an impulse denoting – at least by his present measure – extraordinary resolution; of retracing his steps to the spot where he had turned cold with the extinction of his last pulse of doubt as to there being in the place another presence than his own. This required an effort strong enough to sicken him; but he had his reason, which overmastered for the moment everything else. There was the whole of the rest of the house to traverse, and how should he screw himself to that if the door he had seen closed were at present open? He could hold to the idea that the closing had practically been for him an act of mercy, a chance offered him to descend, depart, get off the ground and never again profane it. This conception held together, it worked; but what it meant for him depended now clearly on the amount of forbearance his recent action, or rather his recent inaction, had engendered. The image of the 'presence,' whatever it was, waiting there for him to go – this image had not yet been so concrete for his nerves as when he stopped short of the point at which certainty would have come to him. For, with all his resolution, or more exactly with all his dread, he did stop short – he hung back from really seeing. The risk was too great and his fear too definite: it took at this moment an awful specific form.

He knew – yes, as he had never known anything – that, *should* he see the door open, it would all too abjectly be the end of him. It would mean that the agent of his shame – for his shame was the deep abjection – was once more at large and in general possession; and what glared him thus in the face was the act that this would determine for him. It would send him straight about to the window he had left open, and by that window, be long ladder and dangling rope as absent as they would, he saw himself uncontrollably insanely fatally take his way to the street. The hideous chance of this he at least could avert; but he could only avert it by recoiling in time from assurance. He had the whole house to deal with, this fact was still there; only he now knew that uncertainty alone could start him. He stole back from where he had checked himself – merely to do so was suddenly like safety – and, making blindly for the greater staircase, left gaping rooms and sounding passages behind. Here was the top of the stairs, with a fine large dim descent and three spacious landings to mark off. His instinct was all for mildness, but his feet were harsh on the floors, and, strangely, when he had in a couple of minutes become aware of this, it counted somehow for help. He couldn't have spoken, the tone of his voice would have scared him, and the common conceit or resource of 'whistling in the dark' (whether literally or figuratively) have appeared basely vulgar; yet he liked none the less to hear himself go, and when he had reached his first landing – taking it all with no rush, but quite steadily – that stage of success drew from him a gasp of relief.

The house, withal, seemed immense, the scale of space again inordinate; the open rooms, to no one of which his eyes deflected, gloomed in their shuttered state like mouths of caverns; only the high skylight that formed the crown of the deep well created for him a medium in which he could advance, but which might have been, for queerness of colour, some watery under-world. He tried to think of something noble, as that his property was really grand, a splendid possession; but this nobleness took the form too of the clear delight with which he was finally to sacrifice it. They might come in now, the builders, the destroyers – they might come as soon as they would. At the end of two flights he had dropped to another zone, and from the middle of the third, with only one more left, he recognised the influence of the lower windows, of half-drawn blinds, of the occasional gleam of street-lamps, of the glazed spaces of the vestibule. This was the bottom of the sea, which showed an illumination of its own and which he even saw paved – when at a given moment he drew up to sink a long look over the banisters – with the marble squares of his childhood. By that time indubitably he felt, as he might have said in a commoner cause, better; it had allowed him to stop and draw breath, and the ease increased with the sight of the old black-and-white slabs. But what he most felt was that now surely, with the element of impunity pulling him as by hard firm hands, the case was settled for what he might have seen above had he dared that last look. The closed door, blessedly remote now, was still closed – and he had only in short to reach that of the house.

He came down further, he crossed the passage forming the access to the last flight; and if here again he stopped an instant it was almost for the sharpness of the thrill of assured escape. It made him shut his eyes – which opened again to the straight slope of the remainder of the stairs. Here was impunity still, but impunity almost excessive; inasmuch as the sidelights and the high fan-tracery of the entrance were glimmering straight into the hall; an appearance produced, he the next instant saw, by the fact that the vestibule gaped wide, that the hinged halves of the inner door had been thrown far back. Out of that again the *question* sprang at him, making his eyes, as he felt, half-start from his head, as they had done, at the top of the house, before the sign of the other door. If he had left that one open, hadn't he left this one closed, and wasn't he now in *most* immediate presence of some inconceivable occult activity? It was as sharp, the question, as a knife in his side, but the answer hung fire still and seemed to lose itself in the vague darkness to which the thin admitted dawn, glimmering archwise over the whole outer door, made a semicircular margin, a cold silvery nimbus that seemed to play a little as he looked – to shift and expand and contract.

It was as if there had been something within it, protected by indistinctness and corresponding in extent with the opaque surface behind, the painted panels of the last barrier to his escape, of which the key was in his pocket. The indistinctness mocked him even while he stared, affected him as somehow shrouding or challenging certitude, so that after faltering an instant on his step he let himself go with the sense that here *was* at last something to meet, to touch, to take, to know — something all unnatural and dreadful, but to advance upon which was the condition for him either of liberation or of supreme defeat. The penumbra, dense and dark, was the virtual screen of a figure which stood in it as still as some image erect in a niche or as some black-vizored sentinel guarding a treasure. Brydon was to know afterwards, was to recall and make out, the particular thing he had believed during the rest of his descent. He saw, in its great grey glimmering margin, the central vagueness diminish, and he felt it to be taking the very form toward which, for so many days, the passion of his curiosity had yearned. It gloomed, it loomed, it was something, it was somebody, the prodigy of a personal presence.

Rigid and conscious, spectral yet human, a man of his own substance and stature waited there to measure himself with his power to dismay. This only could it be — this only till he recognised, with his advance, that what made the face dim was the pair of raised hands that covered it and in which, so far from being offered in defiance, it was buried as for dark deprecation. So Brydon, before him, took him in; with every fact of him now, in the higher light, hard and acute — his planted stillness, his vivid truth, his grizzled bent head and white masking hands, his queer actuality of evening-dress, of dangling double eye-glass, of gleaming silk lappet and white linen, of pearl button and gold watch-guard and polished shoe. No portrait by a great modern master could have presented him with more intensity, thrust him out of his frame with more art, as if there had been 'treatment,' of the consummate sort, in his every shade and salience. The revulsion, for our friend, had become, before he knew it, immense — this drop, in the act of apprehension, to the sense of his adversary's inscrutable manoeuvre. That meaning at least, while he gaped, it offered him; for he could but gape at his other self in this other anguish, gape as a proof that *he*, standing there for the achieved, the enjoyed, the triumphant life, couldn't be faced in his triumph. Wasn't the proof in the splendid covering hands, strong and completely spread? — so spread and so intentional that, in spite of a special verity that surpassed every other, the fact that one of these hands had lost two fingers, which were reduced to stumps, as if accidentally shot away, the face was effectually guarded and saved.

'Saved,' though, *would* it be? — Brydon breathed his wonder till the very impunity of his attitude and the very insistence of his eyes produced, as he felt, a sudden stir which showed the next instant as a deeper portent, while the head raised itself, the betrayal of a braver purpose. The hands, as he looked, began to move, to open; then, as if deciding in a flash, dropped from the face and left it uncovered and presented. Horror, with the sight, had leaped into Brydon's throat, gasping there in a sound he couldn't utter; for the bared identity was too hideous as *his*, and his glare was the passion of his protest. The face, *that* face, Spencer Brydon's? – he searched it still, but looking away from it in dismay and denial, falling straight from his height of sublimity. It was unknown, inconceivable, awful, disconnected from any possibility –! He had been 'sold,' he inwardly moaned, stalking such game as this: the presence before him was a presence, the horror within him a horror, but the waste of his nights had been only grotesque and the success of his adventure an irony. Such an identity fitted his at *no* point, made its alternative monstrous. A thousand times yes, as it came upon him nearer now – the face was the face of a stranger. It came upon him nearer now, quite as one of those expanding fantastic images projected by the magic lantern of childhood; for the stranger, whoever he might be, evil, odious, blatant, vulgar, had advanced as for aggression, and he knew himself give ground. Then harder pressed still, sick with the force of his shock, and falling back as under the hot breath and the roused passion of a life larger than his own, a rage of personality before which his own collapsed, he felt the whole vision turn to darkness and his very feet give way. His head went round; he was going; he had gone.

III

What had next brought him back, clearly – though after how long? – was Mrs Muldoon's voice, coming to him from quite near, from so near that he seemed presently to see her as kneeling on the ground before him while he lay looking up at her; himself not wholly on the ground, but half-raised and upheld – conscious, yes, of tenderness of support and, more particularly, of a head pillowed in extraordinary softness and fainly refreshing fragrance. He considered, he wondered, his wit but half at his service; then another face intervened, bending more directly over him, and he finally knew that Alice Staverton had made her lap an ample and perfect cushion to him, and that she had to this end seated herself on the lowest degree of the staircase, the rest of his long person remaining stretched on his old black-and-white slabs. They were cold, these marble squares of his youth; but *he* somehow was not, in this rich return of consciousness – the most wonderful hour, little by little, that he had ever known, leaving him, as it did, so gratefully, so abysmally passive, and yet as with a treasure of intelligence waiting all round him for quiet appropriation; dissolved, he might call it, in the air of the place and producing the golden glow of a late autumn afternoon. He had come back, yes – come back from further away than any man but himself had ever travelled; but it was strange how with this sense what he had come back *to* seemed really the great thing, and as if his prodigious journey had been all for the sake of it. Slowly but surely his consciousness grew, his vision of his state thus completing itself: he had been miraculously *carried* back – lifted and carefully borne as from where he had been picked up, the uttermost end of an interminable grey passage. Even with this he was suffered to rest, and what had now brought him to knowledge was the break in the long mild motion.

It had brought him to knowledge, to knowledge – yes, this was the beauty of his state; which came to resemble more and more that of a man who has gone to sleep on some news of a great inheritance, and then, after dreaming it away, after profaning it with matters strange to it, has waked up again to serenity of certitude and has only to lie and watch it grow. This was the drift of his patience – that he had only to let it shine on him. He must moreover, with intermissions, still have been lifted and borne; since why and how else should he have known himself, later on, with the afternoon glow intenser, no longer at the foot of his stairs – situated as these now seemed at that dark other end of his tunnel – but on a deep window-bench of his high saloon, over which had been spread, couch-fashion, a mantle of soft stuff lined with grey fur that was familiar to his eyes and that one of his hands kept fondly feeling as for its pledge of truth. Mrs Muldoon's face had gone, but the other, the second he had recognised, hung over him in a way that showed how he was still propped and pillowed. He took it all in, and the more he took it the more it seemed to suffice: he was as much at peace as if he had had food and drink. It was the two women who had found him, on Mrs Muldoon's having plied, at her usual hour, her latch-key – and on her having above all arrived while Miss Staverton still lingered near the house. She had been turning away, all anxiety, from worrying the vain bell-handle – her calculation having been of the hour of the good woman's visit; but the latter, blessedly, had come up while she was still there, and they had entered together. He had then lain, beyond the vestibule, very much as he was lying now – quite, that is, as he appeared to have fallen, but all so wondrously without bruise or gash; only in a depth of stupor. What he most took in, however, at present, with the steadier clearance, was that Alice Staverton had for a long unspeakable moment not doubted he was dead.

'It must have been that I *was*.' He made it out as she held him. 'Yes – I can only have died. You brought me literally to life. Only,' he wondered, his eyes rising to her, 'only, in the name of all the benedictions, how?'

It took her but an instant to bend her face and kiss him, and something in the manner of it, and in the way her hands clasped and locked his head while he felt the cool charity and virtue of her lips, something in all this beatitude somehow answered everything. 'And now I keep you,' she said.

'Oh keep me, keep me!' he pleaded while her face still hung over him: in response to which it dropped again and stayed close, clingingly close. It was the seal of their situation – of which he tasted the impress for a long blissful moment in silence. But he came back. 'Yet how did you know –?'

'I was uneasy. You were to have come, you remember – and you had sent no word.'

'Yes, I remember – I was to have gone to you at one to-day.' It caught on to their 'old' life and relation – which were so near and so far. 'I was still out there in my strange darkness – where was it, what was it? I must have stayed there so long.' He could but wonder at the depth and the duration of his swoon.

'Since last night?' she asked with a shade of fear for her possible indiscretion.

'Since this morning – it must have been: the cold dim dawn of to-day. Where have I been,' he vaguely wailed, 'where have I been?' He felt her hold him close, and it was as if this helped him now to make in all security his mild moan. 'What a long dark day!'

All in her tenderness she had waited a moment. 'In the cold dim dawn?' she quavered.

But he had already gone on piecing together the parts of the whole prodigy. 'As I didn't turn up you came straight –?'

She barely cast about. 'I went first to your hotel – where they told me of your absence. You had dined out last evening and hadn't been back since. But they appeared to know you had been at your club.'

'So you had the idea of *this* –?'

'Of what?' she asked in a moment.

'Well – of what has happened.'

'I believed at least you'd have been here. I've known, all along,' she said, 'that you've been coming.'

'"Known" it –?'

'Well, I've believed it. I said nothing to you after that talk we had a month ago – but I felt sure. I knew you *would*,' she declared.

'That I'd persist, you mean?'

'That you'd see him.'

'Ah but I didn't!' cried Brydon with his long wail. 'There's somebody – an awful beast; whom I brought, too horribly, to bay. But it's not me.'

At this she bent over him again, and her eyes were in his eyes. 'No – it's not you.' And it was as if, while her face hovered, he might have made out in it, hadn't it been so near, some particular meaning blurred by a smile. 'No, thank heaven,' she repeated – 'it's not you! Of course it wasn't to have been.'

'Ah but it *was*,' he gently insisted. And he stared before him now as he had been staring for so many weeks. 'I was to have known myself.'

'You couldn't!' she returned consolingly. And then reverting, and as if to account further for what she had herself done, 'But it wasn't only *that*, that you hadn't been at home,' she went on. 'I waited till the hour at which we had found Mrs Muldoon that day of my going with you; and she arrived, as I've told you, while, failing to bring any one to the door, I lingered in my despair on the steps. After a little, if she hadn't come, by such a mercy, I should have found means to hunt her up. But it wasn't,' said Alice Staverton, as if once more with her fine intention – 'it wasn't only that.'

His eyes, as he lay, turned back to her. 'What more then?'

She met it, the wonder she had stirred. 'In the cold dim dawn, you say? Well, in the cold dim dawn of this morning I too saw you.'

'Saw *me* –?'

'Saw *him*,' said Alice Staverton. 'It must have been at the same moment.'

He lay an instant taking it in – as if he wished to be quite reasonable. 'At the same moment?'

'Yes – in my dream again, the same one I've named to you. He came back to me. Then I knew it for a sign. He had come to you.'

At this Brydon raised himself; he had to see her better. She helped him when she understood his movement, and he sat up, steadying himself beside her there on the window-bench and with his right hand grasping her left. '*He* didn't come to me.'

'You came to yourself,' she beautifully smiled.

'Ah I've come to myself now – thanks to you, dearest. But this brute, with his awful face – this brute's a black stranger. He's none of *me*, even as I *might* have been,' Brydon sturdily declared.

But she kept the clearness that was like the breath of infallibility. 'Isn't the whole point that you'd have been different?'

He almost scowled for it. 'As different as *that* –?'

Her look again was more beautiful to him than the things of this world. 'Haven't you exactly wanted to know *how* different? So this morning,' she said, 'you appeared to me.'

'Like *him*?'

'A black stranger!'

'Then how did you know it was I?'

'Because, as I told you weeks ago, my mind, my imagination, had worked so over what you might, what you mightn't have been – to show you, you see, how I've thought of you. In the midst of that you came to me – that my wonder might be answered. So I knew,' she went on; 'and believed that, since the question held you too so fast, as you told me that day, you too would see for yourself. And when this morning I again saw I knew it would be because you had – and also then, from the first moment, because you somehow wanted me. *He* seemed to tell me of that. So why,' she strangely smiled, 'shouldn't I like him?'

It brought Spencer Brydon to his feet. 'You "like" that horror —?'

'I *could* have liked him. And to me,' she said, 'he was no horror. I had accepted him.'

'"Accepted" —?' Brydon oddly sounded.

'Before, for the interest of his difference — yes. And as *I* didn't disown him, as *I* knew him — which you at last, confronted with him in his difference, so cruelly didn't, my dear — well, he must have been, you see, less dreadful to me. And it may have pleased him that I pitied him.'

She was beside him on her feet, but still holding his hand — still with her arm supporting him. But though it all brought for him thus a dim light, 'You "pitied" him?' he grudgingly, resentfully asked.

'He has been unhappy, he has been ravaged,' she said.

'And haven't I been unhappy? Am not I — you've only to look at me! — ravaged?'

'Ah I don't say I like him *better*,' she granted after a thought. 'But he's grim, he's worn — and things have happened to him. He doesn't make shift, for sight, with your charming monocle.'

'No' — it struck Brydon: 'I couldn't have sported mine "downtown." They'd have guyed me there.'

'His great convex pince-nez — I saw it, I recognised the kind — is for his poor ruined sight. And his poor right hand —!'

'Ah!' Brydon winced — whether for his proved identity or for his lost fingers. Then, 'He has a million a year,' he lucidly added. 'But he hasn't you.'

'And he isn't — no, he isn't — *you*!' she murmured as he drew her to his breast.

NOTES

Four Meetings

New York Edition, Vol. XVI; first magazine publication in *Scribner's Monthly*, November 1877; first book publication in *Daisy Miller* (English edition, 1879).

The title suggests the influence of 'Three Meetings' by Ivan Turgenev (1818–83), the Russian novelist and short story writer whom James admired perhaps above all others.

1. *any assembly*: In the first published version (1877 and 1879) of the tale, this event was described as 'a *conversazione*', but, while revising, James seems to recognize that such a term is inappropriate to 'the depths of New England'.

2. *North Verona*: A more playfully ironic place name than the heavy-handed 'Grimwinter' of the first published version. The European Verona is in Northern Italy.

3. *Her eyes were perhaps just too round and too inveterately surprised*: An improvement on the first published version's somewhat unfortunate 'She had a soft, surprised eye . . .'

4. *'ruche'*: A frill of ribbon or lace, used to ornament some part of a dress or hat.

5. *a person launched and afloat but conscious of rocking a little*: A metaphor, not found in the first published version, suggesting that in her imagination Caroline Spencer has already set sail for Europe.

6. *the Castle of Chillon*: The castle, begun in the ninth or tenth century and given its present form in the thirteenth century, is one of Switzerland's most famous pieces of architecture and a popular tourist attraction.

7. *Bonnivard, about whom Byron wrote*: George Gordon, Lord Byron (1788–1824) wrote, in 1816, 'The Prisoner of Chillon' and a 'Sonnet on Chillon'. François de Bonnivard (c. 1493–1570) has mythic status as a patriot, republican and victim of tyranny. Prior of St Victor's in Geneva, he supported the people of Geneva in their revolt against the Duke of Savoy and was imprisoned twice – in 1519 for two years, and from 1530 to 1536 – in the Castle of Chillon. The iron ring to which he is supposed to have been fettered is still shown to visitors. He was liberated by the Bernese. Byron's sonnet ends:

> Chillon! thy prison is a holy place,
>   And thy sad floor an altar – for 'twas trod,
> Until his very steps have left a trace
>   Worn, as if thy cold pavement were a sod
> By Bonnivard! – May none these marks efface!
>   For they appeal from tyranny to God.

8. *twenty-two months and a half*: In thus revising the first published version's 'twenty-three months', James makes Caroline Spencer even more eagerly precise.

9. *thirst-fever*: Significantly, in James's early novel *Roderick Hudson* (1875), the eponymous young American artist, yearning for Europe, creates a sculpture of a 'naked youth drinking from a gourd', entitled *Thirst*. See *Roderick Hudson*, ed. Geoffrey Moore and Patricia Crick (Penguin Books: Harmondsworth, 1986), p. 59.

10. '*"Everything" is saying much . . . our confident dream*': This important paragraph is largely new to the New York Edition. The first published version reads simply:

'I understand your case,' I rejoined. 'You have the native American passion – the passion for the picturesque. With us, I think, it is primordial – antecedent to experience. Experience comes and only shows us something we have dreamt of.'

11. *dame de comptoir*: Barmaid (French, as are the translations below, unless otherwise indicated).

12. *letter of credit*: Letter written from one banker to another, requesting that the bearer be credited with specific sums of money. The term is used metaphorically here but events soon render the term harshly literal.

13. *circular notes*: Letters of credit used by travellers.

14. *In my cousin's pocket*: James's precise revision of the first published version's 'My cousin has them' augments the ironic chill here.

15. *a beautifully fluted cap*: White, pleated head-dress, part of traditional dress in Normandy.

16. *the ancient fortress . . . Francis the First . . . small Castle of Saint Angelo*: Le Havre was founded, as a port and harbour, in 1517 by Francis I of France (1494–1547). The Castel Sant'Angelo in Rome was built in AD 135–9 as a dynastic tomb and converted to a fortress in the fifth century. The design is essentially a circle surrounded by a square.

17. *slouch hat*: Soft felt hat with a wide flexible brim, described later in the tale as a sombrero.

18. *Rue Bonaparte*: On the bohemian Left Bank in Paris, the site of the École Nationale des Beaux-Arts, established in 1816.

19. *a Raphaelesque or Byronic attire*: I.e. the bohemian attire typical of the artist. The Italian Renaissance painter Raphael (1483–1520) and the Scottish poet Byron are offered here as typical artists.

20. *Je suis fou de la peinture*: I am crazy about painting.

21. *auberge*: Inn.

22. *Salle-à-Manger*: Dining room.

23. *She was a beautiful young widow*: Many of the details of the supposed Countess's past – or what Caroline Spencer has been led to believe that past to be – are new to the New York Edition.

24. *grande dame*: Great lady.

25. *the Levant*: The countries of the Eastern Mediterranean.

26. '*carry-all*': American version of carriole – a light, four-wheeled carriage, drawn by one horse and capable of carrying several people.

27. *a shabby Parisian quatrième*: A fourth-floor apartment, the grander apartments being on lower floors.

28. *à la chinoise*: After the Chinese style, gathered in a knot.

29. *le sourire agréable*: The New York Edition puts into French what in the first published version is described as 'an agreeable smile'.

30. *C'est bien*: That's good.

31. *such parti-coloured flannels*: An addition in the New York Edition, suggesting the motley of the fool or clown.

32. *tant bien que mal*: In the first published version, 'after a fashion'.

33. *sans me vanter*: Without bragging.

34. *La belle découverte . . . la bêtise même*: What a discovery . . . stupidity itself.

35. *me fait languir*: Makes me yearn (for Paris).

36. *Vous avez de la chance*: You are lucky.

37. *hein . . . sous ce beau ciel*: Eh . . . in that beautiful place; literally under that beautiful sky.

38. *hélas*: Alas.

39. *On en a de toutes les sortes*: One can have all kinds of that (experience).

40. *my épreuve – elles m'en ont données, des heures, des heures*: My ordeal (or trial) – I've had hours and hours of it.

41. *comme cela se fait*: As is proper; as is done.

42. *C'est une fille charmante . . . fine*: She's a charming girl . . . colloquially, cognac or brandy.

43. *mon amoureux . . . il me fait une cour acharnée*: My lover or sweetheart . . . he's madly in love with me.

44. *je ne sais quelle dévergondée*: I don't know what kind of shameless, abandoned woman.

45. *my inward sense of the Countess's probable past*: The details of the narrator's speculation are an addition in the New York Edition, matching the addition earlier of the fuller account which Caroline Spencer had been given of the Countess's background.

46. *parages*: Parts.

Daisy Miller

New York Edition, Vol. XVIII; first magazine publication as 'Daisy Miller: A Study' in *Cornhill Magazine*, June and July 1878; first book publication as *Daisy Miller: A Study* (1879); rewritten as a play *Daisy Miller: A Comedy in Three Acts* (1883). Unlike the prose versions of the story, the play ends with Daisy recovered and anticipating marriage to Winterbourne in America.

1. *Vevey*: The chief town of the Canton of Valais. It lies on Lake Geneva and began to develop into a major tourist attraction in the nineteenth century.

2. *Newport and Saratoga*: Newport, Rhode Island, a fashionable resort; Saratoga Springs, New York, another fashionable spa resort. A few lines later James names the Ocean House and Congress Hall, hotels in Newport and Saratoga Springs, respectively.

3. *Trois Couronnes*: The Three Crowns – still a luxury hotel in Vevey.

4. *the Dent du Midi . . . the Castle of Chillon*: The Dent du Midi is a famous peak (3300 metres), south of Lake Geneva. For the Castle of Chillon, see 'Four Meetings', note 6.

5. *the little capital of Calvinism*: Geneva. Jean Calvin (1509–64), the French theologian, fled from Paris to Geneva, making it the centre of Reformed Protestantism in the sixteenth century.

6. *the grey old 'Academy'*: The University of Geneva, formerly an Academy founded by Calvin in 1559 to train Reformed theologians.

7. *alpenstock*: A long iron-pointed staff, for use in mountain climbing.

8. *the Simplon*: One of the main Alpine passes between Switzerland and Italy, and the shortest route between the Valais and northern Italy. Travellers went by horse-drawn coach, the road having been constructed, on Napoleon's orders, between 1801 and 1805. (A railway tunnel was not opened until the twentieth century.)

9. *Schenectady*: Town in upstate New York; an important centre for industry and business.

10. *He don't like Europe*: In the first published versions Daisy says 'He doesn't like Europe.' This is one of many changes in the New York Edition which make Daisy's speech – and that of her brother – less grammatically 'correct', more demotic. This is also seen, for example, in their repeated declarations that they are going 't'Italy' in contrast to the earlier text's 'to Italy' and in the change from Daisy's assertion a little later in the conversation, 'There isn't any society', to her 'There ain't any society' recorded here. The New York Edition also adds Daisy's colloquial exclamations – 'oh pshaw' and 'My!'

11. *the cars*: I.e. railway carriages.

12. *arrière-pensée*: Hidden, ulterior motive (French, as are the translations below, unless otherwise indicated).

13. *courier*: In the eighteenth and nineteenth centuries, parties travelling on the Continent typically employed couriers, servants who made all the arrangements for the journey.

14. *her natural elegance*: The first published version records that Daisy has 'the *tournure* of a princess', '*tournure*' meaning 'bearing' or 'figure'. The New York Edition revision restores the democratic and American in descriptions of Daisy, and does not allow Winterbourne to assimilate her to European models.

15. *in large puffs*: A hairstyle achieved by rolling the ends of the hair to form puffs. Such a style was fashionable at the time in Paris.

16. *Homburg*: Bad Homburg, a fashionable spa town north of Frankfurt am Main in Germany.

17. *constatations*: Findings, statements of fact.

18. *comme il faut*: Proper, correct.

19. *the common table*: The New York Edition's revision of the first published version's '*table d'hôte*' appropriately translates the French into Daisy's American idiom. The more expensive alternative to eating at set times at the public *table d'hôte* was to have meals served in one's rooms, as the exclusive Mrs Costello clearly does.

20. *Mr Frederick Forsyth Winterbourne*: Only in the New York Edition does Winterbourne attain to this full and formal name. In the first edition Daisy introduces him merely as 'Mr Winterbourne'.

21. *city at the other end of the lake*: I.e. Geneva.

22. *oubliettes*: Dungeons, with an opening only at the top, into which prisoners were thrown and – as the name implies (little places of forgetting) – forgotten.

23. *the unhappy Bonnivard*: See 'Four Meetings', note 7.

24. *intime*: Intimate, familiar.

25. *that pretty novel of Cherbuliez's – 'Paule Méré'*: Swiss-born French novelist Charles Victor Cherbuliez (1822–99), author of *Paule Méré* (1864), which has a close relationship to 'Daisy Miller': its unconventional but innocent heroine is vilified by Geneva society, thus destroying any hopes of a relationship with the novel's hero. She dies of a broken heart. It is thus ironic that Mrs Costello thinks of this novel as 'pretty'.

26. *Via Gregoriana*: Near the Spanish Steps, this street, particularly from the seventeenth and eighteenth centuries, provided lodgings for the wealthier visitors to Rome.

27. *the infant Hannibal*: Hannibal (247–182 BC), Carthaginian general and – the point of the comparison here – Rome's great enemy. He was militarily active by the age of nineteen and was following in the footsteps of his father, Hamilcar Barca (c. 270–228 BC), who long campaigned against the Romans.

28. *Zürich*: Scenic city, the largest in Switzerland, and perhaps for that reason an apposite choice for an otherwise unlikely comparison with Rome.

29. *his rough ends to his words*: In *The Question of Our Speech* (Boston and New York: Houghton Mifflin, 1905), Henry James lamented 'our national vocal sound . . . *is* slovenly . . . Nothing is commoner than to see throughout our country, young persons of either sex . . . whose utterance can only be indicated by pronouncing it destitute of any approach to an emission of the consonant. It becomes thus a mere slobber of disconnected vowel sounds' (p. 25).

30. *the Pincio*: Named after the Pinci family, who had a garden there in the fourth century, this hill was laid out as a garden, with walks and avenues, during the Napoleonic occupation (1809–14). The promenade, designed by Guiseppe Valadier and opened to the public in 1828, is celebrated for its view over Rome.

31. *the fever*: Malaria or *perniciosa* or 'Roman fever', so-called because, prior to drainage and the embankment of the Tiber, and the use of quinine, malaria was particularly prevalent in Rome, especially in the summer months, months which visitors, prior to the twentieth century, tended to avoid.

32. *that place in front, where you look at the view*: The terrace of Piazzale Napoleone I in the Pincio, famous for its view, particularly at dusk.

33. *penny-a-liner*: Hack or second-rate journalist, not on a newspaper's permanent staff but paid a penny a line.

34. *amoroso*: Lover, sweetheart (Italian).

35. *the revolving train*: I.e. of carriages driving round the Pincio.

36. *victoria*: Low four-wheeled carriage for two with a folding hood.

37. *true . . . your truth*: In the first published version the talk is of Mrs Walker's desire to be 'earnest' and of her 'earnestness'.

38. *the wall of Rome . . . the beautiful Villa Borghese*: The Aurelian Wall, built by the Emperor Aurelian and constructed AD 271–5, encompassed the seven hills of Rome and was intended as protection against barbarian invasion. The section referred to here which marks the south-west boundary of the Villa Borghese, follows an irregular line and is called the crooked wall (*Muro Torto*). The Villa Borghese is the largest park in Rome, created by Cardinal Scipio Borghese, nephew of Pope Paul V, in the early seventeenth century.

39. *Elle s'affiche, la malheureuse*: She's making a spectacle of herself, poor girl.

40. *my friend in need*: Alluding to the proverb 'A friend in need is a friend indeed.'

41. *as he might have done all the kingdoms of the earth*: A simile new to the New York Edition, and a good example of the later James's often cavalier appropriation of allusion. The reference is to the Devil's temptation of Christ in the wilderness by offering Him 'all the kingdoms of the world, and the glory of them' (Matthew 4:8).

42. *Saint Peter's*: St Peter's Basilica, in the Vatican City, the largest church in the world.

43. *the Corso*: The main street of central Rome, named after horse races organized by Pope Paul II in the fifteenth century, and lined by Renaissance palaces. It was the fashionable place to be seen: from the eighteenth century, it was the custom for a lady to be seen there with her faithful admirer.

44. *barber's block*: Wooden head on which wigs were displayed.

45. *romps on from day to day, from hour to hour, as they did in the Golden Age*: Cf. Shakespeare's *As You Like It* I. i. 107–9, speaking of Duke Senior: 'They say young gentlemen flock to him every day, and fleet the time carelessly, as they did in the golden world.'

46. *scarcely went on all fours*: Did not suit in all particulars; was incoherent. Mrs Costello's finding the Golden Age vulgar suggests her expression has become somewhat entangled and contradictory.

47. *cavaliere avvocato*: A minor official, literally a gentleman lawyer (Italian).

48. *marchese*: Marquis (Italian).

49. *qui se passe ses fantaisies*: Who pleases herself; does what she likes.

50. *the Doria Palace*: The Palazzo Doria Pamphili, famous for the art collection in its Picture Gallery, which includes the portrait of Pope Innocent X by the Spanish painter Velasquez (1599–1660). A 'cabinet' is a room.

51. *du meilleur monde*: Of the best society.

52. *the Palace of the Caesars*: The archaeological site on the Palatine Hill, home of the ancient emperors.

53. *the Caelian Hill*: Or Coelian Hill, one of the seven hills of Rome.

54. *the Arch of Constantine . . . the Forum*: One of the largest of Rome's surviving triumphal arches, built in AD 315 to commemorate Constantine's triumph over his rival Maxentius's troops in AD 312. The Forum is the ruins of the centre of ancient Rome.

55. *the Colosseum*: The largest Roman amphitheatre in the world, begun by Vespasian, the first of the Flavian emperors, in AD 72 and completed by his son in AD 80. A rounded oval, with tiers of stepped seating, it was a place of public entertainment where spectacles included races, gladiators' duels, and gladiators fighting wild animals. It is not certain that Christians were martyred here, but the story has widespread currency and the building was consecrated in the eighteenth century.

56. *Byron's famous lines out of 'Manfred'*: (1817) III. iv. 9–11, 27–41:

upon such a night

I stood within the Coliseum's wall,
'Midst the chief relics of almighty Rome; . . .

But the gladiators' bloody Circus stands,
A noble wreck in ruinous perfection,
While Caesar's chambers, and the Augustan halls,
Grovel on earth in indistinct decay. –
And thou didst shine, thou rolling Moon, upon
All this, and cast a wide and tender light,
Which softened down the hoar austerity
Of rugged desolation, and filled up,
As 'twere anew, the gaps of centuries;
Leaving that beautiful which still was so,
And making that which was not – till the place
Became religion, and the heart ran o'er
With silent worship of the Great of old, –
The dead, but sceptred Sovereigns, who still rule
Our spirits from their urns.

For Byron, see 'Four Meetings', note 7.

57. *great cross in the centre*: Commemorating the Christian martyrs.

58. *perniciosa*: Roman fever; malaria (Italian). (See note 31.)

59. *some pills*: Possibly quinine.

60. *the little Protestant cemetery*: Testaccio Cemetery, at the foot of the Pyramid of Caius Cestius, south of the Aventine, is the first cemetery granted by the popes for non-Catholic Italians and foreigners. It is the burial place of Keats and Shelley.

61. *she did what she liked*: A revision particular to the New York edition. Earlier editions read 'she wanted to go'.

The Pension Beaurepas

New York Edition, Vol. XIV; first magazine publication in *Atlantic Monthly*, April 1879; first book publication in *Washington Square* (1881).

1. *Pension Beaurepas*: Boarding House of the Good Meal (French, as are all translations below).

2. *a letter addressed by . . . Stendhal to his sister*: Stendhal (pseudonym of Henri Beyle) (1783–1842), French novelist and author of *Le Rouge and le Noir* (1830) and *La Chartreuse de Parme* (1839), carried out an extensive correspondence with his sister, Pauline. In a letter to her of August 1804, Stendhal makes the proposal James describes.

3. *Balzac's 'Père Goriot' . . . 'pension bourgeoise . . . autres' . . . Madame Vauquer, née de Conflans*: Honoré de Balzac (1799–1850), French realist novelist and author of *Le Père*

Goriot (Old Goriot) (1834), set in Madame Vauquer's boarding-house in Paris. James quotes the sign outside the Maison-Vauquer, literally 'lodging house for both sexes and others'.

4. *place*: Square.

5. *the 'offices'*: Pantry; servants' quarters.

6. *J'en ai vus de toutes les couleurs*: I have seen every sort of them (French, as are the translations below, unless otherwise indicated).

7. *heads*: Headings, but punning on human heads.

8. *Je trouve que c'est déplacé*: I think it is out of place, inappropriate or in bad taste.

9. *pot-au-feu*: Stew.

10. *chez moi*: To my establishment.

11. *tout compris*: All inclusive; bed and full board.

12. *au sérieux*: Seriously.

13. *priestess of the tripod*: The priestess at the Shrine of Apollo in Delphi seated herself on a tripod, a three-legged stand, to deliver oracles.

14. *French tongue . . . flourish by Lake Leman*: Lake Geneva – otherwise known as Lake Leman – is in the western French-speaking part of Switzerland.

15. *the Academy, the nursing mother of the present University*: See 'Daisy Miller', note 6.

16. *'manquait d'agréments'*: Lacked charm; lacked pleasures.

17. *M. Pigeonneau*: Literally 'a little or young pigeon', an appropriate name given his physical appearance.

18. *cabinet de lecture*: Library; or, perhaps, bookcase.

19. *Galignani*: Daily English-language Paris newspaper founded by William Galignani (1798–1882), an Englishman who became a naturalized French citizen.

20. *this big breakfast*: Mr Ruck's jokes tend to rather laboured translations, here of *déjeuner* (lunch) and *petit déjeuner* (breakfast).

21. *transported*: The character here is joking with the notion of transportation, the deportation of criminals, as a form of punishment.

22. *the cars*: Streetcars or carriages.

23. *pensionnaires*: Boarders.

24. *those framed 'capillary' tributes to the dead*: Compare 'Fordham Castle' where Mrs Magaw's/Vanderplank's hairstyle is also compared to the 'work' – flowers, leaves and tendrils – on mortuary sculpture.

25. *Miss Ruck . . . well out in the open*: Having made her social debut (used exclusively of young ladies), unlike Aurora Church (introduced in section IV), who wants to 'come out' in New York.

26. *the jewellers' windows*: Switzerland is traditionally famous for its clocks, watches and jewellery.

27. *New York Herald*: This famous newspaper, founded in 1835 by James Gordon Bennett, marked the beginnings of modern journalism. It quickly became known for aggressively pursuing news stories.

28. *the Rhône*: The Rhône flows out of Lake Geneva at Geneva, dividing the city.

29. *Salon des Etrangers*: Reading room for the use of foreign visitors, providing newspapers, etc.

30. *Rue du Rhône*: The main shopping street on the south side of the river.

31. *a tournure de princesse*: A princess's bearing or figure.

32. *for my beaux yeux . . . Je vous recommande la maman*: For my sake; for love of me . . . I recommend the mother to you.

33. *a femme superbe . . . Ne vous y fiez pas*: *a femme superbe*: A grand-looking woman; *fraîcheur*: bloom, freshness; *dans l'intimité*: in private; in intimate circumstances; *Ne vous y fiez pas*: Don't you believe it.

34. *Toute menue*: Tiny.

35. *Vous dites cela d'un ton*: You say that in such a tone or in such a way.

36. *maîtresse de salon*: Hostess of fashionable social and intellectual gatherings.

37. *concurrente*: Competitor (in business).

38. *make me des histoires . . . vous allez voir cela*: Make a fuss to me . . . you see if she doesn't.

39. *pour-boire*: Tip.

40. *from Basel*: In the German-speaking part of Switzerland.

41. *si vous me manquez*: If you let me down.

42. *octavo*: Usually a small book, since the paper has been folded into eight leaves (16 pages).

43. *fête de nuit*: Evening party or celebration, with lights.

44. *l'aimable transfuge*: The lovely deserter (from the other pension).

45. *Ça veut dire 'église,' n'est-ce-pas*: That means 'church', doesn't it.

46. *Appenzell*: Pre-Alpine region in eastern Switzerland, south of Lake Constance, its highest point being Mt Säntis (2504 metres). (Appenzell is also a town in this region.)

47. *She wants to go to America*: Aurora Church gets her wish, with comic consequences, in the epistolary tale 'The Point of View', first published in the *Century Magazine*, December 1882, and included in New York Edition, Vol. XIV.

48. *Dresden*: City in Eastern Saxony, Germany, once a scenic and cultural centre.

49. *Dalmatian*: Native of a Slav region in western Yugoslavia, on the Adriatic coast. The joke here presumably refers to the Dalmatian dog and flirtatiously promises dog-like devotion.

50. *tired of Europe . . . tired of life*: A variation of 'No, sir, when a man is tired of London he is tired of life; for there is in London all that life can afford', one of the most famous sayings of Dr Johnson (1709–84), in James Boswell's *Life of Samuel Johnson* (1791).

51. *C'est mon rêve*: It's my dream.

52. *Piacenza*: City in northern Italy, capital of Piacenza Province.

53. *my jeunesse – my belle jeunesse*: My youth – my beautiful youth.

54. *Nous n'avons pas le sou*: We haven't a penny.

55. *Avranches*: Town in Normandy, northern France.

56. *Excusez du peu*: Forgive me.

57. *fauteuil*: Armchair.

58. *de fortes études*: Serious studies.

59. *Sturm und Drang*: Storm and stress (German), usually used to refer to German Romanticism.

60. *vous m'en voulez*: What do you expect of me?

61. *the Hôtel de Ville*: The Town Hall (built fifteenth–seventeenth centuries).

62. *manuscripts of poor Servetus, the antagonist and victim . . . of the dire Calvin*: Miguel Serveto or Servetus (1511–53), Spanish physician and theologian who was arrested while attending church in Geneva, convicted of heresy and blasphemy by the Calvinist government of Geneva, and burned at the stake. He had begun a correspondence with Calvin in 1545.

63. *tapis de lit*: Bedspread.

64. *Mon Dieu . . . c'est un de ces maman, comme vous en avez, qui promènent leur fille*: My God . . . She's one of those mothers who tries to marry her daughter off (literally, who promenades or shows off her daughter).

65. *a mari sérieux*: An important husband.

66. *gros bonnet*: Bigwig.

67. *fine mouche*: Sly one.

68. *courir les champs*: To play the field; have a good time.

69. *Allons donc*: Come along! Nonsense!

70. *pour la partie*: To make up the match.

71. *the Treille*: The Promenade de la Treille, south-west of the Hôtel de Ville, is a walk, reached through a pillared gateway or archway, with views of Mont Salève and the Jura.

72. *the ville basse*: The Lower Town, lying between the old town and the south bank of the Rhône.

73. *the cathedral*: The Cathedral of St Peter, dating from the twelfth century.

74. *Chamouni*: Chamonix, the resort at the foot of the French Alps, close to Mont Blanc.

75. *Grindelwald and Zermatt*: Respectively, the glacier village in the Bernese Oberland, resort and favourite base of climbers; and the mountain village and resort in the Valais.

76. *kind o' foots up*: Mounts up (i.e. bills and expenses).

77. *the English Garden*: The Jardin Anglais, east of the Pont du Mont-Blanc on the south side of the Lake.

78. *Oh la belle rencontre, nos aimables convives*: Oh what a happy meeting – our lovely fellow-guests.

79. *Allons, en marche*: Let's walk.

80. *En morale*: Morally.

81. *elle s'y perd . . . je n'en suis pas folle*: She can't make head or tail of it . . . I'm not crazy about her.

82. *maître de piano*: Piano teacher.

83. *his digne épouse*: His worthy wife.

84. *de leur pays*: Of their country.

85. *the femme comme il faut*: The proper lady.

86. *a closed one*: An enclosed carriage or a carriage with its hood up and thus more private than an open carriage – contrasting with, and rebuking by implication, Aurora's public display.

87. *Que voulez vous, monsieur*: What are you saying, sir?

88. *chaise à porteurs*: Sedan chair.

89. *the Mer de Glace*: Glacier.

90. *Wall Street*: The financial and business district, home of the New York Stock Exchange.

91. *nourriture*: Food, nourishment.

92. *éprouvée*: Tried.

93. *the El Dorado*: The ideal place, the golden city; originally the name given to the fabulous city supposed to be on the Amazon.

94. *au fond*: At bottom.

95. *nous fait la révérence*: Is taking her leave of us; literally bowing (farewell) to us.

96. *elle fait ses paquets*: She's packing.

97. *his adieux to ces dames*: His farewells to these ladies.

98. *Je crois que cette . . . femme austère*: *Je crois que cette race se perd*: I think that breed is dying out; *Ce sera une femme d'esprit*: She will be a lively woman; a spirited woman; *potelée*: plump; *femme austère*: Stern or puritanical woman.

99. *indices*: Signs or indications.

100. *femme de Rubens, celle-là*: She's a woman out of a Rubens painting, that one. The Flemish painter Peter Paul Rubens (1577–1640) is renowned for his paintings of fleshy, generously proportioned female nudes.

The Lesson of the Master

New York Edition, Vol. XV; first magazine publication in *Universal Review*, July and August 1888; first book publication in *The Lesson of the Master* (1892).

1. *in India*: In the latter nineteenth century, part of the British Empire.

2. *the reign of Queen Anne*: 1702–14.

3. *Manchester Square*: Secluded square, built about 1770–88, in Marylebone, London.

4. *Piccadilly*: The large thoroughfare bordered by Mayfair and Green Park, home to the Royal Academy, and at the centre of the fashionable West End.

5. *confrère*: Colleague; fellow artist (French, as are the translations below).

6. *the City*: The business and banking district of London.

7. *Cannes*: Fashionable resort in the south of France.

8. *Il s'attache à ses pas*: He follows her everywhere; he sticks closely to her.

9. *his personal 'type'*: Light allusion to then current theories of phrenology, and notions of 'types', which had their origins in evolutionary theory and allowed character to be inferred from physical characteristics.

10. *dog-cart*: Carriage with two transverse seats back-to-back.

11. *car*: I.e. Triumphal chariot.

12. *his psychology à fleur de peau*: His superficial psychology; presumably referring to thin characterization in St George's later works.

13. *the fine Gainsborough*: The English painter Thomas Gainsborough (1727–88) is celebrated for his portraits and landscapes.

14. *St George and the Dragon*: Jokey reference to the legend of St George of England slaying the dragon, here casting Henry St George's wife as the dragon.

15. *danglers*: Hangers-on.

16. *mot*: Witticism; joke.

17. *crewels*: Embroidery.

18. *bright habiliments*: I.e. colourful smoking jackets.

19. *the very rustle of the laurel*: I.e. the laurel wreath, a symbol honouring excellence in poetry and literature.

20. *Euston*: Euston Railway Station in north London.

21. *Cela s'est passé comme ça*: It happened like that.

22. *jamais de la vie*: Never; out of the question.

23. *hygiene*: Programme for good health and well-being.

24. *to 'have' something*: I.e. a drink, a 'night-cap'.

25. *victoria*: Low four-wheeled carriage for two with a folding hood.

26. *brougham . . . a closed carriage*: Light, closed four-wheeled horse-drawn carriage. Mrs St George's delicate health prevents open-air travel.

27. *Bond Street*: Fashionable street in Mayfair.

28. *a young artist in 'black-and-white'*: An artist using pen and ink, rather than paint. Earlier editors suggest that this refers more specifically to the manner of Aubrey Beardsley (1872–98) but the text pre-dates him.

29. *a père de famille*: The father of a family; a married man who can therefore escort young ladies to functions without social impropriety.

30. *mornes*: Gloomy; dreary; cheerless.

31. *the Park*: Hyde Park, the large park across Park Lane from Mayfair and extending west.

32. *moeurs*: Habits.

33. *the Row*: Rotten Row, in Hyde Park, the sand-track for horse riders.

34. *hansom*: Light two-wheeled covered carriage, the driver sitting above and behind, usually hired rather than privately owned.

35. *C'est d'un trouvé*: He's a real find.

36. *'season'*: The part of the year, May until July, when the Court and fashionable society are in town.

37. *duenna*: Older lady tagging along as chaperone.

38. *the 'fast' girl*: Forward; disregarding of the social proprieties constraining unmarried women.

39. *Comment donc*: What (emphatic).

40. *Marble Arch*: Designed by Nash in 1828, this arch has stood at the north-east corner of Hyde Park since 1851, and formed an entrance to the Park until 1908.

41. *the Serpentine*: An artificial lake of forty-one acres stretching across the centre of both Hyde Park and Kensington Gardens – the latter initially the private gardens of Kensington Palace, but by this time also a public park.

42. *linkmen's*: Men employed to carry torches to light the way for pedestrians, before street lighting.

43. *il ne manquerait plus que ça*: That's the last straw.

44. *carton-pierre*: Papier mâché, made to imitate stone or bronze.

45. *Lincrusta-Walton*: Special type of thick embossed wallpaper, named after its maker, Mr Walton, the patentee of linoleum.

46. *brummagem*: Worthless or inferior articles made in imitation of better ones. The word derives from the local dialect version of 'Birmingham', the city once known for its production of cheap trinkets, imitation jewellery, etc.

47. *Harrow . . . Oxford . . . Sandhurst*: Respectively the famous public (i.e. independent) school, the famous university and the famous military academy.

48. *n'en parlons plus*: Let's say no more about it.

49. *Ennismore Gardens*: Fashionable address in Kensington.

50. *touched a thousand things . . . turned into gold*: Alluding to the legend of King Midas, who requested of the gods that everything he touched might be turned to gold, and who was granted his wish with unfortunate consequences.

51. *the towers of Chillon*: See 'Four Meetings', note 6.

52. *Clarens*: Resort near Montreux in Switzerland.

The Pupil

New York Edition, Vol. XI; first magazine publication in *Longman's Magazine*, March and April 1891; first book publication in *The Lesson of the Master* (1892).

1. *gants de Suède*: Kid gloves (French, as are the translations below, unless otherwise indicated).

2. *Friday . . . superstitious*: Some Christians regard Friday, being the day of the Crucifixion, as an unlucky day.

3. *served on green cloth*: Ulick is either playing billiards or gambling, both such tables being usually covered in green cloth.

4. *déjeuner*: See 'The Pension Beaurepas', note 20.

5. *maccaroni*: The Moreens live, not on pasta, but on a macaronic language – an eclectic mixture of diverse languages, jokingly described by Morgan below, playing on 'ultramarine', as 'Ultramoreen'.

6. *borné*: (Educationally) limited or narrow.

7. *a fourth floor in a third-rate avenue . . . portier*: Not a good address, grander accommodation being usually on the lower floors . . . porter or door-keeper.

8. *the Invalides and Notre Dame, the Conciergerie*: The Hôtel des Invalides, military museum and burial place of Napoleon; Notre Dame, cathedral on the Ile de la Cité in the middle of the River Seine; the Conciergerie, originally part of the royal palace on the Ile de la Cité, most famous for its use as a prison during the French Revolution.

9. *indifferent to his appearance as a German philosopher*: I.e. because the German philosopher's mind is typically on higher, transcendental and *meta*physical things.

10. *the Jardin des Plantes . . . Louvre*: The botanical gardens . . . One of the world's largest museums and galleries, to which Henry James himself made an influential and memorable visit as a child in the company of a tutor. See Henry James, *A Small Boy and Others* (London: Macmillan, 1913), ch. XXV.

11. *calorifère*: Central heating.

12. *on the quays*: There are still open-air bookstalls along the Seine.

13. *immondes*: Disgusting, ignoble.

14. *to filer meant to cut sticks*: Which, in turn, means to leave, to depart.

15. *hauteur*: haughtiness.

16. *a phoenix*: The fabulous bird, there being only one of its kind. Mrs Moreen's implication here is that Pemberton is not special, nor specially gifted, and that hence his sacrifices, in staying with Morgan, are not that great.

17. *n'en parlons plus*: Let's speak no more about it.

18. *modeste aisance*: Modest means, i.e. comfortably well off.

19. *monde chic*: Fashionable society.

20. *as Jews at the doors of clothing-shops*: A simile intent on registering the Moreens' greediness and an instance of casual and cruelly unthinking anti-semitism which shows that the imaginatively generous James was, in some respects at least, very much of his time.

21. *the Bible Society*: The American Bible Society, established in 1816 with headquarters in New York, is committed to the translation, publication and worldwide distribution of the Bible.

22. *tutoyer*: To use, in the case of French, *tu* (second person singular) and its attendant forms rather than *vous* (plural); to speak familiarly.

23. *'sweet sea-city'*: There may be an unidentified allusion here. However, it is also possible that the narrative is merely quoting the term used for Venice by the Moreens, speaking their very odd private family language.

24. *the workaday world*: Echo of *As You Like It*, I. iii. 12: 'O, how full of briers is this working-day world.'

25. *the Grand Canal*: The main canal in Venice.

26. *Saint Mark's*: Famous square in Venice, location of the Ducal Palace and St Mark's Basilica.

27. *sala . . . scagliola floor*: Hall . . . a gypsum-and-glue imitation of ornamental stone (Italian).

28. *the Piazza*: St Mark's Square.

29. *three louis*: A golden coin; in modern usage 20 francs – i.e. Mrs Moreen wants 60 francs in all.

30. *c'est trop fort*: That's too much, too great a sum.

31. *du train dont vous allez*: Where are you coming from? Where did you get that from?

32. *Dites toujours*: Go on! say it!

33. *an homme fait*: A made man.

34. *Balliol*: A college of Oxford University.

35. *Volapuk*: Artificial language, largely composed of diverse European languages, invented in 1879 by a German priest, Johann Schleyer.

36. *the quarter of the Champs Elysees*: On the right bank, one of the grandest, most opulent areas of central Paris.

37. *velvety entresols . . . burnt pastilles*: Expensively draped mezzanine floors . . . small cones of fragrant paste, burnt to scent a room.

38. *n'est-ce pas, chéri*: Isn't that right, dear?

39. *in high feather*: In exuberant spirits, joyous.

40. *making up a 'boy's book'*: Creating an adventure story.

41. *Palais Royal . . . Chevet's wonderful succulent window*: The Palais Royal, bequeathed by Cardinal Richelieu (1585–1642) to Louis XIII, dates from the 1630s, and is located on the Rue St-Honoré, north of the Louvre. The Palais Royal contained (and continues to contain) gardens and galleries of shops – including, one infers, Chevet's shop selling 'succulent' foodstuffs. Oddly, Des Esseintes, the anti-hero of the decadent novel *Against Nature* (*A rebours*) (1884) by Joris-Karl Huysmans (1848–1907), buys a tortoise from Chevet's shop and has its shell studded with diamonds (ch. 4). The galleries or arcades provide shelter in inclement weather and in the past have been heated in winter.

42. *sauve qui peut*: Headlong panic or rout; case of each man for himself.

43. *Bois de Boulogne*: Large wood just west of central Paris, landscaped into an upper-class playground by Baron Haussmann in the 1850s.

44. *Comme vous-y-allez*: That's coming it a bit; how you exaggerate.

The Real Thing

New York Edition, Vol. XVIII; first magazine publication in *Black and White*, April 1892; first book publication in *The Real Thing (1893)*.

1. *a moist sponge passed over a 'sunk' piece of painting*: An inadequately prepared surface can lead to the sinking in of oil paint and a loss of colour. A moist sponge can temporarily restore the picture's appearance.

2. *lappets*: Loose folds or flaps on a garment.

3. *covers*: Area of woods and undergrowth in which game is reared for shooting.

4. *Kilburn*: Suburb in north London.

5. *'Rutland Ramsay'*: There is a curious anticipatory relation here between this grand edition and James's own New York Edition (1907–9), not least because of the similarity in title here to the first volume of James's edition – the early novel *Roderick Hudson*. (Ironically the New York Edition was to make use of the work of a photographer.)

6. *quoi*: What! (exclamatory) (French, as are the translations below, unless otherwise indicated).

7. *Maida Vale*: District in London north of Paddington.

8. *especially for the h*: Speakers with London or cockney accents tend not to pronounce the *h* at the beginning of words. See also 'In the Cage', note 4.

9. *the Cheapside*: Fictitious magazine, with an interesting title, analogous to those magazines in which James published his own tales and novels.

10. *his occupation was gone*: A glance, typical of James's fleeting allusiveness, at Shakespeare's *Othello*, in which Othello, believing Desdemona unfaithful and therefore lost to him, declares 'Othello's occupation's gone' (III. iii. 362).

11. *Raphael and Leonardo*: For Raphael, see 'Four Meetings', note 19. Leonardo da Vinci (1452–1519). Both are Italian Renaissance artists whose figures are immediately recognizable.

12. *bêtement*: Stupidly, foolishly.

13. *profils perdus*: Literally, lost profiles; poses where she is turning away.

14. *the City*: The business and banking district of London.

15. *Saint Peter's*: See 'Daisy Miller', note 42.

16. *the young Dante spellbound by the young Beatrice*: The great Italian poet (1265–1321), author of *The Divine Comedy*. The beautiful Beatrice appears in his verse as his muse.

17. *sentiment de la pose*: A real feeling for posing.

18. *lazzarone*: Italian vagrant or idler (originally associated with Naples) (Italian).

19. *a public school*: I.e. an independent private school.

20. *Ce sont des gens qu'il faut mettre à la porte*: They are people one must show the door; must get rid of.

21. *coloro che sanno*: those who know. In Dante's *Inferno*, IV. 131 Aristotle is described as '*maestro di color che sano*' – 'master of those who know' (Italian).

22. *crush-hat*: Hat, with a spring which can be collapsed, rendering the hat flat; an opera hat.

Greville Fane

New York Edition, Vol. XVI; first magazine publication in *Illustrated London News*, September 1892; first book publication in *The Real Thing* (1893).

1. *hansom*: See 'The Lesson of the Master', note 34.

2. *the lady I had taken down*: I.e. the lady I had accompanied in to the dining room.

3. *the neighbourhood of Primrose Hill*: To the north of Regent's Park, around the park of Primrose Hill. Greville Fane's increasing difficulties have caused her to move from Montpellier Square (note 6) where the narrator had first known her.

4. *the House*: House of Commons. (Sir Baldwin is a Member of Parliament.)

5. *a document not to 'serve'*: A document not to fulfil a public function (as a legal document is 'served'); not to be printed publicly in a newspaper as an obituary article.

6. *Montpellier Square; which helped me to see how dissociated her imagination was from her character*: Superior address near Kensington Gardens, and a very respectable one, remote from Greville Fane's 'dreadful' pictures of life.

7. *from Doncaster to Bucharest*: A very odd pairing of places, perhaps suggestive of Greville Fane's cavalier attitude to fictional plausibility in her efforts to cover all of Europe.

8. *resembled Balzac . . . her favourite historical characters were Lucien de Rubempré and the Vidame de Pamiers*: The improbable comparison is with Balzac (see 'The Pension Beaurepas', note 3). In his *Illusions perdues* (1837–43), Lucien Chardon is the young poet who takes his mother's name, de Rubempré, and sets off to win fame in Paris. There he finds a corrupt literary world where advancement depends on money and a willingness to deride genius and puff trash. The Vidame de Pamiers appears as a minor character in such lesser known works by Balzac as *La Duchesse de Langeais* (1834) and *Ferragus* (1835).

9. *she meant to train up her boy to follow it*: The 'germ' of this story is recorded in James's notebooks:

I heard some time ago, that Anthony Trollope has a theory that a boy might be brought up to be a novelist as to any other trade. He brought up – or attempted to bring up – his own son on this principle, and the young man became a sheep-farmer, in Australia. The other day Miss Thackeray (Mrs Ritchie) [novelist-daughter of William Makepeace Thackeray] said to me that she and her husband meant to bring their little daughter in that way. It hereupon occurred to me (as it has occurred before) that one might make a little story upon this . . . (*The Complete Notebooks of Henry James*, ed. Leon Edel and Lyall H. Powers (New York and Oxford: Oxford University Press, 1987), p. 9; also pp. 48–9)

10. *come out*: See 'The Pension Beaurepas', note 25.

11. *Essex*: The county to the north-east of London.

12. *like Desdemona, wished heaven had made her such a man*: Quoting *Othello*, I. iii. 161–2, which records Desdemona's admiration of Othello.

13. *the story of Madame George Sand's early rebellion*: George Sand was the pseudonym of the French novelist Amandine Aurore Lucile, Baronne Dudevant (1804–76). Her irregular life and habits – including the wearing of trousers – and her many love affairs shocked Paris society.

14. *gagne-pain*: Livelihood (French, as are the translations below).

15. *the price of pension*: I.e. the costs of boarding-houses.

16. *femme du monde*: Society lady.

17. *Rhadamanthus*: In Greek mythology, one of the three judges of the underworld.

18. *premiers frais*: Foremost expenses.

19. *Eton and Oxford*: Respectively the famous public (i.e. private) school and the famous university.

20. *Cheapside*: See 'The Real Thing', note 9.

21. *City*: See 'The Real Thing' note 14.

22. *embonpoint*: Portliness, stoutness.

23. *Flaubert . . . Dickens . . . Thackeray*: A roll-call of great nineteenth-century and, in this context, significantly, male novelists. For Flaubert, see 'The Death of the Lion', note 22. English novelists Charles Dickens (1812–70) and William Makepeace Thackeray (1811–63).

24. *vieux jeu*: Old-fashioned.

25. *feuilletons*: Serialized novels.

26. *Peckham and Hackney*: Suburbs of London, remote from the fashionable society of the West End.

27. *Brighton*: Resort on the south coast made fashionable by the Prince of Wales in the late eighteenth century, and with a reputation – relevant here since Leolin is researching in Brighton how far a novelist may 'go' – as a place to conduct dubious love affairs and amorous liaisons. See also 'The Death of the Lion', note 3.

28. *trouvailles*: Finds; discoveries.

29. *dog-cart*: See 'The Lesson of the Master', note 10.

30. *three new volumes*: In the nineteenth century many novels were published in three volumes.

31. *the Academy soirée*: The Royal Academy, which holds annually an exhibition of recent paintings, etc.

32. '*devil*': Junior legal counsel who does work for his leader.

33. '*Baby's Tub*': Perhaps a sardonic glance at Sir John Everett Millais's painting, 'Bubbles', used to advertise Pears' soap. The painting, originally entitled 'A Child's World', first appeared at the Grosvenor Gallery in London in 1886.

The Middle Years

New York Edition, Vol. XVI; first magazine publication in *Scribner's Magazine*, May 1893; first book publication in *Terminations* (1895).

1. *Bournemouth*: Resort on the English south coast.

2. *the Island*: The Isle of Wight.

3. '*just out*': Just published.

4. *the catchpenny binding . . . the circulating library*: The book has a cheap but eye-catching cover. The circulating library was a commercial establishment lending books, particularly popular novels, to borrowers for a fee. The most famous was opened in London in 1842 by Charles Edward Mudie.

5. '*The Middle Years*': Ironically the third volume of James's autobiography, named by James and unfinished at his death, is *The Middle Years* (London: Collins, 1917).

6. *passed the sponge over colour*: As a painter blurs or weakens watercolours in his painting.

7. *diligence vincit omnia*: Diligence conquers all (Latin). More usually the proverbial 'love conquers all' – *amor vincit omnia* – occurring in Virgil's *Eclogues* X, 69.

8. *Qui dort dîne*: To sleep is to dine (French, as are the translations below).

9. *bergère*: Shepherdess.

10. *the new psychology*: Presumably hypnosis.

11. *a 'type'*: See 'The Lesson of the Master', note 9.

12. *Bath-chair*: Invalid's wheelchair, usually with a hood.

13. *intrigante*: Plotter or schemer.

The Death of the Lion

New York Edition, Vol. XV; first magazine publication in *The Yellow Book*, April 1894; first book publication in *Terminations* (1895).

1. *on a 'staff'*: In contrast to the more precarious existence of the freelance journalist.

2. '*holiday-number*': Special, usually enlarged, celebratory edition.

3. *Brighton . . . Mrs Bounder*: Brighton is a resort on the south coast of England. One part of its reputation being for the louche, it is an appropriate setting for the suggestively named Mrs Bounder and what would then be regarded as the scandal of divorce. See also 'Greville Fane', note 27.

4. *Venus rising from the sea*: The mythological goddess of love and beauty was, according to some accounts, born from the foam of the sea.

5. *passe encore*: Well and good (French, as are the translations below).

6. *The Tatler*: Magazine devoted to upper-class social chit-chat.

7. *having 'a man in the house'*: Bailiffs and brokers would have one of their men take up residence in a debtor's house to prevent sale of the debtor's goods or the disappearance of the debtor.

8. *the larger latitude*: I.e. the degree of explicitness about sexual conduct.

9. *'heads'*: Headings (for his magazine articles) but with an ironic suggestion that Mr Morrow is collecting writers' heads.

10. *Fleet Street*: In central London, then home to, and synonymous with, the newspaper industry.

11. *the king of the beasts*: The (literary) lion.

12. *he circulated in person to a measure that the libraries might well have envied*: Alluding to commercial circulating libraries: see 'The Middle Years', note 4.

13. *the lions sit down . . . with the lambs*: Alluding to the prophecies of Isaiah 11:6–7; and a terrible joke considering what may be on such dinner menus.

14. *Sloane Street*: Fashionable street in Knightsbridge.

15. *a barouche and a smart hansom*: A barouche is a four-wheeled carriage with a driver's seat in front, two double seats inside facing each other and a folding hood; A hansom is a light two-wheeled covered carriage, the driver sitting above and behind. Unlike the privately owned barouche, a hansom is usually hired.

16. *couldn't have worried George Washington and Friedrich Schiller and Hannah More*: Respectively the first American president (1732–99), the German poet and dramatist (1759–1805) and the English religious writer (1745–1833) – all by the time of this tale long since dead.

17. *the Arabian Nights*: The ancient and fantastic Oriental tales.

18. *Albemarle Street*: In Mayfair, off Piccadilly.

19. *seeking him in his works even as God in nature*: A glance at Natural Theology, the philosophy that the nature of God may be inferred from observation of His creation, the natural world.

20. *'specials'*: Special editions of magazines and journals.

21. *Vandyke*: Sir Anthony Van Dyck (1599–1641), Flemish-born English painter, celebrated for his court portraits.

22. *Gustave Flaubert's doleful refrain about the hatred of literature*: Gustave Flaubert (1821–80), French novelist and author of *Madame Bovary* (1857). The *Oxford Dictionary of Quotations* cites Stendhal's letter to Louise Colet, 14 June 1853: 'You can calculate the worth of a man by the number of his enemies, and the importance of a work of art by the harm that is spoken of it.'

23. *valet de place*: Tour guide.

24. *a big building contracted for under a forfeit*: I.e. the contract specifies a financial penalty if the building is not complete on time, and hence the building is being worked on all the time by builders working in relays.

25. *custode*: Keeper, custodian.

26. *the cold Valhalla of her memory*: The hall in Scandinavian mythology where the souls of heroes spent eternity, and hence, by extension, any burial place of the great.

27. *priceless Sèvres*: Fine porcelain made at the French state factory at Sèvres, near Paris.

28. *brougham*: See 'The Lesson of the Master', note 26.

29. *'So are they all honourable men'*: Quoting Antony's funeral speech in *Julius Caesar*, III. ii. 84.

30. *The Family Budget*: Fictitious journal which would have been devoted to recipes, matters of household management, etc.

31. *Le roy est mort – vive le roy*: Proverbial; the [old] king is dead – long live the [new] king.

32. *inédit*: Unpublished work.

33. *confrère*: Colleague; fellow writer.

34. *the Abbey*: Westminster Abbey, traditional burial place, in Poets' Corner, of many famous writers.

The Figure in the Carpet

New York Edition, Vol. XV; first magazine publication in *Cosmopolis*, January and February 1896; first book publication in *Embarrassments* (1896).

1. *the night-mail*: The overnight train.

2. *Kensington Square*: A very fashionable address, close to Kensington Palace and Kensington Gardens.

3. *Chelsea*: A pleasant residential district in the west of London, extending along the north bank of the Thames.

4. *some bedlamitical theory of the cryptic character of Shakespeare*: Bedlam or Bethlehem hospital was, from the fifteenth century, a hospital for lunatics, and by the sixteenth century had become a term for the mad or crazy. Theories that Shakespeare's works were written by someone else – such as Francis Bacon or the Earl of Oxford – were particularly popular at the end of the nineteenth century and continue today. Occasionally those theories have themselves had a cryptic character, discovering the true author within acrostics and anagrams.

5. *Mr Snooks*: Presumably a fictitious critic, although real critics who post-date 'The Figure in the Carpet' and who have argued for the Earl of Oxford as the author of Shakespeare's plays have rejoiced in such names as Thomas J. Looney.

6. *critical laurel*: See 'The Lesson of the Master', note 19.

7. *out-Herod*: To out-shout. The allusion is to *Hamlet*, III. ii. 14 – 'It out-Herods Herod' –

where Hamlet addresses the players and refers to the tradition of representing Herod as a ranting tyrant in the English Medieval and Early Modern theatre.

8. *Monte Carlo*: The most famous European gambling resort.

9. *Vera incessu patuit dea*: 'By her gait the true goddess is made known' (Latin), from Virgil's *Aeneid*, I. 405.

10. *the temple of Vishnu*: Vishnu is the major god of Hinduism. The narrator is remarking that it is odd that Corvick's discovery should have been made in India.

11. *secousse*: Shock (French, as are the translations below).

12. *Rapallo, on the Genoese shore*: In north-western Italy.

13. *Aden*: Major port in the Yemen, by the Red Sea and the Suez Canal; a main stopping place on the sea route between India and Europe.

14. *Tellement envie de voir ta tête*: I long to see your face.

15. *hansom*: Light two-wheeled covered carriage, the driver sitting above and behind, usually hired rather than privately owned.

16. *a Cheltenham aunt*: Cheltenham is a resort town in Gloucestershire, here associated with gentility and propriety.

17. *Meran*: Merano, a health resort in the Italian Alps.

18. *trouvaille*: Discovery.

19. *Torquay*: Seaside resort in Devon in the south-west of England.

20. *dog-cart*: See 'The Lesson of the Master', note 10.

21. *that way madness lay*: Alluding to *King Lear*, III. iv. 91: 'O, that way madness lies'.

22. *Vandyke or Velasquez*: Sir Anthony Van Dyck (1599–1641), Flemish-born English painter, and Diego Rodríguez de Silva y Velázquez (1599–1660), Spanish painter, both celebrated for their court portraits.

23. *phrenological bust*: Model for the instruction of phrenology, the study of the conformation of the skull as a supposed indicator of mental faculties and characteristics.

24. *the numbers on his bumps*: Extending the figure of the phrenological bust, where each section of the skull is differently numbered.

In the Cage

New York Edition, Vol. XI; no magazine publication; first book publication in *In the Cage*, (1898).

1. *the 'sounder'*: Telegraphic device that converts electric code into sound, consisting of an electro-magnet, armature and lever fixed upon a base. The telegraph, as a means of sending messages quickly over long distances, evolved rapidly in the mid-nineteenth century. Although it involved many inventors and experimenters, its invention was credited to the American Samuel Finley Breese Morse (1791–1872). By the late 1890s, there were telegraph connections throughout the world, effected by means of submarine cables. Used by the government, the military and newspapers, the telegraph was also heavily used by business and for social purposes. Telegraphers were often women; in Britain 'usually the daughters of clergymen; tradesmen and government clerks, and were typically between 18 and 30 years old and unmarried. Women were regarded as "admirable manipulators of the instruments", well suited to telegraphy (since it wasn't too strenuous) and they spent the quiet periods reading or knitting' (Tom Standage, *The Victorian Internet: The Remarkable Story of the Telegraph and the Nineteenth Century's Online Pioneers* (1998; London: Phoenix, 1999), pp. 125–6). British private telegraph companies were nationalized as part of the Post Office (PO) in 1869. Telegrams were charged according to the number of words they involved ('count words') – an incentive for the sender to be brief and cryptic.

2. *the poison of perpetual gas*: The smell arising from the use of gas lighting.

3. *the 'Court Guide'*: The directory of names and addresses of nobility, gentry and people in society (i.e. those presented at Court, before the sovereign). The shop is situated in Mayfair, London's exclusive West End district.

4. *more present, too present, h's*: Cockney and other London accents typically drop h at the beginning of words. An attempt to 'correct' this and to speak 'properly' can lead such speakers mistakenly to insert h's where they should not occur.

5. *the far N.W. district*: Chalk Farm is situated north of Regent's Park, and was then a suburban area away from the social centre of the West End.

6. *the place where she borrowed novels . . . at a ha'penny a day*: A circulating library: see 'The Middle Years', note 4.

7. *sitting there in the stocks*: A nice pun, combining the stock of the shop with the stocks in which petty offenders were once confined.

8. *the season*: See 'The Lesson of the Master', note 36.

9. *the charming tale of 'Picciola'*: Novel (1843), popular in England, by Joseph Xavier Boniface or Saintine (1798–1865). Its various subtitles in translation are an interesting comment on 'In the Cage' – *The Prisoner of Genestella, Captivity Captive, The Prison Flower*.

10. *the port of Juno*: The deportment or bearing of Juno, wife and sister of Jupiter, queen of heaven.

11. *Park Chambers*: Unidentified, but clearly intended to suggest a Mayfair address near Hyde Park.

12. *Eaton Square*: Grand address in nearby Belgravia.

13. *Olympian*: Olympus was the home of the Greek gods.

14. *slaveys . . . Buttonses: slaveys*: Male servants or – less likely – hard-worked maids-of-all-work; *Buttonses*: Page or messenger boys, so called because of the profusion of buttons on the front of their uniform jackets. Buttons is a stock character in the pantomime *Cinderella*.

15. *the Pink 'Un*: The nickname may derive from the newspaper, printed on pink paper, devoted to sport, horse racing and betting details. The oddity of the profusion of names used by one sender of telegrams is not particular to this tale. Senders often had nicknames or telegraphic addresses, easier to remember and to send than full postal addresses. 'More than 35,000 telegraphic addresses had been registered at the Post Office by 1889' (Standage, *The Victorian Internet*, p. 162).

16. *like a new Eden*: Mrs Jordan's paradise or Arcadia is – appropriately for a clergyman's widow – a biblical one.

17. *Morning Post*: London daily paper (dating from 1772), and, especially between 1880 and 1900, the principal organ of the fashionable world.

18. *Regent's Park*: The roughly circular park, laid out in 1812 as an aristocratic suburban garden and named after the Prince Regent. For these characters, it is conveniently situated between Mayfair and Chalk Farm.

19. *in the Strand or thereabouts*: The Strand is one of the main thoroughfares of central London, extending east from Trafalgar Square, and part of the theatre district.

20. *Thompson or some funny American thing*: Thompson is perhaps Alfred Thompson (d. 1895), creator of opera-bouffe such as *Aladdin II* and *Linda of Chamouni*; the reference to the 'American thing' may be, on James's part, a wry glance at his own efforts in the theatre.

21. *all Piccadilly*: See 'The Lesson of the Master', note 4. A most desirable area for a grocer to have customers.

22. *'spring meetings'*: Horse racing meetings.

23. *Wesleyan chapel*: Methodist chapel, after the founder of Methodism, John Wesley (1703–91).

24. *in the middle of the day to her own dinner*: The difference in terminology accords with the precise characterization of class divisions in this tale: the upper classes have luncheon in the middle of the day, and dress for dinner in the evening.

25. *Dover . . . Ostend . . . seven nine four nine six one*: A ferry route links Dover, on the English south coast, with Ostend in Belgium. It was quite common to send telegrams in code – which the numbers here seem to represent.

26. *Scotch moors*: The grouse shooting season in Scotland begins on 12 August.

27. *Eastbourne, Folkestone, Cromer, Scarborough, Whitby*: Popular English seaside resorts, Eastbourne and Folkestone on the south coast and the rest on the east coast.

28. *as a Syndicate handles a Chinese or other Loan*: Given China's troubled history in the nineteenth century, loans to China were a considerable risk, to be handled cautiously.

29. *Ramsgate against Bournemouth . . . Boulogne against Jersey*: The first two are resorts on the English south coast, in Kent and in Dorset, while the latter two are in France and in the Channel Islands and hence more ambitious.

30. *pot-hat*: Bowler hat; low-crowned stiff felt hat.

31. *the Park*: I.e. Hyde Park. (See 'The Lesson of the Master', note 31.)

32. *the Swanage boat*: Swanage is a small seaside resort across Poole Bay from Bournemouth.

33. *Saint Martin's summer*: A spell of fine weather late in the year.

34. *Post-Office Guide*: Directory of names, addresses, etc.

35. *Victoria*: I.e. Victoria Railway Station, London.

36. *a French proverb according to which such a door, any door, had to be either open or shut*: First found in de Brueys and Palaprat's comedy, *Le Grondeur* (produced 1691). The general meaning is that the door must be one way or the other and thus, figuratively, that things must be clear-cut (Brewer's *Dictionary of Phrase and Fable*).

37. *the City*: See 'The Real Thing', note 14.

38. *Maida Vale*: District in London north of Paddington.

39. *excessively 'high'*: High Anglican – as indicated by the chants and incense in the service, and contrasting with Mr Mudge's Wesleyan chapel.

40. *thick brown fog*: Before the Clean Air Act was passed in 1956, London was notorious for its 'pea soup' fogs.

41. *Saint Julian's*: No specific church has been identified.

The Real Right Thing

New York Edition, Vol. XVII; first magazine publication in *Collier's Weekly*, December 1899; first book publication in *The Soft Side* (1900).

1. *no smoke without fire*: Proverbial, meaning there is some foundation of truth in every rumour or story.

2. *Mrs Doyne's queenly weeds*: The widow here in black, having not treated her husband well in his lifetime, owes something to Queen Gertrude in the greatest of all ghost stories, *Hamlet*, but 'queenly' may also glance at Queen Victoria, always in mourning for Prince Albert.

3. *a Johnson and a Scott, with a Boswell and a Lockhart*: The great writers, Dr Samuel Johnson (1709–84) and Sir Walter Scott (1771–1832) and their biographers, respectively, James Boswell (1740–95) and John Gibson Lockhart (1794–1854).

4. *Tottenham Court Road rugs*: This road in central London is still a place of furniture dealers.

5. *some 'decadent' coloured print, some poster of the newest school*: After the manner of French poster artists of the late nineteenth century.

Broken Wings

New York Edition, Vol. XVI; first publication in *Century Magazine*, December 1900; first book publication in *The Better Sort* (1903).

1. *'dressing'*: Dressing formally for dinner.

2. *'The New Girl'*: Unidentified and perhaps fictional, the title glancing at the emergence of the more liberated 'New Woman' in the late nineteenth century.

3. *brougham*: See 'The Lesson of the Master', note 26.

4. *Nous n'irons . . . sont coupés*: An old French nursery rhyme, adopted by Théodore de Banville (1823–91) for one of his poems: 'We shall go no more to the woods/ The laurels are cut down.'

The Abasement of the Northmores

New York Edition, Vol. XVI; no magazine publication; first book publication in *The Soft Side* (1900).

1. *'special'*: I.e. special train, in addition to trains ordinarily timetabled. In this case it is presumably laid on specifically for the funeral-goers.
2. *chambers*: Set of rooms shared by a group of barristers.
3. *had thrown, as the saying was, the helve after the hatchet*: Throwing away what remains because your losses have already been so great. The allusion is to the fable of the woodcutter who lost the head of his axe in the river and threw the handle in after it.
4. *a circular urbi et orbi*: Literally, sent to the city (i.e. Rome) and to the world. Usually it refers to the public blessing given by the Pope on the balcony of St Peter's on great occasions.
5. *her one evil hour*: An echo of *Paradise Lost* by John Milton (1608–74), where Eve, tempted, eats the forbidden fruit:

> So saying, her rash hand in evil hour
> Forth reaching to the fruit, she plucked, she ate:
> Earth felt the wound . . . (IX. 780–82)

6. *pour rire*: Joke; sham (French).
7. *the House*: Presumably the House of Lords.
8. *inédit*: Unpublished work.
9. *laurels*: See 'The Lesson of the Master', note 19.
10. *the kiss of Judas*: Judas betrayed Christ with a kiss. See, for example, Matthew 26:46–9.

The Beast in the Jungle

New York Edition, Vol. XVII; no magazine publication; first book publication in *The Better Sort* (1903).

1. *the Palace of the Caesars . . . Pompeii*: The Palace of the Caesars is the archaeological site on the Palatine Hill, home of the ancient emperors in Rome; Pompeii is the ancient city destroyed by the eruption of Mt Vesuvius in AD 79, and is south-east of Naples.
2. *lazzarone with a stiletto*: Neapolitan vagrant or vagabond with a dagger with a slender pointed blade (Italian).
3. *fever*: presumably malaria.
4. *Sorrento, across the bay*: The seaport and resort on the Bay of Naples, south of Naples.
5. *the catastrophe*: The final event or denouement, not necessarily a calamity.
6. *National Gallery . . . South Kensington Museum*: The National Gallery, one of the world's greatest art galleries, moved to its present site in Trafalgar Square in 1838. The first South Kensington Museum, founded in 1856, included both Arts and Science; the

Victoria and Albert Museum, the Science Museum and the Natural History Museum have since superseded it in South Kensington.

7. *her occupation was verily gone*: Allusion to 'Othello's occupation's gone' (*Othello* III. iii. 362). See also 'The Real Thing', note 10.

8. *Dresden*: Fine porcelain, highly regarded since the eighteenth century.

9. *the Park*: Hyde Park. See 'The Lesson of the Master', note 31.

10. *the great grey London cemetery*: Possibly Highgate Cemetery; consecrated in 1839, it quickly became a popular and fashionable place to be buried – and also a tourist attraction, the burial place of many eminent Victorians.

The Birthplace

New York Edition, Vol. XVII; no magazine publication; first book publication in *The Better Sort* (1903).

1. *the early home of the supreme poet, the Mecca of the English-speaking race*: I.e. Stratford-upon-Avon, birthplace of Shakespeare, a figure of such importance that here he acquires quasi-religious status and a capital letter when referred to by pronouns – and cannot be directly named. Even His representatives – They – are deserving of reverential treatment.

2. *a great green woodland . . . this transfigured world*: Suggesting Shakespeare's Forest of Arden in *As You Like It*, and one of this tale's many teasing allusions to Shakespeare's works.

3. *cottage-piano*: Small upright piano.

4. *an old Bradshaw*: The famous railway timetable begun by George Bradshaw (1801–53) in Manchester.

5. *catch-penny publications*: Cheap publications with showy, eye-catching covers.

6. *genius loci*: Spirit of the place; presiding deity (Latin).

7. '*patterns*': Patterns for dressmaking.

8. *Casa Santa*: The Holy House, used originally of the reputed house of the Virgin Mary at Nazareth.

9. *the pound of flesh*: Alluding to the terms of Antonio's and Shylock's bond in *The Merchant of Venice*.

10. *like a thief at night*: Alluding to 1 Thessalonians 5:2, part of James's audacious and comic appropriation of biblical and Christian references in this tale.

11. *Goethe's at Weimar*: Johann Wolfgang von Goethe (1749–1832). German poet and dramatist, lived in Weimar from 1775 until his death and is buried in the ducal tomb there.

12. '*The play's the thing*': *Hamlet* II. ii. 606.

13. *compris*: Included in the price (French).

14. *moreen*: Coarse, stout woollen or woollen-and-cotton fabric, usually watered or embossed.

15. *at Oxford*: I.e. at Oxford University.

16. *hornbook*: Child's primer, consisting typically of a sheet of parchment protected by a sheet of transparent horn.

17. *singing . . . to a Boston audience*: A Boston audience, in Puritan New England, was presumably notorious for being sophisticated and undemonstrative.

18. *Consider it well*: Echoing Lear on Poor Tom: 'Consider him well' (*King Lear* III. iv. 100).

19. *Machiavellic*: Referring to the Renaissance statesman and thinker Niccolò Machiavelli (1469–1527), whose thinking – represented in Shakespeare's plays – included the doctrine that any means, however unscrupulous, may be justifiably employed by a ruler to maintain his power.

Fordham Castle

New York Edition, Vol. XVI; first published in *Harper's Magazine*, December 1904; first book publication in New York Edition.

1. *the entr'acte*: The interval (French).

2. *Peoria*: Town in Illinois, i.e. an undistinguished – or undistinguishable – small town in the mid-western USA.

3. *Wilts*: I.e. Wiltshire, a county, west of London.

4. *Constantinople*: Now Istanbul.

5. *Baedeker*: Karl Baedeker (1801–59) began the publishing of famous guide books bearing his name, much used by tourists.

6. *Castle of Chillon and the Dent du Midi*: The Dent du Midi is a famous peak (3300 metres) south of Lake Geneva. For the Castle of Chillon, see 'Four Meetings', note 6.

7. *car-window*: I.e. railway-carriage window.

8. *the book-agency business*: Selling books on a subscription basis often through door-to-door salesmen. The more modern and notorious equivalent is perhaps the encyclopaedia salesman.

9. *sort of box*: Predicament.

10. *tilleuls*: Lime-trees (French).

Julia Bride

New York Edition, Vol. XVII; first magazine publication in *Harper's Magazine*, March and April 1908; first book publication in New York Edition.

1. *the Museum*: The Metropolitan Museum of Art, in New York City, founded in 1870. It has occupied its present site in Central Park (see note 10) since 1880. James describes his first impression of the new building (1902) on his 1904–5 visit to the United States in Chapter IV of *The American Scene* (1907).

2. *duck*: Closely woven, durable, usually cotton fabric.

3. *between Scylla and Charybdis*: Proverbial; between two equal but different dangers. Scylla was a sea monster, a terror to ships and sailors, dwelling on the rock of Scylla opposite Charybdis, a whirlpool on the coast of Sicily.

4. *wouldn't cast the stone*: Alluding to John 8:7: 'He that is without sin among you, let him first cast a stone at her.'

5. *Qui s'excuse s'accuse*: He who excuses himself accuses himself (French).

6. *the Jersey boat*: The ferry between New York and New Jersey, predating today's system of tunnels and bridges.

7. *the uses, for Julia, in fine, of adversity*: Echoing Shakespeare's *As You Like It* II. i. 12: 'Sweet are the uses of adversity . . .'

8. *Le compte y était*: The sum total of the account was there (French).

9. *downtown*: The business and financial district of New York.

10. *the Park*: Central Park, designed by Frederick Law Olmstead and Calvert Vaux in 1857.

11. *the East Side*: Not then a fashionable address.

12. *sanctum sanctorum*: The holy of holies (Latin).

13. *Nancy and the Artful Dodger . . . 'Oliver Twist'*: Two of the young thieves in *Oliver Twist* (1837–9) by Charles Dickens (1812–70).

14. *not in sympathy with the old American freedom*: Indicating the shift which this later tale represents from the presentation of the 'freeborn American girl' in such earlier tales as 'Daisy Miller' and 'The Pension Beaurepas'.

The Jolly Corner

New York Edition, Vol. XVII; first magazine publication in *English Review*, December 1908; first book publication in New York Edition.

1. *Irving Place*: Street running between 14th and 23rd Streets, near and east of Union Square and Park Avenue; a good *old* New York address.

2. *the inventor of the sky-scraper*: The American architect and engineer William Le Baron Jenney (1832–1907) earned himself the title 'father of the skyscraper'. His method of metal frame construction was first used in his Home Insurance Building (1885) in Chicago and remains basic to the construction of tall buildings.

3. *pour deux sous*: For two cents (French). (A sou is, literally, five centimes.)

4. *ombres chinoises*: European version of the Chinese shadow-puppet show (French).

5. *Pantaloon . . . Christmas farce . . . Harlequin*: Pantaloon and Harlequin have their origins as stock characters in sixteenth-century Italian Commedia Dell'arte and survived into English pantomime, usually played at Christmas.

6. *the trodden worm of the adage*: 'Even a worm will turn.' The most abject of creatures will turn upon its tormentors if driven to extremity.